OFF LIMITS

NEW YORK TIMES BESTSELLING AUTHOR
K. BROMBERG

PRAISE FOR THE NOVELS OF K. BROMBERG

"An irresistibly hot romance that stays with you long after you finish the book."
—# 1 *New York Times* bestselling author Jennifer L. Armentrout

"Captivating, emotional, and sizzling hot!"
—#1 *New York Times* bestselling author S. C. Stephens

"Bromberg is a master at turning up the heat!"
—*New York Times* bestselling author Katy Evans

"K. Bromberg is the master of making hearts race and pulses pound."
—*New York Times* bestselling author Jay Crownover

"Sexy, heartwarming, and so much more."
—*New York Times* bestselling author Corinne Michaels

"Super charged heat and full of heart. Bromberg aces it from the first page to the last."
—*New York Times* bestselling author Kylie Scott

OTHER BOOKS BY K. BROMBERG

Driven Series
Driven
Fueled
Crashed
Raced
Aced

Driven Novels
Slow Burn
Sweet Ache
Hard Beat
Down Shift

The Player Duet
The Player
The Catch

Everyday Heroes
Cuffed
Combust
Cockpit
Control (Novella)

Wicked Ways
Resist
Reveal

The
PLAYER

DEDICATION

This book is dedicated to those women who love sports. The ones who didn't think twice about getting grass stains on their tights as little girls, and now that they're older, have no shame in sitting down to watch a game with the guys.

I've always been a sports girl.

The book is dedicated to nerd girls. The ones who like to sit at home on a Friday night and get lost in the pages of a good book. The ones who always want to learn new things. Never be ashamed of being smart.

I've always been a nerd girl.

This book is dedicated to strong girls. To the ones who would rather help their fellow women succeed rather than try to bring them down.

I've always been a strong girl.

This book is dedicated to the insecure girls. Yes, *you*. I *see* you. I've *been* you. I *am* you. It's okay to spread your wings every once in a while and see how far you can fly. Nothing ventured, nothing gained.

Look at me, I did.

PROLOGUE

Easton

The rush hits me.

The adrenaline through my body.

The roar of the crowd in my ears.

The mixture of scents—dirt, popcorn, leather, pine-tar—in my nose.

They're my lifeline.

My constants.

The only religion I was ever taught to believe in.

The only thing I was ever allowed to be.

For those few moments before the pain hits—the blinding, excruciating, unending pain—when the dust is dancing around me and I can feel its grit sliding beneath my body, I remember why I love the game.

Everything about it.

And then I look up.

Our eyes meet. It's a split-second connection. But I'm reminded of something. Of someone.

And then it's gone.

Because now there's only pain.

It takes over.

Steals my breath.

Kills my streak.

And hopefully doesn't ruin my future.

CHAPTER ONE

Scout

Four months later

"How do you want me?"

Hazel eyes.

An arrogant smirk.

Those are the first two things about Easton Wylder that grab my attention when he peeks his head around the training room door.

I open my mouth to speak but fall silent when he walks over the threshold and comes into full view. And it's not just because he's shirtless—that's par for the course in my job—but rather it's *everything* about him that knocks the words from my lips. The bare, tanned, and very toned chest. The low-slung gym shorts showcasing a perfect V of muscles. The happy trail ever so slightly visible, which draws my eyes to where I shouldn't be looking.

But I *do* look.

And that's a problem. Because even if it's only for a moment, it's still long enough for him to notice. I snap my eyes back up and over his dark scruff to once again be greeted with that cocksure smirk that I swear taunts me and asks if I like what I see.

Another day. Another client. *Another player.*

I shouldn't have expected any less.

He's hot. I'll give him that. Like the mouthwatering, stop-traffic, draw-all-eyes-when-he-walks-into-a-room type of hot. And not only that, but he's a freaking god on the field. One of the best catchers I've ever seen. Batting average, on-base percentage, caught-stealing percentage, pick-offs, pass balls—all his stats say if he stays on this track, he'll be one of the greats someday.

The total package.

But if first impressions are any indication—the arrogant lift of his eyebrows and cocky set of his shoulders—I already know he's going to be like every other *total package* I've worked with before. Great to look at but a bore to work with. Conceited and one-dimensional. If it's not about him, he doesn't want to talk about it.

I hope I'm wrong, or else this is going to be a *long* three months. Not only that, but I've admired his career over the last few years and would prefer to keep admiring the man I perceived him to be, too.

"On my back?" he rephrases his question before I can recover from my thoughts, and takes a step closer. "On my stomach?" He stops and scrubs a towel over his face so that his dark brown hair sticks up every which way, yet somehow it only adds to his appeal.

Give him a chance, Scout. He's baseball royalty. Besides, he might not be that bad. Does it really matter if he's a conceited jerk? There's still a contract, a set timeframe, and he's still your client. So, chop-chop. Get to it and *do your job.*

"Uh," I say as I glance down again, trying not to let that body—the hard, damaged, perfection of it—scatter my thoughts and undermine my professionalism.

"*Uh?*" he repeats, as those multicolored eyes of his laugh at a joke only he seems to understand.

"Sorry, you distracted me." Once the words are out I realize how they sound, giving the implication that his body is the culprit.

"Distracted?" A lift of his brows. A ghost of a smile.

I start over. "I'm the new PT the club contracted to help get you back on the field."

"The *club* hired *you*? I thought they were hiring Doc . . . and you're definitely not Doc."

"Doc's the one who assigned me to your case." My tone is defensive, my soul sagging under the weight of why I'm here and he's not.

"Doc Dalton, Doc?" Disbelief tinges his tone.

"Yeah, Doc Dalton, Doc. I'm his partner."

"*Partner?* Doc's notorious for working solo." He narrows his eyes and studies me unabashedly for a moment. The silent scrutiny has me shifting on my feet, and just as I'm about to speak, he chuckles under his breath at something I'm obviously not privy to. "Which one of the guys hired you?"

"Your general manager. Cory Tillman."

"Cory?"

"Yes. Cory." *Why is this so hard for him to understand?*

"And she even has the name right," he mutters, more to himself than to me, only furthering my confusion. "Nice try, though. My bet's on Drew or Tino. They covered all of their bases with you, didn't they?"

What in the hell is he talking about?

"Not that you care, but I don't need my bases covered. I'd really like to get started."

"No."

"No?" *Is he being serious?*

"You think I'd let *just anybody* touch my arm?"

"Excuse me?" The insult hits me harder than it should. It's one I've learned to expect—the assumption that I can't be as good as Doc—and yet my temper still lights. "I assure you my touch is every bit as magical as Doc's is." *Asshole.*

"I'm sure it is," he murmurs, drawing the words out, while his eyes roam down the length of my body. The look in them—one of pure male appreciation—sets my nerves, already tinged with temper, abuzz. And I don't want them to be abuzz. I don't want them to feel anything when it comes to him and how much of a prick he is proving himself to be right now.

"Try it on someone else, Hot Shot. Your charm isn't going to work on me."

"My charm?" I love the little startle to his head. The one that says he's not used to being called on the carpet.

"Yeah. The 'I'm a cocky bastard' charm. Do you really get women when you act like that?"

"I wasn't aware I was trying to get a woman." His eyes lock onto mine. There's humor in their hazel depths, but all I feel is stupidly hurt as if he'd just rejected me, when I didn't want to be wanted by him in the first place. "And for the record, it works all the time."

What I'd give to knock that smug smirk off his face right now.

"So, what? You just walk up and throw some stats at her? 'Hey, baby, I'm having a killer season, batting three seventy-five with a twenty-game hitting streak. Wanna go out?'"

"Nah." He fights back a laugh, and I hate that even though I know I'm being mocked, that sheepish smile of his draws me in to take a step closer. "I just tell her I have a big stick and I know just how to use it."

"Seriously?"

He shrugs. "No, but you're going to think what you want to anyway, right?"

"Sure am."

"And you have a thing against big sticks, I take it?"

He's taunting me. Seeing how far he can push me. Little does he know, I push right back.

"Nothing against big sticks, but they're worthless unless you know how to use them. And guys who drop cheesy lines like the one you just did definitely don't take the time to learn how to use them properly."

"Are you speaking from experience? Do a lot of men try lines like that on you?" Our eyes war across the small space.

"Not men I'd give the time of day."

"That's a pity. Maybe you haven't met the right one, then." He just stares at me with an unrelenting gaze that asks questions and makes assumptions I'd rather he not make. This conversation has veered way off course from where it needs to be.

Back to him.

Focused on him.

And the irony isn't lost on me that this is the exact opposite of what I wanted moments ago.

"Look, I'm here to do a job. It's probably best if we stick to that," I say in an attempt to reset this conversation for the second time.

"You sure you want to? Your hostility screams how much you're enjoying my company."

"Liking you is not a necessity. I'm good at ignoring people who rub me the wrong way." I follow the dig with a sickeningly sweet smile. "Let's get to it." I motion to the padded table behind him.

He looks at the table and then back to me. "What if I tell you thanks, but no thanks."

"And what if I tell you, you don't get a say? I'm getting paid to do a job, and I intend to get that job done." I take a few steps closer to him and make sure my voice is as authoritative as possible. "On your back."

"Gotta love a woman who knows what she wants." There's no mistaking the suggestion in his words, and it's only reinforced by the intensity of the way he stares at me, as if with each passing second, another layer of my clothing is falling off. "But you'll learn soon enough, I rarely do what I'm told."

"*Pretty please.*" Sarcasm rings through my voice as we wage a visual war of wills, but I'm unsure over what. I'm here to give him exactly what he wants—to be back on the field—and so his defiance is both frustrating and confusing.

Because while I may have been questioned by players in the past—underestimated because I'm a woman, tested because I'm not as experienced as Doc—it's so very different this time around.

This time I have Doc Dalton's benchmark career riding on rehabbing Easton Wylder. I have my father's last wishes to fulfill. I have my reputation to solidify.

"Feisty, gorgeous, intelligent, *and* polite," he muses, crossing his arms over his chest so his biceps flex with the movement. Eyebrows lifted, he gives me a full-blown smile to boot. "Because of that, I'll obey . . . but just this once."

Quit staring at me. "Let's get to it." *Quit smiling at me like that.* "On the table." *Quit flexing your biceps.* "Shirt off." *Quit unnerving me.*

"My shirt's already off."

"Oh. Yes. Sorry." Crap. *Nothing like showing you're capable and in control by completely missing the obvious.* "Do you want to tell me where it hurts the most, so I can start there?"

"I've got a lot of hurts." He laughs, and it irritates me that I find the sound of it sexy. "But I'm curious, how do you plan on fixing me if touching the clientele is off-limits?"

"I touch, Wylder. There are no limitations. I throw my hands and my body into it until I've made the pain go away. Then we move on to your next ache and start the process all over again." Ignoring the disbelief on his face, I point to the table behind him. "I thought you were going to obey this once?"

"On one condition."

Condition? *Is he serious?* I have no choice but to play along. "What's that?"

"Stop pretending like you know what you're doing when it comes to my arm." He arches an eyebrow in challenge.

The surest way to piss a woman off is to question her abilities and yet he just did again. "Don't be an ass. You're irritating me. And wasting my time." I raise my eyebrows. "I don't like my time wasted."

"Isn't the customer always supposed to be right?"

"Sit. Down."

"What the lady wants, the lady gets." Resigned, but with a lopsided smirk that says somehow he's getting what he wants anyway, he scoots his ass onto the padded table behind him, eyes still locked on mine. "One more condition?"

"No more conditions." The man is positively frustrating.

"What's your name?"

"Scout," I answer, already exhausted from this game I'm a player in but don't quite understand.

"*Scout?*"

"Yes. Scout." I opt to leave out my last name. There's no need for him to question my abilities any further.

"That's not exactly the type of originality I was expecting. What happened to Star or Trixie or *Kitty*? Were those all taken?"

What in the hell is he talking about?

"Sorry to disappoint you, but it's just Scout."

"Damn. My bet was on Kitty."

"Nope."

"Scout. Hmm." He nods his head, eyes narrowing as if he's trying to figure something out. "I was wrong. It wasn't Tino. It was Drew. He's the one who hired you, coached you on what to say, and told you what to do, right?" He swings his legs up onto the table, and I swear he says something about there being *no Velcro* but when he props himself up on his elbow and meets my puzzled gaze, all he does is give me a perfectly innocent, choir-boy smile.

"I'm sorry, am I missing something?" *I'm so confused.*

"Don't you worry that *pretty little head of yours*," he says with a smirk. "You're not missing a thing."

I hear him—the mockery in his tone, the alarm bells telling me something's going on that I don't quite understand—but I'm momentarily distracted by our proximity. By the scent of the shampoo in his hair. By the sight of faded scars on his body, more visible now that I'm closer to him. By the unique color of his eyes, which are a mixture of brown and gray with a ring of blue around the iris.

But it's his wince that pulls me from la-la land. It's a simple motion, the lift of his arm behind his head, but I catch the grimace on his face. My eyes home in on his shoulder. On the vibration of his muscles as he shifts and adjusts to get comfortable and the mask now in place trying to pretend it didn't hurt.

My training kicks in. Takes over. Throws that unwelcome pang of insta-lust I was momentarily mesmerized by out the window. I itch to put my hands on him so I can knead and stretch and try to give him relief from his nagging pain.

But right as I'm about to touch his shoulder, he shifts to look at me and asks, "Don't you need music or something?"

My hands freeze as his words break through my concentration. They hit my ears, and my synapses fire for what feels like the first time since he stepped in here. Everything clicks into place. The hints that have been niggling in the back of my mind suddenly link together and make sense.

The throwback baller.

The All-American do-gooder.

And the notorious prankster.

How could I not have connected the dots earlier? That the man who is known in locker rooms around the country for pranking his teammates—like the ones he named moments ago, Tino and Drew—thinks they are pranking him. Getting him back for the legendary stunts he's done to them.

And he thinks I'm in on it.

Velcro. Music. The ridiculous stage names.

Yep. He thinks I'm a stripper.

Or a hooker.

Lovely.

And while I should be insulted that he thinks I'm here because his buddies hired me to dance for him, at least our conversation makes some sense now.

Why does the thought relieve me? Because it redeems him? Not in the least. But maybe he's not the asshole I pegged him to be. Maybe, just maybe, he was reacting to the situation he assumed and not to me.

But then again, he's still lying down, still letting this play out, still letting me—the woman he thinks is here to strip for him—touch him.

And while I may have worked in enough clubhouses to know this prank is tame in the scheme of things, I also know there is no better way to get a prankster to take you seriously than to prank him right back. So, I make the split-second decision to ride this ruse out. I'll play the part, and then when the time is right, I'll tell him the truth. Perhaps his disappointment that I'm not a stripper will knock some of the cockiness from his smile.

When I meet his eyes again, I hold them just a touch too long, smile a little more seductively. "Do I want music? It's your preference. Do you prefer that I . . . *do it* to music? Or would you rather we do a dry run first—see what feels good to you, what doesn't, and then we can take it from there?" I don't believe my voice has ever purred before, but right now I feel like I deserve the stage name Kitty.

Those thick lashes of his shock open at my sudden change in demeanor. He glances at me and then out of the training room's windows to the empty locker room beyond. He must be wondering where Drew and Tino are, because no doubt they'd be standing by to watch their prank play out.

No dice, Hot Shot. The joke's on you.

"There's no one else here, Easton. Just you. And me." I put my finger on his forehead and push so his head rests back. "And the little workout I'm about to give you."

"A workout? Is that what you call it these days?" His chuckle says it all. So does the quick inhale of breath and the tensing of his muscles beneath my fingertips as I press on the skin atop his rotator cuff to feel for the presence of scar tissue. The first step to try and assess why it's taking his arm so long to heal when it should be far past the wincing stage.

His skin is smooth. Hot. And there's a zap of electricity—a hum of something—when our bodies connect in this most innocent of ways. It's so unexpected and unlike anything I've ever felt before that I have to stop myself from pulling my hand away in reaction.

"I appreciate you pretending to know what you're doing and all, but—"

"Oh, I know what I'm doing, no worries there," I croon to stop his protest. "Let's try this now. Does that hurt?" He resists when I try to lift his arm over his head. At least he has enough sense to question letting a stripper work on his million-dollar arm.

"No. It's just . . . I don't think you should—"

"I assure you I'm more than qualified." There's panic in his eyes, fear over how far this stripper is going to carry on the I'm-a-physical-therapist-routine. So I carry on. "A torn labrum isn't anything to mess around with. Only a professional will know how to make it feel better. And rest assured, I'm a professional."

"Handling me is one thing, Scout," he says with a bit of bewilderment, "but my arm is a whole other matter."

"You don't trust me to fix it?" I walk my fingers up his biceps, and his Adam's apple bobs in reaction as he debates what to do next.

"I highly doubt that's what you're here for."

"No?" I feign innocence. "Then why don't we get down to exactly what I'm here for?"

In a move I use daily to stretch my players, and before I lose the element of surprise, I hop onto the table so that my knees cage the sides of his hips.

"Wait. *Whoa.*" Easton's face is the picture of surprise—eyes wide, mouth opening and closing, eyebrows arching.

"I'm ready if you are." The purr is back as I lean forward so I'm on all fours with our torsos parallel and my eyes locked with his.

"Yes. No." He blinks rapidly as if it will help him grasp the fact that what was all fun and games a minute ago is now very real. A part of me likes that he's hesitant and not all grabby-hands and raring to go with some random woman. The other part of me wonders if I really were a stripper here on a prank, just how far would he let this ride out. "My rehabber—Doc. He'll be here any minute." He stutters out the protest.

"No, he won't."

"*He won't?*" His voice rises in pitch.

"Nope." I shake my head and lift my eyebrows.

"I knew it. I knew Drew and Tino were behind this." He breathes out a laugh that's part disbelief, part relief, but when he starts to sit up, I remain right where I am.

"Nope. Not a prank." That stops him cold.

"What do you mean? You're a . . ."

"A physical therapist," I finish for him.

"That's a good one. Cute. But I call bullshit."

"Actually, it's not." I reach out with one hand, and just as I'm about to touch his shoulder, he yanks it out of my grasp. His hiss from the pain, the kneejerk reaction, is audible. "*And you need me.*"

His eyes bore into mine—gauging, judging, questioning—before that cocksure grin of his returns. "I'm sure a lot of other guys need you . . . Scout, *is it?* But I'm not one of them. I don't need to pay to see some skin."

"First, you're not paying me, the club is. And second, I'm fully clothed."

"Drop the act, sweetheart. The club's not paying you shit. They're paying Doc, and right now, he's somewhere waiting for me, and I need to find him. So, time's up. It was cute, you had me going for a bit, but it's time for you to head out."

I nod in mock resignation as I slowly climb off the table, but my eyes never leave his as I lean down close to his ear. "You get a pass today, just so you can wrap that *pretty little head of yours* around the fact that I'm your new physical therapist. Be here tomorrow. Same time. Same place. Don't let my appearance fool you, because I'll work you out all right, but only so I can get you back on the field." I step back, take in his wide-eyed expression as it morphs slowly from arrogance to the realization that I just might be telling the truth. I smile. "Oh, and leave your assumptions at home. I may not be Doc, but I sure as hell am a *Dalton.* It's been a pleasure."

And with that, I turn my back and head for the door. My hands are trembling, and my body is riding high on something akin to adrenaline, but I'm satisfied that he'll take me seriously from here on out.

"Hey, *Kitty*."

Despite every urge in my body to keep walking and not acknowledge the stripper alias, my feet stop. And I hate that they do, but at least I don't give him the satisfaction of turning around to face him.

"The name's Scout. And, for the record, I'm not sure whether to be flattered or pissed off that you'd think I'd accept money to dance for you *or* sleep with you."

"So, you'd do it for free then?" The chuckle that follows is smooth as silk, full of suggestion, and twists my insides with a potent combination of disgust and lust.

"Not hardly," I lie.

"Good thing I didn't take the bait then. I was ready to kiss you senseless just to call your bluff and prove you were a stripper."

"Good thing I didn't knee you in the nuts because you had."

His laugh is warmer this time around. "Lucky for me, I practiced restraint."

"Remember that term—practice restraint," I say, feeling like I've made some headway. "I won't be easy on you, you know."

"I'll count on it. And Scout? I knew you weren't a stripper."

"Way to try and save face, Hot Shot." *Men and their egos.* "But if that's the case, then why'd you let me keep the act going?"

"Only a stupid man would stop a beautiful woman when she's straddling his thighs."

"And here I thought you'd redeemed yourself," I mutter through the smile he can't see.

"Redemption's boring. I prefer excitement," he goads.

"Great."

"Tomorrow, Scout."

"Yeah. Yeah."

I walk out of the locker room, the echo of my footsteps down the concrete corridor nowhere as loud as his voice on repeat in my mind. *I was ready to kiss you senseless just to call your bluff.*

If that would be my punishment for being wrong, why the hell would I want to be right?

CHAPTER TWO

Easton

"It's just pain. I've played through it before. I can play through it again."

"And risk ending your career?"

"Look. I know my body better than anyone. I'm not going to risk my career by pushing myself too early, which is why—"

"Which is why the club hired Doc."

"Don't remind me." My laugh is loaded with sarcasm but my thoughts are already back on the athletic brunette with challenging gray eyes and a smartass mouth. The one I've probably thought about more times in the last few hours, while waiting for my agent to call back, than I care to count. "And for clarification, it's not Doc doing my rehab. It's Scout. Whoever the fuck Scout is, because I've made some calls, been asking around, and I can't find shit on her other than she's his daughter. *His daughter*, Finn? Not some topnotch professional who is scheduled out for months in advance because she's everyone's go-to. Look, I'm not one to knock taking up the old man's profession because . . . well, *because pot meet kettle*. But taking over and actually being as good as him are two entirely different things. The club promised they'd get me the best physical therapist after the bullshit I had to put up with from the other one. Second best isn't the best, Finn. This is my arm we're talking about here. My career, so—"

"The same arm you want to chance by thumbing your nose at the club's protocol and declaring yourself ready to go without the therapist's consent, right?"

Fuck. Finn's got me there. I roll my shoulders in reflex and hate that there's that slight stab of pain when I do—my constant reminder that I'm not ready to play, and yet that's all I want to do to get my life back to its norm.

"Easton." He sighs. "You agreed to the terms and have to abide by the parameters now."

His disapproving tone grates on my nerves. "We've gone over this." *What feels like a million times.*

"Well, you're the one who signed the papers—"

"You're goddamn right I did. They carted me off the field and the pain was so brutal I would've signed anything for them to get the oxy quicker to dull it some; so don't chastise me like I did something stupid. You would've done the same exact thing."

His silence is more irritating than his disapproving tone. "I would have at least read the papers first."

"Yeah. Yeah. I know. But I didn't, and now I'm forced into their rehab guidelines. Can they really put a deadline on when I have to return? It's not like everyone heals the same."

"Should they? No. Can they? Well, you signed the paper that said you'd be back by August first, so yes, now, they technically can."

I roll my shoulders, pissed at myself for signing it, at him for his constant nagging over it, and at all the shit that can't be changed. "And if I'm not ready by then?"

"I told you, they can trade you."

"And you also told me during the last negotiation that I had an iron-clad contract, Finn. Eight years with an extension option."

"It is iron-clad. . . but then you went and signed the first papers they put in front of you without reading them, and—"

"It wasn't like . . . you don't understand." Frustrated, I pinch the bridge of my nose and close my eyes to shut out the stadium laid out before me, taunting me. "It doesn't matter. I don't quite understand this new general manager yet, but I guess it's his new protocol."

"What is?" he asks. "Making a player sign something when his arm was just ripped apart? Sounds pretty callous if you ask me. What's the purpose? Is dotting all your I's and crossing all your T's really that important in that moment?"

"You're preaching to the choir, dude."

"Everyone says he's the best there is when it comes to this kind of thing, and there's no way they can all be crazy, so hang in there."

"Easier said than done," I gripe.

"Yeah well, the bright side is that it typically takes him three years to successfully restructure an organization before he moves on to the next one."

"Three years?" *Fuck.*

"Let's just hope all these new policies and strategies are worth it. I expect to see a pennant won before he leaves."

"Always looking for the diamond in a pile full of cow patties aren't you, Finn?

"One of us has to."

"Strategies are one thing, but treating your players with respect is another. Giving me a finite amount of time to rehab and return to the starting line-up is definitely not a way to show me respect." Everything about the situation pisses me off and rubs me the wrong way.

"I know. The timeframe is most likely Cory's way to add a bit of pressure so you get back on the field as soon as possible. After all, you're their star player."

"He does know this is my job, right? Star player or not, I'm a big boy who's well aware of what my fucking obligations are."

"He does. I promise you I gave him an earful over this. But look at the positive, he listened to you and brought in Doc—hired him exclusively for your rehabilitation. That shows just how much the club wants—no, *needs*—you back to help them win that pennant he's promised the city."

"Perhaps. But if they wanted me back so desperately, it would be Doc here, not his daughter."

"She wouldn't be here if she wasn't qualified. You sound like a prima donna. You wanted a different physical therapist and you got one. Suck it up, Wylder. You've got less than three months to get your spikes back between the chalk lines, so use the resources they got for you and quit—"

"My bitching," I finish for him as I scrub a hand through my hair and look out at the empty stadium. "You're right. Sorry."

"Don't be."

"This is getting fucking old. I'm stuck on the DL, being pressured to return on a timeline by the club I've played for my whole career, and all because I decided to go for home and try to score the extra run? Santiago didn't even have the goddamn ball when he blocked the plate. So what? He fucks over me and my arm both in one goddamn dirty play, and all the fucker gets is a hundred-grand fine and a four-game suspension? You want to know why I'm in a crappy mood? It's because I'm getting the shit end of the stick here, with no damn clue why he did it."

I know he's heard it all before. My bitching and moaning over the injury. Over being taken from my game, my life, and forced to sit here on a daily basis and watch it play on without me.

"I can't tell you why Santiago has a beef with you . . . but he does. That's pretty damn evident."

"No shit. Sorry," I say for what feels like the tenth time. "I'm just having a pity party."

"I get it, East. You want back out there."

"Like fucking yesterday."

"I know dude, but I can't make your arm heal any faster. You've had the best surgeons, the best resources, and now you'll have the best physical therapist there is in baseball."

"But—"

"You think Doc's going to risk his career by ruining yours? If he sent his daughter to rehab you, then no doubt she's qualified to get you back. Just ride it out. Put your earphones on if you need to, listen to one of those damn audiobooks that I can't for the life of me understand how you listen to, and tune her out . . . but put in the hours. Get better. And you'll be back before you know it."

Easier said than done.

"Yeah. Sure."

I end the phone call, lean back into the hard plastic of the stadium seat, and prop my feet on the empty row in front of me.

And I dare to look at what I'm missing out on. The nets of the backstop fade away as I stare at the place where I've lived my life—between the chalk lines and behind home plate.

It's fucking beautiful. A blessing and a curse. My pleasure and my pain.

The only thing I've ever known.

The only thing I've ever wanted to do.

I lose myself to my thoughts. Time passes, minutes ticking down to the next Aces' game tonight that I won't be playing in. And like every night my team plays without me, I fight the rage of helplessness that corners my mind.

I know he's there. I can sense him before I hear the creak of the seat a few down from mine, followed by the clearing of his throat. I don't glance his way—unsure if I want to deal with his bullshit just yet—so I nod instead of speaking.

"By the length of time you've been sitting out here, and the fact that you're not in the team meeting right now, am I right to assume you haven't gotten cleared to play yet?"

"Hi, Dad. How're you doing today?"

"I take that as a no?"

"What do you think?"

"Don't be a smartass." There is no humor in his tone. No smile warming his voice.

"I'm not. I'm here. They're there. And it's been two days since the last time you asked the same exact question you asked me three days before that, so do you really think that I've miraculously recovered since then?"

Definitely not in the mood to put up with his shit.

"The team—"

"Dad, there are more things in life than baseball." I look his way for the first time. I give no smile, no nod, just a lift of my eyebrows behind my sunglasses in a half-hearted attempt to mask my need for him to just be my dad and not the baseball great, Cal Wylder.

"Like what, son? Do you have a family you go home to every night? *No.* This club is your family. Your teammates are your brothers. And you're currently letting them down by not showing up to the table with dinner every night."

Ah. Tough love, Wylder-style. Gotta love that. But then again, I shouldn't expect any less. It was always one more fly ball, one more throw down to second, one more *let's do it until you get it right, son*, before we could eat lunch, eat dinner, or go home.

In an effort to avoid the recurring fight between us, I look away and rest my head on the seat back. It's much easier to focus on the blue sky above and feeling sorry for myself than deal with him. "Sorry, Pops. While I inherited your skill with a ball, I sure as hell didn't inherit your godlike ability to heal."

"Maybe you're not putting in enough time at the gym, then. It takes dedication to come back from an injury. You know, if you get the muscles strong around the tear, they will help take the pressure off the cuff."

"Got it." I clench my jaw.

"Every day you're off the field gives another player an opportunity to steal your starting position. You have to be vigilant against that."

"Sure thing."

"I'm serious, Easton. This is important, so you better start treating it that way." Funny how no matter how many times he's used this phrase over the years, it still jolts me back to being eight years old and on the mound in Little League, the tears of frustration in my eyes because I couldn't make the ball hit the strike zone, and him telling me I wasn't trying hard enough. And how, well over an hour after the last inning ended, he sat on the bucket behind home plate and demanded ten strikes in a row before we could go home.

I hated him that day.

I respected him later for it, but I hated him that day.

Kind of like now. Not much has changed.

"I get you're serious. No doubt there, Dad. Good thing the front office is, too, since they just brought in Doc to help my rehab."

"Hmm," he murmurs, and it takes everything in me to keep my eyes closed and wait for whatever I've got coming next. That sound from him is never followed with a benign statement. "Doc, huh? Let's hope you don't blow off three sessions with him like you did the trainer you had before. That'd be grounds for the club to cut you."

"They're not going to cut me, Dad." But he's planted the seed, and I know it will haunt me tonight when I can't sleep. "Besides, I skipped out because I didn't have a choice. I had to take care of Mom."

I wait to hear the disapproval that always falls from his mouth, but it doesn't come. In fact, nothing does, and I'm not sure if the silence makes me grateful or worried.

"It's a shame your mother's . . . *problem* . . . is affecting your career."

I grit my teeth and hold back the sigh I'm certain every child of divorce knows by heart when one parent disses the other. "Yeah, well . . . her *problem* was a result of things beyond my control. She was alone and fell. Someone had to take care of her. And, for your information, I didn't skip out on my appointments. I called in, got my training, and did it on my own time."

He clears his throat, his universal sound for "not buying it," but I don't really fucking care right now. I love him more than anything, but most days I loathe him, and his demanding expectations, too.

"It's not the same. You have to be present, be seen. The club isn't happy, Easton . . ." He lets his phrase fade off, but it will still fertilize the goddamn seed he planted. "Your bat was on fire. You had the streak going, you were picking off runners left and right, and your pitch calls were perfection. Every day you're gone is another day those facts are forgotten, and in a game of statistics, that's worrisome."

"And here I thought you were going to pay me a compliment and just leave it at that. I should have known better."

"Easton." My name is a warning. A demand for respect. One I've heard more times than I can count. And yet there is something underlying it that I can't quite pinpoint.

"Such a shame my rotator cuff was ripped apart. Must have been my fault that prick yanked it backward on the tag. Should I have called time-out on the way down and asked him to hurt something else instead? Break a bone because that heals easier than tendons? Is that what I was supposed to do, Dad? Would that have met your expectations?" My voice escalates with each word, my frustrated anger loud and clear. And fuck, yes, I'm being disrespectful, but so is he, and I'm sick of hearing it.

Silence descends around us in this house I grew up in, under the shadow of the iron giant sitting beside me, who ruled this stadium his entire career. I look out to where his number, twenty-two, adorns the center field wall in retirement, and wonder if I'll ever live up to the expectations he set out for me that day on the mound when I was eight.

I'm not quite sure.

"Look, you're right." He sighs instead of apologizing. "I just want the best for you, Easton. I always have. I hate that you're injured. I hate that your shoulder's not coming along as quickly as it should. And I hate that I'm here and there's nothing I can do to help you."

I look over to him, see his dark hair with silver at the temples and his eyes that match mine, and know he means well. The hard-ass with a son who can carry on the legacy he left when he retired.

"You can just be my dad. That will help me."

And yet I know there's no separating Cal, the three-thousand-hit player, from Cal, Easton's father.

They're one and the same.

Always have been.

Always will be.

CHAPTER THREE

Scout

Each thump of his stride on the treadmill irritates me more than the last. Every grunt of exertion adds to it.

And then there's the beep. The one that tells me his thirty minutes of high intensity running is complete, and now it's my turn to get hands on and complete the session.

Lucky me.

I'm irritable. Pissed off. And I'm not sure if my current mood stems from exhaustion after spending too many hours last night Googling Easton Wylder, or the fact that it seems he was doing the same about me.

"So are you actually going to touch my arm today, or is the expertise you bragged about yesterday limited to telling me *treadmill, thirty minutes, level ten*? If you wanted to avoid me, then maybe you should call in sick for the next few months." Sarcasm drips from his voice. His obvious disdain for me makes that even keel I thought we might have found yesterday seem nonexistent.

I need to turn around, to face him, but I stall. The images from Google are seared in my mind. The charity calendar where the month of April is a picture of him wearing nothing but a strategically placed baseball glove. The ESPN body issue where he's batting—naked—the twist of his legs hiding his package. The ESPYs with him looking dashing in a three-piece suit. All of them are there, floating around, reminding me how all those hard lines and toned edges look in person.

And it would take a dead woman to not be affected by him.

So, I steel myself for the visceral impact of looking at him—hot, sweaty, relaxed—but it doesn't help when I turn around. I'm not sure anything could. Because even in his sweat-dampened T-shirt, he's still breathtakingly handsome with his mixture of all-American and rugged outdoorsman. He still exudes that tinge of arrogance. And the odd thing is how today when I look at him, after I've stared at pictures of him for hours yesterday, somehow the arrogance adds to his appeal.

And then he smirks, and I shake my head and question my own sanity.

"So you actually want me to look at your arm? You mean you'll trust me with it? And here I was under the impression you thought I was just a *trophy trainer.*"

"Come again?" He chuckles.

Time to clear the air between us. Being handsome doesn't override being an asshole. "You know, *trophy trainer*—someone good for you to look at, but incapable of much else."

He shrugs. "If the shoe fits."

I take a step closer to him, his sarcastic comeback igniting the embers of my temper he lit yesterday. "Don't be a jerk. If you want to find out if I'm qualified for the job—capable of getting you back in top form—then you *ask me* for my credentials. You want a resume? You want references? I'd be glad to hand you a list of them, so don't go snooping around, making phone calls, and questioning everything about me without talking to me first. *Got it?*"

Our eyes hold as he worries his bottom lip between his teeth to combat the smile he's fighting. "You want me to take my rehab seriously, right? Then don't chastise me for making sure the person charged to do it is up to par and has the right experience. I don't trust my body with just anyone, let alone a rookie trainer still learning the ropes. *Got it?*"

"Touché," I murmur as we wage a visual war of defiance and misunderstanding. "We're wasting time. Let's get started."

Maybe if we begin, I'll forget about the phone calls I received last night. The ones from previous clients and personal friends I'd rehabbed informing me I was being vetted. I was thankful for the heads-up, and at the same time, I was pissed that he was questioning my qualifications.

But he did just make a damn good point.

I grab the ultrasound cart and wheel it toward the table, but he's still standing there like yesterday, still questioning me. Obviously, he doesn't believe I'm experienced enough to do the job, but I shrug it off, knowing after my rebuke of him, he was bound to either respect me or test me, and by the current standoff, I'm guessing it will be the latter.

"Yes?" I finally ask when he doesn't budge.

"You wanna tell me where Doc is?"

"He's got a packed schedule on the East Coast right now. As you know, injury happens without warning." I hold his gaze and hope he doesn't see through the lie.

"Uh-huh." He just nods, but I can tell he's not convinced. He's the one who made the calls last night, so I'm certain he has pieced together that it's been a while since Doc's been around. But there must be something in my eyes he sees—the something I'm trying desperately to keep together—that prevents him from digging deeper. "He's the best there is," Easton says.

"Agreed."

"Should I be worried then?"

"About?" I prompt.

"If he's the best, then doesn't that mean you're second best?"

His remark hits closer to home than I'd like, but it's his body, his career, and his right to ask.

"Second best to Doc Dalton isn't a bad place to be. I learned everything I know from the man. I assure you, he's the last person I want to let down, and you're the beneficiary of that fear, so . . ." I quirk my brows. "Lucky you."

"Lucky me," he murmurs but still doesn't move. "The problem is I still don't know shit about you, and yet you're standing there ready to work on my arm."

"What do you want to know?" I'm getting impatient. Another day, another round of bullshit, and once again, time is wasting. But at least he listened and is asking me instead of snooping around for answers.

"What were your stats in the major leagues?"

"*What?*"

"I asked your stats. Errors. On-base percentage. Batting average. Fielding percentage. You know, statistics."

"I know what statistics are," I respond dryly.

"But if you've never played in the majors, how do you know how my arm's supposed to feel so that you can get it back to one hundred percent?"

He's neglecting the fact that no other trainer has played in the major leagues either . . . but I have a better way to shut him up. "Have you ever been a woman?"

"*What?*" It's his turn to be surprised by an unexpected question. "Of course not. I've got plenty of proof that I'm all man."

I roll my eyes, half expecting him to grab his crotch and equally relieved that he doesn't. "Well, if you've never been a woman, how is it you know how to please one in bed? How do you know if you're hitting the right spot? Getting her off?"

He fights back a bark of a laugh, but eventually lets it escape as he just shakes his head. "Touché," he repeats my word back to me.

"If you're going to bust my chops, Wylder, you should know that I can give as good as I get."

"Point taken. But since you're the one singlehandedly charged with busting my balls in rehab over the next three months, you've gotta admit, it was a valid question."

"It was," I concede, "but it's your job to talk to me, tell me how it feels, where it hurts, and when it feels good, so I can make it better." An unexpectedly shy smile slides onto his lips when he gets the correlation between my question about how to please a woman and my answer.

"Just like sex."

"Perhaps." I smile; it's all I can do as heat flushes my cheeks and the room around us becomes too small for him and this innuendo-laced conversation. "Some men have all the tools in the world, but if they don't know how to use them, they're useless. It's the same with my job. You've gotta know how to use your skills, and I assure you, I do. So, if the I-don't-trust-you-because-you-have-a-vagina-card has been exhausted, can we get started, please?" I lift my chin toward the table behind him while I adjust the settings on the machine.

"You drive a hard bargain, *Kitty*." He chuckles as he sits down and pulls off his shirt.

"You ain't seen nothing yet."

Nothing more is said between us as I apply the ultrasound gel and then the wand to his shoulder, despite being all too aware that he's still staring at me.

I welcome the silence, using it to concentrate on the task at hand as I move the wand over the joint of his shoulder, across the angry red seam there and back, several times over. Players enter the locker room beyond where we are. I can hear their chatter—the low whistles, the suggestive laughs, the one-off comments—but know better than to give them attention. It may be a different clubhouse, but it's basically the same reaction I typically get.

I knew I'd have a tough crowd to win over when I followed in my father's footsteps. I knew being a woman in this male-dominated world wouldn't be a walk in the proverbial ballpark. And so I ignore the comments like I always have and choose to consider them compliments, while letting the more suggestive ones go. In a practiced move, I keep my eyes focused on the player I'm working on and my back to the lockers to avoid any pecker peep-shows, which I learned long ago are inevitable.

It saves me embarrassment and preserves the respect I have to command to be taken seriously.

"Relax," I murmur as I run the ultrasonic waves back and forth to reduce inflammation. For some reason, he keeps tensing up, and it's counteracting the therapy I'm providing.

There's another comment behind my back. Something good-humored about another wand in his jock I could put to better use.

If the guy's going to be a chauvinist, at least he's witty about it.

I stifle a laugh. It's all I can do. But it's Easton who visibly tenses in reaction.

Apparently, he can dish it out, but doesn't want anyone else to.

Interesting.

And sweet.

He seems to be upset on my behalf, and yet yesterday he was the one who thought I was a stripper here to entertain him.

Good thing I didn't take the bait, then. I was ready to kiss you senseless just to call your bluff and prove you were a stripper.

His words come back to me—the ones that repeated through my mind at random times yesterday, which then led to my Google search on him. My hands touch him now, but my mind recalls the charity calendar I found—him in all his gorgeous, naked glory.

Another comment somewhere in the locker room.

Another bristle by him.

And the irony isn't lost on me. He's getting pissed on my behalf, and I'm thinking of what he looks like naked. Well, almost naked. My imagination fills in exactly what is beneath the baseball glove.

And, of course, now *I* blush.

"Where did you leave off with your previous trainer?" I ask to try and break the tension that's becoming more and more evident in the tightening of his muscles.

"We were throwing the ball."

"All out?"

"At about fifty, sixty percent."

"Hitting any?"

"A bit, at about seventy percent."

"Okay." I draw the word out, pleased he speaks my lingo. "Tell me how it felt when you did those things."

"Frustrating."

"If you're going to make love to me Wylder, you're gonna need to do a helluva lot more than that to get me off." His head whips up, shocked hazel eyes meeting my gray ones, and I know I've got his attention now. I continue. "Explain. Why was it frustrating? Did it hurt? Was there a pinch, or was it just tight from not being used? Or was it mental? It's bound to feel different, so is it the fear of reinjuring yourself that's holding you back?"

He struggles with what to say, his eyes narrowing as he looks away. I lower the wand and wipe the excess gel from his shoulder. "How about all of the above?" he finally says.

"That's a fair answer. I tell you what—how about we stretch it today, go through some new exercises that you might not have done yet, and then tomorrow we take it to the field and get a ball in that hand of yours?"

"Really?" He sounds like a little boy finding out he gets to play after sitting on the bench for the last six innings. It breaks my heart and fills it simultaneously.

"Really." I walk around to the back of him and begin to move his arm to feel for any clicking or popping with the movement in his rotator cuff. "Let's get started then."

"So, I think it's on the right track," I say with a conclusive nod, needing to step away from him and the connection that our bodies have had for the better part of ninety minutes.

I've worked his arm every which way and now have a better grasp on what I need to do to strengthen it. How to make a plan of attack.

"It might be a bit sore later and tomorrow. Your hissing tells me I pushed you a little further than your previous trainer did, but I'm pleased with how solid the repair feels. We just need to get you back into the routine slowly, and then the motions will begin to feel natural again."

"Does that mean I get to throw a ball tomorrow?"

"It does, indeed." His smile is lightning-quick in response, and completely disarming.

I've seen Easton-the-skeptic's smile. I've even seen the Easton-thinks-he's-being-played smile. But Easton's I-get-to do-what-I-love-tomorrow smile is bright enough to light up the room.

"Easton. My man. You doing good?" Luckily we're interrupted so I stop staring at him. J.P. Gaston, another player, walks into our training room. He grabs hands with Easton in some kind of handshake and pulls him in for a manly hug before slapping him on the back in greeting.

"Hanging in there. Way to kick ass last night. Your bat's on fire, man."

"Don't jinx me, dude. Bad juju is everywhere these days."

"Look who you're talking to," Easton says with a shake of his head. "I feel like I've been swimming in it for months. My luck has to return soon."

"Fucking bad juju," J.P. says with a laugh before leaning closer to Easton and murmuring so I can barely hear it, "But dude, the DL has never looked as appealing as it does right now."

"Watch Guzman's slider tonight," Easton says, talking right over the comment as if he didn't hear it. "I was studying him against the Yankees the other night, and it's starting to float some."

"Ah, the beloved hanging curveball," J.P. says as he takes a few steps backward toward the door. He slides his eyes my way and offers up a smile before looking back to Easton. "Good thing I know how to swing my stick."

Easton picks up his shirt sitting beside him, balls it up, and throws it at him, just as he darts out of the doorway and past the windows, into the depths of the now-full clubhouse. I avoid the natural inclination to watch him, because the pregame ritual has started out there, and that means men in varying stages of undress, shooting the shit as they mentally prepare for their night of work.

"Hot damn. She's as hot up close? Shit," someone says loud enough for me to hear. Seems that J.P. was the one elected to come on in and get a closer look at the new female trainer.

There's one in every clubhouse.

"Hurt me, baby," someone else cries out.

"Oh, Easton. Let me stretch you and bend you and do naughty things to you," another teammate mimics in a high-pitched voice.

Without glancing up, I lift my middle finger to the men, who I'm more than sure are watching and waiting to see my reaction from their schoolyard ribbing. Laughter rumbles through the locker room at my response, but I hear a muttered, "Goddammit," beneath Easton's breath.

"Let me guess? Tino and Drew?" I ask, completely unfazed.

"Yep," he sighs with a roll of his eyes.

"Good to see they've matured since high school," I say lightheartedly as I continue to put the ultrasound machine away. But when I turn back around, I'm stopped in my tracks by the look on his face. His expression is guarded, and yet there's something about it—a hint of surprise maybe—that holds my feet still and my attention hostage. "What is it?"

"Just trying to figure you out, is all," he says with a shake of his head.

"There's not much to figure."

"I disagree."

"Well, you're wrong," I say as I spray disinfectant on the table and start to wipe it down, anything to avoid the softening of his eyes and the questions I don't want to answer. "I'm boring. A what-you-see-is-what-you-get kind of girl."

"Except you wear your heart on your sleeve." My hand falters mid-motion then I continue to clean with a renewed vigor, but he doesn't turn to leave like I had hoped. "You come off tough as nails, like you don't let shit get to you, and yet that heart you're wearing says there's a helluva lot more than the tough exterior does."

"And your point?"

"Nothing. Just making an observation."

Those words scrape nerves already raw after the last few months. Comebacks and rebukes all swirl in my head, but every single one of them is on the defensive. And while the defensive implies he's right—*and he is right*—I sure as hell don't want to let him know that.

This is work—the reputation I'm trying to establish. And he's a client who holds the ticket to achieve two of my goals.

"Scout and Easton sitting in a tree, k-i-s-s-i-n-g," someone sings above the fray outside the door.

"Let it rest, guys," Easton shouts over his shoulder.

"It's fine," I say.

"Of course it is. Anything to save you from having this discussion, right?"

"There's nothing wrong with wearing your heart on your sleeve." I may say the words to play it off, but my tone doesn't sound as forgiving.

"Sorry." He sighs. "For what I said . . . and for the assholes."

"Don't be. I'm here for you. Not them." I risk a glance their way and smile. "Hopefully none of them get hurt, because I'd be a lot less gentle if I have to rehab them." I get the chuckle from him I was working for and hope the discussion is now buried.

"Good to know, but I'm sorry, anyway. We can train somewhere else if you want. Or if it bugs you, I'll have a talk with them."

"No need to . . . but thank you for the thought. Besides, it seems like their ribbing is minor compared to the legendary pranks you've pulled on them."

"True." His lips break into a smug smile. "But it's not fair to you."

"Don't worry about me. I'm a big girl. I can handle myself. I've got a sword tucked in my purse in case I need to slay any dragons."

"Your purse?"

"Yeah, it's big and roomy." I smile, more than glad to change the subject, as I grab said purse from the cupboard I stashed it in.

"Keep anything else in there besides a sword?"

"High heels," I joke, earning a raise of his brows. "This girl likes her heels when she's kicking ass."

"Gotta love a woman who's multidimensional. You heading out, too?" he asks, but neither of us makes a move to leave as his eyes continue to ask more questions than I want to answer or even acknowledge.

Suddenly flustered by the intensity of his stare, I begin to ramble. "So, alternate ice and heat every twenty minutes or so for the next few hours. That will help with the swelling and inflammation I caused today. Okay?"

I take a few steps, as if the conversation is over, but Easton doesn't move out of my way. He just stands there, eyes still searching, continuing to pull at parts of me that need to stay put.

I lick my lips. I shift my feet.

"I know the drill," he finally says.

But we still don't move.

"Same time tomorrow."

"Okay."

Quit looking at me like that.

"And depending on how the week goes, we might bump up our sessions to twice a day."

"Okay."

You've run out of things to say, Scout. Time to go now.

"Well, I'll see you then. Tomorrow, I mean." I roll my eyes at myself.

"Obviously. Tomorrow, I mean." A half-cocked smile turns up one corner of his mouth.

Move. Go. Walk.

"You're nothing like I expected." I cringe once I realize I've just blurted my thoughts out and hate myself the minute I do. My cheeks flush with heat, but my embarrassment gives me the motivation I need to take the first step away from him.

"I'm never what anyone expects. It's a blessing and a curse."

His comment begs me to ask more, but I don't. Can't. This space is too small for us—it feels like there's not enough air when he looks at me that way.

"Good night."

"'Night, Scout," he says as I reach the doorway. "Hey . . ."

"Yeah?" I turn around, one hand on the doorjamb, my eyes falling back on him.

"For the record, how is it you know that I know how to please a woman in bed?"

Crap. I walked right into that one.

The cocky grin he flashes me is the lasting image burned into my mind as I walk away without a word.

Because I know.

CHAPTER FOUR

Scout

"Hi. How are you doing?"

"What's the assessment?"

I fight back the tears that burn at hearing his voice again and knowing, even now, he's still putting the business between us. I take a deep breath to control the emotions spiraling out of control, because I know he'll get upset if he hears a waver in my voice when I answer.

"Scouty?"

"Yeah, Dad. I'm here." He may only be a two-hour drive away, but right now it feels like a million.

"And?" he presses.

How are you?

I miss you?

Are you in pain?

Are you getting worse?

I'd rather be there with you than here.

"Clear mind. Hard heart."

I clench my jaw when he repeats the mantra he expects me to live by, and I sense the rebuke is because he knows I'm about to fall apart. Of course he knows. He knows me better than anyone.

I clear my throat, compose myself, and then try my best to be what he needs me to be right now. "Easton Wylder. Four months post-op from a torn labrum. The onset of injury was due to a questionable play by the opposing team when the patient was sliding into home plate. He was tagged unnecessarily, arm hooked by the opponent and yanked backward with force. The injury presented immediately and surgery commenced within twenty-four hours. Easton completed his initial three-plus months of post-op rehab, but was not cleared for play by the previous physical therapist. Upon initial observation, he seems to have good mobility. I'd say he's at eighty-five percent. The joint seems stiff, as is to be expected after restricted use, but during stretching would allow me to push its limits, which indicates that full mobility is within reach. The patient has indicated that in previous attempts to bat and throw he has felt pain. I plan on getting a ball back into his hand as quickly as possible to work on the mental aspect, because I feel he is holding back for fear of re-injury. Prognosis is good, but I need more time with him to know if my assessment is accurate or not." Confident I've covered the bases, I wait for my dad's feedback.

His rattle of breath reaches through the line and draws out my need for approval.

"You mean *the player*, right?" It's all he says, and I die a little inside.

"What?"

"You said Easton."

"I did?"

"Yes. Twice."

"Yes. Once for the patient introduction and the other was a simple mistake."

"Scout. How many times do I have to tell you that you're to remain impartial?"

"I am. I was. His name's in my notes. I was looking at them and accidentally repeated what I saw."

"Don't let it happen again."

"Yes. I won't."

"And questionable play. Why add that in? It's not your job to decide what's questionable or dirty or accidental. It's your job to get your player back to optimum performance, not to pass judgment."

"I know, but the play was dirty, Dad. You can't argue that."

"Do you like him, Scout?"

The question catches me off guard, and I'm uncertain what exactly he means by it. "I've only just met him." It's a safe answer.

"But do you like him? Is he going to work hard? Does he want to return? Or is he a prima donna riding his dad's coattails with no respect for the sport?"

"You're kidding me, right?" I stutter. "The man plays with more heart than anyone I've seen in a long time. He's a throwback. A real gamer. The guy you want at bat when you're bottom of the ninth, full count, with the World Series on the line."

"You're too close, Scout." It's all he says, but it's enough to make me realize how ardently I just defended a man who, seconds before, I said I barely knew. Did I just prove my dad's point that maybe I'm already too close, because Easton's just another player and it's my job to get him ready.

But he isn't just another player.

He's the player who can give me what I need to fulfill my dad's wishes.

And he's the man who has invaded my thoughts and taken residence there.

"That's the player you're talking about. What about the man?"

It's the oddest of questions for my dad to ask, and yet I feel like there is more to this conversation that I'm not quite getting the gist of. I take my time to respond. "Like I said, I've only assessed him twice, so I don't know him that well. First impression is that he's a good guy. I mean, he stood up for me when the guys were doing their usual bullshit about me being in the clubhouse."

"*Really?*" It's a leading question, but I don't buy into it. If he wants to ask me something, then he needs to ask it.

"Dad, what are you—"

"What's your plan of action with him moving forward?" he asks, as if I never even spoke. And while I hate being disregarded, this razor-sharp focus of his on a player has been gone more days than not, and so I acquiesce.

I sort through my thoughts, explain them point by point, and then outline what I plan to do with *the player*. My dad makes suggestions, and I take notes, heeding his advice on possible drills.

But I catch myself holding the phone to my ear with two hands and just listening. Memorizing the sound of his voice. The timbre of it. The little inflections only he has. I lose myself in the presence of the only person who has ever been a constant in my life.

"Sounds like a good plan, Scouty. You'll need to adjust as he does, though. Nothing good ever comes from setting your plans in stone."

"I know," I whisper, thinking of all the plans we'd made over the years for when he retired. And now that he unofficially has, we'll never get to fulfill them.

"Scout." It's a warning. A reprimand. A plea for me to toughen up.

I clear my throat. "He seems eager to return," I say to save face, in the hope that he'll see I'm unaffected by Easton. But before I can finish my thought, he erupts into a fit of coughing.

It sounds worse than last week. That's all I can think as that rattle makes chills race across my skin and dread sink in my stomach. The questions I want to pepper him with, but know he won't allow, are getting harder to bite back. The need to jump in the car and drop my foot like a lead weight on the gas until I'm beside him is getting tougher to resist.

"Daddy?" The word slips out in a whisper just like the lone tear that escapes and slides down my cheek.

"I'm fine, Scouty. Just fine. It's just the damn cough," he finally says when he catches his breath.

But it's so much more than that.

"What did the doctor say yesterday?" I ask, prepared for the rebuke.

"Did Sally tell you I had an appointment?" he barks.

"Someone has to." *Please. Talk to me.*

"Everything's the same. Nothing's going to change, so it's ridiculous to be worrying about me when you need to be worried about getting *the player* back up and behind the plate. It's a rarity to have a cuff tear when it's not a pitcher, so make sure you heed caution. And make sure to learn from it."

"Okay," I agree, but my mind is lost searching his voice for what he's not telling me. Did the doctor tell him he has less time left than he thought? Is that why he won't talk about it?

The notion stuns me when I've already been stunned enough over the past few months. And I'm so lost in my fear that I almost miss his soft words when he speaks them.

"I'm counting on you. I know it's a lot to ask . . . and I'd do it if I could . . ."

Words escape me as the tears slide freely down my cheeks, and my heart twists inside my chest. "Dad." It's all I can say through the onslaught of emotion I'm trying to hold back.

"We'll talk soon. Clear mind, hard heart, Scouty. Remember that and you'll be fine."

But I won't.

I'll be far from it.

And that's why I'm more determined than ever.

CHAPTER FIVE

Easton

I nod my head and lift the neck of my beer in thanks to the knockout blonde across the bar who just sent it over.

"You need to jump all over that," Tino says with a little hum of appreciation to follow.

I smile at her—doe-eyed, legs for days, with a skirt pulled up and a shirt plunging down—and fuck, I could use a good lay right now. "Nah," I murmur, my mouth contradicting what my dick is agreeing to as I raise the bottle to my lips and look back to the guys at my table.

"Nah?" Drew sputters. "Since when do you say *nah* to a betty like that?"

Images flash through my mind. Challenging gray eyes. Muscular little body. Brown hair pulled up in a messy ponytail. A woman who isn't trying hard at all and is still sexier than the blonde baseball betty trying to add a notch to her *how many Austin Aces have I fucked* tally she most likely displays prominently on her bedpost.

"She's all yours, D. I'm sure she'd take you as a consolation," I tease as J.P. barks out in laughter at the fuck-you look Drew is trying to kill me with.

"Second is better than third," Drew replies with a direct dig at J.P., since he plays third base and Drew plays second.

"Fuck off." J.P. laughs but flips us off.

"Gladly. But I want to know why East here is passing up parting her sweet thighs when he obviously needs to get good and laid," Drew says with a lift of his chin to the blonde again.

"How do you know I need to get good and laid?"

"You've been on a permanent home stretch, which means your forearms are getting a workout, but not in the baseball sense." He demonstrates making a jacking-off motion.

"Fuck off." I roll my eyes.

"Dude, a homestretch like yours is enough to make anyone itch for some action, and since you can't get any on the field, you might as well get some between the sheets," Drew explains with perfect sense.

"Boredom makes your dick need action," Tino affirms, and I can't help but laugh at their fucked-up logic.

Fucked-up, but pretty damn accurate.

I catch Blondie's eye again, consider her, but know any chick buying me beers in Sluggers, our team's local hangout, is looking for more than a thank-you.

Could be fun.

"Ah, it all makes sense now."

J.P.'s murmur pulls me from making a mistake that I suddenly want to make . . .

"It's that fuck-hot trainer of yours that's grabbing you by the balls, isn't it?"

And knocks it out of the park, putting the image of Scout into my mind. Not like it was very far to begin with.

"Nah," I murmur. Hell if I'll give him the satisfaction of knowing he's right.

"Bullshit. Dude, I'd let her rub me down in a second. Add in some oil . . . and we could have our own slip and Drew-slide," Drew chimes in.

"You're fucked in the head," I laugh.

"That's the hope," he muses as he raises his eyebrows, "just a different kind of head."

Over my dead body.

My own thought knocks me back a step. Forces me to suck down my free beer and reconsider Blondie's unspoken, no-strings-attached offer, but now I can't. Not when Scout is in my head, and my dick's reacting to the thought of her more than the thought of the woman down the bar.

"For some reason I don't think Scout's into screwing the starting line-up," I say with an arch of my brow. "So hands to yourself, you grabby fucker." I hope my thinly veiled threat is heard, and at the same time not heard. Them knowing I have the hots for Scout will only make life in the clubhouse worse for her.

"I agree. If she was into that, she'd be out in the locker room flirting with everyone. Sucks for you, though." J.P. taps his beer against mine.

"Depends who's doing the sucking," I say, getting a laugh for the distraction.

"Well, rumor is you're her ticket to getting the Aces' contract," Drew says.

"Really?" He has my attention now.

"I heard that Doc's worked in every clubhouse in the majors except for ours. Supposedly by fulfilling this contract and getting you back on the field, he's angling for the club to sign him to run the team's PT program. Word is, he's never had a long-term contract with a club, but after a lifetime on the road, travelling from team to team to rehab their stars . . . a la *you*," he says with a nod, "he wants to end his career this way. Getting to stay in one place for a while."

"The perfect game to close out a pennant-winning career," I muse. Makes sense.

"Exactly."

"And how does his daughter play into all of this?"

"Not sure." Drew shrugs. "But if she's half as good as he is, it'd be more than good enough. Plus, dude, are you going to complain that you get that hot little body pressing up against you every day?"

My smile is automatic. "Not at all." I laugh.

"That's what I thought," he says as he motions to our waitress for another round. "Lucky for you, our lovely GM has given Sumo Sam his written notice. He's got ninety days and his contract is void."

"Thank Christ," I murmur, recalling the last time I let the team's lead physical therapist, Sam, touch my shoulder. At about three months post-op, my shoulder was nowhere close to where it should have been. Frustrated and feeling like I was spinning my wheels, I demanded to know why we were doing the same shit every day rather than try the new methodologies other clubhouses were using and having success with. I think back to how pissed he was that I questioned him. How he told me I wasn't healing because I wasn't putting in the time when in fact I was putting in so much time I was overdoing it. Such fucking bullshit.

"Sam doesn't know an elbow from an asshole," J.P. says.

"You're telling me."

"Yeah, Miller told me he overheard Cory tell Sam that the Aces are a forward-thinking organization and that from here on out he expects every member to subscribe to the idea or some bullshit like that. And how since Sam refused to educate himself on the newest trends—your shoulder rehab—then he was in breach of the fine print of his contract and would no longer have a position with the Aces."

"Asshole," I mutter.

"Which one? Sam or Cory?" Tino asks.

"Take your pick." I roll my eyes. "Look, I get bringing a new GM in to restructure the Aces' organization. It's always good to switch things up and trim costs after having the same people running the club for so many years. What I don't get is Cory. There's something about him I can't quite put my finger on."

"He's a bean counter." Drew shrugs. "He's a live by the contract, die by the contract, even when the words in the contract don't make any fucking sense, kind of guy. I get his job is all about dollars and cents, but this is *baseball* we're talking about here." He takes a long swig of his beer. "Then again I'm buzzed so what the fuck do I know?"

"A lot."

"I'm with you, East," Tino says. "The jury is still out on Cory. I mean . . . take Doc Dalton. The man has a legendary record of success. How fucked up is it that Cory is making him vet himself for the new long-term contract by getting an ugly fucker like Easton here back on the field?"

"Vet himself? Doc Dalton?" J.P. laughs in disbelief. "That's kind of funny."

"The man with the golden hands," I murmur, thinking of all the times I'd be on the road with my dad and watched Doc work his magic on opposing players.

"No doubt his daughter's hands . . . *and thighs*, are just as magical."

I hear the comment but my thoughts are on what Drew just said. On the fact that the club's new general manager is thinking of bringing Doc's team on board to run the club's physical therapy regimen. It's fucking great news, since I'll need the continued rehab.

But it's also daunting to have the final piece to this man's renowned career rely on whether I return to the roster within the mandated timeframe.

Nothing like adding a little more pressure or anything.

"If that's the case," I interject into the conversation that's moved on to the questionable call from the game earlier, "wouldn't Doc be here rehabbing me instead of Scout?"

Three pair of eyes angle my way. "You want man-hands on you instead of woman-hands?" Tino asks, and the table erupts into laughter.

"T, you're so hard up you'd take any hands at this point."

"At least I'm not a picky bastard like you," he replies.

"East has a point," J.P. says. "But considering I was thinking about pulling a groin tonight just so Scout could rub it out for me, my vote is to keep her around."

"Fucker," I chuckle. "You're vote's no good, though. Scout's here for me. *Only me*," I taunt. "So you're shit outta luck. Be my guest, though, and pull that muscle. I'm sure Sumo Sam would love to rub out your groin and maybe take a quick detour to find your dick while he's at it."

"Gonna need a magnifying glass for that," J.P. mocks.

Phones ding around the table and interrupt the conversation as we all move to see what's going on.

ESPN Alert: Trade rumors are swirling that Jose Santiago will likely be traded in the coming weeks.

"Fucker." My comment is repeated around the table as I stare at the name of the person responsible for my stint on the DL.

"God help whatever team he lands on," Drew says.

My phone alerts me again, and when I look at the screen, I sigh but for a completely different reason. *Not again.* "Sorry guys. Put mine on my tab. I've gotta head out."

"You good to drive, man?" Drew asks.

"Yeah. I only had two. I'm good."

Too much damn time to think.

About Santiago.

Scout.

If my arm's fucked up to the point of no return.

And only one of those thoughts on the hour drive to the outskirts of town is welcome. So, by the time I pull into the familiar gravel lot, tires crunching beneath me and the silver moonlight around me, I'm in no mood to face this. It's not like I have a choice though.

The slam of my truck door echoes as I stride up the pathway I know all too well.

"Sorry it took me so long, Marty," I say as I walk through his plume of cigarette smoke to where he's standing outside the rundown bar.

"No worries. She's not hurting anyone. Sissy called in sick tonight. I'm flying solo so I can't leave the bar to take her back to her place."

Same old song and dance. Just a different day.

The air, stale with cigarette smoke and cheap liquor, hits me the minute I open the ill-hanging wooden door and walk into the dimly lit bar. I spot her immediately. She's slumped in *her booth* with empty glasses littering the table in front of her.

"Mom."

She jumps at the sound of my voice, her eyes painted with too much makeup look up at me, and her lips, a bright red, turn up in a smile. *"Easton."* She says my name like it's the first time she's seen me in months—excited, grateful, and hopeful.

"Hi, Momma. You've gotta stop doing this," I tell her as I fake the same level of enthusiasm, my insides fucking exhausted from this dance.

"I know, but I was so excited that you won tonight!"

"I didn't play tonight. My arm's still hurt," I explain as I help her scoot from behind the table and wrap my arm around her waist to get her out the door.

"But you were playing on the TV. I was watching it. My handsome boy. You went three for three and picked two people off base. . ."

"Good night, Marty. Thanks for calling," I say as we pass by him.

"And I was so proud of you I thought I'd go and celebrate and wait for you to join me . . . and here you are!" She throws her hands up, her happiness sincere, as I usher her inside the cab of my truck.

We drive the quarter mile to her trailer in silence, but her smile remains wide. There's nothing else I can do other than squeeze the hand she's placed in mine, so giddy that I came home to her.

"You were watching a replay of one of my games on the DVR again," I tell her gently as I push open the unlocked door of her mobile home to find the TV on and the lights blazing.

"I was?" she asks, as if it's complete news to her, and a small part of me wonders if it's the alcohol making her forget, or if something is wrong with her mind. Both options scare the shit out of me.

"Yes, you were. I wish you'd let me move you out of here, Momma." I look around the double-wide mobile home she refuses to leave. The furniture is threadbare, the new pieces I've bought her returned time and again, and the wall opposite of us is lined with stacks of boxes filled with brand new things I've given her she refused to open.

"I don't need anything. I love it here," she murmurs as she sits on the edge of her bed and I wonder if she really does or she just believes her own lies. It takes me only a minute to find the makeup wipes and remove the paint from her face.

"There's my girl." I smile when she looks up at me, face bare, lips still in a smile to match mine. "So much prettier without all that gunk."

"A lady likes gunk, East."

"I know. I know." I take her shoes off, one by one. "I could move you near me. It would be so much nicer and safer for you, and I'd be able to keep an eye on you."

"Not gonna happen. I'm not gonna leave here. He'll come back for me some day, and I want to make sure he knows where I am when he does . . . much the same way you know where to find me each time."

"Who, Momma? Who is going to come back for you?" I reiterate the same question I've asked countless times over the years.

"The love of my life." Her voice is dreamy when she says it, and the sound tugs on my heart. What is it like to hold out hope for someone for this many years?

"And who's that?" I ask again, knowing she won't tell me, just as she never has in the past.

"Some things children aren't supposed to know," she says with a laugh. Her eyes are tired, but her smile remains. "You are always so good to me. I don't deserve you."

"You're talking nonsense now. It's time for you to get some sleep. You'll feel better in the morning."

"Are you gonna leave me?" she asks, voice wavering in panic.

"No. You know I'll never leave you. I'll be right here when you wake up."

I help to pull the covers over her, wipe her graying hair off her face, and stare at her for a few minutes as her smile slowly fades into sleep.

My sigh is heavy as I turn off the television, the lights, and then sink down on the lumpy couch she won't let me replace. Pulling the blanket she made from all my various team jerseys up to my chin, I listen for the soft rattle of her breath and wonder how many more years I'm going to allow myself to continue to do this.

"Night, Momma," I whisper like I used to when I was a little boy. And yet, this time I know no one is going to answer.

I'm the parent now.

Even when most days I still feel like the child.

CHAPTER SIX

Scout

"**F**aster. Faster," I shout as I watch pure male perfection move across the field.

Honed muscles ripple with pristine performance. His grunt echoes off the empty plastic seats around us. His cleats hit the base with a thump of sound.

When I click the stopwatch, I'm more than impressed with his time. "Not bad," I muse as I watch him from behind my mirrored lenses and wait for him to trot back over.

"Are you trying to kill me? What did I do to piss you off?" He pants the questions and then lifts a bottle and squeezes some water into his mouth.

"No and nothing," I answer as I hold up the stopwatch so he can see the display. "That's an impressive time."

He grunts in response as he swallows more water. "Not bad. But not my best. Are you going to explain what running bases has to do with rehabbing my arm?"

"When you run, you swing your arms without thinking about it. And swinging your arms moves your shoulder joint," I say, placing my hands on his arm to swing it and demonstrate the point. "And when you move your shoulder without tensing up, you also break up any scar tissue that might have built up in the joint. And that scar tissue is most likely what is giving you that pinching feeling when we toss the ball around."

"Huh."

"That doesn't sound like you're convinced, but I don't need you to be convinced, I just need you to not feel the pain."

"I'm still sticking with the 'you're pissed at me' theory." He angles his head and takes a step closer. "Or at the world. I just haven't decided which one you're taking out on me right now."

I bristle, hating that he can read me so easily when I've put an enormous amount of effort into trying to appear perfectly fine these past few days. But I haven't been fine. I've been far from it. I'm pissed at my dad, angry that he's shutting me out when all I need is to be closer to him. I despise that I have to hear secondhand from his caretaker, Sally, that the cold he's caught has set him back a few steps. I hate that my brother's birthday is coming up, another year gone by, making the memories even fuzzier.

So, yeah, Easton's right; I am pissed at the world. Obviously, I'm doing a shitty job of hiding it.

"C'mon, let's get you stretched out." *Conversation over.* I turn my back to him and walk to the foul line on the outfield grass. I could have stretched him perfectly fine where we were standing, and yet I needed the distraction to avoid him looking at me more closely and seeing that he's right.

"Classic avoidance. I get it."

"No, you're just *the player.*" The comment slips off my tongue, more a reminder to myself than meant for him. The disdain tingeing my tone is intended for my dad, but I'm taking it out on Easton instead.

How can you be mad at a man who is dying?

"*The player?*" Easton's voice is right behind me, and I cringe. He definitely heard me.

Crap.

"Don't ask."

"No, please. I'm intrigued."

"It's just a classic Doc Dalton idiosyncrasy." I keep my back turned to him as tears burn in my eyes. Moments ago I was mentally lashing out at my dad, angry at the world, and in a matter of seconds, I'm smiling bittersweetly at the quirk so representative of my father.

I can hold it together most days, push the grief aside, not believe the prognosis, but for some reason, this week it has hit me hard.

Clear mind. Hard Heart.

Shove it away, Scout. Not here. Not now.

"Isn't that how all fathers are?"

There's a surprising bite to his tone, and yet I'm too preoccupied with my own world to delve deeper into his. I clear my throat, push the emotion away, and turn around to face him.

"How does your shoulder feel?" *Time to change topics.*

His laugh rings out across the empty field and gets lost in the vastness of the stadium. "You really don't like talking about yourself, do you?"

His smile is genuine when I meet his eyes, and I hate that it pulls on me to say more. But I can't. I won't. "No."

Without another word, I begin his routine. I work in silence—my hands on his body, his heartbeat against my palm—feeling for the bunching of muscles as I pull and push and work through the tightness in his shoulder. The hiss of his breath is my only gauge to know when I've pushed him too far.

"How does this feel?" I position myself behind him, our bodies pressed against each other's, enabling me to manipulate his larger frame.

"What's bugging you?"

I ignore his question. "Is it tight? Sore? Is that pinch still up in the top part of the cuff?"

"You're upset. That much is obvious."

"I'm fine. Can we get back to you and your shoulder? To my job." My tone is clipped. "What's hurting you?"

"I don't know. What's hurting *you*?"

I falter, trying to grasp that he's really going to push the issue, and just when I realize I've stopped moving—one hand resting atop his shoulder, the other on his bicep—he turns to face me.

Now we're body to body, my breasts brushing against his chest while his eyes search mine for the secrets I keep. And we're close, too close, but neither of us step away. It's just him and me inside a sunlit stadium with thousands of empty seats as bystanders.

His breath catches. My pulse races. I look away in a desperate attempt to avoid his question and ignore the sudden hum of desire snapping within me like a broken power line twisting in a storm.

Not desperate enough, though, to step back.

"Uh-uh." Easton's finger is on my chin, lifting my face so that my eyes scrape over the day-old growth on his chin, up to those lips, and on to the curiosity in his eyes. "What is it, Scout?"

Our gazes lock. Hold. Question without speaking. Sympathize despite not knowing what the other needs.

And it's odd because we've stood like this dozens of times over the past week. When I'm stretching him in warm-up, midway through our exercises, after we throw the ball around for a bit, and again after our routine is completed—but for some reason, this time there's an intimacy to it.

It's unnerving. It's exciting. *It can't happen.*

Seconds pass before it hits me where we are, what might be happening— *what I think I want to happen*—and I push away from him as quickly as I can. The connection is broken.

But the desire remains.

"Sorry." I shake my head, and without another word, I jog into the dugout toward the locker room, needing space from everything he makes me feel—and from making a *huge* mistake.

Stupid. Stupid. Stupid. You're in the freaking stadium, where anyone from the front office can see you, and you're standing there like a teenager begging to be kissed. Are you actually going to risk this job for a guy who will be gone and done with you before the post-season begins?

"Scout?"

"You're good for the day." Keep walking. Keep moving.

He curses behind me, and then his footsteps fall into pace with mine when I just want them to walk the other way.

Or maybe I don't want them to.

Hell if I know, because that little moment was enough to mess up my head. Sure, Easton hits all my buttons: hot, athletic, funny, and a bit of a mystery. But in this job, those buttons are pushed all the time. There are plenty of players who fit that bill. It's everything else that he just made me feel that's confusing me.

It's the fact that I wanted him to lean in and kiss me.

It's the notion that I press up against hard, male bodies all the time—so much so that I'm rarely affected by it—but right now, my body is reacting and wanting and pissed off that it *is* reacting. Easton Wylder just affected me.

It's the acknowledgement that for some reason he can see the things I think I'm hiding from the world. He sees them, and has no problem calling me out on them, either.

It's that right now I feel exposed and raw, and I hate that I am, but at the same time I feel relieved that someone sees it. That I'm not invisible, when lately, that's all I've felt as I've worked to secure this job. To succeed in getting the long-term contract. *Anything* to try and keep my dad holding on.

My footsteps echo down the concrete corridor, the clubhouse all but vacant of players since the team is traveling. I need a minute to clear my head and push away the sudden vulnerability I feel because of everything going on with my dad.

Clear mind, hard heart, Scouty.

Maybe it's the toll of my emotions, maybe not, but when I enter the empty locker room, my feet falter at the sight. It's eerie and beautiful and bittersweet all at the same time.

This is how I remember it from when I was a kid. Ford and I would tag along with my dad to work and we'd sit in the empty locker room while he got everything set up for whoever he was in charge of rehabilitating. When the team straggled in, we'd be relegated to the office with a vending machine full of candy we weren't supposed to eat but would stuff our faces with anyway. We'd giggle at the Mad Libs made naughty with words we weren't allowed to say in front of our dad—like *hell* and *damn*—and then grumble over our homework, which Ford would help me with when it was too hard. It was my dad's way of keeping us with him—our fear he'd leave us was a constant in those early years after my mom left—but making sure we didn't get in the way, or hear the cursing, or see the players as they changed.

And every once in a while, depending on how long he worked with a club, the players would come in, kid with us, give us high-fives, and make us feel like we were part of the team.

"What is it?" Easton pulls me from my thoughts. When I look his way I realize his hand is on my upper arm, his head dropped down so he can look into my eyes.

"Isn't it magical?" I whisper. *Oh my god. Did I really just say that? I'm so lame.*

His laugh is amused, but the expression on his face as he looks around us— the empty lockers, the hanging jerseys, the nameplates on them—says he has a love/hate relationship with this room. And for a guy who probably grew up here more than anywhere else, the expression, and the curiosity it raises, surprises me.

"Some days it is. Some days it isn't," he finally murmurs, confirming my assumption of his mixed feelings as his gaze lands back on mine.

And we stand like this for a few seconds, his hand on my arm, his eyes asking me what's wrong, and mine questioning why this room evokes the conflict I see hiding in his.

The clearing of a throat has me jumping back like we're two kids caught doing something we shouldn't be doing.

"Sir," Easton says with a slow nod as I meet the eyes of the giant who is standing a few feet away from us, an indecipherable look on his unmistakable face.

"Easton." He looks down to his watch and then back up, with hazel eyes that are a mirror image of his son's. "Cutting your rehab time a bit short, aren't you?"

The laugh that falls from Easton's mouth is one I haven't heard before. It's void of any humor. "This is my second session today, so no, actually, I'm not."

The man's gaze shifts from Easton's to mine as he angles his head and studies me. "We haven't officially met."

I snap to attention, suddenly cognizant of what the situation looks like— Easton and I alone in the locker room, with his hand on my arm—and stride toward him with my hand outstretched. "Scout Dalton. So nice to meet you, Mr. Wylder."

"The pleasure's mine," he says, brows drawing together as he looks me in the eye. "So *you're* the one charged with getting my boy back up to speed."

"Yes, sir," I say as resolutely as possible, a little star struck and a lot aware that Cal Wylder has a ton of pull in the front office of the Austin Aces organization. "We're making good headway."

"What seems to be holding him back?"

The question throws me. Why wouldn't he just ask his son, who is standing right beside me? He's searching, when he knows I can't tell him. Discussing Easton's status with anyone other than the GM is off-limits for me, not to mention completely unprofessional.

I glance over to Easton, who gives me no indication that he wants me to answer, and then back to Cal. Is this some kind of set-up? See if the new girl can handle both confrontation and keeping her mouth shut at the same time?

"Nothing that I can tell," I say with caution, trying to feel out the situation. "Just creating a routine for stretching and strengthening, and giving Easton the time to learn what his repaired shoulder should feel like. It'll most likely have a completely different feel for him, so he needs to learn what each pinch or pain is telling him now."

"Good. Good." Cal finally looks back to Easton again. "From where I was watching in the press box, you seemed to have lost some time on your run to first. Don't let him fool you. He's faster than that, Ms. Dalton. He just has a habit of slacking a bit if no one is pushing him."

"Most players wish they had his time." I laugh, thinking Cal's joking until I notice the look on his face, eyebrows pinched as his eyes shift back toward mine. And now I'm under the impenetrable stare.

"Hmm." He doesn't say anything else, but rather lets the sound hang in the air as if he doesn't believe me.

"The stopwatch never lies."

"Well, he can do better," he says with a disapproving shake of his head quickly followed by the flash of a dazzling smile almost as if he remembers he has an audience. "But I'm glad to hear you think the shoulder hasn't slowed him down too much."

And even though the words sound sincere, I'm not sure there isn't the hard edge beneath them of a father pushing his son beyond his limits.

"Not at all, sir," I say to keep the peace and my respect in place. I glance over to Easton, noticing the strong set of his jaw, the visible tension in his shoulders, and his eyes locked on his father's, despite the tight smile on his lips.

There is suddenly a palpable tension between the two of them that grows with each passing second. I try to deflect.

"It was a pleasure to meet you, Mr. Wylder."

"Cal," he says, finally drawing his eyes away from Easton.

"Cal," I repeat. "I'll get him back on the field, but only because he's busting his ass to get there himself."

He gives me that look again, hazel eyes searching, just like his son's. "Good to know," he murmurs. "Keep up the good work."

And with that, a man I watched break every record in the book when I was a kid, turns on his heel and heads out of the locker room.

Cal may have shut the door in his departure, but the tension he brought with him still lingers.

"We need to get the fuck out of here," Easton mutters as he turns to face me. "Get changed if you want, and grab your shit. We're going for a drive."

I stand there, mouth agape. Easton takes a few steps and turns back to look at me like I've misheard him. The look in his eyes is just as demanding as his words. I want to tell him to go to hell, that I don't take orders from anyone, and yet for some reason, I do just as he asked.

This time.

CHAPTER SEVEN

Scout

We drive in silence as Easton maneuvers through the streets of downtown Austin. He's still pissed, that much I can tell, but it seems to lessen with each mile we put between us and the ball field.

Curiosity over the exchange between him and his father owns my thoughts. The picture-perfect father and son. Both uber-talented. Both a rarity in this game because they spent their careers playing for only one ball club. Both obscenely handsome.

But after the meeting in the locker room, I'm left to wonder how everyone else has failed to see what I glimpsed. The smooth and personable Cal Wylder is not so easy-going, and not so complimentary of his protégé of a son.

"Sorry about that," Easton says after some time, his voice resigned.

"'Bout what?" I turn to look at him from my seat in the front of his truck, asking my question but not really meaning it.

"My old man can be . . . a little overbearing at times. I'm sorry if it made you uncomfortable."

"I'm good. My choice of career has taught me how to handle even the most overbearing of people." I eye him up and down to let him know I'm including him in the generality. "Thanks, though."

"I've noticed." He chuckles with a glance my way before turning his attention back to the road, smile fading, and lips twisting as he loses himself back to his thoughts.

I use the time to study him. The line of his profile, the flex of his biceps as he turns the wheel, the pulse of the muscle in his jaw. He knows I'm watching, and yet he just carries on, checking his side mirror, his rearview mirror, and using his turn signals.

There are so many questions I want to ask him but don't. About the relationship with his dad and the obvious tension between them. About whatever it was that happened between us on the field earlier. If I put a voice to my curiosity, I'm only inviting his questions about my personal life in return. And while we've developed a pseudo-friendship the past two weeks, there are secrets I need to keep.

So I bite my tongue and try to quiet my head so I can enjoy the comfortable silence we've slipped into. And no sooner than I do, it hits me: I *like* Easton. And not just that lusty kind of indifferent attraction I feel occasionally with players I've worked with. The kind where, hell yes, they're hot and probably would be a willing candidate if I wanted a temporary good-time, but not good enough for me to cross that fine line of mixing my professional life with my personal life.

I've never crossed it. I have no intention to.

My studies, my softball team, graduating at the top of my class had always come first. Then I threw everything I had into working my way up the ranks to prove I'm worthy to help run Doc Dalton's business. Sure he was my dad, but I wanted to earn the position. And thankfully I did, because there's no way I could have known what the future would hold for us.

Did I have fun with men? Of course, but since I started working for my dad, no player has ever tempted me to cross that professional line like the mysterious and attractive man beside me does.

And that's a major problem.

But then again, it's not. I'm a big girl. I can handle my lusty urges. He's charming and attractive and funny and so much more than I'd assumed. Even with all of that, I think I've barely caught a glimpse of the real him. I'm intrigued, to say the least.

Wait. The truck has stopped. And I'm still staring at Easton. And he's staring back at me, smirk growing wider by the second as he waits for me to realize it.

"I'm sorry." I shake my head with a laugh, embarrassed and flustered.

"Don't be. I sure hope it's me you're thinking about that intensely." His grin is lightning quick as I try not to die a thousand deaths.

"Of course I was. Just trying to think about what to do with you next," I say with pursed lips and a shrug, and then realize that it sounds exactly like how I didn't want it to sound. I stammer to correct myself. "I mean, your rehab. On the field. For training. About your arm."

"Uh-huh." I'm certain I turn every shade of pink, all the way to red, as he just stares, and that huge grin morphs into a lopsided smile.

"Where are we?" *Smooth, Scout. Real smooth.* You're a master at changing the subject. To reinforce my attempt, I glance around to our surroundings. We're on a residential street with a park on the passenger side and a row of houses on Easton's side.

"Sorry to drag you along, but I have to do something real quick. I hope you don't mind, but feel free to turn on the radio if you want. I'll leave the keys here."

"Okay. Sure."

He turns to face me, hand pushing open the door, smile and sunglasses in place. "Hey, Scout?"

"Yeah?"

"I'm leaving now."

"Okay?" I draw the word out to let him know what he's doing is pretty self-explanatory.

"That means you can carry on thinking about whatever you were thinking about me and not get embarrassed, since I won't be sitting two feet from you."

Dear God. "I was thinking of your arm. *Your arm*," I emphasize.

He darts his tongue out to wet his bottom lip. "That's not all you were thinking about."

His laugh fills the truck before he shuts the door and leaves me with the echo of it through the open window.

I follow his very fine backside as he jogs across the grass field toward a small crowd of people. There are tables dotting the playground, with bunches of green balloons at every other one. There looks to be a group of kids seated in rows on the grass and some kind of costumed character in front of them holding up an oversize book.

I'm more than fascinated with what is going on and just what Easton is doing here. Especially after he reaches the crowd of people and shakes hands with several of them, while hugging a few of the others.

After observing for a few minutes, I conclude that this is some kind of school function, and somehow Easton is a part of it. I'm distracted momentarily from watching him when the teddy bear character throws his hands (or is it paws?) up in the air. Despite the distance, I can hear the roar as the kids shout out loud in response.

Their enthusiasm brings a smile to my lips. And when I see Easton walk up before the rows of kids, their cheers grow even wilder. Some of them jump from their seats and run to give him a hug. Despite the distance, I can see the wide smile on his face and the sincerity in his expression as he hugs them back, ruffles their hair, and then does some kind of silly routine with the bear.

The kids shift to the next activity, the next station, and yet I'm left staring into space once again, acknowledging that Easton Wylder is getting to me. That hard heart my father taught me was a necessity to get through life is slowly softening.

And I'm not quite sure how to feel or what to even do about it.

My thoughts are too loud in the confines of this truck when all I crave is some peace and quiet. I don't want to think about my dad, the stress of the contract, or how I'll be letting both Easton and my dad down if I don't succeed. Instead I just want to sit parked on the side of the road in the hometown I feel like I barely know. As a kid we were always moving on to the next city, the next injured ball player, so much so that tutors became our teachers and our beds at home felt unfamiliar.

I've missed Austin—the sights and sounds and beauty that I haven't really gotten to enjoy as an adult—and being back for this short amount of time has only reinforced the thought.

The desire to make a life here is suddenly strong. To win the contract, find a place of my own, and grow roots. I need something of my own, somewhere I can belong.

Because pretty soon . . . I'll be all alone.

The pang of grief is crippling, the swell of emotions inescapable.

Desperate to stop thinking, to stop feeling, I turn the key in the ignition and push the radio on. Music is what I need. Music will let me close my eyes, lean my head back, and get lost in the beat.

Except when the radio comes on, I'm startled when a man's voice starts talking to me. Or not me, rather, but the reader, because it sounds like he is narrating an audio book.

An audio book?

I know it's shallow, but an audio book is the last thing I ever expected to hear coming through Easton's speakers. The man keeps throwing me for loops every time I think I have him pegged.

I should turn it off so he doesn't lose his place, but there is something so soothing about the narrator's voice that I snuggle into the seat with a soft smile on my face and just lose myself in the words he speaks.

A little more than a chapter later, I'm jolted from the story when the truck door opens. Feeling like a kid caught with her hand in the cookie jar, I look over to Easton with wide eyes and cheeks flushed with embarrassment.

He doesn't say a word but just stares at me from behind the dark lenses of his sunglasses for a moment before climbing into the truck, turning the radio off, and then pulling away from the curb.

We drive in the silence that has seemed to plague us today, and I'm left to wonder why he seems embarrassed when there's nothing to be embarrassed about.

He listens to books. *How can he think I'd judge him poorly for that?*

And yet I sense his discomfort, so I try to ease it the only way I know how. "Stephen King, huh? I kind of figured you more for a romance novel kind of guy."

"Bullshit." His laughter breaks the awkward silence in the cab.

"What's wrong with romance?"

"You seriously have to ask me that?"

"What?" I mirror the posture that got me into trouble earlier: body shifted, knees angled, eyes on him. "You don't like a feel-good story? Or is it that you don't believe in true love? Maybe you just haven't found a good baseball romance to pull you in and steal your heart."

"See! That's just it. Those books give women unrealistic expectations about what a relationship is supposed to be like."

It's my laugh that fills the truck now. "Maybe our expectations are spot on, and it's the men who are unreliable." I purse my lips as he looks at me from over the frames of his sunglasses.

"That's such a crock."

"No, it's not. What are you afraid of? That you might actually like the story and maybe get a few pointers to help *better* your game?" My tone is coy, smile playful as he looks over at me.

"Are you telling me you don't think I have game?" he asks, mock offended.

"On the field? Yes. Off the field? I couldn't tell you."

"I've got game all right. No worries there, *Kitty*. Just you wait and see." His voice may sound irritated but the smile on his lips says different.

I roll my eyes while trying not to read into his comment. *Just you wait and see*. Was he saying it off the cuff? Or is he interested in me? And more importantly, do I want him to be?

"No game," he mutters under his breath and then laughs. "That's hilarious."

Twenty bucks says he's listening to a romance sooner rather than later.

A man's ego can't handle being called into question.

He'll have to find out the truth for himself.

CHAPTER EIGHT

Scout

"**S**o what was that all about back at the park?"

I glance around the hole-in-the-wall bar where we've ended up. It's downtown, somewhat near the ballpark but outside the area of the city's revitalization efforts. Texan memorabilia lines the walls, and country music plays softly on the speakers.

"It was nothing. Just an obligation I had to fulfill." He's nonchalant in his response and makes a point to avert his eyes from mine.

"Whatever, Wylder." I roll my eyes. "You don't get to act like that was nothing, because whatever it was, those kids loved that you were there, and that's pretty freaking awesome. So, 'fess up. What was that all about?"

"Why were you so upset earlier?" His eyes meet mine, searching and questioning, as he lifts the bottle of beer to his lips and takes a sip.

I shake my head. "We're not going there again."

"Then I guess you're not going to know what I was doing at the park, now, are you?"

"You're a pain in my ass, you know that?"

"It's a mighty fine pain you've got there, too, then." The words come out of a mouth turned up in a smile, but with eyes loaded with suggestion.

"Flattery doesn't make me spill my secrets."

"It wasn't flattery. It's the truth."

"Well, in that case, flattery will get you everywhere," I respond, our smiles wide but the unanswered questions still lingering between us. "You're really not going to tell me what was going on?"

He shrugs. "Seems that way, doesn't it."

"I don't think I've ever played show-me-yours-and-I'll-show-you-mine, and I doubt I'm going to start at the age of twenty-five," I say dryly.

His laugh carries over the noise of the bar. "That's a pity. You should definitely play it once in your lifetime. You never know, it might be fun." That gleam is back in his eye, highlighted by a lift of his eyebrows, and once again I'm aware of how he captivates me without even trying.

"Tell me something about you." He changes the topic, his expression daring me to refuse him.

"I never played in the major leagues."

He narrows his eyes and purses his lips. "That's the best you can do?"

I shrug and mimic his posture. "How about this," I murmur as I lean in a little closer, "you tell me what you were doing earlier, and I'll tell you something about me."

His laugh is quick but telling. "I see I've been outmaneuvered. You're a tricky one, turning that back on me, Scout Dalton, but I'll bite. God knows if I don't, your stubborn ass will have us volleying the same question back and forth all night."

"I'm so glad you have me all figured out."

"Not hardly." He shifts in his seat and looks down at the label on his beer he's playing with. "I run a literacy charity," he says softly, lifting his eyes to meet mine. "We run programs at all of the local schools to encourage reading and to make sure any kid struggling with reading, or who has dyslexia, or just needs extra help or tutoring gets it."

And there he goes, surprising me again.

"Who knew the man who's got a wicked arm and swagger for days also has such a huge heart?" I murmur, more to myself than to him, but I am thoroughly impressed. Not just because he has a charity, because a lot of players pay it forward somehow, but after watching him—his interaction with the organizers, the kids, the good mood it put him in—it is obvious this is more than just a tax write-off to him.

I love that his cheeks flush some and hate that he's embarrassed at all by it.

"I meant that as a compliment, Easton. It's nice to see someone paying the community back, and in such an important way. Don't ever be embarrassed by it. Please."

"Your turn," he says after a beat, effectively shifting the focus back on me. "Spill it."

I suck in a breath and debate how to be honest with him while keeping my promise to my father. "I have an uncle who is pretty sick. It's just hitting me harder than usual today."

"Scout." The way he says my name—apology laced with compassion—causes a lump to form in my throat. "I thought I was being so smart, tricking you into telling me something, and now I feel like a complete asshole. I'm sorry. The only thing I can say is I hope he gets better soon."

I don't know why I chuckle, but I do. The tone of it is anxious and sarcastic, and I know it's because I'm afraid if I say the words out loud, they'll come true. "Yeah, well, thank you, but he's not going to get better." I focus on shredding my cocktail napkin—anything to avoid seeing the sympathy in his eyes. I can't handle sympathy right now. I can deal with anger. I can handle disbelief. But I absolutely cannot deal with sympathy.

Sympathy will break me, when I can't break.

It will make me confess the secret I've been keeping. The one that's been eating me whole—bit by bit, day by day—because I'd give anything to talk about my dad's diagnosis. It would be so much easier if someone else knew so I could let all this bundled emotion out instead of letting it implode.

But I can't tell Easton. I promised my dad I wouldn't, so I sit in the booth across from him, staring at where I'm pushing the tiny pieces of shredded napkin around with my finger instead of looking at him.

Somehow, though, he senses that I need a connection, a something, and he reaches across the table and links his fingers through mine. I look down at our hands entwined; I study the scars on his from a lifetime of playing, and hold on to the little bit of comfort he has no idea how much I need.

"Thank you," I say after a moment to regain my composure. A huge part of me likes this—our fingers linked—but knows it's a bad idea all around. And yet, when I lean back in the booth, try to create an opportunity for him to withdraw his hand, he doesn't.

"I used to play ball," I say, feeling the need to reciprocate with something else about me, considering I wasn't completely honest with my first confession. Anything to change the topic and relieve the depressed atmosphere I unexpectedly created.

"You did?" he asks with a tone so full of warmth that it pulls on me to look up to him. There's a surprised gratitude in his eyes that tells me he wasn't expecting me to let him in any more than I did, and for that look alone, I'm glad I did.

"Yep. So, I may not have played in the majors, but I won a few collegiate championships."

"You're fucking with me now."

I laugh. "Why is that so hard to believe?"

"Because you're completely unpredictable. First a stripper and now a ball player."

"Very funny." I roll my eyes as he narrows his in thought.

"Let me guess . . . you were a second baseman."

"Uh. Please," I say in mock offense because I know he won't guess in a million years what position I played.

"C'mon. With that compact little body of yours, I bet you would've been a kick-ass second baseman."

"I like to get a little more action than second base," I say, fully knowing the innuendo that goes with it, but with the first drink down, I'm feeling a bit more daring than I normally would.

His eyes hold mine for a prolonged moment, and I know he wants to say more, but he doesn't. Instead he begins to name every position on the field while I reject them until there are only two left.

"What's left?" he asks, knowing damn well the answer.

"Pitcher and catcher."

"No fucking way," he murmurs.

"Yep." I quirk an eyebrow, and the smug smile on my lips tells him I'm enjoying the fact he's underestimated me.

"And twice in a matter of minutes you make me feel like a complete heel." He releases my fingers and drops his head into his hands, his laugh ringing out as he scrubs them through his hair. The simple mannerism makes me smile, even more so when he looks at me again, eyes intense, smile bewildered. "*Seriously?*"

"If I was gonna play, I wanted to play the best position on the field. The one that holds all the control."

"Control freak."

"Ditto." I murmur back, my smile soft, the alcohol warming me from the inside out.

"Incredible." His voice is part awe, part surprise, and it makes every part of me stand tall with pride.

"My dad used to say the best place in the park to sit was behind home plate. And so when I was about ten, I figured if I was going to play, I wanted to make sure I had the best seat in the house."

I can hear my dad's voice saying it now, the memory bittersweet.

"And my dad told me to play first base instead," he says with a shake of his head, "because catching caused too much wear and tear on your body and could shorten your career."

"So you've always rebelled against him, then?"

His laughter is quick and his smile arrogant. "That noticeable, huh?"

"There was just a touch of tension in the locker room."

"A touch? Was that all?"

Relieved he can laugh now at what upset him earlier, I put my thumb and index finger half an inch apart. "Just a smidgen."

The soft smile on his lips does nothing to ease the conflict in his eyes as he lowers his gaze to watch the condensation run down the side of his beer bottle. He collects his thoughts before he looks back up at me to explain. "He means well. He's just very particular and extremely determined that I live up to the Wylder name. He doesn't want me to disgrace the legacy he left behind, especially since I play for the club he spent his entire career playing for."

"That's a lot of pressure." I can't imagine.

"I'm sure the situation you're in is no different, living up to the legendary Doc Dalton."

I twist my lips and consider his statement. "Pressure, yes. But it's something I want to do, love to do . . . to make him proud." But I get the feeling that while

Easton feels similarly about his situation, at least I had the choice whether I wanted to follow in my father's footsteps. For some reason, I don't think he did.

"Every kid wants to make their parents proud," he muses as he angles his head to the side. "But every parent holds a different standard for what exactly it is that will achieve that."

And that comment confirms my assumption that Easton feels like he's never been good enough to live up to his father, the legend. My heart hurts for him, working as hard as he does, playing a game he is more than gifted at, but living a life to earn someone's approval.

"True. That must be hard for you."

He shrugs again. Averts his eyes. Takes a swig of his beer. "When I'm playing good, it's not." He laughs, and I can tell he's uneasy with the topic of conversation.

"Tell me something else about yourself," I say, more than curious to find another piece to complete this puzzle of a man.

"You sure are full of questions," he teases.

"Please," I say drolly. "I'm sure you'd prefer to talk baseball or stats or something scintillating like that."

"Scintillating?" He laughs.

"It's a good word."

"It is," he says with a nod, "but I don't talk stats."

What? "I thought all players liked to talk about the game."

"I'm not all players, though."

"So it seems."

"First off, I'm *the* player." He quirks an eyebrow, and all I can do is smile at the reference.

"And second?"

"Second," he mimics, "I may be wrong, but I think it takes a helluva lot more to impress you than a list of above-par stats."

"True." I draw the word out while my mind is a flurry of thoughts. *Is he flirting with me? He wants to impress me? Or am I reading into the comment when he means nothing by it?*

"Stats are boring. They're my work. And while most days I live and breathe baseball, on and off the field, they're the last thing that comes to mind when I'm in the company of a beautiful woman."

That's twice. He is flirting with me.

"What *does* come to mind, then?"

Oh, crap. I'm flirting right back.

He flashes me a megawatt smile that lightens his dark features and brightens his eyes. And if I doubted whether we should continue this exchange or not, that smile right there pulls me in hook, line, and sinker.

"Right here? Right now?"

"Mm-hmm."

Our eyes lock as we gauge each other and try to figure out the next step in this unfamiliar dance we're moving to.

"Dance with me."

I stifle a laugh. *Is he reading my mind now?*

But my laugh is short-lived when he rises from the booth and extends his hand to me. He can't be serious.

"No way!" I laugh, batting his hand away. "I'm not letting the King of Pranks make a fool of me."

"I do love a good prank but dancing with me isn't one of them." He puts his hand out for me to take again.

"I don't know how to dance, let alone to country music."

"Neither do I. We're quite the pair, aren't we?" he asks, that boyish smile on his lips winning me over. "A pair of Texans who can't dance to country music."

"We should be ashamed of ourselves and hide in this dark corner here."

His laugh tells me he's not buying it. "No time like the present to learn."

"We'll be the only ones on the dance floor." I scramble to think of any other excuse to avoid this situation—not avoiding the limelight part of it but the dancing body-to-body with Easton part—because he's already lowered my defenses, and dancing with him might be too temptingly disastrous for me—in more ways than one. "Everyone will be staring at us."

"I live my life under the lights, baby," he teases as he grabs the hand I've refused him. "You think these dim bar lights are going to intimidate me?"

"People are going to stare."

He pulls me to my feet.

"Good."

"*Good?* We're so out of place in here."

"I've never cared what people think of me, and I sure as hell am not going to start now. Besides, there's nothing wrong with getting a little attention now and again."

He tugs on my arm for me to follow.

"Ah, you can't handle being out of the limelight now, can you?" I tease.

"I can handle it just fine. And it's not me people are going to be looking at, it's you."

"Me?" I say, but the word comes out in a whoosh of air when he stops and turns without warning, causing me to bump solidly against his chest.

"Yes. *You.*" His smile is a juxtaposition of shy and suggestive, and it tugs on so many things inside of me. Want. Need. Denial. Desire.

We're standing in the middle of the empty dance floor, and all I can think about when he looks down at me is that I need to remember to breathe.

Because chatting at a table is fine. Stretching his shoulder on the field, I can handle. But this, face-to-face on a dance floor with nothing between us, only serves to reinforce my epiphany in the truck earlier—I really like him.

And as if the universe is trying to cheer this mistake on, the music suddenly becomes louder and the lights become dimmer, prompting Easton to slide one hand against my lower back and lift my hand with his other.

Breathe, Scout.

And then he begins to move.

"Relax," he murmurs against my ear as he guides us in a mismatched array of steps that make no sense and perfect sense all at the same time. But it's not like I can concentrate on the movement with the heat of his body against mine, familiar and so very different.

It's his tutelage I'm under now. It's not me working him or stretching him. It's him guiding me. Commanding me. And the ripple of his muscles beneath his shirt is not for me to study this time around, but rather to feel. To react to. *To want.*

I'm normally one to avoid the spotlight, but Easton has just thrust me right into it. Attention shifts. Eyes observe. And there's something about knowing we're being watched that magnifies everything about the moment.

More specifically, everything about Easton.

The scent of his shampoo. The strength in his hand as it holds mine and the heat of his other splayed across my lower back. The vibration of his voice against my hair as he hums along with the Luke Bryan tune. The rhythm of his hips as they move against mine.

"You lied to me, Scout."

The heat of his breath against the side of my face.

"About what?"

The sensitivity of my nipples as they rub ever so gently against the firmness of his chest.

"You damn well do know how to dance."

I chuckle in response but don't look up to meet his eyes because I don't want him to stop whatever it is we're doing. There's something intimate about the moment that has me wanting to breathe him in a little more before it's lost.

His reaction to my laughter is to press his hand against my back and pull me closer. "I was always taught lying comes with punishment." His voice has a sing-song quality to it that only serves to draw me deeper under whatever spell he seems to be casting on my impenetrable shell.

"Punishment?" Somewhere deep down, the word awakens the parts of me curious about but inexperienced in anything of the nature, and I'm suddenly nervous.

And excited.

"Mm-hmm." His voice sounds as seductive as his body feels against mine. "Something that causes you pain."

I gulp over thoughts as my insides begin to heat up, and I'm well aware of the attention still turned our way.

And before I can take my next breath, Easton spins me out with a laugh until our arms are fully extended, fingertips barely still grasping each other, before pulling me back so I land solidly with a thud against his chest.

"See?" he says, prompting me to look up at him, the one thing I was telling myself not to do. And now that I have, I'm fully aware that our lips are only inches apart.

"*See?*" I laugh, trying to comprehend what I'm supposed to see when my body is still reeling from the feeling of our bodies colliding into each other and the mortification of being twirled in a public display.

"Being the center of attention." His voice is barely a whisper, but I hear every word. "Dancing with me isn't too painful of a punishment now, is it?"

Normally I would laugh at him—at his version of a punishment—but all I can think of is how much I want him to kiss me right now. With his lips right there. And our bodies like this.

Breathe, Scout.

"You've got a heavy hand there, Mr. Wylder." My head is so scrambled I'm not even sure how I manage to sound so witty.

And breathless.

It's in that moment that I realize we've stopped moving completely. Our feet. Our bodies. We're standing alone in the middle of the dance floor in a crowded bar, staring at each other.

"Excuse me?" At a woman's voice to our left, we shock apart like two kids getting caught for the second time today. "May I cut in?"

I look over at the attractive—and much older—bottled redhead beside us, whose smile is as evocative as the clothes she's wearing, and then back to Easton, a man no stranger to women hitting on him, I'm sure. His smile is fixed and eyes wide as he tries to figure out what to do.

"Of course. He's all yours," I say as I step back, despite every part of my body wanting to move closer. He sputters a protest, but his manners get the best of him when the woman, who must be at least thirty years his senior, has absolutely no qualms about stepping into where my shoes just were.

I twist my lips to fight my smile as he sends me a visual SOS when the woman begins to lead him around the dance floor. He's all smiles to her while shooting playful I'm-gonna-kill-you daggers across the room at me.

And as I sip my fresh drink, sent compliments of Easton's dance partner, for the first time in forever, I realize what jealousy over a man feels like.

CHAPTER NINE

Scout

"**S**he *so* wanted you." My laugh is louder than normal, a bit giggly, and I don't care because I'm a little tipsy and a lot relaxed, and I can't remember what it feels like to be relaxed.

"Some wingman you are. Throwing me to the wolves so you can go drink all the alcohol, which could have helped to put me out of my misery."

"She was sweet, though," I explain.

"Of course you thought that. You were getting buzzed on the drinks she sent your way, while I was busy moving her hands off my ass. And I won't even get into her thoughts about the team's chances this year, or how much she kept asking if it's true that son is like father."

"If it's true that son is like father?" I look at him, wide-eyed, and cover my mouth with my hand.

"Yeah. Exactly."

"Are you telling me she's slept with your dad?"

"I have no clue, and I don't want to know," he says dryly, mock shivering.

I stifle a laugh. "And to think you were so generous with your time for her."

"What was I supposed to do? Cause a scene? I tried to escape, tried to explain I was on a date with you, but she wouldn't let me go."

"She just wanted to see if the apple fell far from the tree," I snicker, earning me a stern glare.

"Funny."

"Well, it was nice of you to stick it out." His glare is back, and I try to smother my laughter. He just walks ahead of me and shakes his head. "Look, I'm sorry. You were being very kind to her. She is probably lonely, and you just made her night."

"And that's why I wasn't rude. She just wanted to feel important."

And so you let her have that moment.

It's one surprise after another with him, and the revelation only makes me want to get to know him further. "You better watch out, or I might change my opinion of you."

"You have opinions of me? What might those be?" he asks, voice playful but eyes serious as he takes my hand to stop me. We're standing on a sidewalk in the middle of downtown Austin, his truck left in the bar's parking lot and mine a few blocks ahead in the stadium's parking lot. We decided to walk off the alcohol, but we're not walking now.

We're standing with my back to the brick wall of the building and this surprise of a man standing in front of me.

"I've been around ball players my whole life, Easton."

"And?" He says the word as if I've insulted him.

"They're *players*. They come and go on a whim. They typically need the high of the attention they get on the field to thrive. And if they can't find it, then they'll seek it out somewhere else . . . and that's never good for a relationship."

"So you've had a relationship with a ballplayer, then?" His eyes narrow.

"No. Never. It's my personal rule." And even though I said it myself, I know I'm already justifying in my head why I might make an exception for him.

"It's arrogant to brush your opinion in broad strokes across all of us players." The dark night prevents me from seeing what else his eyes are saying.

"True," I muse, "but I've heard enough locker room talk to know the truth."

"So you think that's how I am, too, then?"

"No. Yes." I tighten my ponytail and tuck the loosened strands behind my ears. "It's just . . . *they leave.* Night after night. Day after day. Game after game. And when the season is over and the limelight is gone, they seek the attention of someone new, someone who gives them that adrenaline rush. That thrill of finding someone new, or the high that comes with the risk of being caught cheating."

"Scout—"

"I've had enough people in my life leave me, Easton. I'm not walking willingly into a situation that sets me up for that hurt." And I hate that I just gave him that part of me. That glimpse into my past. I blame the alcohol for lowering my guard, but I fear it's so much more than that.

I fear it's because of him and how he makes me feel.

"You're wrong." He steps into me and out of the street's light. The shadows on his face give him an edge that's sexy, reckless, and daring. "I've played on grass my whole life, Scout. There's no need for me to see what's out there when it's green beneath my feet."

"There's turf nowadays. Everything is green," I fight back.

"If there's turf, then there's no point to your argument. No one's going to be looking for greener pastures when they're all the same color." He lowers his head so our eyes are on the same level, to reinforce what he's said.

They're just words, Scout. Declarations that have no basis. He's just a man trying to defend his own gender. His own ego.

Yet, I want to believe him.

I want to think he's not like those guys.

And God, how I want him to kiss me. Call my bluff. Because with the alcohol in my blood and the memory of his body against mine in my brain, it's all I can think about.

I spring off the wall and away from the slowly closing gap between us. "Is there a bathroom around here?" I ask the first thing that comes to mind to give me an escape, hands gesticulating animatedly, and nerves humming recklessly. "All of those drinks are catching up to me."

He steps forward under the light of the building and just stares at me. He can see through me right now—my nerves, my fear, my confused desire—and so I hold his gaze, pretend to be unaffected by him, and wait to see if he's going to let me off the hook or push the issue.

"My place is just around the corner," he says, giving me a pass, but with a look telling me we'll be revisiting this discussion where I called his character into question. "I'll take you there."

I should say no.

I should reject the offer and walk away from everything that he represents for me.

But I don't speak. Instead I fall into step next to him.

We walk through the newly revamped downtown area, past couples holding hands and hordes of college kids making their way from one bar to the next, the night still young. Our silence only feeds my insecurity and the knowledge that he's mad at me because I insulted his character. I know I should apologize, tell him that based on his actions today I can tell he doesn't fit my generalization, but I don't say a word. I can't. Because, deep down, I have a feeling that it's probably best if he stays mad at me.

It's safer.

By the time we enter the lobby of a glossy high-rise, I really do have to use the restroom. Easton laughs at me as I dance from foot to foot during the long elevator ride to the penthouse. The doors open to the foyer of his home, where a lone lamp lights the space as he ushers me to a door to my immediate left.

I take a few minutes after I use the facilities to check my mess of a reflection—hair falling from my ponytail, lipstick long gone, and eye shadow all collected in the crease of my lid. There's no way I can fix this. Not here. But I try.

I pull my ponytail out, let my dark brown hair fall, and fluff it with my fingers. And now I look like I just woke up. Shit. Is it so bad to want to look like I didn't just wake up?

I spend a few more minutes trying to look a bit more presentable, but when I check my reflection one last time—hair fluffed and cheeks pinched pink—I immediately grab my hair tie and pull my hair back up into a messy bun. This is how Easton knows me—in work mode—with my basic makeup and my hair thrown back. Anything else comes off like I'm trying too hard.

And I'm not trying too hard.

Keep telling yourself that, Scout, and maybe you'll start believing it.

When I exit the bathroom, Easton is nowhere to be found. Hesitant to overstep, but wondering where he is, I walk past the foyer and start making my way through the vast and still darkened condo. It's all hardwood floors and slate grays and blues. Or I think it is from what I can see as I move through its spacious layout. I only see that much because there is a wall of windows straight ahead of me, where I'm met with Easton's silhouette, highlighted by bright lights beyond.

Both pull at me. Tempt me to look closer. Dare me to want what they are showing me.

It's a sight—his darkness against the light—and I can't help but stare at him for a moment. Study his lines. The broad shoulders and trim waist. The wide stance and arms relaxed at his sides.

I fool myself as I take the first step toward him, past the gourmet kitchen on the left, with its white cabinets and granite slab, that I'm just here to use the restroom.

I lie to myself as I walk past the huge living room, with its oversize couches and state of the art electronics, that wanting him to kiss me was only a passing fancy that has come and gone.

I push away the notion as I pad past the massive dining table, that I'll be leaving here in a few minutes to head home and get a good night's sleep. *Alone.*

The worst part about telling yourself lies is you know the real truth.

And the truth is I want everything I just tried to convince myself I didn't.

The realization echoes in my head as I prepare myself for his irrevocable pull, because it's pointless to pretend he doesn't affect me when my body is already humming at the sight of his silhouette.

"Your place is gorgeous. The only thing missing is a scruffy . . ." My words trail off before I can say *mutt to snuggle up with,* because when I step beside him, I'm rendered speechless by the sight before us—the source of the bright lights beyond.

"*Wow.*" It's all I can say, and I sound like a little kid seeing Santa Claus for the first time—astonished. Mesmerized. Staggered. "You're forgiven for not having a mutt," I murmur, my words barely audible as I stare.

"*A mutt?*"

"Shush and let me enjoy the view." I swat at him to reinforce my words, transfixed by a sight that's as beautiful to my eye as the man standing beside me.

Like mouth-dropping, chill-inducing incredible.

Beyond this wall of windows high above the city, the buildings dotting the darkened skyline paint a uniquely beautiful picture, but they're nothing compared to what lies directly below us: the home of the Austin Aces.

The lights are on, bringing the ballpark to life despite the fifty thousand vacant seats. They highlight the brilliant green of the outfield grass and its mesmerizing mowed crisscross pattern. They brighten the brown of the infield's dirt, the white of the chalk lines, and the blue uniforms of the grounds crew who seem to be working on the pitcher's mound.

He chuckles and pulls me from my trance. "I'm glad I'm forgiven when I wasn't even aware you liked dogs."

"Mutts. I prefer mutts. Preferably the no-one-else-wants-them kind of mutts. And I want one desperately, but with traveling for work and . . . *just wow* . . ." I'm rambling because my attention is engrossed elsewhere.

And for the first time tonight, it's *not* on him.

"*I know.*"

I appreciate the fact that he doesn't say anything else. That he just allows me to appreciate the view before us—the only diamond this girl has ever dreamt of. And right now I'd challenge anyone who told me this diamond doesn't sparkle as brightly as the rock you wear on your finger. With empty seats or with a sold-out crowd, this one outshines jewelry any day.

"It's your church," I whisper, not even certain I say it out loud until I glance over to Easton and find him watching me. There's a look on his face. His expression is part awe, part disbelief, and a whole lot of little boy mixed together, and it steals my heart when I had it firmly protected under lock and key.

But he's stolen it nonetheless.

"This is the place, isn't it?" I murmur like he should know what I'm referring to—the fabled house I've heard some players talk about, with its sparkling views and the private field in its depths, twenty-something floors below. And because I've never heard them say who owns the place, I thought it was a legend of sorts, a fantasy home some players aspire to have, and yet here it is.

And, of course, it's Easton's.

"It is." He nods his head, eyes intense, and I can't figure out which thing I want to look at more: the field or him.

"Is it true?"

"Mm-hmm."

"There's really a personal batting cage and mini-field beneath the building that came with your place?"

"There is." He nods again, but his eyes say so much more. I'm drawn to look closer but am afraid of what I might see because deep down I already know it might be something I won't be able to walk away from.

"Why would you need that when you have *this* in your backyard? Your office?"

He shrugs and diverts his eyes back to the stadium. It's almost as if he's embarrassed or uncertain of his answer. "Because that view, right there . . . the power of it, the strength I draw from it when I'm having that kind of game where you can feel the humming in your bones that tells you something indescribable is about to happen? This is the only place I get to have that alone. The only place where I can quiet my head and listen to what the humming is telling me without the fans or the front office or my teammates or the media watching me home in on it." He scrubs a hand through his hair and snorts. "Never mind. That just sounded completely ridiculous."

"Not in the least." I stare at him until my silence urges him to face me, meet my eyes, and see that I'm nowhere close to laughing at him. "Please. Finish what you were going to say."

"I don't know. I guess some nights I like to sit here when the lights are out, with this ghost of a stadium below me, and go to church, if you will. Think about my game." His exhale is audible and his discomfort with being so open is suddenly palpable.

"See? I knew you loved to talk about your stats."

"You and your statistics." He laughs with a shake of his head, but his discomfort is gone and his smile is genuine when he glances my way. "When they were building the new stadium, some eccentric billionaire bought this place while the building was still under construction. He was obsessed with the game and paid some stupid amount of money to build the field in the basement. The place went up for sale a few years back, and I bought it. How could I not? But I've tried to keep that it's mine on the down low. It's the one place I have that's truly mine, that's completely private and removed from everything that comes with this game."

"It's perfect."

"You haven't even seen the place with the lights on," he teases.

"These are all the lights this girl needs to know it's a perfect fit for you," I say, motioning to the ballpark's towers.

"Sometimes I'll just stand here like this after a brutal game or bad home stand, staring, thinking, and I'll suddenly get inspired to go work on what I did wrong. Sometimes I'll gear up, other times I'll head down in my pajama pants, and I'll work on it until I can't see straight and the clock reads four in the morning."

I shouldn't be surprised by his dedication, and yet I find it so refreshing to know he actually has to work at something, when he seems to be such a damn natural at everything.

"Plus, I'm super competitive so it's nice to be able to put in the extra time without anyone else knowing. Never underestimate the element of surprise."

"Never," I murmur. "And there's never a rain delay, either."

"Lately, I feel like there's been a permanent rain delay on my career." His chuckle transitions to a heavy sigh. The resignation in it tempts me to ask him more about the toll this has taken on him, but I'm startled from the thought when, without a word, he reaches over and hooks my pinky with his.

And just like I found comfort in the touch of his hand earlier, I wonder if maybe he needs the same from me right now. So I don't interrupt the moment. Instead we settle into the silence, touching and watching and trying to figure out what we are doing here.

"I'm doing my best to get you back out there," I say after a bit, letting him know I heard the frustration and defeat in his previous statement. *His permanent rain delay.*

"Is that the polite way to say you're busting my ass?"

And within seconds, we go from serious to playful, and I love that it's so easy to do with him.

"You ain't seen nothing yet, Wylder."

"Oh really?" He tugs on my pinky so that I'm forced to face him. "You've got more moves up your sleeve, Dalton?"

My smile is automatic when our eyes meet. The slow, sweet ache of want is, too. How can it not be when we're standing in the dark, he's framed by a halo of baseball stadium light, and that electric charge between us is snapping with an unfathomable current from just our pinkies touching?

There's something about Easton that makes me want when I shouldn't, need when I needn't, and desire when I know it'll be disastrous.

But damn the fallout to hell, because more than anything, I want to *feel* right now. Alive. Wanted. Desired. Like a woman.

Is that such a bad thing?

I'm sure it's not. I'm sure it's normal for most women, but not for me.

And not like this.

"I'll show you what's up my sleeve if you show me your secret baseball fort downstairs."

His laughter echoes off the glass beside us and back to my ears a second time. "Aha! So that's what it takes to impress you."

"Perhaps."

"My big bat doesn't do it for you, but my home plate downstairs does?" He shakes his head, but when our eyes meet, his laugh fades as the air between us shifts and charges with an unmistakable energy.

"Scout." All he says is my name, but in its timbre I hear so many things that I can't comprehend over my head shouting that I need to step back.

I step toward him.

Time feels like it stops.

His gasp is soft but audible.

Then starts again in slow motion.

A soft squeeze of his pinky around mine.

Then slams into fast forward.

Within a heartbeat, exactly what I both wanted and feared happens: his lips are on mine. The kiss is slow and breathtaking, with soft lips and gentle tongues and murmured sighs and guiding fingertips.

This is wrong, Scout. So wrong. But how can it be wrong when it feels like this and tastes like him?

"Easton." I tell myself to step back. To resist. To not want to kiss him.

And then our tongues meet again in a soft dance of sighs and need.

"I think we should go check out—"

His lips smother the words on mine.

"—your field—"

He nips my bottom lip.

"—your bases—"

His tongue taunts again.

"—your—"

"Will you shut up, please?" He laughs against my lips. "You've been fighting this kiss all day long, and I practiced restraint like you told me to do . . . but right now? *Right now*, I'm going to kiss you senseless, Scout, and I want to fucking enjoy it. So, for the love of God, woman, use those lips of yours on me and not on words."

His sexy-as-hell reprimand evokes a flood of emotions within me, and yet there's only one of them I can name: want.

And God how I want.

So I lean into him and take control of the kiss. I talk without sound this time. With lips and teeth and tongue, I let him know I want to enjoy the kiss just as much as he does.

I throw my concerns out the window. Tell myself to worry about them later, be mad at myself later, but for now just enjoy this virile and attractive man who wants me just as much. I slide my fingers up his chest, touching him the same way I often have to when I stretch his shoulder, but now there is no thought of anything other than how much I want to feel his weight on top of me.

He runs his hand down the line of my neck to the curve of my shoulder and then down until it rests on the small of my back, where he'd placed it earlier tonight. But this time when he pulls me in tighter against him, I don't resist. This time I welcome everything about it. The heat of his body. The flex of his hand against my back in tangible restraint. The bulge of his erection as it pushes against my lower belly.

And damn if knowing he's already hard for me doesn't add fuel to my firestorm of want.

"Scout." It's my name again, but this time I know exactly what he's asking me.

"Yes." One word. It's all I say, then that need and desire simmering between us ignites into a combustible wildfire where first-kiss-caution is consumed by unfettered lust and reckless abandon.

That hand on my back slides under my V-neck and runs up the side of my torso, thumb rubbing ever so gently over the underside of my breast on its way to help unclasp my bra.

My body burns with the expectation of his touch.

And then it lights on fire when his fingers trace their way back—skin to skin—beneath my loosened bra and over my nipples. They harden instantly as his thumbs rub circles over them—they tease and pleasure—all the while his lips and tongue launch another assault with a renewed vigor that only makes me want more.

And he gives me that *more* when he lifts my hands above my head, pulls my shirt off, and dips down and takes my nipple in his mouth. The warmth of his tongue mixed with the scrape of his stubble adds an element of contrast, soft versus rough, that twists my insides and leaves me wanting to know if he's as slow and thorough with every other part of his sexual attention.

My hands are in his hair as he teases one breast and then the other, and I'm not sure if I want him to stop and come back to kiss my lips, or if I want him to keep stoking that fire bright.

Emitting the sexiest growl I've ever heard, Easton makes the decision for me when he puts his hands on my waist and lifts me like I'm a feather. There's no hesitancy on my part, only need, when I wrap my legs around his waist, thread my fingers through his hair, and lose myself under the haze of desire his kisses are unleashing on that sensitive spot beneath my jaw.

And then he begins to walk.

His mouth is on my neck. His unshaven jaw tickles my collarbone. The cool air of the room slides over my breasts. His hips rest deliciously between my thighs.

All of those things tempt and taunt me, but it's when he lays me down on the bed, when I'm so desperate for more from him, that my own control snaps.

We reach for the waist of each other's jeans at the same time. Without any finesse, we fumble and bump hands, our laughter forcing us to come up for air, making us realize it would be so much quicker if we undress ourselves.

So in a rush of movements we strip and shimmy and step out of our clothes until we are naked, laughing in panting breaths, hungry for more and eager to have it.

But it's when I look up from where I lie on the bed to where he stands at its edge, my laughter falls off. He's watching me, wanting me, and everything about him, from his expression to his eyes to his body, is breathtaking. He's hard lines and tanned skin. He's confidence with a half-cocked grin, and he's desire restrained with the tense set of his shoulders. His fingers flick, ready to conquer and claim, and his lips part, ready to lead the assault.

But it's his eyes that command my attention.

They ask and demand and want as they slowly scrape their way up my legs, pausing at the apex of my thighs before continuing up my abdomen to my breasts. When they finally make their way back to mine, they are darkened by a desire I'm desperate to sink whole-heartedly into.

So many things about him—the look in his eye, the set of his shoulders, his impressive dick standing hard and thick between his muscular thighs, and the sexual tension snapping in the air around us—has me craving more of him and willing to beg for what comes next. The push and the pull. The give and the take. The need and the greed. The wish and the want. The climb and the release.

Lost in the haze of lust and expectation, my mouth waters. My body aches. My fingers beg to run over every dip and dent and curve of his body.

"Easton." It's his name on my lips this time. My turn to ask, to demand, *to beg.*

My knees fall apart in invitation.

His breath hitches.

My body hums, and chills chase over my skin.

He licks his lips. Steps. Stares. Admires.

And then he's on the bed, crawling over me and dipping down to take my nipple in his mouth again.

"Oh, that feels good," I murmur as my back arches and offers.

His chuckle vibrates the sensitized flesh. "I'm about to make it feel a whole lot better. Time to fuck your pretty kitty, *Kitty.*"

I manage to laugh through the sensations his skilled tongue is evoking, but it turns into a gasp of welcome pleasure when his hand slides between by thighs. His fingertips dance over my seam, taunting with a feather-light touch before slowly parting me to brush ever so slightly over my clit. Warmth. Heat. Electricity. The current of desire jolts my system, and my hips buck into his hand and beg for more.

"You like that?"

"*God, yes.*"

"I don't think God has anything to do with this, but feel free to call his name." He chuckles and looks up at me over the rise of my breasts, his eyes sharp with desire and contradicted by a cocky flash of a grin. "'Cause we're about to get biblical."

"Oh, please." I laugh, but it's lost to him as his lips claim mine and his fingers rub and tease and work my clit into a frenzy of overwhelming sensations. I writhe and lift and tense, wanting to prolong this onslaught of ecstasy and reach my climax all at the same time.

"Greedy girl," he murmurs, kissing his way down the line of my neck and up to my ear where he nips on my earlobe. "I kind of like that."

His simple praise and the soft chuckle that follows only adds to the riot of hormones racing to my every nerve as his fingers continue to work me to my brink.

"East . . ." A pant of his name is all I can manage as my hands grip tighter onto his forearms, my body edging that fine line before climax. "*East.*" Another pant. Another warning that I'm going to come.

My nails score his skin. My body vibrates with tension.

And then nothing.

His fingers stop. His hand stills. My head snaps up so I can look him in the eyes. And once our eyes meet, once he knows he has my attention, he takes the pads of two fingers and slides them ever-so-tauntingly-slowly down the line of my sex. He teases me, wetting them with my arousal before just as leisurely sliding them into me.

My exhale is unsteady, nerves already strung tight and primed to snap. But it's his eyes on mine—unwavering and intense—that dare me more than anything. To come for him. To please him.

He hears every hitch of my breath. He watches the arch of my neck. He notices when I bite into my bottom lip. He feels each clench of my muscles around his finger. And it's this complete attention that creates an unexpected intimacy and encourages me to slip under that veil of pleasure.

The orgasm slams into me, hijacking my breath as the explosion of desire morphs into a flash of white-hot heat.

My hands grab the sheets. My hips buck into his hand. My lips part, but no sound escapes. My body is seared by the sensations he's just brought to life.

The bed dips as he moves, and I can just barely hear the telltale rip of foil over the thunder of my pulse in my ears. And before I have any chance to recover from the orgasm still pulsing through me, Easton's hands are on the back of my knees, pulling me toward the edge of the bed.

He meets my eyes as he steps between my legs and wastes no time making that first carnal connection when he runs the crest of his dick up and down my slit to prepare both of us for what comes next.

And oh, how I want it to come next. Especially if it feels this incredible already and we haven't even gotten to the good part yet.

He groans, his struggle to take this slow written all over his face. But I don't want slow. I want him. Now. And I'm desperate to have him, so in an attempt to snap that control of his and get what I want, I spread my thighs as wide as possible in invitation.

His eyes flash up to mine, a ghost of a smile on his lips that tells me he knows what I'm doing, but he holds on. Resists. And then he taunts me right back by pushing just the tip of his cock inside me so I can feel that burn that is *oh so good* before he slowly pulls back out.

I lift my hips to try and prevent him from withdrawing completely but he just steps a foot back with his cock in his hand, and smiles at me.

Smug bastard.

We wage a visual war of wills, but when he looks back down to where I'm wet and waiting for him, he caves.

But if I thought this time the wait would be over, that he was going to give me what I want—all of him—I was wrong. Because he continues to toy with me, tease me, arouse me by rubbing his tip just inside of me until I moan with want, before pulling back out.

And the best part is his expression. Not just the taut lines in his neck telling me he's struggling through the denied pleasure like I am, but the widening of his eyes and how his lips fall lax in pleasure each time he enters me.

The next time he pushes his hips forward, I prop myself up on my elbows so I can look between my thighs and see what he sees. How my arousal—visual proof of what he does to me—glistens on his shaft. How each time he pulls out, he slides a little deeper into me the next time, uses his hand to guide his cock so it rubs expertly around all of the nerves within me, and then withdraws.

Before starting the process all over again.

It's arousing. Heady. Intoxicating. To see my body accept his hard girth. To watch how I stretch around him, adjust to him, and then take him in a little more. To see how when he pulls back out, my pink flesh clings tight like I don't want him to part from me just yet. To know that, even after coming once, my body is more than willing to go again with him.

His patience is admirable. His determination to stretch me bit by bit, escalate our desire inch by inch, is frustrating and erotic and leaves me vibrating with need.

And then finally, with one final thrust he bottoms out, fully sheathed, root to tip, within me. Our mutual groans fill the room as we each allow the other to savor the moment, the feeling, our first time coming together like this.

Seconds pass. Anticipation steals our breaths. And then he reaches out, puts his hand on my shoulder, and holds me in place so he can grind his hips against mine, seating his cock even further into me.

And holy fuck does he feel incredible.

We both gasp, caught up in the slow circle he makes with his pelvis and the absolute eroticism of the moment.

And then he begins to really move.

Our foreheads are pressed against each other's. Our lips kiss and then pant and praise. Our hips move, grinding and bucking in that first-time dance as we find the friction we both need to drive us to the edge. Our hands tense and grasp and grip as Easton picks up the pace.

We crash together in a torrent of lust and lips and tongues, where wants now become needs. Where greed becomes the game, and satisfying it becomes a by-all- means-necessary type of strategy. Where bodies mesh and meet and tease and pleasure.

The room fills with sounds.

Fuck, that feels good.

Right there.

Scout.

Yes. You're incredible.

Oh god.

I can't hold back much longer.

Harder.

Good?

Faster.

Scout.

His hands grip tighter.

"Scout."

His hips buck harder.

"Scout."

A second warning. His restraint is gone.

"I'm coming." I can barely get the words out. The second orgasm that hits is ten times more intense than the first. My body, my breath, my thoughts, my sensibility is all lost as I buck and writhe and take and claim every single ounce of what he gives me while he races to claim his own.

I'm barely coherent, lost in an unforgiving sea of bliss, but when Easton's fingers dig into my thighs, I'm pulled back just in time to watch his climax slam through him. His groan is guttural. His head is thrown back. My name is on his lips. His hips grind violently against mine.

It's sexy as hell to watch him come undone. To know I did this to him. To see his muscles, taut from release, slowly relax, one by one. And when his fingers loosen their grip on me, murmurs of praise are on his lips until he leans over and fuses them to mine for one last kiss.

And then we collapse onto his downy soft bed, his weight on top of me, his dick slipping out of me, and his head resting on my chest.

Seconds turn to minutes as we catch our breath and let our heartbeats calm.

"Well, it wasn't the private field downstairs, but I guess it'll do," I tease as I lazily run my finger up and down the line of his spine.

His laughter rumbles through his chest into mine. "*It'll do?*" he asks in mock disbelief; and that alone—the scrape of his scruff and the heat of his breath from speaking—causes chills to chase over my already sated body. "I played your field all right and slid perfectly into home."

"*If you say so.*" My voice is coy and playful as I shrug and fight the smile on my lips. "This field is pretty impressive."

"I guess I'll have to try harder next time to outrank it then."

"I'm a hard girl to please."

He props himself up on his elbows and just stares at me. But there's something different about the look, the kind of different that suddenly makes me panic and feel fluttery and like I need to go but want to stay.

So I do the only thing I can think of to quiet the chaotic thoughts and prevent them from ruining the moment—I lean up and brush my lips ever so gently against his.

"A demanding woman indeed," he murmurs before giving me that tender type of kiss that reverberates to your toes and then all the way back up until it slams into your belly. *Or heart.* "Good thing I've got a big bat and know how to use it."

CHAPTER TEN

Scout

The sun is blinding. It takes me a minute to adjust to its brightness, and when I'm able to fully open my eyes, Easton's face is inches from mine, dark features half hidden in a sea of light blue pillowcase.

My first reaction is to run my fingers along the scruff on his jaw. To touch him again. To make sure he's real. And to validate every single thing I felt last night as we came together, again and again and again.

My second reaction is *oh shit*.

The buzz I had long into the early morning hours vanishes, gone with the rising of the sun. But with its disappearance comes that groggy awareness of what I allowed—what I wanted to happen—but know can't happen.

Realization hits.

Oh. My. God.

I slept with Easton Wylder.

Hot, delectable, just-as-talented-in-the-sack-as-on-the-ball-field Easton Wylder. The one lying naked beside me in bed, his tanned, sculpted body nestled beneath these pristine sheets.

The player.

A client.

My ticket to getting the Austin Aces' long-term contract. The last wish left on my dad's bucket list, to put the cherry on top of his incredible career.

The wish I just risked by breaking the rules of my ironclad contract.

My head dizzies with the possible consequences if someone were to find out.

My stomach flip-flops over the sight of him sound asleep, so peaceful, so mouthwateringly gorgeous.

Then the panic returns. Not over breeching my contract, like it should be, but rather over how last night made me feel. And man, *how I did feel*. But now that the sheets have cooled and the haze of lust is gone, I'm not sure what to make of these newfound feelings. Or what do to with them now that they still linger.

Oh crap.

What am I thinking?

There can't be feelings.

There can't be anything.

There wasn't even supposed to be sex.

There was supposed to be rehab.

There was supposed to be me getting Easton back up to par, *athletically*, so he could play again and I could tell my dad I did it. Make him proud of me. Give him something more to live for.

Staring at Easton only makes my emotions riot that much louder, but I know what I need to do.

With guilt eating at me like acid, I slide out of the bed slowly so as not to disturb him. How could I be so selfish? So reckless? I search for my clothes, all the while desperate to push these feelings away and crawl back into bed with him. Let him wrap his arms around me and kiss me again just like he did last night when we finally decided we were too exhausted to go another round.

Conflicted in heart and head, I pull on my jeans as quietly as possible and pad out into the condo to find my bra and T-shirt. They're lying on the floor, a scarlet letter of shame to slide on as a reminder of what I'm about to do: leave as silently as possible.

The elevator ride down feels like it takes forever.

It gives me too much time to think. To regret. To realize Easton lifted me up last night. *And I let him do it,* when I definitely weigh more than he should lift with his shoulder. Did he hurt it? Did he reinjure anything?

No. He's fine. It's my panic talking.

Because there was no pain in that moment. There was only want and greed and need and selfishness and selflessness. Definitely not pain. That sexy growl of his fills my head and begs me to stop the elevator right now and press *penthouse* instead of *lobby.*

Go back.

I can't.

Go back.

I press my hand to the row of buttons illuminating five random floors. The elevator stops abruptly at the next floor, its doors open to an empty hallway lined with expensive carpet and doors to other condos.

I stare at the emptiness as my heart fights against my mind.

Duty wars against desire.

Promises made battle against personal wants.

Responsibility clashes against recklessness.

Selflessness is pitted against selfishness.

The doors slide shut, and I close my eyes then press **L** for lobby.

When the doors open, my composure is held together by a thread. I need to get out of here, need time and space to think. Blinded by emotions I can't process just yet, I accidentally run straight into a young coed, knocking her binder to the ground. I scramble to help her pick up the papers that have fallen out, focusing on the words on the pages—teaching credential requirements and adult development something or other—because it's so much easier than meeting her eyes. Embarrassed, frazzled, and moments away from crying, I mumble an apology to the polka-dotted sorority letters printed on the front of her sweatshirt.

"Sorry," I mutter, trying to sound sympathetic when all I feel is responsibility heavier than the weight of my world.

To my dad.

To the Aces.

To Easton.

And as I push open the doors to the street and suck in a huge breath of morning air, the first tear slips down my cheek.

I hate myself for it.

But I hate myself more when my phone vibrates in my purse. The panic I felt upstairs pales in comparison to how I feel when I look at the screen of my phone.

And in an instant, every reason I had for sneaking out and leaving Easton upstairs becomes validated.

The ring through my Bluetooth swallows the silence of my car. I startle at its sound, then cringe, because without even looking at it, I know who's calling.

I ignore it.

He calls back.

I ignore it again.

He calls back again.

After three more rounds of *ring, ignore, repeat*, I'm more aware than ever that sneaking out was total chickenshit. And as much as I'd like to push ignore again, I can't. I have to face him, I have to try and smooth this over without damaging our working relationship, so I bite the bullet and answer.

"Hello?"

"Where the hell are you?" Easton's voice fills the line. Its confusion laced with disbelief mixed with anger and a touch of rejection.

"Good morning." Keep it professional, Scout.

"It would have been an even better morning if you were still here. But you're not. And I'm a little confused as to why."

"Easton." His name is a sigh. An olive branch. It's anything to explain what verbally I can't.

"Don't 'Easton' me, Scout. Where are you? Because you sure as hell aren't in my bed."

My dad's sick. Sally texted five times while I was lying in your bed, trying to tell me he was having a hard time breathing. Asking me if I could come home and visit with him, not only to brighten his mood, but to remind him why he needs to fight harder to get over the funk he's in.

"I had some errands to run," I lie.

I'd rather be with you, too. I'd rather have met you under different circumstances. That would have made all of this ten times easier.

"Errands? Wow. That's a way to make a guy feel confident in his abilities. 'Hey Easton, it was so great last night, but I'd rather go to the store to pick up some toilet paper than have sleepy morning sex with you,'" he says, but his attempt to sound like me does nothing to hide the irritation lacing its edges.

I glance over my shoulder then change lanes as I work up the courage to say the words I need to say but don't really want to say. "Last night was a mistake," I whisper as if I don't want him to hear. Because I don't.

It's a lie.

"Come again?"

"We can't do this."

"Well, we did do this, and it was fucking incredible, so tell me something I'm actually going to believe."

I'm afraid of what I'm going to find when I see my dad for the first time in a month.

I clear my throat but lose the battle against tears for the second time this morning, and it takes everything to sound unaffected when I speak. "If Cory were to find out, he'd fire me."

"Bullshit." He says the word, but we both know it's true—the silence hanging on the line tells me, so I take advantage of the moment to try and reason with him.

"I'm contracted by your employers, Easton. I *have* to remain unbiased . . . and I sure as hell don't look unbiased if I'm sleeping with you one minute and telling them to reinstate you the next. Call me crazy, but they'd second-guess every opinion I have when it comes to you. My credibility would be shot to hell when it's a vital, necessary part of my job."

"Credibility is one thing, Scout. Sleeping with me is another. Now find another way to spin this so you can avoid having to explain why you tip-toed out like you were some one-night stand. *I'll wait.*"

I hate that his words make every part of me sag in relief and in sadness.

But they do, because he didn't consider me a one-night stand and because I know it can't happen again.

"I just can't right now. If someone found out, then . . ."

"No one's going to find out. Are you going to tell someone? Because I'm not. Who else knows about last night and is going to say something?"

My mind scrambles for an explanation, a validation. "What if someone recognizes me leaving your place? Another player? The media? The damn girl in the lobby? And they go and tell the press?"

"Girl in the lobby? What are you talking about?"

"Nothing. No one." I shake my head and grip the steering wheel harder, knowing I sound schizophrenic but unable to stop. "Just never mind."

"There's something you're not telling me."

"No." My voice breaks, and I clear my throat. "There's nothing. It's just . . ."

"It's just? That's all you're going to give me?"

"I've gotta go."

"This discussion isn't over, Scout."

Yes, it is.

I hang up the phone just before the sob breaks free. I know I'm being overly emotional. I know that everything with my dad is making me sensitive. But I also know that there's something about Easton that I can't let go of just yet, but I have to.

Is he the type who'd leave?

Of course he would. *All men leave, Scout.* All people leave. That's what they do.

But what about last night? What about how he made me feel? And not just the sex—because that was pretty damn incredible—but all of the other feelings I went to bed high on and woke up still swimming in. Do they mean anything? And more importantly, do I want to *let* them mean something?

I fight the urge to call him back. To ask him if we could table this for another place and time. Tell him that my dad's sick, explain why this contract is so important, and let him know I'm scared, because if I feel this much after spending only one night with him, how would I feel if we were to spend more together?

But I can't call him back.

Because it all comes back to my dad.

To the promise I made him.

To the fact that anyone I've ever truly loved in my life has left me.

And the one I've loved most will be gone soon, too.

CHAPTER ELEVEN

Scout

"He's going to be pissed that you took the time to drive all the way out here, Scout."

The lines of worry etched on Sally's face warm my heart. "I know he will, but two hours isn't that long of a drive. Besides, I'm sick of him being the one to dictate the visitation terms. And don't worry, I won't tell him you called." I pull her into me for a hug and then chuckle. "Why, I just needed to take a drive to clear my head, Sally, and lo and behold I ended up here." I bat my lashes and smile to reinforce the lie.

She smiles, but it does nothing to ease the weariness in her eyes. "He doesn't want you to see him like this," she whispers. "He's got a lot of pride, and it's hard for him to know you see him as weak."

I sigh. "He's the strongest man I've ever known. Even now. How can he—"

"Who are you talking to Sally?" My dad's voice booms through into the kitchen where we stand.

My smile is as automatic as the drop of my heart into my stomach as I prepare myself for the unknown. What will he look like? Weaker? Bedridden? Gaunt? Has he gone downhill quicker than expected so that I'll be shocked at the sight of him?

With a fortifying breath I walk into the living room where his hospital bed has been set up to make it easier for him to get around, for Sally to tend to him, and because it allows him to stare at one of his favorite places in the world, the endless fields of tall grass that stretch to the horizon.

Relief overwhelms me when I see him out of his bed, sitting in his favorite chair by the window. "She's talking to me."

"Scouty?" Love floods into his voice as he turns and sees me standing there, but it's quickly replaced with upset. "Why are you here?"

"Because I needed to see you." I've never spoken truer words. And while he doesn't look any feebler than the last time I saw him, I know from Sally that he is. The cold he can't shake has knocked him on his ass and taken its toll on his already weakened immune system.

"Nonsense." Irritation litters the edges of his voice. "I told you that you could come to see me once you've won the Aces' contract."

I grit my teeth and bite back the hurt his disregard causes. "Well, you may want to shut me out, Dad, but you don't get to control me." My tone is no-nonsense while my heart aches. He must know that Sally called me, updated me on his rough week, but I refuse to let her take the blame. "I wanted to take a drive today. Clear my head, think about some things. So I ended up here. What are you going to do, kick me out?"

I hold his glare and tempt him to do just that, and I hate that for a minute I wonder if he actually will. He's been so stubborn and difficult in the past six months that a part of me wouldn't put it past him.

"You're not going to prevent me from seeing you. If you try, I'll let *the player* figure out his recovery on his own and take up residence here in my old room."

"Your old room's full of stuff."

"I'm a big girl, I know how to throw *stuff* out." And I know that will get him, break through his obstinacy—the fear that I'll sneak in here with black trash bags and clean out his clutter of memories stacked in boxes in my old room. Newspaper clippings on giants of the sport he helped rehab. Articles highlighting Ford's pitching stats and my softball career. Trophies and jerseys for the teams he's worked for. It's a treasure trove of memorabilia any baseball collector would die for.

He eyes me again, but I can see his lips fighting the smile I know he wants to give me for doing just what he taught me: giving as good as I'm getting. "You can stay for a bit, but one sign of waterworks and I'm kicking you out."

I nod, understanding the hard-ass is giving me a mulligan so long as I don't cry. Stepping beside him, I place my hand on his shoulder and squeeze, needing to touch him. And when he lifts a hand to place on top of mine, I'd give anything to be a little girl again. Then I could crawl into his lap like I used to do and listen to the rumble of his voice as he told me stories about a mom I never really knew, but who he swore loved me. The stories I now know to be lies, because a mom who walks out on her two children getting ready for bed while her husband's washing the dishes without ever looking back never really loved them at all.

This house holds too many memories for me, good and bad, and I wonder if maybe that's why my dad's forcing me to distance myself from it.

"Tell me about how Easton is coming along."

The pang in my chest is real at the mention of his name. The images of him last night—his smile when he was dancing with me, the adoration on his face highlighted by the bright lights of the stadium beyond, and the moonlight across his face as he sank into me—all flash through my mind and force me to act like none of it mattered when every single thing did.

Forced to switch mental gears, I try to care about work right now.

A safe middle ground for us. Well, safe for my dad, but not so much for me.

"The player is doing well," I murmur, knowing damn well Easton's cologne still lingers on my skin as I go into the details of his therapy, what still pains him, what I think he's hiding, before I listen to the master of the trade tell me what he thinks I need to do differently or add to my regimen to help. "What I don't get, besides the obvious—that the team needs him on the field because he's just that good—is why rush it? Why give a timeframe for recovery on a franchise player?"

My dad angles his head as he contemplates the question. "Beats me, Scout. I learned a long time ago that front offices rarely do things that seem reasonable to the public, but in the long run make perfect sense."

"Yeah, well, how about they make common sense instead of aiming for perfect sense," I grumble in defense of Easton when there's no need to defend him.

And it's the look in my dad's eye that unnerves me. The one that tells me he's reading my thoughts when I sure as hell don't want him to. "You like him, don't you?"

"Yeah, I do. He's nice, easy to work with, and wants to recover. What's not to like about that in a player?" I figure that's as safe as anything.

"True." He nods his head again and chews the inside of his lip. "Is this going to be a problem?"

There are so many ways I can take his question, so many ways I can answer it, and so I don't say anything. Does he mean am I going to be able to get Easton back on the field in the allotted time? Does he mean that he can see right through me, knows something happened between Easton and me, and is wondering if it will jeopardize my standing with the club?

When he chuckles at my lack of response, it's music to my ears. *He's let me off the hook without answering.*

"How is it you can have two kids, raise them exactly the same, and they turn out so completely different?" he asks, and I know now that he didn't let me off the hook at all. His chuckle was just prepping me for the schooling he's about to give. "You were always pushing boundaries while Ford was . . . he was always so concerned with making everyone happy. You were always willing to take risks, and he was always the one who would stay the course. You were always so hard to read, and he was the open book. You were opposites in so many ways, and yet so very much alike it scared me some days."

I watch him. The lines in his face may have changed over time, with age and illness, but he still looks the same, still seems the same, and it's hard to believe he's really that sick. That he's mortal and not the invincible man the little girl in me still sees.

"But you changed, Scouty girl. After Ford died, I know you tried to be both for me. That you stepped into his shoes—tried to give me pieces of both of you—even though some days I know it killed you to be someone you weren't . . . but you did it for me. So, thank you. I wanted you to know I appreciate that."

"Dad . . ." I fight back the emotions his acknowledgement churns up. Hearing he knew how hard I'd worked to try and fill the hole Ford's death left in our family—and in his heart—means more to me than he'll ever know.

And at the same time, I hate hearing it. I hate wondering if he's slowly checking items off his mental list of things left to say, and that this is the slow, winding path of him starting to say good-bye.

"You promised you wouldn't cry."

"I'm not." I sniffle and swallow what feels like a boulder in my throat. "I just don't understand why you insist on not letting me—"

"I have my reasons," he barks, and stuns me into wondering what the hell just upset him so much.

I stare at him, wanting to question him, to finish my thought. But I shift my gaze to the field outside again, to the good memories of playing hide and seek with Ford for hours, to try and abate the tears sobbing silently within me.

"He'd be thirty, this month, you know."

"I know." The silence stretches between us, interrupted only by the rattle of his breath. "No father should have to bury his son," I whisper, not sure if it's to remind me or to reassure him.

"And no daughter should be left all alone to bury her father."

CHAPTER TWELVE

Easton

A fucking *text*?

That's how she's going to play this bullshit game with me? Leave me to do my rehab by myself because she can't face me or the fact that the other night was incredible and she left without a word?

"I just can't." Seriously? Those three words were all she could give me before hanging up, followed by a text detailing my rehab routine for the day? Four reps of weighted arm swings and the rest of the regimen?

Total bullshit.

Fucking women.

But I should be happy about this, right? She's not Doc. She's nowhere near as skilled, experienced, or knowledgeable as him. So maybe if I bitch about her, tell the GM, then they'll demand Doc come here instead. He's the best after all.

If that's the case, then why do I want her? How come I keep thinking about that look in her eyes and the feel of her body and the sound of her laugh?

She's frustrating.

And sexy.

She's stubborn and unrelenting.

And goddamn beautiful.

She's fucking irritating is what she is.

She doesn't want to pick up the phone? Then fine. I've got this. I'll bust my ass on my own. I don't need her. I knew that the first day I met her.

But I like her.

Fuck if that isn't perfect. And fitting. Wanting a woman I can't have.

Wanting a woman who could cause trouble if others found out.

Wanting a woman who made it clear she doesn't want me back.

Scratch that. There's nothing clear about it. She's about as clear as mud, because she wants me. A marathon of sex is about as good a validation as any.

Now I just need to figure out how to make her admit it.

Damn woman.

I grit my teeth as I prepare for the pain that typically begins with the fourth set of repetitions, and then startle when it doesn't.

There's no pinch. No burn. There's fucking nothing.

I repeat the movement. I lift and twist and turn a few extra times.

And still nothing.

I try one more time, push my shoulder farther than I should, until I feel a faint pinch before dropping the weight. And when I look in the mirror, I have a stupid grin on my face. It's been so long that I forgot what it even feels like to not hurt.

And, of course, I immediately want to call Scout and tell her so she can celebrate with me over this tiny fucking milestone that shouldn't feel like a victory but does.

But I can't. Because she won't pick up. And I know this because I've called and texted—enough times that I lost count—without getting a return response.

Someone did a number on her. That much I can tell from all her talk about players moving on and leaving her behind, but fuck if I can figure out who it was. No one I've talked to can remember her ever dating anyone. Her social media accounts show shit other than pictures of her in other team clubhouses posing for the camera with various players, arms hanging casually over her shoulders.

Fucking lovely. Isn't that her term? Lovely? Well, that's the first thing that came to mind when I saw the picture of her sandwiched in between Rizzo and Bryant after she worked with the Cubs last year. Or of a shirtless Posey laughing with her in the Giant's clubhouse.

Not a single personal picture. No mutts. No weekend out boozing it up with girlfriends. No inspirational sayings that you want to roll your eyes at and scroll past. *Nothing.*

But she can go out dancing with me. She can stare at my stadium from the darkness of my condo and put into words everything that the sight of it makes me feel. A woman who can understand that shit is not normal.

And now she won't talk to me? Can't face me?

The other night was not a mistake. No way. No how.

"Where's Ms. Dalton?" The voice of the club's GM startles me from the other side of the training room. "Are you on her clock or are you putting extra time in on your own?"

I'm not sure why I hesitate to respond, but I do. He's hard to get a read on, and so caution is the name of the game until I can.

"Hey, Cory. How's it going?" Wiping the sweat from my face with a towel, I walk toward him.

When he steps into the room, I'm surprised to see my father right behind him. *The best-buddy squad. Great.*

"Good. And you? How's the arm?"

"I'm feeling great. The shoulder's feeling the best it has since surgery. I'm anxious to get back out there."

"I'm sure you are. Is Scout around?"

"She caught a bug. I told her to stay home, but we've talked and gone over my regimen so I can stay on task." The lie comes out smoothly, but I can't for the life of me figure out why I feel the need to cover for her at all.

And yet I did, the need to protect her unexpected, but there nonetheless.

"I'm impressed that you came in on your own to get it done," my dad interjects.

I stare at him, trying to comprehend why he'd think it was anywhere near okay for him to say that. And around my boss, no less. I'm not a child. This is my job, and I'm damn good at it, so he needs to leave me the fuck alone. The thought manifests into words, but I bite my tongue so hard it hurts.

It's not worth it. Besides, Cory's expression is guarded, making it nearly impossible to gauge his thoughts. And since professionalism is always the best route, I play the part they expect me to play.

"Like I said, I'm anxious to get back on the field. I miss contributing to the team." I spout the company line, and even though they smile in response, there's something off here. Something I can't put my finger on but can sense nonetheless.

"The guys miss you, too. The Aces don't quite feel right without a Wylder on the field."

My dad laughs and slaps me on my good shoulder. "Keep up the good work, son. I have no doubt you'll be back to fighting form soon enough."

"Neither do I," I say.

"Make sure to tell Ms. Dalton that I'd like a report in the next day or two on your progress."

"Will do."

I watch them leave and blow out a breath as I try to figure out what the little visit was all about. I don't want to care but have to. He's my boss.

"Everything good in here, Easy E?"

My smile is automatic, the irritation vanishing in a heartbeat at the voice I've known since I was eight years old. I turn to find the familiar face of our clubhouse manager, the man who used to entertain me with stories and jokes when my dad was too busy being the public persona.

"Hey, Manny-Man," I say in the same exchange of nicknames we've done for over twenty years. "How're you doing today? You staying to watch the game tonight?"

"Pretty damn good. And nope. You know me. I only stick around when the greats play."

"Are there no greats playing today?" I ask with a shake of my head.

"Greats are few and far between, son," he finishes his typical retort and surprises me when he continues. "I've watched enough baseball in my life to hold off watching another game until it's someone who's going to dazzle me with his talent."

"Picky. Picky."

His grin just widens, and I love that even though I'm injured, he's still Manny-Man.

"I see the old man is still as hard on you as ever," he says with a knowing nod, just like he used to do when he'd find me alone in the locker room, sniffling away tears in secret after I was hurt by something my father would say.

"Yeah, well. Why change now, right?"

He just nods, never one to be disrespectful, but a man I'm glad to have on my side.

"True." He laughs, contrary to the gravity in his eyes as he searches to make sure I'm okay. "Look at me—forty years, and I'm still doing the same goddamn thing."

"Taking care of us pretty boys?" I tease.

"There's nothing pretty about you, son." I bark out a laugh at the good-humored dig. "But that tough cookie who's been working you over? Hoowee. Now, she? She's definitely pretty."

"She sure is," I murmur before I catch myself, and wonder why nearly every conversation of late seems to come back to her.

Because she's the one in charge of the decisions.

And the one currently clouding up and fucking with my head.

CHAPTER THIRTEEN

Scout

My lungs burn.

My legs ache.

And all I can think is one more side of the stadium before my nerves are calm and emotions dulled enough to be able to face Easton today.

Because how do I keep things professional when every time I have to touch him, I'm going to be reminded of the other night?

So, running the stadium steps I go. Up one section. Lower loge to loge to upper loge, across the top row of empty seats, then down the other side.

I replay my meeting with Cory. His insistence that I answer whether I think Easton will be up to speed by mid-August. His pressure on me to say if he'll be back to one hundred percent, or if he will slowly slide down the slope of injured and irreparable that sometimes happens despite all rehab efforts.

Frustrated with their businesslike attitude when it comes to a human being—to tendons and muscles and soft tissue you just can't superglue back together—I push myself harder. To the next section, to the upper loge, to the loge, to lower loge, and then to the next.

Forget about it, Scout. It's his job to get good players on the field and win pennants. Players are commodities.

I sprint across a row of seats.

Screw that. Players are people.

My lungs burn, but I need more.

Martinez hits a ball over the left field wall in his early morning batting session on the diamond below, but the crack of his bat is silenced by my ear buds. And I need it to be. I may be in the stadium, but I need to forget about baseball for a few more flights. And, in particular, a specific baseball player.

So, I continue to push myself. To use the physicality to burn my mind and ease my soul. To eat away at my anger. To calm me the hell down when all I feel is uncertainty.

When all I want is something I can't have.

So, I climb. Section by section. Step by step. Trying to shed the burden of my emotions with the sweat that drips off my body.

But the clearer my mind becomes, the more room I have to think, and of course I veer to where I shouldn't. To Easton and everything about him. The contrasts. The unexpected. The disarming smile and the intense eyes. His soft groans in the dark and his baseball-bat-roughened hands on my skin. The vulnerability he pulls out of me, when I'm tough with everyone else.

This is not a good sign—me thinking about him.

Not at all.

And, of course, when I turn to run down the next section of seats, he's right there, running behind me. Matching me step for step.

I ignore him.

I still get thirty more minutes to myself before I have to deal with him.

I still need thirty more minutes to figure out how to look at him and not want to feel how I feel.

I still want thirty more minutes to calm the flutter in my belly just from knowing he's near me.

So, I run faster. I take the steps two at a time.

He does the same and double-times it so that he's now running beside me instead of behind me.

I push harder. Irritated. Competitive. Not wanting him to think I'm weaker or less than or both, even though he's never made me feel that way in the first place.

But having feelings for him does, and so that makes it his fault. All of it.

And so, I run. But this time, instead of turning to cross over to the next section, I run straight through the exit to the concourse beyond.

One of my earbuds has fallen out, and my shoes squeak on the concrete as I run in an all-out sprint down the empty corridor, past the vacant concessions stands and team merchandise kiosks.

His shoes slap the concrete behind me, and his labored breathing echoes through the space.

I know he's fast. Having clocked his time, I'm well aware he could be ten steps ahead of me in seconds if he really wanted to be, and the fact that he's not grates on my already irritated nerves.

And at the same time, I'm out of gas—my legs, my lungs, my everything—and so I have no choice but to stop when I'd rather keep running right on out of the stadium instead of having to face Easton.

"Scout."

Keep running.

"Scout."

I can't even breathe, let alone talk.

"Hey."

I can't do it anymore. I can't run another step, and so I stop, knowing I'm going to have to face him—right here, right now—with a mind and body so exhausted it's going to be tough to keep my guard up.

With my hands on my knees, sweat stinging my eyes and lungs heaving harshly, I glance over at Easton, strangely satisfied to see he's just as winded as I am. Hands braced behind his head, elbows out, he walks around this mecca of gray concrete to cool down.

"It's not your time yet. Go away." I know I'm being mean. I know he doesn't deserve it. And yet I need to catch my breath so I can think straight.

"I have just as much of a right to be in this stadium as you do, *Kitty*." The nickname is a taunt I try to ignore. He has a way of pushing my buttons, and that damn name is just one of them.

Especially when I remember how he was pleasing my body the last time he called me that.

And that pisses me off more. I hate that I'm supposed to feel like I don't care when all I want to do is care.

"I'm not on the clock yet, so this is my time."

"Like hell it is."

If he was looking for my full attention, he just got it. And not only that, but my temper to go along with it.

"Excuse me?" I stand to my full height and look at him for the first time. And when I do, every part of my body wants to move toward him instead of rail against him.

"You heard me," he says, meeting me glare for glare as he takes a few steps toward me. "I never figured you to be the love 'em and leave 'em type, but hey, you've already underestimated me . . . so I guess we're even. Right?"

There's a bite to his tone. A defiant rejection edged with bruised ego. And all of that and more is reflected in his eyes as he takes another step closer while I glance around frantically to see if anyone is within listening distance.

"No one's close enough to hear me, Scout. Or to save you from having this conversation."

"We're not having this conversation, so it's a moot point." I begin to walk away, and he sidesteps to block me. I'm forced to stop, or else I'll end up face first in his chest, and touching him right now is not exactly the smartest thing.

"We are having it because there're a few things that we need to get straight. First one: I've had plenty of fun in my life, in and out of the sheets. But not once have I ever snuck off in the early morning and not faced what I did or didn't do the night before. I'm a bigger man than that, and something tells me you are, too. So, you want to tell me what's going on?"

His dig is real. His hurt breaks through the spite in his tone. I hate that my immediate urge is to apologize and explain . . . but I can't. I must stand my ground with him. I have no other option.

"Like I said, I'm not on the clock."

"You're damn right you're not. But I'm not your clock, sweetheart."

"Leave me alone." The comment is quick off my lips, my temper flaring and body on fire from his words. The ones that make me want to step into him and let him taste the anger on my lips.

"What? I thought you weren't on the clock. Remember? So, that means you don't get to tell me what to do for about . . ." He looks at his watch then back up to me with amusement in his eyes. "Fifteen more minutes."

That grin of his is maddening. And sexy as hell.

"Exactly. So, if you'll excuse me."

His hand is on my arm in a flash, and now my back is against the corner of two walls, and he is directly in front of me.

"You're determined. I'll give you that." He nods and squeezes my arm ever so slightly as he steps farther into my personal space. And now when I breathe in, it's him I smell. His shampoo. His cologne. His fabric softener. *Him.* "But I'm wondering where that fast-talking, loud-laughing, carefree girl I was dancing with the other night went because, while you're still goddamn gorgeous, all the rest of her is nowhere to be seen."

"Everyone makes mistakes, Easton."

His chuckle is a low rumble that fills my ears and echoes in my head as he moves so that our bodies are merely a whisper away. Heat. Want. Need. All three dance a troublesome tango inside of me as he leans in so his lips are by my ear when he whispers, "It wasn't a mistake. You know what I think? I think I got to you. I think when you close your eyes, you think about me. I think you don't want to, but you do, because God knows I think about you, Scout. About what we did. About how I want more of it. With you. And you can give me the company line all you want, about how you are under contract and so we can't pursue this, but fuck that. I don't like to play by the rules. A contract is business, Scout. But this? You. Me? This is pleasure."

His words ignite every ember of desire within me. "You don't understand."

"Then try me." The honesty in his words combats the promises I've made outside of this. When I refuse to meet his eyes, he provokes me. "I never figured you for a coward, Scout."

"You know what? You're right," I state with an enthusiastic nod and a shrug of my shoulders. A ruse to mask the truth. "The other night was fun. Incredible. The best sex I've had in a while, but that's all it was—sex. A little fun to let off some steam, and now that we've got each other out of our systems, we can forget about it. As you can tell by the way I left, I don't do commitment. I don't do more than what we did. So, thanks for the good time. Now let's get to work."

I try to dart past him, and end up with his hand back on my upper arm, refusing to let me run again.

"Thanks for the good time?"

"Yep. *Thanks.*"

His hazel eyes narrow, the edges tinged with green today as he squeezes my arm. "You're scared." And he makes the statement so matter-of-factly that my denial is automatic.

"No."

"How did I not see it before? Why do I scare you?"

Mayday. Mayday. I avert my eyes. Shift my feet. "That's such bullshit. Make sure to flatter yourself while you're at it."

"It's not flattery if it's the truth," he quips, trying to get a smile out of me, but it's kind of hard to smile when your heart feels like it's beating out of your chest and your first instinct is to sprint but your feet refuse to move. "Besides, there was no need for you to run unless you were spooked."

"What, so now a woman can't have a one-night stand without a reason?"

"Nice play, but no dice. You knew this wasn't a one-night stand, Scout. You knew we were going to have to see each other for the next few weeks. So you can try to convince yourself, but I'm not buying it."

My thoughts fly out of control, and none of them manifest into words, so I just stand there looking at him, mouth opening and closing, like more of an idiot than I already feel.

"Then why push the issue? If you don't believe what I'm saying, then why don't you walk away?" There. I said something.

And yet I feel everything.

He chuckles, but it is anything but amused. "Because talk is cheap, Scout. Your lips are saying one thing, but your body and eyes are telling me something completely different. Did you already forget how incredible the other night was? How good I made you feel?" His eyes pin me motionless with a dare to refute him. "So go ahead and lie to yourself—stand by your one-night stand excuse—but just know I don't buy it for one minute. I was there. I know the truth."

"Maybe I'm just a girl who likes to see how many major leaguer notches I can add to my belt." *Deflect. Divert. Distract.*

"You're full of funny today, aren't you? Do you think the other night would have happened if I thought that you were a baseball betty trying to charm me into the diamond between your thighs?"

"Then why *did* it happen?" The question is out before I can stop it, and I know it's surprised him because I can feel his fingers stiffen on my arm. I immediately want to know and don't want to know the answer.

"Because you're incredible? Is that a good enough answer?" He angles his head and just stares at me for a beat in a way that has heat spreading from my center out to my toes and back in. "Because we had a day."

"A day?"

"Yes. It wasn't good. It wasn't bad. It was just a day filled with a little bit of everything, and you don't share *a day* with someone you don't like." His reasoning is simple enough, and sounds so sweet coming from this gruff baseball player who is a mixture of so many things. "And because we danced. We drank. We sulked. You stood in my apartment and looked at a symbol representing my whole life and summed up how I feel but can never put into words. You got me. And then *you seduced me.*"

"I what?" I cough the words out as that soft smile of his turns big and bright.

"You seduced me. A beautiful woman with a sharp tongue, a sharper mind, and a look in her eye that said she was scared and confident, haloed by the light of a baseball stadium . . . I mean, a man only has so much restraint when it comes to that kind of perfection."

And I'm a puddle. A big, messy puddle of feelings that are so foreign I'm not sure what to do or say or how to act other than to reject the words. But for some reason nothing comes from my lips because . . . because, look at him. Complete virility mixed with sincerity. Everything a normal woman would fall into the arms of when all I can think of is running away.

But my feet don't move. They don't listen to my head because they are too busy listening to Easton. They are too busy letting his words break them down and give them an ounce of hope when hope was supposed to be lost.

All I can do is stare at him—wage a war with everything I've conditioned myself to believe—and try to trust what he's saying.

"Or maybe you were just using me so you could see my private baseball field." He delivers the joke with a soft smile, but his eyes tell me he knows I'm freaking out inside and is trying to add some levity to calm me.

"Perhaps." I give him an inch and secretly wonder if I do so because I want him to take the mile.

"See?" He shakes his finger at me as his smile grows. "You forget I can read you. And you like me, Scout Dalton. So, pretend all you want that you don't. Tell me the other night was a mistake. But I'll be over here chipping away at whatever is preventing you from admitting it, because that night was incredible. And not just the sex. That was phenomenal, too. But you . . . . You *get* me. In a world of people wanting the throwback baller they see on the field, you understand there is more to me than just *him.* For some reason you seem to understand the things no one else does, the parts of me I'm not sure I even get, and yet you're able to put words to it. So, yeah . . . the sex was great. You can stick to your guns, tell me it wasn't, tell me it was a mistake, tell me you don't feel a damn thing when we touch . . . but I do. And I want to go out again."

He leans forward and kisses me. I'd like to say it's against my will, but I'm all in, despite trying not to show it. Because we're here. At the stadium. And I can't kiss him.

But I do. With lips and tongue and heart, while his hands hold my shoulders still and my body motionless.

I missed him.

The single thought runs wild in my head over the few seconds I allow myself to be kissed senseless and reminded of how incredible he tastes.

And how amazing our chemistry is.

I want. And don't want.

I know we should stop. But I can't make myself step back.

Sensing my sudden hesitation, he does it for me. He tears his lips from mine and stares at me with a vigor I've not seen from him before.

"Easton—"

"You can refuse me all you want . . ." He laughs, stopping the rebuff on my lips. "But I should warn you, I'm a determined man. I'll win, Scout. I'm a gamer, remember? So I'll get that date. That next kiss. Earn them from you, including the halo of stadium light in your hair. And I'll wear you down until you figure out there's no need to be scared of me."

He lets go of my arms and steps back as the arrogance returns to his grin. "It's going to be a bitch, isn't it? To have to stretch me. Body to body. To have your hands on me. To have to watch me get hot and sweaty. To hear me groan when I lift weights and not remember that's the same sound I made when I came. To rub me out—nice and slow. To be around me so much you're sick of me, all the while denying there's something here worth figuring out." He takes another step back, adjusts his baseball hat and lowers the sunglasses resting on its bill to his eyes. "Have fun with that. I know I will. You've got five minutes before I'm on your clock. Tick. Tock."

And with one last flash of a grin, Easton turns on his heel and jogs down the corridor like we didn't just run a race.

Or he didn't kiss me senseless and then leave me speechless.

I'm breathless.

I'm stunned.

God, I'm fucked.

CHAPTER FOURTEEN

Scout

"**H**ey, Scout?"

"Hmm?" I murmur as I busy myself pulling my glove out of my bag, anything to keep my distance from him.

"I need to be stretched." His sing-song tone, laced with the promise of his words from the corridor, floats from where he's sitting on the right field turf and hits me squarely in the gut.

"Start your warm-up."

"I already warmed up," he says, prompting me to turn his way and see his grin in full effect and aimed whole-heartedly at me.

"Lovely," I mutter as I make my way over to him, more than aware of the trio of players working out in left field with their conditioning coach. No rest for the weary, even on an off-day in their insane schedule.

"What was that?" he asks, cheer infused into his voice because I know he's pushing those buttons he mentioned upstairs.

"Nothing." I put my hands on my hips and stare down at him where he sits on the turf. He's changed into his baseball pants, cleats, team T-shirt, and a new baseball hat. Add to the mix that grin on his face and he's irresistible, but hell if I'm going to let him know I think that.

"How do you want me?" he asks, and I know he's trying to pull me back to that first time we met. We're around each other so much it feels like that was months ago, but in reality, it has only been weeks.

I don't give him the satisfaction of an answer, but rather motion for him to stand up. Stepping behind him, I begin our routine—stretching, working through the stiffness, and feeling for any click in his shoulder.

I work in silence, trying to listen to his body and ignore it all at the same time. His taunts from earlier replay in my mind, challenging me to disregard them, despite the ripple of his muscles and heat of his skin beneath my fingertips that only validate them. Because with each touch of his arm, each rotation of his shoulder, all I can think of is what his biceps looked like when he braced his body over me. When he sunk into me. When he made me come.

"Can you do that one again?" he asks softly.

So focused on his shoulder, I repeat the stretch without skipping a beat.

And when I press his arm up, I'm met with Easton's waiting eyes and knowing smile.

"Seriously?" I say, dropping his arm instantly, pissed that I just willingly walked right into his *extra stretch* so he could maneuver me closer to him without questioning it or him.

He blinks his eyes a few times and feigns innocence. "It's gonna be a bitch, isn't it?"

"You're a pain in my ass." I laugh, wanting to maintain a hard line but unable to because I know he's right. I step into him, jab my finger into his chest, and try to discipline myself anyway. "If *this* is contract, and *that* is pleasure, then let's keep it that way. Don't bring it on the field. This is my job. *You're* my job. So, suck it up, Hot Shot, get your gear on, and meet me behind home plate," I say the words that I know will stop him from saying anything else.

"What?" His excitement is heartwarming.

"You're throwing down."

"What did you just say?" I can hear the hope in his voice as he jogs up beside me, and it tugs on every heartstring that he hasn't already tugged on.

"You heard me."

"I know you didn't just say that to distract me from the conversation and not plan on following through."

"I wouldn't do that. Not when it comes to your arm. This is contract, remember?"

"Then say it again." His grin is contagious, and I smile at his reaction, my bipolar emotions on overdrive.

"Please don't tell me you forgot what throwing down is." I toy with him, speaking to him like a teacher does to a child, fingers pointing to each location as I explain. "I know it's been a few months, so I'll explain. Throwing down is when the catcher, *that's you*, sits behind home plate—that's the white thing over there behind the batter's box. And when the pitcher—that's the person on the mound—throws the ball to you, you throw the ball down to second base—that white square *way* out there—to try and get the runner out who's trying to steal."

"Thanks," he says drolly as he gestures to the glove in my hand and then stops when he notices his gear already laid out in the dugout. Thankfully Manny was around and helped me get that part done. "You're serious, aren't you?"

"As a heart attack."

The look on his face will forever be etched in my mind as one of those times my job is incredible. Reverence. Awe. Gratitude. Relief. All of them are reflected as he slides on his armor. The barely visible inscription *Thou shall not steal* written in black sharpie around the edge of his chest protector makes me smile.

I'm reminded of the times I've watched a game on TV, stared at his inscription, and wondered what kind of cocky asshole would taunt a runner by wearing that. But then within a few pitches he'd pick the runner off the base with such ease, I'd know that if anyone could pull off wearing that chest protector, Easton Wylder could.

Waiting for him at home plate, I give him a moment to enjoy feeling semi-normal again, putting his gear back on for the first time in months. It's a milestone—physically and mentally. And I love that when he walks out of the dugout, he's greeted by hoots and hollers from his teammates still in left field.

"'Bout fucking time, Wylder!" one of them yells, which earns him a middle finger from Easton, but his huge grin doesn't lie about how this makes him feel.

"So, here's the deal . . . we'll start off slow. We'll warm up tossing the ball, and then once you're warm enough, I'll take a few steps back—we'll throw some at that distance—and then I'll step back farther, keep going until you feel any pain or discomfort."

"Sounds good, but why the gear?"

"Because you throw different with your gear on. You might not think so, but you do. Slow and steady wins the race here, Easton. There's no prize for coming out hard."

"Fitting." His laughter is loud and rich and hits me about the same time I realize the innuendo in my words. All I can do is shake my head and step down the first base line. "I know all about slow and steady, Kitty. Don't you worry there."

I turn to glare a warning at him. "This is contract, Hot Shot," I say knowing damn well he's enjoying this. "We'll start working our way to first base, and then, depending on how you're feeling, we can move on to second."

Thankfully, he lets that innuendo slide with only a snicker as I lift my glove and motion for him to throw the ball.

"How is it feeling?" It's been about thirty minutes since we started, but the grin on his face tells me all I need to know.

I think.

"Good. Better with each throw."

"That's good." My hands go automatically to his shoulder, pressing, kneading, feeling. "Was there any tightness or pinching or—"

"A little tightness, but this is the most I've done in months, so it feels good."

"Mm." I stare at him, wishing he'd take off his sunglasses so I could see his eyes and know if he's being truthful or not. But this is where I have to trust him. He knows his body best, after all.

"So, do I get to play with second base?" he asks, hopeful that I'm going to let him throw the full distance.

"Wouldn't you like to know." I laugh because all of this—his lack of pain, how good his arm looks and feels, our flirty banter—has put me in a good mood. Add to that working with Easton out in the sunshine and making progress has given me time to think.

"You're looking good," Drew Minski says as he jogs over on his way to the dugout from the outfield.

"Feels fucking great to have leather and laces in my hands again," Easton says.

"Hi, Drew." I greet him when he nods my way. "Great at-bat last night."

"Thanks." He glances over to Easton and then back to me. "Hey, man, some of us are thinking about going out tonight if you want to hang with us."

"Thanks, but I have plans," Easton says, and I hate that regardless of how much I've pushed him away, a little part of me is jealous of whoever he has plans with.

"Your loss. I know it's your thing to keep them all strung on a line, but that pretty little blonde keeps asking for you." He chuckles in that way that says, *go for it.* I've been in enough clubhouses to know the sound of encouragement when I hear it.

And the sound of it pisses me off.

He's got plans with one woman, is stringing the blonde along, all the while making promises to me. Done with the conversation, and not wanting for him to read the emotions I can't seem to hide from him, I turn without saying another word and head over to grab my bag.

I try to be rational. I try to not care, and I hate that I've lowered my guard enough, let myself hope enough, that I thought he really liked me. Believed he was different. Not a player.

And the idea of other women liking him irritates me because I know thousands of women would way more than just like him; they'd hop in bed with him without a second thought.

"Scout?"

"You're done for the day." I try to hide the hurt, try to hide the fact that I might be overreacting, because I should know better. Hope is a dangerous thing, especially when you're pinning it on someone else.

One step forward and five steps back in the *How Fucked-up Is Scout's Head* game.

CHAPTER FIFTEEN

Easton

Cool down like normal. Ice for twenty minutes on, twenty minutes off. Text me if you have any problems.

-Scout

A note?

She left me a fucking note?

Whoever did a number on her is a fucker. Grade A asshole. But I don't have time to worry about him because I need to find her. Talk to her. Wear her down. Figure out what the fuck spooked her again.

I run out of the locker room—cleats still on—and see Manny. "Hey, Man. Did you see which way Scout went?" A grin spreads slowly on his lips, and I know he's assumed I'm looking for her for more than just my cool down instructions. "Save the lecture, old man."

His grin grows wider, and he points down the tunnel that leads out to the parking lot. "No lecture at all."

His laugh echoes after me as I hustle down the corridor and out the side entrance of the ballpark. It only takes me a few seconds to spot Scout and jog after her.

"A note, Scout?"

She freezes midstride for a split second before she begins walking again. "Yep. A note. You worked out. You can cool down with my instructions. I'm your trainer, and—"

"If you're my trainer, then do your goddamn job!" I shout at her, frustrated in every way imaginable by this woman who continues to test me, push me away, run away, when I can see in her eyes that she wants me just as much as I want her.

"I was. You got your instructions. You know what to do. Didn't know I had to hold your hand, Wylder."

"I know what to do, all right," I mutter as I glance around to make sure no one from the team is around. *Throw you over my shoulder and take you up to my place so we can figure this the fuck out. And then I can lay you down and we can make this all better.*

"Once a player always a player, *right*?" she sneers.

"Drew." His name is all I have to say to know what she's pissed about. I'm a dumbass for not putting two and two together.

"String 'em along? Is that what you're doing to me, so you can keep a woman in every city, ready and waiting for when you pass through town?" The hurt in her eyes is undeniable, and I hate that I put it there.

"What the fuck did he do to you to make you think so highly of men, Scout?"

Emotions flicker through her eyes before she can clear them and avert her gaze. "Never mind. Forget I said anything."

I jog after her, pissed at myself for chasing her, and at the same time wanting to figure out what exactly is going on. "The blonde is no one."

"Mm-hmm." She keeps her eyes focused straight ahead and refuses to look my way.

"Seriously. You want to keep this all secretive—"

"There is no *this*."

"And Drew is part of the club," I explain, completely ignoring her remark. "What did you want me to do? Correct him? Tell him to shut up when normally I just laugh at all the guys' ribbing over the women in bars? Then he'd really know there was something going on between us. And there *is* something going on between us," I say, cutting her off before she can argue with me again. "So save yourself the argument."

"You're an arrogant asshole, you know that?" she spits out as she turns toward me, arms folded across her chest as if that will protect her from the truth she can't seem to face.

"Maybe, but you're fucking adorable when you're angry at me."

There's a slight crack in her anger. A bit of a smile.

"And I kind of like that you were jealous."

"I was not."

"Ah, Kitty, but you were." Another crack in her smile. "A woman only storms out when she's jealous, and while the sight of your ass swaying as you stalked away was almost enough to let you keep being pissed, you needed to know the truth. There is no blonde in the bar waiting just for me, because she waits for anyone. There are no strings of women. There is no one else in another city."

She stares at me. Searches to see if she believes me, and fuck . . . not only can the woman stand her ground, but she can take care of herself too. Tell me that's not sexy as hell.

And frustrating all at the same time.

"Tell me what you're thinking, Scout." There's too much silence. Too much time for her to doubt and poke holes in what I said and bend it to match whatever insecurities are banging around inside of her.

"I just . . . you're just . . ."

"I think you're thinking how much you want to kiss me right now."

"Too much," she says at the same time I speak, and we both smile softly as it feels like the explosive wave of her temper may have just blown over.

"So you want to kiss me *too much*?" I say, combining our comments and garnering a huff from her.

"I don't know what to do about you," she finally says, softly and full of trepidation.

"Nothing, Scout. There's nothing *to do*. There's just *us* going out to have a good time. There's just *us* figuring out if there's anything here. There are no commitments. There's no need for anyone to know anything. It's just us getting to know each other and enjoying each other's company."

"What if I don't want that?"

There's that doubt again. The insecurity I don't understand.

"You want this."

It takes everything I have not to lean in and taste those bee-stung lips that tempt me every single time I look at them. Not to lean in and remind her of how it felt earlier when we'd kissed.

There's just something about her I can't let go, and I don't even know her that well yet.

Because there are women who are good for a quick fuck. There are women you would fuck, but are better in the friend zone. And then there are women like Scout. They make you wonder, make you crave them, and drive you absolutely fucking crazy because you want them when you shouldn't. They're an enigma. Confusing, alluring, tempting, and fucking perfection.

I stare at her, with her ponytail whipping around her face on the downtown sidewalk, and have never wanted so badly to pull a woman against me and soothe the trouble in her eyes as I wait to hear her response.

You want this.

"Easton. The contract. My dad. It's just—"

I look around for space. For privacy. For what I need to prove a point that she needs to feel, not just hear.

"Complicated? Messy? Welcome to life, Scout. Mine's all of those and then some, and you don't even know the half of it."

Her smile tugs at me. Makes me want to take care of her when I've never wanted to take care of anyone in my life other than my mom.

"Easton."

"You keep saying my name like that and I'm going to think you like me."

She laughs. The darkness clears from her eyes some, and I know I've made an inroad.

And at the same time, we pass a little alleyway behind the stadium, out of view of the public, and I push her backward into it. Before we even clear the sidewalk, I have my lips on hers.

God. Damn.

She's fucking addictive.

I want her.

Her taste.

Must have her.

The scent of her perfume.

Say yes to this, Scout.

The softness of her lips.

Say yes to me.

The tentativeness of her tongue as she fights her will to dive right in.

Let me the fuck in.

Even her temper turns me on.

And so I take what I want from her. What I need from her. My dick hardens from the kiss. From the way her fingers twist in my shirt. From the feel of her tits rubbing against my chest. From the goddamn moan that sounds like the white flag waving as she surrenders herself to me.

I don't want this to end. But my dick is hard and I still have my cup on, and fuck, that's a miserable feeling. Plus, we're on the street. Near the stadium. And while I'd love to relieve the ache in my balls by doing a variety of things with her—right here, right now—it pains me to have to end the kiss.

To pull back and try to hold tight to my control that's hanging by a thread.

But I don't release her from my grasp when I lean back and look in her eyes. I try to catch my breath, try to quiet the caveman side of me, and then she speaks.

"Well, I guess that's getting to know each other as good as any other way."

The smile is there, but it takes a few seconds before the cautious look in her eyes reflects the same confidence reflected in her voice.

But fuck. I'll take it.

I'm putting myself out on a limb for a woman who wants to run, when for the life of me, I've never been one to stay.

But I'm not going anywhere.

Chapter Sixteen

Scout

Nerves rattle around within me when they shouldn't.

"This is . . . unbelievable." I look around the facility. There's a state of the art batting cage with a multi-pitch batting machine set up on one end, and a sloped floor to collect the balls and refeed the machine. The turf beyond houses a complete infield. The walls are littered with sports memorabilia from some of the greats—signed jerseys, bats, and balls from Mickey Mantle, Babe Ruth, Jackie Robinson, Hank Aaron, Ted Williams . . . and a few from Cal Wylder.

I walk along the walls, stare at the living history lining them, and am in awe of the mini-museum of men I grew up hearing my father talk about.

"It's my wall," he muses quietly, allowing me to take it all in as I turn from the legends beside me to face one that I feel has equal potential.

"It's a good wall," I muse, heading over to the rack of bats all sized and weighted to match his preferences. "I've never seen anything like it."

"Yeah, well . . ." He shrugs and blushes and it's rather adorable. "The machine is having issues, or else I'd tell you to hit a few."

"I haven't touched a bat in what feels like years." I run my fingers over the butts of them and then continue to explore the space. We both fall silent, but I know he's watching me, and I'm not quite sure what to do about it.

I asked to see the field because it was safer than going into his condo where I will be reminded of the other night when I need to still process the events of the day and how I feel about them. How I let him wear me down, kiss me senseless twice, and then manage to get me to admit that maybe I want to see where all of this leads us because me agreeing to come here means it is, in fact, going somewhere.

And that scares the hell out of me.

There's a wall to the left of a bathroom. It's lined with framed jerseys in different colors and sizes, and it takes me a minute to figure out what they are. "These are all of your Little League jerseys, aren't they?"

I stare at the simple idea and can't believe how touched I am by the sight of them. The history he has with each one. The memories from then that made the man he is now.

"Yes. My parents kept them all." He says nothing more, and the silence prompts me to wonder more about him, his family, but I have a feeling it's an off-limits topic.

"Have you always wanted to play baseball?" It's a simple question, one I expected him to answer immediately, and his pause piques my curiosity.

I turn to look at him while he's looking at his history on the wall. I take in his profile—the bill of the baseball hat shadowing his face, his thick lashes, straight nose, and full lips. His scruff is longer today than normal, and there's something about it that's incredibly sexy.

"It was what was expected of me." The honesty in his voice is haunting. His exhale is uneven. "I mean, I'm Cal Wylder's son."

There's an unreadable emotion in his tone, and I sense there is so much more beneath the surface, but I'm afraid to pry, even though I want to.

"Were you always good at it? You're such a natural, but I'm sure it had to be hard living in the shadow of your dad."

He chews the inside of his cheek as he continues to stare at the wall. He points to one of the smallest jerseys up there. It's a faded dark green with the number ten on its back. "That was my first year playing. I remember I got in a fistfight with Joey Jones. He told me I had to have been adopted, because there was no way Cal Wylder's son could be so horrible at playing baseball. I cried for days. My dad was on a road stretch and I dodged his phone calls, too embarrassed to tell him what had happened. I knew he was going to be so disappointed in me—not because of the fight, but because of how bad I was. I spent days sick to my stomach and worried about what he was going to say when he came home and saw for himself."

I want to walk over to him and hold his hand. I want to tell him I'm sorry. Tell him I understand about living in shadows of giants and the weight those shadows bear. I want to do anything but hear the sadness in his voice. Yes, he has the last laugh now, being as successful as he is, but even success can't erase the scars of childhood memories.

"That must have been hard."

He nods, shifts his feet, and then points three jerseys down to a dark blue one with the same number on it. "That was the year everything clicked for me. I was eight. My hand-eye coordination suddenly matured, and I learned to read a ball out of a pitcher's hand. All of a sudden I went from zero to hero. And, of course, that meant my dad came to more games when he could. Suddenly I was Mr. Popular. Kids who wouldn't give me the time of day before now wanted to be my friend in the hope that they'd get some pointers from a major leaguer when he showed up."

I close the distance between us and step up beside him, our arms touching, and let him get lost in his thoughts.

He points to the next frame over, a red and white jersey; this time the number on the back is eighteen. "That's the year my parents divorced. I lived at the field that season. It was so much easier than being at home where my mom cried nonstop, or being with my dad when he was in town and feeling guilty for leaving my mom home alone. Baseball became my escape that year. I put everything I had into it. It was the first time I really fell in love with the game."

"So, back then you played to escape. Why do you play now?"

He laughs. "Because I make a shit ton of money, and who wouldn't want to play baseball for a living?"

"True." I nod, but can sense the unspoken words and the underlying hint of sarcasm. "Do you still love it?"

"Some days."

"If you have a shit ton of money, then why do you still play?" I know I'm pushing, but I'm intrigued how a man who is so incredibly talented and oozes respect for the game has misgivings about saying he loves it.

"For my dad."

"For your dad?" His answer surprises me. "Not for you?"

"No."

"Do you love it?" I ask the question again, forgetting that I already have, and before I can tell him to disregard it, he responds.

"Yes. No. Fuck, Scout, most days I don't know." He turns to face me for the first time, and I can see the conflict in his eyes, the uncertainty in his expression, and the tension in the set of his shoulders. "It's all I've ever known. All that's ever been expected of me. It's hard to explain without sounding ungrateful because I'm extremely blessed in talent and luck when I know there are a million others who would kill to fill my shoes. It's just complicated. I have a love-hate relationship with the game just like I guess I do with my father."

Reaching out, I link my fingers with his. I don't say a word. I try not to judge. All I do is just listen, because the pain in his expression says that's exactly what he needs from me.

His laugh is unexpected and loaded with sarcasm. "Fuck," he says as he lifts his hat, runs a hand through his hair, and then sets it back down. "When I said we needed to get to know more about each other, I sure as hell didn't mean this. We're a far way off from learning if the other likes sushi."

I smile and squeeze his hand. For a man who seems pretty open, I can tell he's a bit exposed and uncomfortable. "Sushi? It's all right, if you count California Rolls as legitimate," I say to try to get a laugh from him. "I'm not very adventurous with it. And this conversation is okay. This is real, Easton. I assure you, I have more *real* than I care to think about in my own life right now, so this is okay."

"Yeah. Thanks." He looks down at our joined hands and shakes his head as if he's trying to convince himself of something I can't understand.

"It's admirable to play for your dad, but have you ever wanted to do anything else? For yourself?" I leave the unspoken question hanging out there. The one I think I know the answer to: do you think your dad won't love you if you don't play?

"I'm good at this, though." He lets go of my hand and paces to the other side of the batting cage to stare at a picture of him and his dad on the wall. "I sound like such a pussy saying that. Like I don't have a backbone, or I don't like to play, but I assure you, I do . . . there's just a history that . . .. My dad is fucking Cal Wylder. He's perfect in every way. The Iron Giant of baseball who broke records and is still the public darling of the club. He's never had a blemish on his career. In fact, the only mark he's ever had against him in his perfect life has been his divorce from my mom."

"Nobody's that perfect, Easton."

"He is." There's bitterness in his tone.

"We all look at our parents through rose-colored glasses. Those lenses make you miss their flaws, overlook their shortcomings . . . and still be able to love them unconditionally." He turns to look at me and narrows his eyes in thought. "God knows my dad is far from perfect, and yet when I see him, I see the person I want to be when I'm his age. I overlook his grumpiness and stubbornness and his need to have opinions about everything, even when I don't ask for them. So I'm sure your dad is not perfect."

"He's pretty damn close to it, Scout. And even if he's not, he demands it from me."

I have no comeback for him because I saw it for myself the other day in the locker room. I wonder if Cal Wylder has always been that hard on his only child.

And I hate that I think I already know the answer.

CHAPTER SEVENTEEN

Scout

I'm sorry I don't have a place to invite you to," I apologize as I take a seat at the large island and watch Easton move with ease around the kitchen.

"Did you just move here?"

"I've kind of been on the move since I graduated college, shifting from clubhouse to clubhouse with my dad over the past three years. Learning from him so I could finally make sense of the things I watched over and over as a kid but didn't understand. So, I'm currently living a few blocks over, on the other side of the stadium, in a furnished apartment until I figure out what comes next."

Easton looks at me for a beat—something fleeting in his eyes I can't quite pinpoint—before uncorking the bottle of wine and pouring two glasses in silence. He slides one across the counter to me and then meets my eyes. "What is next, Scout?"

"I get you rehabbed, get your arm to one hundred percent, and get you off the disabled list, for a start."

"You think that's going to happen?"

"Yes." I nod my head for emphasis. "Today was a huge start. How does your shoulder feel? You really should have some ice on it."

He laughs as he turns and grabs a medical ice pack from the freezer and presses it to his shoulder. Then, with a skill that tells me he's done this more times than he can count in his career, he begins to expertly wrap an ACE bandage around the pack to hold it in place.

"So rehab me, and then what's after that? Are you off to another club? Another city? Moving on?"

A part of me hates the lump that suddenly forms in my throat when I realize what he's asking. The woman who's afraid of getting too close to someone because everyone leaves her is now being asked if she's going to leave. And the other part of me breathes in the feeling of having someone care enough to ask. Someone I want to care.

I take a sip of my wine and meet his eyes above the rim of the glass. I'm afraid to respond, uncertain of this next step between us. Downstairs was easy.

We talked baseball, we talked about him, and we avoided the topics that had ruled our afternoon so far.

But now, the tables have turned. Now, the spotlight is on me, and I wish I could answer him, but I'm not sure what that answer is just yet. Or if I want to even have one, in case I get spooked again and need to leave.

"I'm not sure." My voice is barely a whisper when I finally find it to speak.

"Rumor has it Doc is vying to get the permanent contract with the club-house for the team's physical training. Is that true?"

I nod. "Yes. It is. It's the only clubhouse he hasn't held any sort of contract with over his career."

"And so that's why he wants it? Just because?"

"He's kicking around the idea of retiring," I lie, repeating the story he's asked me to tell.

"Retiring? I don't see him as one who'd want to retire."

"Yeah, well . . . there are a lot of things about my dad that I don't under-stand, so your guess is as good as mine."

"What I don't understand is . . . hasn't he already fulfilled that goal then? I mean, technically he already has a contract with the Aces, since you're here for me. So, once you're done with me, you can move on to the next clubhouse? The next team? The next injured player?"

He doesn't relent. Not the intensity in his eyes . . . or the searching ques-tions . . . or the unspoken ones. The ones that say: tell me if you're leaving.

"That's the typical MO, but this time around, he's looking for a term con-tract for the season and beyond. A multi-year agreement."

"Hmm."

"What does that mean?" I wish he'd just come out and ask me what he wants, because I feel like he's leading me somewhere.

"Well, if Doc has done things one way for all these years . . . why change now?"

"Because of me." The answer is automatic, and I realize that I've given him the truth, but can't give him the reasons why.

"You?"

"Yeah. He lived this life. He knows how hard it is to feel settled when you aren't anywhere long enough to let roots grow, let alone have a family . . . and he doesn't want that life for me, so he figured if he got a contract for a team as a whole, then that would give me a place to settle for the first time since I graduated from college."

And because he knows I'd rather quit than not be near him in these last months.

"So you'd be the one to stay then?" He leans a hip on the kitchen island

and digs deeper. I nod slowly and concentrate on tracing the lines in the granite on the countertop.

"You wouldn't move on to another team?"

"Not if I get the contract."

He's quiet for a beat. "Is that what you want, or are you just doing what your Dad wants?"

The irony in his words is not lost on me. He's turning my questions back on me. I lift my gaze to meet his, suddenly very aware of how similar our situations are.

"It's what I want," I say softly.

"And it's dependent on me, right?"

I stare at him, see the curiosity in his eyes, and wonder if, when it comes to why I want to stay in town, we are speaking about my career, or about whatever this is between us.

"In a sense." I chew on the words, not wanting to put pressure on him to heal quicker to get me the job when I've already seen the amount of pressure his dad puts on him.

He nods and then swallows the rest of his glass of wine without saying a word, leaving me wondering what he's thinking. The mood between us suddenly turns uneasy, both of us with questions to ask but unsure how to ask them.

If I were to stay, how would this change the dynamic between us when I'm no longer just in town for a few months?

"What does your mom think about all of this?" he asks, throwing me for a loop.

I stutter to answer as a part of me hides in shame over my own mother not wanting me. Then again, he's shared so much with me tonight, been so open, how can I not be honest about the one thing I can?

"I don't know. I haven't seen her since I was five."

"Scout . . ." His voice trails off like most people's do when they hear that news, uncertain what to say.

"Hey, it's not sushi, but that's my bet-you-didn't-know-about-Scout fact of the day," I joke, trying to quell my immediate defense to shut down after letting someone in.

It's my thing. It's what I do. And every part of me revolts at my need to avert my eyes and change the topic.

And so, when I lift my gaze and meet his, I see compassion there. Understanding. Acceptance. All of them cause a flutter of anxiety to fly in my belly, and yet the feeling is a far cry from the all-out panic that usually consumes me.

Once again, Easton is making me feel instead of shutting down, and I'm not quite sure what to say now.

"Did you say sushi? I think that's exactly what we need." He smiles softly, giving me the reprieve he somehow knows I need. "I'm starving. Want to order some takeout? I know a great place that delivers."

Saved by sushi.

"Perfect."

"Can you grab that?" Easton calls from his bedroom when the buzzer on the elevator rings.

"Sure." My stomach rumbles at the thought of food being on the other side of the sliding doors.

I hit the button to open the elevator and am startled when I'm met with the hazel eyes and curious expression of Cal Wylder.

"Ms. Dalton?" He says, as calm as can be, all the while subtly looking me over—for what, I don't know. Probably wondering why Easton's trainer is making house calls.

"You're not sushi." The words fall from my mouth as the panic I had averted earlier comes full circle and slams back into me. And then I realize what I just said to him. To Easton's dad. To the club's liaison. The man who now is probably putting two and two together when he can't. That I'm here. Off the clock. What if he tells Cory? *Fuck.* "I mean food. You're not food. Chinese food. I mean Japanese food. You were . . . it was supposed to be delivery."

Someone please kill me now before I make an even bigger ass of myself.

"Dad?" Easton walks out to the foyer, and the sound of his voice helps to calm my rioting nerves. But when I turn to look his way, I want to die. He's wet from a shower I didn't even know he was taking, wearing gym pants slung low on his hips, and he's running a towel through his dripping hair.

"Well, now that I know your shoulder's feeling good and iced, I should get going," I say and scurry from the room like the petrified mouse I am.

"Scout," Easton calls after me, resignation and agitation mixed in his voice.

"Typical, Easton." Cal's voice, followed by a heavy sigh, stops me dead in my tracks just as I step into the kitchen area and out of their line of sight. "I should've known."

"Should have known what, Dad?"

"Always playing the women, getting distracted by a piece of ass, instead of playing the field like you should be."

I straighten my spine where I stand, needing to leave but knowing damn well that would mean having to walk right past them. Every part of me bucks the idea of giving Cal Wylder the satisfaction of my running away, tail tucked between my legs.

"A piece of ass? Really, Dad? What I do off the field is none of your business or the club's. Not if I have a friend over for some dinner and a movie. Not if I have a woman over and she's more than a friend. Not if my fucking trainer stops by to check my shoulder and make sure I've iced it, since I was throwing down to bases today for the first time since my surgery and she was concerned about how it was doing. So, don't you fucking dare walk into my house and judge a situation when you have no clue which of the three it is."

There's a tense silence I can feel all the way in the kitchen, and I realize I'm holding my breath.

"You have a habit of getting distracted."

"Distracted? Really? I put in six hours today between the gym, conditioning, and rehab. And I put another two in first thing this morning at Children's Hospital visiting sick kids . . . so please, tell me what else I was supposed to be doing when I'm on the damn DL?"

"Easton." There's a pause, and my mind runs through the image of them standing face to face, mirror images separated by twenty-five years. There's a sigh, and I can imagine Cal looking just like Easton does when he runs a hand through his hair and tries to figure out what he's going to say next. "You're right. I'm sorry. I just want the best for you, son. I want you back on the field showing everyone you're good as new and one hundred percent."

"Fucking Santiago," Easton mutters with vitriol.

"There's always going to be a Santiago in your career, son. Always." There's a sadness to his voice that pulls on me and makes me wish I could see his expression. "Another player who's jealous of your success or pissed at a pitch you called against him and is going to try to bring you down."

I wish I could hear Easton's response, but he speaks it quietly.

"So you threw today? How'd it feel? What did Scout say about it?"

"It felt so damn good to be back in my gear." I can hear the smile in his voice, and, silly or not, I love knowing that I helped to put it there. "And it feels good. A little stiff, and I'm sure it will be sore tomorrow, but right now, I can't complain."

"And Scout?"

Even though there has been a mood shift in the conversation, I sense a hesitation in Easton to respond. I can't deny that I breathe a little easier knowing he's just as cautious about others knowing I'm here—that there is, in fact, something going on between us—as I am.

And it takes this moment to hit me square in the solar plexus and knock the wind out of me. *I want to stay in town.* I want to get to know Easton better. I want to know what it feels like to wake up next to someone in the morning without freaking out that I'm too close, too attached, and I need to create some space to protect myself for when he leaves.

I reach for the glass of wine I left on the counter and finish it off, stunned by the realization but liking the good kind of flutter it puts in my belly. The same kind of flutter I get when Easton cocks his head and stares at me with that knowing smile on his lips.

And now cue the fear. The worry that we both work in a volatile business where there are no guarantees where you'll be from one year to the next, and that means he could still leave me. He could still move on.

I could still be left behind.

Take it day by day, Scout. Enjoy the time; don't think about tomorrow. But, I want tomorrows with someone. I want yesterdays, tomorrows, and next years with someone because I've never gotten that chance before.

And that's why I can enjoy Easton, but can't get attached to him.

"Why are you pushing me so hard to get back on the field?" Easton's irritation breaks through my thoughts, pulls my attention away from my fear and back to his conversation.

"Because nothing is guaranteed," Cal says and unknowingly confirms my resolve. "Contracts are contracts, son. When you sign on their dotted line, you become a commodity."

"Meaning?" Frustration resurfaces in Easton's voice.

"Meaning this is a business. While you may play for the love of the game, the team is in it to make a profit. And you not on the field is not helping their bottom line."

"Do you know something I don't know, Dad?" His voice escalates, disbelief vibrating in its timbre.

"No. Not at all. I just know how clubs operate. Four months is a long time to be out."

"Yeah, well, it's not like I'm a pitcher, coming in for one game, and then getting five days off. I play every day. My arm returns almost every pitch, so I'm not being a pussy here. I've played through the pain before. A cortisone shot and some oxy and I'm good to go for a big game . . . but this isn't just a strain, and for some reason I don't think you get that."

The physical therapist in me wants to give him a standing ovation for understanding the seriousness of his injury, while the child in me understands Easton's plight in wanting his father to comprehend where he's coming from.

"I know you're not. It's just . . . I can't quite get a read on Cory yet. And while I may be the face of the club, first and foremost I worry about you as my son."

"I know you do."

The elevator dings and the forgotten Chinese food delivery arrives. When

Easton walks into the kitchen with the bags in his hand, his father is not behind him.

He doesn't say anything at first—just sets the food on the island as he gathers plates and silverware from drawers I'm not familiar with. I watch him, wondering if I should leave and let him have time alone with his thoughts, when he surprises the hell out of me by grabbing my waist and pulling me against him.

Strong arms wrap around me, and his chin finds its way onto the top of my head. My arms snake under his and around his torso, unsure what else to do other than be here for whatever it is he needs right now.

I can feel him breathe in deeply, can feel him clench and unclench his jaw, can hear his heart beneath my ear where it rests against his chest. The stirring of desire that is always a constant when he's around smolders to life, but I know this is so much more than that, so I hang on and let the moment be.

"It's been a day," I murmur, drawing a rumble of a laugh from him.

"Yes, it has," he sighs. "Let's eat."

CHAPTER EIGHTEEN

Scout

"You will be hungry again in one hour." Easton laughs when I read my fortune. "Very cheeky, but probably true. What does yours say?"

I glance over at him reading his, and he hands the little strip with his fortune to me. "Here."

"*The fortune you seek is in another cookie.*" I roll my eyes. "These are funny. Someone was definitely in a mood when they made these."

"Seems like it."

I'm sitting in the corner of the couch, my back against the armrest and my arm propped up on the back. He's beside me, leaning forward with his elbows on his knees, turning the uneaten fortune cookie over in his hand. He's here, but still a million miles away. My eyes wander over the definition of his torso, admiring the obvious work he's put into his physique, and my fingers itch to reach out and touch him.

"You've been quiet. You okay?"

"Yeah, just thinking," he says with a sigh as he tosses the cookie onto its bag and leans back beside me. He rests his head against the couch pillows, then turns it to the side so he can meet my eyes.

"Care to share?"

"A lot of things."

"Mr. Forthcoming," I tease.

"You want a rundown, then?" His smile is wide, and I can sense his playful side emerging.

"A rundown?"

"Yep," he says with a nod.

"I'm a 'list girl' so you're talking to my heart right now."

He shakes his head and rolls his eyes. "You want a list?"

"Only if you want."

"She wants a list," he teases as he reaches out and squeezes my knee like it's the most natural thing in the world. The casualness of it causes a welcome discord. "Let's see. The first thing is how you definitely like more than California rolls, but I have to lie and tell you it's shrimp in order to get you to try it."

"Oh, God. What did I eat?" His smile is contagious, and even though

I'm suddenly alarmed that I ate something off-the-charts odd, I can't help but smile with him.

"Just a little of this and a little of that."

"I'm not liking the sound of this."

"Sometimes the less you know the better," he muses, and I try not to read into the comment too much. "What else? Hmm. I wondered what you used to be like as a catcher. If you were the quiet but commanding type or the smack talker who annoyed the hell out of the batters."

"A little of both." I blush but allow a smirk to play on my lips.

"Ah, so you *were* a smack talker. That's good to know. I'm taking notes here on my list."

"You should. I can be troublesome if you get on my bad side." His laugh is rich and calls to every part of me. "What else was on that intriguing mind of yours?"

"You're a damn good runner. I was winded today trying to keep up with you."

"Oh, please. You could probably run circles around me."

"Perhaps . . . but if I did that I'd miss the spectacular view of your ass from behind you."

I swat at his arm while my insides melt a little . . . and my insides don't melt. Ever.

"Nice. You get to run in front next time so I can watch your ass, then." I laugh.

"Mine?"

"In baseball pants. That's a requirement," I murmur, knowing damn well how fine his ass looks in his pants because I was more than checking him out when he was behind the plate today.

"Oh really? Making demands, now, are we?"

"I can be very demanding. I mean, you said you want to get to know me better. So now you know." I purse my lips and lift my eyebrows at him. "And I'm stubborn . . . also a stickler for rules. I can't cook at all. And I have a slight obsession with wintergreen Life Savers, biceps, and romance novels. Oh, and I've been known to snore. Horribly."

"I love that you have no shame." He throws his head back and laughs before narrowing his eyes as he takes in my smirk. "But why do I get the sense that you're trying to make me not like you?"

He shifts on the couch and leans toward me, framing my thighs by putting his hands on each side of them. And holy biceps. Right there is exactly why I like them. Firm, sculpted, and so damn hot.

"Who, me?" I feign. "I'd never do something like that."

"Let's add manipulative, too." He quirks an eyebrow and doesn't relent with his stare, despite his smile disarming me in every way imaginable.

"Only the good kind of manipulative."

"The good kind? There's such a thing? Well, I think it's time we get a few things straight," he murmurs, his lips so damn close I can smell the wine on his breath and see the flecks of green in his eyes. "I like demanding and stubborn. It means you don't stop until you get what you want how you want it. You're a rules girl, huh? I'm good with that. Rules are fun because I like to break them, so keep telling me things I shouldn't be doing, Kitty . . . like wanting to date you . . . and I'll keep doing them. And cooking? I'm a bachelor, so I've got every damn take-out menu in town in the top right-hand drawer in the kitchen, and I can make a mean grilled cheese, if need be, so nice try with that one. Wintergreen Life Savers? I prefer the taste of cherry, but as long as I can put it in my mouth and work my tongue into its center, then I'm pretty sure I can compromise." His lips quirk and his eyes bore into mine as every single drop of blood in my body ignites from his insinuation.

My breath hitches as he reaches up and takes my hand that's still holding the fortune and brings it up to the bicep of his other arm. "And biceps. Is this what you're talking about, Scout? Is this what you like?"

He wraps my fingers around as he flexes so I can feel every muscle beneath twist with the movement. I force a swallow and make myself meet his eyes again. "And what is it about you and romance novels? Is it the happily ever after? Is it the man who's too good to be true? Because I assure you, we all have our flaws, even the fictional ones. But the happily ever after depends on what you put into it. The hard work, the listening instead of talking, the laughing instead of crying, the sticking it out instead of running away, the knowing that sometimes silence is best but having her wrapped in your arms can still solve a lot of problems. So, you can have your romance novels while I have my King and Follett and Patterson because I don't want to read about having that kind of love someday. I'd rather be over here trying to take a chance at it in real life."

I open my mouth to argue, but nothing comes out because I don't know what to say. He effectively just stole a little piece of my heart when it was still under padlock and steel.

"Oh, and snoring? When you're with me, we'll both be too damn tired to even worry if you're snoring, so that's a moot point. But, uh, nice try."

"Oh."

"Yeah. *Oh.*" His grin is lightning quick as he leans in and brushes his lips ever so tenderly against mine. It's achingly soft and causes a warmth to spread from my center out, seep into every fiber of my being, and then leave me a little shell-shocked and wanting more. "You smell good," he murmurs.

"Ewww. I haven't showered since my run today. I was sidelined by the same person who's telling me I smell good, so I'm quite sure something is wrong with you."

He chuckles, and then surprises me by placing an open mouth kiss on my neck and then licking a line up to just beneath my earlobe. The sensation, the act, *the everything* about it is like a livewire exposed to water. "You taste salty. And all I smell is your shampoo." He tugs on my earlobe with his teeth, and that slow, sweet ache between my thighs burns bright. "Sweat on you is sexy."

"Men." I laugh and push against his chest, all the while enjoying the feeling of him sinking against me.

"I offered you the shower."

"Yeah, well, good thing I didn't take it, or else I'd have been standing in your kitchen in a robe or one of your T-shirts when your dad showed up, and we both know how that would have looked."

"He won't say anything to anyone."

"Uh-huh."

"And I kind of like the idea of what you'd look like in my T-shirt."

I can't resist. I lean forward and take the initiative by kissing him soundly on the lips. It surprises him. But I love that he lets me take the lead. I love that he allows me to control the depth and the demand and the softness of it. I pour everything that I'm feeling but can't express into our connection.

We shift some, but the pace never quickens, the urgency nonexistent; it's just us, with a setting sun at our backs and the fortunes from our cookies crinkling on the couch when we move. No hands wander, no fingers itch to touch more, because our lips, and everything their connection evokes, is simply enough.

It's intoxicating. It's unexpected. It's everything in a kiss I never knew I needed, and yet somehow knew was missing.

It's not a means to an end, but rather a slow, sweet seduction of the senses, and when it finally ends—when he leans his forehead against mine, with our breaths feathering over each other's lips, and our minds trying to process the moment—he speaks.

"I'm going to hate myself for this the minute the words are out of my mouth," he murmurs.

"Then don't say it and just kiss me again," I tease before I lean in and bring my mouth to his.

His groan sounds tortured when after a few seconds he tears his lips from mine , sits back on his haunches, and squeezes his eyes tight before looking back at me. "I don't think I've ever said these words before in my life."

Now he has my attention. "What words?"

"No."

"*No?*" I laugh; the pained look on his face is more than comical. "No to what?"

"No to what I want to do to you right now. *Desperately.*"

"What do you want to do to me, Easton?" My voice is coy, my eyes inviting.

He clenches his jaw, and the muscle that pulses at its corner is so damn sexy. He laughs, a sound like audible restraint. "I want to fuck you, Scout. I want to take you in my bedroom and make you so tired your body forgets to snore. Okay?"

And now it's my turn to clench my jaw—and my thighs—together as he stares at me with an intensity that only adds to his allure. "So, why don't you?"

His smile is half-cocked when he speaks, "Because I made a promise to myself and to you. I told you we were going to get to know each other better, build up some trust, and see where this thing takes us . . . and so that's what I'm trying to do. Even though, currently, where I really want it to take us is my bed."

"I don't know what to say." I'm flattered. I'm dumbfounded. And, holy hell, how I'm turned on from that kiss and the feeling of his thighs caging mine.

"Tell me you understand the sacrifice I'm making, because right now, all I want is you. Under me. On top of me. Any way with me."

"Then let's—"

"You don't get it, do you? I can see it in your eyes, Scout. I can tell you're spooked, with one foot out the door and one foot in my bed because it's easier to be in either of those places than it is to be in this position. The one where you have to talk to me, where you have to let me get to know you better, instead of shying away from it. So even though it's said under serious protest, the answer is *no*, we're not having sex tonight."

"That's admirable," I murmur as I lean in and tease his lips with mine, "but we've already slept together, so does it really matter?"

He chuckles. "Yes, it does matter because you're trying to distract me with those lips of yours when all my mind keeps thinking of is all of the other things you could be doing with them."

"Like what?" I purr.

He leans back and shoots me a warning glare. "I told you, Scout. We're getting to know each other."

"So even if I go like this . . ." I run the tip of my fingernail over the more than obvious outline of his hardened cock through his jogging pants.

He groans my name, his body tenses, and his head falls back as I complete one long stroke of my fingertip. And just when I think I might have won the battle, his hands flash out and tighten like a vice around my wrists to prevent me from tempting him any further. "Not going to happen," he grits out.

I try to move my arms, but he doesn't let them budge. And there's something about his reaction and the strength of his hands on mine that urge me to try again.

"And I couldn't persuade you if I did this?" I lean forward and circle my tongue around the flat, bronzed disc of his nipple before sucking on it gently.

"Goddammit, woman." His tone is sharp, but the groan that follows it is so damn sexy I grow wet between my thighs.

"What?" I feign innocence as I look up at him and bat my lashes with my lips still pressed against his chest.

His grin is full of warning, and yet his erection is pressing against my thigh. With our gazes locked, I lean forward to lick the other nipple, knowing I've put him in a quandary.

And just as I make contact, he makes his move. The element of surprise, and probably my own escalating desire, gives him the opportunity to pull me onto his lap, twist me around so my back is to his chest, and wrap his arms around me so that I can't move mine.

"There."

"You bastard." I chuckle because now his cock pressing against my lower back is his reciprocated torture.

"Is something the matter?" he teases, hot breath against my ear.

I wiggle my ass over his dick and feel his thighs grow tense. He repositions and adjusts so his arms are tighter around me, and he brings his legs over my calves to quiet my wriggling.

All I can do is laugh.

He sighs. "See? Perfect position to watch a movie together."

"A movie? That's the first thing that comes to mind right now?"

"Yep." He shifts so that he can hold the remote in one hand and me between both of his arms. "We're going to sit here and watch the first movie I come across on the menu."

He scrolls through the on-screen guide. "Your hair is in the way . . . what's that one say?" he asks, and I smile, knowing exactly what movie it is. *Perfect.*

"Click that one."

And when he does, and the guide cuts to the movie, the screen fills with a very involved sex scene. Moaning and nudity and thrusting and licking. How was I to know it would be at this scene already?

"Jesus fucking Christ," he mutters with a laugh. "Perfect."

"It seems fate is trying to tell you what you should be doing."

"Fate or a manipulative and determined woman."

"Maybe a little of both. But this is actually a movie adaptation of a hugely bestselling romance novel, I believe," I say, tongue in cheek, while my body is reacting to the visual porn in front of me and tangible porn against me.

"Ah . . . and now it becomes clear why you like romance novels." He laughs.

"It has a great story line," I say in jest.

"I can see that."

"Seriously. You can have hot sex and a great story line." I try to gesture to the television, but my arms are still restrained. "Or we could just have the hot sex, instead."

"I'm not budging, Scout. You told me I needed to read a romance novel, so no time like the present to watch one. With you."

"I thought you only liked King and Follett and Patterson?"

"I do, but I've recently been told that romances are where it's at."

"Oh, please." I roll my eyes and laugh but only get a kiss on my shoulder in response.

So, we sit like this and watch the movie.

And another one after that.

But more memorable than the movies that I can't quite pay attention to is the fact that when I fall asleep in the late hours of the night, my last thought is I've never let myself fall asleep in the arms of a man before without there being sex first.

But this time I did.

And when I wake up the next morning with his body behind mine on the couch, and his arm still holding me tight against him, I realize this isn't so bad.

But more importantly, as scared as I am to let him in, I'm more scared of walking away.

CHAPTER NINETEEN

Scout

"I just needed to hear your voice." It's all I say but it's the truth.

"I'm here, Scouty-girl. I'm here." His voice rumbles through the connection and soothes my heart that was having a mini-panic attack over needing to talk to him for no other reason than to know he was still there.

I sag against the wall beside me and close my eyes, willing away the tears that threaten.

"You okay?"

No.

"Yeah. I'm good." I clear my throat and look around the empty hallway outside of the locker room. "Sometimes a girl just needs her dad."

"Understood. This time of year is always tough for you," he murmurs. "I'll sit here on the line as long as you need me."

"Thank you." My voice is almost a whisper as I try to contain my emotions. We both sit on opposite sides of the connection, we don't speak, and yet I find comfort in knowing he's there.

"I need to get to work," I say after a few minutes even though I'd stay like this all day if I could. "Thank you for . . ."

"Anytime." He clears his throat. "Remember, clear mind, hard heart."

"I know," I say before the line disconnects and then whisper, "I love you." I know he's no longer there, but I say the words anyway.

I take a moment to pull myself together—frazzled female emotions make gruff men uncomfortable—before I head into the locker room to prepare for Easton's first of two training sessions today.

But it's when I walk into my office to grab the notes on my desk that the fake smile plastered on my lips becomes genuine.

Sitting on top of my notes is a mess of wintergreen Life Savers, crudely arranged to look like a flower. There are three white mints making up each petal, and they all connect into the center Life Saver. Except the center candy isn't wintergreen white.

It's red.

Cherry red to be exact.

And there's a Post-It note beside it that has '*Have a day*' scrawled across it.

It's a simple something that at a glance looks like candies tossed on a desk but speaks volumes to me. It says *I'm thinking about you.* It says *remember what I like to do with cherry Life Savers.* It says *I'm still here, still determined to prove you wrong.* It says *remember that first time we* 'had a day' *together? Well, here's to more of those.*

My heart does a little flip flop in my chest. There's only one person who could have done this. One person who had no clue that I needed something like this right now but who gave it to me anyway.

I pull the wrapper off one of the wintergreen Life Savers and look up through the training room window to see Easton standing at his locker, looking my way. Our eyes connect for the briefest of moments so as to not give away what's happening between us, but it's long enough for me to slip the candy between my lips and offer a ghost of a smile. His nod is ever so slight before turning to say something to J.P. as if our exchange never occurred.

But it did.

And as I look down to the flower (less one Life Saver) I'm left struggling with how to accept all of the good things happening in my life—the rehabilitation contract, my time spent off the field with Easton, the prospect of a long-term job that will allow me to stay in one place for more than a few months—when I should be thinking about my dad instead.

The guilt eats at me when I know I can't let it. I just have to take things one day at a time.

Another quick glance Easton's way drives the point home because while I may not want to admit it to myself, the time I spend with him is the highlight of my day.

CHAPTER TWENTY

Easton

"Where've you been lately?"

I glance over at Drew and wait for him to say what his eyes are insinuating. "You guys have been on a road trip, so I've been here, and you haven't." I snap my towel at him to emphasize my point.

"It wouldn't have anything to do with that hot little trainer you've got rubbing you down, now would it?"

"Fuck off, Drew. You're just jealous I get a female."

"Damn straight, I'm jealous. Please tell me you've tried to round the bases with her, because, dude, I'd be worried if you hadn't."

Heads have turned our way, ears listening, the locker room full of players as they come back in from batting practice, the game's first pitch a little over ninety minutes away.

"Shot down, brother," I lie, and he bumps my fist and laughs. "She's all business, all the time. Last week I thought I had a shot when she showed up at my place after I threw hard for the first time . . . but nope. I had my phone off and hadn't answered her, so she swung by to make sure I'd iced my arm. Not exactly the kind of front-door service I was hoping for."

"There's hope for me yet if Wylder still gets shot down."

"That's cold, man."

Comments ring through the room right beside the disbelieving laughter at the fact that I'd been rejected by Scout.

Little do they know the damn woman has owned my thoughts more than I'd fucking like to admit. It could be that I get to see her every damn day of the week. That I've badgered her into having a few dinners with me. That getting drunk on her kiss is what I look forward to.

But hell, this "getting to know you" shit has to end soon, because a man only has so much restraint and his balls can only get so blue. Besides, there's only so much satisfaction in jerking off when the one you're fantasizing about does something like she did today, showing up in a tank top that makes you want to cave on your promise.

Oh, fuck, how I'd wanted to cave. And not because it was revealing, but rather because every time she rubbed against me during our stretching routine, all I could think about was that I know what her tits look like beneath it. Perky. Pink. Suckable.

The drought definitely needs to end.

And soon.

But isn't that the damn problem? Just when I thought we've gotten to know each other better, that sex is just what the doctor ordered, she showed up today with that fucking spooked look in her eyes. The one that had her so antsy she left right after we cooled down and she was done with me.

I play it off that she's having a bad day. Maybe her uncle is still sick. Who knows, though, because she won't say shit to me about him.

Then again, maybe she's just freaked.

Fucking women.

"Well, one thing for sure," Stanza says from across the locker room, "Santiago is going to get some chin music tonight."

I meet his eyes across the distance and just nod—a quiet thank you for letting me know that when he pitches tonight, he's going to throw a few inside to push Santiago off the plate. A little "fuck you" for hurting me.

Those who say there's no retaliation in baseball have never played. A pitch aimed a little too close to the head. A tag thrown just a tad too hard. A shoulder lowered or cleats angled up when going in to slide at a base. You fuck with my teammate, we'll fuck with you back, is the motto for most teams.

Especially mine. Especially for me because the play was dirty.

"Fuck that fucker," J.P. mutters, getting a rise out of the guys.

"You staying to watch?" Drew bumps my shoulder and asks.

I pull my shirt over my head and chew over the idea I've considered more times than I'd like to admit. "Probably not. Last thing I need to do is run into him in the hallway. A few months isn't long enough for me to not want to rip his goddamn throat out." The guys around me laugh. "Besides, if I did, I'd probably just fuck my arm up further . . . so, nah, I'm gonna watch from home."

"Gonna meet us after?"

I glance over to the empty training room. The one Scout ran out of earlier. She's the one person I'd rather hang with tonight, but fuck it, going out is probably just what I need to feel like my old self again instead of this overthinking, whiny bitch I'm feeling like right now. "Got nothing better to do than hang with my boys."

And then I see him. The rookie who was just called up from the Triple-A team outta Bum-fuck, Nowhere. He's sitting on his stool, staring in awe at the locker with his name placard on it, much the same way I did my first time here, all those years ago.

"Hey, Gonzo!"

The kid startles as he turns around and sees me across the room. "Yeah?"

"Thanks for filling in for me. You'll do great. Knock 'em dead tonight." I smile at him and nod. A little something to ease the pressure of his first time in the big leagues, and a subtle reminder not to get too comfortable in the gear because I'll be back.

I'm not sure who I'm trying to convince more, him or me.

"Thanks," he stutters, eyes as big as saucers.

"We'll see you at Sluggers after the game. The guys'll show you where to go. It's not every night you make your major league debut."

His smile widens, and he nods. And I'm left sitting, staring at my own locker, contemplating what it would be like to have that feeling back—the awe of walking into the stadium for the first time, the nerves that roll your stomach, the jog of your knee as you sit in the dugout for the first time, and the knowledge that when you hop over that chalk baseline there are thousands of people in the stands who would kill to take your place.

All of it is a reaffirmation of how damn lucky I am, when I've been sitting here feeling goddamn sorry for myself.

The chatter begins to die down as the guys head for the dugout. Some slap me on the back as they leave, some give a fist-bump. Good lucks are given. Shit-talking is required.

And when I'm the only one left in the locker room, I head out, hating the feeling that I'm missing all of this with them. That they're moving on—the next game, the next play, the next city in this long season—while I'm still sidelined and going fucking stir crazy over a game I love but can't play and a woman I want but can't seem to get.

Talk about being majorly fucked.

I laugh at myself as I stand in the tunnel and decide if I want to go to the right and past all the VIP fan events happening, where I'll get wrangled into PR, or asked to head up to the announcer's booth for a bit and add some color commentary, as I've done a few times over the past few months, or if I want to veer left and take the long route.

Left. Definitely left.

I'm not in the mood to deal with fans right now. Not when I'm pissed and just want the hell out of this stadium that suddenly feels like a prison I can't escape from fast enough.

My shoes echo against the concrete as I make my way through the maze of tunnels. My thoughts are all over the place. On my shoulder. On Scout. On watching the game today, the first time Santiago has been in the starting line-up against us since he fucked me over.

"Don't you go anywhere near him."

The voice comes from the next hall up, and the threat in it resonates down to where I am. By the time I wrap my head around the notion that it sounds like my dad, I'm standing in the opening of the passageway, staring at him and Santiago.

Standing side by side.

My dad's hand fisted in my enemy's shirt.

There's a tense second where it takes everything I have not to close the distance and smash my fist into his smarmy fucking smirk that has never said anything near an apology.

"What the fuck is going on here?"

He's suited up to play. Just like I should be, but can't.

Because of him.

"Dad?" I address my dad, yet I can't help but stare at Santiago and try to figure out what in the hell his deal is.

Santiago turns to look back to my dad, eyebrows raised. "Thanks for the chat, Cal, but I've got a game to play. See you on the field, Wylder?" he says as he looks toward me. "Oh. Wait. *My bad.* You won't be there."

And with a fucking chuckle that is like acid in my gut, he pats my dad on the back and jogs the other way down the tunnel. We both stare after him without saying a word.

"What the hell was that all about?" I grit the words out, clenching and un-clenching my hands to prevent me from punching the wall.

"I saw him walking down the hallway toward your clubhouse. I asked him where he was going. When he wouldn't answer, I figured he was coming to see you. I told him he better not go near you or I'd have him thrown out of the ballpark."

I stare at my dad, but rage clouds my judgment to the point that I'm ques-tioning whether he's telling me the truth. And of course he is, he's my dad, but it's so much easier to listen to the anger and pick a fight with him.

"You should have let him come at me," I mutter as I scrub my hands over my face and pace a few feet past my dad, toward the opposing clubhouse's locker room and then back the way I came.

"For what, Easton? So you can get hurt again and piss the club off be-cause your DL stint just got extended? Nothing good ever comes out of anger. Nothing." He walks up to me, puts his hand on my shoulder, and squeezes. "I know you're frustrated. I know it's taking everything in your body right now to not storm in there and kick his ass. And I know more than anything you just want your norm back. Keep doing what you're doing, and you'll be back in six weeks' time, according to the report that Ms. Dalton gave the front office."

Six weeks? How did I not know that?

I push it away. The thought. The excitement. Because I was given a return date before and never hit it. A man can't recover on a clock.

But something else becomes clear. For the first time in what feels like forever, my dad is being my dad, not Cal Wylder. It's just what I needed right now, even though he might not know it.

"I'm going fucking stir crazy."

"It's hard being cut off from what you love."

I look up to him, meet eyes that mirror mine, and see the concern. "Yeah, well, thanks to *him*." I pace back and forth once more. "You know what I don't get, though, is *why*? Why take me out? Why hurt me? Why any of this?"

My dad clears his throat and chews the inside of his cheek as he thinks it over. "I just don't know, Easton. The guy's bat is on fire. He has a helluva on-base percentage. His arm's flawless, and no one dares steal with him behind that plate. His style reminds me a lot of yours, yet he's probably making a third of what you make."

"You think this is a jealousy thing? There's no way. I mean, there's hundreds of us taking the field every night across all pay grades and starting positions. If that's the case, then why single me out? It just doesn't make sense."

"Nothing seems to these days, son."

"The fucker went three-for-three tonight. What the fuck is up with that?" Drew mutters as he takes a nice long drag on his bottle.

"Bad juju, man," I mutter, tired as fuck but with zero desire to make it the few blocks down the street back to my place.

"Yeah, but we won, so it couldn't have been too damn bad," Tino chimes in with a clink of his bottle to mine. "I think I deserve to get laid for that homer, though."

"Then go home to your wife," I say, the same as I do every time we go drinking. It's innocent enough, I know, because Tino worships the ground his wife walks on, but he never fails to say it.

Almost like a routine.

Pretty much the same as the four of us sitting here after a home game, reliving the highlights, bitching about the ball that wouldn't drop, or the shitty call that cost us the game, and taking time to unwind for an hour or two before we head home to our non-baseball lives. Tino, his wife; Drew, his three dogs; J.P., his girlfriend; and me to my empty bed.

"I plan on it," Tino says with a quick grin, "but I was waiting for Gonzo to get here so we could buy him a beer and fuck with him a bit."

"Yeah. Where is he?" J.P. says, craning his neck around the crowded bar to look for him.

"He's probably still sitting in the dugout, sporting wood and trying to be-lieve he actually just made his debut in the show," Drew says, and the image has us all thinking back to that first time and the rush of nerves and adrena-line that lasted for days.

"The kid did good." I nod. "Real good."

"Not as good as you, East," Tino says. "When're you going to get your ass back on the field?"

"Soon. Four, five weeks. It's up to Scout to clear me."

"Ah, the mysterious Scout," J.P. taunts, but I don't take the bait. Because fuck yes, I've thought about her tonight. When I was sitting at my place watch-ing the game, shouting at the television, and flipping off Santiago every time the camera panned to him, it was her I imagined laughing at me. Even when I came down here to grab our table in the back and wait for the guys, sure, the women who approached were attractive, but all I kept doing was comparing them to her.

I've got it fucking bad. Christ. Talk about feeling pussy-whipped when you aren't even getting any pussy.

"You mean *that* mysterious Scout?" Drew asks with a tilt of his beer to-ward the far side of the room.

I look immediately, hating that my heart fucking slams into my chest as violently as confusion does when I see her on the other side of the dimly lit bar.

"Dude, is she with . . .?"

"Well, we definitely know what team she wanted to win tonight," J.P. mur-murs, just above the chatter of the crowd.

I shift in my seat to see better and try to wrap my head around why she's sitting with Penski and Cameron, whose asses we just kicked tonight. I think of her Facebook page. Of picture after picture of her with other players.

It's her fucking job, Easton. Dealing with other men is her job.

So why didn't she say anything to me about them when I asked her if she wanted to do something tonight? If there was nothing to hide, then why fuck-ing hide it?

And if you're trying to hide something, then why come to Sluggers when you know that's where the whole team goes after a game to blow off steam?

You don't own her, East. She's not yours. You don't have the right to know what she's doing when she's not with you. You don't get to lay claim to her.

Fuck that. I damn well do.

I've put the time in. I've gotten to know her. I've taken more care than I ever have with a woman, and so, fuck yes, she's going to be mine.

Wasn't that the whole point of this?

And it's not lost on me, I can't do shit about any of it. I can't stare long enough to see that she has on a denim skirt, with some sexy ass cowboy boots on her feet. Or that her hair is curled and down, when usually it is thrown up in a ponytail. Or that she has some top on that makes my mouth water thinking about what's beneath it.

She gets dressed up for them, but not for me?

My blood boils knowing that they're over there enjoying the sight of it, getting turned on by her, when I'm over here trying to figure out what the fuck is going on, because I can't do anything about it.

Not with three guys staring me down. Hell, the guys wouldn't give a shit if I was sleeping with her; the only reason they'd care is because that means they can't get with her. But if they knew and accidentally told someone, and it got to the front office, then that could cause problems for Scout and Doc's contract.

Besides, I promised her I wouldn't say anything. And with a woman who has a hard time believing promises, this is one I need to keep.

The problem is, it doesn't seem she's keeping her word, either.

Her *word*? Have another beer. She made no promises. All she agreed to was getting to know each other, to seeing where this might take us . . .

And spending every day together on and off the field doesn't qualify as that?

What is going on here?

"You okay there, Wylder?" Tino bumps my shoulder with his and pulls me from my thoughts, and I realize I'm still staring at her.

"Yeah. Sure." I down my beer and lift my hand to the waitress for another. "Just trying to make sense of it."

"She didn't say anything to you during rehab today about knowing them?" Drew asks, glancing over to her again, and I hate that I want to follow suit, but can't without being way too obvious.

Because every time I look her way, my temper burns brighter. I try to justify that she knows I'm here. Christ, they weren't sitting there an hour ago when I got here to save our table, so she had to have seen me when she walked in. Why hasn't she acknowledged me? I get keeping a public distance to protect our professional relationship and her damn contract, but a simple nod of her head wouldn't scream "We've fucked," either.

"Did she tell me she knew them? Not a word." I thank the waitress for the new beer and take a long swallow of it.

"You'd think she'd have said something about sleeping with the enemy," J.P. jokes. He gets the laugh he was going for, but all it does is piss me off even further.

I lose sight of her through the crowd and tell myself that's a good thing. The conversation moves on like it should, even if all I can think about is what she's doing here. With them. And why she didn't mention it to me.

"I'm gonna hit the head." Drew stands, and when I glance Scout's way, she's staring at me.

There's a shot glass up to her lips, but she doesn't offer me a smile, doesn't acknowledge me at all; her face is expressionless—distant. And my fists clench in reaction to the fleeting thought that she's ferreted. That she somehow got spooked and didn't have the balls to tell me to my face we were over, so instead she came out tonight and sat where she sat on purpose, so I'd see her with them. And then I'd know.

But as she tilts her head back and downs the shot in one impressive swallow before slamming it down on the table among the countless empties I can now see, all I can think is that there's no way she's moving on without me getting to have a final say about it.

"Where're you going?" Tino asks as I tilt my own beer back and down its contents.

"Gonna buy the lady a shot, since it seems to be her poison of choice tonight."

CHAPTER TWENTY-ONE

Scout

The burn of the shot numbs the significance of today's date and yet does nothing to ease the shock to my system when I glance around and meet the ice in Easton's eyes.

I should have expected him to be here. It's the postgame hangout, after all. But I could have handled him if things had stuck to the plan—just Penski and Cameron and me taking a few shots in my brother's honor on his birthday. Yet another piece of my history that I keep tucked away.

But things didn't stick to the plan.

Because now I'm seated across from the one man I want to be nowhere near but can't ask to leave, considering he's Penski and Cameron's teammate.

"That was two," Cameron says with a nod. "Two more and Ford would be pleased."

"Pour me one."

I look across the table, and just the sight of him disgusts me. "No." I snap the word out, causing Penski to nudge my knee under the table.

Santiago just stares at me. The mixture of his dark features, the dim light of the bar, and the fact that he's in the corner of the booth (thank God) so the shadow of the wall falls over his face makes him seem like the asshole I've conjured up in my mind.

And keeps him out of Easton's line of sight.

Because if there is ice in Easton's glare at seeing me here with members from the opposing team—or maybe just men in general—then seeing Santiago here would set him off.

No doubt.

Because it sure as hell set me off when he walked in and sat down with us. I protested, told the boys that this was a ritual we've always done with just us—the only ones who really knew my brother—but they said it was harmless for Santiago to stay.

But he's anything but harmless. Not with his curious eyes always watching me. Measuring me. Making it clear he wants me.

The neck of the bottle of tequila clinks against the shot glass as Penski pours Santiago the shot.

"To Ford," Cameron says, lifting his glass. "It's been three years without you, brother. It feels like a fucking lifetime since I've heard that laugh of yours. Fuck you for leaving us. We miss you."

"Fuck you, Ford," the three of us murmur in unison, and then we toss back the shot. This time, the burn is a little less, but the memories are still painful as ever.

In fact, something about this year's get-together to remember and curse Ford for leaving us behind seems so much harder than the last two.

Maybe it's because what started out as a promise one drunken night when they were trying to make me feel better over my brother's death is tonight reminding me that next year I might have to perform two of these memorials instead of just one.

I raise my shot glass. "To my brother," I whisper as the tears threaten. "You have no idea how much I miss you right now. How much I need your friendship and advice. How, if you were here, I wouldn't think everyone leaves. What I'd give for one more hour to lie in the long grass at Dad's and pretend we were the only ones left on Earth. I miss you."

"Fuck you, Ford," we say in unison, but when I finish my shot, as my head grows fuzzy and a lone tear slides down my cheek, I add in a whisper, "I love you."

"I guess shots are the order of the night." Easton's voice snaps me from my melancholic fog, and for a split second I forget we have eyes on us. I forget that we are supposed to be trainer and player. Relief floods through me from the presence of the one person I've unknowingly started to need.

But just as quick as the relief is the reality that slams into me like a wrecking ball. That Santiago is here. Across from me.

This is trouble.

But Easton's eyes hold mine, search my face, and when he notices the lone tear sliding down my cheek, he shoots an accusatory glare to Penski and then Cameron. But when his gaze shifts, when he comes to the person cloaked in the shadows of the bar, his expression morphs from curiosity to rage.

"What the fuck is he doing here?" His voice is a growl of unrestrained fury as he pushes his way to the table, testosterone raging and temper raw.

"It's not what you think." The words blurt out of my mouth as Penski shoves up from the table, sensing chaos is about to unravel, and steps between Easton and Santiago just as Tino and Drew arrive.

"Not what he thinks?" Santiago chuckles in a low, baiting tone that makes me realize what exactly I'd just implied.

"Leave her the fuck out of this." Easton tries to push Penski out of the way, his fists clenched and body vibrating with a rage so palpable it rolls off him and slams into me.

"Easy now, Easton." Penski pushes against Easton's chest as Drew pulls back on his good shoulder. They can try all they want to prevent the fight, but it's been brewing for so long I'm not sure anything can stop it now.

"You fucking the trainer now, Wylder?" Santiago baits Easton, his name a marred sneer loaded with disdain. "A little locker room lovin'?"

Easton lunges at Santiago, the empty glasses on the table crashing to the ground as Penski uses all his strength to keep them separated. "You fucking bastard!" Easton grits out.

"You got that right, pretty boy," Santiago taunts, his chuckle grating over my nerves.

"Are cheap shots the only thing you're good for?"

"You'd know, wouldn't you? Too bad your lady was planning on going home with me."

"Bullshit!" I shout in the confusion that's now causing a crowd to form.

"Shut him the fuck up!" Penski barks to Cameron as he lifts his chin to Tino and Drew, silently asking them to get Easton the hell out of here, because it seems Santiago is going to keep provoking until he gets just what he wants.

In seconds, Drew and Tino have flanked Easton and are forcibly pushing him toward the door. There's a mass of chaos and confusion swirling around me, but it's the look on Easton's face when he meets my gaze before he's shoved out the door—the look that says, "What the fuck, Scout?"—that sticks with me more than anything.

"We'll get him home," J.P. says before looking at me and shaking his head in disapproval. "Not the brightest of moves, Scout."

With that reprimand, J.P. walks away, leaving me standing in the middle of Sluggers with the man I want more than anyone being escorted out one side of the bar, and the man I despise for his nasty demeanor and the stunt he just pulled being shoved out the other door.

I sink back down into my chair, the remaining shots of tequila looking damn tempting. But they're not the answer.

"I'm sorry." Cameron's voice is behind me, resigned and apologetic as he scoots into the seat next to me. "Not exactly how we'd planned to remember Ford tonight."

I glance his way, at my brother's best friend and college teammate, and know he misses Ford just as much as I do. That this annual ritual means as much to him as it does me. And that neither of us will go back on the promise we've made my dad to always celebrate Ford's birthday to ensure his memory stays alive.

But how would we ever forget the boy with the goofy grin, obnoxious laugh, and heart as big as the ocean?

"I know," I sigh. "The timing was perfect though. How the three of us were in the same city, the same time, on his birthday. Besides, Ford always liked a good fight so . . ."

"We should have made Santiago leave. I wasn't thinking. Not with you working with Wylder or us coming to Sluggers . . . it's my fault."

I toy with an empty shot glass, wonder how Easton's doing, and worry that one of the guys may have wrenched his bad shoulder.

But more than anything I just want to see him. Need to see him.

"You want me to walk you back?" Cameron asks, and I'm so grateful that he knows me so well.

I nod.

CHAPTER TWENTY-TWO

Scout

"Scout?"

I look at Cameron. "It's fine. Thanks for walking me back."

"You sure?" His eyes dart over my shoulder and then back to mine.

I nod and welcome the huge bear hug he pulls me into. "It was good to see you again, even if the night went to shit."

I laugh, the tears threatening, as I squeeze him back. "It was. And it did."

"Fuck you, Ford," he murmurs and causes me to hiccup out a laughing sob. "Thank you for never forgetting."

"Never," he says as he gives me a peck on my cheek, squeezes my hand, and glances one more time over my shoulder before walking away.

I draw in a deep breath before I turn to face the dark silhouette highlighted by the lone light still on in the parking lot. He's leaning against the side of my car, his arms folded, his body tense. We stand there with distance between us and discord roiling around us.

"You want to tell me what the fuck that was all about?"

And the funny thing is, as much as I wanted to see him, as much as I feel like I need him tonight, he just pushed every wrong button possible by coming at me with anger when I did nothing wrong.

"Excuse me?" My voice is a quiet steel as I take another step toward him and his irrational temper.

"You heard me, Scout. What the fuck were you doing with Santiago?"

"First of all, I wasn't with Santiago. And second, did I miss a point in time where you laid claim to me?"

"Not. At. All." He rolls his shoulders. He shifts his feet. But between the dark night and the brim of his ball cap, I can't see his eyes when I desperately wish I could.

"Great. Then you can move out of the way. I can leave. And tomorrow, when we meet up for your training, we can forget all about this whole *getting to know you* shtick and move on."

His laugh fills the night, but falls flat. "It's just that easy for you, huh? Run. Dodge. Avoid. Nice try, Scout, but I'm not letting you use that on me."

"You don't get a say in what I do or don't do, Hot Shot." I take a step closer to him, partly hurt, partly relieved that whatever he's pissed about isn't deterring him from whatever is happening between us.

"Nice skirt," he says, completely throwing me for a loop with his change in conversation. There's an underlying edge to his voice, though.

"Your point?"

"Can't a man tell a woman who got dressed up she looks nice? I mean, I sure as shit know you weren't dressing up for me. I get Nikes and sports bras, but Penski or Cameron or fucking Santiago gets a short skirt, long legs, boots, and fixed hair. 'Dress to impress' must have been the motto for the night, huh?"

My temper snaps.

"I don't have fucking time for this. Or you." I storm over to my car, hands on my hips. "Move."

He doesn't budge, just stands there with a clenched jaw and murder in his eyes that reflects how I feel. "You talk to Santiago with that mouth, too?"

"Fuck you!" I shout. He's pushing for a fight, and you know what? I'm so game for one right now. I have a tornado of emotions whipping around inside of me—grief, loneliness, desire, need, uncertainty, fear—and it's so much easier to be angry than to face any of them.

Or to admit that I'm hurt he could think I'd want Santiago when the only person I want is him.

I want him.

It's a fleeting thought, one my temper overrides, but it's loud enough to add fuel to the fight. Because if I fight, then I don't have to acknowledge that, though I'm used to shutting everyone out, he might be the first I want to let in.

"Come on, Scout. Are you playing me?" I can hear the hurt in his tone, know he's had a few drinks, like I have, and know that nothing intensifies bravado like alcohol. "Are you using the contract as an excuse to keep this your little secret? Do you keep pushing me away, holding me at arms' length because you're really dating one of them and you don't want either of us to find out?"

What? My temper's too far gone for me to think rationally, and so I do what comes next in line—lash out at him.

"Playing you? Glad to know you think so highly of me." I step into him, our bodies inches away from each other.

"Well, you sitting there with Santiago tells me exactly what you think of me." His words are guarded armor when he grits them out, quiet but loaded with vitriol.

"The way you're acting, I shouldn't think of you at all."

We glare at each other. Hurt waging against hurt. Anger swirling in the cool night air. And neither of us attempt to back down.

"You know what? Fuck this," he mutters, looks at me one last time through eyes laden with sadness, shakes his head, and strides out of the parking lot.

It takes me a second to process what's happening. To realize he's walking away from me. And at first, all I can think is that with him gone, I'll be able to breathe for a second. Have a clear mind.

Let him go, Scout. If you do, then you can't get hurt any further. Because people leave. They all do. Ford. Mom. At some point soon, Dad will, too. Chalk up Easton to *having fun while it lasted.* Some good sex, a new friend, but nothing harmed in the end. He's too close. You're too close. Push him away or you're going to end up devastated. And alone.

Walk away now, like he will from you.

Clear mind. Hard heart, Scouty-girl.

But what if I don't want a hard heart anymore?

My feet move. Toward him.

My heart, hard as it may be, jolts into my throat.

And I really wish I had my damn Nikes on instead of my cowboy boots.

"Easton!"

His shadow's up ahead, the streetlights hitting his hair a beacon for me to follow.

"Easton!" I call as I chase after him.

"Forget it, Scout. Just forget it."

"No, wait."

"At some point, it's not worth the trouble anymore."

Tears burn and my vision blurs as I catch up to him, just as he hits the lobby of his building. Conscious of the other people, I don't yell like I want to for him to stop. Instead, I move a bit faster. He steps into the elevator and turns to face me with shoulders square, body tense, and eyes that say everything he doesn't speak.

Step in now or turn around and keep walking. Now or never.

My pulse pounds, knowing the answer but fearing it at the same time.

I step in.

Easton blows out an audible breath as he pushes a button, and I'm not sure if that's a good sign or a bad sign, but it doesn't matter because my heart urged me to step in when every sensible thought screamed for me to stay out.

The elevator jerks and then surprises me when it begins to descend. I glance over at him, but he's just staring straight ahead—jaw clenched, hands fisted, face intense.

So damn handsome.

I want him.

In more ways than *let's have fun 'til it ends.*

Because I want to take a chance on this. On him.

Sure, we've known each other for a couple of months, but when I look at him now, when I think about him when I'm alone, when I anticipate seeing him, it makes me want to push all fear out the window. It makes me want to step into him rather than step away. It makes me realize it's okay to want more, when before, I've never even allowed myself that chance at all.

And I get it now. What he said the other night about making your own happily ever after. His implication that it's not easy. That sometimes it takes time and patience and shutting up instead of shouting louder. That it might be the hardest thing in the world, but it can also be the most rewarding.

We just fought in the parking lot. He walked away, and I chased, for the first time ever. That should tell me something . . . but it's bigger than that. There is the notion that, even though he was livid, even though he told me he wasn't doing this, he still stood in the elevator with his finger on the open-door button and gave me a choice to be with him. The idea that he was mad at me, but still wanted me. That he walked away, but that didn't mean he was leaving me.

This all hits me in the few seconds we have during the elevator ride down—it's suffocating and invigorating.

When the doors open to the private field, I follow as he steps into the lighted entry, the rest of the space still in the muted dark. The elevator dings, the doors close behind us, the silence returns.

"Easton." It's a plea. A question. A "talk to me."

"Don't 'Easton' me," he says as he turns to face me, eyes alive but posture guarded.

So we stand and stare but don't speak. My heart is in my throat. My emotions a train wreck inside of me.

I expect him to tell me to leave.

I expect him to shake his head and say no more.

Wouldn't that be fitting, considering I now want more?

But he does neither. We just stand there as the air around us shifts and changes, reacts and charges. It's hard to draw in a breath, and yet I know damn well it's not the air that's making me feel that way but rather the look in his eye.

Then in the space from one beat to the next, he has me against the wall, his lips on mine, his body pressed against me in the most delicious of ways. Our hands grab and pull and squeeze and *feel*.

He wages an all-out assault on my senses with his lips alone. There is nothing gentle about the kiss. There is nothing passive. It's packed full of greed and need and hunger and a violent desire that ignites every nerve inside my body.

I react in kind. My anger at his accusations earlier, my sadness over Ford's birthday, and the realization of my feelings—they all curl into an explosive ball of harbored energy that gives just as good as it gets.

There are sparks of hunger on his tongue when it brushes against mine.

Each connection is like a livewire hitting water—evocative, incendiary, inescapable.

And just when I feel like I can't catch my breath—when I'm drowning in everything that is Easton Wylder—he tears his mouth from mine, hands fisted in my hair, knee between my thighs, and eyes a burning kaleidoscope of colors.

"Fucking Christ, I'm so mad at you right now."

And that's all I get—the growl of his anger—before I taste it on my tongue as he dives back in, catching me off guard and taking what he wants, what I offer him, once again. His stubble scrapes my skin, his fingers tighten in my hair, and his teeth nip my lips, swollen from his.

I fight against him. Not because I don't want more, but because I need to explain.

"I wasn't there for Santiago," I pant as he lets us resurface for air. His eyes narrow, his tongue darts out to lick his bottom lip, and his fingers twist in my hair so he can pull my head back.

He struggles with words. I can see them form, then fade, and so he speaks with his lips again, but by putting them back on mine.

But it's not enough. As much as there's no hesitation in his actions, I can still feel it from him and know he doesn't believe me whole-heartedly.

As hard as it is to stop him again, I can't do this without him understanding the truth. "I was there for my brother," I explain between kisses.

His lips move for a few seconds more, but as soon as the words sink in, his hands still in my hair he leans back to look at me. "You have a brother?"

I swallow loudly and realize there's hurt in his eyes that I never expected to be there. I don't understand it. Moreover, I choose not to because if it's there, then I'm responsible for it being there.

So, I lean in to kiss him again. To try and pretend like I didn't see it, or the confusion in his features. To absolve myself of being the asshole I suddenly feel like I've been.

"No, Scout. No. You don't get to hide behind your sweet fucking kiss. You don't get to hide your life from me when I keep giving you more of mine. Jesus fucking Christ." His growl of frustration echoes around the concrete walls as he paces a few steps away from me, shoves his hands through his hair, the distance between us reinforcing how far away from me he feels right now. "You don't get it, do you? This. You. Me. *This*. It goes both ways."

His words fade and die in the space around us. The look on his face—resigned, uncertain, disappointed—causes the panic to flood full force through me. And the panic this time isn't because he's getting too close, but rather because I fucked up. Because I didn't give him the benefit of the doubt and just assumed he'd run.

"What do you want from me?" I've never spoken a truer statement and been more afraid of the answer.

"More than I think you can give me." His voice is even, but it feels like he just shouted at me at the top of his lungs. The rejection is blindingly real and scary and overwhelming to a point that fear speaks for me this time. Shame carries the tune.

"What do you want to know, Easton? That I had a brother who was two years older than me? That he was my best friend, my everything, and three years ago he died? That I had a mother who went to get milk when I was five—left my dad washing the dishes and my brother in the bath and me in my Strawberry Shortcake pajamas waiting for her to come back and read me my bedtime story—and never came back? That we were too much work for her? That we weren't worth coming back for?" I yell, each word escalating in pitch, my body vibrating from the words I hate to admit but now can't stop from tumbling out. "Or let me see . . . What other juicy secrets can I tell you that no one else knows? What can I confess to prove to you that I really am trying to let you in instead of push you away?"

"Scout. Please. Stop so—"

"Nope. Just giving you exactly what you want." The catharsis is real and frightening and feels like a thousand-pound boulder is being lifted from my chest with each word. "Like how my dad is sick. He's dying, Easton. Is that what you wanted to know? Or how it's taking everything I have to get this goddamn contract with the Aces that I don't give a fucking rat's ass about, but have to get because that was his one request? And once I do, he's going to leave me, too? Is that what you want to know?" I scream the last words at him, tears sliding down my cheeks, anger burrowed in my heart, and all of me laid on the line. "Is that enough for you? You now know that every single person I've ever loved, who I've ever let in to know the real me, has left me. How I'm cursed, and petrified that if I let you in, I'm just dooming myself because you'll leave me, too?"

My voice is hoarse. My heart bared. My fears exposed.

My shoulders shudder with the sobs I won't allow to come. My mind reels with my confession as the dust settles, and I realize everything I just said.

Oh. Shit.

Those two words are the only thing running through my head like the tears running down my cheeks as Easton just stares at me, his face a picture of shock, his eyes a sea of compassion.

"Scout." His voice is broken when he says my name, much like how I feel.

"Don't. Please don't," I beg of him.

I can't do this right now. I don't want to hear the sympathy in his voice. I don't want any pity. But more than anything, I just can't take the hurt anymore.

There's a reason I've locked all this emotion up and not touched it for years. This is the explanation for my hard heart.

So, I shut it out to shut him up and step into him. With my hands in his shirt, I yank him down to me and bruise my lips on his, needing to feel him. Needing to feel wanted. Needing to know that, even though he knows my fears, he still wants me.

He kisses me back, but I can feel his hesitation, sense his discomfort, his wondering what in the hell I'm doing. My heart falls, and his hands lift to frame my cheeks. He holds my face still as he leans back. "Scout." Our eyes meet, and I see honesty so raw I can't handle it. I also see the pity. The sadness.

And I can't see any more of that.

I shake my head back and forth, and he leans forward and brushes his lips tenderly against mine, almost as if he thinks I need nice and sweet right now, to go along with my sadness.

"No." I need the exact opposite from him. "No," I reiterate, gripping the back of his neck, not allowing him to back off, adding some urgency to our kiss. And he lets me take the reins again. Allows me to pour my unsettled emotions into the kiss until I'm breathless and the tears have started to dry on my cheeks. "Make me feel, Easton. I don't need sweet. I need real. I need to know you're here. I need to know you want me. I need to forget. But more than anything, *I need you.*"

He leans back again. I watch his Adam's apple bob, see the clenching and unclenching of his jaw, and watch the realization sink in.

"I need you," I mouth the words to him, and it's like I've just thrown kerosene on a lighted match.

We meet each other in the middle, a mass of hands and tongues and commands and haste. We move to our own music: shirts over heads and bra unclasped and jeans unbuttoned and shoved down while he pulls my skirt up and his fingers find their way beneath the lace of my panties.

"God, yes." His fingers part me, play with me, enter me. There's no niceties. There's no seduction. There's just him doing exactly what I asked him to do—make me feel. Push my mind into the free fall of orgasmic oblivion so I can't think.

He's everywhere at once, hands and teeth and lips and skin, and it's nowhere near enough. We shift backward somehow, our feet moving as our hearts race, until I bump into the net of the batting cage behind me. My feet tangle in it until I fall against it, leaving my body supported by the net itself. My laughter at the predicament shifts into a moan as his teeth nip at my jawline and his thumb slides over my clit.

"Mmmm, hold tight, Kitty," he orders as he pulls his fingers from within me and moves my hands to hold onto the woven rope above my head. "You holding on?"

My eyes flash up to meet the salacious look in his, and I nod and try to comprehend why he's asking; he shakes his head in warning and slides his fingers into my mouth. I taste my own arousal, suck on them, as he slides them back and forth between my lips.

"Don't talk, Scout," he murmurs. "Don't question. Don't move your hands. *Just do.* Just let me. *Just feel.*"

I nod as my breath grows shallow. His teeth are biting into his bottom lip as he watches, his free hand working back and forth over his cock. But it's the look in his eyes, desire personified, that makes my back bow and beg for more.

"You want me to touch you?" He leans in and murmurs against my ear, his body close enough that I feel the crest of his cock bump against my lower belly as he strokes it in his hand. Talk about the sweetest torture, knowing the havoc that cock can wreak on my system, having it just within sight, and being told not to touch it.

I moan when he rubs it against my clit, and push my hips forward to get the feeling again. He half laughs, half groans as I take his dick between the tops of my thighs and show him what I want.

"Mmm, that feels good," he says as he pushes between my thighs and adds to the friction on my clit.

But it's not enough.

Nowhere near enough.

And he must agree because, unexpectedly, he lifts my hips and sets my ass back in a framed alcove of the netting. The moment my butt is settled on the shallow shelf, Easton drops to his knees, spreads my thighs, and looks up at me.

"You want to feel? Well, I want to taste you. Hold tight, Kitty."

Without another word, and with his eyes fastened to mine, he uses one hand to part me and then licks a line from my clit all the way down to my opening and then back up. And with the perfect amount of pressure and frequency, he begins to flick his tongue over the hub of nerves there. Soft and slow at first, and then faster and a bit harder.

I writhe beneath his touch. I sink into the pleasure and soar in its haze. Every sensation works my nerves—the warmth of his tongue, the tickle of his breath, the pressure as he slides his fingers inside me to give me the one-two punch of tongue on my clit and fingers rubbing my G-spot.

I moan and buck and pull on the netted ropes, all to ease the mounting pressure inside of me. To hold off my orgasm so that the pressure can build even stronger. I'm a mess of contradictions, and yet every one of them feels so damn good that the moan from my mouth can't even express how incredible they are.

I'm aroused. Needy. Greedy. Desperate for more. Selfish. Eager. And every single one of those feelings is amplified by the hunger in his eyes as he looks up at me with his tongue buried between my thighs, my arousal glistening on his skin, and his fingers buried deep within me.

A lick of his tongue. A rub of his fingers. The groan from his lips. The carnality in his eyes. The rope biting into my skin.

My breath grows faint. My body pulls tight. My head grows dizzy.

And then lightning strikes—from my center, out to my toes and fingers, and then all the way back in until the reverb slams back for a second, more powerful wave.

My cry fills the room as he laps at the wetness between my thighs, his groan of pleasure sounding as good as the orgasm feels. He milks it out for me, the licks of his tongue grow softer, and his palms slide up my belly to cup my breasts, gently tug on my nipples, and sustain the ecstasy pulsing through my body.

And when he stands, when he brings his mouth to mine and takes my lips with as violent a desire as when his tongue brought me to climax, I'm immediately desperate for the feel of his dick sliding into me.

I can't speak, even if I wanted to, and so, with my taste on his tongue, I suck on it. His groan, broken and begging, is all I need to hear to know I'm going to get my wish.

"Fuck me, Easton."

I broke the rules. I spoke. But I don't give a damn because when he lines his cock up and dips the tip inside of me, my head is already rolling back against the net, and my lips are already falling open into a garbled sound of *yes, please, now, and thank you.*

He fists his hands in the net beside my hips and pulls it to him so that he stands still but I slide slowly onto his rock-hard shaft. When he's sheathed root to tip, our mutual groan is the only sound in the room, as he lets me enjoy the feel of him filling me before he pushes the net back so he slides out.

And then, without warning, he yanks the net back toward him, and I slam against him, and him into me. The action sends shockwaves through my already hypersensitive nerves.

This time, when we're as close as can be, his lips find mine and devour them, murmuring, "Hang on, baby."

"Please."

And before the plea is even finished, he already has me pushed back and then pulled back into him again. He sets a bruising pace by manipulating the net around me to control the depth and the angle of his thrust. All I can do is hold on and watch how damn sexy he looks as he works himself up to his own release.

Those biceps of his flex and release with each pull and push. The tendons in his neck grow tight. His teeth bite into his bottom lip, and his nose scrunches up as he concentrates. But his eyes stay steadfast on mine. All the way up until the very end, when his head bucks back as his hips thrust forward, his hand holding me as close as I can be to him as he grinds his hips against mine and loses himself.

Completely.

And I don't think I've ever seen anything sexier than Easton Wylder come undone. I can't take my eyes off him. I can't stop thinking how I did that to him.

With my words.

With my confession.

With my body.

And when he lowers his chin and meets my eyes, everything I was fighting against the past few months dissipates.

I surrender.

Heart.

Body.

Mind.

Fear.

CHAPTER TWENTY-THREE

Scout

"We can go upstairs, you know." Easton's voice is murmured satisfaction as he speaks a full sentence for the first time since we moved from the nets to lay naked atop our discarded clothes on the turf baseball field.

"I kind of think this is fitting," I muse, grateful to hear his laugh. His silence has been eating at me, because I know I unloaded a ton on him, and now that our tempers have cleared, I must explain more, but need a few more minutes before I do.

I appreciate his patience. I am grateful for his silence. But with both of those also comes the unsettled quiet in my head that riots around on how to begin, since this sharing thing is all new to me.

"It would be more fitting if we were lying on home plate," he chuckles as his finger trails lazily up and down the length of my spine, pausing to smooth over the curve of my ass before starting the whole process all over again.

"So, why did you bring me down here, anyway?" I ask to buy more time. His hand pauses, then continues.

"Because, if you were going to walk away, I didn't want you in my place. Memories are a bitch, and the last thing I needed was to make more of them there on the kitchen counter."

"The kitchen counter?"

"I figured that was as far as I'd get you in the door before I had to have you, and the kitchen counter is the closest horizontal surface so . . ."

"Do you always want to sleep with someone when they make you that angry?"

"Only you, Kitty. Only you." Silence descends again. He plays with a strand of my hair while my fingertips draw aimless circles on his chest.

I feel at peace. It's such an odd feeling for me. New. Foreign. And yet the panic I've lived with for so very long is nonexistent. It's unsettling but also so very welcome.

"My mom is an alcoholic."

His confession into the peaceful silence has me shifting so that I can see his face, but his eyes are staring at the ceiling above us.

"Easton, you don't have to do this."

"Yes, I do. You shared your secrets with me, and so you deserve mine," he says with a nod. I watch his Adam's apple bob. I hear his unsteady exhale. And he continues, "She's not a mean drunk, but she's a drunk nonetheless. There's no gentle way to pretend she isn't. She's stuck back in time, not wanting to let go of the past, so much so that most days she doesn't know what day it is."

"Does she live close?"

"Mm-hmm." He falls silent, but I know there is more, so I give him time. "She lives about an hour outside of town. Seventy-eight minutes to be exact. I know because I often get late night calls when she won't leave the bar in the trailer park that she lives in and refuses to let me move her out of."

"That has to be frustrating for you."

"So many things about it are," he sighs. "It would be different if she were a mean drunk. It would be easier to hate her for it then. But she's not. She's sweet and lonely and just wants me around more. And I feel guilty that I don't spend more time with her . . . but at least sleeping on her couch a night or two during the week is enough for her. She deserves the world, but her world is her double-wide trailer, cluttered with her things and my games on replay on the TV, and so that's what I give her."

My heart swells at the audible love transparent in his voice. The measure of a man is often unquantifiable, and yet, with Easton, it's everywhere. In his love for his mother. In unpublicized visits to Children's Hospital. In his charitable organization for literacy. In his patience with a spooked woman.

"You love her." It's a stupid statement but so very true.

"Yeah." I can hear the smile in his tone. "You know, my dad wasn't around much when I was a kid. Sure, he was here in the offseason, or I got to spend time in the clubhouse with him, but she was the day-in, day-out parent. It would be easy for me to be mad at her for her drinking. It would be easy when the bar calls to let them get her home . . . but that's my job as her son. She took care of me, now it's my turn to take care of her."

Emotion clogs his voice, and all I can think to do is to press a kiss to his chest to let him know what I think of him.

"Was that the reason she and your dad divorced?"

"I don't know. I don't remember her drinking back then, but it's easy for parents to hide things from their kids when they're that young."

It's easy for them to hide things from their kids when they're old, too. Like my dad has for the past year.

"My parents never discuss their divorce. I don't remember them fighting. I don't remember any ill will. I just remember coming home from practice one day and my dad sat me down and told me that things were going to be changing a little. That was it. Later, I learned from friends how weird it was that neither of my parents tried to pit me against the other . . . but they just didn't."

"Lucky for you . . . I guess," I amend, realizing how wrong that sounds.

"No, you're right. I understood what you meant." His finger begins to trace over my back again.

"You're a good son. A good man."

"I'm all she has, Scout."

I press another kiss to his chest. "She's lucky."

"My biggest fear is a trade. She'd have no one to take care of her."

Easton shifts some and rolls onto his side, head propped onto his elbow, and looks at me for the first time since the conversation started. "Why didn't you tell me about your dad, Scout?" The compassion is back in his eyes, and I can't hide from it this time.

I sigh, shrug, and squirm under the intensity of his stare. "Because he made me promise not to tell anyone. Hell, he only told *me* a few months ago." I shake my head and remember the defeat I felt when he'd told me. "His heart is failing him. Heart disease, which sounds so weird to me because he's always been so healthy, but I guess he's had it for a long time and never took the steps to slow it down. He's on a donor list, but so are a million other people who have stronger bodies that can withstand a transplant, while doctors have determined that at this time his can't. Why waste a precious heart on someone who might not make it through the surgery, when they have ten other matches who can?" The tears threaten and burn, but I keep them at bay. Hold them back like I do the acknowledgement that this is all happening and real and my dad really is sick.

"I'm so sorry." Easton leans forward and presses a kiss to my forehead, the gesture so natural, so sweet, that one of the threatening tears slips out and slides down my cheek.

"When he first told me, I argued with him. Told him he was lying. And to this day, I still hope that's true, but he's living proof you can't recover from a broken heart." Easton's eyes narrow as he links the fingers on his free hand with mine and waits for me to explain. "My mom leaving was hard on all of us, but especially him. He had to figure out how to travel for weeks at a time for his job while giving us as normal of a childhood as possible. And then when my brother Ford died, I don't think his heart ever recovered."

I can see his eyes jolt as everything starts to connect for him. "Wait. Ford? As in *the* Ford Marsden drafted from UCLA? The wonder boy who used to play with Cameron and Penski?" he asks, sounding more shocked with each word.

I nod, my smile bittersweet. "He didn't want any show of favoritism because he was Doc's son, so during college and the MLB draft, he decided to use my grandmother's maiden name."

"I remember when he collapsed on the mound." The dreamlike quality reflects how I feel about it still today. Like I wish the whole thing were a dream instead of the nightmare it is.

"Hypertrophic cardiomyopathy." I murmur the term I'd never heard before I received the hysterical phone call that afternoon. "A massive heart attack from a condition he never even knew he had."

"All of us players had always thought we were invincible. We ran every day, ate healthy, were in top physical form, and then that happened to him. It freaked a lot of us out for a while. Like, if it could happen to him, then . . ."

"It could happen to you. Yeah, I know. I think I've had my heart checked every which way possible to make sure I don't have the same condition." I nod, the nagging worry just something I live with. "And obviously, my dad was checked too . . . but his situation is a different issue all together . . . and now it's going to take him from me, too."

Easton reaches out and pulls me into him. And this time, I let him. I accept the warmth and comfort and reassurance of his arms around me. I listen to the beat of his heart and memorize the feel of his skin beneath my cheek as I nuzzle his neck.

"When Ford died, it broke my dad. He was his pride and joy. He was the light in our house, the one we looked to for our laughter. And then, like that, he was gone. I was left to try and pick up the pieces and fill the holes that seemed to surround us constantly. So, I changed my major in school. I'd always been interested in following in my dad's footsteps, but my dad wouldn't let me. He told me I had to go take the world by storm and do my own thing. But when Ford died, it was like he wanted to keep me close to make sure I was okay, and so he finally agreed to let me learn the trade. Once I was given the chance, I threw myself into everything about it to make him proud. To try and make him happy."

"He's proud of you, Scout. I have no doubt about that," he murmurs into the crown of my head, the heat of his breath hitting my hair.

"Pride doesn't mend a broken heart, though." I speak my thoughts out loud and am grateful that he doesn't refute them, doesn't disagree with my opinion, no matter how irrational it may seem. "So that's why I'm here in Austin. Securing the last job for him, so he can know he fulfilled the one career goal he still had remaining."

"That's honorable and selfless."

"I'm terrified that I'm going to let him down."

"You won't," he murmurs. "Not if I have anything to do with it."

I snuggle further into him, appreciative of the reassurance, but more than aware that the front office has the final say. Not him.

"Is there anything else we need to lay on the line before we get up from our naked ball-field confessional?" I tease. His chest vibrates against mine with his laughter, but when he doesn't say anything, I'm suddenly paranoid. "What is it? What else do you need to tell me?" When I try to lean back and look into his eyes, he just holds me still.

"For a girl who spooks easily, you sure ask a lot of questions. Didn't anyone ever tell you to not ask questions you can't handle the answers to?"

"Easton." His name is a playful warning, but my pulse quickens with his comment. "Please tell me you don't have a wife in every city, or I'm going to be royally pissed."

"Hardly."

"Then what?" Impatience rings in my tone as my body comes to life with the feeling of his naked body and dick slowly hardening against me. I try to tickle him to get an answer. We wiggle and squirm away from each other, but he has the upper hand in the strength department.

"Let's just say, you're not yet ready to hear what I have to say," he laughs out amid my tickle torture, but the simple statement knocks all the fight out of me as my mind races with possibilities. Good possibilities, ones I never dared to think could even be possible but which flicker and fade through my mind nonetheless.

And he uses my momentary lapse in attention to scoot away from me. I scramble on all fours to go after him.

"I know how to make you talk, Wylder." My voice is full of suggestion, and my body is renewed with desire as I crawl slowly toward him.

"Naked batting practice?"

It's sad that there's hope in his voice when he says it, but I burst out in laughter. And it feels good to laugh after everything tonight—my trip to visit my brother at the cemetery, the tension with Santiago, our fight, my confession, him making me feel, the last hour we spent talking—that I welcome the humor.

"Mmmm," I murmur with a raise of my brows. "That's not exactly the bat and balls I was thinking about using right now."

"They weren't?" He fights his grin but lets his eyes roam over my breasts as I crawl over his legs so my face is perfectly poised above his cock.

"Nope. Besides, I'm more fixated on making you talk than proving I can swing a decent stick."

Easton shifts his hips beneath me. "Fixate away."

It's my turn to give him a lightning quick grin as I slowly dip my head and take him into my mouth and all the way to the back of my throat.

His groan fills the room as his taste assaults my senses in the most intoxicating of ways.

"Good God, woman. You're going to be the death of me."

CHAPTER TWENTY-FOUR

Easton

She's gorgeous.

An absolute mess of gorgeous chaos with her hair fanned around her, pillow creases in her cheeks, a soft smile on her lips, and a well of emotion in her eyes.

God. Damn.

Chaos has never looked so damn inviting.

I won the battle last night, but I know there's a war still ahead of me. She's been left, is going to be left again, and there's nothing I can do to protect her from it.

But it all makes sense now. Her not wanting me to get too close. Her closing herself off. Trust being a hard thing and fear being a reality.

Her fears are valid. I get them but don't understand them. And yet I need to figure out how to make her not feel them when she thinks of me.

Last night was the first step in a long journey, but fuck if I don't want to take it with her.

Look at her. She's fiery. Beautiful. Funny. Intelligent. But more than all of that, she gets me—my thoughts and my love/hate relationship with this game. She gets this career I have, which to most others is exciting but disruptive as hell to relationships.

I reach out a hand and wipe a strand of hair from her face as those lips of hers spread into a sleepy smile and she snuggles a little deeper into the covers.

What in the hell am I letting myself fall into?

If she doesn't scare the hell out of you, East, then she's not worth the trouble.

And last night she scared the hell out of me. When I thought she'd moved on. When I thought she'd played me. When I thought I'd lost her.

"Morning." Her eyes light up at the sound of my voice, and I'm a fucking goner.

Toast.

"Morning," she murmurs, in a rasp of a voice that feels like fingernails scraping ever so gently over the underside of my balls. It makes me want. She makes me want, when I should be so damn exhausted after last night that even my dick should be fast asleep.

"Just because my cleats will hit the dirt again, doesn't mean I'll move on from the people in my life." The words are a truth she needs to hear the morning after confessing her secrets, her fears, to help reassure her that I heard her and I'm still not going anywhere. I run my hand down the line of her torso, rest it on her hip, and squeeze it for emphasis. "You're not one who can easily be forgotten, Scout Dalton."

Her eyes cloud with emotion, but it's her shaky inhale that catches my attention. "Uh-uh. I'm not going to let you do it, Scout. I see that look in your eye. After last night . . . you don't get to spook anymore. I know why you're scared. I get it. But you don't get to shut down, you don't get to shut me out. Talk to me. Tell me what's going on in that beautifully, scared mind of yours."

"You can't control our lives, Easton. I may not get the contract with the team. You could get traded. There are no guarantees." Her voice is soft, the emotion I couldn't read is obviously fear.

"You're right, I can't. But it's the possibility that should keep you going, not the guarantees. And I can tell you this—you're going to get the contract. I'll do whatever it takes to get back on that field so Cory sees you got your job done, and I'll put in every single good word I have for you to get the job." She shakes her head, starts to refute, but I just lift my finger to her lips to quiet her down. "And as for being traded, that's always been my biggest fear because of my mom. So, I hear your spooked-ness, Scout, but I'm matching your bet, so what else are you going to throw at me that I can debunk."

Our eyes hold, and I'm shocked to shit when she reaches out, wraps her arms around me, and snuggles into me. The woman who keeps pushing me away has finally pulled me in. And fuck does it feel good.

The only thing that rivals the feeling is her body snuggled up against mine.

My dick stirs to life—how can it not—and every little move she makes, combined with the scent of her shampoo in my nose, makes me want to have her all over again.

"I need to get to work," I groan, hating my own lips for even speaking it.

"I hear you have a mean, wretched trainer who likes to crack the whip." Her lips move against my neck, their heat only making the urge to bury my dick into her tight, addictive pussy that much more enticing.

"You have no idea," I murmur, and press a kiss to the crown of her head as my hands slide down to the curve of her ass, pulling her thigh up and over my hip to open her up for me. "She's demanding."

"And manipulative," she chuckles, and then sighs as my fingers touch ever so softly over that perfect, pink flesh between her thighs.

"Mmmm." Fuck. She's already wet for me. I can feel it and I haven't even slipped my fingers in yet.

"Or we could go bat another round downstairs." She spreads her legs farther, granting me access as my fingers slide inside.

Her hands tense on my shoulders. Her teeth nip into my collarbone.

I chuckle at her comment. "It's not the same. It will never be the same again," I murmur as her breath hitches.

"What won't?" I love how she's trying to act unaffected, but when my fingertips hit that little rough patch inside of her slick, wet pussy and her nails dig in reflexively, I know I've got her.

"Every time I set my helmet in that net shelf, it'll be my face between your thighs I think about." Rub, stroke, slide. Her moan fills my ears. The heat of it sears my skin. "Every time I stand at the plate to take a swing, it'll be you I picture. Naked. Swinging the stick like you own it and hitting that line drive back at me."

"East." A sigh of pleasure. My thumb to her clit. Her coming all over my hand.

"And then your little happy dance as you jogged around the bases." Tits bouncing, hair down her back, laugh filling the gray space.

I angle my body, open her wider, and line the head of my dick up right where I want it.

"No, it will never be the same."

I push into her. Become consumed by her.

Her feel.

Her touch.

Her sounds.

And I'm well aware that when I speak the last words, when her hands tense on my back and her mouth finds the curve of my neck, I'm not just speaking about my field downstairs.

I'm talking about me.

CHAPTER TWENTY-FIVE

Easton

"**L**ooking great, Easton. I don't see anything in the X-ray or otherwise that would impede your recovery any further."

If I could kiss my doctor, right now, I would.

"Whew." I blow out a sigh of relief. "That's good to hear, because it's getting stronger every day."

"Still stiff?"

"Less and less each day."

"I don't feel the click anymore when I move it. I don't feel any resistance either. Your surgeon must have done a wonderful job, if I do say so myself." He winks at me and chuckles.

"No complaints here."

"I'll file my report with Cory. Let him know I see no reason why you shouldn't be able to move to the active roster by the end of the month."

"Music to my ears."

"It's up to your PT though. He has the final say, since he's the one working with you, day-in and day-out. Does the club still have you working with Doc?"

I smile automatically. "I'm working with Scout Dalton." Images flash through my mind of her earlier. At least I know I was right about the kitchen counter theory.

"I hear she really knows her stuff."

"Seems to." I meet his eyes. Hope he doesn't see that I'm talking about a helluva lot more than just her job.

"Haven't heard much from Doc though, lately. Rumor is he's planning on retiring."

"I've heard the same," I murmur as I stand and pull my shirt back over my head. I think of Scout yesterday, and the tears she tried to hide when she hung up the phone with him. She won't talk about it, and I won't push her. That's her dad. It's her frustration over wanting to be with him and him being a stubborn cuss and telling her to finish the job first.

To get me back on the field first.

Fathers and their unexplained actions.

I shake Dr. Kimble's hand and say good-bye.

Let's hope he's right. That my arm should be good to go. While the X-rays may be clean, sometimes it's the things you can't see that are waiting to bring you down when you least expect it.

I'm on fucking cloud nine.

Dr. Kimble gave me his clearance.

The Literacy Project just got approval for a huge grant that's going to help us expand our reach to more inner-city schools.

Scout and I practiced throwing down to second base yesterday and not a single fucking thing hurt.

Then, of course, Scout rewarded me for my progress. Surprised me with a little takeout on a picnic blanket on the private field, gave me a full body massage to work out any muscles that may be tight, and then let me work *her* out.

And Christ did we work out.

So, I add a few extra reps in while I'm down here putting my time in and take advantage of all the things that are falling in line for me.

"You should be activated by the end of the month."

Kimble's words echo in my head as I scrub a towel over my face and head toward the locker room.

Three weeks.

Looks like my stint in hell—the disabled list—might be coming to an end.

"I thought you'd already put your time in?" Miguel says as he passes me in the tunnel, an odd expression on his face that I chalk up to surprise.

"Yeah. I did. But Mathers told me I could come in and catch bullpen if I want to warm the pitchers up and help get my reflexes up to speed."

"*Nice*. That close, huh?"

"I want back on the field so bad I can taste it. I might even give up sex at this point." He looks at me like I'm crazy and we both laugh. "Nah. I'll never give that up." I laugh as we pass each other.

"Hey, Wylder?"

"Yeah?" I turn around to face him. He's standing in the middle of the tunnel, the daylight from the field at his back as he just stares at me.

"Nah. Nothing. We'll be glad to have you back."

"Thanks. Me, too."

Pumped to be getting my gear on and be part of the game in some way, I head into the locker room, ready to shower and check my phone to see if Scout's going to swing by.

"Hey." I lift my chin in greeting as I pass Drew. He startles when he sees me and flicks a glance over to J.P. across the locker room, a concerned look on his face when he meets my gaze again.

What the fuck is going on?

Is this the prank I've been waiting for? Are they finally going to man up and get me back for that stunt in Cleveland? Bring it on, boys.

But when I meet J.P.'s eyes and he glances across the room, I start to doubt it. I follow his line of sight and see a group of guys, some with towels wrapped around their hips, others with just their jock on, some in sliders and their jersey shirt.

Something's up.

Gonzo's locker is empty and the placard with his name is gone. Poor kid. He had a good run but has probably been sent back to Triple-A. Dr. Kimble was quick with filing his report if they already sent him back.

But then who's behind the plate for now?

Just as the thought crosses my mind, I notice the bag on the floor in front of the locker, about the same time the entire room falls silent. Fucking bad juju. I can feel it instantly but have no clue why . . . until a man strolls through the center of the square room. His head is down, he's using one white towel to shake the water out of his hair, and another towel is around his waist.

But I'd know that tattoo on his bicep from anywhere.

And as if he can sense the whole locker room is staring at him, he lowers the towel from his head and looks up and straight into my eyes.

It's not a prank.

Santiago.

Mother. Fucker.

"Tell me it's not fucking true, Finn," I grit the words out.

I keep my head down, the bill of my hat pulled low over my face as I weave my way against the flow of the crowd milling around the ballpark, here to catch batting practice.

I don't know where I'm going, but I know I need to walk. Run. Fucking punch something. Anything to abate the rage controlling me right now.

"I'm trying to get answers."

"That's not fucking good enough."

"It's fucking bullshit is what it is," he sneers, and thank fuck for that because I need him to be just as livid as I am. He was about to be fired if he wasn't.

"Cory wasn't there. The front office was the first place I went for answers."

Neither was my dad. "And no one had any answers for me other than 'Cory will be back late tonight.'"

"It's probably best you didn't talk to him right now."

"He's a chickenshit fucker to make the trade and not give me a heads-up."

"I'm in agreement with you there."

"They know the history here. He's the bastard who took me out of their starting roster, and then they go and sign the fucker?"

"I know, Easton. It's not making sense." I'm so angry I start to walk one way, and then start back the other way, not sure where I'm going, what to do now, or what to do next. "How bad was it?"

My laugh fills the connection but sounds anything but humorous. "I didn't land a punch, if that's what you're asking. Not from a lack of trying, though." I scrub a hand over my face, my feet eating up the squares of the sidewalk like they're endless. "Tino and Drew were on me before I could throw it. The other guys grabbed him. It was a clusterfuck."

"I've got calls in. I'm hearing it was Gonzo and two other Triple-A players plus Maddox."

"Maddox? They traded fucking Maddox?" My head spins at the news.

"He had a big salary and isn't having that great of a year."

"Fucking Cory."

"This is what he's known for, playing moneyball—he comes in, cleans up, tightens budgets, and he wins pennants."

"We win them. *Not him.*" I pinch the bridge of my nose, trying to process how the hell Santiago is an Ace. "Please tell me I'm ironclad."

"With that book of a contract we negotiated, you're solid."

"Finn . . ." I sigh as I cross the street and cut right, far enough from the stadium to breathe a bit freer, where I can talk a little less guarded, but am conscious that I'm still in the city I play for.

"I don't know," he murmurs, answering my unspoken question: why trade for another catcher when I'm getting my clearance soon? "He's a damn good left fielder, too. Circe's been weak this year. Maybe they're thinking of shifting him there when you come back. This is a business, East. You know that."

"Bad juju, man."

"Fucking juju," he mutters. "Just tell me you can handle being in the same clubhouse as him and that I'm not going to get a call to come bail you out."

"I'm not making shit for promises."

"Good to know and glad to hear it. I'll text you when I hear something."

I look at the blank screen on my phone for a minute, wanting to call my dad but at the same time not wanting to. And when I look up, I realize where my feet took me.

Scout.

I stare at the front of her little townhome for who knows how long, trying to make sense of the trade and the club where I've devoted my career.

And all I feel is defeat. I've busted my ass for months to get back, and just as I get there, my team trades my enemy to my team? To play my position?

I should go have a few drinks.

I should turn around, head back toward the stadium, find a dark hole-in-the-wall bar and drink myself into oblivion while I watch the game. While I watch Santiago in my position. In my team uniform.

Fuck me.

I should leave Scout out of this. I'm not at my best, not what she needs to deal with.

I look around. Spot a bar across the way and down a little bit to the left.

Drink.

Scout.

Drink.

Scout.

I need both.

CHAPTER TWENTY-SIX

Scout

"**E**aston? *Where have you been*? I've been trying to get ahold of you for the past hour!"

Relief courses through me at the sight of him standing in my doorway, still in his practice uniform, almost as if he heard the news I found out about a little bit ago and walked right off the field. He's a little bleary eyed and a lot unsteady on his feet but it's his face that etches itself into my mind— part lost little boy, part defiant teenager, and a whole lot of pissed-off man.

"I needed a drink. I needed you first, but figured I should have a drink first." He half slurs, half laughs and shakes his head. "I'm not making sense. Welcome to the motto of my day: nothing makes sense."

"Come on. Come in." I grab onto him, pull him inside, and lead him by the hand over to the couch. "I flipped on the TV to catch the game, and he was an Ace. I've been out of my mind trying to get ahold of you."

He plops on the couch but doesn't say a single word as I prattle on, trying to ease the anxiety I've had for the past hour and a half over whether he was okay.

"Talk to me. Please," I beg as I look down at where he's sitting in front of me. I need to know what to do to help him.

The silence stretches except for the low hum of the announcers' voices in the background of the game, and I debate whether or not I should turn it off. His discord is more than obvious, magnified by the drink or ten he's most likely had, and I feel helpless standing here staring at him while he's staring at his hands clasped in between his legs.

"I'm going to get you some water," I say, and just as I take a step, Easton takes me by surprise, grabbing me by the waist and pulling me into him so that his arms wrap around my hips, and he rests his forehead against my belly, his hat falling backward off his head.

My heart breaks for him, for what he must be thinking, because I've been thinking the same. So I do the only thing I can: I thread my fingers through his hair and just let him hold on to me and take whatever it is he needs from me.

Half an inning expires while we stay like this and I try to figure out what it is I can say to make it better. Then I laugh at how stupid that sounds. So I say the next best thing I can think of.

"I talked to Dr. Kimble today. We'll give Santiago three weeks to rent that spot behind your plate and show his skills. Then you'll be back, and when you step on the field, the difference in your skill level will be so obvious, everyone will realize how much they missed you."

He chuckles. The heat of it hits my belly as his fingers tense and flex against my hips before he slowly leans against the back of the couch. His hands pull on my hips and guide me to straddle him. I follow his lead, my eyes steadfast on his, waiting for him to look up so I can get a glimpse of what he's thinking.

He doesn't.

Instead, he rests his head back and closes his eyes; his thumbs, now resting on the sides of my hips, rub circles against the denim of my jeans. "I turned my phone off. Sorry I didn't pick up, but I thought it might be best to not talk to anyone for a bit."

I nod my head, and then realize he can't see it. "Understandably. I'm sure your dad is worried about you. Did you talk to him at all?" He doesn't reply, just gives a half-hearted shrug that doesn't give me any insight.

"You know what gets me?" he asks with an audible skepticism I can understand. "What did I ever do to him? Get a better contract with a better team? There are a hundred guys out there who have better contracts . . . so why pick me to fuck with? Is it just because I'm the privileged legacy son, so he doesn't think I deserve it? Is it because he thinks I was born with a silver spoon in my mouth and a gold bat in my hand when he had to struggle? Doesn't he get that it wasn't all fucking cherries being Cal Wylder's son? That I'd give my eye-teeth to have one moment of my baseball career that wasn't overshadowed by the fact that I better perform as expected from the Iron Giant's son?"

He lifts his eyes and looks at me for the first time, weary and a little lost.

"You know what's even more fucked up? You know what I thought about as I sat in the bar across the street?"

"What?" I ask gently.

"I love this game, Scout. I told you the other day that I played because of my dad, and fuck yes, I do . . . but I also play because I *love* this game. Baseball is so much more than just a game to me. It's sights and sounds and smells—the roar of the crowd when you crank a home run, the tack of the pine tar on your bat, the smell of the popcorn in the air, the pop a glove makes on a screaming fastball, the sting of a broken bat vibrating through your fingers and up your forearm, the awe on the little boy's face standing above the dugout when you toss him the game ball as you jog off the field . . . Shit, Scout. I could go on forever, but that is the soundtrack, the movie, the everything of my life. *It is my life.* How stupid was I that it took Santiago showing up to reaffirm the love I have for something that's been a part of me before I was even born?"

There are tears in my eyes that I don't even bother to blink away. The reverence in his voice speaks louder than all the things he just said, and they were pretty damn loud.

I lean forward, bringing my hands to frame his cheeks, and press a tender kiss to his lips before resting my forehead against his.

"I promise you that we'll have you back in top form. You're already there—we just need to work your arm up to playing a full game."

He nods, his breath hot against my lips, and the scrape of his stubble rough against my fingertips.

"Santiago being on the team means nothing. Maybe there was an old trade that linked to this one. The 'a player to be named later' kind. Maybe they brought him on to spur your ass into gear."

"Or maybe Cory's an asshole and just wanted to fuck me over."

I know that's the alcohol talking, but he still has a point. "I get why you feel that way, but at the end of the day, you're Easton Wylder. The Aces' franchise player. You're not going anywhere, so why cause trouble just to add strife. There has to be a valid reason."

"And I'm sure if I listen to my thirty messages, there will be, but right now I don't care. Right now, I just want to feel sorry for myself, have another drink, sit here with you, and figure out how exactly I'm going to see that fucker every goddamn day and not break his nose."

I chuckle and press my lips to his before shifting and nuzzling my forehead against the side of his neck. "Ignore him."

"Easier said than done."

"True, but the best way to get back at him is to come back and blow him out of the water. The assumption is that you're injured and won't be one hundred percent. Won't it be the ultimate 'fuck you' to be just the opposite?"

"The mother fucker deserves it."

"He does."

"Do you really think I can get there?"

The cautious hope in his voice digs its claws into my heart and doesn't let go. "I know you can."

"There are no guarantees."

"You're right, there are no guarantees," I repeat his words back to him, "but it's the possibility that should keep you going."

When the guys call him after the game and ask him to meet up for drinks, I encourage him to go. He needs their camaraderie right now. He needs their reassurance that they have his back.

And I need time to myself.

To think.

To process.

To reread the email that Sally forwarded, explaining how they've pulled my dad's name from the transplant list.

It's not like I didn't expect this. A new heart was out of the question. His body is too frail, his immune system too weak to accept a foreign organ.

But while his name was on the donor list, there was a false sense of hope.

And now there's not.

My heart just needs more time to accept what my mind already knows.

But there will never be enough time to accept this.

CHAPTER TWENTY-SEVEN

Scout

My feet stop the second I spot Easton.

The moms pushing strollers have to swerve around me and a little boy bumps against me, but I stand still, trying to comprehend how the mere sight of him eases the stress of my day.

He's lying on a slope covered in grass beyond the left field fence, his legs are crossed at the ankles, his hands are braced behind him, and an Aces baseball hat sits low over his brow. His attention is focused on the Little League game playing in front of him where little boys about five or six years old are trying their hardest to master his game.

The boys are adorable and the man observing from his incognito spot in the outfield even more so, and yet I can tell something is bothering him. He's never missed a training session like he did this afternoon, and the simple text he sent me offered no explanation.

I should leave. The fact that he didn't reply to any of my texts should be a big enough indicator that he wants to be left alone and me being here is anything but leaving him alone.

But I don't move. Can't. And I'm not blind to the fact that my inability to walk away stems from so much more than wanting to know why he bailed on his workout today. The kind of *so much more* that often wakes me up in the early morning hours and challenges me to pull up a thought that doesn't involve Easton in some way, shape, or form, all the while being lulled back to sleep by the even rhythm of his breathing beside me.

The kind of *so much more* that has me standing in the middle of some recreational park a few blocks away from the stadium questioning why I chased after a man when normally I'm the one running the other way.

But there's something about seeing him in this element, watching the game he loves in its purest form that tugs on my heartstrings and has me making my way over to him.

"You just can't stay away from the game, can you?"

"Seems like it," he muses without so much as a look my way as I take a seat on the grass beside him.

We sit in silence as the inning plays out and watch the extremely patient dads trying to coach their sons on how to swing the bat or field a ground ball. I can't help but wonder what Easton's thinking about. Would he trade his experiences for ones like this? Ones where the game was about having fun and absent of the pressure that came with realizing you're expected to live up to the standard of play your father has set? Is that why he's here?

Another inning ends. Another round of high fives is handed out as the teams enter or leave their respective dugouts. And I'm still in the dark about what's going on with the man beside me.

"You blew me off today," I say after a bit.

He nods. "I did."

"Everything okay with your mom?" I ask, fishing for a connection with him when he feels so far away right now.

"Yep."

"Just needed to get some fresh air?" I ask, scrambling for anything to keep him talking.

"Yep."

"Care to elaborate?"

"Nope," he says and then hangs his head for a beat before scrubbing his hand over his jaw. When he lifts his head up, he glances at me momentarily, expression guarded, before he looks back to the game, but I can see he's upset now. It's in the sag of his shoulders. The defeat in his posture. The stress etched in the lines on his handsome face.

"You want me to leave?" *Please say no.*

"Nope."

My sigh of relief is audible. All I want to do right now is rest my head on his shoulder, make a connection with him somehow, but know I can't because of the ever-prying eyes of the public. It only takes one person to recognize the man in the outfield is Easton and take a picture with their phone and . . .

"Manny?" he asks pulling me from my thoughts with his guess on how I knew where he was.

"Yep," I say, taking a page out of his book of one-word responses and earn a soft chuckle from him.

"My first season with the Aces was rough," he begins to explain. "I had a few games that really tested me and messed with my head. Without confidence, skill can only take you so far in this game, and my confidence was shot. I was this huge prospect surrounded by all of this hype and I wasn't delivering. Teammates and coaches were throwing advice my way but all I heard was white noise. After one particularly shitty game, Manny walked into the locker room and told me to follow him. I thought he was crazy. It was almost midnight and here I am traipsing after him through the streets of the city until we ended up here. He made me sit in the middle of the empty field and told me to tell him what I remembered about playing as a kid."

"He brought the fun back," I murmur. I can picture the two of them in the darkness out here and it brings a smile to my lips.

"He did. He made me remember all those first moments when I finally fell in love with the game. And then he told me to come back the next day at ten o'clock. I did." He smiles and shakes his head at the memory. "There was a T-ball game starting. The kids were running to the wrong bases, swinging the bat backwards, and playing with the weeds in the outfield. It sounds stupid, but watching those little guys drowned out the white noise for a bit."

"It is oddly relaxing," I admit.

"It is," he murmurs, "and ever since that night, this is where I find myself when I need to clear my head."

"It's a good place."

"It is."

Easton falls silent again, while I replay the story in my mind and wonder what he's trying to clear from his head today.

Another inning passes. The red team scores a run, and Easton belts out a loud whistle in congratulations.

If they only knew the random bystander with the Aces hat on sitting in the outfield was Easton Wylder.

"I just couldn't do it today," Easton says unexpectedly.

"Do what?"

"Be in the same space as that fucker. The locker room. The field. The gym. He's everywhere. I'm sick of having the guys babysit me. I'm sick of not being able to walk in my own clubhouse without wanting to throw a punch every time I hear his voice." He pauses but his frustration continues to resonate. "I'm sorry for bailing on you, but I just couldn't do it today."

There's nothing I can say to make him feel better. Honestly, I don't know how he's occupied the same space as Santiago for this long without a serious fight breaking out between them.

So, I don't say anything.

Instead I move my hand to rest in the grass beside his and then hook my pinky around his. He looks over to me, his eyes a well of unexpressed emotion, but when he tightens his pinky around mine, it's all I need to know that my silent show of support and little bit of affection is enough for now.

So with the sun slowly moving toward the horizon, we sit and watch the rest of a Little League game while trying to remember what life was like as kids. Back when my dad wasn't sick and his shoulder wasn't injured. Back when there were no contracts to abide by and we could just be a girl and a boy sitting on a grassy slope enjoying the warm Texas evening together.

We don't feel the need to talk just to fill the silence.

Our pinkies are linked.

And the simple connection is all we need right now to reassure each other that we'll get through this.

CHAPTER TWENTY-EIGHT

Easton

"**S**hit. Maybe I need to get a shoulder injury, if that's how you come back and swing the stick."

The next pitch comes. I swing and connect. The crack of the ball against the bat is the most satisfying sound in the world. And even better, there's still no pain. No pinch. *Just like new*.

"He's the only lucky fucker who could pull it off, though."

"Bunch of fucking cackling women. Leave the poor man alone. He needs to reacquaint himself with his balls right now."

I laugh as I take a swing and miss the fat pitch Coach Walton lobs from the mound. All three guys say, "whiff," in unison.

I hold a batting-gloved middle finger up to J.P., Tino, and Drew standing behind the portable backstop as I take my hacks. The Santiago Brigade. Following me around like the three musketeers anytime I hit the field at the same time as Santiago.

They're trying to keep my nose clean and my temper at bay. It doesn't look too good when the unofficial team captain goes fist-fucking his replacement's face. But shit, how satisfying would that be since the asshole seems determined to annoy me every chance he gets.

Another pitch. I channel my anger at Santiago, my drive to return, my need to prove to Scout that I'm good to go.

And when I hit the next pitch—a line drive that goes right through the five-point-five hole between third base and shortstop—I know I'm back.

"What do you think she's telling Walton out there?" Drew chimes in, trying to get in my head as I watch Scout lean in and say something in Walton's ear. He nods.

"Oh, Walton, you handsome devil. If you hit that pain in the ass Wylder in the nuts, you can take me out to dinner tonight," Tino says in a high-pitched voice. I step out of the box, my hand up to hold the pitch.

"Fuck you, Tino," I laugh as both Walton and Scout look to me from the mound, wondering what the hell is going on.

"It's just the asshole brigade," I shout to them and wave for them to pitch.

Used to our antics, Walton winds up, throws the pitch, and when I let loose on my swing, the crack echoes in my ears as I watch it clear the wall into the stands in left field.

Hell yeah, I'm back.

"Looking good out there, Hot Shot," Scout says as I walk into the training room.

"Felt damn good." I roll my shoulders and smile at her.

"I can tell," she laughs. "You got your swagger back."

"My swagger?"

"Yep. That cocky little smirk you used to get before you stepped into the batter's box was there today. It's the first time I've seen it since I started training you."

"I don't get a cocky little smirk when I step in the box," I say with a chuckle as I slide onto the table. *Do I?* She steps up behind me to work the muscles in my shoulder as I try to think of my batting routine and smiling is not something I do.

"Yes, you do. It says, you better bring your best stuff, Mr. Pitcher, or I'm gonna take you downtown," she murmurs. And there's no way I should find what she says sexy, but the fact that she can talk baseball terms while her fingers slide over my shoulder is definitely a turn-on. It doesn't matter how many times she touches me—here in a rub down or at home in my bed—because every fucking time she does just makes me want her more.

It doesn't hurt that that murmur of hers reminds me of when she climbs on top of me, straddles my thighs, leans forward, and says in my ear to *get ready* before she takes my cock for a ride.

"You're all kinds of swagger and arrogant when you play. It kind of turns me on," she says under her breath, but I catch every damn word.

"You know what I like more than hearing you say that?" I reply with a groan as she digs her knuckles into the knot in my shoulder.

"My magic hands?" she laughs.

"Well, those, too, and that's not the only thing on you that's magical . . . but I like knowing that before you were my trainer, you were watching me. That you knew I had a cocky little smile."

The hitch in her movement tells me she didn't realize she just gave that little fact away. "You also wiggle your ass two times."

"I do not," I deny, but know damn well that I do. It's unintentional but always there.

"Yes. You do. Everyone knows your routine."

"Oh please." I roll my eyes, even though she can't see it.

"I'm serious. Everyone stops and watches you when you walk to the plate, Wylder. They can't wait to see what you're going to do next. The lightning in the bottle you create. You're just that kind of player."

"*The player*," I murmur more to myself than her, remembering that first week we worked together.

"We've come a long way since then," she says, knowing where my thoughts have gone.

And yes, we have. I laugh, though, playing it off, because just like she gets spooked easily, I am, too. This has been too easy, how we've fallen into sync with each other, and I don't want to jinx it.

Don't want any bad juju fucking this up.

I tilt my head back so I can look at her. "I'm still waiting for that lap dance, Kitty."

"If you play your cards right," she murmurs under her breath, "you just might get one tonight."

Hot damn.

"You looked good out there today, East."

I glance back to the doorway of the press box where my dad stands, arms braced on both sides of the doorjamb with a proud smile on his face.

He's looking old. It's my first thought when I see him. The lines in his face are deeper, his eyes serious, his trademark cheer muted.

"Thank you. It felt good." I angle my head and study him closer.

"You looked stronger than I've seen you. The time you've put into your rehab has paid off." I wait for the 'but' from him—in classic Cal Wylder back-handed compliment fashion—but it doesn't come. He just stands there for a beat, shoulders square, with pride on his face. "I'm proud of you and how you've handled everything."

The implication behind *everything* is there, and I smile softly and nod my head, knowing he went to bat for me against Cory, even though I never asked him to and knew nothing about it until after the fact. The Iron Giant, Cal Wylder, tried to throw his weight around and let it be known that you don't run a front office or win a pennant by making a trade that divides a team when they're mid-season.

Luckily Manny had let me know about the conversation he'd overheard between Cory and my dad, or I would've never known. To say it shocked the shit out of me is an understatement. The fact my dad hasn't said a word about it to me even more so.

But knowing he tried without wanting glory for it makes it mean that much more.

"Thanks. Someone once taught me I can only do my job to prove them wrong."

His smile is slow to spread from his lips to his eyes—the sadness not fading completely—as he nods his head when he hears his own words repeated back to him.

"You want to join us for a bit, Mr. Wylder?" Bruce, the Aces' on-air sports announcer asks him, pulling me back to what I'm about to do. An on-air, pregame chat with the team's broadcast network to update the fans on my progress, how I'm feeling, and when they can expect me to return. I wait for my dad's answer, already scooting my seat over as I adjust my headset because he's never been one to turn down talking about baseball.

"No, thank you. Easton, here, has the team covered. The fans want to hear about him, not me. I'm old news." He winks with a soft smile before meeting my eyes and nodding to me.

"Maybe another time, then."

"Maybe," my dad says before turning and walking out of the press box, leaving me to look after him and worry why he seems so subdued.

"Okay, let's get started, Easton. Here is the list of questions in case you want to prep for them ahead of time."

"Nah, I'm good." I don't even glance at the sheet of paper he hands me. "There's nothing you're going to ask me that I can't answer on the fly."

"Even about Santiago?"

I look over to him, and his eyes tell me that he's behind me and my displeasure with the team's bullshit move.

"Let's leave Santiago off the table," I joke. "This is a PG show after all."

He laughs, shakes his head, and pats my back. "You could always knock him out and leave him on the floor if it's easier."

"I like the way you think, Bruce."

"Thought you might. You ready?" I nod. "We're good to go in five, four, three, two, one."

CHAPTER TWENTY-NINE

Scout

"**G**oddammit, Wylder!" The voice rings out and then a few more curse words, followed by a riot of laughter rumbling through the clubhouse.

I peek out of my training room, and once I see that all of the guys are covered and decent, I head out to see what's going on.

"Where is that asshole?" I think it's Tino's voice, I'm not sure though because the players are all standing together and blocking my view of what's going on.

"That's one way to sparkle and shine on the field, Tino," J.P. says through the laughter that doubles him over.

"Aw man, this shit is *everywhere*." It's Tino again and the guys around him slowly begin to back away as they laugh and shake their heads. "*It's like I'm fucking Tinker Bell.*"

"You always said you were light on your feet, now you just have the fairy dust to prove it," Drew says drawing another round of laughter from the guys.

This time when the crowd parts, I can see what they are all laughing at. Tino is standing at his locker in just his undershirt and sliders on with his baseball cap in his hand, and every inch of him is covered in sparkly blue glitter. From the amount that is concentrated in his hair and down his back, it appears to have been put in his hat so when he put it on his head it fell all over him.

"Tinker Bell Tino," someone chimes in and when Tino looks up to glare at them, he sees me standing there.

I can't help but laugh as he moves toward me, his whole body shimmering and shining under the locker room lights.

"You're a girl," he says.

"Way to state the obvious, Einstein," Drew says earning him a death stare from Tino before he looks back to me.

"Yes, I am," I say fighting the smile on my lips. Now that he's closer, I can see the glitter is that very fine type of powder that's basically impossible to get rid of.

"How do I get this shit off me? The more I wipe it off, the more it sticks." His eyes plead with me, but it's so hard to keep a straight face when I notice even his eyelashes are coated blue.

"Why would you want to wipe it off? I think blue's your color." I bat my eyelashes and feign innocence as the guys hoot and holler in response around me.

"Why you gotta be like that, Scout? Wylder's starting to rub off on you isn't he with his . . ." His voice fades off as he looks down to his hands coated in blue sparkles and does the only thing he can, laugh.

"You can shower, Tino . . . but you're still going to sparkle under the lights for the next few nights, if not weeks," I tease as I turn to head back to my training room.

There's more ribbing as I walk away but there's one comment that rings louder than all others to me. "Wylder's almost back, boys. That much he just proved."

He sure did.

The thought makes me smile more than anything has all day long. Well, since the last time I saw him that is. Because if Easton's pranking the guys again, that means he's getting back in his groove—mentally and physically.

"One scoop of chocolate peanut butter in a cup, please," I say to the girl behind the counter waiting for my selection with her ice cream scooper in hand.

"Make that three scoops." I yelp at the sound of Easton's voice and before I can turn around, his hands slide around my waist and pull me back against him. "Hi." His breath is hot against my ear, and after a long day it takes everything I have not to sink against him and just close my eyes.

"Hi." My smile is automatic when I turn to face him and take a step back, ever conscious of being noticed together in public. I take him in and wonder if there will ever be a time that I look at him and don't feel that flutter in my belly. "Blue glitter, huh?"

His lopsided grin turns full-blown, eyes light up with mischief, and he gives a little boy shrug in his grown man's body. "Peanut butter and chocolate, huh?"

I nod. "Yep."

"Treating yourself for anything in particular?"

My day flashes through my mind. The update from Sally on my dad. My double training session with Easton. The frantic call from my dad's long time client, the Red Sox, asking me to drop everything and fly there to evaluate their ace pitcher who hurt his arm last night. My refusal and then agreement to hop on a video conference call so I could help develop a regimen for them to follow. Then there was the report I had to put the finishing touches on for Cory—my proposal for how I would handle the players' day to day routine if I were to get the Aces' long-term contract.

"Yeah. I survived." My smile is soft when I respond. "It's been a day."

"That bad, huh?" He asks as he steps forward to pay for the ice cream despite my protests.

"Not bad, just crazy."

"I like that you treat yourself to ice cream," he says with a smile as we sit across from each other in the small seating area.

"I like that you chose glitter to showcase Tino's talents under the lights tonight." I raise my eyebrows and take a bite of the heavenly ice cream.

"If you're trying to get me to admit I did something today," he says as his shoe taps mine beneath the table, "then you're barking up the wrong tree. The first rule about pranks in the clubhouse is that there are no pranks in the clubhouse."

"Oh, please." I laugh and roll my eyes. "Well, it was pretty damn funny and the poor guy is going to be scrubbing that off himself for the next few days."

"Good. I'm glad to hear because the Nutella he hid inside my back pockets at the start of the season really sucked ass." My eyes widen as the gasp falls from my lips. "Yeah. It was that bad. I was late getting changed after an interview ran long. I threw on my clothes and hauled ass to the field. First inning, I go to put something in my back pocket and all I feel is this gooey stuff. So now I'm behind the plate with a crowd at my back and something that's the color of crap on my fingers. Where exactly was I supposed to wipe it? On my pants? That would be a great story for the announcers to create as they try to explain why Easton Wylder is crouched behind the plate with these mysterious brown smears all over his pants that appeared out of nowhere from one pitch to the next."

I laugh so hard my eyes tear up because between the disdain in his voice and the image he's painted in my head, I can see it all perfectly. And he's totally right. "So what did you do?" I ask when I can finally speak through the giggles.

"I rubbed my hands in the dirt to try and cover it up some," he says, the devilish look returning to his eyes again. "So . . . glitter."

"Did you just break the first rule of the clubhouse?" I tease, realizing this was the perfect way for me to end the day. His only response is to take a big spoonful of ice cream and shove it in his mouth so he can't talk. "Whoa. Wait. How did you know I was going to be here?"

"I was taking a walk toward your place to see if you wanted to grab a bite to eat and saw you in here."

"You could have just called, you know?"

"I know, but I figured if I came in person, you'd have a harder time saying no." His smile turns shy and it takes everything I have to not lean across the table and brush a kiss against his lips.

Doesn't he realize he's the only one I say yes to?

CHAPTER THIRTY

Scout

"Will he be ready?"

I startle at Cal's voice beside me, but try to keep my cool, forget the *she's a piece of ass* comment, and turn my attention from where Easton's currently crouched behind the plate in full gear.

"Mr. Wylder." I nod and go to turn my attention back to his son but the look in his eyes—the genuine concern—stops me.

"He's looking good, like his old self, but do you think he's really back to where he was? The top of his game?"

"Are you asking me as his father, or as the club's liaison?" I ask, trying not to sound disrespectful, but at the same time needing to protect Easton.

He narrows his eyes and angles his head as he looks at me, lips opening and then closing a moment before he nods as if he gets what I'm saying. "I deserve that."

"I'm not trying to be disrespectful, sir, nor am I trying to overstep my boundaries. I'm just asking so I know which report to give, because with all the crap that's happened over the past two weeks, I think he needs you to be his dad more than be on the side of his employer."

He nods and then looks back out to where Easton makes a perfect throw down to second base that clearly beats the runner trying to steal. Yes, it's just a practice. Yes, it's his teammates helping him get back in the groove. But his talent is unmistakable. His natural ability is phenomenal.

"I know you must think I'm a pushy asshole. A guy who only thinks about the game, about his own image, and not his son who plays it." He pauses, watches Easton throw to third base with laser perfection. "Easton's the best thing I've ever done. I only want the best for him."

The emotion in his voice stuns me and is such a contradiction to the hard-ass I've seen bits and pieces of.

"What's best for him or what's best for your legacy?"

He whips his head my way, and I know I've overstepped here, but it's Easton, and he deserves to have a relationship with his dad. The kind I have, which I'm going to lose soon.

"For him." He says the words, but I can see he's questioning himself by the furrow in his brow and swallow in his throat. "This is a hard business, Scout. It's not your right to judge me." His tone is stern. The features on his face tell me he's offended.

"You're right. I don't. I overstepped." And I hate that a part of me feels the need to back down to make sure I don't screw up my chance at getting the club's contract, since he's such an integral part of the front office. "But I've grown to care about your son, sir. You don't spend all this time rehabbing someone, training them, celebrating their small victories to get them back where they can play the game they love without caring about their continued success. And I do care about it with Easton. He has more talent in his pinky than most guys would dream of having."

"He's definitely more talented than I ever was," he murmurs, both of our attention pulled back to the field. To the man we both care about, whose swagger is back and unmistakable. We watch him for a few minutes, the silence settling between us.

"Maybe you should tell him that."

In my periphery, I can tell Cal has turned his attention back to me. "He knows it."

"Does he, though?" I meet his eyes. "He's clawing his way back from an injury that was so severe it would be career-ending for most players. His team, which he's been a part of for most of his life, traded for the man who caused the injury, currently in his position while he's on the DL. Physically, he's getting ready to take the field and kick ass . . . but it's his mental game I'm worried about now. It takes a lot to come back from an injury and not be timid of re-injuring it and suffering through the pain again. Add to that the bullshit with Santiago, and a father who is the Iron Giant of baseball, perfect in every way. That's a lot to swallow all at one time."

"I was and still am far from perfect," he murmurs, in a faraway voice that tells me he's speaking of way more things than I am.

"Not in your son's eyes."

There's a crack in Cal's armor as he blinks away tears that well in his eyes.

There's a commotion on the field that pulls our attention. The guys are practicing bunt plays, so that Easton has to run out from behind the plate, bare-hand the bunted ball, dying in momentum right in front of the plate, and then throw it in an off-kilter stance down to first base.

It's a hard play for sure. One that makes you throw with your arm at odd and often inconsistent angles. It'll be a test to his arm's range of motion. If there is any scar tissue that's going to cause a problem, he'll notice it now because the guys are watching him, the adrenaline is pumping, and he's nowhere near thinking about how to properly throw the ball. He's acting on instinct, falling back on the motion he's done hundreds of times over his career.

I cringe as he scrambles out from behind the plate, calls the other players off so they know he has it, picks up the ball with his bare hand, and then throws down to first base on one foot and off balance. And the throw is perfect, beating the runner by a few feet.

But more important than the ball's placement is Easton. I watch him as he walks back behind the plate, raising his hand to acknowledge something that was said to him by J.P. before pulling his mask back down on his face.

"He's an iron giant in his own right, too, you know." Cal speaks so quietly, but the emotion packed into every word is unmistakable. "I never pulled his kind of stats. I never had his strength or understood the game like he does. I just used my natural ability, but Easton . . . he has the ability and then some. He'll surpass every record, every career high I ever had, way before he retires from this game."

"And how does that make you feel?" If I'm going to overstep, I might as well clear the line with a flying leap. I turn to watch him as he watches his son play the game he no longer can, and wonder what that does to a man's ego when their ego has been on one of the biggest stages of the sports world for so many years.

He doesn't turn to look at me, and I'm more than surprised when he answers. "Every parent wants their child to have more than they did. More opportunities. More success. More happiness. More life. More love."

"It's hard constantly living in the shadows; maybe it's time you helped him step out from under them. Telling him what you just said to me might just do that."

CHAPTER THIRTY-ONE

Scout

"**A**re you going to tell me where we're going?"

I glance over at Easton in the driver's seat and take him in. And I'm just as knocked back by how attractive he is now as I was when he unexpectedly knocked on my door forty minutes ago with a bouquet of handpicked daisies and a request that I get dressed because he was taking me on a proper date.

"I'm not going to tell you, but I will say I like the skirt," he murmurs as he reaches out and rests his hand on my bare knee and slides it slowly up my thigh, the fabric bunching with it. "And the boots."

Without thinking about it, I slide my hand on top of his and link our fingers. It's a natural gesture, so indicative of how he makes me feel. Comfortable. At ease. Okay with whatever this is.

We drive for a bit longer, leaving the city behind us with each mile. The houses grow farther apart. The wispy grass grows longer. The trees grow bigger. It's so different than the brick buildings and high rises of the revamped downtown district around the ballpark. And while I love the new, trendy feel of the buildings the developers tried to make look aged, this is real. The country around us. It's peaceful and idyllic beneath the blue sky, sitting beside Easton with Sam Hunt playing softly on the stereo.

"*Scout and Ford*. Did your parents have a thing with cars?" he asks out of the blue, and I laugh at the random but very valid question.

"Says the man named Easton," I tease.

"No mystery what I was named after." He laughs.

My smile widens as the country whips by outside my window and the memories come back. "Ford was conceived in . . . well, in the back of a Ford truck, from what my dad has told us. I guess he and my mom were having a hard time with names, and on the way to the hospital, he racked his knee on the bumper in excitement. As he was leaning over in pain, hand braced on the tailgate, there was the Ford decal, and so Ford was named Ford."

"Logical," he muses. "And you?"

"My brother loved the neighbor's car. It was a bright yellow Scout International, but being two, all he could say was Scout. So, when my parents told him he was going to have a little brother or sister, he said, 'No, I want Scout,' and would point to the car next door." Easton laughs. "And I guess he continued to say that all the way through my mom's pregnancy, so at some point it became a joke and they would refer to me as Scout. Needless to say, they thought I was going to be a boy and thought Scout would be cute with the name Ford."

"But you are definitely not a boy," Easton says playfully, that hand of his sliding a little farther up my leg.

"No, I'm not, but the name stuck."

"I like it. It suits you."

"Yeah, well . . . people think my parents had a thing with *To Kill a Mockingbird* and named me after Scout Finch. I always disappoint them when I explain that my name has much less significance than that."

"It's unique. Just like you."

I glance over to him and smile. "Thank you. I used to hate it but now I love its originality. I'm glad my mom went along with my dad's suggestions."

"Do you miss her? Shit. Fuck. I'm sorry. Don't answer that."

It's cute watching him stumble all over himself. "No, it's okay. People always want to know, but then don't know how to ask."

"Yeah, but it's kind of a shitty thing to ask. I'm sorry."

I nod to accept the apology and wonder exactly how it is I feel when it's not something I think about much these days. "Do I miss her? Hm. I guess in a sense I do, because she's my mom, and I hear other women talk about how they do this and that with their moms and how lucky they are . . . and I don't have that. In fact, I have the exact opposite. I'm close to my dad. I work in a business dominated by men . . . so maybe subconsciously I've surrounded myself with people who won't remind me constantly and unknowingly that I don't have a mom."

"It has to be hard, though. I mean, I have a mom. She makes things hard for me, makes me have strings most grown kids no longer have . . . but she's my mom," he says, the love evident in his tone, just as sincere as the look in his eyes two nights ago when he received a phone call at one in the morning, crawled from my bed, and went to take care of her.

"I think. . ." I begin, and then pause before I start again. "I've spent a lot of time over the years wondering if I'm glad she left when she did or if I wish she'd waited and I'd gotten more time with her. And I think I'm glad. If she'd stayed, then I'd have gotten used to her. I'd have missed her more. The way she did my hair, or the way she made me lunch for school. I remember the songs she'd sing me good night, but I don't remember much about the predetermined ways she did things, and that means I couldn't miss them. I couldn't compare them to my dad trying to fumble his way through them and learn . . .

it was harder for Ford since he was older. And it may sound strange, but if she was going to leave, I'm glad she did it when she did. As much as I missed having a mom around, I think it would have been harder if I'd known what I was missing, if that makes any sense."

He rubs his thumb back and forth on my thigh in reassurance. "Yeah, it makes sense. Thank you for talking about it. I know it hasn't been easy . . . there's no way it could have been, but it also tells me that your dad is as good of a man as I always pegged him for. Raising two kids on his own, giving them as stable of a life as possible, all the while being the best of the best in his job. I respected him before, but now . . ." He shakes his head, and his kind words about the best man I've ever known make me smile.

"Yeah, he's pretty fantastic. I'm a lucky girl."

We fall into our own thoughts again, our fingers linked as we hum mindlessly along to the music and just enjoy the comfortable silence between us.

"Speaking of dads, mine paid me an unexpected visit yesterday."

His words ring out, and while I'm immediately curious, I'm also unsure whether I should tell him about my conversation with his dad, too. "Hmm. Is that not normal?"

"Not this kind, no." He squeezes my thigh, and when I look over at him, his eyes are hidden behind his sunglasses, but his smile is soft. "He said you two chatted the other day."

"You were on the field, and he asked me if I thought you'd be ready to play by the club's date. That's all." I hate that I lie, but think it's important for him to think whatever Cal may or may not have said was because of his own recognition, not because his son's lover said something to spur it on.

"I'm sure that's not the half of it," he murmurs.

"What do you mean?"

"He told me that if I were smart, I'd figure out how to keep you around . . . after your rehab assignment is over."

"Oh."

"Pretty much." He laughs. "And then he told me how proud he was of me. How it must have been hard growing up in his shadow, and that I need to handle the transition back into the game, with Santiago being on the team, with the exact same amount of grace as I did growing up as his son."

He clears his throat, and there is nothing I can say to express how thankful I am that Cal heard me and actually said something. I can tell that it touched Easton, even though he's trying to play it off in his gruff way. The fact that he's not speaking right now is saying it all.

"Here we are," he murmurs as he turns down a tree-lined drive set back from the road. Dust plumes up behind us as we drive, and my neck feels like it's on a swivel as I try to take in my surroundings.

When the trees part, we pull up to a two-story brick house that spreads in all directions over the plot of land. Dogs are barking, I can hear a lawnmower somewhere in the distance, and cottonwood seeds dance all around us in the breeze.

I narrow my eyes at Easton as he hops out of the truck and rounds the front to open my door. He takes my hand in his, and the minute he shuts the door of the truck, he pulls me against him, into a kiss to rival all kisses. It's soft and sweet and tender and has the heat, desire, and need that's never too far from reach.

"We're not in the city," he murmurs against my lips. "There's no one to see me kiss you, so I'm taking advantage of it."

I laugh, loving that he's so protective of our little bubble, and put my free hand to the back of his head to pull him back down. "Me, too." I brush one more kiss against his skillful lips before letting him tug me along by my hand toward the house.

He has the cutest grin as he pushes the doorbell and just stares at me, shoulders against the wall behind him, one foot angled and resting against it. His eyes dare me to figure out what we are doing, and I honestly have no clue.

The door opens, and a slight woman with long, gray hair stands inside. Her smile widens to epic proportions when she sees Easton. "Mr. Wylder. Thank you so much for making your way out here to come and visit us."

"The pleasure is mine, Melinda. Thank you for letting us come out on such short notice."

"It's such a long way from the city."

"It's a beautiful drive," he says as he steps in, kissing her on the cheek in greeting.

"And you must be Scout." Her voice is full of warmth as she wraps her arms around me in a brief hug. "So nice to meet you."

I'm a little startled by her overly friendly welcome but follow Easton's lead and hug her back, still so in the dark about what we are doing at this woman's house. "You, too."

"Let me show you to it," she says as she leads us through the large but cozy family room of the house. "I had to kick Timmy out with the boys, or else they would have just gawked at you—the real live Easton Wylder in our back-yard. Noses smashed to the windows. Eyes wide as saucers. They'd grab at any reason to head out back and interrupt you, and I couldn't have that."

"You shouldn't have. They would have been fine," he says with absolute sincerity. I get that this is Easton's public persona, have seen it time and again at the field, but this is also the real him. "Maybe they'll be back before we head out. Meeting them is the least I could do after you so graciously let us come here."

"Are you kidding me?" She laughs, her fingers nervously fidgeting with her hair. I want to put her at ease and tell her we all get that way around Easton. "Your generosity is enough to keep the sanctuary fed for the next year. It's us who should be bending over backward for you."

"It's well deserved," Easton says as Melinda pushes open the door to the backyard. The sound of dogs barking hits us immediately, before I even clear the threshold, and when I do, my eyes widen and the smile is instant on my lips.

"You brought me to see dogs?" I ask, my voice escalating in pitch with each word. I look around the yard, where, organized in a hexagonal type fence, there are about fifteen dog kennels angled off one large play space. And the play space is currently occupied by about ten dogs of different colors, breeds, and sizes. Tongues loll, tails wag, and bodies wiggle in excitement.

"Not just any dogs," he says with a laugh, "but mutts."

My feet move on their own, down toward the fence where the fur babies are all vying for attention, hopping on top of one another, trying to lick my hands through the fence. "Can I go in?" I ask as I turn to look at Easton and Melinda, who are both smiling at me.

"That's the whole point," Melinda says as she walks the short distance toward me and directs me to go in the first set of gates that closes me off from the rest of the free yard, before opening the second set that leads me into the play pen. "These babies need some extra attention, and Easton said the two of you would love to come out and give it to them."

"Seriously?" I look over to her and then glance at Easton as the gate is opened, but my attention is diverted as I'm assaulted in the best of ways by licking tongues on my hands and tails whacking against my legs. There are grunts and whines and a few growls.

Time passes in wiggles and pets. The pack slowly calms down; their interest and eagerness is still there, but not as desperate. And I'm so lost in giving and receiving attention that it's a while before I notice Easton standing inside the play area, staring at me with a beagle snuggled in his arms.

There is a soft smile on his lips, a quiet awe in his eyes, and there's something about his expression that makes those butterflies in my stomach take flight, tickling my insides as they flitter about. His face is typically all hard lines with his dark features, but right now, with the sunlight on his face, all I see are his soft edges—soft edges that call to me to push myself to my feet and let him know how much this means to me.

And he must sense that I want to be near him but am currently serving as a chair to Lola, the slobbery pit bull with a scarred face and the sweetest disposition of the lot. As I nuzzle Lola with my forehead against her back, Easton makes his way over to me.

I laugh when he's overrun by the wags and licks like I was when I first sat down, but when our laughter subsides and I look his way, those butterflies hit me again.

"What is this magical place?" I ask as I reach over and squeeze his forearm as he pets the belly of a scruffy three-legged mutt.

"It's a dog sanctuary for abused and abandoned dogs. Melinda used to work for the ASPCA . . . and she wanted to do more after she ended up adopting some of the dogs she'd nursed back to health herself. She couldn't turn them away, so she started with one, and then another, and then . . ." He shrugs. "You get the picture."

"That's incredible. This *place* is incredible." I laugh as I get nudged by a fluffy brown dog demanding attention. "Such a good girl," I coo, but my next words trail off when I look up to see Easton's head cocked to the side, eyes on me. "*What?*"

"Nothing." He shakes his head as if he's trying to rid it of a thought, and links his fingers with mine. We smile like goofy teenagers for a moment, like there isn't a care in the world and this is the only thing that matters.

"I just thought, with how hard you've been working to get me back on the field, and everything with your dad, that you could use some extra loving."

"It's perfect." I feel like I've used that word a million times while we've been here, and I'm not sure if I have, or if I've just thought it, but it's true. The trees. The sun. The clear sky. The furry flurry. And Easton. How much better could it get?

"I guess Melinda typically has some high school kids come out and volunteer to help her here at Pet Haven. They give the dogs some extra attention or give them baths when people are coming out to possibly adopt them, but there's some big school function this week, so they're not available . . . and so I volunteered us."

"How long have you been involved with the organization?"

"Since about two days ago." He laughs and goes to lean back on his elbows, quickly realizing what a huge mistake that is as he's smothered in canine tongues and pawing paws. His laughter carries over the landscape and sounds so carefree, so relaxed, it makes me smile. When he can finally sit back up, after giving equal loving to the dogs around him, it hits me what he just said.

"Wait. Just two days ago?"

He nods. "The night I had to head out to take care of my mom? Melinda was there to help rescue a dog who broke free one street down. I ended up helping her get him back, and we started talking. I told her about you and how you were missing puppy love."

"But wait . . . didn't she just say something about a donation that would help feed the animals for . . ." I narrow my eyes as I put two and two together, and he nods slowly, trying to figure out where I'm going with this. "Easton Wylder, how much money did you donate so I could pet dogs?"

"I love when you get all *Easton Wylder* on me." He laughs at the same time I realize how ungrateful I sound. I begin to backpedal and explain that I don't need to be impressed, because I already am—with everything about him—but he just shakes his head, takes my hand in his, and brings it to his mouth, pressing a kiss to the backside of it, which cuts me off before I can get the words out. "First of all, Kitty, I never donate to charity to impress a girl. I donate because I want to. Because I've been blessed beyond measure in my life. It didn't hurt that I know you love dogs. And it definitely doesn't hurt that bringing you here might get me extra brownie points I can cash in for my benefit." He lifts his eyebrows and one corner of his mouth curls up. "But I did it because I wanted to *and* because they need more love than most to prove that not everyone is going to hurt them or leave them behind."

I look at him for a split second, hear the subtle parallel he's drawing to my life, and wonder what man does this. What man would pay enough attention to what I need and then go out and find a way to reassure me the one way he knows I'll hear?

I scoot next to him, the grass cool beneath my skirt and the sun heating my skin, but it's the man whose shoulder I just put my head on that keeps on warming my heart. And so we sit there for a bit and just enjoy our canine company and the fact that we don't have to speak to fill the silence. We can just sit here in a field of grass with the breeze on our cheeks and let the idea of there being an *us* settle between us.

"You brought me to see doggies," I finally say, and there's no other way to describe my voice other than completely enamored with him and what he did for me.

"I figured it would tide you over until you can get one for yourself."

If it were possible for my heart to break free of my rib cage and flop onto the ground, then that's what it would be doing right now. That hard heart of mine doesn't seem so hard any more. Not when it comes to Easton Wylder, at least.

And as much as I want more of this with him—as much as I think I'm ready—it still scares the shit out of me. The idea that I'm cursed is still alive in my mind, despite the most incredible past month.

"I love this."

I love you.

The thought is there. And once it's there, it takes hold and won't let go, no matter how hard I push it away, try to run from it, try not to be freaked by it.

Because I am.

"Thank you so much, Melinda, for letting us come out here today."

"Thank you, sweetie," Melinda says to me, but I don't think she's heard a word I've said, because her attention is on the field to the left of the house. Her two boys, ages ten and twelve, are standing there with bats in their hands while Easton gives them pointers about their stances. The looks on their faces are priceless, complete idolization, and yet Easton continues his lesson, making them laugh and kidding around with them.

He's good with kids.

And with dogs.

And with his sick mom.

And with spooked women.

Is there anything this man can do to make me not like him?

Because I'm beginning to think he might need to do that, so I don't start believing he hung the moon.

Or stole my heart.

CHAPTER THIRTY-TWO

Easton

"**Y**ou smell like dog." She laughs, leaning over to kiss me on the cheek before settling in the passenger seat.

"You're one to talk. Lola got more kisses than me. It seems she claimed you as hers," I tease as I push a hand playfully against her face when she comes close and makes a show of sniffing at me. She grabs my arm, her laugh ringing out above the warm night air rushing in the windows, and she tries to wrestle it away.

I let her win. Let her grab my hand and link her fingers through it, tangle us as if we're not already entwined. Am I a sap if I admit I like this? A relaxing day, a casual dinner at a roadside diner, and a beautiful woman in the cab of my truck. There's only one thing that could make this day better, and I sure as fuck plan on making that happen once we get back home.

A skirt and cowboy boots? What sane man says no to that?

"What are you thinking about?" she asks.

"Today."

"What about it?"

"How it was just what the doctor ordered."

"How so?"

"It was good to get away from the city."

"It was." She nods.

"And it was nice to get to do something for you for a change." She squeezes my hand in response as I roll up the windows. "You have spent so much time and effort on me."

"That's sweet. Thank you for being so thoughtful."

"You deserved a proper date."

"You just wanted to see me dressed up in my skirt and cowboy boots again," she laughs.

"Now that . . . I won't deny." Images of her laid out in the batting cage with her legs spread, skirt pushed up around her hips, and her hands wrapped around the netting fill my mind. "Seeing your legs in anything is a turn-on."

The truck falls silent as I check my mirrors and take a right on the lone highway back to town.

"You mean these legs?"

I glance her way to find her shifted in her seat, back against the door, with one leg bent so her thighs are spread. But with the dimming sky and the shadow of her skirt, I can't see shit.

And fuck how I want to see what's beneath it, even though I already have the taste, the scent, the feel of her pussy imprinted on my damn mind.

"Yes. Those. Legs," I murmur, as desire fires my blood and my dick hardens at just the thought of her. I glance up to find her eyes trained on mine. The damn woman is testing me, taunting me, and it's hot as hell.

"About those brownie points . . ."

Music to my ears.

"Yeah? What about them?" I may feign nonchalance, but fuck if she can't hear that restraint in my voice snapping string by string.

She doesn't answer, not with words, anyway. It's the hitched sigh of hers that catches my ear and almost makes me jerk the truck off the road when I find her with legs spread wider and fingertips moving in the darkness I can't see between her thighs.

God. Fucking. Damn.

The road, Easton. Look at the road.

I glance to the straightaway then look back to her. To her fingers hidden beneath the white pair of panties. To her teeth sinking into her bottom lip. To her nipples pressing against the thin fabric of her shirt. To her panting breath that turns into a moan as she fingers herself.

"Eyes on the road, Hot Shot," she murmurs.

"Now, that's just not fair," I groan, but obey only for a second before my eyes are back on her.

On her eyes. On that slow, seductive smile with her teeth still biting into that lip.

"Straight ahead," she orders, and damn it's hot being ordered around by her.

"Fuck me," I mutter under my breath, but I obey under protest. Because those fingers are still in her panties. The scent of her is filling the cab of the truck.

"That depends if you're a good boy and do what I say." She chuckles, cranking up the seductress role and turning me on even more.

I groan.

She laughs. Fucking foreplay if I've ever heard it. Deep and suggestive and throaty.

Her seat belt clicks.

I move to look her way, and her hand is right there, guiding my face forward so I remain looking at the road. I start to protest, but I'm met with two of her fingers slipping between my lips.

They taste like her.

Sweet.

Damn.

Perfection.

I suck on them and fight the urge to yank the truck to the side of the road and fuck her hard and fast right here for all to see. Because it's Scout. That's what she does to me.

She pulls her fingers from my mouth and slides them down to my lap. She scrapes her nails up and down my thigh and over my cock pressed against the seam, pushing my thighs wider so she can tease my balls. I groan out loud and struggle not to close my eyes and drop my head against the headrest because it feels so damn good.

"Here's what's going to happen," she murmurs against my ear, the heat of her breath tickling my skin and hardening my dick. "I want your cock, Easton Wylder. I want it right now. I want to wrap my lips around it. I want it hitting the back of my throat. I want all of it. To suck you off. To fuck you with my mouth. I want every last drop you have to give me."

That's about the hottest thing I've ever heard.

"You're going to help me get your cock out of your pants, then you're going to put both hands on the wheel and concentrate on not crashing. Understood?"

My hips are already lifted, my zipper undone, and my pants shoved to my knees before she even finishes her sentence.

"Good God, woman." It's all I can say as she wraps her lips and one hand around my shaft and then takes me all the way to the back of her throat on the first suck. My hips lift to give her as much of me as she can take. My hands squeeze the steering wheel like a vise grip. My teeth grind together as I force myself to keep my eyes open and watch the road.

It's a mixture of sensations. The heat of her breath warming and staying on my skin. The wetness of her mouth as she slides up and down. The suction of her lips as she pulls to my tip, and the little pop I hear and feel as she releases me from her mouth. She twists her hand as she works over my cock in a varying pattern; just as I start to get used to the feel of it, think I'm at the point of no return, she changes the angle, the grip, the movement, and builds me up all over again.

Nice and slow, East.

"You taste so good," she murmurs around my dick, the vibration tickling down to my balls and then back up.

Keep the gas pedal steady.

She goes to town, holds nothing back as she sucks and fucks and licks and tongues every inch of me until I can't hold back any more. I'm either going to crash or come, and fuck if I want to do the former.

Remember the road.

The sensation rushes from my balls and then through my cock. Her moan as she tastes my precum is the final straw that pushes me over the edge.

I break the rules. I put my hand on her head to keep it still as I buck my hips and fuck her lips. And she doesn't fight me. She doesn't do anything more than pump my cock faster and suck harder as I shoot down the back of her throat.

Her name fills the cab. *Scout.* It's a broken moan as she does what she promised—sucks every last drop from me.

And I can't take it anymore. I can't not have my hands on her. My tongue in her.

I jerk the truck to the side of the road. She shrieks in surprise and sits up just as I slam on the brakes. And then I lean over the console in a flash.

My one hand is back in her hair, the other is sliding to the wet heat of her pussy, and my tongue is between her lips.

I taste me.

I taste her.

The two of them together are a drug I can't get enough of.

I need more.

I want more.

I'm going to take more.

Right here. Right now. On this rural country road with fireflies outside the window and the scent of her everywhere.

And just before I lose my fucking mind to lust again, just as I shift in the confines of the cab to slide down and taste the heaven between her thighs, a single thought owns my mind.

I'm so fucked.

I'm so far gone.

Damn, does it feel good.

And I'm not sure if I ever want to come back.

CHAPTER THIRTY-THREE

Scout

"**D**ad?"

"Scouty-girl!"

I sigh in relief. He sounds good. Stronger than he did the last time I spoke with him. And I'll take that any day.

"How are you doing? Are you comfortable? Is—"

"Sally's taking care of me just fine. Stop hovering, child. I'm the parent. I'm supposed to be the one hovering, so knock it off or I'll hang up on you."

"Yes, sir." I laugh and feel so good hearing him do the same. I know it means nothing more than he's having a good day, like Sally already told me, but a good day is a good day and that's what I'm holding on to.

"You're five days out. How's the player looking?" he asks as Easton walks into the room with timing so perfect, he could never have known. I enjoy the visual—the towel slung low on his hips, the water still beaded on his skin, and the flex of his biceps as he runs another towel through his wet hair.

"*The player . . .*" I say, meeting Easton's gaze. He stops on his way to his dresser and narrows his eyebrows at me, a silent inquiry as to how my dad's doing. When I nod my head and give a thumbs-up, his smile chases the concern away. "Appears to be at or above one hundred percent."

In my periphery, I can see the little fist-pump that Easton gives in response to my comment, his grin a mile wide. And I share the same sense of satisfaction knowing that, in a big way, I helped him get there.

"So you're ready to give your recommendation?"

"Yes."

"You need to make sure you have a written report. Type it all up. His range of motion. What percentage you think his arm strength is. If you think he can last a whole game or if he needs to take a few innings at a time."

My cheeks hurt from smiling. You'd think he forgot I was around to watch him do this so many times in his career. But I'm just so thankful to be getting a lecture from him.

So I let him ramble on.

I let him advise me.

I let him feel like he's still in the game when his feet will most likely never touch the field again.

It's the least I can do after everything he's given me.

CHAPTER THIRTY-FOUR

Easton

"**H**ey, Easton?"

"Ignore him, Easton," Tino warns.

"I see him," I mutter as we line up on the left field line, jog a few feet, and then sprint the remaining ninety feet of baseline. We turn to jog back, and there he is, Santiago, with his arms crossed over his chest, his hips leaning against the left field railing, and that goddamn smirk I want to punch off his face. "The asshole doesn't know how to leave good enough alone."

"He's just trying to fuck with your head. He knows in three days you'll be back behind the plate and he'll be relegated to riding pine or being bat boy."

I laugh. It feels good to know these guys have my back. But when we hit the line again, he's still there. Still smirking. Still goading me.

"Was that your trainer I saw you with the other night? Heading into your building with you?"

My feet stop.

"Easy, E," Tino warns.

My blood boils.

"If that's the type of personal PT the Aces provide, then this is one helluva club. Count me in. I'm gonna request her now for any future injuries."

My body vibrates with anger.

"What's her name again? I need to write it down on my request form."

My temper snaps.

I turn to charge him, but Tino holds me back, and just as I break free, Drew is there. Then J.P.

The goddamn Santiago brigade.

Santiago's laugh fills the air. "Was it Scout? Or Slut?"

I see red.

Fucking blood-red.

And just as I'm about to punch my own friend to get a piece of the mother fucker, I hear one of them mutter, "He's all yours."

Their hands are off me.

And I'm charging.

I lower my shoulder and tackle him to the ground.
All I think about is Scout.
We roll back and forth on the ground.
All I see is fury.
I fist a hand in his shirt. Yank him up.
All I feel is satisfaction.
When my fist connects—
All I feel is pain.
Then there are hands.
And shouts.
Ripping us apart.
Pinning us down.
Damage control.
But I don't fucking care. I've had enough.

And when Tino and Drew push me off the field, it's my dad's face I see in the stands before they usher me down the dugout steps, and I can't quite read what it's saying.

CHAPTER THIRTY-FIVE

Scout

"How stupid could you be?"

All this work—months of healing, hours of strengthening—and Easton risks all of it by fighting Santiago.

"You should have seen the other guy," he jokes, then hisses when I push his hand with the ice pack back up to his cheek.

"It's not funny."

I slam stuff around the training room. The door is shut so no one can hear us, or the drawers I shove open then close, or the cart of the ultrasound machine as I bang it against the table where Easton's sitting. I hate that I'm pulling out the shit I used when I first started his rehab, because who knows what he just did to his shoulder other than just telling me it hurts.

"It's a little funny."

"Don't. Just don't!" I smack my hands down on the counter and brace them there as I let my emotions roil through me.

The confusion when I first heard the shout of "I'm gonna kill him."

The shock of seeing Tino and Drew physically restraining Easton from running back onto the field.

The bewilderment when they shoved Easton toward where I stood in the training room, when I saw his knuckles on one hand were bloody, his T-shirt was torn, and his cheek had an angry red mark on it.

And then the fury, the goddamn fury, when I saw him wince as he moved his shoulder.

"Scout." He sighs my name, and the resigned defiance mixed with apology only infuriates me further.

"What? What could possibly be your excuse?" I shout as I throw my hands up and turn to face him. "You couldn't control yourself? You couldn't be the bigger man and walk away? At least for a few more days?"

"Ah. Now it all makes sense. You don't give a fuck about my arm right now. All you care about is the meeting. The goddamn contract and what's in it for you."

His words punch out into the small space and slam into me harder than his fists probably did into Santiago's face. Because if he is aiming to lash out at me, he just got a direct hit.

Why am I fighting him? Why? Santiago deserved to get punched weeks ago. Better yet, he deserved it months ago, when he hurt Easton and was only fined and given a four-day suspension.

So why are you so pissed at Easton for actually doing it?

Why are you fighting him so hard?

Because I'm scared.

Over what this means for him and his position here. What this means for me and working with the team in the future. What this means for the two of us as a couple. And most definitely what it means to my dad's final wish.

It's so much more than the contract. Doesn't he see that? And yet, that's how highly he thinks of me right now—that I value the contract over him?

Add some more hurt to the anger, Scout.

"Excuse me?" My body trembles with restless fury. The kind you can feel deep down in your bones and have no clue how to get rid of.

"You heard me." Easton stands and squares his shoulders. His rage toward Santiago is still there, still raw, but right now it is directed at me.

Well, bring it, Hot Shot, because I'm primed for a fight, especially when you say bullshit like that.

"Glad to know that your precious fucking contract is your number one concern right now. Doesn't anything else matter?"

"Yes. Of course other things matter."

"Betcha can't name one." He stares at me, eyes searching and a muscle pulsing in his jaw. For the life of me, put on the spot like this and with his anger misplaced on me, I can't think of one when I know there are tons.

"Are you kidding me?" I screech, hating that I can't answer him, and lashing out in return. "You're going to turn this on me? Was it that hard to keep your testosterone in check? To walk the fuck away from him? Did you even think once that maybe when they reinstated you, it would cement his fate? You'd step back into your position, they'd see you side by side and know your talent blows his out of the damn water, and—"

"And you'd be awarded the contract." His voice is quiet and even now, and I hate the tinge to its edges—disappointment, sadness, hurt . . . I'm not sure what, but it digs deep down in me and makes my stomach churn.

"It's not about the goddamn contract! Don't you get it?" I walk from one side of the room to the other. I'm so angry, so confused, I can't seem to say the words I need to get out. It's like I have so many I'm suffocating on them, and yet at the same time, I don't have any. "It's about the time you put in. It's about getting you back on the damn field. Back to the game you love." My voice hitches. The tears well. "What's more important to you than that?"

He glares at me, the tendons in his neck taut, his mouth pulled tight, his body like a rubber band about to snap. "You just don't get it, do you?" He shakes his head, his voice vibrating with resigned frustration.

"Get what? That you couldn't control your temper. That you just risked everything we've worked for?"

"There you go again." He blows out a sigh.

"Whatever, Easton." I'm done. He wants to act like the asshole, then I don't want any part of it. I turn my back to try and hide the hurt, the confusion, the unsettled feeling that things just changed majorly between us, even though it had nothing to do with us.

"Whatever?" he shouts, grabbing my arm and spins me around so we're face to face, body to body, temper against temper. "*Whatever?* There are more important things than getting the goddamn contract," he growls, his finger poking against my chest.

"Like what?" I challenge.

"Like doing what's right."

"What's right is keeping your nose clean and getting reinstated. There's nothing more important than that right now."

"Jesus fucking Christ, you're frustrating." He steps back from me, shoves a hand through his hair, blows out an audible breath, and then steps back up to me. "What's right, Scout, is defending what you care about."

"And what's that?" Our eyes are locked, tempers bouncing off each other's in the space between us.

"Not what, but who." He pauses, squeezes his eyes shut for a beat, and when he opens them back up, the anger is still there, but there's something else, too.

"Who? What in the fuck are you talking about?" Did something happen with one of the guys? With his dad? What?

"*You.* I care about *you.* And I'd fucking punch him and fuck up my shoulder a thousand times over than ever let him talk shit about you again. You got it?"

"Oh." I stand there, stunned. Never in a million years did I think that Easton and Santiago would get in a brawl, on the field, with the fans there to watch batting practice, *over me.*

How could I have been so stupid when he was saying it all along?

We stand a foot apart, and all I want to do is put my hands on his cheeks and kiss him senseless. Reassure him. Reassure me. Anything to make a connection with him and thank him and tell him in the only way I know how that I care.

But I can't. There's a room full of teammates at our backs, who I'm sure were watching our fight unfold from the room's window. I'm certain assumptions have been made over why we're fighting. I know Easton's had his hands on me one too many times to come off like trainer and player.

And, right now, I don't really care, because he's upset and I want to soothe him. I can't touch and I can't kiss. I can't wrap my arms around him or press my lips to his hurt cheek—the punch he took for me—and kiss it better.

I step forward out of instinct, and he steps back.

"No, Scout." There is so much emotion in my name, I know he's feeling the same way I do, but the look in his eyes tells me his control has been snapped once, and it's best not to test it again.

He's so amped up on adrenaline and need that one touch and he won't be able to stop.

So, I use the only thing I can to reach him: my words.

"There will always be men talking shit about me, Easton. It's part of my job. I know it comes along with the career I chose. There will always be a guy who thinks I'm a Kitty or a Trixie." He sighs, and my heart does, too, right along with him. "Thank you for standing up for me, but you can't slay every dragon I face. It's a full-time job these days, but I'm strong and can handle it."

He cracks a smile. One full of regret, apology, but more than anything, filled with love. It's the first time I recognize it, and I stand there, so overwhelmed with emotions, I don't know what to do about it.

"You may be able to handle it, but that doesn't mean I'm going to stand by and put up with it."

I nod my head, acknowledge it, and know it's a battle I'll have to fight another day, but right now, I need to look at his shoulder.

"Come on, let me see if you did any damage." I direct him to the table and start checking out his shoulder. I can't see his face any longer, but the look that was in his eyes is all I think about.

About how it's ingrained in me to want to run.

But one thought keeps repeating over and over in my mind.

He tried to slay dragons for me.

CHAPTER THIRTY-SIX

Scout

The condo is quiet.

There's traffic in the distance, and the windshields glint from the early morning sun.

The stadium is empty. The grass is groomed in its crazy crisscross pattern that mesmerizes the eyes from this distance, and the dirt of the infield is dragged to perfection.

The coffee is warm in my hands, and the chair I'm sitting on is sink-into-it-and-never-want-to-get-out-of-it comfortable.

Easton, too amped up about getting to hit that groomed dirt later today, for what feels like the first time in forever, is somewhere in this city, jogging mile after mile to ease some of his restlessness.

Everything seems storybook perfect.

But inside I'm a nervous wreck.

Three hours.

That's all the time I have left before I willingly turn our world upside down. Our quiet nights at home. Our seeing each other every night. The day-to-day routine we've somehow established in this relationship that we haven't admitted is a relationship.

Or maybe we have, and I'm just choosing not to see it for fear of cursing it.

But in three hours, all of that will change.

CHAPTER THIRTY-SEVEN

Easton

"**S**hould I be worried about what I'm interrupting?"

Fucking Finn.

"I'm running, you jackass," I pant.

"Oh," he laughs. "I was going to say, she must not be that important if you're stopping to pick up the phone mid-stroke."

"I love you, man, but there's no way I'm stopping mid-stroke if my phone rings." I lean over and brace one hand on the streetlight to try and catch my breath.

"Smart man. It's D-day . . . how you doing? You good?"

"Dude." I chuckle as I look around and judge; I'm about five miles from the house. "I'm so amped up, even crossing paths with Santiago couldn't fuck it up."

"Well, that says it all." He laughs, then gets a little more serious. "I know you're ready, but how's your arm feeling? Is it still sore from your stunt the other day?"

I roll it out of habit, wait for pain to come, but know it's not going to. Scout was right when she said I'd be at one hundred percent. *Even after throwing a few punches.* "I'm ready, Finn. It feels like it's been for-fucking-ever since I had the crowd at my back. Just get me on the field."

"That's Scout's job to decide for them. Not mine. Are you confident she's going to tell them you're good to go? That your arm is able to withstand the pressure?"

Images flash through my mind. The shower. Scout's soapy hands sliding over my skin, down to my dick. Being tested and taunted. Picking her up and holding her against the wall as I fucked her.

Can it withstand the pressure?

I believe it did about six hours ago.

"Easton," he groans, mistaking my silence for uncertainty, and causing my smile to widen. "Please tell me you thought to ask her."

I laugh—can't help it. Torturing him is part of my job as his client.

"I'm not feeling as confident about this as I was when I picked up the phone to call you. I thought you two were close. Why the hell would you not flat-out ask her?"

His torture has gone on long enough. I can hear his anxiety ratcheting up. "Relax. There's no need to worry. It's just fun listening to you carry on like a little old woman."

"So your arm's good, then?"

"I love how you just completely ignore me." I laugh, needing the comic relief this phone call has brought with it.

"Easton," he warns as I laugh again.

"We had one . . . uh . . . final workout last night. It felt great."

If he only knew what I was talking about.

"No side effects or anything?"

Not the kind you can quantify. "Nope. I slept like a baby."

"Good. Good." I can hear his agent's mind start to turn now that he knows I'm ready. "Just promise me from here on out you won't do anything stupid like sign a document that says you'll agree to be back on the field by a set date."

"Are we back to this again? I was in pain. They pushed papers in front of me, and I signed. Does it matter? It all worked out, and I'm back with one week to spare on their deadline."

"We dodged a bullet is what we did."

"Quit being a worrywart. I'm fine. You're fine. We're all fine."

"You're going to kill me one of these days, Wylder."

"No, I'm not. I'm your most favorite client."

His silence makes me smile.

"Just make sure you're in the locker room getting ready to help catch bullpen like you've been doing. That way, when I get the call you've been taken off the DL and reinstated, you're at the field."

"Already planned on it."

CHAPTER THIRTY-EIGHT

Scout

"Wow."

Easton's voice startles me. I've been so lost in my own mind, so busy rehearsing what I'm going to say, what my dad advised me to say, that I didn't hear Easton come back.

"What?" I turn to face him, watch him pull his sweat-soaked Under Armour shirt over his head and toss it in the hamper.

"Work-out-clothes Scout is hot. Cowboy-boots-and-skirt Scout is sexy. But dress-up-for-a-business-meeting Scout is gorgeous."

"Thanks. I'll be in a room full of men. Work-out-clothes Scout makes them think I'm a college intern getting my hours in. Cowboy-boots-and-skirt Scout makes them think I'm there to giggle and flirt and maybe date a baseball player," I say as he lifts his eyebrows. "And dress-up-for-a-business-meeting Scout tells them I take my job seriously, and I'm a professional who wants what's best for the team and the player."

"What if what's best for the team, for you, and for *the player* are all different things?"

"In this case they are the same, so it doesn't matter," I say, knowing he needs the reassurance that I technically can't verbalize due to my contract but have told him in a hundred different ways anyway.

"But what if they were, though?"

I don't like the feelings the question evokes, because they very well could have been when he punched Santiago the other day. But that was a different day, a stupid fight, and we've moved on, so I try to shift from this topic.

"Well, since you said *wow* when you saw me, I'd use my wily feminine ways to woo them into what I thought was best."

"Ahh, there comes that manipulative side of you."

"Not manipulative." I laugh as he takes a few steps toward me. "Just determined."

"You're sexy when you're all business," he says as he slides his arms around me and goes straight for my ass.

"Eww, you're all sweaty." I try to bat his hands away, but half-heartedly.

"You didn't say that last night when I was all sweaty." He leans in, and all my doubts disappear with the brush of his lips and the taste of his kiss.

"Well, that kind of sweaty is welcome," I murmur and then physically remove his hands from my ass before they move to undo the zipper.

He laughs and swats me on the ass as I turn to put my makeup, curling iron, and dirty clothes into my overnight bag. When I turn around, Easton's smile is still there, but he's just staring at me with that look in his eyes like he had at Pet Haven.

My pulse speeds up.

"*What?*"

"You don't have to do that, you know."

"Do what?" I glance around like I don't understand, but the sudden echo of panic within me tells me I do.

"Pack up your things." He waits for a reaction, and when I don't give one, other than not saying a word, he continues, "You can have a drawer here, Scout. You can have a whole side of the closet if you want. Better yet, why don't you just stay with me. You're in that temporary place with furniture that's not even yours . . . when I have all this space."

I just stare at him, eyelids blinking and panic slowly clawing its way in to squeeze my heart. "I . . . we . . . it's not . . . how can . . ."

"Scout." Easton says my name as he takes my hand in his and looks at me with those hazel eyes that are loaded with storm-cloud-gray today. "Don't you get it?"

"Get what?"

"This is the next step for us. Some sort of permanence. We're doing it anyway, so why not just admit to it?"

My chest constricts. It hurts to draw in air. The fear I thought I'd chased away is the weight making it hurt. "Easton."

"No, uh-uh," he says as he steps into me and frames my cheeks with his hands so that I'm forced to look up and into his eyes. "You don't get to spook right now. You don't get to hide from me."

"But things are going to change." I finally find my voice. "You're going to start travelling. You're going to leave."

He shakes his head and smiles. "Just for a few nights at a time. And most nights you'll be there, too, since you'll have the team contract. It's not that big of a deal, Scout. Me getting back on the roster doesn't mean this has to stop between us."

He leans forward and reinforces his words with his kiss. To try and combat the fear. To ease my anxiety.

When he ends the kiss, his eyes are back on mine. "We can make this work."

And I see it before he says it.

Maybe I've been seeing it all along and have just been denying it.

But then he says it.

Out loud.

Concrete.

Can't take it back.

"I'm falling in love with you, Scout."

The elevator doors open, and I step to the side and stand there for a beat. I try to pretend I'm okay. I wave to the doorman. I smile at the college girl with the sorority sweatshirt on, doing her homework in the lobby chairs like she often is. And I concentrate on breathing.

On collecting myself.

On telling myself that Easton confessing he was falling in love with me was not a curse for us. I repeat his words in my head. "Just because I said the words doesn't mean I'm going to leave you, Scout. You're not saying it, but I can see it in your eyes. And I'm going to prove to you that you're wrong. That you're not cursed. That's one dragon I'm going to slay for you, and there's nothing you can do to stop me."

Clear mind.

Believe him, Scout.

Hard heart.

He's slayed them for you before.

Clear mind.

He believes in happily-ever-afters.

Hard heart.

Isn't it time you deserve one, too?

Yes. It is.

CHAPTER THIRTY-NINE

Easton

"**Y**ou ready?" My dad's voice booms through my cell.

Did I just royally fuck up?

"Yeah." My response sounds flat even to my own ears, but I'm too preoccupied second-guessing myself as I stare at the elevator doors Scout disappeared behind minutes ago. *Should I go after her and make sure I didn't just spook her?*

"*Yeah?*" he asks sounding just as confused as I feel.

Because sure as shit, I just spooked the hell out of myself.

"Yeah," I snipe, irritated that he's questioning me.

I told her I was falling in love with her. How fucking stupid could I be?

"Easton?"

It's not stupid when it's the truth.

"Are you okay, son?"

The genuine concern in his voice breaks through my thoughts. It brings me back to the present. "Yes. No. Sorry." I chuckle as I take a deep breath, rattled when I'm never rattled. "I'm good. Just preoccupied with something and anxious to get the call later saying that I've been reinstated."

"Well, I'm glad you have something to keep your mind off things," he says. "Since you're coming off the DL, it's probably best if you have a strong presence tonight. You need to go three for three and—"

"Thanks, dad, but I've gotta go." I don't wait for his goodbye to end the call because I've got more important things to do than listen to what my dad expects from me in my first game back.

Like processing how Scout was standing in my room like she does more mornings than not lately, and my only thought was how perfectly she fit there. How seamlessly she's become a part of my day to day. Then of course, how the words rolled off my tongue.

The offer for her to move in with me.

Telling her I was falling for her.

Damn straight I saw the fear in her eyes, but I was too busy trying to manage my own panic to do anything to help quiet hers. Because thinking you're falling for someone is one thing, but saying it out loud is another. *You can't take that shit back.*

But now that she's gone, I know I don't want to take the words back. Who needs grass that's greener on the other side when you're a huge fan of how green the grass is beneath your feet?

Let's just hope I've proven that to her.

CHAPTER FORTY

Scout

"**G**entlemen."

Nerves rattle and shake through me, and I realize this is fear. This is panic. This is not wanting to screw up.

So very different than how I feel with Easton. So very different than how Easton makes me feel.

And I know I'm ready to slay dragons for him, too.

Starting now.

I meet the eyes of the six men surrounding me at the table, and begin, "I was brought on board to facilitate the rehabilitation of *the player*, Easton Wylder, and assess his ability to return without limitation to the starting line-up. I'm here to report my findings. Shall we wait for Mr. Wylder's agent?"

"He won't be joining us," Cory Tillman says with a resolute nod of his head.

"Oh, I assumed—"

"Let's begin."

CHAPTER FORTY-ONE

Easton

I see it the minute I walk into the locker room.

My pinstriped jersey.

Wylder 44

Pressed and hanging in my locker where it hasn't been in what feels like forever.

A hand slaps me on the shoulder. "Welcome almost back, Easy E."

I turn to see Manny and the twinkle in his eyes. "You better not be jinxing me, Manny-Man." I laugh and shake his hand. "I don't need any bad juju today."

"No jinxing. No bad juju. Maybe I wanted to give ol' Santiago a subtle reminder when he walks in here today who was first. And who will be last."

I shake my head and laugh. Good ol' Manny. He had my back way back when, and he still has it now.

"God, I love you, old man."

"I've missed watching you play. I can't wait to sit in the stands tonight."

I stare at him, eyes wide, mouth open. Did I hear that right? "The stands?"

"Yep." He nods. "That's the only place I like to watch the greats play."

I clear my throat. Such a simple comment means so much to me.

Because it's Manny.

And it's what today means to me.

All the hard work.

All the pain.

All the doubt.

I'm so close I can taste it.

CHAPTER FORTY-TWO

Scout

"**A**nd so it is my professional opinion that Mr. Wylder—"

"Shit!"

Cory says the word but it takes me a minute to process the dark brown pool of liquid sloshing across the conference table in all directions. The room erupts into momentary chaos as we shove our chairs back and try to save the pile of documents littering the table from being ruined by the spilled coffee.

Cory curses again as he furiously blots the liquid off the keyboard of his laptop with a wad of Kleenex while his assistant rushes from the room for paper towels. The gentleman who was seated to Cory's right adds to the litany of curses as his hip hits a stack of file folders right on the edge of the desk and knocks them to the floor.

"Get the stuff on the table," I direct as I drop to the floor to help out. "I'll get these." There's so much bedlam, no one argues or notices that in a room full of men, I'm the one in the skirt and heels kneeling on the floor.

Papers are everywhere. Manila folders are lying open and their contents scattered on the carpet beneath the table. I note the labels on the folders as I collect them—Easton Wylder, Dalton Rehab, Long-Term PT Contract, Options—but am too preoccupied grabbing everything to process exactly what they mean. Or rather, what their contents might be.

And it's only when I have all the documents haphazardly stacked in a pile and am about to crawl out from beneath the table that I notice what the topmost paper has on it. The words. The figures. The implications.

There's no way.

Can't be.

Trying to make sense of it all, I flip to the next page but with the papers being out of order, I find nothing.

I look at the next one. Nothing.

Cory's loafers come into my view a few feet from where I'm kneeling and pull me back to reality—to what I'm doing snooping through his files and to the ramifications if I were to be caught.

It's when I look back down one more time to bury the first page in the stack so no one knows I saw it, that I'm blindsided for a second time.

My mind scrambles to process what I'm reading and why Easton's signature is scrawled across the bottom of it in acceptance.

My hands tremble.

I scan the words again.

My pulse thunders in my ears.

Holy. Shit.

"Do you need any help under there Ms. Dalton?"

CHAPTER FORTY-THREE

Easton

"**Y**ou're just wasting your time suiting up, Wylder." Santiago's voice rings above the chatter of guys shooting the shit and silences them instantly.

Every bone in my body vibrates with the need to smash my fist into his face to shut him up, but I ignore it. I grit my teeth and just stare at my jersey hanging in my locker in front of me. He's just not worth it anymore.

"Why's that?" I ask, more than aware that the entire team is on edge waiting to see how this plays out.

"Because it seems the team has one too many Wylders on the roster these days."

"Hmpf. Thanks for the heads up." I don't take the bait. I don't let him know I haven't got the call yet informing me I've been reinstated so technically, there's no Wylder currently on the roster at all.

"Sure thing. Did you hear that joke that's been going around? What's ten-times worse than a shitty catcher?" he asks and then answers without skipping a beat. "A Wylder one."

Every muscle in my body is tense when I turn around to face him.

"Cool it, Santiago," J.P. warns, sick of hearing his mouth like we all are.

"What?" he shrugs and smiles. "I'm just having a little fun with my new teammate."

I take my time crossing the distance, stopping when I'm about a foot from the bastard. I stare at him for a few seconds before I speak. "You know what, Santiago? I don't know what your deal is and I sure as hell don't know what I've done to make you hate me, but honestly, I'm beyond giving any fucks. I'm a part of this team, have been for years—we're one big, happy family—so every time you fuck with me, remember you're fucking with them too." I jerk my thumb over my shoulder toward the guys and take another step closer to him. "And I guarantee you that life will get awfully hard for you as an Ace if you keep this shit up. *Capisce*?" I stare at him for a beat longer, wait for him to nod his head, and then turn on my heel and walk away.

CHAPTER FORTY-FOUR

Scout

What if I'm wrong?

What if the information on that paper didn't mean what I thought it did?

But what if it did?

I glance around to the pairs of eyes staring at me, waiting for my response, and wonder where the hell Easton's agent is. None of this makes sense to me and I *need* him to help me make sense of it.

The image of Easton's signature flashes in my mind.

I learned a long time ago that front offices rarely do things that seem reasonable to the public, but in the long run make perfect sense. My dad's voice rings loud in my ears and I'd give anything to call him right now and ask him what to do but the gentlemen waiting impatiently across the table from me wouldn't think too highly of that. In fact it would only serve to undermine my credibility.

My stomach churns. There's too much at stake.

For Easton.

And for me.

The whole situation feels off somehow, and I can't help but think it's because I'm still rattled by Easton's confession this morning.

You're too close, Scout. My dad was right, I am too close.

"Ms. Dalton?" Cory prompts.

What if what's best for the team, for you, and for the player *are all different things?*

It's Easton's voice I hear now. His question from this morning comes back to haunt me.

What. Would. You. Do. Scout?

"In your informed opinion, is Easton Wylder completely rehabbed and ready to return as a contributing player to the Aces' line-up?"

CHAPTER FORTY-FIVE

Easton

"**F**irst Santiago and now the carpet. Take it easy there, turbo, and save some energy for the game tonight."

I glance over to Drew as he tightens a spike on his cleat while I wear a hole in the carpet of the locker room. "What the fuck is taking them so long?"

"Maybe that lady friend of yours is spilling your deep dark secrets."

I halt midstride and glare at him and his half-cocked smirk.

"You think those of us who know you well don't know you've got the hots for each other? Dude, the way you look at her is enough to make me get a boner."

I roll my eyes. "Fuck you."

"I got you to laugh *and* stopped you from making me dizzy watching you walk back and forth like a caged animal."

"Whatever." As soon as I say it, I realize I'm already pacing again. Shit. All I can do is hang my head and laugh at proving him right.

"My job here is done."

"Such an asshole," I mutter.

"You wouldn't want me any other way." He pats me on the back. "She better hurry the fuck up because if I have to see Santiago behind the plate one more night, instead of your ugly mug, you're going to owe me more than just a round of beer."

"Agreed," I laugh as he heads into the tunnel and out to the dugout where I want to be.

My phone rings.

I can't get to it fast enough.

"Finn. I've already got my jersey on. Tell me I'm good to go."

"Easton."

"Sweet."

"Easton." His voice is harsher. It begs me to stop moving. "I just got word."

"Finn?"

"You've just been traded."

THE END

HARD *to* HANDLE

Cover design by Perfect Pear Creative Covers
Cover Image by Rafa G. Catala
Editing by Marion Making Manuscripts
Formatting by Champagne Book Design
Printed in the United States of America

If life can remove someone you never dreamed of losing,
It can replace them with someone you never dreamt of having.
—Rachel Wolchin

Prologue

Hunter

"YOU HAVE NO CLUE WHAT YOU'RE TALKING ABOUT!" RAGE FIRES, AS I stare at my agent and verbally reject every rebuke he's throwing at me while silently agreeing he's right.

"I don't?" he yells. "What the hell was that stunt then? Fighting against the opposition is one thing, Hunter, but punching your own damn teammate?"

"Is it that he's my teammate or that he's another one of your clients you're trying to pimp and sell to the next highest bidder? My guess is, it's that. My gut tells me it's because he's your newest golden ticket to a higher commission and, since the press already caught wind of the fight, that pristine reputation of his might be a little tarnished." I shift on my feet and move a step closer. "Ever stop to think how the press already knows? Huh? Ever think that maybe Dyson picked a fight with me, staged the bullshit so he could get his name out there on social media? It's hard to live up to your self-proclaimed wonder-boy status when someone like me outperforms him every damn night, hands down, and steals what he thinks are his headlines. What is it they say? No press is bad press? Seems to me like he's looking to play off that."

Finn Sanderson chews his lip as he stares at me. His hair, his clothes, his everything, are in their usual styled perfection, but there's a flicker of uncertainty in his expression that I can't quite read. His dark eyes never leave mine as they stare and assess and scrutinize.

He draws in a deep breath and purses his lips as the silence falls stagnant. "What's going on with you, Hunter?"

Here we go again.

"What do you mean, what's going on with me?"

"Exactly what I asked. What the hell is going on with you? You're about to smash three long-standing records within a ridiculously short time frame. That's unprecedented. You used to play with finesse and poise, and now you play like a feral cat about to—"

"About to what? Seek and destroy? What does it matter? My numbers are better than ever."

"I was going to say you play like a man ready to win at all costs. Even if those costs include collateral damage."

"Sometimes winning requires that."

His chuckle is low and condescending at best. "At what expense though? Your teammates? Your club?" He shows his frustration with a subtle shake of his head. "They're putting up with it because you're winning, but that'll only go so far. You've been in this game long enough to know that losses happen and the tide can turn."

"I know, a whole twelve years in the league, and knocking on records it took others a lot longer to hit makes me a relic." I don't hide the sarcasm. Instead, I play it up so he knows how ridiculous he sounds.

"Winning will create tolerance . . . but your antics off the ice are going to cost you in ways you've never imagined."

"Fuck this." I say the words, but I know he's right. The problem is, I can't find a flying fuck to give right now.

"If that's how you want to be, fine." He shrugs in indifference. "Then no one is going to be cleaning up your messes in the press. Not the brawl you started at that hole in the wall. Not airing your grievances to the press about the bullshit in the locker room. Not the snubbing of fans as you walk by—"

"Glad to see you believe the press over your own client," I say.

"It was on video. It's kind of hard to dispute the fact that you walked right past a kid in a wheelchair holding out a sign for you to autograph." *Fuck. I never do that. Never.*

I used to be *that* kid. In many ways, I still am, so the fact I missed seeing him makes it all the worse. The notion that the press is using it against me only adds insult to injury.

I replay the scene he's talking about. My mom on my cell freaking out about Jonah and refusing to let me talk to him because she said I'd upset him. Her insistence laced with guilt, the ever-constant reminder of what happened, whose fault it was, and how it made us into the people none of us wanted to be. How I was ducking my head down, finger to my other ear, so I could hear her. The flash of the cameras still in my eyes like a thousand bright lights glittering at once. The weight of the game still heavy in my mind highlighted by all the opportunities I couldn't convert into goals. My teammates behind me, Dyson with his loud mouth and shitty attitude, which I was trying to tune out completely.

And I didn't see the kid.

I wish I had.

I know how it feels to hope and want and dream . . . and then to live that dream but at so many costs.

"Once the public turns the tide against you, you'll have a helluva time getting them back."

"And what about you, Finn? Has the tide turned against me with you?"

His eyes hold mine as he chews his gum with vigor, but he doesn't voice the fucking thoughts I can see in his eyes.

"Really?" I ask, exasperated and disappointed when I shouldn't be either anymore. "You've been with me since the get-go. Represented me right out of college through the trades and renegotiations of my career. It's been twelve years and now . . . now, you want to walk away because I'm having a tough time?"

I walk toward the window. There's a world beyond this hockey arena, but it's not like I can see it. I've lived my life with one goddamn goal since the accident, one goal since being traded to the LumberJacks two years ago, and now with time running out, it's the only goal I can focus on. It fuels the anger that's always been there but has now surfaced. The guilt that owned me but now eats away at me. The tears that threaten burn bright, but I blink them away as I try to find my way back to the man I used to be months ago, all the while knowing he doesn't matter.

He never has.

"And that history is why I'm standing here asking what's going on with you."

"I didn't snub that kid intentionally. You know that's not me. I wouldn't have—"

"I don't know much these days other than it seems you have your head up your ass," he says and folds his arms over his chest.

"There used to be a time you defended me. There used to be a time when you stood up for your clients. Seems to me you now love chasing after everybody in a jersey with potential to maintain that name of yours instead of taking care of those who you stand on top of to make that name of yours glow in neon."

He winces, but he doesn't bite with the anger I was hoping for. "I've got three sponsorships waiting to be yanked from you with one more fuck-up, Maddox. I have management calling, asking me why their captain—*my client*—is the problem and not the solution here. They want me to tell them what's eating you and to figure it the fuck out because if you don't, your upcoming contract negotiations won't be pretty."

"Ah, the threats. The bait and switch to lower my contract when any other team out there would kill to have me." My words are straight bullshit, because I don't want to play anywhere else. I want to be here, with the LumberJacks. I want to be on a team where hockey rules the management's decisions instead of money like so many of the big teams.

And more than anything, I want to be known as the star who turned down those huge contracts to play for the *Little Engine That Could* Team and then helped win that team a Stanley Cup.

I have my reasons. But he's never cared to ask what they are.

As if on cue, my phone alerts a text, and I don't even bother to look. I don't acknowledge its buzz. I already know the gist of what it's going to say and *fuck*, the last thing I need right now is to see how I've disappointed one more person.

"If you don't like the threats, then how about Hunter fucking Maddox shows back up, huh? He's been missing for the past three or four months and this angry, spiteful asshole in front of me is someone I can't quite figure out."

"Can't figure out or don't care to so long as I'm bringing in the cash? There are guys out there doing far worse with a lot less threats and consequences."

"But you're Hunter Maddox. You're the guy the National Hockey League hung its hat on to bring it back from the strike and subsequent lockout."

"They sure as fuck did," I counter, "so how about you remember that and start giving me the benefit of the doubt."

"When you start jeopardizing my other clients with your acts of stupidity like a roid-raged asshole, I have no choice but to put them first."

My hands clench and the unrelenting anger and hurt and confusion that's toyed with my mind over the past few months, hell, *the past season*, fights just beneath the surface.

Obligations.

Guilt.

Responsibilities.

"Good to know where you stand. Is this conversation over? Is the *let's tell Hunter he's an asshole lecture* complete?" I ask, not giving a shit if it is or isn't.

"Sure. It's done. Let's not make it a *let's tell Hunter if he pulls more shit like this again, I can't be his agent* lecture."

His words hit my ears, their gravity, their *everything*. "You threatening me, Finn?"

He holds his hands up. "Just telling it like it is."

It's my turn to laugh. The sound is riddled with disbelief and a healthy dose of *fuck you*. "I'm one of the first clients you ever signed—one who took a chance on you when you were wet behind the ears and no one else would— and you threaten to drop me after all these years, just like that?"

"Something has to snap you out of this funk." His eyes are clear, his voice serious, but he has no clue *this funk* feels like it's permanent.

"Threats don't do it for me."

"Everyone has a line they have to draw in the sand, and one more stunt is mine."

"Good to know." I stare at my agent, the person I thought was my friend, and wonder when the fuck he became a greedy asshole who was only out for himself.

Then I wonder if I even care, because it's hard to find any emotion these days other than anger.

And without another word, I leave.

Chapter
ONE

Dekker

MELODRAMA AT ITS FINEST.

It's the only thought that runs through my mind when I take a seat at the conference table in the back office of Kincade Sports Management.

Brexton sits with her arms crossed over her chest, and her resting bitch face in full effect. Her foot bounces where it's crossed over her knee, and she scrolls through her phone with complete disinterest.

Chase sits ramrod straight, her business suit crisp and pressed and everything else about her perfectly styled to match. Christ, even the leather cover of her notepad matches. Perfection in a sickening fashion.

Lennox inspects her fingernails. They're too long and too red, but I'm sure she has her reasons for looking like she wants to claw someone's eyes out with them.

Let's hope this time, it's not mine.

I sit back and wait and watch and wonder.

Aren't we all the perfect picture of disdain? I'd rather be anywhere—anywhere, like even shopping—than sitting right here with them right now. I'm more than sure they feel the same way.

Thrilled was the last thing we all probably felt when we got the call to be here.

My competitors.

My rivals.

"Ladies." Kenyon Kincade's voice rumbles when he walks into the room. Our heads turn and only two of us nod in response, but all of us watch him.

The same paranoia that has me questioning why he'd invite the chaos by inviting us all in here at the same time, has me eyeing his movements closely. Is he moving slower? Is there something wrong with his health?

Fear tickles its way up my spine in a way I've never known before.

"Thank you for coming." He clears his throat and takes his time taking a sip of his coffee, hissing when it scalds his tongue. "I know it's a rarity for you to all be in the office together, but humor this old man in wanting his four daughters in one place, at the same time."

Brex bites her tongue while waiting for him to get to the point. Patience has never been her strong suit, and he takes note of it with a nod of his own.

"Why did you ask us to all be here, Dad?" Taking the lead as per usual, I ask the question we're all wondering.

"I've made a lot of mistakes over the course of my life. Even more so when your mother died, when I was left alone at thirty-something to raise four girls without much experience. I did the best I could, but by the way you guys prefer not to be in the same place together at times, it feels like my best wasn't good enough."

"That's not true."

"Then what is it, Lennox?" He calls her out. "Why can't the four of you get along?"

I think of the years of competition for his attention. A single dad with clients we felt were more important than we were at times. Not by any fault of his own, but more because of his caring nature. We wanted his attention. We lived for it.

And the bittersweet taste of being the oldest still stings. Stepping in to be a mom at fifteen when you're not the mom, fosters a lot of resentment. Telling your siblings what needs to be done inside a house ruled by estrogen doesn't exactly make for long-term peace.

Lennox flips a lock of hair over her shoulder and meets his eyes for the first time. The only man who can tame her constant snark and fiery temper. "We can get along just fine." There's a muffled snort somewhere, and I fight not to look up and glare down whoever it is . . . because I'm not the mom, and I never wanted to be.

"You fight like cats and dogs," he says.

"And we love like lions," she says and we all snicker. "We're just very different people."

His laugh is boisterous and takes us all by surprise. "Maybe it's because you are all so much alike."

When each of us physically bristle at the thought of actually being like the other, he holds his hands up to stop us. "Sanderson is killing us."

The name of our rival agency.

"As in Finn Sanderson?" Brex asks. "What do you mean?"

He purses his lips and takes his time meeting each of our eyes before he speaks. "Twelve clients over the past year. That's what he's taken from us. I'm not sure if he's undercutting our commission or if he's stroking more than just their egos, but it's not acceptable to me."

And my father's tone says it all—he's worried.

Shit.

"Are we in trouble?" Brexton asks, concern weighing down her voice as she sits forward in her seat. "Is something wrong?"

He looks to where his hands are clasped in front of him and his pause in response sets the mood.

"Dad? Is everything okay?" I ask, my voice shaky as worst-case scenarios fill my head. Is he sick? Is he hiding something from us? He's been the unbreakable pillar of strength to this family. Slayer of Boogie Men and the King of Bear Hugs for teenage broken hearts. He's been my strength in dark moments, and I can't imagine him anything other than redoubtable . . . larger than life. But not now.

When he looks up, his smile is forced, his eyes somber, and that feeling of dread settles in me again. "It's fine. I just . . . this is all I have to give you girls—this company, my reputation . . . *each other.*" He twists his lips and nods. "And lately, it feels like I've done a bad job at fostering and preserving all of it."

We all meet eyes across the table. While the four of us may be fiercely competitive, Brexton was right—we love like lions and will fight to the death to protect each other. By the looks on my sisters' faces, right now is one of those times.

"Is it because of your doctor's appointment the other day?" Lennox asks, disquiet flooding every syllable, as she voices the one thing I think we're all wondering but are afraid to put words to.

"We need to take care of Sanderson." It's all he says, and a quick glance at Lennox tells me she's just as worried as I am.

"I think your meaning to that term and my meaning are very different," Chase says, blasé as can be, when I know the simple mention of her ex-boyfriend has what he did to her flooding back and boiling her blood.

"Don't worry, Chase. We'll post your bail," Brexton murmurs.

While we all laugh, it's our father's lack of response that's most noticeable. He takes his time sweeping his gaze around the table, making sure to stop on each one of ours in that way he has that tells us he's about to say something profound like he used to do when we were kids and he wanted to make us feel like adults.

He stops when those bright blue eyes stop on mine. "What is it, Dekker?" he asks as I twist my lips in thought and mull over my assumptions.

"*Of course, he asks Dekk,*" Lennox says to the singsong tune of my other sisters murmuring, "His favorite one," like they used to do when we were kids.

"You're just jealous," I say with a megawatt grin to annoy them.

"Jealous of your shoe collection, maybe," Chase teases.

"Ladies," my dad warns. "You have the floor, Dekker."

I clear my throat and speak. "Obviously the gloves are off when it comes to stealing our clients. Sanderson doesn't give a shit about decorum or professional courtesy or—"

"—or anything else other than money or how far her legs are spread."

If I were taking a sip, I would have spit out the water in reaction to Chase's remark. It's a rarity to see any kind of emotion from her, so I nod slowly in response. She's still hurting all this time later. "That too."

"You're the dork who dated the competition," Lennox says and rolls her eyes as we all laugh. I nudge Chase, hoping Lennox's comment will ease some of the anger in her eyes, and am glad when a smile creeps onto her lips.

"What are you thinking?" my father asks me, attempting to bring us back to the topic at hand.

"If he has no morals and he's a prick—"

"A savvy prick," he adds.

"Exactly. So why can't we be the same way? As much as I want back the clients he stole from us, we need to think bigger than that." I tap my pen against my pad. "Maybe we all work together and try to land a huge name."

"As much as I'd like that"—he shakes his head and chuckles softly—"I'm not quite sure you four working together in that capacity is a wise move. Remember the last time we tried that?"

Brexton shifts uncomfortably, as Dad glances to the wall to his right where the hole in the drywall from her fit of rage has long been patched up. We've since banned paperweights from the office.

"I think we should steal his clients in turn," I suggest.

Lennox snorts, and the sound about sums up everything about the suggestion: it's impossible, it's ludicrous, *it's freaking genius.*

Plus, it's the easiest thing to say—I'm going to steal some of the top athletes in the world away from their current representation as a *fuck you*—but implementing it is a whole other ball game.

But the slow crawl of a smile across my dad's mouth tells me he was thinking the same thing. "Agreed. Fighting fire with fire is the only option . . . especially when it comes to him."

"What did you have in mind?" Brex asks.

"I think we should tackle this on four fronts. Each one of you with an athlete to win over to our side," he says.

"Besides more clients, what's this going to prove?" Lennox asks, despite it being obvious to me.

"People look at you and they can't help but notice your overall appeal. They see the former beauty queen"—he looks at Lennox—"the Olympic athlete"—then Brexton—"the girl who graduated top of her MBA program"—then Chase—"and the lawyer"—he meets my eyes—"and they forget the most important thing of all, that my four girls are just as damn dogged, professional, unflinching, and successful as their old man was."

"*Was?*" I catch the word immediately.

"*Is.*" He waves a hand my way without meeting my eyes. "Slip of the tongue."

"Dad—"

"You have all been successful recruiting clients thus far, but it's always been under the umbrella of my name. It's always been my company. Now I think it's time you make Kincade Sports Management yours."

Silence falls as each one of us wonders why this sudden push, and I hate the answers I assume.

"Should we assume you have it all planned out as per usual?" Chase asks, making Dad's smile widen and the sadness clear from his eyes.

"Of course, I do," he says. "We divide and conquer. When have you ever known me not to have it all worked out?"

He always does.

"What do you need from us?"

His grin is lightning quick, and it's the first true glimpse I've seen of my tenacious, work-addicted dad since he walked in here.

"You're up first, Dekk." He looks to my sisters as they start their singsong "you're the favorite one" again. "I'll get to you next, but yours"—he points a finger my way—"might be making it easier on us with his current antics."

Current antics?

Words no sane agent ever wants to hear.

Shit.

This is not going to be good.

Chapter
TWO

Dekker

"Hunter Maddox."

Definitely not going to be good.

Every single nerve in my body reacts viscerally to the two words that fall from my father's lips.

Thoughts run rampant as I try to process what he's implying. As I try to fathom how he could think I'd be the right person for the job when Hunter's the one who broke my heart.

But how would he know? Texts late at night telling me where to meet and when. Quick romps in hotel rooms when we happened to be in the same city at the same time. Zero promises given of anything more than the physical. How would anyone know when I played our whole sexcapade off as a casual thing I had no attachment to?

Even to Hunter, himself.

But I'm looking at my father, and he's not backing down.

"This is a joke, right? You're playing with me?" I ask in a half-laugh, half no-damn-way tone.

"I wish I were." At least there's contrition in his voice when he says it, and I wonder if in his father-sense he has an inkling that my casual dating of Hunter had grown into something more in my heart. "I know you two had a thing a way back and—"

"A *thing*?" I snort, realizing I'm reacting off my own emotion and not from something he knows. His lifted eyebrows say as much. "Yes. Sure. Something like that."

"I saw you talking to him at the ESPY's a few months back. I didn't realize there was bad blood between you."

Not bad blood.

More like unresolved feelings.

"This is just a bad idea all around."

"Personally or professionally?" And it's that tone—the one that says I need to suck it up, be tough, and professional—that's a reprimand in itself, but I don't respond. I'm busy wondering how I'm going to make a man, who despite aggravating me in all other ways, devastated me sensually and brought out an explosive sexuality I never really knew I had, come over to Kincade Sports Management. "Any way you look at it, Dekk, he's one we have to have."

"Why?" It's one word but it's loaded with so much tension.

"Because this is his year."

"His year to what?" I snort. "Be an ass and ruin what he has going for him?"

"To win the Stanley Cup."

"I disagree—"

"Hear me out," he says with his hands up. He speaks quietly, and that tells me he's put way more thought into this than I have. "Hunter's been in the NHL for twelve years. Ten with various teams and then the LumberJacks came along and decided to build their hopes on him because he's that freaking good."

"They can build their hopes on whoever they want, but it doesn't mean it's going to happen." I rise from my seat and pace the room as I think. "There's that thing with the kid in the wheelchair the other day. The one he snubbed. There are rumors about fights in the locker room with teammates. That management isn't happy. That—"

"So, you have been keeping tabs on him."

My feet falter as I let his words settle in the room, because anyway I respond means I'm on the defensive when I shouldn't be about a man I don't care about.

"I keep tabs on a lot of athletes."

"I see," he says in that fatherly way that is part all-knowing, part maddening, and nothing I want to address. "The question is why is he acting out? Why has he had an excellent career with a pristine reputation for almost twelve years and then all of a sudden he doesn't?"

"I'm not a psychologist, Dad."

"No"—he leans forward in his seat—"but you know him better than anyone else in this office."

Shit.

He's right in every aspect, and yet I want to argue and reject his theory because I've moved on and don't want to revisit a man who broke my heart.

"Make Lennox go after him," I say, offering up my sister while at the same time hating that she might. "Give me a different athlete to bring over." Panic flutters in my chest at the mere mention of Hunter and the vivid memories of him that might still fill my fantasy bank.

"Hunter and Lennox?" He chuckles. "The two of them together would be oil and water."

"Well, so were we," I throw back as I attempt to fathom why my dad would ever assume I'd be the right one to go after Hunter.

More like a match to gasoline.

But oh, that one time with oil was so damn fun.

"We can use your history with him to our advantage."

"Using it to *our* advantage is one thing. What about what it means for me?" I ask, giving away what I was hiding—that he meant more to me than casual.

Snapshots of memories flicker through my mind like a tape reel. Volatile and deliciously addictive sex always highlighted—or rather lowlighted—by our inability to remain civil to one another. And despite that, I still fell for him. I still wanted to try to have something more with him.

He still let me walk away from him without a word.

"He's who we need, kiddo," my dad says, ripping me out of the documentary in my head. "Statistically speaking, he's phenomenal. He's angling to surpass records—goals, assists. He's one of the fastest on the ice out there and his stick-handling skills are unrivaled."

"You forgot that he's an asshole." I smile sarcastically.

"Aren't we all in some way or another?" He raises his brows and returns the same smile. "Look, if he stays injury-free, he might just be one of the next greats. And having him as a client could be a huge draw for us."

"Or he could implode and we could be stuck scrambling to salvage his career."

"Then let's swoop in and save him from doing that because, sure as hell, Sanderson isn't."

"It's not that easy."

"It is, Dekk. He's coming up for a contract negotiation after this season that could net him a substantial pay increase. Pair that with his poor conduct and his closing in on some long-standing records, and we could help him get there. *You* could help him get there. I've watched him, admired him, for a lot of years, but lately, I can tell he's struggling."

"I am not a nursemaid, Dad."

"Don't I know it." His chuckle fills the room. "I'm not asking you to be one. All I'm saying is visit him. Talk with him. Travel with the team during their next road stretch and see if you can figure it out. Sell him on the fact that you understand him when it seems Sanderson is just a stat chaser these days—picking up clients with the brightest stars, not necessarily the most talent. And you know what happens to bright stars."

"They burn out."

He nods, his eyes holding mine as they turn serious. "We can assert that he'll receive more by going with us. Drop names, and give him examples of the contracts we've increased during negotiations."

"And that's why you think he'll leave Sanderson?" I snort. "The only effect my appearance will have is him walking the other way."

Or wanting to have sex. And that just can't happen, not if we're to have a professional relationship as my dad is sitting here telling me we need to have.

"You underestimate yourself, Dekker. You always have."

Silence falls as our eyes hold. The hum of my sisters chatting in the main office filters through to us in muffles, but it's him that holds me rapt.

"Dad? What's going on? Is the business in trouble? Was everything okay at the doctor's the other day? I mean . . . where is this all coming from?"

His smile is slow and soft, much like his voice when he speaks. "It's just time for you guys to step up. Nothing's wrong," he says, but I don't believe it. "Make sure you go in with a game plan. Don't underestimate Hunter. You need—"

"Trashing bars, fights with teammates, snubbing kids . . . *can't wait.*" I sigh.

"And he's been the NHL's MVP two years running, so I think this year is his to win the Hart Memorial Trophy. You keep pointing out the bad, but none of it is affecting his success on the ice. Find out what has affected his behavior off the ice. That's not like him, and you know that."

He's right. I do know that. *I've never seen him ignore a fan before. Especially a kid.* But I can't get emotionally involved. Not again.

"Right now, you need to focus on getting your stuff packed and making travel arrangements," he says as he pushes his chair away from the table.

"*What?*"

"You heard me. You'll have plenty of time to think about how you're going to approach him on your flight to Chicago tonight."

"Tonight?" I say the word but it takes me a second to digest it.

"Yes, tonight."

"You expect me to just pick up and go, like that?" I ask, like this is something new and I haven't done it before in the past. But this is Hunter we're talking about. This is my secret weakness and my silent heartbreak. "I have plans with Chad tonight. His work event is a very big deal. I can't just—"

"Yes, you can. I'm sure he'll understand." His smile is tight and his expression is stern. "It's not like he bends any of his business obligations for you."

"And there's the dig," I mutter.

He stops in his tracks and turns to face me. "Not a dig, at all. He's just a man who'll never commit, and for the life of me I can't figure out what you see in him. He's successful and handsome if you go for that sort, which you usually don't—"

"Which sort is that?"

"The kind who doesn't like to get his hands dirty." He holds my glare. "He may look the part, honey, but I don't see a single ounce of fire in your eyes when you're together. If you want to be friends, be friends, because he sure as hell is *friends* with a lot of people."

"My life. My business," I say in warning, but hate the pang I feel knowing he thinks I'm settling. Companionship should be okay in any form . . . even if it's a few nights out a month, some nice dinners, some mechanical-esque type sex. The kind of relationship—and I use that word very loosely—where commitment has never been discussed nor really wanted.

"True. Your business. I'm sure Chad will understand. It's not like he hasn't done the same to you for his job before." He grabs the handle to the door. "Like I said, you should have no problem making that flight tonight to catch the LumberJacks game." He opens the conference room door and looks back over his shoulder. "Good luck."

Chapter
THREE

Hunter

Dad: Sloppy play tonight. You're not controlling the team like a captain should. Your shot percentage has taken a nosedive. Your assists went up but nowhere near what your brother's were.

Chapter
FOUR

Dekker

It never fails me.

The excitement of a game and the roar of the crowd never fails to boost my mood, clear my mind so I can think, and give me that rush of adrenaline to remind me why I love my job.

The crowd bustles inside the sports bar, The Tank. Drinks flow freely while all the TVs are tuned to ESPN. The talking heads on SportsCenter are promising highlights of the game I just watched in person after the break.

"Is it true the teams come hang out here after games?" a twenty-something asks as she sidles up beside me on the barstool. Her dress is Lycra and hugs every glorious curve of her body, no doubt in the attempt to catch the attention of one of the players.

Someone will definitely bite, especially after the high of tonight's win.

"It's rumored this is the bar the visiting teams frequent, yes," I murmur and give her a smile, when I know damn well they'll show. Callum already confirmed he'd meet me here. Where he goes, they all go.

"Have you ever met them? I mean, I love hockey—like, *love it*—but the players are a whole other sort of obsession. And the Jacks have so many hot guys. I mean, what I'd give to . . ." Her words trail off as her desperation comes through. Every part of me wants to let her know they'll use her for the night and never call despite the promise to. But one look at her again and I realize she already knows this and is okay with it.

There's no use being overprotective when she's obviously walking in willingly.

"They're pretty cool guys. Fun to party with, not so much fun to date."

A raucous cheer goes up in the bar followed by a cold rush of air as the doors open. I don't turn to look but between the rise in chatter and Lycra girl's sudden fluffing of her hair, I know the New Jersey LumberJacks have arrived.

I don't turn to watch them give high fives to their overeager fans hoping for a few seconds with their heroes or the women hoping to get more than that with their short skirts and tight tops. They'll make their way to the back corner where they can monitor those coming in and out of their space so if fans get a bit overeager, security can cut it off.

The Tank is known for its dark beer, its unfettered access to the hockey players, and its carefree atmosphere.

All those things good and bad, depending on the night.

I keep my attention on SportsCenter and appreciate the quick service of another glass of wine.

"Should I worry that you're showing up in person?" a deep tenor says beside me as a hand grips my shoulder and squeezes.

"Callum Withers." My smile is genuine as I take in my client's grin and the red mark marring his cheekbone from his fistfight in the game tonight. "Someone has to come and scold you for getting in schoolyard fights."

"Just part of the job, *Mom*." His chuckle is infectious and at complete odds with the severity of his features—dark colors and sharp lines.

"Is that so?"

"Yep." He holds a finger up to the bartender and doesn't have to even say what he wants, his regular status here when they're in town ensuring immediate service.

"You enjoy all that time in the penalty box?"

"Dickman's a dick. It's even in his name," he says, referring to the member of the opposing team he traded punches with on the ice earlier. "He had it coming to him for blindsiding Hunter on that play. It was uncalled for and total bullshit slashing him like that."

"It was definitely dirty," I say, glancing over his shoulder to where the rest of the team is, looking for the man in question.

"Everything that asshole Dickman does is dirty." He snorts and takes a sip of his beer. "So, tell me why you're making house calls when we're on a road trip. There has to be a reason."

Yeah. One I don't want to acknowledge.

Chapter

FIVE

Hunter

UNABASHED.

Unyielding.

Uninhibited.

Those three words describe the woman sitting at the end of the bar to a goddamn T.

I take in her black high heels, her pale pink sweater and black slacks, and the sweep of her pale hair sitting atop her head. She's elegant but feisty, gorgeous but unassuming, composed but so damn infuriating . . . and nothing if not all-business.

And not a single one of those things diminishes the firsthand knowledge I have of every inch of her body.

Dekker Kincade.

Jesus, even my balls draw up at the thought, sight, and memory of her.

But I stop mid-sentence, mid-lift of my beer to my mouth, mid-everything when I catch sight of her sitting at the bar, talking to Callum. Sure, her back is to me, but I would know that curve of her shoulders in a heartbeat.

"There a problem?" Frankie asks.

I shake my head and turn back toward him, trying to remember what the hell I was saying but find myself at a loss.

Damn Dekker.

She always did have a way of owning my thoughts when I'm not a guy to be owned by much of anything other than hockey . . . and family.

But my eyes slide back to where she's sitting. I hate the way Callum's hand rests on the back of her chair and how he throws his head back and gives that cheesedick laugh that's too loud and not real.

Yeah, he's her client, but it's not a hard jump to assume he'd fuck her if given the chance.

Hell, every damn guy in this place would.

I know. I'm one of the lucky bastards who have.

Lucky? Is that the right word, because I've seen her for a whole five minutes and the shit that the sight of her has stirred up is insane.

Over-the-top sex. Hours on end of never being able to get enough. An intensity as she stared at me from the hotel doorway and told me our . . . *friends with benefits* had run its course.

I convinced myself it was because she had found someone new.

I pretended I didn't care.

But fuck if seeing her sitting there right now doesn't tell me otherwise. It's been almost three years since . . . since the end of whatever we were, but seeing her now, I remember every sigh, every moan, every goddamn thing.

And hell if I'd complain about getting lost in her again for a few hours.

I try to focus on what Frankie is bullshitting about, but my mind and eyes keep going back to her. Back to what we left unfinished and to my sudden need to see her again, talk to her again . . . to see if she's feeling that same damn attraction still.

"Right?" Frankie asks, pulling my attention back to him. Fuck I'm being a prick to him.

"Yes. Right. I—uh . . . I see someone I need to talk to."

Without waiting for a response, I make my way across the bar. It's packed tonight with an abundance of puck bunnies wanting attention and lots of guys buying us drinks to celebrate the victory.

It should be sad the visiting town is excited when we beat the hometown team, but our run has been insane lately, and fans always like bandwagons to jump on.

"Hell of a game, Maddox," is yelled to my right, and I lift my beer in acknowledgment but keep my course.

"Withers." Callum looks up when I call my teammate's name and lifts his chin in greeting before continuing whatever it is he's telling Dekker. "Maysen needs you," I say when he finishes.

"About?" He meets my eyes, but I don't give Dekker a glance.

"Hell, if I know, but he's looking for you," I lie.

Impatiently, I wait a few seconds for him to wrap shit up with Dekker, all small talk, and then slide onto the barstool beside her after he vacates it.

Lifting my finger to Donnie, the bartender, I motion for another beer and then tip the bottle toward Dekker's glass to ask for a refill for her too.

"You're a long way from home it seems," I murmur as her subtle perfume—summer and sunshine—fills my nose.

"Just doing my job." Her voice, *Christ*, it's soft with a hint of a rasp and feels like fingernails faintly scraping over my skin.

"What? No, *go to hell*? No, *drop dead, Maddox*? No, *what hotel room can we find so we can use every surface?"* I turn to look at her now. Those dark brown eyes a little too big for her face but in all the right ways. Her soft lips and straight nose with a row of freckles dotting across the top of it. But I know better than to be fooled by those freckles. I know Dekker Kincade is a straight-up sex goddess that may have on occasion made me want to beg for more. I'm not ashamed to admit it. "You feeling all right?"

"Funny," she says with a roll of her eyes.

"I try." I hit the side of her knee with mine. "You're here for work and not pleasure, then?"

She lifts a lone eyebrow and a ghost of a smile paints those lips of hers. "It's always about work."

"Not when it came to us, it wasn't."

"There was no us," Dekker asserts, and I snort in response.

My chuckle is low and knowing and the way she adjusts her shoulders tells me she knows what a lie that is. "You're right. There was no incredible sex. No nail marks down my back. No bite marks on my collarbone." I shrug. "I don't know about you, Dekk, but I think we did pretty good in the pleasure department."

"Too bad we couldn't seem to master the playing nice part when it came to everything else."

"Maybe volatility is our thing," I say, the adjective the only way to describe us in the bedroom. Volatile in desire. Volatile in need. Volatile in temper. "Remember that rooftop bar in Los Angeles?" I ask, knowing she does. "It was a hot summer night. You were in that little sundress and we stowed away to the corner of the patio. I had to put my hand over your mouth to muffle your moans so we didn't get caught." I hum in appreciation of the memory. "God, that was hot."

She averts her eyes and shakes her head ever so slightly, but she doesn't refute me. She remembers how incredible that night was—the sex on the rooftop, the thrill of not getting caught, the sex at the hotel that followed. It was the only time we had met someplace other than a hotel room, and it left me wondering why we didn't do it more often.

She ended things the next time we met up.

"You played well tonight."

Her voice draws me back to the present. I smirk at her attempt to change the topic and lean down so my lips are near her ear. "You can sit here looking all prim and proper and professional, but I know your panties are getting wet and the ache is burning a little brighter, because you remember just how damn good it was and how damn good we were."

She clears her throat and shifts in her chair to unsuccessfully gain some distance from me and turns to look at me without an ounce of fluster in her expression.

"You played well tonight," she repeats.

My grin widens. *That's how she wants to play this?* She wants to act like seeing each other doesn't cause old embers to spark? She wants to act like a tiny part of her doesn't want to revisit that? Then again, she's the one who walked out and ended things, not me. And yet . . . the fact that she's acting like there was nothing between us bugs the shit out of me. I've never forgotten her.

Has she forgotten me?

I lean back and cross my arms over my chest and take my time responding as I struggle with the need for her to remember. "How I played? That's subjective."

"Subjective?" She laughs and the sound slices through the sexual tension that's as automatic now as it used to be when we shared the same space. "Two goals. Three assists, and you had one hell of a block to help Katzen when he was recovering from his first block. But you know, it's *subjective*." She rolls her eyes and pulls a laugh from me as my eyes roam down the sweater and its V-neck that shows nothing but hints at everything.

Damn.

"But I missed more than I made," I say and realize we're actually being civil to each other when normally we're at odds.

The crowd cheers as a highlight of one of my goals is shown on the closing credits of SportsCenter. I glance around at the crowd, at my teammates who are milling about, and try to figure out why she's here.

Because I know it's not for me.

"So you're here, why?" I ask. "You miss me that much?"

A shadow glances through her eyes and as quickly as it's there, it disappears. "Don't flatter yourself."

"Oh, it's official business then." Our eyes hold for a beat. "I can help you mix pleasure with that business."

She tips her glass toward me. "Thanks for the drink, but—"

"Keep your money." I push the cash she's sliding across the bar top back toward her. "And your attitude."

"That was a new record. Us being civil." Her smile in response is all snark. "It was good seeing you."

I grab her wrist to prevent her from walking away. "Back to that again?"

"Back to what?" She pulls her arm back but remains where she is.

"You walking away without an explanation."

Her glare is enough to tell me she gets the dig. That she remembers just as clearly as I do that last time we were together. "I wasn't aware my presence here in Chicago meant I owed you an explanation."

She's sexy when she's stubborn. She always has been. Maybe I forgot just how much . . . or maybe the years have added to her confidence and her confidence merely adds to everything about her.

"So let's see," I say, completely ignoring her comment and loving that it's pushing her buttons. "You're working, but you weren't in the clubhouse before or after the game like I've seen you do in the past." I lean back in my stool and study her. "You have clients on the team, but you're not partying with the team." I chuckle. "You're flying under the radar. That means you're here trying to steal someone."

"Who died and made you the Jacks' official detective?"

"Private Dick reporting for duty." I give a mock salute and earn a glare from her. "And, babe," I say, strictly because I know it pisses her off, "you forget that I know you."

"I'm not your babe, you don't really know me"—I lift a brow at that but she just continues—"and I prefer the word *recruit*."

"Recruit. Got it. Isn't that kind of like using the word borrow instead of steal?"

"More like asshole instead of prick," she says, but I don't buy the innocent flutter of her lashes for one second.

"I always did like that mouth of yours," I murmur as I tip my bottle of beer, but keep my eyes on hers.

"Are we done here?" she asks but makes no attempt to move, which answers my question. She *is* here for a player.

"So, you're not after Callum, since he's already your client." I stand up and crane my neck. "Maybe it's Heffner." I tip my beer to the other side of the bar where our burly defenseman is chatting it up with a few ladies. "Nah. He's not easily swayed and has a perfectly solid and long-term contract. Finch, then?" I ask. "He doesn't seem too happy with his agent, so I'm pretty sure if that's why you're here, the struggle to get him over to your side wouldn't be too tough."

"Thanks for the intel. I'll file it away in my need-to-know, but uh, who says I'm here scouting anyone?"

"You're here to get laid then?" I flash a grin and hold my arms out to my sides. "If that's the case, here I am."

"Don't flatter yourself." She takes her time uncrossing and then recrossing her legs, and I take in every long inch of them as she does.

"You're just here for the night then? Flew in from New York to catch a game, then sit at a bar and talk to the guys afterward, but you're—uh—not recruiting?"

There's the slightest hitch in her movement and it's her tell. She's definitely here to steal a client.

"Just came here to enjoy the atmosphere of a winning team, a player who's on top of his game"—she lifts her chin to me—"and get a break from the monotony of things for a bit."

"How's what's-his-name?" I ask, thinking of the guy I saw her with the last time I was in New York. Or was it at the ESPYs? Regardless, he was too slick, too pretty, and nothing like who she needs.

She was on his arm but her eyes were firmly on me.

Definitely not a match made in paradise, and I'm a dick for being happy about it.

"Well, considering I was supposed to be at his work event with him tonight." She shrugs with a lift of her eyebrows . . . but there's something more there she's hiding.

"So what? He can't adjust to his girlfriend's successful career because it reminds him he has a little dick?" The words come from nowhere, and I'm surprised by the pang of jealousy that hits me over the thought of them together.

She opens her mouth to defend him but her hesitation speaks volumes. "When my dad ordered me here, Chad decided—"

"Chad?" What kind of name is Chad?

"Yes. Chad," she says with a resolute nod. "He said he was sick of me putting work before him—"

"Probably like he does to you."

She takes a gulp of her wine. "So, he is no more."

"I'm sorry," I lie.

"No, you're not." She forces a smile. "You hated him."

"I never met him."

"But you still hated him. I could tell in the way you glared at him during the Corporate Cares Charity Gala when we ran into each other." She eyes me above the rim of her glass.

I laugh and tilt my head to the side. "You're right. I did hate him. He wasn't good enough for you."

That and I can't stand the idea of any other man touching you.

"Says the man who doesn't know him."

"I don't have to meet him. No one'll ever be good enough for you, Dekk," I say, our eyes holding. *Including me.*

"Not your business," she murmurs and her words hang in the unsettled air because fuck if there isn't so much unsettled between us. Like why she walked away. Like how I let her. "Besides, you know me, I suck at relationships."

"It wasn't relationship status, was it?"

She snorts. "Not even close."

And there's something about the way she says the words, almost as if she'd been trying to talk herself into believing it was more than whatever they thought it was for so very long, that she almost feels a relief that she can stop bullshitting herself now.

"So you came all this way to take a spin around my cock for old times' sake, then?" My words are meant to ease the tension—*partially*—and to see that gorgeous smile of hers.

"Yes. That's it." She sighs. "Do you really get women with lines like that?" she asks dryly.

"I don't have to speak and I get women."

"*Jesus*. And you wonder why we fought all the time." She rolls her eyes for good measure.

"We fought all the time, because you could never get enough of me and because I . . ." I falter over my words, because I prefer not to finish the thought. Maybe because I can't. Maybe because the truth is I was starting to feel things and those things were feelings . . . and feelings are bullshit.

"Because you, what?" she asks, her interest piqued. That slow crawl of a smile does things to my insides that shouldn't be legal.

I take a moment and let the topic die. The last thing I need to do is to get into shit that doesn't matter. How her walking away fucking sucked and was the closest thing I've ever felt to regret. How seeing her here right now is like a slap in the face of how good we were when we were good and how bad we were when we were bad and everything in between.

But more than anything is how she makes me feel, when every other fucking thing in my life is on dull fucking mute.

I look at the label on my beer as the crowd erupts into a Happy Birthday song on the other side of the bar, moving for a change in topic. "You're smart as hell, Kincade. You know if you're sitting in a bar full of Jacks, no one will think twice if any of us talk to you."

"That's your first mistake," she says, her voice low as she shifts to turn and face me. "No one is paying any attention to where I am or who I'm talking to."

My eyes drag over every seductive inch of her before returning to those eyes of hers. "You're a hard one to miss."

"I doubt that, considering half the women in this bar are showing about ten times more skin than I am."

"You don't have to show skin to be sexy, Dekk." My voice deepens and lowers with the words, and once again memories flicker to the forefront of my mind. Tangled bodies and unattached hearts. "We both know that."

She clears her throat and shifts in her seat. "You look good too."

"I look like something the cat dragged in. My cheek is sore from that stick I took to it. I'm limping like an eighty-year-old man from my knees hurting so bad . . . and I'm just all-around exhausted. This beer doesn't help with that, but you being here does."

Chapter

SIX

Dekker

I STARE AT HIM. AT HIS DARK HAIR THAT'S A LITTLE LONG, A LITTLE shaggy, but fits the man as a whole. At his bright blue eyes that look too closely, and his five o'clock shadow dusting across his jaw. Sure, his cheek is red from the hit he took, but there's something about him that makes you stare.

And savor.

All man, all arrogance, with a hint of boy beneath the surface who's living out his dream.

And he knows me way too well.

This beer doesn't help with that, but you being here does.

I choose not to acknowledge it.

I opt to ignore how it tugs on those feelings that seeing him—*and talking to him*—have drummed up.

The ones I feared would rear their ugly head when my dad told me who my client to win was.

"You do look a little rough around the edges," I say, because it's so much easier to notice the shadows under his eyes and the tension in his posture than to admit the punch in the gut I felt the minute I laid eyes on him. *As always.*

"Candor always was your blessing and curse," he murmurs as he shifts in his chair, and I take in the abrasions on his knuckles from tonight.

"It's why I'm good at my job. I know when to coddle versus when to push."

He chews the inside of his cheek as he surveys the members of his team on the other side of the bar. "So who are you here to push?"

"What's going on with you?" I ask, pushing his comment to the side and his need to know why I'm here. "Things good? Life outside of hockey good?"

He purses his lips and lifts his brows, but it's there for the briefest of seconds—a stutter. Was Dad right? Is Hunter's behavior of late unrelated to him simply being an asshole?

"What is it, Hunter?" I ask, reaching out to put my hand on his arm, sensing something is bugging him.

But his rare drop in his guard is replaced almost instantly. He makes a show of removing my hand, as he stands and places his own on the back of my barstool. My breath hitches as his fingers sweep ever-so-subtly against the skin on my neck. Chills chase over my flesh and I hate the visceral reaction my body has to it—to him. It's as if I still want him even though I know the havoc he'd wreak on my system.

He leans in so the heat of his breath feathers over my ear for the second time in this conversation, but I stand my ground and don't move. "How about I'll tell you what it is, when you tell me why you're here. And I know you won't do that . . . so my secret's safe for the time being."

I stare at him, at the cocky smirk that quickens my pulse, and shake my head. Now is not the time nor place to proposition him about KSM. I knew that coming tonight. I thought I'd hate him on sight after how we left things. But, no. It's not hate I'm feeling. *It's lust.*

"Hunter. I—"

"Ah, if it isn't the Ice King and the Frigid Queen," Katzen, the LumberJacks goalie says as he stumbles over and hangs an arm on the back of my chair where Hunter's just moved his from.

"Hey, Katz," I say but my eyes go right back to Hunter.

"Drunk as always," Hunter says and presses his palm against Katz's chest to push him back.

"Fuck yes, I am. We won. You rocked. I got a little playing time." He laughs at his own joke considering as their goalie he was protecting the net, saving goals left and right, the entire game. "And shit—you are looking mighty fine tonight, Miss Kincade," he slurs as he draws out the word Miss.

The muscle in Hunter's jaw ticks, and I shake my head to try and stop him from acting on whatever darkness I see in his eyes. With his recent antics, I'm not exactly sure I trust he won't use force to move Katz away from me.

"I'm looking fine every night," I say with a wink, knowing the rumors about him and his drinking are more truth than fiction. Guys like Katz are a dime a dozen and working in this industry has taught me how to take care of myself and push back. "A good agent would remind you that hockey is your job, and that hangover you're angling for isn't going to help your stats any."

Katz makes a hissing sound. "Did you just burn me?" He laughs. "See? That's why we call you the Frigid Queen, cold as ice and not afraid to burn anyone at the stake."

"Dramatics get you nowhere." I chuckle to play off his moniker, but hate that it irks me.

Katz sets his empty glass down and looks from me to Hunter and then back. "You know? You guys make a cute couple. You should really do something about that. The two of you together. You and your captaining," he says, pushing on Hunter's shoulder then turning toward me, "and you and your bossiness." His laugh is obnoxious and over the top. "Like sleep together or make a porn or something hot like that . . . but then again, *coupling* isn't really Hunter's strong suit . . . but it could be *mine*."

In the morning he'll feel like an ass for hitting on me. I know this, he'll know this, but the tightening of Hunter's fists tell me his temper is flaring regardless. His forgiveness isn't as readily available as mine. And I'm not sure if I should be flattered or pissed at his overprotectiveness when he has zero claim on me.

"Hey Katz," I say and rise from my seat, going for shock value to deescalate the tension. "I'd say Hunter is the type to be more into *fucking* than *coupling* . . . and uh, how do you know we haven't already? Those memories of us together. On the kitchen counter. In the nightclub at Mandalay Bay. In the press box before a game." I groan overdramatically. "Those are what keep me satisfied on those cold, lonely nights."

"What?" Katz screeches, body jolting, as I put an arm around his shoulder.

"*Get real*," I say and push him away playfully, refusing to meet Hunter's eyes, knowing one glance and Katz will know the truth. "I'd *never* sleep with a hockey player. They're all stick and no finesse. A discerning woman likes slow. She likes skill. She likes to know that once the goal is scored he still has more in the tank."

"Stick. Skill. Finesse," Katz murmurs.

"Damn straight. Stick. Skill. Finesse." I stand on my tiptoes and press a kiss to his cheek, my voice lowering as I say, "I've yet to find a hockey player who can deliver that."

"Maybe you've dated the wrong hockey players, then," Katz replies.

"Maybe I should be worried that you're more concerned with Hunter's between-the-sheets tendencies instead of his on-the-ice skills."

"Fuck off," he says with a wave of his hand but with a grin a mile wide. "I like you, you know that?" He nudges Hunter and shakes his head. "She gives as good as she gets."

Hunter bristles at the double entendre that Katz probably has no clue he managed.

"That's no way to talk to a lady, Katz. Remember what I said. *Finesse*." I look around the bar and then back to the two men—one drunk and careless, the other tense and on edge. "It was a pleasure, gentleman, but I must be heading out. I expect to see that finesse on the ice next game."

"And you're here why?" Hunter asks with just the hint of a smile curling his lips. One that screams arrogance and sexiness and makes me wonder if he's trying to figure a way to get me back in his bed tonight.

No way.

No how.

This will be a strictly professional trip.

"I'm traveling with the team for the next however long. Call it customer maintenance." I shrug coyly. "That's why."

And without another word, I walk out of the bar with my head held high while holding on to tonight's small win.

Hunter Maddox came to me.

That's a start.

Chapter
SEVEN

Dekker

I FEEL SO ALIVE AS I WALK THE STREETS OF CHICAGO. I STAY AMONG the crowds, milling around on my way back to the hotel.

My cheeks are cold but the chill isn't enough of a sting to ease the hurt from Chad's rant, which I really haven't had much time to process. I've been in go-mode since I left the office, what feels like days—not just hours—ago.

But his words linger. *"For what it's worth, you're cold-hearted, Dekker. Lack the sort of passion I want in a woman."* They hurt more than I'd like to admit.

First, him calling me cold-hearted and then Katz calling me the Frigid Queen. What the hell?

I haven't always been unresponsive. Uninspired. Passionless. But, I did realize that while I wasn't in love with Chad, I also wasn't *in like* with him either.

Maybe the thing with him was more of convenience.

Who knows.

I'm done.

We're done.

Life moves on.

The doorman to the Thompson Chicago greets me as I step into the lobby of the luxury hotel. The dark brown décor is the perfect mixture of modern and old-world with its reception desk on one side and its elegant bar on the opposite end of the massive space. Classical music plays softly in the background, accompanying the soft hum of chatter from the bar's occupants.

Glancing that way, I recognize a few players relaxing at the tables off to the right, and wave in greeting when one of them recognizes me.

"You good?" Heffner calls out.

"Yeah, thanks. Just tired. Good night, guys."

With my coat wrapped tightly around me, I head toward the bank of elevators and push the up button. It dings within seconds and after I enter the car and push my floor, a hand stops the door from closing.

"Hold up."

When I look up, I'm stayed by the intense eyes the color of the sky. I despise the thrill that shoots through me at the sight of him—at the complication of him—but it doesn't make the ache it leaves me with any less potent.

Crap.

He doesn't say anything as he steps beside me, but rather holds my eyes and leans a shoulder against the wall. I refuse to retreat.

The doors finally slide closed.

"You don't date hockey players?" he asks, repeating my words back to me, as he cocks his head to the side.

"Nope."

His chuckle is a low rumble that's equal parts smooth and rough and reminds me of what his hands on my body used to feel like.

"Nope?" He reaches out and tucks an errant lock of hair behind my ear. "I seem to remember you dating a hockey player before." He lowers his voice so it's a seductive whisper and takes a step closer to me. "The one whose memory and stick skills keep you satisfied on lonely nights."

I open my mouth and then close it, knowing there's absolutely nothing I can say to take back those comments. Even worse, I can't pretend those words were a lie . . . because they're not.

"Stick. Skill. Finesse." His eyes light up with so much more than humor when he stares at me. Desire swims with lust, and the sight of it shouldn't surprise me, but it unnerves me.

"I was just . . . I was putting Katz in his place."

"Was it true though? How exactly did my memory keep you satisfied on those lonely nights?" There's a ghost of a smile on his lips with an intensity in his eyes that demands an answer.

Sexual tension thickens in the elevator as a floor dings, the door opens, but no one gets on.

It doesn't matter if someone did though because nothing would break his focus on me.

And I feel it all the way to the apex of my thighs.

Memories of him—his skill, his prowess, his finesse—own my mind, and I can't divorce myself from them and the man standing before me.

No matter how much I tell myself I need to.

The urge to reach out and touch him is real, which I hate.

The door shuts.

"Not true," I murmur.

"Ah, that's where I think you're lying, Dekker." He closes the distance with another step. Our chests are all but touching as he braces himself, placing one hand on the wall beside my head. "Your lips and eyes aren't matching up there.

Sure, you're telling me you don't think of me, but your eyes"—he emits a guttural hum in the back of his throat—"they're telling me you can't stop thinking about me . . . because as you know, I'm the triple threat."

"Triple threat?"

"All stick, all finesse . . . all *stamina*."

I roll my eyes at his macho, chest thumping. "See? That's why whatever it was between us never worked—"

"You mean sleeping together?" he asks.

"Yes. That."

"Can you not say it? Can you not say 'having sex with you,' because that's what we did." He leans in so his lips are near my ear, so one hand can trail a finger down the line of my jaw, and whispers, "We had a *lot* of sex. *Incredible* sex. *Mind-blowing* sex. *Incomparable* sex."

"Sex is sex," I lie as my nipples harden at the thought of us together, the palpability of our attraction still volatile in nature even all these years later.

"Not ours."

I lift a lone eyebrow to meet the dare in his eyes and know it's a mistake.

"Then I'll remind you."

His lips are on mine before I can process his words, a torrent of desire owning my thoughts—*and* my body.

Good sense tells me I should resist him, but the heat of his body and warmth of his tongue fires everything inside me that dear ole Chad never could.

Funny how I never noticed it until now.

Hunter's hands don't touch me, but stay positioned on either side of my head. His body doesn't meet mine, but brushes ever so subtly.

But his lips own mine. How they move, how they possess, how they control.

And as much as I want to say I'm helpless to the onslaught of desire they bring me, I also want to own every damn sensation they summon within me. The chills chasing, the adrenaline coursing, the ache simmering, and the desire mounting.

There's comfort in the familiarity and a thrill of newness simultaneously.

Need wars against want as he launches an all-out assault on my senses with his mouth.

The man can kiss.

How did I forget how devastating his lips were when they connected with mine?

"Dekker," he murmurs. The strain in his voice mirrors how I feel—flustered and aroused, dashed with a mix of regret.

I lose track of my senses, of my resolve, and with lust leading my thoughts and the memory of him urging it along, my hands are on him. His chest. The back of his neck. His ass.

And it's maddening that his only reaction to my touch is to push and hold the door close button on the elevator so we're not interrupted. To pause this from ending but to do nothing to further it along.

Does he not feel this? The unsated need? The desperate desire? The damn *everything* that makes me want and need and not be ashamed in the least?

My hands are on the buckle of his belt.

On the button of his waistband.

On the zipper of his pants.

When I cup him, he groans into my mouth. When I slide my hand between the fabric of his underwear and begin to stroke the thickness of him, his entire body tenses, his hands fisting against the wall beside my head, and his lips faltering momentarily in their sensual destruction of mine.

I crave the feel of his hands on me.

It sounds so simple yet stupid, but Hunter knows how to touch a woman. My body remembers.

Because I've missed it.

His touch.

Him.

Touch me.

I stroke my hand up him and rub my thumb over the crest of his cock.

Want me.

The nails of my other hand score down his back through his shirt.

Take me.

The ding of the elevator shocks me to my senses, and the way that Hunter jolts back, has me looking toward the door in fear of being caught by a guest.

When I look back to him, he's tucking himself back into his pants, and the smirk on his lips is almost as taunting as his words. "Now you'll know how it feels. Now you know what it's like to watch *me* walk away." His chuckle is low.

"*What?*" I look up to meet his eyes, curious and darkened with desire neither of us can deny.

"Good night, Dekker. It was good to see you again."

When he strides out of the elevator, I stare after him with shock etched in every muscle of my body.

That shock morphs to embarrassment. The embarrassment churns to anger. That anger fuels self-loathing.

The dig is real, and the sting from it hits harder than it should.

But I caused this. He kissed me, yet I overstepped every damn line there is.

You almost just gave him a blowjob in the elevator.

I didn't, but my mind *was* there. The want *was* there. The goddamn urge *was* there.

I let the door close. I let the car ride to my floor. I let the doors open. All the while my mind reels, and my temper simmers from the utter mortification of what I just did.

Each step I take toward my room is emphasized by my thoughts.

How could I be so unprofessional?

Step.

How could I let him play me like that?

Step.

How could I let those unrequited everythings *I feel when it comes to him* resurface?

Step.

How could I be so weak?

Even worse, how can I stand here trying to put my key card in the door and question how I'm going to carry out my dad's professional wishes when they clash with my personal desires?

This is bad.

So very bad.

"This can't happen. You can't let this happen," I mutter as I move into the room. "We're not good together. We can't be good together. Not even for a night." *Shit. Shit. Shit.* "This was a huge mistake. Christ, the last time . . ."

I kick my heels off and fling them carelessly into the hotel room as my mental chastisement for what I almost let happen reigns.

For what I wanted to happen.

The last time . . .

I undress with trembling hands, and my need to take back everything that just happened owns my every thought.

But I can't. I know, I can't.

And I hate that a small, unprofessional part of me doesn't want to.

The last time . . .

Those three words keep repeating in my mind as I climb into the shower. As I crawl into bed.

As I try to clear my head and not think about him when the taste of his kiss still lingers on my tongue.

The last time . . .

The last time almost broke me, because it was only after I walked away that I realized I'd fallen in love with him.

Chapter
EIGHT

Dekker

3 years earlier

"Dekker." Hunter groans my name and every part of me aches as he pushes his way into me.

Our fingers link and our bodies churn with a deep-seated burn that neither of us can put out. Time after time. Hookup after hookup.

We may be in a new hotel, in a different city than usual, but dammit, Hunter knows exactly what I need, and how I need it.

It's been a shit day. An even shittier week. And the only thing I looked forward to was this.

Him.

That thought scared the shit out of me but didn't deter me from showing up, and it sure as hell didn't prevent me from holding myself back when my heart constricted in my chest when he opened the door.

There's something different about tonight, though.

"Fuck. I needed this." A kiss to my lips. A grind of his hips. "I needed you." A pull out as his teeth nip my collarbone and the head of his cock slides along every damn nerve.

Something's definitely different.

Sure, the carnal hunger was there for our first round tonight. The clothes yanking, hands possessing, can't-get-in-me-quick-enough desperation that we thrive on.

But now—this second round—is so very different.

The sex has shifted. Less greed, more need. Less fervor, more finesse. Less guardedness, more vulnerability.

He moves in and out of me with silent strokes. His lips are on my skin, the heat of his breath against my ear.

When he pushes up and meets my eyes, gone is the usual cocky smirk.

Gone is the humor that usually lights up his face. He's intense and serious, and my breath catches when our eyes hold and he moves.

There's an intimacy I'm not used to from him.

An intimacy I've slowly begun to crave and fear at the same time. One that spooks me and fulfills me in ways I'm too overwhelmed to contemplate in the moment.

So I avert my eyes. I lean up and take my own nip of his collarbone as I move my hands from his and scrape them up his flanks. "Let me ride you," I murmur into his ear as my hand slides between us and my fingers circle around him at the hilt of his cock and squeeze.

I take control, pushing us back into familiar territory. Into the physicality of our motions. Into the carnality of our movements.

He emits the sexiest groan when I turn my back to him, straddle his hips, and lower myself painstakingly slowly on top of him. He's heaven, hell, and everything in between as the stress of the week releases with each inch of him I accept until he bottoms out inside me. When I begin to rock my hips, I lose myself to him.

I lose myself to him.

His hands grab my hips and help guide me up and down.

I ignore the look in his eyes from moments ago and how being with him has made me feel lately.

Our moans fill the room, one after another.

And how wanting more from him scares the ever-living shit out of me.

I let my head fall back and we give ourselves over to the pleasure and desire and fall under its all-consuming haze.

Getting close to someone means getting hurt.

There are no sweet words whispered afterward. No soft kisses or snuggling.

This is how we are. We are *let's meet in a hotel somewhere*, work ourselves into an exhaustion of sexual satisfaction, and then part ways before we fight or spar or whatever it is we do that makes us want to get away from each other. But as I stare at myself in the bathroom mirror, there's a churning in my stomach and an ache in my heart.

This doesn't feel like enough anymore.

The question is, why?

I see my flushed cheeks and swollen lips. I see the truth staring right back at me.

I've fallen for Hunter Maddox. I've fallen for him when we agreed this was casual, when I don't let myself get close to anyone, and when he doesn't do relationships. I've fallen for him when we agreed to meet at hotels instead of our places so we'd prevent this from becoming routine or take the excitement out of it. I've fallen for him when I've never allowed myself to fall for anyone.

I'm an emotionally unattached girl. It's easier this way. It prevents the hurt of knowing it's going to end badly.

But his eyes . . . the way he looked at me. The tenderness in his touch when we're typically fire and brimstone and bruises and teeth marks . . . there's something more on his end too.

Panic sets in.

Full-blown panic . . . because this isn't us. This isn't what we agreed to. And hell, I'm looking at his actions through love-colored goggles so of course I'm going to read too much into everything. Of course I'm going to when I'm the one who went and fell.

I bring a hand to my chest as if it's going to allow me to catch my breath, when I know it's not going to do shit.

When I know falling for Hunter isn't going to make him want any more from me than the hot sex we find ourselves in. Even if he did, we'd crash and burn into an ugly mess before we even began.

How did I let this happen?

I take my time getting dressed. Each item of clothing I put on, I talk myself out of my revelation. I haven't fallen for him. This is just sex. We'd never work. He doesn't do relationships.

I almost believe it, until I walk into the room and see him. His pants are pulled on but unbuttoned, his chest is bare, and a bottle of beer is in one hand when he looks up to meet my eyes. Every part of me wants to go and kiss those lips, run my fingers through his hair, and tell him I want more with him. Six months flew by and doesn't seem like enough.

And then the truth is clear. My heart already hurts. My head is already spinning. The words I need to say—to tell him I've fallen for him—die without ever finding sound. He's not in this like I am. He's not ready for more.

His eyes narrow. "Where're you going?"

"I've got stuff to do," I stammer.

"Like . . ." He takes a few steps toward me.

I want to wake up next to you. At my place. At your place.

"Just things I forgot I needed to do. Deadlines."

I want to learn about what it is that clouds your eyes and makes you go quiet.

"Deadlines?"

I want quiet nights with a glass of wine and you beside me.

"Yes." I gather my things in measured movements, when all I want to do is shove them in the bag so I can rush out of here and let the tears fall. Even worse, I can feel the weight of his stare at my back, and I know he's standing there watching me and wondering.

"Hey? What's wrong?"

With a deep breath, I turn to face him. Standing a few feet before me, he's throwing a shirt on, his hair has fallen over his forehead, but his eyes home in on mine.

Tears burn as my thoughts tumble and fight against the want to say them and the knowledge that they'll only end in being hurt.

"Nothing." I offer a tight smile.

"Dekker?"

I shake my head and swallow over the lump of emotion lodged in my throat. "This was a mistake. *Again.*" He chuckles over this ongoing banter we always have. I don't sell the lie as well as I think I do, because his head tilts to the side. "But"—I look down to my purse strap in my hand and take a deep breath—"I don't think we can do this anymore." *Because I hate saying goodbye to you.* "We always said we'd know when this had run its course, and I think it finally has. You know, you and me and this." *Because it's easier to walk away now than to confess my feelings for you and be destroyed when you reject me.*

"What do you mean this has run its course?" He takes a step toward me.

"Just what it sounds like." I offer a laugh that has no resonance. My smile warms but only by sheer force when I take a step toward him. "Don't you think it's better to part ways now, like it is with us . . . actually liking each other?"

Confusion etches the lines of his face as he leans his hips against the dresser behind us. "If that's what you want."

Ask me to stay.

"I think it's for the best." I nod to reinforce my clipped words.

Tell me this is more than sex.

"Okay then." He runs a hand through his hair and blows out a breath that fills the room and suffocates my heart. "If you're sure. I mean . . ."

Agree that I forgot our rules—no emotions, no obligations—and tell me you want more than this.

In what feels like the hardest thing in the world, I step up and press a kiss to his cheek. I let his arms slide around me and pull me into him. It's the kind of bear hug that you can lose and find yourself in. It's the kind that tells you you're loved and that the person cares for you.

But his words don't come.

Not when he leans back and gives me that lopsided smile that makes my heart melt.

Not when I walk toward the door, my heart screaming to tell him the truth.

Not when I turn back one more time and look at him.

There's something in his eyes I can't make out, something I wish I could read, but I know I'm staring through jaded eyes. Eyes that want to believe he doesn't want me to leave for more reasons than the incredible sex. Eyes that want to believe he has feelings for me too.

Isn't that the irony though? I want him to feel about me how I feel about him, but if he did, if he professed how he wanted more, I'd run the other way.

I learned about love the hard way.

I learned how you could love someone more than the whole world but that doesn't save them from death. It won't save you from being alone.

My soul knows that love always ends in pain and loneliness.

Chapter
NINE

Hunter

THE PUCK HITS THE PLEXIGLASS THAT SEPARATES THE CROWD FROM the ice with a *crack*. The arena is a ghost town at this godawful time in the morning, so the sound ricochets off the walls and echoes back to us.

"You losing your touch, Maddox?"

I swing my stick back and then let my arms jerk forward without responding. The puck hits the upper left corner of the net, and I glare at Maysen.

"Does that look like I'm losing my touch?" I ask.

One after another, I land puck after puck into the back of the net, but nothing abates the anger and restlessness I feel. Nothing diminishes the feeling that I'm a hamster on a wheel. Nothing eases the goddamn ache Dekker left me with last night but that I refuse to admit.

But walking away was the right thing. Putting her in her place so she doesn't think I'm naïve about why she's here, or that I'd fall right back into how things were when she's the one who walked away.

Was that the whole point of last night then? A subtle stab at revenge? I can't make sense of it—my need to talk to her in the bar, to remind her I was there, and then leave her hanging in the elevator.

Shit. I'd be lying if I denied it wouldn't have been a hardship to fall right between her thighs.

Groaning at my own stupidity, I go back to my practice shots. Trying to work myself into a frenzy so my head can go to that silent place where I don't think and just do.

There's a rhythm. Grunt with the swing. Smack the stick to the puck. Thud as the puck hits the net.

Grunt. Smack. Thud.

Maysen lifts the bottle of beer to his lips, and my eyebrows lift.

"Hair of the dog?" I ask.

Grunt. Smack. Thud.

"Shit, if it were the hair of the dog, I'd be sliding back between Sadie's . . . or was it Sandy? Maybe Shelby. Fuck if I remember what her name was, but if that's the case, I'd be all up in her because she straight wore me out. I need this shit," he says and lifts the bottle of beer in the air, "to simply get me through the morning."

Fucking Maysen.

Normally I love the asshole. Right now, not so much.

Perhaps it's because he got some and I didn't.

Then again, after seeing Dekker last night—after tasting her—just any ole puck bunny wouldn't have satisfied me. Not that they've satisfied me for a long time.

Since Dekker.

Stopping to catch my breath, I rest my hand on my stick and take in the arena around me. Years upon years of blue and red pennants hang from the rafters while images of the team's history play out over the uppermost walls. Defining moments in the franchise's history. Defining moments in the league's history. And while I shouldn't care about any of it, it's a history I never thought I'd get to be part of and now hope to leave my own mark on as well.

And that, in and of itself, makes me a prick.

How can I be grateful to play here when Jonah can't? How can I be happy when I'm the one who took his place?

Christ. Isn't that why I play for the Jacks? I could have been on any play-off-contending team but he told me to play here. He told me this was the decision he would have made. And since I play for him, I did what he suggested.

Who knew it would work? Who knew I'd be the starting block management built the franchise around and that in my second year here, we'd be in playoff contention?

Always the big brother, always looking out for me.

Even after what I did to him.

But that's why this is so fucked. Sanderson is already threatening that contract talks are going to be brutal when they were the ones who begged me to come here . . . and then not keep their promises. *Why can't I just play the game I train every day for?*

I close my eyes for a second and breathe it in. It's by far my favorite time in any arena, when the nineteen thousand or so seats are vacant, and it's just me and the ice and a game I'm lucky to be gifted at.

Nothing can beat the roar of the crowd as you're dancing down the ice, weaving between defenders while trying to control the puck, but there's something about the silence that is more profound. Almost as if the silence reflects the magnitude of it all.

So how come I'm feeling that less and less?

How come most days, this gift feels more like a curse?

Why have I come to rely on these early morning sessions with just me and the puck and the silence of an absent crowd to attempt to keep my head in the game?

"What is it?" Maysen asks.

I shake my head and eye his beer. "That shit better be cleared out of your system before game time."

Grunt. Smack. Thud.

"Relax, Captain. The game is over twelve hours away and I've got an IV set up at noon. You know, I feel like I'm coming down with something"—he fake coughs—"so I already set it up with the doc to give me more fluids to re-plenish—er, flush my system."

"How are you even any good?" I joke, knowing full well, I'd never pull a stunt like that.

"It's in my genes."

"You wish it were in your jeans." I roll my eyes.

"*Jealous?*" he asks, when we both know my stats run circles around his.

"Drink the fuck up," I mutter.

Grunt. Smack. Thud.

"Mind telling me what the hell is up your ass, Maddox?" he asks again, his skates cutting across the ice the only other sound between us.

"I do mind and it's nothing," I grumble, refusing to look his way, but swipe his beer from his hand as he skates past and help myself to the rest of it with-out asking. As much as it tastes good, it also isn't what I want.

It seems I don't know what I want these days.

"Nothing?" His chuckle resonates.

"Yeah, nothing. Why?"

He moves his jaw from side to side as his eyes question me with things I don't quite understand. "Just trying to figure out what's going on with you."

His words cause me to pause. "What the hell is that supposed to mean?"

"We just thought—"

"*We?*" I bark the word out. "So that's what this is? The team designated you to come play the shrink with me?"

"Not like you couldn't use one," he mutters under his breath.

"What the fuck is that supposed to mean?" Now he has my full attention.

"It's . . . we're concerned."

"About yourselves? About the team? About me? What exactly are you con-cerned about?" I demand, the stick in my hand and the pucks lined up waiting to be shot now forgotten.

"You're playing dangerously. Over the past two years, you've become the man we look to for leadership—*to lead us*—and now in the past four months, you're like a one-man show out there. While that's great for your stats and the scoreboard, it fucking sucks for team morale. You're not better than us"—he pauses and emits a laugh of contrition—"well, maybe a little . . ." He chuckles. "We're on your side, Cap, and when you're on the ice, your play suggests you don't know we're even there. Sure, we're winning, but at what cost? So again, what's your fucking deal?"

His words are like a slap to my face. A slap I've anticipated but that doesn't lessen its sting. "Good to know my team thinks so highly of me."

"No one thinks more highly of you than you do yourself."

My hands tighten on the beer bottle. "Where the fuck do you get off . . ." My words fade as I check myself before I say something I'd probably regret. Hell, I'm the leader of this team. I shouldn't be the one being put in his place.

But can you fucking blame them, Maddox?

"We all have a stake in this. That's where we get off talking to you." He blows out a breath in frustration. "You're the big shot the Jacks took on to build this franchise to its full potential. And it's fucking working. We're tearing up the league and closing in on a playoff berth for the first time in this club's history."

"And the problem with that?"

"What the fuck is your endgame? You *were* here for the long haul. The franchise player, but now . . . now it seems you want the fuck out. You went from being our captain who pulls us together, who's led us to this point, to acting like you're a one-man show."

"Bullshit."

"That's exactly right. It is bullshit, but on your part. Hell, if you put as much effort into the game as you do your anger, we'd already have a fucking playoff berth clinched."

"Or maybe you should do it without me." I throw the baseless threat into the air between us but have never felt as strongly about the statement as I do right now. A man can only keep going for so long.

"That's how you're going to be, Hunter?" He shakes his head and I feel his disappointment—and fucking hate it. "Come on. We're just concerned for your well-being."

We hold each other's stares for a few seconds as I try to process why I'm so pissed off by this. As I try to figure out why I should expect them to have my back when I've been a selfish prick for the past however long.

The hardest part about processing it all though is knowing how I should feel and still giving a shit less.

"Tell me something, Maysen . . . if I'm playing like a one-man show, being selfish but we're still winning. . . which one do you want me to be?

"Because I assure you, if I started passing the puck more and shooting less, I'd have one of you on my ass asking me what the hell was going on in the opposite way."

"Oh, so none of us have earned our own spots on the team, Maddox? That what you're saying?" And when I don't answer, I hear him mutter, "Asshole."

Yep. That's me. Grade-A asshole.

I throw the empty bottle across the ice in frustration and turn back to my row of pucks without saying another word.

My head is filled with so much shit I can't see straight, think straight . . . anything. It's so fucked.

You're the one who fucked up, Hunter. You owe it to him to fulfill his dream. You owe him.

I'll never stop owing him.

Grunt. Smack. Thud.

His talent was unmatched.

Grunt.

My one-man show isn't even good enough for him.

Smack.

My dad's words . . . they fill my head, fuel the anger, feed the rage, expose the hurt. The goddamn everything.

Thud.

"Since when do we drink when we work?"

Catching me off guard just as I hit the puck, Dekker's voice rips through my flustered concentration, and the puck goes sailing into the stands.

I hate that I don't want her here.

I despise that I do want her here.

And when I turn to where the sound of her heels clicking on the concrete of the tunnel leading up to the ice, I hate myself even more for *remembering*. How good we were in bed, how explosive—almost violent with lust.

Fucking incredible.

She stands with the beer bottle I chucked onto the ice in one hand, her other hand on her hip, and rocking a pinstriped pantsuit that looks part *time to party*, part *don't fuck with me*.

Totally in control when last night she was anything but.

Maysen is behind her as he walks down the tunnel toward the locker rooms. I was so pissed, so focused, I didn't even realize he'd left.

Lucky for me, now I don't have to address the bullshit he was hoping to resolve. Unlucky for me, I'm being stared down by a much tougher opponent, and the look of disappointment on her face isn't one I really care to acknowledge.

I already have a mother.

I already own guilt.

"Should I be worried there are more bottles hidden elsewhere?" she asks and shifts her weight.

"You know us hockey players, Dekk. If there's a rule, we're going to break it. You want to strip search me?" I lift my hands above my head. "I might have a stash somewhere on my body you can find."

"Drinking on a game day? At eight in the morning?" She lifts a lone brow and ignores my comment.

"What? Last night you were all about touching me and today you're not?" I tsk. "My, how things change."

Anger fleets through her expression, followed closely by embarrassment, but just as quickly as it's there, it disappears.

Hmm. Seems what I did last night got to her more than I thought.

"The beer?" she asks, giving a stoic glance from the beer bottle in her hand and then back to me.

"Sometimes you just need to relax." I shrug. *What does it matter? What do I care what she thinks of me?*

Why is she here?

"You going to call the LumberJacks management police on me?"

Chapter

TEN

Dekker

I STARE AT HUNTER. AT HIS SHIRT PLASTERED WITH SWEAT AND HOW it clings to his body, despite the chill of the ice his skates are standing on. He has his warm-up pants on and is without a helmet, his hair curling at the ends from the sweat.

And all I see in his eyes is anger I didn't put there. Or maybe I did. Rejection can do that to a man . . . but there's something more here. Something I walked in on that doesn't make sense.

"Don't give me that look, Kincade," Hunter mutters as he skates over to the penalty box where his electrolyte drink sits.

"What look?" I ask.

He half laughs, half snorts and meets my gaze across the distance. "Disappointment. Disproval. Disdain. I'm the king of all of them, so save your breath—or in this case—your glare, because it's not going to work with me."

"Are we working on emotions that start with the letter D today?" I ask. A hint of my embarrassment and anger over how I acted last night creeps into my voice, but I mask it with sarcasm. "If that's the case, I'm more than impressed with your answers thus far."

He clenches his jaw in response and then skates back over to line up more pucks so he can shoot them. And he does, one after another, each shot taken with laser precision and a healthy dose of fury behind it.

He goes through the first ten lined up and then stops to catch his breath.

His talent and skill are undeniable, but so is the beer bottle in my hand.

"Just because you're the captain and star of this team, doesn't mean management won't frown upon this," I say, unable to let this go.

"Fuck the management."

His comment surprises me. Always a team player and public mouthpiece for the team, I've never heard him talk like this.

"Those are some strong words," I say.

"The iron fist they seem to hold me with is even stronger."

"Iron fist?" *Where is this coming from?* "I believe they pay you a healthy sum to put their jersey on every night and play a sport that you love, so unless they're handcuffing you to a locker afterward and forcing you to not eat or drink for days, I think you're being ridiculous."

"Handcuffs, huh?" His eyebrow quirks up, and his constant need to distract from the gist of our conversation tells me I'm hitting too close to home.

"What's going on?" I ask again.

"We'll just say we're not seeing eye to eye at the moment," he mutters and then slaps a shot off and hisses when he misses.

"No one likes a player who's hard to handle and honestly, Hunter, you're becoming hard to handle."

"No one likes unsolicited advice from someone who has no bearing on his career, either," he counters, the rebuke stinging but deserved.

The problem is, I do care about him. Doesn't he get that's where my hostility stems from?

And only a crazy person would say that, Dekker.

I put my hands up in surrender to both him and my own thoughts. "You know I only want the best for you." I take a few steps in his direction in the first row of the stands. I'm close enough to catch the hitch of his movement and to see uncertainty flicker in his eyes. It's almost as if he needs to talk but doesn't see me as someone he can trust. *I hate that.* "What is it, Hunter?"

"Nothing. It's . . . never mind."

But I see it, and he knows I see it. The question is what do I see, though?

"Twelve years in the league. You're thirty-two, in the top twenty of all-time best scorers and you still have years left to play. Made it there faster than anybody else."

"You make a habit of studying people's stats who aren't your clients?" he asks.

"It's my job to know who the best of the best is." I only speak the truth but hate that it probably comes off like I'm kissing his ass.

"What's your point, then?" he asks, but his tone is different, quieter, more reserved.

"No point. I just know you've been running full steam since you entered this league. Straight off NCAA championships, where you still hold some records, right into the NHL."

"Every kid's dream, right? So many would kill to be in my shoes. Save it. I've heard it all. I've thought it all, and I leave everything out on the ice every damn time I play."

I nod slowly, letting him know I hear him, but I don't buy what he's saying. I'm missing something. "But you're angry."

"And your point?" he snaps.

"It's affecting your game. Your life."

"You don't know the half of it," he mutters as he skates past me.

"I know a change of scenery is sometimes needed. I know that stars can sometimes burn out. From what I've seen—"

"You don't know what you're talking about," he says, his skates cutting into the ice as he stops right in front of me, the plexiglass the only thing separating us.

"I make a living knowing what I'm doing. Just like you do." I shrug, trying to act as unaffected as possible by his nearness. Trying to pretend my pulse isn't racing as my body remembers his kiss last night. Trying to hide the flush on my cheeks over how I overstepped.

"I'm sorry about last night," I say quietly. "I overstepped. I . . . your point was made. Again. I apologize."

Our eyes hold, question, dismiss, and right when I think the conversation is over, his lips turn up in the slightest of smirks. "Same hotel as the team?"

The mental whiplash lasts only seconds as I refuse to give him the satisfaction of knowing he threw me. "Why am I staying in the same hotel?"

"Yeah."

"Convenience."

That cocky grin spreads wider as he just shakes his head ever so slightly and takes a step closer so his skates hit the barrier between us.

"What?" I ask, relieved by the sudden levity. This verbal sparring is exhausting.

"Just trying to figure you out."

"Didn't you know? I'm an open book," I tease.

"An open book inside a block of ice."

"Amusing," I mutter, unnerved by his intense scrutiny and hurt by his dig, even though it's more accurate than not. Those eyes of his hard to look away from.

"I'd say it's amusing too, but I'm the one who's always on the other end of whatever game you're playing."

"What the hell is that supposed to mean?" I shift on my feet. This is the last place I need to address why I'm here in Chicago. The mood has changed, the moment lost to speak to him. "You know what? I'm not going to be your verbal punching bag. By the way Maysen stalked out of here, you're pissed at him. Fine. Be pissed at him, but not me. I know that look in your eyes, and I'm not going to be the one you toy with so you feel like a man in control again."

I stalk toward the players' opening, the click of my heels only rivaled by the slice of his skates on the ice. And just as I reach the entrance to the tunnel, Hunter is there, his hand on my bicep pulling me back toward him.

"A man in control again?" he asks, his fingers adjusting his grip as his chest brushes over mine. "I'm always in control."

"That one seemed to touch a nerve, did it?"

"Maybe you should ask yourself how in control you are, huh?" His eyes flit down to my lips and back up to mine, the warmth of his breath hitting my lips. I can all but taste his kiss again but know that mistake will not be repeated.

No way.

No how.

Not after last night.

"Let's move on to adjectives that start with I. Irritable, much?"

His chuckle is that low rumble that tells me he's ready to play. That's the last thing I want right now. "*Irritable*? How about *indecisive*?"

"Who, you?"

"No, you," he sneers and takes a step closer.

"Not in the least."

"No?" His eyes flicker from my eyes to my lips again. "This was a huge mistake," he says, pretending to sound like me last night before clearing his throat. "Right back to that phrase, huh?"

"What do you mean?" I tug on my arm to no avail.

"I mean, it's amazing how convenient it is for you to fall back on that line. You said it the last time I saw you and you said it last night."

I did? I try to relive the moments, knowing I said it in the elevator but not remembering the time before. All I remember is trying to keep my emotions under check so Hunter Maddox had no clue I'd failed at the casual dating—er, sex situation—we'd found ourselves in. Sure, we fell into bed that first time, then verbally fought our way out of it, only to fall back into it more often than not over the course of six months.

But we weren't dating.

You could have asked either of us and we would have confirmed that. We were benefits buddies. The call we'd make when we were in the same city, at the same time—hell, even when we weren't we'd arrange to be. That's how great our sexual chemistry was.

The problem? Even though we couldn't be in the same room longer than thirty minutes without fighting—unless we were having sex—I became addicted to him. His gruff way, his cutting sense of humor, and his . . . well, his cock and fingers and oh-so-gloriously skilled tongue. But I can't see that in him now.

"Cat got your tongue, Dekker?" he asks, and leans in so I panic he's going to kiss me. Panic I'm here in the arena with the team nearby and Hunter is body to body with me. But I don't move. I don't back down. I refuse to let him feel like he has the upper hand again like last night. "Because the way I see it, this is your MO. We'd have incredible sex, you'd get up and say, 'Shit, that was a mistake,' and then collect your clothes or kick me out of wherever with a lame excuse about how you had somewhere to be until we'd see each other again. We were always a mistake. Every time. Until the next time that is."

I hate that the boyish smirk and arrogance in his eyes owns my every reaction—even after all this time.

I hate that I know he's right. If only he knew why . . . but he didn't stop me from walking out three years ago, so he has no idea what it took to leave.

"Are you saying we weren't a mistake?" I ask through a laugh to try and find my footing.

"'Till next time." He releases my arm and runs his hand down the length of it.

"There will be no next time."

"Yes, there will," he says and begins to put skate guards over his blades.

"No, Hunter, there won't." I straighten my spine. "Last night was completely unprofessional of me. It was—"

"That's never stopped you before," he says, and I swear to God I see the moment it clicks, because his body falters in motion moments before his eyes flash up to meet mine. "And here I was thinking you'd come here to finish what we started last night. Have an early morning of brunch sex for old time's sake before telling me what a mistake we were . . . but it's *unprofessional* of you. Let me guess, you didn't come here for that part of me . . . you only came for the other part of me. The part that would make us sleeping together unethical."

"You're crazy," I mutter and wave a hand at him as I backpedal.

"It'd only be unprofessional if I happened to be the person you were here to recruit. It would only be immoral if you were sleeping with your client, because that would mean others might worry that you're giving me preferential treatment . . ."

"You need a new agent." It's the closest I'm going to get to telling him the truth in this environment.

He throws his head back and laughs. "And why's that? Why the concern all of a sudden?"

"Because Sanderson isn't doing you any favors."

"And how would you know what he is or isn't doing for me? Unless of course you were asking around and trying to figure out how to woo me over to your side."

"I'm here to check up on my clients," I say and glance over my shoulder as the trainer walks past with Katzen following closely behind, no doubt to work on that hamstring that's been giving him trouble. "And you're reaching."

"Am I?" Hunter asks as he walks up to me, our bodies back in the same position as last night in the elevator—almost touching.

I nod, not trusting my own words and hating that he's the only man who can make me tongue-tied. The one thing my dad always emphasized to us was time and place. Never make an offer, a proposition, an anything to a potential client if the timing is off or if the place has you at a disadvantage. I walked into the arena this morning thinking I'd have a chance to talk to Hunter alone, since everyone knows he prefers his mornings solitary and his practice hard.

What I didn't expect was to walk in on whatever was happening between him and Maysen, a beer bottle on the ice, or Hunter to have me on the ropes so to speak with his comments.

Ones I have to figure out how to maneuver.

"Yes," I reiterate. "You're reaching."

"So then why not give in to what we both want?"

My mouth is as dry as his eyes are intense. "What's that?" I barely get out.

The groan he emits might as well be for both of us because it rumbles in the space between us. "Shall we finish what we started last night?"

"I told you, we're not sleeping together. Things have changed. I've changed from who I was three years ago."

"You may have changed but the chemistry is still the same. Time didn't put a damper on the want."

"You're being ridiculous." I take a step back only to bump against the wall. Of course, it's there, because why wouldn't it be, right?

"I am? Because I mean, if you're not here to try and steal me from Sanderson, then there would be no reason for us *not* to walk down memory lane."

"You mean sleep down memory lane?" I ask.

"There's that smile."

Shit. Don't do that, Hunter. Don't be playful. Don't be charming. Don't be nice.

"While this has been amusing—"

"There's that word again."

I sigh in exasperation. "I have work to get to."

I expect Hunter to stop me—he's a man who typically gets what he wants after all—but he doesn't, so I walk down the hall toward the visitor's section in the bowels of the arena.

"One thing, Dekk."

"Yeah?" I turn to face him. He's standing in the opening, the rink at his back, his stick in one hand, and the smug expression on his face fitting perfectly. If I could take a picture, the image would be him to a tee.

"Why'd you come this morning? If it wasn't to steal me or fuck me . . . why waste the trip?"

Shit.

"I told you, I'm traveling with the team for the next stretch."

"That didn't answer my question of why you came looking for me."

Bastard. He wants an answer? All right.

I walk back toward him and stop as he strips his shirt over his head. Where there would normally be an undershirt and pads, there is nothing but skin. Defined, sculpted muscles beneath his olive-toned skin with a tattoo on one shoulder and a war story of scars on the rest.

Scars I've traced with my fingers. Tattoos I've nipped with my teeth.

When I drag my eyes away from the sight in front of me, I'm met with a raised eyebrow and that damn amusement again painting every single muscle of his face.

Definitely a bastard toying with me.

"I wanted to come here and thank you."

"We've talked all this time and those words haven't graced your lips so I doubt that's the reason."

"No. Maysen was here. I was thrown with the beer bottle," I fumble.

"Beer bottle is in the trash. Maysen is gone." He puts one hand on his hip and raises his eyebrows. "What did you want to thank me for?"

I clear my throat. "For reaffirming that Chad wasn't right for me."

"How'd I do that?" he asks.

And what I meant as a completely innocent comment on the fly—one I somehow didn't get out correctly, now just screwed me. How do I answer this? How do I tell him that I felt more alive in the few moments his lips met mine than I did the whole damn time Chad and I dated? *Dated?* Maybe more like were companions.

Because now I'm stuck staring at his blue eyes that are questioning me and I can't really give him an answer without showing my cards. *Professionally and personally.*

"Because . . . I . . . uh missed his call last night when we were in the elevator," I lie. And internally roll my eyes. *I missed a call?* Pfft.

"I'm not following you." His smile widens.

Shit.

"Um, a man who wanted to fight for me would have called back. He would have—"

"Kissed you like I kissed you? Is that what you were going for?"

"No. Absolutely not." *Yes. That's exactly why.*

"You keep thinking that," he says and then holds his hand up to someone over my shoulder. "Hold up. I need you to look at something." He takes a few steps so that he's shoulder to shoulder with me. "It was definitely the kiss."

"Hunter—"

"You're welcome."

Without another word, his skates clomp down the carpeted hallway toward the visiting team's quarters, while I watch after him wondering how in the hell he just got the upper hand in this conversation when I'm the one holding all the cards in a game he doesn't even know we're playing.

But isn't that us?

Well, him and me.

There is no *us*.

There won't be an us.

There can't be an us. Not even a one-night-stand us.

Hell, Hunter maneuvered me right where he wanted me to be—me answering his questions while I forget to get answers to mine.

Something is going on with him.

The agent in me wants to figure it out so I can manipulate it to my advantage—take care of the problem, negotiate the issue away, and show him just how good I am at my job.

The woman in me worries about *him*, because you can only push so hard, so long, without burning out.

Chapter

ELEVEN

Dekker

KINCADE SPORTS MANAGEMENT
Internal Memorandum
New Recruit Status Report

*denotes urgent status

Athlete	Team	Sport	Agent	Status
Carl Ryberg	n/a	Golf	Kenyon	Meeting set up
Jose Santos	D-Backs	Baseball	Chase	In talks
Lamar Owens	Bulls	Basketball	Lennox	Negotiating
Michelle Nguyen	n/a	Soccer	Brexton	Negotiating
*Hunter Maddox	Jacks	Hockey	Dekker	

I GLANCE AT THE FIRST PAGE OF THE WEEKLY STATUS SHEET IN MY INBOX and twist my lips. What do I type? What answer do I give? Haven't approached him? He doesn't know? I kissed him?

I want to kiss him again?

Shit.

Instead of typing anything, I close the email and don't respond. It's too soon for me to type anything.

Chapter

TWELVE

Hunter

"Hey Mom. Just calling to see how Jonah's doing." I lean back against the pillows propped against the headboard behind me. Different day. Different hotel. Same life.

Her nervous chuckle unnerves me. "He's fine. Just has a cold. Probably from all the germs. I went to the store to buy things to prepare us to come and see your game. I probably got the germs there and somehow brought them home to him."

Christ, it's always my fault he's sick, one way or another.

"There are germs everywhere. You can't really avoid them."

"When it comes to Jonah though. He's fragile and—"

"Can I talk to him? Can you put his headset on him?"

"You know sometimes that thing doesn't work."

"Then can you put the phone up to his ear?" I ask, running a hand through my hair as I stare out the window.

"Your father asked if you've been getting his texts. He says you're not responding."

Another no when it comes to Jonah. I shouldn't be surprised, but I am. *Thanks, Mom.*

And my father's texts? I don't think I've responded in ten years, and yet he keeps sending them as if he doesn't notice otherwise.

Then again, it's not like they notice me much at all.

"How should I respond to his texts?" I ask. "Thanks for the negativity? The criticism? How exactly should I respond?" I chuckle, the toxicity I endure to talk to my brother is ridiculous.

"He means well. He's the reason you're there, you know."

"Jonah, Mom? Can I talk to him?" Exasperation hits an all-time high.

"Yes. Sure. I can't remember the last time you called for him."

Two days ago.

Two fucking days ago. And two days before that.

There's shuffling on the other end of the line as she goes through the process of connecting his headset to the phone line so he can hear me.

"Okay, it's connected," she says, her voice distant.

"Hey J." I suddenly feel calm and pause after my greeting because in my head, I can hear him talking back, I can feel my twin responding. *God, I miss him.* "Just wanted to call and check in. I'm sure Mom is driving you crazy with her fussing and repeating the same thing over and over. I get it. I totally do." I close my eyes and listen to the ventilator for a beat. "We're playing Rampage tonight. Those guys are fucking assholes but yeah, I'll keep my stick up like you taught me. It's going to be a tough one. Ferguson knows how to play me. It's like he knows which line I'm going to take before I even know myself. And their double team defense is strong. We've been working on a way to overcome it. It's like a play you would have made up. Perfect in every way for them and harder than fuck to defend against for me."

So I talk to my brother for the better part of an hour like I always do, caught in that indecision that I'm being an ass for talking to him about things he'd kill to be doing and treating him like he's gone completely.

The worst part about it is that I call him because I want to, because he's the only person that quiets the anger. But as I hang up, I wonder if my calls only feed his.

Chapter

THIRTEEN

Dekker

SOMETHING'S OFF.

I can't put my finger on it but watching Hunter play, the difference is noticeable from the last game to this one.

There is none of his intuitive anticipation of where his opponents are going to play several passes before it happens. There's no showmanship as he dodges defenders left and right while keeping the puck in action. There's a loss of the ferocious determination to get the puck in the back of the net.

Normally I can't take my eyes off him because his ease of play enthralls me. Tonight, I'm all but cringing every time he gets the puck. It's almost as if he's the star kid on the first-place hockey team that's creaming the last-place team so the coach has told him to hold back and pass twelve times before he attempts a shot.

But he's not shooting.

No, instead he's passing it off and then falling back when normally he's the heart of the offense.

If the Jacks were in their own arena, the crowd would be booing him after every pass. This crowd here senses something is off and has been cheering each and every one, because it's to their advantage.

Someone has knocked the king off his reign-of-terror throne and it's not pretty.

I welcome the distraction from the scoreboard when my phone buzzes at my hip.

Lennox.

It's sad that I'm immediately on the defensive before I even answer the phone.

"Hey, Len," I say, walking toward the back of the press box and pushing a finger to my other ear. "What's up?"

"Just checking in."

"For?"

"No reason," she says, but a lifetime of living with her tells me she's fishing for information.

"So you just called to say hi?" I can't remember the last time one of my sisters did that.

"Yes . . . and, never mind."

And here we go.

"What is it?" I honestly don't have the bandwidth to deal with her today.

The crowd goes wild as the opposition scores, and I crane my neck from where I stand huddled in the back to watch the replay on the Jumbotron overhead. Lucky shot.

"Who scored?" she asks.

"The Patriots."

"Boo," she says, and I smile but then remember she's playing coy.

"What is it you needed, Len?"

"I just wanted to see how it was going with Maddox."

"I've talked to him but haven't *talked* to him yet about us."

"*Us?*"

"KSM," I explain in annoyed exasperation.

"Yes. Sure," she says but doesn't sound anything like she does. "It was pretty shitty of Dad to make Maddox your recruit."

I open my mouth and close it, wanting to say so much—agree, commiserate, talk about what it felt like to see him for the first time—but don't. "It's business. I can handle it."

"Keep that in mind."

And now my back is up.

"Excuse me?" I snort.

"You two were more than sex."

"Thanks for the analysis, but you're wrong. That's all we were." *Were my feelings for him really that transparent?*

"That came out wrong. What I mean was I know he hurt you."

"I've been hurt a lot. It's not a big deal."

"Easy to say, hard to do," she murmurs.

"Your point?" I ask, ready for the conversation to be over.

"If you sleep with him, this whole thing is over." I should be stunned by her direct nature, but I'm not. Subtlety is not Lennox's strong suit. Silence is my response. "Not to be the party pooper . . . or should I say pretty kitty pooper, but if you sleep with him—"

"No worries there."

"—then our other clients will think he's getting preferential treatment—"

"Are you actually lecturing me?" I ask through a laugh. "After you slept with Hardy and that entire debacle? Seriously?"

"It's not the same. This time it matters."

She pauses as the arena plays a song that the crowd chants along to and I welcome the distraction.

"And who exactly are you busy trying to woo over to Kincade?"

Her pause has me leaning over as if I can hear the words she's not saying . . . and I wait.

"I don't exactly know yet."

"What do you mean you don't know yet?"

"I mean, Dad said we need to recruit one at a time so it looks more subtle than a hostile takeover, or some weird father analogy like that."

I stare at the game unfolding before me—at the loss the Jacks are being handed, no thanks to Hunter. "So I'm the only one who's—"

"Teacher's pet always gets to have fun first," she says in a singsong voice. She called to gloat . . . or to make sure I'm not fucking up things for her because let's be honest, when's the last time she thought about anyone or anything but herself?

If KSM were to fail as a business, how would my sister survive without all the fancy social functions that go hand in hand with being a sports agent? God forbid, it would thrust her out of the limelight she thrives on.

I'm far from naïve and know her concern is genuine but skewed for selfish reasons.

But what the hell is my dad pulling here? While he has some logic to avoid an all-out war with Sanderson, why was it so pertinent that I pick up my life on the fly and do this?

"I've got to go," I murmur.

"No. *Wait!*"

"What?" I snap. "What more can you possibly have to say that's not duplicitous in its meaning?"

"Look, all of that came out wrong. All of it."

"I don't care anymore, Len. I've got a game to watch and a client to schmooze."

"Hear me out." It's the tone in her voice and the fact that I've been like their mom that prevents me from hanging up.

"You've got two minutes."

"I know you like him, Dekk. And I know how you get when someone gets too close to you," she says. I'm still not following her. "Because of Mom, because of the hurt we experienced, it's easier to push someone away when you love them than to see where it leads."

"There is no talk of love here." I snort at her ludicrousness.

"But there was when you walked away from him last time." Her voice softens and she speaks before I can interrupt her. "You can interrupt me all you want, you can tell me you didn't have feelings for him, but I was staying at your place that night when you came home. I know that look you had, and I know you were hurting and maybe, just maybe, it's because you were too chicken to tell him how you felt. You were too scared that if he said he had feelings for you too you'd have to face your fears. That you'd have to let someone in."

I forgot about that. That she was there at my place when I got home. The twenty questions she peppered me with asking what was wrong. The twenty shrugs I gave, telling her I was perfectly fine. The scrutiny of her stare and how irritated I got when her voice turned compassionate, because it only made the tears I was fighting burn brighter.

Damn my father for giving me him to recruit.

Old feelings are better left dead and buried.

"Len—"

"All I'm saying is if you choose to sleep with him—if you choose to risk him as a client and what Dad's asked of us because of it—that it better be for more than just sex. It better be because you're going to put yourself out there and tell him how you feel this time."

"I have to go."

"I'm sure you do," she says quietly but doesn't argue.

I end the call.

I sit back in my seat but don't see a minute of the game before me.

It better be because you're going to put yourself out there and tell him how you feel this time.

I'm used to the panic that comes with the thought, but I'm not used to someone else seeing it or knowing it . . . and I'm not sure how I feel about that.

What I do know is that what started out feeling like a wild goose chase to acquire Hunter has turned into so much more.

I knew that the minute I laid eyes on him.

I knew that there was going to be a casualty in all of this.

And most likely, it was going to be my heart. *Shit.*

Chapter

FOURTEEN

Hunter

"WHAT THE FUCK WAS THAT, CAP?" FRANKIE ASKS AND DELIBERATELY bumps my shoulder as I stride past him in the locker room.

I keep walking and ignore the inferno raging within me to take a swing at any of these fuckers. Guys that were friends—teammates—and now calling me out. I did exactly what they fucking wanted—became a pansy-assed passer instead of myself—and of course, it's not fucking good enough.

"You not feeling good?" Katz asks.

"Your ankle bugging you again?" Callum questions. "Your knee?"

But I keep my focus on my locker, because it's so much easier than facing the bullshit in here and their subtle digs at how I played.

Maysen's shoulder hits mine and I refuse to respond to the look in his eyes that says, *this is how you let us down.*

"You trying to throw the game?" another voice yells from the back just as I hit my locker. "How much money'd you bet against us?" There's laughter that follows the joke, but I know it wouldn't have been said if it wasn't thought of first.

Do they really think I'd bet against my team?

Screw this.

Like fucking clockwork I don't want to acknowledge, I open my locker and the first thing I see is the screen of my cellphone lit up like a goddamn Christmas tree. Text after text after text telling me what a disappointment I am to the Maddox name, no doubt. How Jonah would have never played this poorly. One after another hit the screen and goad me like the eyes of my teammates at my back.

I don't pay any attention to them. I never do.

At least that's what I tell myself.

I round on the locker room to find every teammate staring at me, defeat in their postures, and fury in their expressions. They're sweaty and spent in partial stages of undress but all of them are laser-focused on me. In anger. This isn't right. This isn't how it was when I decided to come here two years ago. They had welcomed me and my aggression, knew I was here to lift the game—the team—to Cup level. And now the bastards think I could throw a game . . . *fucking pisses me off.*

"What's the problem?" I shout, hands out, fight welcome. "Is that not what you were asking for when you sent Maysen to talk to me today? Be more of a team player? Pass to make sure every goddamn one of you got to put their stick on the puck? You wanted a fucking Kumbaya session, boys, and you got it." I stand on the bench. "What? You don't have a right to stand there and look like someone pissed in your Wheaties when you got exactly what you asked for."

They all gawk at me, the rookies on the team shrinking into themselves, the hardened fuckers like me standing their ground.

"What do you all have to say now?" My voice reaches a fever pitch, and I hate the fucking tinge of panic in it. I hate that even though I did exactly what I set out to do, I'm still sick to my stomach over it. Staring at the people I've devoted blood, sweat, and pulled muscles to, I loathe the look of disappointment in their eyes and that it's directed at me.

"Mad Dog—"

"Don't Mad Dog me. Don't act like you guys didn't send Maysen to lead the charge in telling me I'm too selfish, too aggressive, *too me*, because guess what? When I'm not, none of you stepped up to the fucking line and played the damn part." I throw my gloves into my locker with a thud. "Maybe you all oughta start asking yourself the question, why the fuck not?"

My hands tremble with anger, and I need to get the hell out of here before I do something I'm going to regret. Before I fuck up more than I already have.

I'm losing control and there's no worse feeling in the world.

None.

"Maddox. In my office." The voice of Coach Jünger booms through the locker room and while I look at him, everyone remains staring at me. "*Now.*"

"This is total bullshit." I jump off the bench, kick the foot of my locker, and stride toward the door Jünger is holding open for me.

When it slams behind me, I stand there as he takes his time walking to the other side of the desk before resting his hips on the counter at his back. He looks at me with the same disappointment that everyone else did.

"You want to tell me what the fuck that was all about?" he asks and tosses his clipboard on the desk with a thud.

"The team thinks I've been showboating. Had a delegation deliver a talk to me this morning over it . . . so I gave them what they wanted." There isn't an ounce of fucks given in my voice, but inside is a goddamn hurricane of emotion. "I gave them mediocre Maddox."

"And you think you're paid the big bucks by the big dogs upstairs to deliver mediocre Maddox?" He crosses his arms over his chest.

"It's not our arena so I'm not quite sure where the big dogs are, but I'm pretty sure they're not upstairs."

"That's how you want to respond, smart-ass? Let's try again."

"Just trying to keep the team chemistry alive."

"The fuck you are," he shouts and walks over to snap closed the blinds that allow everyone in the locker room from seeing in before turning to face me. "I don't know what the fuck is going on in your life, and it sure seems like you don't want anyone to know, so you give me one reason why I shouldn't go against the GM's request I received five minutes ago to bench your ass for the next three games."

"Because you want the Stanley Cup as much as they do and benching me isn't going to help a goddamn ounce with that. We're running out of games now and without me on the ice, the team's just not the same. *You need me.*"

"We don't need what you did tonight."

"My half-ass is better than some of their full bore."

"Your arrogance isn't becoming." He says the words but nothing else, because he knows I'm right.

"Withers is in a shooting slump, Frankie is in his own head too much after that suspension, and Maysen, God love the fucker, but shooting isn't his strong suit right now . . . so yeah, I've been an asshole. I've got shit going on that no one needs to know—"

"Who'd you get pregnant?"

My laugh echoes off the walls. "Hilarious."

"You off the oxy?" he asks, his face suddenly falling some to match the gravity in his voice.

"I'm good."

"You sure? You've had injury after injury this year without taking a day off. Cortisone shots help, but I know Oxy is even better to take the edge off. Is that it? Are you hooked on—"

"It's not drugs, it's not women . . . fuck, Jüng, it's just *shit*, okay?"

"Things okay with your brother?" he asks, his voice lowering as sympathy edges his gruff tone.

"Of course," I lie. Because what else can I do? Tell him, no, things are shit? That Jonah's struggling more and more, getting sick time and again and doctors think his time is limited? That I'm the reason Jonah's there, and dealing with it is more bullshit than he could ever imagine? I walk toward the window and back before he can see the reality of my thoughts, before he realizes that this sport I've been *blessed* to play has single-handedly saved me and ruined me simultaneously. "He's fine. It's my teammates pulling crap like they did this morning that isn't exactly helping."

"And what about the crap you've pulled the past few months? The lashing out. The fights. The thumbing your nose at the people who sign your checks? The you're too good—"

"I've never said I'm too good!" I shout and take a step toward him, realizing more than ever that everyone around me doesn't understand, and it's making me feel even more suffocated. I lace my fingers at the back of my neck and exhale a loud sigh in frustration.

My exhale fills the room as he settles in his spot against the counter again. "You're too valuable to be fucking up like this. It looks like you don't give a shit about anyone but yourself."

I'm the last person I care about, I want to scream. *The last person. Don't you see that? Don't you see I'm punishing myself? Don't you see that no one gives a fuck about me, and I've never felt so goddamn isolated in my life?*

"I'm not going to bench you, Maddox. Whatever you're dealing with needs to be dealt with though, or else I'm not going to be able to protect you from the people signing that gigantic check of yours or the teammates who can make you look even worse if they start talking to the press." He holds his hands out to the side. "It's your call."

I nod, unsure what else to do or say because my head feels like it's not connected to my body. The thoughts are there but the normal emotions I should feel—shame, grief, chagrin—aren't attached.

"That's all." I can't get out of there fast enough, but the minute my fingers are on the door handle, he speaks again. "Hey, Cap?"

I turn to face him. "Hmm?"

"You need anything, I'm here, okay? It's never as bad as it seems."

Yes, it is.

"Thanks."

"I'd avoid the main exit on the way to the team bus. I've made the locker room off-limits from the press tonight. Wasn't sure what was going to happen in here and we like to keep our fights within the family. But uh . . . the press is out there in droves, clamoring for answers."

"Noted."

Chapter
FIFTEEN

Hunter

Dad: Such a waste to have ability and potential and refuse to use it.

Dad: Disgraceful. Absolutely disgraceful.

Dad: You get a chance that should've been your brother's and that's how you play?

Dad: You're lucky they don't boo you out of Jersey when you get home.

I STARE AT THE TEXTS. AT THE CRITICISM AND NEGATIVITY AND AM REminded, as I am after every game, how I'll never be Jonah.

How I'll never live up to my father's standard of perfection even when I bust my ass day in day out and he criticizes from the sidelines.

With a swipe of my thumb, I clear the display. I know the words will eat at me as I fall asleep tonight.

Sleep.

That's what I want. To fall into an oblivious sleep and to put this fucking piss-poor night behind me. To try and forget. Just fucking forget.

I take a glance around the locker room. Most of the team has cleared out by now. Thank God they left me alone after Jünger's dress-down. I'm in no mood to talk to them, or anyone, so I head to the back tunnel just like he suggested and hope everyone continues to stay away.

Chapter
SIXTEEN

Dekker

"I HAD A FEELING YOU'D BE COMING THROUGH THIS SIDE OF THE TUN-nel," I say the minute I see Hunter walk out of the doorway. His head is down, his sweatshirt hood pulled out to shadow his face, and his posture can either read absolute defeat or unfettered anger.

Or a mix of both.

His feet falter as he stands in the middle of the tunnel. We're in the bowels of the arena, and there is no one in sight but the two of us.

He lifts his gaze to meet mine and words, emotions, everything seem to fall when they do. He looks beaten down and confused, and I want to reach out and hug him, even though I know that's so inappropriate. It's like the fire in him from earlier this morning has been extinguished, snuffed out.

We stare at each other in the dim light for longer than we should as a mil-lion things I should say come to mind and then fade. He won't listen. It'd be unwanted, unheard, lip service.

And I have never given lip service to clients just to make them feel better, so why would I attempt to with him? If I lie to them about things we both know aren't true, how would they ever trust me when it really matters?

"Leave it, Dekker." His voice is a soft rumble as he walks past me.

"Hunter!" I hate the desperation that rings in my voice but can't help it.

But he doesn't stop.

He keeps on walking.

⌒

"That sigh of yours is heavy, Dekk. It always is when you're overthinking things. What's on your mind, kid?" My dad's voice sounds like comfort coming through the line and as much as I'm frustrated at him, a smile turns up a small part of my lips.

"Are you trying to set me up?"

"What?" he asks. "Don't be ridiculous."

But I'm not being ridiculous.

It's all I thought about as I wandered through the tunnels of the arena waiting for one of my clients on the opposing team to finish with his press interviews so I could have a quick check-in with him.

My conclusion was this. "I'm the only one of the four of us you sent to recruit, Dad. Lennox told me you haven't given the rest of them clients to steal yet."

"Because it's not the right time."

"I call bullshit." I fold my arms over my chest and stare out the window of my hotel. The skyline of the city is dotted with buildings and lights in the moonless night.

"Hunter was the most urgent. He's up for a contract negotiation in a few months and with them so close to competing for the Cup, it's a good time to be ready to poach."

"Uh-huh."

"What?" He sounds like the voice of innocence. "Did you piss him off? Is that why he played like shit tonight?"

"That right there!" I all but jump. "You never watch hockey, it's not your sport, but you watched tonight's game? That's suspect."

"It was on the TV while I worked through some contracts." His chuckle fills the line. "And, sweetie, I watch all sports."

I chew the inside of my cheek as I listen to him turn the water on and then off, now wondering if my thoughts ran away with me earlier. "You're up to something." *I know it.*

"How about you be *up to* telling me what's going on there?"

"Nothing to report," I say, willing to give him a reprieve momentarily, because I do want to talk to him about Hunter.

"But your silence says you have thoughts."

"I do." I nod. "I think he's definitely burned out and can't see the forest for the trees."

"Meaning?"

"Meaning, there's a catalyst that's causing it."

"Like?"

"Getting to the playoffs? His future with the Jacks? Something," I murmur more to myself than to him.

"So what are you going to do?"

I lean my hip against the back of the couch and eye the sandwich I brought back for a very late dinner and think for a second. "Make him fall back in love with the game somehow. He's too important to the franchise and maybe he's feeling the pressure."

"That's what I would do."

Is it stupid that such simple affirmation from my dad still makes me grin ear to ear?

"Now to figure out what to do."

"You'll sort it out. You always do," he says. "It's getting late—"

"Not so soon, Kincade. Nice try. Now about you picking me to go after Hunter." I purse my lips and wait for an answer.

"I promise you, it's because I know you're the right one to handle him."

My mind flashes to the other night. To my hand wrapped around his cock and my tongue slipping through his lips. To how bad I screwed things up and how much Hunter called me on it.

My cheeks fill with heat as I fumble over what to say to my dad. "I'm not one hundred percent sure I believe you."

His laughter fills the line. "Good. Then it'll keep you on your toes. Night, Dekk." Without another word, he hangs up on me.

All I can do is laugh into my empty hotel room and shake my head. The worst thing about my dad is also probably the best thing about my dad. I can never stay mad at him.

I'm spending too much time with my thoughts.

Way too much time.

But the one lingering thought remains as I eat my sandwich. If Lennox saw how I felt about Hunter when I rarely acknowledged that we were together, wouldn't my dad have too?

That's the million-dollar question.

Chapter
SEVENTEEN

Dekker

KINCADE SPORTS MANAGEMENT
Internal Memorandum
New Recruit Status Report

*denotes urgent status
***denotes Dear Dekker isn't answering us and we're going to raid her chocolate stash while she's gone until she does.

Athlete	Team	Sport	Agent	Status
Carl Ryberg	n/a	Golf	Kenyon	In talks
Jose Santos	D-Backs	Baseball	Chase	face-to-face mtg
Lamar Owens	Bulls	Basketball	Lennox	Contracted. YES!
Michelle Nguyen	n/a	Soccer	Brexton	Coming to KSM Tues.
*Hunter Maddox	Jacks	Hockey	Dekker	***Hello? Anybody home?*

Chapter

EIGHTEEN

Dekker

"WHEN YOU ASKED ME TO TAKE A RIDE WITH YOU, SHOULD I HAVE known you were planning on kidnapping me?" Hunter asks from his place beside me in the passenger seat. "Or is this your attempt to finish what you started the other night?"

As much as I want to make a witty comment, I just flip the blinker and smile.

It took me half the morning to figure out how to make Hunter realize he was burned out. Even trickier is showing him without mentioning the words.

Athletes are superstitious. They don't shave if they're winning. They don't step on lines when they walk on the field. They wear the same, but washed (hopefully), undergarments if they had a great game in them. And they never speak aloud certain terms: no-hitter, perfect game, burnout, etcetera.

So I had my work cut out for me to show and not tell.

Even more so, I don't know if Hunter even knows he's burned out so if I did tell him, I'm assuming he'll fight me on it.

And fighting me is exactly what I don't want.

When I asked him to take a ride with me, I'd already made the promise to myself that no matter what he did or said to antagonize or irritate me, I was going to smile and let it go.

We could get along outside of the bedroom.

I was determined to prove that to myself on a personal level and to him on a professional one.

That's the only way I have any chance of convincing him I know what's best for him and once he knows that, trusting me as an agent would fall into line.

Heading east on Wheelock Street, I glance his way. "I never said how far the ride was going to be."

"Good thing it's an off day or else I'd be missing my game," he mutters, but there's humor in his voice as the lights of the college come into view on our left and the arena is just coming into our sights on our right. It's dark outside, but co-eds mingle on the sidewalk and common areas as the streetlights cast their glow around them.

"When in Hanover, right?"

"When in Hanover, what? Kidnap a hockey player and take them to . . . where in the hell are we exactly?" he asks.

"Dartmouth. We're at Dartmouth College to be exact."

I see the jolt of his body. "Okay." He draws the word out as I pull into a packed parking lot and get lucky and find a space right off the bat. "I was never good at school, Kincade. You're making me get all itchy just thinking about having to sit in a classroom."

"What? You hate having someone tell you what to do and how to do it? That's a shocker." I shift the gear into park. "Here, wear this." I reach into the back seat and toss a baseball cap at him and wait for his response.

"No way!" He shakes his head and throws the LA Kings hat off his lap like it's a hot potato. "Are you crazy?" His laughter fills the cab and I pause and take it in. It's not a sound I hear often from him. "I can't wear that."

"Why not? You'd be supporting the NHL." I pick it up and try to put it on his head.

"No," he cries and grabs my wrists as I struggle with him playfully. "I will not be a traitor. I will not."

"I'm going to take a picture and post it all over social media."

"Never," he shouts as he begins tickling me to distract me from my efforts. I squeal as I fall awkwardly across the center console so that my chest is on top of his.

Breaths panting and lips inches from each other in the small space, our eyes meet and hold as the protests die on our lips.

"Dekker." My name is a quiet assault to my ears even after all the shouting. In those two syllables, I hear so many things. Are they real or am I making them up?

Kiss me.

The thought is in my head as I struggle to slow my thoughts. As I fight the urge to lean in and taste him.

But his lips are right there. His body is warm and inviting beneath my hands pressed to his chest. And the memory of just how good we can be together is front and center in my mind.

His eyes flicker to my lips and then back to my eyes.

A horn blares in the aisle behind us and we both jump back like two kids caught necking in the school lot.

"Saved by the bell," he murmurs into the silence of the cab as he turns the

Kings hat over in his hand. I sit with my back against the door and watch his fingers play over the embroidery.

"You ready?" I ask the question, but neither of us move as we sit in the silence.

"Why are we here again?"

"Here as in the car or here as in more of a philosophical way?" I dodge.

"Dekker?" he growls, and I laugh.

"Because sometimes a change of scenery is good for perspective." The comment is innocent but the insinuation is there, and the way he looks over at me, blue eyes shielded in the shadows, says he caught it.

"What exactly are we talking about here, Dekker?"

Chills chase over my skin as we stare at each other. Nerves. They run rampant as I debate how honest to be with him.

We're talking about you needing to remember why you play the game.

We're talking about you needing a new agent who appreciates you.

We're talking about you and me deserving a second chance.

But none of those reasons fall from my lips. Nope. Instead, I chicken out and give him the answer that will satisfy him. For now.

"I need to watch a prospective client's game. I thought you might want to watch him and provide some feedback."

He narrows his eyes and shakes his head. "What?" The word comes out in a disbelieving laugh.

"Humor me," I say and turn to look in the back seat. "I think I have a beanie. Would a beanie work?" I ask as I begin to rummage through the travel bag I have there.

"Why do I need a hat?" he asks as I produce a nondescript black beanie.

"Voila!" I hold it up. "You need a beanie because you're not here to be Hunter Maddox, the hockey god. You're here to be Hunter, an average guy with an even more average-sized dick who's going to enjoy a game simply to enjoy a game."

He eyes me for the longest time and I wait for him to say something, for him to express the caution fleeting through his eyes, but he nods and slowly slides the beanie over his head. "But it's more than average in size. This beanie-wearing guy might be average, but his dick definitely isn't."

I laugh. "I should've known you'd say that."

He shrugs. "Average guys need all the love they can get."

"Let's go, bigger-than-average Hunter," I joke and open the door, needing the blast of the cold air to shock me to my senses from realizing that we're actually getting along. And from thinking how much I want a second chance with him . . . despite how he hurt me the first time.

But is it hurt when you both go into a situation with the same expectations and yours change? How is he to blame for that?

Jesus, Dekk. Get over it. *Get over him.*

But it's been three years and obviously, I haven't. What exactly does that mean?

Our shoulders bump as we walk through the lot like other college co-eds on their way to one of the biggest games of their season against Dartmouth.

"Wait." Hunter tugs on my hands and stops me so I can look at him. "Why in the hell do you have a Kings hat in your car?"

"I have clients on most teams."

"So, what? You dress the part at their games?"

I shrug and offer a coy smile. "Sometimes."

"You've been on the road with us this whole stretch. I've yet to see you wear a LumberJacks hat."

"I'll only wear one once they've won the cup."

"Ohhhhhhhh," he says and then bursts out laughing. "Fucking brutal."

But his laughter as we head toward the arena is all I focus on.

It's all I hear.

It's all I want.

Chapter
NINETEEN

Dekker

"YOU SURE YOU DON'T WANT ONE?" HUNTER ASKS AS HE SLIDES A PINT of beer onto the table. The tavern is dim with Dartmouth paraphernalia lining its walls and teeming with college students excited after tonight's win.

We found a seat in the back corner where we can blend into its dark edges and hopefully have a drink incognito. I'm surprised we've skated by this far, pun intended, without anyone recognizing him.

"You drink. I'm the designated driver tonight." I take a sip of my Diet Coke and laugh.

"What?" he asks

"I'm just thinking of how confused that poor lady was until we convinced her you're Hunter Maddox's twin."

His smile is tinged with sadness and I hate that I put it there. Maybe I was too caught up in the moment during the game to see it then, but I definitely see it now. "I'm sorry. I didn't mean—how is your brother?" I ask, feeling like a heel. There's not much I know about Jonah Maddox other than Hunter thinks the world of his twin, and that he became a quadriplegic after a car accident in their teens.

His brother is a topic Hunter rarely speaks about. In interviews and relaxed conversations, he keeps anything about Jonah close to his vest. I'd probably be the same if it was one of my sisters, let alone a twin.

"He's fine." He takes a sip and looks around at the patrons having a good time. "You were quick on your feet with that lady, Kincade," he says. "Thanks."

"You have to be in this job."

A cheer goes up in the bar as some of the Dartmouth hockey team walks in and Hunter's face lights up at the sound of it. He watches the Dartmouth forward I was scouting walk in and shakes his head ever so subtly.

"Give that kid a couple of years and he'll be getting the same reception when he walks into The Tank after a game."

"You think?" I ask, even though I already know the answer—the kid's that good. But more than anything, I'm happy Hunter's engaging with me on this.

"Yeah. The kid has it. Skill and that star quality that has you on the edge of your seat waiting to see what he's going to wow you with next."

"Kind of like another forward I know," I murmur with a lift of my brows. I catch the hitch in his movement as he brings the beer to his lips. But he lets the comment go. He doesn't push or prod or live for the praise that many athletes I've repped need to continually boost their egos.

Hunter's different. He'd rather fade into the background than be the center of attention. I've always been curious why a man so brash in personality and bold in his play, hides from the limelight. As if he's not worthy of such praise. Ridiculous.

"Your dad doing good?" he asks. "Your sisters still a pain in your ass?"

I nod, surprised he's asking. Small talk was never our thing and this feels surprisingly normal, but maybe we're stepping into new territory. "They're always pains in my ass but isn't that how it goes?" I laugh and think of Lennox and our conversation the other night about the man in front of me, and I have a sudden pang of homesickness. Sure, we fight and annoy each other, but there's a comfort in knowing they're there. In knowing we might tell each other we hate each other one moment, but the next, they'd have my back if I needed them to. "We're all just super busy, always all over the place to tell you the truth."

He chuckles. "Is that your polite way of saying you guys still don't get along?"

I run my fingers up and down the condensation on my glass and let the water pool around the coaster. "It's not that we don't get along." I sigh and try to put it into words so that someone on the outside of our family dynamic might get it. "I mean, we all care about each other but there's a lot of resentment there. I—it wasn't my choice to be the mom when my mom died. I was the oldest, so with my dad off all the time with clients, trying to provide for us . . . sure, we had a nanny, but the discipline and rules and shit fell on me for some reason."

"That had to have been hard losing her when you were young."

I avert my gaze from his and look at the bubbles moving up the side of my Diet Coke. What no one truly understood was that I was never allowed to grieve. To have her be there healthy one day and the next be gone when the aneurism hit without warning. I remember feeling so damn lost and alone. I had responsibilities and emotions way beyond most teenagers, but no one knew I cried myself to sleep every single night. No one saw me turn over the pillow because the case was soaked from the tears I shed.

No one knew how desperately lonely I was.

"It was devastating." I scrunch my nose to abate the tears and then push away the sadness as I've learned to do. "For all of us."

When he meets my eyes, there's a compassion I've never seen before from him and as welcome as it is, I'm glad when he breaks the moment by speaking. "Why haven't your sisters realized you were just stepping up?" he asks. "They're old enough to know better."

"I'm sure they do . . . and we're all working on healing from the trauma of it all, but we're so damn different. It's like each one of us are different directions on a compass that will never see eye to eye except in those rare moments. For us though, it worked. I mean, our individualism was good because it gave our dad something to have with each of us . . . but it also caused a competitive dynamic that was toxic in a sense."

"Something will happen that will make you all realize none of the differences mean shit. You'll realize the fights are love disguised. The competition is fate's way of making you want more. The laughter is something you'll hold on to in your darkest moments. And eventually, you'll reach a point where you appreciate each other and the rest will be white noise."

I stare at him, his poignant words so unexpected, and wonder where this wisdom comes from. There are so many things I want to say to him, least of all how beautiful his comment is . . . but I know that's not something he'd readily accept. "Maybe we should already realize that after losing our mom. Then again, maybe we're just a houseful of stubborn women who'll figure it out someday."

"Hey man," a waiter says as he slides a fresh beer across the table before patting Hunter on the shoulder. "It's on the house. Your secret's safe with me. Enjoy your beer in peace."

Hunter laughs and shakes his head. "Thanks, man. Appreciate it." They shake hands and then the waiter moves to another table.

But when I look back to Hunter, he's leaning back in his seat, more relaxed than I've seen him this whole road trip, and a soft smile is on his face as he studies me.

"What made you think to bring me with you tonight?" he asks after a beat.

"Just a hunch."

"A hunch?"

"Yeah. Like I said earlier, sometimes it's good to get a different perspective on things."

"You're talking in circles, Dekk. You tend to do that when you don't want to answer something."

"Tell me," I say. "From the last few hours, what's the first thing that comes to your mind?"

"Besides the fear you were kidnapping me?"

"Besides that," I say with a nod.

"Tennis balls," he says through a laugh.

The same laugh I've heard all night. While he pointed things out to me about the game. Insights I might never have caught as I wouldn't have known. When he took the tennis balls the people sitting next to us offered and tossed them on the ice as is the school tradition upon the team's first goal against their rival Princeton.

He was booing and laughing and pointing at the torrent of balls bounding around the ice. It was the most carefree I've heard him, and another clue that I might just be right about him being burned out.

"It's the craziest thing I've ever seen, and that's coming from a man who's had the damn octopus flung within feet of him during a game against the Red Wings."

"I've been to the Dartmouth-Princeton game a few times. Sometimes for fun, others for recruiting purposes. It's the best when those tennis balls get tossed. Chaos and comradery. There's nothing like a rivalry, like playing a sport simply because you love it, like being a part of something so steeped in tradition."

"Ah," he says and tips his glass up, but his eyes don't leave mine. "Is this where we return to talking in circles?" His tone is playful but his eyes warn me to tread lightly.

I could have figured as much.

"No circles. I just thought after the last game, you needed a night away from the guys."

"So you took me to more hockey." There's amusement in his voice.

"I did." I shrug unapologetically. "It was an off night before the team moves on to Boston, I had to check out that kid, and so I thought . . . why not bring one of the best along."

"The best? You keep complimenting me, Kincade, I'm going to start thinking you actually mean it."

"Maybe I do." Our eyes meet, hold; there's a silence between us that stretches with equal parts comfort and flirting.

"That's why you kidnapped me?" He reaches out and tucks a piece of hair behind my ear. "And here I thought it was for you to use me for your own devious pleasures."

"Devious pleasure?" I laugh, but hell if that slow, sweet ache doesn't come to life at the apex of my thighs thinking about Hunter and pleasure.

"So good it's dangerous."

"Jesus!" I laugh. "Yes, that's it. I kidnapped you and then twisted your arm so I could take full advantage of you."

"Tasered me too."

"Was it that bad? Is going with me so brutal that tasering is the only option?"

He leans forward and puts his elbows on the table, and for a moment

I think he's going to kiss me. I freeze and then feel ridiculous when he does nothing more than murmur, his voice a low rumble. "You want to know the best part of the game?"

"Hmm?" I'm surprised by his sudden change of topic but entranced not only by his voice, but by how content he seems.

"Everything I do, everywhere I go, someone wants something from me. Time, talent, notoriety, you name it. Do you know how nice it was to go to a game and just enjoy it? To be amazed by talent and laugh at tennis balls and to sit in the stands where no one knew who I was or demanded something of me?"

"I can't imagine," I murmur and feel like a traitorous asshole, because *I* want something from him.

"Part of it's the Cup, you know."

"What do you mean?"

"That's why Ian and the Jacks gave me such a huge contract," he says, referring to the LumberJacks general manager. "It's on my shoulders to deliver the Cup in return."

I laugh at the ludicrousness of that. "Any agent worth their salt wouldn't agree to those terms." I shake my head and place another mental tic next to why Sanderson is an asshole. Commission, first. Client's well-being, second. "What happens if you don't deliver?" I ask, and the only response I get is the twitch of that muscle in his jaw. Curiosity owns me, and while I understand that companies acquire benchmark players to build on, no one can guarantee a Stanley Cup.

"It doesn't have to be written in the contract to know what's expected of me," he says answering my unspoken question.

"Winning is expected of every player." I laugh, but it falls when I see the gravity in his expression. "That's why you play the game, right? That's why every player is out there on the ice. No one forms a team hoping they'll be mediocre."

"The teams without the big purse strings do."

"You're missing my point, Hunter." I shake my head and lean back and stare at him. Now, he looks like the weight of the world is on his shoulders, and I wish I could take it all away. "Do you know how many exceptional players never won the Cup? I can list a ton of them."

"So can I, and my name would be one of them."

"Your career has been phenomenal. Even if you never win the Cup—"

"Don't bullshit me, Dekker. You can be the greatest there ever was, but if you don't ever win, it doesn't mean shit. The greats win the Cup. More than once. So that was our deal. He paid me a ridiculous amount of money, and expects me to build the team around me that will help win the Cup for the first time in franchise history."

"You're staring down your first playoff berth. I'd say the team you built around you is working just fine." But at what cost, I wonder. "What is there, fifteen games left in the season?"

"Yes."

"That's a hell of a lot of pressure," I murmur more to myself than to him.

"You have no fucking idea." He sighs. "And we're almost there. We're so close I can all but taste it . . . but, fuck if I know if we can do it."

"What do you mean?" I ask, reaching out and putting my hand on his to stop him from pulling away.

"Never mind. It's nothing." His smile is tight as he downs the rest of the beer. "It's late. We should get going. It's a long drive back."

I sigh as he scoots his stool out and goes to close out his tab, because I feel like we were making genuine headway. The positive in this? My hunch was right. Hunter Maddox has reached his emotional limit, and he doesn't know how to admit it to himself.

Instead, he's angry. He acts out. He burns the candle at both ends. For a man who prefers to fade into the background, he's the face of a team who I think is going to take center stage in the coming weeks.

How is he going to handle it? Because if his reaction to the pressure he's under now is any indication, it's not going to be good.

Will helping him realize he's burned out help the situation or hurt it?

Chapter
TWENTY

Dekker

"JUST SAY IT."

The fight he's angling for, the one I can sense in his tone of voice and how he's pulled into himself and thoughts since we parked, I don't really have the energy to give.

"Say what?" I ask as I glance over to Hunter as we walk through the parking lot toward the hotel entrance. It's been a long drive, it's late, and I'm beat.

"Whatever the fuck it is that has been on your mind since we left the bar."

"Who said I had anything to say?"

"You've always been shit at hiding your emotions. You think you're so good at it—a hard-ass—but they're on your sleeve when it comes to me."

"You're such a liar."

"Huh. Then I guess the last time I saw you *before*, when you walked out of the hotel, I misread you and had you pegged all wrong."

"What's that supposed to mean?" Caution vibrates through me.

"It means you walked out because you broke the rules."

My feet falter, and I have a hard time swallowing as his words hit my ears. "Broke what rules?" I feign ignorance.

He takes a step closer to where I've stopped and stares at me. I'm glad for the cover of the night, but I don't think it's going to mask the sudden anxiety I have about where he's going with this. "You tell me."

Our gazes hold in an awkward dance where it seems he doesn't want to follow through with whatever accusation he'd planned. I don't want to open Pandora's box.

I'm not sure what's worse, him telling me he knew I had feelings for him or me realizing he knew *and* let me walk away without saying a word.

I shake my head when I realize why he made the comment. Such a Hunter thing to do. Dodge. Deflect. Turn the topic around to the opposition by changing the subject so he doesn't have to answer and be the one to open himself up. Classic fucking Maddox.

I'm glad I didn't say anything. I'm glad I didn't give him the distraction he was angling for and answers he might not have realized.

"Tell me something," I ask, bracing my hands on my hips.

"Nothing good ever came from a sentence starting like that." He crosses his arms over his chest, already on the defensive.

"You're the one who came after me, so why can't I ask you a question in turn?"

His exasperated sigh fills the silence around us. "Look, it's been a good night. We had fun. We didn't kill each other, which is always a bonus when it comes to us, and while it's a good thing, it's also kind of unnerving because *it's us*, right?" He chuckles but there's an exhaustion to it. "Just let whatever it is go that you need to know and don't ruin the night, okay?"

"What do you do in the off season?" I ask.

He laughs in protest. "I'm not doing this, Dekker. This isn't the discussion we're having."

"Just . . . humor me. Please. I . . . please." I reach out to grab his arm to stop him when he begins to walk, but I see the minute his shoulders fall and know he's going to give me an inch here. "It's not a trick question. It's just . . . what do you do in the off season?"

"Practice. Work out. Practice some more." His arms fall to his sides.

"And in your downtime?"

"Study hockey, film, opponents, weaknesses." He says the words like I should know this—*and I do*—but I need him to hear it. I need him to listen to himself and realize his single-minded focus.

"And what else do you do besides hockey?"

"What is it I do?"

"Yeah, besides twenty-four/seven hockey, what else do you enjoy doing?"

The crooked grin that crawls over his lips and the way his eyes scrape down the V of my shirt and back up has me shaking my head.

"We could go upstairs and I could show you exactly what I enjoy."

While my body reacts viscerally to his words, my head remembers his complete rejection from the other night.

"I'm sure we could, but that's not part of this conversation." I shake my head. "Seriously. What do you do besides hockey and the one-night stands?"

"Two-night stands."

"Funny. I'm serious."

He stares at me. "Plenty."

I bark out a laugh but the sound settles as he stares at me.

"You asked me why I took you to the Dartmouth game tonight. You asked me to stop talking in circles . . . so I've stopped . . ." Every part of me prepares for the fallout from what I'm going to say. My shaky inhale reflects it. "You're burned out, Hunter—fucking fried—and you need to recharge your engine somehow—"

"No, I'm not." He physically rejects the words as if taking two steps back from me is going to help do that.

"It's okay to say it. There's no shame in it."

Another partial laugh. An opening of his mouth and then shutting it, but I see the sudden panic in his eyes. I hear it in the vibrato of his laugh.

"This is the last thing I need right now. Do you know that? Do you get the shitstorm I'm about to walk into tomorrow?"

"Tomorrow?"

"Do you know—fuck," he barks, his body tense, the can of worms I've opened expected but unknown. He walks a few feet away and laces his fingers on the back of his neck. "This is the last damn thing I need. Why couldn't you leave well fucking enough alone, huh?"

"Hunter. I'm sorry. I don't know what you're talking about, but I—"

"You're goddamn right you don't," he thunders as he glares at me, probably oblivious to the couple on the other side of the parking lot. But I care and hate to know what they're thinking as they glance our way several times. "Do you know how stupid that sounds?"

"How stupid what sounds?"

"That I no longer *love* hockey."

His words stagger me. Burning out because of the relentless nature of the sport and trying to be your best versus hating that sport are two completely different things. But standing here, seeing him struggle, I know he can't see the difference or separate himself from it . . . and it breaks my heart. There are tears in his eyes weighted with a mixture of shame and confusion and anger. It's almost as if uttering those words—that he's lost his love of hockey—is an admission that his identity has been stolen, and he's not sure how to navigate his way back to it.

I struggle between offering him tough love or sympathy and know that it seems that neither is going to cut it. Taking a step toward him, I try to reason with hm.

I no longer love hockey.

"You don't mean that—"

"You're goddamn right I do," he shouts, arms out to his sides. "But it's so much more than that. So much more than I could ever explain."

It's that little break in his voice on the last word—and the defeat that eats up his posture—that nearly undoes me and makes me want to wrap my arms around him to take away the hurt that owns his eyes.

"Try me." I take a step closer. "I'm here. I'm—"

"You're what? You're going to waltz in here with your positive attitude and magic wand and put everything back to fucking perfect again? No offense, Dekk, but it's the last thing I want or need from you. The shit that's broken can't be fixed. The damage done can't be reversed. All I can do is ride the fucking wave and make the best of it."

"At least let me be there for you." His laugh is hollow and raw and eats away at me. I get he's a man not used to talking about feelings, but he needs to know. "Just know it's a normal thing that most professional athletes experience at one time or another during their career. I mean, how can you not burn out? How can you play day after day and—"

"That's enough!" His voice thunders through the parking lot. His words suggest he's not listening, but the expression on his face—fear and uncertainty—shows me that he hears me. He knows I'm right. He's just too proud and stubborn and masculine, too scared to admit defeat. Like many, he sees it as a sign of weakness.

As a sign of failure.

But failure of what is the question?

"Who do you think you are, playing shrink with me?"

"I'm the furthest thing from a shrink." I take a step toward him. "We need to help you remember why you loved the game in the first place."

"Who's this *we*, crap?"

"You. I mean you. I just thought I could help—"

"So that's what tonight was about, right? It wasn't about just letting me go watch a game. It wasn't about letting me get away from the guys for a bit and be me, and not just a captain. It was to show and make me see that I can love the game in a different way." The protest dies on my tongue when I see the tears of frustration glistening in Hunter's eyes. "Like I said, there are always strings attached. Always an ulterior motive. Always something someone wants from me and this time, no fucking surprise, it's you—"

"Will you listen to yourself?" I shout.

"What? The alternative is listening to you?" His voice beats mine out.

"I don't want to fight. All I want to do is help you however I can. Saying you're burned out isn't an admission of—"

"Isn't an admission of what? You don't think I know millions would kill to be in my shoes? You don't think I know how fucking crazy it sounds for me to complain about living the dream? Who the hell needs a break from the game or thing they love? Who the hell says fuck you to the thing that has defined and saved them?" He walks a few feet the other way and the low, guttural chastisement he emits is heartbreaking. "I'm thirty-two years old and every goddamn day is a grind. Every day is me chasing a ghost I'll never surpass in certain eyes. Each day is me faking it for the fans that I'm the person they think I am. *Christ.* How many days will it be until they see I'm a fraud? Until they realize I'm smoke and mirrors and only trying to live up to the expectations others have of me?"

He's saying things I don't understand now, but I don't interrupt. I close my mouth and let him rant on things I can only partially comprehend but emotionally can fathom.

He's like a little boy. One who hears the truth but rejects it on principle.

"Hey." My voice is calm and soothing as I step beside him. My hands itch to pull him into a hug, to touch him somehow, to calm him. "I know you don't want to hear this, but I really need you to. I understand everything that you've said. The why. The how is it possible. The *what an ass* I *would be to feel this way*. And all of that's valid to someone on the outside . . . but you're on the inside looking out, Hunter, and what you feel is valid too. I mean, isn't that why you're struggling? The *how can you complain* or be sick of it when it's most people's dream job . . . but it's just that, *a job*. You can be the best in the world at something, be on top of your game, and still burn out. It's human. It's—"

"And I'm sure you have the cure for it, right?" Gone is the emotion etched in the lines of his face. His mask has been put back on, feelings under lock and key. The anger replaced by sarcasm. The confusion traded for denial.

It takes everything I have not to grab his shoulders and shake him to make him listen to me. I'm frustrated and hurt that he's shut down.

"I don't have any answers. All I can say is that you need more balance. You need to be Hunter Maddox, the guy who likes to watch movies or cook or I don't know what it is you might like to do, but you can have an identity that's outside of hockey while still being Hunter Maddox the hockey star to everyone else."

"Oh, don't look now, but here comes Detailed Dekker and her perfect answers for everything to the rescue. Well, news flash, I don't need to be saved. I don't need them or their pressure. I don't need fucking anyone, and I sure as hell don't need you."

His words hit me one after another. Most making sense, some not, and I concentrate on who he means by *them*, but refrain from asking.

His shoulders heave with anger as our eyes hold. The white smoke from his breath disappears.

When I speak, my voice is the antithesis of his. It's calm, even, unemotional. "That's not what I was trying to do. All I was—"

"Save it, Kincade. Fucking save it." He waves a hand at me and shakes his head. "I've had enough of this shit. Thanks for ruining tonight when I told you to let it go."

Without another word, he turns on his heel and heads to the entrance of the hotel.

That whole conversation was a disaster. Total and utter disaster.

And I'm not a single step closer to figuring out what it is that weighs so heavily on his shoulders.

Chapter
TWENTY-ONE

Hunter

"We didn't get a chance to speak to you after the other night's game, any comment on the marked difference in your performance or were you just having an off night?"

The game feels like light years ago already. What was it? Only three days? Four? Fuck if I can remember.

Through the blinding lights I can just make out my agent, Finn Sanderson, at the back of the press briefing room. His arms are crossed over his chest, his back is against the wall, and it seems like his eyes never leave me.

Management called in the big guns to control me. Jünger must be worried I'll let him down and not heed his threats.

Hell, maybe they were smart considering we're in my hometown and avoidance is at its finest.

"Everybody has an off night. Apparently that game was mine," I say, giving the company line Sanderson drilled in my head right after his numerous threats about how if I keep my shit up, I'm going to be benched or suspended and lose him as an agent. While I'm pretty sure his warnings about losing endorsement deals are a load of crap said to instill fear in me, the benching me part might be true enough. "Let's hope I can shake off the bad juju and get back into the groove tonight."

"Are you worried how that loss is going to matter to the Jacks in the standings?"

I move the microphone back and try to find who asked the question but have a hard time seeing through the lights.

"Every game matters. Every win, every loss. I've been playing in this league long enough to know a one-goal loss in the first week of the season can be the determining factor to how your season ends when you never realized it. Lucky for us, the Nomads lost too so we had an even night on paper."

You're burned out, Hunter—fucking fried.

Dekker's words replay in my head for the millionth time since they passed her lips, and I try to shake them off. I know it's true. Obviously, she knows it's true.

But goddamn it, the reason why is something I can't fix.

I've tried.

Jesus, have I tried.

"Mr. Maddox, over here." The female reporter's voice rings out and knocks Dekker's voice from my head. I blink a few times into the light and then hold my hand over my eyes so I can look in her direction. "Hello. Hi."

Rookie reporter. They always ramble when they're new.

"Hello."

"Um, yes. Um . . . Vida Henson with Sports Worldwide. You seem to have been on a tear lately. You're closing in on two NHL records in rapid time. Are you doing anything different this year to make such strong improvements to your game?"

Yeah, my brother's dying.

"Good question."

And I helped kill him.

I stare at the lights and shake my head as I fight back the truth that haunts me every day of my life. At the crushing weight of it.

"I've been . . . training differently," I lie. "I added on some new members to my team outside of the club to help bring out my potential, and I—uh—guess they deserve a raise because it seems to be working."

I say a few more things, but I'm distracted.

Maybe it's being back in the same city I grew up in.

Maybe it's knowing I have to go home and face reality.

Maybe it's because . . .

"Mr. Maddox? Randy Girdley with Headline Sports. You grew up not far from here, are there any places you like to frequent when you get to come back home?"

The stretch of road where my life changed forever.

The cemetery to pay my respects.

Dekker wasn't completely right.

It's so much more than being burned out.

I blink a few times as the room shifts and moves around me, and I try to fight those first few terrifying moments when the path my life was on changed forever.

Your game is shit tonight, son. You should be embarrassed of how you played.

Facing my dad.

Yeah, that's another place I can't fucking wait to go, *home.*

I force a smile and let a laugh fall. Anything to draw them away from the truth. "Everyone has their places when they return home." I scoot my chair back and stand.

"Like?" he counters.

"My schedule is always packed when I come here, so I rarely have time to venture from it. Of course, my training and the team comes first, but then there's a visit to Boston's Children's Hospital, some time spent with the kids at the Elite 9 Rink to answer their questions. A few other things to help pay it back or help the game move forward. Busy. Busy." Another smile to sell the lie. "Thank you for your time. I hope to see you all at the game tonight."

I'm through the door to my right as more questions are fired off, my feet moving from one side to the other while I try to settle the discord eating me whole.

Why is this so hard this time? Why does it feel like all the oxygen is being sucked out of every breath I try to take?

Within seconds, Sanderson comes through the same door I just did. "Everyone has their places?" He chuckles. "It came off like you meant a brothel or some shit."

If he only knew.

"I danced in the dog and pony show you set up, isn't that enough? You want me to focus on the game tonight and play my hardest, then isn't it time I go so I can prepare for it? I did what you said and you're still crawling up my ass."

"I asked you this the other day when your GM called me and told me to straighten your shit out and you dodged it, and I'm going to ask you again: what the fuck is going on with you? You answered their questions, but your smile said *fuck you*. The bad-boy act only flies so far. Are you trying to throw away your career, the stats, and records you've almost reached?"

"I played nice. Now I'd like to go study films. The Fishers have a new defense they've been toying with and I need to make sure I've got it figured out," I say of the team we're playing tonight.

He nods as he studies me. "Good to see your head is back in the game."

"It never left it."

"You're the face of this team, Maddox. A lot is riding on you."

My face is, but it should be Jonah's heart and body.

"So you've said," I mutter and look out the window of the otherwise empty room.

"Mind answering why you seemed so distracted? Why you keep moving around like you can't sit still? Jünger was concerned the Oxy you were taking for your knee is—"

"Fuck this." Fed up with the accusation, I go to walk past him and he reaches out and grabs my arm. I yank it the hell away. "Get the fuck off me, Finn. You think I'm using? Then drug test me. I'm clean. You think I'm drinking?

Hell yeah, I overindulge a time or two, but not any more than anyone else on this team. Maybe my problem is you guys putting your nose in my shit when I've told you to back the fuck off."

"My job is to have my nose in your shit and right now, it stinks. Straighten the fuck up."

"Noted." I move toward the door.

"I'm riding out the next few games with you, because I fear what you'll do if I don't, so I suggest you make sure we don't have to have a talk like this again."

When I exit the room without a response and turn the corner, I come face to face with Dekker.

Fucking hell. First him and now her. Both on my ass.

"Whoa! You going somewhere in a hurry?" she asks as we spin around so we're in opposite positions now, and she puts her arms on my bicep to steady herself.

"Yeah. I've got shit to do." A ton of it, in fact. Having too much to do gives me an excuse why going to my parents' house isn't an option until after the game.

That and being busy prevents the ghosts this place conjures every time I come back here from haunting me too much.

"Hunter?" I meet her eyes and it's for a split second too long, because I can tell the minute she sees them—the ghosts—because her hand tightens on my arm. "Hey?"

"Yeah? What?" I take a step back.

"I've texted a few times. You're not responding."

Because if you're the only one who's noticed I'm burned out, I'm afraid if you look any closer you'll see the rest of the truths I hide.

"Been busy." My tone is clipped and my feet shift with impatience.

"I just . . . I wanted to apologize for the other night. I didn't mean to push you. I—"

"Done and fucking over with." I offer a tight smile and hate that seeing her makes me feel so damn rattled. Hating her presence and not wanting her to leave. Frustrated, because it feels like a burden has been lifted that someone else knows and unsettling that she does. *That she can see me.*

She worries her bottom lip between her teeth and shakes her head, her eyes loaded with concern I don't want to see. "Got it. Done and over with. Discussion never happened. Night never happened. No need to repeat it."

But it did. The laughter. The Kings hat. The tennis balls. The beer. The comfortable silence. The solidarity.

"Did you need something else?"

"Just know I'm here for you. If there's anything I can do to help—"

"Do you know what would help? If people stopped fucking telling me that. I'm not a cancer patient. I'm not dying. I'm fine."

She stares at me, her jaw clenching and eyes firing with anger.

I'm reminded immediately of three years ago when she stood in that hotel room, her chin quivering but held high as she fought the emotion in her eyes. As she told me our fling had run its course and that it was best we didn't meet again. As she saved me from having to break her heart that was starting to grow a bit too attached to mine.

Because mine was already fucking there too.

The memory is the last thing I need. To be reminded of what it felt like to be cared for by her. To remember how I had spent too much time convincing myself I didn't deserve someone like her—the feelings, the comfort, the simplicity of it all—only for her to save me by doing it for me.

Only to prove to me just how much of an asshole I am. I never chased her, told her she was wrong . . . because I let her walk away.

She struggles momentarily with her emotions before the businesswoman façade slides back into place and she takes a step back.

"It makes sense now."

"What's that?" I ask.

"You don't want to hear what I said the other night, but you want to play the victim. News flash," she says, mocking what I said to her. "You—"

"Christ, Hunter." I look up to see Sanderson over Dekker's left shoulder, disbelief and disgust etched in the lines of his face. "You told me you were leaving to get your head in the game. Yet here you are, trying to score a cheap fuck like a desperate john."

Before I can respond with the fury that streaks through me, Dekker spins to face him.

"A cheap fuck?" she asks, and Sanderson's face pales when he sees who I'm speaking with. "I'm sure your clients get great publicity when their agent talks to their fans like that." She takes a few steps toward him, a tsk on her tongue. "For the record, Finn, I'm nowhere close to being a cheap fuck, but you'd never know because I wouldn't touch you with a ten-foot pole."

With that, Dekker Kincade saunters down the hotel hallway without looking back. I chuckle quietly. And then I wonder why she's the only person who can put a smile on my face these days.

Chapter

TWENTY-TWO

Dekker

SKATES CARVE UP THE FRESHLY RESURFACED ICE. THE SOUND IS LIKE A symphony of skills and maneuvers you can hear just as easily as you can see.

I watch the LumberJacks go through their warm-ups as the diehard fans arrive early to make sure they catch every second of hockey they can.

A few times I catch Hunter glancing up to where I'm standing in the visiting team's suite. While a small part of me hopes it's because he feels bad for being an ass to me earlier, the rest of me knows he doesn't care.

Hell, the only time Hunter Maddox cared about how I felt was when it came to sensations to get me off.

But I think about his press conference today. About the disconnect I saw him have in his answers and the way he acted when I ran into him afterward.

Guess nothing much has changed about him in that aspect either . . . Even now, I can't figure him out.

"Such a surprise to see you in Boston."

I glance in my periphery to see Finn Sanderson step up beside me, arms folded, the suit he's wearing ridiculously expensive.

"We all have jobs to do," I murmur, not exactly wanting to engage with him, and not just because of his *cheap fuck* comment. I simply don't like the man.

"And some of us are better at those jobs than others, right, Dekker?" His voice is smooth as silk but I know it's laced with arsenic.

He's pushing buttons.

I don't give him the satisfaction of responding.

"What client are you here to babysit?" he asks.

Every word he utters is a reminder of the clients he's taken from us. How he's slowly chipped away at our foundation and it strengthens my resolve that much more. The Kincades will win this fight.

Now, if I could just approach Hunter to see where I stand.

Then again, if Finn keeps sticking his foot in his mouth like he did earlier today with his *cheap fuck* comment, I'll just keep my mouth shut and let him do the convincing for me.

The guys switch drills, and I watch Callum move through the line. He swears his change to a plant-based diet has made all the difference in the past couple of months and a part of me agrees. It seems to have assisted in the fluidity of his movement and his increased stamina. Regardless of the reasons behind it, I'll take it, because his contract is up at the end of the season and I'd love his stats to inch up to help those negotiations in our favor.

I watch them and Finn watches me.

"Should I be worried you're here to steal my clients, Dekker?" he finally asks.

He's pushing buttons.

I snort in response and check a text that came across my phone to play him a bit.

"Is that a yes?" he pushes.

I turn to face him for the first time. I take in his perfectly styled hair and dark gray eyes and all I can think is how he's too perfect, too polished.

I bristle over how much I despise him but the smile on my face shows nothing but indifference.

"It's a nothing. It's a maybe you should be a better agent and then you wouldn't have to worry if your client might jump ship, because you already know they're satisfied."

"Like yours are?"

"I'll let you stand here and be a petty, insecure agent while I go stand over there in shoes I'm more than comfortable in and with a conscience that lets me fall asleep perfectly fine at night." I start to move to the opposite end of the box.

"Tucking your tail between your legs already, Kincade? I thought you'd fight harder than that to keep your clients."

"Prick," I mutter under my breath and welcome the ringing of his cellphone to interrupt this less-than-stimulating conversation.

There is a commotion at my back, and I turn toward the entrance to see a high-tech-looking wheelchair being moved into the suite. I smile at the person who's strapped into the chair out of kindness, but I'm unaware if he sees me or not. Fearing I'm staring, I offer a similar greeting to the woman pushing it. She's older in age, her hair stuck to her cheek and frustration lining her face.

"Do you need any help?" I offer and move toward them, noting the awkwardness of the chair since its occupant is lying back.

"No. I've got it. Thanks," she says with a slight grunt as she moves him to the end of the aisle where the chair can fit with an unobstructed view of the arena.

And it hits me.

That's Jonah. It's Hunter's brother.

I digest the information, trying not to look their way so I can make the connection completely.

Then I debate walking over and introducing myself to them, but figure I should let her get them situated first so my presence doesn't make him feel like I'm there to ogle or so I'm not in the way.

And the whole time I stand there waiting for them to get settled, eyes watching the Jacks warm-up and their actions in my periphery, she murmurs words to who I assume is Jonah as if she's making sure everything is okay.

"Here we are. You comfortable?" She adjusts his arms. "How exciting. Aren't you excited to be here, Jonah? I know you've been waiting forever for this." She flips a switch on the chair and it sits up some. "The Jacks are going to win tonight. I mean, you're here. You're their good luck charm."

She talks to him in a soft, singsongy voice, each sentence of hers competing with the gentle hum of his ventilated breaths, as she fiddles with things on the chair.

"Carla. So great to see you," Finn says before stepping around me.

I turn to watch Carla's face light up as she moves toward him and embraces him in a quick hug. "Mr. Sanderson. I didn't know you'd be here tonight. So good to see you."

Finn moves toward the man in the wheelchair. "Good to see you, Jonah. You excited to watch the game tonight? Your brother has been slaying it. I bet he's going to play like a madman tonight knowing you're here."

Carla reaches her hand out and pats Finn's arm, her eyes and the slight shake of her head saying something I don't understand.

Feeling like I'm eavesdropping but forced to due to proximity, I turn my attention back to the ice, my moment to introduce myself lost.

"Are you taking care of my boy?" she asks.

"You know he doesn't need taking care of." Finn laughs. "I'm sure you saw that for yourself."

"We haven't seen him yet. He said you had him scheduled all day. Maybe after the game tonight." There's sadness in her voice that replaced the excitement from moments earlier.

"Maybe."

Hunter looks up my way again and raises a hand in greeting.

"Hi, honey," Carla says loudly as if Hunter can hear her. "Jonah, Hunter says hi."

"Dekker? Have you met Carla and Jonah Maddox yet?"

I take a few steps to where they're set up. "No, I haven't. I've heard so much about you though," I say with a smile and extend my hand, hoping Sanderson just caught the implication that I'm close with Hunter. "Such a pleasure to meet you."

"Aren't you a pretty little thing," Carla says in the warm and most non-condescending way as she shakes my hand.

"Thank you." I turn to Jonah and suck in a breath. And it's not because of his pale complexion or the trach tube or anything to do with his disability, but rather the fact that he's identical to Hunter. Like exact. The hair, the eyes, the nose . . . it's simply stunning. I force myself not to stare at him for that reason alone and offer a smile. "Nice to meet you, Jonah."

He doesn't respond verbally but his eyes meet mine, and I nod in greeting.

"Carla, this is Dekker Kincade. She's the agent trying to steal your son away from me."

Carla barks out a laugh while I try to figure Finn's angle with the comment. "Well, she already has one up on you," Carla says. "She's a hell of a lot prettier."

Chapter
TWENTY-THREE

Hunter

HE SHOULD BE THE ONE OUT HERE.

The thought is on replay in my head with each pass.

Each shove of the opposition.

Every whack of the puck toward the goal.

He should be the one out here.

The anger in my blood hums with a potency stronger than any drug I've ever been given. It surges and pushes me to take risks I don't even register and beats the shit out of me when whatever I try to do on the ice fails.

He's not doing well, Hunter. Another chest infection. Another blood infection. He's not able to speak anymore. Dr. Masterson says it's only a matter of time, really.

My mom's comment from months ago echoes in my head and causes the split-second fumble of my thoughts and the puck is stripped away from me. *Shit.*

My head.

It's way too fucking busy to be on the ice. Way too much shit going on.

How can I be down here doing this when he's up there like that?

When he damn well knows what ice feels like beneath his skates? When the roar of the crowd was more his drug than it was ever mine? When life ended that night for him and finally began for me?

He should be the one out here.

The thought is the cadence of the fists I throw at Brighton for no reason at all—other than he plays like Jonah used to and it pains me to defend against him and remember—and then later at Vladkin for pushing me from behind like so many others have in my years playing this game.

But tonight is different.

Tonight, I can't deny the pain that burns within. I'm the reason he's not in my skates right now.

The reason hockey feels more like a prison than a job. A game.

The guilt.

Shame.

Self-loathing.

C'mon, Hunter. Tonight's your night.

Those words from my twin so very long ago echo in my ears and ring true now.

Tonight is my night.

Every night is.

And I hate every minute of it.

Chapter
TWENTY-FOUR

Dekker

I WATCH THE GAME FROM THE NOSEBLEED SEATS.

It's where I prefer to sit. My AirPods are in, the local announcers are giving the play-by-play in my ear, and the game unfolds in front of me while I'm wrapped in my own world.

"Look, Bob. I'm not going to complain that Mad Dog Maddox showed up to play tonight, but it does look like there's a little trouble in paradise. Unless I'm mistaken, when Withers came up on him before that last period, I thought Maddox was going to take a swing at his own teammate."

Shit.

Announcers are noticing.

How can they not? When Callum came up to get his attention from behind, Hunter whirled on him with his fist cocked back and so much anger etched in his face, his intention was all but unmistakable.

Management has to see it.

Fans won't be far behind.

"Or maybe you read it all wrong," Bob says.

"I know what it looked like to me and that, mixed with his poor performance last game, has me wondering if he's losing his edge."

"Losing his edge? No way. Not Maddox," Bob counters. "Everyone has an off game."

"An off game is one thing, but there have been rumors during the past few months about discord in the team over Maddox," Steve says.

"Of course there is. The tension is just as high as the expectations over us gunning for the Cup. It's bound to surface somewhere. Besides, you said it yourself, they're just rumors."

"Let's hope the boys can keep it together and bring this thing home for us . . . if not, I'm afraid of the fire sale that might happen."

"Fire sale? Are you implying the Jacks will get rid of Maddox if they don't reach the playoffs?" Bob gasps. "That's blasphemy. Boo, fair-weather fan."

Steve laughs. "That wouldn't be my option of choice, but seriously, how much longer can a club like the Jacks keep a player like Maddox?"

"Let's hope forever." Bob chuckles.

"To be the voice of reason—"

"Fair-weather fan," Bob coughs, and they both laugh.

"Seriously. We're a small-time club with only so much money for salaries. If we're not winning and the seats start going half-empty, we'll never be able to afford a player like him."

"I see what you're saying, but he's a sure thing," Bob says. "He's going to get us that Stanley Cup . . . and he's a Jack now. He's one of us and dammit, we love him."

"Sometimes sure things don't pan out."

"The season's not over yet. Give him time."

Yeah, time to succeed or to fail.

"Action coming back in two minutes, folks. In the meantime, I'll hit Steve over the head for those of you already doing it at home for throwing out into the ether that we might have to trade Maddox away."

"Oh, please. All I'm saying is we—the Jacks—are like the little engine that could. We're having a hell of a season. For the first time, everything has clicked and a huge part of that is because of Maddox's leadership and star power— off games like the other night not included. At what point will a club like the Rangers or the Red Wings with their abundance of cash be able to woo him away?"

"Woo him away?" Bob laughs.

"It's a legitimate question."

"He'd stay here. Lucky for us, he chose to leave one of those big-name teams two years ago to come here. I'm sure he has his own personal reasons why, and yes, while he's had a rough patch these past few months, he's brought this team and our city to life like no other player has in recent memory. My money's on the Jacks on this one. They won't let him get away."

"Yeah, well, let's just hope whatever is going on with him sorts itself out. The subpar game the other night against the Patriots where he played like he was handcuffed, and now this game tonight where he's a one-man wrecking crew . . . it's like night and day."

"You can't have him both ways. He's an all-or-nothing guy."

"Food for thought," Bob says. "We're back in action, Jacks fans. The third period is about to get underway with your Jacks up an impressive four to one."

They drone on as the game picks back up while I lean back in my chair, cross my arms over my chest, and try to figure out what to make of today. Of

Hunter's press conference, of my conversation with Sanderson, meeting Hunter's family, and how he's playing tonight—somewhere between out of control and brilliant. He's a very rich man, but is out there playing like he's starving. He's been in the penalty box more than I've ever seen him before. There's more of an edge to him tonight, and I guarantee that's part of the reason.

His family.

His brother.

Is that part of the drive for him?

I don't need them or their pressure.

Is he living out this dream . . . for the both of them since Jonah can't? The relentless schedule is enough to burn a man out, let alone have the added pressure of trying to do it for another person. Even his family, perhaps.

Is that what he meant by *them* the other night? Or am I way off base and he just meant *them* in general?

With a sigh and needing a break from my own thoughts, I figure it's a great time to stretch my legs. Standing from my seat, I walk back toward the general manager's box to get a refill on my drink. I'm just about to its entrance when I overhear Finn's voice.

"How can you complain? He's tearing it up tonight. The team's winning and we're one step closer to a playoff berth," Finn says. "Fourteen games and counting, but I think you'll have the playoff spot clinched before then."

"He may be tearing it up tonight, but he's also tearing up the team," the unique voice of the LumberJacks General Manager, Ian McAvoy, echoes off the concrete walls and has me perking my ears up. I'm not one for eavesdropping, but I'm definitely one for getting as much information as possible to do my job and the task I was sent here to do.

Even I understand how lame that sounds—standing here in the hall of an arena when I've had several times to tell Hunter exactly why I'm here but have balked every time.

"After the stunt he pulled the other night, Finn, I'm at my limit. The press conference was a Band-Aid, but don't kid yourself into thinking it fixed everything. The calls I received from the commissioner of the league asking me if he was purposely throwing the game tell me they're watching him."

"He wasn't throwing the game. I spoke in depth with him about what that game looked like to everyone else, and I promise you, it won't happen again."

"It better not. I wasn't too thrilled having to explain to the commissioner that Maddox isn't betting against his team, nor is anyone else for that matter. The last thing we need is a full-blown investigation into the club and whether or not they're betting money on game outcomes."

"That's preposterous," Finn sputters.

"It is, I agree, but can you see what it looks like to the outside world? The guy goes from a precise, calculated player, to a selfish madman on a scoring streak, to being all but listless the last game, then to whatever you want to call the man down there who we're seeing dominate tonight. I'm all about showmanship, but this is more than that," Ian says, and I can't help but agree.

The crowd's chants echo in the corridor and I miss some of what the men are saying.

"We're nearing the end of the season, Ian. He's probably just running out of gas. I know you're paying him to be who he is, but between all the publicity you're pushing on him, you're taking time away from his game . . . and from some much-needed downtime. He's been pushing hard for months through injuries and without a break—"

"And we're paying him handsomely for his time." He laughs. "Don't try to act like we're not. He's your player, manage him or I will, and you're not going to like how I handle it."

"Is that a threat?" Finn huffs the words out as if he's not buying Ian's warning.

"That's up to you to decide."

They move back into the press box and their voices fade, but I'm left leaning against the cold cinderblock wall stunned at what I just heard.

Why in the hell are they talking about this right now, in the middle of a game? Did something else happen that I don't know about?

As much as I hate to admit it, Finn gave the perfect, placating response.

But shit, is this what I'm walking into if I win Hunter as a client? Threats by his GM and the inability to respond with conviction because Hunter refuses to let me in?

I lean my head back against the wall as the crowd roars and sigh.

There's a lot of time between the end of a game and when the players leave the locker room to head to the team hotel. Time is spent with coaches, with teammates going over certain plays, with physical therapists treating injuries, interviews with the media in the locker room, and then finally showers and cleaning up.

I know other female agents stride into the locker room not caring that they're going to be hit with a bare ass or better yet, someone's dick, but not me.

I prefer to keep things on a professional level, and I've found that the minute a player knows I've seen him naked, the dynamic changes. It opens the door to the crude jokes and innuendos and those can sometimes ruin a working relationship no matter how nonchalant you are about them.

So, I stand outside the locker room as players begin to trickle out. Some dressed up to go out for their night on the town in Boston, some a whole lot worse for the wear with ice taped to knees and know they are definitely headed to the hotel to order some takeout.

"You ready?" Callum asks as he tosses something in the trash can.

"Sure am." I push my shoulders off the wall where I'm standing. "It's about time I get some time with you."

"Sorry. My schedule's been crazy."

"I get it. Mine always is. Great game, though."

He snorts. "They almost came back."

"But they didn't." I pick up my briefcase off the ground and wonder how a 5-2 score is almost coming back, but let it go. "What do you feel like eating?"

The door to the locker room opens and there's a shout that sounds off before it shuts.

"Party starting early?" I joke with a lift of my chin to behind the door.

His chuckle says volumes but he waits until we round the corner, away from any ears. "It's Maddox. He's . . . I don't know what's going on with him, but it's pulling all of us into it. I don't know if it's family or life or shit . . . I figured you knew since you guys, *you know* . . ."

"Since we . . . *you know*?" I brace myself for the frigid air when he opens the door to the outside for me. "What does that mean?"

"Everyone knows you guys had a thing a while back."

"Is that so?" I laugh outwardly . . . and cringe internally.

"Yeah. Rumor was you were leaving a hotel together."

"So nice to know my personal life is fodder for rumors," I say, playing it off. "We had drinks a few times like three years ago," I lie, neglecting to divulge the sordid details of our quick but fulfilling sex life. "But our interaction didn't give me any more insight on why he's acting how he is than you guys have."

"Yeah, but with you—never mind," he says as we reach my rental car.

"With me, what?" I stare at him over the roof of the car, our breaths turning white with each breath.

"With you, he's just different."

Chapter

TWENTY-FIVE

Hunter

Dad: Is that seriously all you had in you? Piss poor performance.

I STARE AT THE TEXT, AT THE BLINKING CURSOR TAUNTING ME, AND fight the urge to hurl my cell against the wall opposite me.

It's not his words that get me this time. It's the sudden emptiness that follows them. It's the hurt I felt when I looked up to the box between periods and didn't see him there. It's the knowing he never missed a single one of Jonah's games, but he won't take the time to make mine no matter how fucking effortless I make it for him.

I squeeze the phone and grit my jaw and struggle to control my temper.

Then I type.

Me: I didn't see you at the game tonight, Dad. I had a ticket saved for you.

I hit send and lean back against the wall, my eyes closed, and my disappointment heavy.

But why, Maddox?

Why are you disappointed he wasn't here? So he could criticize you face to face?

You need to stop wishing he might care as much about your game as he did Jonah's. You need to stop thinking he's going to be proud of you. You need to stop hoping for miracles.

I look down at my phone again as if he'll respond, when I know he won't, and then reread Dekker's text again.

Dekker: Great game tonight. That first goal was tennis ball-throwing worthy. Heading to dinner with clients then to Sculler's Jazz Club after with some of the team. Come celebrate.

I'm not sure how long I stare at the text before deleting it and heading toward what I know will be a clusterfuck.

Visiting my parents always ends in one.

It doesn't matter that we won the game or that I've taken time out to visit my brother.

It doesn't make a difference that we're running down the playoffs or that my personal bests are beating past ones by miles.

Nothing does.

All that matters is that I'm not Jonah.

That's what it all comes down to.

Chapter
TWENTY-SIX

Hunter

I STEEL MYSELF WITH A DEEP BREATH BEFORE I WALK INTO THE HOUSE. Everything is the same—the flooring, the furniture, the curtains. It looks like time stopped the day of the accident and has never moved on.

It's hard for me to breathe.

It's difficult for me to think of anything other than how, already, I need to get the hell out of the house with its walls lined with images of a life Jonah and I never got to live together. Because that life—that future we always talked about—never happened.

Reminders of that life we used to have are plastered on every surface as if to remind us all how perfect it used to be.

As if to forget the accident ever happened.

"Hunter? Is that you?" My mom's voice calls out from where she no doubt is sitting with him in his room.

I've offered to buy them a new house a million times, even put deposits down on a few. I explained how much easier it would be having a custom suite built for Jonah and his needs. How it would make their life—and his—so much easier, how it would give him some autonomy when he already feels trapped, but after numerous rejections of the offers, I gave up. They'd preferred to stay here where they can be reminded daily of the ghosts of that day and the butterfly effect I created.

"She's in Jonah's bedroom," my father mutters from his La-Z-Boy where he folds his newspaper with a crisp snap and reveals the blood pressure cuff on his arm. His eyes move from the newspaper in his hand to the television on the wall beside me, but he never looks at me. "Sloppy game tonight, son. Your skill fell by the wayside to your aggression. You need to work on keeping both at the same time."

"Yes, sir." I choke over the words and the resentment they cause. I played a damn good game by any player's standards, and as much as I know it, I also know he's nowhere near finished.

Just like the nights he kept me on the ice way past midnight. My body would be exhausted, my fingers numb, my stomach growling, but dammit, I was nowhere near good enough.

I wasn't Jonah.

And the way he looks at the picture of Jonah in front of him tells me just that: he sees everything Jonah could have been and more. He sees everything I caused. He sees everything I'll never be.

"You're weak on your left side, you know that? You were beat every damn time. You're not checking your shoulder enough like Jonah did, and it's getting you in trouble. You're partying too much. It doesn't seem like you're practicing on your shot and that's for mornings. You're out drinking and hungover. It's showing."

"Yes, sir." I nod—my feet shifting and lips pursing—and take the ridicule without talking back, because whatever I say doesn't matter. It won't be heard. His head is too preoccupied with another star forward, the one lying paralyzed in the next room, who I'll always be compared to.

I take the criticism, I accept the disdain, because I know my dad is hanging on by a thread. I know this is the only way he can cope with the dreams that were killed that day and the future that was robbed from us.

But it doesn't prevent my resentment from festering. It doesn't prevent my hands from fisting.

"There was a ticket there for you, you know. I didn't see you in the box. I thought maybe you'd like to come."

He nods, his eyes never leaving the television. "You know I like to watch my hockey from home."

Not with Jonah, you didn't. You were at every damn game up against the glass cheering and yelling.

In the fifteen years since the accident, you've sat and pushed me, but criticized and judged and disapproved from afar.

I swallow over the rejection that tears into me like it does every time, and let it settle in a place where someday I'll deal with it. *Maybe.* "Your health? It's okay?"

Forced words in a strained relationship.

"Yes. I can't be going anywhere, now can I? Jonah needs me too much."

So do I, Dad. So do I.

But that's irrelevant—I'm irrelevant—because Jonah does. Only one son survived that night and in my parents' eyes, it wasn't me.

I need a dad too, but not according to the man in front of me.

If only I had truly died that night. Anything but a walking ghost who once had a family who loved him.

"Of course." I stare at him for a beat. The blue of the television casts an odd glow on his skin, and I wonder if he really loves this life he lives, or if he's merely going through the motions.

"Maybe I'll see you in the stands at the next game?" I ask like I always do. My, *I love you, Dad, and still need you as a father* plea that never seems to be heard.

"Maybe." The lone word is all he says. All I want is for him to tell me to stay and sit with him, but I take off down the hallway toward Jonah's room.

The old, oversized den we used to sit in for hours playing Nintendo as boys and then later making out with girls as teenagers, looks like a hospital room now. My mom has tried to dress it up, but there's no hiding the reality.

The quiet hum of the television hides my footsteps as I stand there and take it all in. There's a bed on the far side of the room with a lift that hangs on a boom off to one side that helps my mom get Jonah in and out of bed.

The room is decorated in light colors that do nothing to disguise the medical equipment dotting its perimeter. A wheelchair is parked against one wall while on the opposing one a curio cabinet showcases his old trophies like shrines to an era gone by.

Like reminders to Jonah every single day of what he's missing out on in this shitty deal fate handed him.

My mom's back is to me as she fiddles with something beneath the hospital bed, her soft talking a constant, soothing sound she somehow adopted after the accident—almost as if one of us were a little boy complaining about an upset stomach, not a quadriplegic depending on her for his every need.

The last thing I look at in the room is my brother. I'm petrified almost as much as I am desperate to see him. It's been several months but it feels way too long since I have, and every part of me misses everything about him in a way I've never been able to express or understand.

It's the twin thing. The connection that's inherent.

I bite back my gasp when I finally look. He's withered away to nothing now, the shape of his body beneath the sheets barely noticeable. His lungs rise and fall with the help of the ventilator fastened by the trach tube at his throat, and the sound of the machine fills the room in a steady rhythm. His face is pale and his eyes are closed, but there's a small smile on his lips in reaction to something my mom has said.

My chest fucking caves in like it does every time I see him. Guilt and sorrow and anger and so many other damn emotions ride a roller coaster through me until they strangle all the words I normally say.

I feel awkward, as if I'm invading his privacy, while at the same time feeling at home and comfortable with the one person I know better than anyone.

Or used to.

"Hi guys," I say and walk toward them. My mom gasps, her startled smile following right after.

"There you are. You were so busy today I wasn't sure if we were going to see you before you moved on to the next city."

"I'd never miss the chance to see him." I accept the arms she wraps around me, and I fucking hate that I hold her tighter a little longer so I can keep the tears welling in my eyes hidden behind my closed lids. I don't want him to see how I see him. I don't want him to know how bad he's gotten.

And yet, I feel like he already knows. How can he not?

"It's been too long." Her words are barely audible.

I breathe her in. She smells of citrus and vanilla, but she feels so very frail and incredibly strong simultaneously. "I missed you too," I murmur as she pulls away and puts her hands on my cheeks to look at me.

Tears glisten in her eyes but she blinks them away with the sadness that falls momentarily over her countenance.

"Jonah, look who's here."

"You don't need to announce me. I'm not a guest," I tell her as I step to the bed and meet my brother's eyes.

He garbles something unintelligible that I know is a greeting, his attempt at pronunciation seeming worse than the sounds he was making last week when I spoke with him. Even with the speaking valve . . . It feels like everything is on a constant decline.

"Yeah, yeah." I lean down and give him a pseudo hug and rest my forehead against his for a moment, almost as if I'm recharging my twin meter. He's the same but so very different. "You're still the better looking one," I say as I stand back up with my jaw clenched to fight the helplessness I feel.

He gives a partial laugh that ends in a coughing fit. My mom pushes me out of the way as she pulls him up so he doesn't choke.

"You sanitized?" she asks, her voice going into panic mode over me bringing germs into his room.

"Yes," I mumble, feeling inept as I step back and let her help him in ways I can't. Ways that have changed and evolved over the fifteen years he's been a prisoner in his broken body and mind.

"Just rest, Jonah. You're fine now," she says after fixing something on his ventilator. He draws in a deep breath and calms.

"Rrrr," he says for my name with the next struggle of breath.

"Yeah?" I lean down closer so he doesn't have to fight so hard to be heard, and grab his hand even when I know he can't feel it.

But I can.

And I need this connection with him more than anything right now.

"Good." He takes a second and closes his eyes as if each word is a battle to be won. "Gm."

My smile is soft and sincere and hides the emotions clogging in my throat. Our eyes hold—one twin to another, two halves of a whole—and I know his is the only praise I need. His is the one who matters the most.

"I miss you, J."

Tears well in his eyes and slip from the corner to the pillow beneath his head. I hate that he can't wipe them away. I hate that it'd kill him if I did it for him. He may be paralyzed, but I'm still his little brother by four minutes and two seconds and even like this, he holds tight to that tiny bit of pride.

"He's exhausted, Hunter," my mom says as she steps up and adjusts his pillow for him. "His sleeping pills are kicking in and he needs to get to sleep. It's way past his—"

"Yes. Fine." I don't need to be reminded of the Ambien he takes nightly to combat the anxiety that's caused him to have nightmares in the past few months.

The anxiety I wonder is because he fears he's dying.

She steps in front of me to fuss some more while I struggle with what to say like I always do, caught in that need to pretend like everything is normal when nothing is.

It's so very different when we're face to face.

On the phone, I feel like I'm filling him in on the world outside of this damn prison cell—almost as if I'm letting him live vicariously through me.

But when we're face to identical face, it's brutal.

Face to face, I can see his reactions and feel the guilt. If I talk about hockey, I feel like the asshole who's talking about the one thing he loved more than me. If I talk about women, his other favorite love, then it's a stark reminder of the things he'll never get to feel again. And if I talk about trivial bullshit to fill the air, he knows I'm at a loss of what to say to him—my twin—and isn't that worse?

So when my mom clears out of the way, I sit there with him and hold his hand he can't feel and connect without words he can't speak, but still feel a sense of peace. Nothing can rob the two of us of that. *Except of course, death.*

His exhaustion from leaving the house and going to the game is evident in the bags under his eyes, and it's not long before he succumbs to it. His eyes fall heavy and the muscles in his face relax as I whisper to him that I love him.

But even with him asleep, I don't look away. I can't. All I keep thinking is how I packed my schedule today to avoid this emotional bullshit and how wrong I was to do so. This is my brother. He deserves better from me . . . and I should be able to deal with my parents, because this time with him is what matters most.

How many moments like this will I get? How many more times will I be able to tell him I love him face to face? How many more times will I be able to find my calm with him?

Not enough. And yet my pride has kept me away.

As if guilt didn't rule my life already.

Fuck.

I close my eyes and shake my head, knowing I fucked up. Knowing I should have figured he'd be worn out from the game, and that I'd get so little time with him.

"Love you, J," I whisper as he settles into slumber. "Love you more than you know." I can't take my eyes off him. I need to memorize the lines on his face. The same ones we should share. But where I have laugh lines and crow's feet from the sun, his are less pronounced or not even there. Mine show a life lived and his show a life lost. So I visually trace the lines he does have, over and over, needing to map them. Needing to commit them to memory.

The problem is, the longer I sit here, the calm Jonah gives me is slowly eaten away by resentment.

At my parents. At the world. At fucking God and fate and everything in between, because why is he there and I'm here?

Knowing he's completely asleep, I turn to face my mom. She's sitting in a chair at the foot of his bed, her eyes focused on the television show that's on but that I can barely hear.

"You didn't show up before the game like you were supposed to today. I had everything set up for him."

"Hunter." My name is an apologetic sigh that snaps my anger like a livewire.

"I had plans to empty the arena so I could push him on the ice. So I could let him skate again—"

"He's too sick now to let him—"

"He can't get much sicker, Mom." I stand and move to abate the anger.

Or try to.

There's no abating shit right now.

"Let him have whatever fucking joy he can. Christ." I shove a hand through my hair and turn my back on the damn case of trophies.

"Oh, you know Jonah," she says with a wave of her hand, as if we're talking about the weather outside. She stands and moves to the seat I just vacated. She takes her time tucking his arms beneath the covers so he doesn't get cold. "He has his routines and when we step outside of the routine too much it's hard, and he gets upset—"

"*Upset?*" I chuckle without an ounce of humor. "Robbing him of the experience would make him upset." I look out the window to the streetlight's orange glow and try to compose myself. "Next time, I'll just pick him up and take him myself."

"No, you won't." Defiance edges her tone and does nothing to soften the tight smile she gives me. "We're his guardians and will do what we think is best for him."

All I can do is stare at her and her subtle but stinging rebuke and wonder if she hears her own words. If she realizes she may have lost two sons that day, because she gave up on me too. She devoted her life to him, forgetting that I need her too, just in different ways.

My chest aches in a way it never has before. "Maybe I wanted you there early, Mom. Maybe I wanted you to stay after. Maybe I wanted you or Dad to see—" My voice breaks and I fucking hate that it does. "You know what? Fuck it. Just fuck it."

"He has to come first. He needed his medication and I had to get him back and—"

"I know." It's futile. I lost the right to need anything from them the night of the accident.

"We need to keep our voices down. He needs his rest," she says, trying to usher me out of the room.

"I wanted to see him tonight, Mom. And you and Dad." I turn to face her in this house that no longer feels like home to me. "I don't get the time to have with him and you didn't come early like you said you would. You didn't let him meet the guys. You didn't—"

"You just don't understand how things are, *Hunter.*" And there it is. My name is spoken with so much derision that I don't think she hears it anymore.

"Yeah, I do. You see me and you see who he could have been. You look in my eyes and know everything changed—your life, his life, my—"

"You don't get to feel sorry for yourself," she bites out, and again, I'm reminded why I kept busy all day with publicity stints for the team. Why I hope every time I come home things might change and then hurt when I realize they never will.

"What about you, Mom? You've fired every nurse I've hired to come in here and help you out."

"No one will take care of my son but me."

"You need to get out more. Go back to teaching or something." Maybe I say the words I know will cause a fight like every other time so I have a reason to leave. Maybe I poke the sleeping bear so I can find my way out of this house. So I can breathe again.

"We've had this discussion a million times. You may have run away . . . but we didn't."

"Ran away?" I cough the words out. "Is that what you called it? Pushing me to be everything Jonah was supposed to be? Letting me know every damn chance you had that I would never be him. That I would never be enough." I clench my fists and resist the urge to punch the wall. "Look at me." I throw my hands out to my side, my voice rising. "I'm one of the best goddamn NHL players on the ice right now and neither of you can see it. Neither of you can acknowledge I've lived up to every one of your fucking goals. And yet, it's still not enough. It's still not Jonah."

"Hunter." My father's voice comes as a low warning from the other room. His constant aversion of anything about to show.

"Honey." My mom repeats the tepid warning in her placating tone. "Don't upset your father. His heart . . . it's fragile."

"It seems everything is fragile in this house," I grit out, running a hand through my hair and blowing out an unsatisfying sigh.

Nothing fucking changes.

"It's been a long day," she murmurs.

"Got it. I know. You're tired. He's tired. It's been a long night, and I should get going because I'm upsetting the balance here." I walk back toward my brother and look at him one last time before leaving. She turns the lamp off so the light from the open door paints a swath across his cheek.

All I can do is stare at him. At his face that was once the mirror image of mine. At the hands tucked away that I used to play catch with. At the memories I hold closer than anything in the world while hating them all too. At the person I've tried the hardest to become.

And wonder, for the millionth time if I'd have been better off being the one in the bed instead of being the one who lives with the guilt for putting him there.

Chapter

TWENTY-SEVEN

Hunter

16 years earlier

EACH NAIL I POUND INTO THE FENCE DOES NOTHING TO ABATE MY RE-sentment.

You think you deserve to go, Hunter? You think with sprint times like that I'm going to reward you for slacking and let you go?

Another nail.

Jonah has your time beat by a full second. Christ. There's a reason he's being scouted by the top schools and clubs in the country and you're not.

I drop the next nail as I try to hold it in place with hands shaking with anger. When I bend over to pick it up I realize my jaw is sore from clenching it so tightly.

He's got everything going for him. School. Hockey. That Terry girl. What do you have going for you? What do you do that doesn't require me asking you to do it twice?

I pound the head of the nail so hard into the shitty shed at old man Watson's house that the face of the hammer leaves a round circle in the weathered wood.

So no, Hunter. You can't go to junior prom tonight or whatever the fuck it's called. You'll fix Mr. Watson's shed while he's out of town. You'll pick up your mom from work for me since Jonah's using the other car. Then you'll meet me at the rink at seven o'clock, and you better be ready to skate. Your whole class will be at the dance, and you'll be here making up for slacking off. Maybe then . . . you'll learn your lesson.

I drop my arms to my sides and raise my face to the late afternoon sun, trying to catch my breath that keeps getting robbed by the emotions I don't want to feel.

Hatred.

Resentment.

Fury.

Fucking jealousy.

It's not Jonah's fault he's perfect. It's my fault I'm not the fucking golden boy.

He's the one set up with a full-ride already, Hunter. Full fucking ride to Boston College, one of the best hockey programs in the country. And what are you going to do, huh? Stay here and be a bagger at Stop & Shop? Why can't you apply yourself and make us proud? You'll never be Jonah, but you can at least be something.

My hands ball into fists. I fight the urge to punch the stupid wall of the shed, because I'd either break my knuckles or the whole damn thing will collapse, and then I'll be stuck here for even longer.

My cell rings and I sigh.

"What do you want now?" I snap at Jonah.

"Mom's getting off work early and she needs you to pick her up," he says. Laughter in the background has me gritting my teeth. Nothing like a pre-dance beer or two while the girls are at the salon getting ready.

"Get her your fucking self," I mutter.

"Dude. I can't." He laughs at something someone else says. "Please, bro."

"You're the reason she doesn't have her car tonight. You fucking get her," I say. "I'm the one finishing the shit you didn't at Watson's."

"I'll finish it tomorrow. Don't worry about it."

"Can't. It's part of Dad's punishment for me. You know, picking up your shit while you're busy being perfect."

He sighs. I know it's not his fault. I know he's stood up for me with Dad more times than he should have. I know he hates the difference in treatment between us just as much as I do.

But it doesn't change a fucking thing.

He's perfect, outstanding, everything my dad wanted in a son and hockey player.

I'm mediocre, insignificant, the son my dad has never needed.

The failure.

"C'mon, Hunter. Don't be a dick to me. Dad's just being Dad. I'm sure if you turn it on after a few suicide sprints, he'll be wowed by how fucking fast you are. He'll think he's taught you a lesson and then tell you to meet up with us." He shushes people around him and their noise fades. It sounds like he walked into a different room. "Hunter?"

"If only it were that easy."

Easy to what though? Live in your twin's shadow? Never be enough? Love your brother like he's a part of you while hating him from jealousy?

"Look." His voice lowers as someone yells, *I need another brewski,* in the background.

"Nah. I'm out. Get Mom. Don't get Mom. She called *you* to get her, so figure it the fuck out on your own." I end the call and toss my phone on the ground, then squeeze my eyes shut to push the tears back down.

Jonah doesn't fucking care.

No one does.

And when I go to pick up the hammer to finish punishment number one, I catch movement out of the corner of my eye.

I look over to where Terry Fischer plays with the ties of the bottom of what could be called a T-shirt if it had more fabric to it as she walks toward me. Her shorts are short, her legs are sinfully long, and her sandals high. When she rocks back on her heels as she licks her lips and bats her eyelashes, every damn ounce of blood in my body heads south and my mouth goes dry.

"Hey. I thought you were going out to Rick's house for some beers before we meet up for pictures and then head to the dance."

I stare at her—I mean how can I not—eyes blinking and lips parting, before I realize she thinks I'm Jonah.

There's a split second where I hesitate and she continues—her hips swaying, her fingers accidentally twisting her shirt tighter over her boobs—and I keep thinking about my brother.

How much he thinks he loves her.

How he's already lost his virginity to her. (*Hasn't everyone at Hillman High?*)

How he has fucking everything without trying, while I have to work so damn hard at everything . . . *but for what?*

"Jonah," she croons as she stops within a foot of me, laces her fingers with mine, and swings our arms. "What's wrong?" Pouty lips. Cleavage right there. Perfume. "Your daddy make you finish this since I distracted you the other day from finishing?"

Her giggle fills the air and her tits jiggle when she does. I'm mesmerized.

"Yeah." I smile and emit a nervous laugh. No wonder Jonah keeps volunteering to come over here and work on Watson's property.

"You gonna answer that phone?" she asks. I didn't even hear my cell ringing again.

"It's probably Hunter." I roll my eyes. "You know how he is."

She laughs again and twirls a lock of hair on the finger of her free hand. "So . . . you're not out with the guys?"

"I had to finish this. I'm meeting up with them in a bit." I wrack my brain to remember what was supposed to happen this afternoon. "I—uh—thought you were getting your hair or nails or whatever done," I fumble.

"Why?" She leans up against me. "You don't think I'm pretty just like this?"

Jesus. Hell. Fuck. Nerves vibrate through me just as fast as the adrenaline does, and I swear I can smell it coming from my pores.

I've dated girls. Lots of them. I've been to second base a few times, while the guys think I've all but slid home.

But this is Terry Fischer, innocent sweetheart to parents and blowjob queen to the boys of Hillman and the almost-men at the local junior college.

"Pretty?" I lick my lips, my mouth dry as cotton, my dick harder than it's ever been before and my balls ache. "You're so much more than pretty."

"Jonah," she says in a singsong voice as her lips meet mine. The hammer drops to the ground with a thud right beside the cellphone that starts to ring again as her fingers slide around my neck and thread through my hair.

Terry Fischer is kissing me.

Our tongues touch, and she moans loudly as she presses her body against mine.

My thoughts are frantic. What am I supposed to do now? I'm going to hell.

Oh my God, this feels so fucking good.

She thinks I'm Jonah.

Oh shit.

Oh shit.

The kiss grows greedy, if that's even a thing. Like I can't get enough of it or her, and it's easier to get lost in her kiss than to acknowledge the tinge of guilt over how I'm kissing my brother's girlfriend.

"Is old man Watson still not home?" she asks as she looks around the empty backyard before pulling my hand up and pressing it against her breast.

"No." I gulp. I try not to move, because if my jeans rub too hard or she grinds again against me, I swear to God, I'm going to come in my pants.

Gretzky. Crosby. Lemieux. Roy. Howe. Orr.

I try to recite the hockey greats. Anything to get my focus off what her nipple feels like beneath the thin fabric. Hard and soft and her breast the perfect weight as if I know what that is.

"He—he's still out of town."

"Should we do this now? Like you and me? So my hair doesn't get messed up later and my parents don't wonder?"

Jesus.

I'm not Jonah.

Oh my God, he's going to kill me.

She runs a hand over the outside of my pants and my eyes all but roll back in my head. If a cool breeze on any other day is enough to make me stand at attention, her hand is doing so much more than that.

"I—sure—I—"

"I mean, we can do what we did before—with me sucking you and you licking me . . . but, I brought a condom." She holds a foil packet up and my eyes bug out of my head, causing her to giggle as my breath all but stops.

"Yes. Please. Um—"

"You're acting funny," she says as she pushes me toward the patio furniture and grabs my shirt, pulling me toward her to meet my tongue again.

My pulse pounds in my ears. My breathing is shallow as I try to process what's happening. As I realize the next closest house is half a mile away and Terry Fischer is here and wants to *do it* with me.

I guess the rumors were right.

I guess Jonah wasn't lying.

Don't think about Jonah. Don't think about—

"C'mon, J. Feel my panties. Feel what you do to me."

She guides my hand between the flimsy cotton shorts to where it's warm and moist and—

Gretzky. Crosby. Lemieux. Roy. Howe. Orr.

"Ohhhh." My own moan is all I can hear as her hands slide inside my jeans and circle around me.

Gretzky. Crosby. Lemieux. Roy. Howe. Orr.

Chapter

TWENTY-EIGHT

Dekker

THE SAXOPHONE FLOATS THROUGH THE AIR ABOVE THE STEADY DRONE of chatter. Sculler's Jazz Club is crowded for a Thursday night and by the looks of my company—Finch and his wife, Maysen, and Callum—the few drinks have settled and the exhaustion from the game tonight is setting in.

Finch with his uniquely good looks—longer hair with almost clear blue eyes—has his arm hooked around his wife's shoulder. For the life of me, I can't remember her name and am too embarrassed to ask, so I've spent the better part of the conversation making sure to avoid saying anything where I need to use it.

For a businesswoman who prides herself on remembering names, I just don't have it in me tonight.

Regardless, Callum was right. This place that the guys usually meet up at after wherever their adventures take them in the city, is just what I needed. Relaxed and sufficiently off the beaten track that it offers privacy away from fans. The guys can enjoy a drink or two without interruptions for autographs or fear that pictures will be posted online of them when they've had a little too much.

The lounge is dim, and the furniture is dark, save for the stage across from us with its red velvet backdrop and lights angled at the lone man sitting there playing the sax. His tune is melodic and seductive and begs you to relax . . . or make love. I'm angling for the former. We're in the top of the three tiers of seats, and the bar is behind us with its clinks and clanks of glass as it buzzes with business.

Taking a sip of my martini, I close my eyes, and lean my head back to listen and unwind, but as per usual, my head never quiets. Everything I need to do sifts through my mind. Contracts and negotiations and endorsement deals. I understand my father's reasoning in sending me here to recruit Hunter, but in the meantime, I feel like I'm neglecting my other clients who need my attention.

Sure, I can work most crises remotely, but not being in my office makes it difficult. Living in a hotel room that changes every other night makes it even harder.

I tune into the conversation in front of me. Comments about the game tonight, including a few snide remarks about one of my clients on the opposing team, make me smile.

"It's true, isn't it, Dekker? The fucker must eat lemons the way he's so damn sour," Finch says.

I belt out a laugh. "Client info is confidential, but uh, he's got some killer lemon trees at his house," I say with a wink.

He throws his head back and laughs while Maysen stands suddenly, the expression on his face causing us all to turn and see what has his attention.

Hunter stumbles near the entrance of the other side of the club. His shoulder falls into a guy and much like Maysen, we can see the fight coming a mile away.

Unlike Maysen, though, I overheard the conversation tonight between the LumberJacks GM and Sanderson.

The last thing Hunter needs to be doing is getting into a fight.

But before I can react, Maysen leaps over the back of the couch on legs that don't look like he just played sixty minutes of high-intensity and brutally physical hockey, and jogs over to his teammate.

Between the distance and the music, I can't hear what's being said, but body language—Maysen's hands are up and his smile is broad as he talks to the guy Hunter is staring down. A few tense seconds unfold where I'm sure Maysen offers to buy a round of drinks or something to that effect, before he wraps his arm around Hunter's waist, and starts veering him our way. Situation handled.

Thank God.

But what the actual fuck?

What the hell is Hunter thinking?

Disgusted with his immaturity, I turn back to the company in front of me, down the rest of my delicious and much-needed martini, and choose to ignore whatever the hell is going on with him, because I'm off the clock.

At least that's what I tell myself.

I should be prepared for Hunter's flop on the seat beside me a few seconds later, but I still emit a startled yelp when he does.

"It's Dekker the pecker wrecker," he says with a huge grin that would be charming if he weren't drunk or his words weren't shitty. His cheek is red where a punch was landed in the game tonight, and his hair is falling in his face. I can't deny that small tug that hits me at the sight of him.

And I hate everything about that admission.

I have just enough of a buzz going that I'm primed to pick a fight with him. Despite his behavior, how he's shutting me out, the way he's turned me on, the fact that I haven't told him why I'm here, and the career he's trying to throw away with his bullshit antics.

Reason would tell me I shouldn't engage. The last drink I had encourages me that I should.

"Oh, look. It's out-of-control Hunter who's going to get his ass kicked off his team if he keeps his bullshit up," I add with an equally charming smile as I meet his eyes.

"Bullshit?" he scoffs. "Nah, it's just me getting warmed up."

"I'm sure your teammates are thrilled to hear that."

I don't back down from his glare, so the silence settles between us as we stare at each other.

"Where've you been, man?" Callum asks, trying to ease the tension, as he leans back in his chair.

"Just taking care of some business," Hunter says and dismisses him.

"Old friends?" Finch asks.

"Something like that." He stands abruptly. "Can't an asshole get a drink in this place?"

I push myself up. "I'll get it," I say, knowing if I get it for him, I can ask the bartender to make it light. Hunter's so drunk he probably won't notice. "What'll you have?" I ask when I already know the answer.

"Good. I'll have a Bombay and tonic. And uh, glad to know you know how to do your job properly," Hunter says, and I see Finch's wife wince at the comment.

"At least someone does," I say, and he grabs my arm as I start to walk past him.

"Hey," Finch says and stands to reinforce his warning. He glares at his teammate.

"It's fine," I say and shrug out of Hunter's reach before anything can escalate. Getting in a fight with a random person is one thing, but fighting his own teammate is even worse.

The bar is crowded and it takes a few minutes before I can belly up to it. "Another?" the bartender asks.

"No. A gin and tonic. Bombay. And a lot more tonic than gin," I say with a wink.

He nods, understanding what I'm saying. "Got it."

Right when I go to turn around and check on Hunter, he slides into the spot beside me and leans his elbows on the bar top. Our eyes meet and the million questions I want to ask him surface and die right along with my want to tell him about the conversation I overheard tonight.

"Let me guess, you're watering down my drink," he says, his lips beside my ear.

"Should I worry about what kind of trouble you got in tonight before finding yourself here?"

Something flashes through the blue of his eyes, but it's gone before I can decipher it. "I'm not your problem to worry about. Just looking after some fans. Surely you know what that is." He looks at me with such an unexpected bitterness as if to test me. "How much do you want to bet I could walk away from this place tonight with five different phone numbers?"

"If your goal is to be a phone book, then by all means." I roll my shoulders and refuse to give him what he wants. *Another fight.*

"What is it with you, Kincade?" he murmurs just above the music. "All of a sudden you're here, there . . . fucking everywhere. In my face."

"Not what I'm here for. But I'm sure any of those numbers you collect would be willing to be whatever you need for the night." The bartender slides the drink in front of me, and I thank him as I push it toward Hunter.

"You're right. They would." He turns around so he's still beside me, but so his back is against the bar. He makes a show of giving a hum of appreciation when he spots a woman who catches his eye.

I can't figure out if he's being serious or just trying to get a reaction out of me.

"Have at them, Hunter." I choke over my own words. "You sure seem like you're at peak performance tonight."

"What?"

"Nothing." My buzz is gone, and there's no point saying another word.

His chuckle is a low rumble that I can feel more than hear as he turns to face me, but I keep looking straight ahead at the mirrored wall behind the bar. "Why are you here, Dekker?"

"Same reason you are. To have a drink. To unwind after a long day. To have a little downtime."

"*To get laid.*"

"Yep, that's me." I shake my head in frustration. "My every waking goal is how I'm going to end up on my back with my legs spread."

"It used to be."

A million things run through my mind—*fuck you*, being the one that rings the loudest and *only with you* running a close second—but I know Hunter Maddox. He wants to stay angry.

But his words still sting. They still ignite my temper. They still hurt, when I shouldn't care.

Hunter seems determined to ruin or sabotage every part of his life. Why bother being his agent? Then I'll be the one being warned by McAvoy. *And why do I want that?* Surely my dad *doesn't* want that.

"That's a class-act thing to say, Hunter. Be a dick to me." *I don't deserve that from him, and I hate that his drunkenness has disconnected his filter and allows him to be so scathing.*

"Not being a dick, just trying to figure out why the hell you're following the team around like a puppy dog waiting to get a scrap of bone."

I take a sip of my drink, let the alcohol swish around on my tongue before I swallow it, and turn to face him. He remains looking ahead, his profile strong with pride and marred with a disdain I can't figure out. "Let's get one thing straight, Maddox. I chase after no one. I'm a damn good agent who's simply doing my job. If I choose to go out for a drink with one of my clients after a game, that's my own business, not yours."

"Is that what this is, Dekk?" The muscle in his jaw feathers as the melody being played changes.

"What?"

"We fizzled out so I moved on, and now you're back to exact revenge?"

For fuck's sake.

We never fizzled out.

The thought screams to a halt in the front of my mind and sits there in blinking neon lights.

We never fizzled out because if we had, those feelings I had wouldn't have sparked to life the minute I saw him. They would have had me sneering and disgusted. But then I hear the other part about him moving on. I *had* tried to avoid looking up pictures of Hunter after I left him. To see how quickly and how easily I'd been replaced. *How he'd moved on.* I'm not naïve enough to think that I walked away and he's pined after me all these years.

So yeah, I'm sure he moved on. But I've never wanted that reminder.

Hell.

"News flash. What happened three years ago is dead and over," I say.

"Yes, I forgot. No-nonsense Kincade can move on without ever looking back."

"God, Hunter. There are way more important things you need to be focusing on than me."

"Yeah," he murmurs just loud enough for me to hear, "like that hot brunette over there."

That dig hurts.

"Just like old times, huh?" I ask, staring at him until he slowly turns and faces me, that cocky smirk that usually makes my insides simmer, instead now irritating me.

"Depends on what you mean by old times." He reaches out to move a piece of hair off my shoulder, and I slap his hand away.

"Hockey. Party. *Repeat.*"

"You forgot the most important part." He leans closer so I can smell the alcohol on his breath just above the scent of his cologne.

"Meaning?"

"Hockey. Party. *Fucking.* Repeat."

"Screw you, Hunter," I say, refusing to show that those words and his cavalier attitude are hurtful.

I toss some cash on the bar and head back to our table, needing space and distance from him and his destructive behavior. *Why?* Why does he keep coming to me when it clearly bothers him that I'm here? Why can't he just go after his hot brunette on the other side of the bar and leave me the hell alone?

More importantly, why do I keep engaging?

I think the answer lies somewhere between the two of those answers.

"You jealous?" he calls after me as I step past Finch and his wife on the way to the open seat on the couch. I turn to face him, confusion no doubt etched in every line of my face, as he stares at me above the rim of his glass, his eyes challenging me as much as his words do. "You're the one who moves from man to man, night after night."

"Man to man? Really? It's called entertaining clients, you ass." I laugh at his ridiculousness and when I try to walk between him and the table in the way, I realize now that putting myself in this corner was a bad idea.

"Sleeping with clients is part of the job now? No wonder Chaddy-boy was so pissed that you dropped him to come see me," he says, reaching out to grab my arm.

Finch and Callum both stand instantly with his name falling from their lips.

But I'm faster, my hand stinging as it connects with his cheek.

We glare at each other—his teammates and one of my clients—staring at us, gauging the situation and whatever it is that's happening between us. Patrons on the outside of our seating area turn to watch too as the music picks up in pace.

Hunter may have a ghost of a smile on his lips but there is a host of pain in the depths of his eyes, but I'm past wanting to listen to him now. A moment passes before I see him tuck it all away and that smile falls lopsided and his snark returns.

"This is what this is all about, isn't it? You. Me. Years ago. Relationships aren't my thing, Dekker."

"No shit." I pull my purse strap back up to my shoulder that fell off with the action.

"Not between me and a woman. Not between me and an agent." He chews his cheek momentarily. "Not with anyone."

"Good to know." I angle my head, stare at him, and then go out on a limb with a hunch. "Why are you here? Hockey. Party. *Fucking*. Repeat? Is that why? I figured you'd be spending time with your family. But *you're* out drinking and being an asshole."

Muscles tic in his face as he clenches his jaw.

And there it is.

A reaction that is as sincere as it is threatening.

"Leave my family the fuck out of this," he growls, his shoulders squaring, as he takes a step toward me. "Where do you get off—?"

His teammates take a protective step forward, but I shake my head to tell them it's fine. In fact, I turn toward them and say, "It's late, and I have an early conference call. Thank you for inviting me. It was a great time"—I glance to Hunter—"until it wasn't."

"Do you want me to take you back?" Callum asks, and I shake my head, not wanting to add fuel to Hunter's accusation.

"No, thank you. Enjoy the rest of your night. It'll probably be your last one for a while with the next few games being tough ones . . . so enjoy it while you can." When I go to leave, Hunter won't move so I can walk out of the small space between the table and the couch.

"Just admit it," he says.

"Admit what?" I ask.

"Why you're here."

"Lay off, man," Finch says and tries to pull Hunter by the arm out of my way, but he shrugs off his teammate's arm without a look his way.

I shake my head subtly, the gravity in my voice matching the look in my eyes. "Honestly? I'm not sure why I'm here anymore." More than a small part of me wishes I wasn't. I've been his verbal punching bag one too many times since I came here, and I'm done.

It's one thing when it's just the two of us, but now he's doing it in front of his teammates and all that does is undermine my professionalism. If I stand by and take it, I look like I have no backbone, and they'd wonder how that would translate to me fighting in contract negotiations for them.

On the other hand, when I do engage him and stand up for myself, it just devolves into an insult-fest that looks unprofessional and immature.

I feel like I'm in a no-win situation, especially when I see he's not going to change.

Before I showed up here, I thought I could fix whatever was going on with him and win his trust in doing so, but now . . . now, I don't think anything I do will help him.

Is this where I call my dad and tell him to pick someone else for me to recruit? That I refuse to put up with Hunter and his constant picking of fights to prevent us from having any real conversation? Or do I stick it out to prove to my dad that I'm tough and can handle even the most difficult of clients? *But this isn't about my father's lack of faith in me . . . because I know he believes in me.* KSM needs a Hunter Maddox in its client list.

I feel like I'm at a loss either way, but my dignity is stronger than my pride, and I'm done.

I look at Hunter one last time, and his expression falls as I stare at him a second longer before skirting around him and walking out of the club.

Chapter

TWENTY-NINE

Hunter

"WHAT?" I SNAP AT THE GUYS WHEN THEY STARE AT ME AFTER SHE WALKS out.

"What the fuck, Cap?" Finch asks and the look on his face—disgust and disappointment from a man I'm supposed to lead—hits me harder than his words.

I don't wait for them to say anything more or rebuke me or what-the-fuckever it is they want to malign me with and head to the bar.

It's much easier to drink to cope than to stand here and replay everything that happened at my parents' house—the things I know will never change—and the fight I got into at the first bar I stopped by on my way here.

When will this pain and guilt and need to destroy everything go away?

When will the things I do ever be good enough to outrun the clusterfuck of emotions that have been running rampant over the past few months?

It's simpler to down the first shot of gin. To focus on the burn instead of the argument I had with my mom and the disinterest and then criticism from my dad. From the words I wanted to shout at them—that I'm still alive and still their son, and isn't that enough?

But I know why they are how they are.

I know why our lives have all changed.

I know that I'm the one who set forward the events that caused all of this.

The second shot I swallow in one gulp burns just as bright as the first.

Thoughts of Dekker fill my head. I can't get them out. Not her before. Especially not her now.

Her presence is torture. It's showing me something I thought I wanted. Something I forced myself to walk away from because I knew I didn't deserve her.

And just when everything is turning to shit, she's back again. A sinner and a saint, and fuck if I know which one of those parts of her I'd love to drown in.

You're a piece of shit, Hunter.

I think of the words I spewed at her.

Grade-A piece of shit.

Not like that's anything you didn't already know, but now you can't deny it.

The accusations I made just so she wouldn't look too closely or see the truths about me.

Hockey player. Royal fuck-up. Commitment-phobe. *The reason Jonah's dying.*

I scrub a hand through my hair and down the third shot in as many minutes, landing the glass back on the bar top with a slap for emphasis.

Fucking Dekker.

I shake my head but she's still there, still owning my thoughts, still making me want her.

But she's here.

And I think she's recruiting someone.

But who?

Me? She's ballsy enough to make that kind of move without a blink of an eye.

Maybe the rumors are true that Sanderson is fucking people over. It's not like he's doing me any favors right now.

Would I move over to KSM? Would I let Dekker represent me? Her track record's phenomenal . . . so why is it people are jumping ship to Sanderson? What exactly is he promising these new clients that us old ones aren't seeing?

The question is, if she represents me, how is it going to work when I sleep with her? Because I *am* going to sleep with her again.

That was a forgone conclusion the minute I saw her standing in Tank's last week.

And with her by-the-book attitude, I'm going to enjoy every damn minute of bending her to my will.

I chuckle to myself and look around, catching the eye of a blonde at the end of the bar. Tall, nice rack, good smile, *come fuck me* eyes.

She'd do for the night.

But Dekker would be so much better. We may be oil and water, but between the sheets, hell, we're a goddamn masterpiece.

I rest my hips against the bar and watch the sax player do his thing—fingers pressing on keys, sunglasses shading his eyes, body moving to the rhythm he's creating—and let myself fall under the haze of the shot I've just downed.

I'm still watching him while the blonde studies me, and all I can think about is a different woman: Dekker Kincade.

The fourth shot is much smoother, simply because I no longer taste it. I'm distracted though. Preoccupied.

You better stop thinking about her, Maddox.

The question is, do I really want to?

Maybe she's the distraction I need right now.

Perhaps she's the something I can get lost in—the chase and the challenge and then the reward—that will get me out of my own head.

But I know more than most, a little bit of Dekker was never enough. Nights of wanting and needing and pretending, are my proof of that.

But why would she want you after the bullshit you put her through tonight? The crappy comments and accusations?

Surprise, surprise. You fucked up again, Maddox.

I pull bills out of my wallet and set them under an empty shot glass. Time to go. To stop thinking. To sleep this off even though my thoughts have already sobered me enough.

Shit. What a waste of good alcohol.

"Hey there." The smooth voice belongs to the blonde from the corner of the bar and as much as I need to get lost in something for a while, she's not her.

"Have a good night." I take a step away but her hands grab one of mine and pull it toward her as she tries to lace her fingers with mine.

Interest doesn't even flutter to life.

"Don't be a party pooper." She pouts and then paints a siren's smile on those glossed lips of hers. "I saw you looking. I know you're interested."

Doesn't she know that subtlety goes a hell of a long way?

I laugh a few notes. "I'm interested in a lot of things. Going to my hotel right now is one of them." I pull my hand from her grasp. Her fury can be heard in the stomp of her foot.

"I could give you a lift."

"I'm more than capable of getting there. Thanks though." I give her a smile and take a step back.

"You're the first guy to say no, you know."

I turn back to look at her. "That line in itself is the reason I'm walking away."

She mutters something I can't hear and don't fucking care because the sudden movement tells me I'm still buzzed enough. I laugh as I push the door open and breathe in the frigid air.

That's a slap to sobriety right there.

It's when I step a few more feet under the covered entrance that I see Dekker near the carpark. She's standing with her arms crossed over her midsection, shivering from the cold, as she looks from her phone to the car that's pulling up and back again in what I can only assume is checking the Uber drivers.

The shit feeling I had inside about what I said returns at the sight of her.

But so does my resolve to want to lose myself to her—in her. *Please don't say no to me.*

Chapter THIRTY

Dekker

"DEKKER."

His voice is the last thing I want to hear right now. I'm tired, have had enough alcohol, and more than enough of his bullshit, so I pretend I don't hear him. Besides, I've already decided I'm done with this. Done with him. Turning my back to the entrance of the bar, I check the ETA of my rideshare again.

It's almost one o'clock in the morning. How in the hell is the only driver checking in to pick me up over five minutes away?

"Dekk!" Snow crunches beneath his boots at my back and my hands fist in response. "Look. I'm sorry." His words slur and I hate the sound of it. Hate that in the fifteen minutes max that I left him at the bar, he's drunk more to shut out whatever the hell is going on with him. And even worse, I hate that I care. "You know how I get. You know—"

"No," I shout as I whirl to face him. "I don't know how you get and I don't care how you get. Even if I did, that doesn't give you the right to—"

"Come on," he says and tries to put his hands on both of my arms.

I shrug out of his grasp and step back. "Let's get one thing straight. You are not allowed to talk to me like that. Ever. It's bullshit and demeaning and nowhere near close to the man I used to lov—know."

His head startles as my words hit him. "Maybe you didn't know me at all, then."

There is no thought to my next action other than anger and hurt and frustration. The three mingle and meld in the second I reach back into the planter filled with snow at our side, scoop up the biggest heap of snow I can find, and throw it at him.

He mutters a curse as the handful hits him squarely in the face. It falls like powder to his chest and pieces stick to his eyelashes as he blinks it away—but there's no expression on his face, no rebuke on his lips, just eyes staring at me with an intensity that makes me question what his reaction will be.

"Mature, Kincade," he finally says as a car pulls into the drive at his back. "That's my car."

"You're not going anywhere until we get a few things straight," he says with a stream of white from the cold highlighting his breath.

"Like you have any right to tell me what to do."

He grabs my arm as I walk past him and I get lucky, because when I swipe the planter again, I come up with another handful of snow. We stand there with his hand on my arm and my other arm cocked back, ready to fire.

"You wouldn't dare," he taunts, his smile finally returning, even if it's just a trace of one.

"You don't know me very well, then," I say, seconds before I launch the snow at him.

When it's midair, he lunges for me, but I don't see how much hits him because I'm off running down the sidewalk like a ten-year-old kid without a care about slipping on black ice or wet clothes or waking anybody up.

"Paybacks are a bitch, Kincade." He laughs as his footsteps thump behind me.

"You've got to catch me first." My screech fills the air as I jump over the small hedge that borders what looks like a park area under the blanket of snow. It's desolate at this time of night—morning—whatever it is—and I'm just grateful that Hunter is drunk. Otherwise, he could have easily caught me by now.

"It's an all-out war," he shouts as the first ball of snow hits my shoulder. Another yelp escapes as I swoop down to make a snowball of my own while trying to hide behind a piece of the play equipment.

"I'll win." I peek my head up and duck just in time to avoid being hit by a massive snowball. It lands with a thud behind me and pieces of it hit against the leg of my pants.

"Like hell you will."

I toss two in a row to where he's hiding behind a bench and shout in excitement when one lands on his back.

"Son of a bitch!" He laughs as I prepare more ammo. "That one's going to cost you," he says as he runs in my direction.

"No," I shriek as I run to the opposite side of my hiding place that now is his and throw two more blindly at him.

"Missed me. Missed me!"

Now you have to kiss me.

The childhood taunt repeats on my mind as I run to where I think he is . . . only to find him gone.

"Hunter," I call in a singsong voice as I look behind a shrub where I swear he is. Crap. "Hunter?" I follow footprints in the snow but am not sure if they're mine or his. "Come out, come out wherever you are."

I turn around when I hear a sound to be met with a snowball in the middle of the chest. "Argh!" I laugh as I brush it off my jacket only to look up and see him walking toward me, grin lighting up his face, and another monster-sized snowball between his hands where he's toying with it. "Do you really want to throw that?"

He nods and takes a step closer. "Do you surrender?"

"*Never.*"

He takes a bite of the snowball in his hand and there's something about him right now—the soft yellow of the park's lights overhead, the boyish grin on his lips, and the careless snowball fight—that momentarily lessens the insult and injury of the crap he said earlier and reminds me why I find him so damn irresistible. "I'm still furious at you."

"And you're even prettier with all that snow in your hair."

Shit. Don't do that, Hunter. Don't . . . break down my defenses that are weak enough already.

"You owe me an apology." I make a stand with my hands on my hips and my feet firmly planted, more than sure there's no way he's going to throw that at me.

"That's what you want to say right now when you're at my mercy?"

I've been at your mercy since I first laid eyes on you at Tank's.

Another laugh falls from my lips—nerves mixed with an anticipation I can all but feel—as I take a step in retreat. "One hundred ninety-two goals in this season alone. Twenty-three shy of Gretzky's single season record. One hundred twenty-four assists. That's fourth all-time in a season and you still have over ten games left to play. Too bad you weren't a baseball player, because all of those pretty stats don't do shit to bolster my confidence that you're going to actually hit me when you throw it," I tease, his arm pulling back faltering slightly.

"All-state third baseman right here." He lifts a finger and points to himself. "I'd have probably ended up hating it too though in the long run. *Tag.* You're it."

I'm distracted slightly by his comment about *hating it too*, so my reaction time is off.

Shit.

I cry out in shock as the snow hits my cheek and explodes in a puff of dust all over my face and down the collar of my jacket.

"That's it. You're mine now, Maddox."

The war begins. One snowball after another, we act like little kids having a snowball fight in the front yard instead of two adults in the dead of night in some random park in the middle of Boston.

"Time out," I finally pant as my lungs burn and toes numb, my hands going up to form the time-out sign.

Hunter stops in his tracks, hands on his knees but eyes trained on me and a smile owning his face. "I never figured you for a quitter."

"I am not a quitter," I say and then wait for him to get a few feet closer before I launch the snowball I'm hiding behind my back at him.

He charges after me. I shriek and run, but I'm no match for him before he tackles me to the ground.

"No!" I laugh out, as he takes a handful of snow and tosses it on my face. "You play dirty."

"Always." I giggle as he cuffs both my wrists. "No," I groan as he pulls himself up to his knees so he's sitting astride me with my hands pinned to both sides of my head. "Get off me." There's no heat behind my words, because as fun as the snowball fight was, as exhausting as our wrestling match becomes, all of a sudden awareness hits both of us as I stare up at Hunter, inches from my face. There's clarity in his eyes that I haven't seen in forever.

The cold of the snow beneath me begins to seep through my jacket but the smile on my lips feels so very good. The heat and weight of his body against mine even more so.

"Where's that cocky mouth of yours now?" he asks as his gaze flickers from my eyes to my lips and then back up.

"This wasn't part of the snowball fight," I all but whisper.

I hold my breath as he leans forward, his lips near my ear. "There aren't rules to a snowball fight. You don't get to control it, Dekk."

"I know . . . I just—" But I'm at a loss at what to say, and then can't find any words as Hunter brushes his lips over mine.

"Missed me. You missed me," he whispers. "Now you've gotta kiss me."

He leans down to kiss me again. It's gentle and tender and unexpected, since there has never been anything like it between us before.

Hunter isn't gentle when it comes to kisses. He's possessive and demanding and steals the breath from your lungs with the dominance everything about him holds over your senses.

But he just stole my breath with the simplest of kisses, and I'm not quite sure how to feel when I know I want to feel everything.

So when he releases one of my hands and runs his fingers down the side of my cheek before kissing me again, I don't fight him like I should.

I don't think of KSM and what's right or wrong professionally. All I think about is wanting to forget.

Who I am. Who he is. The possible repercussions, and the throwing my own principles out of the window to just enjoy the moment.

The warmth of his lips.

The tenderness of his touch.

The taste of him on my tongue.

The sense of calm mixed with desire that he's evoking in me.

How is it possible to want all of this without there being any fallout—professionally or emotionally?

The kiss ends, but the whirlwind of emotions sparking back to life inside me doesn't.

"Now who's playing dirty?" I murmur, my mind as scrambled as my hormones.

But when desire darkens his eyes and turns up the corners of his lips, I realize what we're doing. Here. In the snow. One hundred feet from where his teammates could be coming out of the club at any moment.

I'd like to think reason takes hold, but it doesn't. Nerves do. Pure, flustered nerves have me saying, "Snow angels," in a spontaneous burst of words as I roll out from under him.

"What?" He laughs the word out as he runs a hand through his hair to shake the snow out of it and shifts to sit on the ground.

"Snow angels," I repeat, "Come on"—I tug on his arm—"make an angel with me."

"There are a million things I want to make with you right now, Dekker Kincade, and making snow angels isn't one of them."

Our eyes hold as I'm mid-angel—arms above my head, legs spread out—but I love watching his defenses crumble. I love that he gives in to the moment and plays with me when he flops on his back and starts making angels.

Our laughter is loud as it rings through the night, dotted only by the sound of buses air brakes and a horn way off in the distance.

The sound of our swishing stops and silence descends over the park. We stare at the stars in the sky above, clouded intermittently by the curl of white from our pants of breath.

"Christ," he sighs, as his frozen hand finds mine at my side in the most casual of ways. "Why was that so fun?"

"Because being a kid again is always fun." I giggle without caring how stupid it sounds.

"It's easy to forget."

"You know . . ."

"And here it comes," he says. How easy it is to get his defenses back up.

"Nothing is coming." I pause to choose my words as best as I can. "In fact, you don't even have to respond, but if you need a friend, I'm here."

His silence is deafening, but then again, I didn't expect him to up and spill.

But I said it and I'll let it rest. I know by the tightening of his hand on mine that he heard me.

"Truth." One word. It's all he says, and a part of me dies at the sound of it.

"Nah. I'm not playing this game with you. I remember what happened the last time you asked me that," I say, and I do. It was the first time we hooked up. He asked me if I thought people could do friends with benefits. I told him no. He told me I was stubborn and questioned my resolve. The insults we flung at each other were heartless, the angry sex we had afterward, mind-blowing.

Truth.

That one word was the start of our six-month benefits-only affair. The one I walked away from with a broken heart he may or may not have known about.

So why would he say it now? Is he trying to get us back on an even footing? Or is he trying to cause a fight to push us further apart?

I'm not sure which I would be more surprised at.

"It's not what you're thinking"—he chuckles—"although that might be fun too, considering we're actually being civil to one another."

"At the moment," I murmur. "You forgot to add that we're being civil with each other *at the moment.*"

"Truth," he says again, ignoring my comment. "Why are you here, Kincade?"

"Truth?" I murmur, knowing we need to have this conversation but afraid if I admit what he already knows then the moment will be ruined. I improvise. "Only if you tell me what's going on with you first."

His sigh is long and drawn out and is at odds with how relaxed and comfortable we are with each other . . . excluding how cold we are. "Is this all there is, Dekk?"

I open my mouth and then close it as I hunt for the words to appease or soothe or commiserate. But all will sound placating. Nothing will answer a question I'm not quite sure he's getting at. "What do you mean?"

"You said it earlier. Hockey. Party. Fucking. Repeat. Is that all there is?" I want to brush away the pain I can hear, but know I don't have the right to.

"No. It's not. Maybe it's what there is for you right now—what you want there to be—but there is so much more."

"Says who?" he asks. God, he sounds lost.

"Says . . . says whoever it is you listen to, I guess." My answer is stupid and feels inadequate at best but without knowing more, I don't know how to help him. I don't know how to put to rest whatever it is he's struggling with. "Maybe you just reach a point where hockey, party, sex, repeat, isn't enough anymore. Maybe that's when you realize you want more."

"Maybe I don't deserve more." His words fade off as my surprised laugh breaks the silence.

"That's ridiculous. Why would you even say that?"

"You were right."

"About?"

"Being burned out."

My breath catches. I exhale as softly as I can so he doesn't hear it. I know how hard this admission is. "Okay."

"It's . . . it's a long story, but you were right."

"I never needed to be right. I just needed you to know it's okay if you are." I squeeze his hand to reinforce my words. "If you ever want to tell the story, I'm a good listener."

I focus on the swirl of white from our breaths above as a small part of me sags in relief inside. Not because I'm an agent trying to make a breakthrough with a client, but because I'm a woman finally being let in by a man I can't help but care about.

Finally, a breakthrough.

"Hey?" he says after a beat.

"Mmm?"

"I appreciate the romp in the park, here . . . but uh, there are parts of my anatomy I'm fearing I'll lose to frostbite." His laugh is forced, but I also know this conversation has given more of himself than he's ever given me before, so I don't push.

I let him help me up to a standing position. We laugh and threaten more snowballs as we dust the snow off each other's backs and admire our sloppy angels.

But it doesn't go unnoticed to me that he doesn't ask for my truth in return.

It only makes me wonder. *What is he afraid of?*

Chapter

THIRTY-ONE

Dekker

"You're kidding me?" My teeth chatter and my body shivers.

Even with the heat on high, the constant blowing of my breath into my hands, and Hunter's arm around me in the rideshare, I still can't feel parts of my body as I stand in front of the reception desk in the lobby and stare at the after-hours clerk.

I'm sure we look like drowned rats—hair plastered from the snow, clothes wet, boots making squishy noises on the expensive floor.

"We're so sorry, Miss Kincade," the clerk repeats, as I stand where he stopped me to tell me the news.

"What seems to be the problem?" Hunter asks as he comes in behind me.

"It shouldn't be more than an hour or two," he explains as his eyes grow wide when he realizes who he's speaking with. "I'm sorry, Mad Dog—er, Mr. Maddox. A pipe has leaked on Miss Kincade's floor. The rooms are fine, but the hall is closed off so we can fix the problem quickly."

"Then move her to a suite," Hunter demands, and I should be miffed he's speaking for me, but I'm too freaking cold to care.

"We're completely booked. I don't have any vacant—"

"You don't have rooms set aside for emergencies like this? You don't—"

"We do, but they're all taken already. We can try to find and comp you a room at a neighboring hotel. Just give me a moment to—"

"It's fine," I say with a tight smile, on which I'm more than certain are blue lips.

"My room then," he says.

"No, I can wait," I stutter, more than cognizant of the unrequited sexual tension continuing to reverberate between us, even when we're half frozen.

"Don't be ridiculous." He rolls his eyes and puts his hand on my back to usher me to the elevator as the clerk stares at me, waiting for me to tell him anything more. "You can at least get out of these wet clothes so you can warm-up."

"That's what I'm afraid of," I say drolly and lift my eyebrows.

"You're a pain in my ass," he mutters and then turns to the clerk. "She'll be in my room."

"How should we inform you so we don't wake you up in case you're asleep?" the clerk asks.

"Text her cell," Hunter says as he gives him my number from memory that has me quite surprised. He wraps an arm around my shoulder and runs a hand up and down my arm.

"Please," I finish for him when he doesn't say it.

And without waiting for a response, Hunter directs us to the elevator. We're in his room within minutes—top floor, great view of the city, but all I can think about when he closes the door behind us is getting warm.

He turns the heat on as high as it can go. I'm stuck in that dilemma between wanting to take my jacket and my wet clothes off and not being in my own room.

"Sooooo cold," I say as I rock back and forth under a vent with my face tilted up and eyes closed.

I hear the click of something and then the sound of ringing. "Hi. Yes. This is room eight-oh-five. I want to order two hot chocolates, two grilled cheeses, um . . . and any dessert you have that's hot." He murmurs something. "I don't care if the kitchen's closed. Figure a way to get it made and I'll make sure to tip accordingly."

"Hunter—"

"No. It's the least they can do after not having access to your room." Then he turns back to the voice on the other end of the phone. "Yes, we're one of those rooms . . . thank you so much for your help. I appreciate it." He hangs the phone up. "It'll be about thirty to forty minutes."

"What are we going to do?" I ask with a chattering laugh as the heat stings my face. "Have a frozen picnic?" It does sound perfect though.

"Why not? Get out of your jacket," Hunter says as I hear a zipper and then a thud as his falls to the floor.

He moves into my line of sight, and of course he didn't just remove his jacket, but his shirt too. Him standing before me shirtless in all his chiseled ab perfection doesn't do anything to help erase the kiss on my lips and his taste on my tongue from the park.

At least he's sobered up now. There's that.

Refusing to give him the satisfaction of staring at him or acknowledging that he's half-naked, I focus on undoing the buttons of my jacket. "Crap," I mutter, my fingers so numb I keep fumbling with them as my teeth chatter and my body begs for some hot water to sink into.

"Let me."

"I've got it." I slap at his hands when he reaches out to push mine out of the way and help me, but it does nothing to deter him. Within seconds, he has the front of my coat opened and is yanking it off my shoulders and then fighting to get my hands out of the bunched ends of the sleeves as if I'm a little kid.

"There," he says as it drops to the floor before enveloping me in his arms. I accept the warmth—even though his body is as cold as mine—and accept the rare moment of magnanimity from him after the night we've had. It feels like an apology without words, and I didn't realize how much I needed this from him until now.

I close my eyes momentarily and absorb the feel of it.

This is a bad decision all around. Me. Here in his room. Our past. Our future.

Christ.

It's a double-edged sword that reminds me just how good the good is when it's with Hunter and how there's no way I can let myself fall back into this trap when I have to try and win him over as a client.

"I can't. Hunter, I can't," I say as I push against his chest and step back even when he tries to keep me close.

"You'd rather freeze?"

I eye him. "Last time—we weren't—"

"Shh," he says and holds his very cold finger to my lips. "Don't ruin the moment. More civility is afoot."

A sigh falls from my lips that matches the shake of my head. I stare at him. At the breadth of his shoulders and the wave to his hair. At the blue of his eyes and the lopsided smile. At our past, and what I'm trying to make our future. I take in the whole and let his words from earlier hit my ears again. *Is this all there is?*

"This is too complicated," I say when I finally find the words.

"What is? You standing here in my hotel room? It's only complicated if you make it," he says, batting around words with double meanings that I try to ignore. "Besides, you're the one to blame here."

"Me?" I laugh the word out. "How am I to blame?"

"You're the one following us from city to city on this road stretch."

"Okay." I draw the word out and toe my shoes off one by one, trying to buy time to figure out where he's going with this. Is this his way of realizing what he said to me in the park and being uncomfortable that he had a moment of vulnerability?

"You're the one who hit me with a snowball."

That's definitely what this is.

"I'd do it again." I laugh and play along. "And your point is what?"

"Why exactly do you know my stats?"

"What?"

"My stats. In the park you recited them off the top of your head like you'd been studying them, so I wanted to know . . . why do you know my stats?"

Here's my chance. To finally be honest . . . professionally. But because he just opened up to me, was real, I loathe to ruin it. I'd be lying if I said I didn't want him to share more. He's standing there shirtless. We just shared a kiss that's still very fresh in my mind and on my lips.

Shit.

How did we just go from a fight in a jazz club, to a snowball fight full of laughter, to a kiss loaded with things I don't want to acknowledge . . . to this? I answer with caution. "I know your stats because it's my job to. I told you that the other day when you asked me the exact same question."

"But I'm not your client."

"I know a lot of athlete's stats who aren't my clients."

He takes a step closer to me. "Why?"

"Because what you're paid is commensurate with your stats and status and draw to a crowd, and that affects all my clients. If you're the benchmark, we know where to go from there."

He cocks his head to the side and stares at me as he says, "Hmm. I thought maybe you were following the team because you missed and wanted me. Because you were sick of those memories keeping you satisfied on lonely nights and wanted the real thing as a refresher." A slow, steady grin slides onto his lips as his eyes reflect thoughts I'd be better not to remember.

"I do like you. Like this," I explain, pointing to him and then me. "But with you clothed and me clothed and—"

"Liar." He unbuckles his belt.

"I'm not lying. How can I be lying?" My words tumble out in a frantic mess as my libido and my head argue with my visceral reaction to it.

He unbuttons his pants.

The body is definitely winning out over the head right now.

"What are you doing?" I practically shout because yes, I may have seen him in all his glory many times before . . . but I've also experienced what that glory feels like and holy hell, I do *not* need to be reminded with a high-definition visual.

"I'm freezing," he says as nonchalantly as possible as he shoves his pants down his hips so he's standing before me in his boxer briefs and a body gorgeous enough to want to reach out and touch and feel its realness.

"Hunter?"

"What?" He chuckles. "You can stand there in your wet clothes and freeze to death because you don't trust me . . . but I'm getting in the shower."

Heat. It sounds so damn good as my teeth chatter. I suddenly forget him standing before me and remember the wet clothes I'm still swathed in.

"No one said I didn't trust you." *Liar.* "But I'm not taking a shower with you."

"Suit yourself, but oh, it's going to feel like heaven sinking in a nice, scalding hot bath."

"Bath?" My ears perk up. "I thought you said shower."

"Plans change. Now it's a bath."

"Oh," I moan the word out.

"Yep. I plan on filling it until it starts to cool and then refilling it again."

My eyes virtually roll back in my head at the thought. "That's wasteful."

His chuckle is a seductive sound. "But it'll feel oh-so-good," he hums.

"And bad for the environment."

"Currently, feeling my toes and my nuts trumps my inefficient use of water."

I take a step toward him as my body shivers. "You're keeping your underwear on, right?" I ask, shoulders straightening as if the thin cotton will be a deterrent from us touching each other.

Or wanting to.

"If that's what you want. I mean"—his eyes roam up and down the length of me—"you'll need to do the same because there's no way I want to see you naked either," he teases.

I stare at him—my body begging me to accept and my head knowing it's the worst idea ever . . . but I'm so damn cold.

"Fine." I strip my shirt over my head and do everything to ignore the hungry way his eyes scrape over the black lace of my bra beneath, the muscle twitching in his jaw. "Quit looking at me like that," I scold.

"I'm not looking at you in any way. Not your curves or your ass or . . . God"—he mock shivers—"why would any man be turned on by you?" His words are playful, his smile even more so.

"Go turn the water on like you promised." I flick my finger in that direction as I question whether the wet clothes or fighting my attraction to him is worse torture. "I'll be right there."

He gives me one quick flash of a grin before heading toward the bathroom, giving me a view of his ass, hamstrings, and back. I have no shame in staring at and appreciating it.

When the sound of the water echoes out of the bathroom, I shimmy out of my jeans in record time and thank fate that I wore some lacy boyshort panties instead of the thong I originally grabbed.

That decision just made my life a whole lot easier.

Or at least I think it did until I enter the bathroom to find him standing to the side of the massive tub, bubbles starting to form in the water, and the lights of the sleeping city twinkling outside the wall of windows the bathtub is positioned in front of.

Hunter glances up, and I'm not going to lie when I say it gives me the slightest thrill to see the hitch in his motion when he sees me standing there in my bra and panties.

"No funny stuff," I warn as I head toward the tub.

"No worries, Kincade," he says, but I don't believe him. "I'm well aware you're on the straight and narrow."

"I have to be. It's my business."

"What is?" He takes a step toward me. "You being here in my bathroom is business?" He gives a frustrated shake of his head. "It's always business with you. Every time. It used to not be that way. You used to take every ounce of that pent-up perfect professionalism you wear like a shield of armor and destroy me in bed with it until we were spent. Until we were satisfied. Every damn time. You used to like to walk on the wild side with me. You used to—"

"Not anymore." I shift my feet, needing to stop his words, the memories I can all but taste, and the poignant ache they create. "I have too much at stake now."

"And what exactly do you have that's at stake?" he asks as we stand a few feet apart, eyes warring and bodies wanting.

Too many things.

Way too many things.

My company.

My heart.

My dignity.

He takes a step closer and dips so we're eye to eye. "What is it, Dekk? What happened to change you? What is it that dimmed your fire?"

You.

The answer pops in my head without any hesitation, and I stagger because how can I say that? How can I think he's the reason I've become cautious when before I would have jumped in with both feet with him without a thought?

"My fire's still there." I offer a smile that I don't think he believes.

"Prove it," he breathes, as he closes the remaining distance between us. It feels like it's in slow motion as he reaches out to brush an errant strand of hair off my cheek, and I almost let myself sink into him.

"Whatever," I say as an out and stride past him toward the tub, simply to avoid his touch, and the dare I can already see him trying to set me up with. Nerves dance beneath the surface as I stare at the world beyond but somehow end up meeting his eyes in our reflection in the glass.

It hits me how much I'm flirting with danger.

In my standing with my clients.

In the reality of my life.

In what the hell I'm doing here in my bra and underwear in Hunter's room, when I know even if we did do something, he'd wake up in the morning without anything changed when everything would have for me.

He turns the water off but his chuckle at my lack of answer snaps me to the here and now. To the want and the need sparring against the reason and sanity.

I take an even breath and turn to face him and his inflammatory comment.

Walk away and make a stand, Dekk, or stay here and know what's going to happen.

His hand is on the nape of my neck in an instant and pulls me to him so his mouth meets mine the same time our bodies slam into each other's.

And every damn thing I felt in the park is magnified times a million.

Where the gentleness of the park confused me, the violent desire of right now is the Hunter Maddox I remember.

This is the one I can feed off.

This is the one that's purely sex, only need, and completely animalistic.

One hand holds my neck hostage to allow his lips to take what they want, while his other fists in the back of my panties and twists tightly so the fabric cuts against my skin.

Push him away.

He tugs on my bottom lip with his teeth.

Tell him no.

The hardness of his erection grinds against me.

Oh my God.

The firmness of his chest beneath my palms.

I missed this.

The hunger in his every action.

I missed him.

His breath is ragged when he rips his lips from mine, eyes blazing into mine, as we stare at each other, hands still owning the other's body in some way or another.

"Goddammit, Dekk," he groans. "Don't fucking toy with me. Tell me you want this. Tell me you need this as much as I do."

His voice sounds like how I feel—desperate, needy, ready to detonate.

The knowledge that I can break the control of a man like him, is beyond explanation. I want him. How he sates all desires. How he devastates all reason.

Him.

More of him.

Now is the time to feel every ounce, every inch, everything, he's willing to give me.

Chills chase up my spine as I stare at him and anticipate and debate and throw caution to the wind.

Who cares about hot chocolate and grilled cheese now?

It's my lips that meet his this time. It's my teeth that nip the tattoo on his shoulder. It's my fingernails that score their way down the side of his torso. It's my hand that slides inside the waistband of his boxer briefs and encircles his rock-hard cock. It's his body that tenses beneath my touch.

There's intensity to our actions, an urgency. A need to hurry up to the endgame and slow down at the same time.

I ache and burn and yearn every place Hunter's hands touch and his stubble scrapes.

We are a mass of hands and lips and grinds as we stumble the few steps to the bed. His underwear comes off as we walk. His fingers unclasp my bra as I shove down my panties.

I lied the other night.

I don't care about finesse when it comes to Hunter. I care about his hands gripping, his hips thrusting, his teeth nipping, his cock sliding.

My body vibrates as his hands take and claim and knead my breasts, my hips, my ass.

"Dekker," he groans, his lips against my breast, my skin vibrating under the strain of how he says my name. His hand fists in my hair, and he pulls my head back so I'm forced to look in his eyes as he stands back to full height.

My body is raw and wanting, and the seconds we waste as he stares at me, as his eyes wander up and down every inch of my body, has me itching to reach out and take what I want.

I open my lips, swollen from his, to speak, to tell him to destroy me in the most delicious of ways, but there's something in his look that tells me he needs this as much as I do . . . but for such very different reasons.

"Turn around," he orders and I obey, anticipation held with bated breath.

He puts a hand on my waist as he pulls me back against him, my ass meeting his thighs, the firmness of his dick undeniable against my lower back. He moves the hair off my neck with his free hand and his teeth scrape over the skin there as his other moves between my thighs.

"Fuck, Dekk. You . . ." He kisses the juncture of my shoulder to my neck. "This." His fingers slide between my thighs as one of his feet knock mine wider. "I'm going to fuck this sweet pussy of yours." He parts me, and his groan when he finds me wet for him has my nipples hardening. "With my fingers." He tucks them into me and my body convulses in reaction, anticipation for the next touch already building. "With my tongue." He slides his tongue up to my ear and dips inside, the combination of his coarse stubble and warm tongue making me gasp.

"With my cock." He uses his hand to slide it between the cheeks of my ass and I tighten around his fingers in response.

My body is strung so tight, my need at fever pitch, my want dancing across my skin in goosebumps.

His hand grips the back of my neck again. "Tell me you're ready for me. Tell me you want me. Tell me to fuck you," he growls into my ear.

But I don't speak—can't—as his fingers continue their slow, delicious torture to the nerves and pleasure points between the apex of my thighs. My head falls back on his shoulder as I moan with another maneuver of his fingers. "Hunter." His name is a long, drawn-out plea to give me what I need and to never stop.

"I know this body. I know what you need. So goddamn wet," he groans. "I've wanted you from the moment I saw you. Now, bend over."

My pulse races as I do as I'm told. His hands caress down my hips before one slides up and down my slit, allowing the room's cool air to hit my most sensitive flesh.

But more arousing than his touch is his hum of approval, of desire, of greed that owns the room around us.

I rest on my elbows in eagerness and then jolt when I feel the soft swipe of his tongue over my clit, stopping to dip in my center, before moving up over the tight rim of muscles atop, before going back the way he started.

He's deliberately slow, and his tantalizing torture has me squirming and widening my legs so he can have whatever part of me he wants.

I'm his.

Completely.

"Please," I moan.

A chuckle is his only response as he withdraws all touch from me. Then I yelp as his hand connects firmly with the side of my ass.

But the sting is quickly forgotten, the temporary pain gone as I hear the telltale rip of foil. He takes a moment to protect us before he slides the head of his cock up and down my slit.

"Sweet hell, Dekker," he moans as he slowly pushes his way into me.

My muscles resist with the sweetest of burns until they heat and accept and tighten from the fullness. It's my moan in the room now. It's my command for him to move. It's my ass pushing back against him telling him I'm ready.

With both hands on my hips, he begins to move in and out of me in measured, controlled strokes.

Each one a slow seduction to my nerves.

Each one an assault on my senses in the best way possible.

Each one another stroke closer to his control snapping.

And I can feel it happening, just as surely as I can feel my own orgasm begin to build.

His grip becomes tighter on my shoulder. His thrusting is more powerful, the slap of his thighs against mine louder. The sounds he emits more guttural, more unhinged.

Combined, they turn me on in a way no one else has ever been able to before, but I push the thought out of my mind and fall into the moment. Under the haze of pleasure. To the sensations he evokes.

I reach my hand between my thighs and brush my finger over my clit. The drag of his cock inside. The tease of my fingers on the outside. The gruff groan of my name. The ability he gives me to feel, to be, to give in.

It's heady and powerful and damn it to hell, he allows my body to build and soar and ache until the sensations reach a crescendo that I can only close my eyes, bow my head, and hang on to for the ride.

My body detonates—fractures into a million pieces as the orgasm slams into my every nerve, my every muscle, my everything.

My hips buck.

"Take it all."

My hands grip the comforter beneath me.

"Come for me, Dekk."

I cry out as my body tenses with pleasure and then sags with its release. I'm awash with warmth and bliss as my knees buckle, but Hunter's hands hold my hips up as he continues to drive into me. As he milks every ounce of pleasure out of me before picking up his pace.

I'm still under the fog of my climax, still trying to catch my breath and gain my faculties, but I don't have a chance to because it's Hunter's turn now.

His hands bruise and hips slam against me until his feral groan echoes as he empties himself into me.

"Hell," he murmurs as he bends over and kisses my shoulder before wrapping his arms around my waist and holding me into him.

We stay like this for a few moments as our breathing evens and our hearts decelerate. Just as I'm trying to figure out what happens next, he slips out of me when he straightens up, and heads for the bathroom without a word.

Chapter
THIRTY-TWO

Dekker

THE KNOCK ON THE HOTEL ROOM DOOR HAS ME JOLTING TO ATTENTION like a kid caught doing something she shouldn't be doing.

"*The food,*" we both say in unison as if that singular idea can suddenly bring back the disjointed feeling we both have in the aftermath of what happened between us.

"Here." He tosses a robe my way as he strides past me to where his suitcase is. "Just a second," he calls to the room service person on the other side of the door. Within a few seconds, he's stepping into a pair of jogging pants, as I slide the robe on.

"I'd kill for anything hot." He laughs the words out, his hand tapping my ass, before he opens the door. "What do you have for us . . .?"

Hunter's words fade while my hands still tying the knot in my robe.

Callum.

Eyes wide, jaw lax.

Shit. Shit. Shit.

"I'm—I'm sorry." He jerks back a step. "It's late." His eyes go between the two of us again as he stammers. "I didn't mean to interrupt—"

"You didn't. Nothing happened." More than flustered, I take a step forward, well aware that the room behind us suggests the contrary. Our wet clothes litter the space, landing wherever we took them off, and the bed is a rumpled mess. "We had a snowball fight. We were wet." The words come out messily as I gesture toward the clothes strewn about. "Freezing. There's a pipe leak in my hallway. On my floor. We thought you were room service bringing us food to warm us up."

"Relax, Dekk," Hunter says as he reaches up and puts a hand on my bicep. "You're a big girl. You don't have to explain."

But I do have to explain, I want to say. Callum is a client, and now that he thinks we're together, my integrity and reputation are at stake.

"I just . . . it's not what he thinks it is," I mumble, hating that Callum can't even meet my eyes.

"I wanted to make sure you got back okay," Callum says to me, eyes lowered. "I tried your cell but didn't hear anything." He pauses and then turns his attention to Hunter. "And you, Maddox. You took off from the club without a word and were drunk as shit . . . Forget about it." He looks from Hunter to me and then back. "You're obviously okay. Both of you."

"Yep. Sure am," Hunter says, that half-cocked smirk on his lips not doing me any favors to dispel the situation.

"I'm just waiting for my room to be ready."

"In a robe," Cal purses his lips and nods. "Got it."

"Cal, wait," I say and step past Hunter. "I promise it's not what it looks like."

"It's your business, not mine."

"Perfect timing," a voice says behind Callum, and we all startle at there being someone else in the hallway at this odd hour of the morning. There's a rattle of dishes on a tray—glasses and silverware, before the room service person steps forward, pushing the tray in front of them. "Mr. Maddox?" he asks as he looks at the two men.

"Yes. Thank you." Hunter steps forward.

"Some hot chocolate. Grilled cheeses. Some hot apple turnovers. And I think a few more goodies. It's all on the house of course for the inconvenience we've caused you, Miss Kincade."

"Thank you." I nod and give a tight smile, more than relieved to have an innocent bystander back up my story with Callum.

"Maintenance just told me your room will be ready in five minutes. I was asked to escort you down there to make sure all your things are okay and to your liking."

"Oh." I hold the top of the robe closed and wonder if this is a blessing or a curse.

The blessing being that Hunter and I have never done that after part of sex before. It used to be sex, clean up, exchange a few words, maybe not . . . and then one of us would leave. Sure, we enjoyed each other, but there was nothing else between us.

The *curse* being that we've never done the after part of sex before either.

I glance back to the clothes on the floor and wonder how I retain my dignity while I scramble to pick them all up.

Callum assesses the situation and nods. "It's late," he says before shuffling down the hall toward his room, a few rooms down.

Hunter moves a hand to my lower back as the server moves the cart into the room. "Stay and eat?"

I shake my head, suddenly in a state of limbo—embarrassed, worried, confused. "I'm fine. I've got to go to my room—he said so—and . . ."

"Dekker."

"No, It's late. I should go make sure my room and things are okay."

"I'll walk you down there."

"No. I've got it." I step away from him, suddenly uncomfortable in everything. Needing space to clear my head and the emotions I know are most likely one-sided. At the situation I've just put myself in.

Shit.

"Dekker?" he asks.

"It's fine."

"I'll take her down," Hunter reasserts.

"No," I say with more force than I should before turning to the hotel staffer. "Can you give me a minute? I'll be right there."

The staffer nods and I shut the door to buy me a few minutes to gather my stuff.

"Dekker?" Hunter says as I move around his room like a madwoman gathering my wet clothes and shoes.

"It's fine. We're fine," I mutter and smile.

"So you've said."

"If Callum talks—"

"Then what?" Hunter asks, his voice resonating around the room. "If he talks, then what's the big deal? You're a grown woman who can have sex with whomever she chooses. Why does it matter?"

"Because it does." I fight the sudden burning of tears and hate that they're there. Because I don't cry over men. I don't cry over things that can never be. And I certainly refuse to cry over Hunter Maddox.

"Gotcha." He sighs as he moves with me through the room. "Ah, I forgot." He tsks as I survey the room one last time. "This was a mistake, right? It shouldn't have happened. It can't happen again. Yadda, yadda, yadda."

I expect to meet his eyes and find amusement in them, but there's nothing but a gravity that unnerves me. I can't tell if he's angry or confused, but it's something I've never seen before, and that in and of itself has me needing to get some space from him to figure out why there's an awkwardness here.

"Hunter . . . I'm here for work and—"

"I wasn't aware you were on the clock at two in the morning."

"It's not that. It's just—"

"Just like old times, huh? Great sex. Poor communication. It's best you leave before the fighting starts." He takes a step forward and presses a kiss to my forehead. "Good night, Dekker."

I stare at him as he opens the door. The second course of rejection from him tastes just as bitter as the first time. Maybe even worse.

The hotel clerk in the hallway rocks on his heels as he senses the discomfort between Hunter and me. I give him a half-smile and then turn back to face Hunter. Our eyes hold unspoken words exchanging between us—I'm sorry. *Why is it like this? Why can't we figure out how to do this right?*

At least that's what I think they say, because I second-guess every single one of them as I head to my hotel room.

Maybe this was the best way to end tonight.

Hockey.

Callum knocking on the door. The room service man shortly after.

Party.

Maybe a quick exit where neither of us had to talk about what's next, and how we move on from here is for the best.

Fucking.

Because I just screwed up by sleeping with Hunter.

No *repeat.*

And the worst part? I know that I did, but I wish I was still in the hotel room with Hunter right now.

Chapter
THIRTY-THREE

Hunter

THE CURL OF STEAM COMES OFF MY COFFEE AS I SIT SLUMPED IN THE chair where I moved it in front of the windows of my hotel room.

The city of Boston waits to wake up as I replay the last twenty-four hours in my mind and anticipate the sun to light up the sky.

Sleep was hopeless.

It is most nights as of late.

I've watched film of last night's game twice. My notes are taken. My critiques of my performance ten times worse than my father's. Maybe next game I can prove him differently.

Who can sleep when the world is burning down around them? When my brother's dying, my parents live in an alternate reality, and I'm constantly fucking up one thing after another.

When I simply don't want to care anymore.

It's the white noise I've grown used to living with. The constant. The things I'll never be able to change but will always try to.

"Christ," I mutter and roll my shoulders, my body exhausted but my mind going a million miles an hour.

The lone difference tonight in my thoughts is Dekker. For the first time in as long as I can remember, the shit in my head is quieter. Or maybe not quieter, but not as choking. The anger, the guilt, the unease . . . they took a backseat for a snowball fight, her hand holding mine in the rideshare, and then the incredible sex soon after.

Or maybe it's the relief in finally admitting to someone an ounce of my truth.

Either way it—us together—was *like* old times and yet so very different.

Is that what's bugging me? The *difference* between us this time?

I already knew having sex wasn't going to sate the hunger I had for her. I already knew one taste of her, one thrust into her pussy, and I'd only want more.

That's how it has always been with her. That's how it always will be.

What I didn't expect was for the same damn heartache I had when we broke things off last time to return with a goddamn vengeance. The heartache I didn't have to admit to last time because she walked out before I could.

But there was something different than that tonight. Something new.

I let the coffee scald my tongue when I drink it. I let it hurt and burn, as I force myself to acknowledge the one thing I pretend I don't notice. *Experience daily.*

I have women at my fingertips, fans are everywhere I go, and I have teammates around me almost every waking minute of each day, but fuck if Dekker walking out of here tonight without a glance back didn't make me realize how fucking lonely I am.

How alone I feel.

Daily.

"You're crazy. Fucking crazy, Mad," I say to the empty room as I acknowledge that tonight was most men's dream. Hell, it used to be mine too.

Great sex with a gorgeous woman who walks away after it's over and doesn't ask for anything more—not even a kiss goodnight.

Sex without strings.

But fuck if I don't feel invisible strings tying me up in the biggest fucking knot I've ever seen or felt before.

One that has her at the goddamn center of it.

Get over it, Maddox. Get the fuck over it.

I don't get attached.

I don't get the privilege to have feelings for someone.

I don't ever allow myself to want more.

But hell if what she did for me tonight—made me laugh, made me feel carefree, and then fucking owned every urge and need and want and inch of my body—doesn't make me wonder what it would be like to have that on the ready. If it's something I could get used to.

Drawing in a deep breath, I swear this room still smells like her—her shampoo, our sex—and that makes it hard to stop thinking about her. To stop wishing she were still here. To stop replaying her bullshit ghosting act and the way it felt watching her walk away.

"Let it go," I murmur and lean my head against the back of my chair, willing sleep in any form to come.

I close my eyes and try to quiet everything. All thoughts. All hopes. All dreams.

And in that limbo state between being awake and falling asleep, I have a moment of clarity I'm sure I won't remember once I wake in the morning.

She slept with me tonight and bailed.

Why?

To get back at me like I did her that first night in the elevator? To show why I should have chased after her three years ago? That's not like her, though.

Then what could it be?

Because Callum saw us? Because what had just happened between us was more than obvious?

Why the fuck does that matter?

He's her client, I'm not.

There's no line of professionalism that was crossed when it shouldn't be. There were no favors promised. Just pure, insanely incredible sex.

So why . . .

Shit.

Because Dekker Kincade is here to recruit *me*.

That has to be the only logical answer.

And I say logical, because I can't swallow that she bailed because she's embarrassed for people to know we were together. For Callum to know we had slept together.

The question is: is that why she slept with me? To maybe slide into my life between some bouts of good sex, some pillow talk . . . where she convinces me to leave Sanderson and change to KSM?

That would mean she just slept with a potential client. That would explain why she bailed right after.

I reject the notion but hate the thought that lingers. The one that screams all I am is a client to her.

A number she wants to nail to her wall, a fat commission check she'll win over to her side and then forget to pay attention to. First the Dartmouth game and then tonight.

It's the easiest thing to believe.

So much easier than believing maybe I deserve her. So much easier than believing she cares for me.

Because the last time she blew me off like this was after a bout of sex, when she got dressed and walked away, visibly upset without divulging why.

I didn't chase her. I never asked what the hell happened but just figured our time was up. It was probably a good thing because the minute I feel things, I bail too. And I was starting to feel things.

But now I'm remembering the shitstorm it made me feel and hating it.

And that's a sign that I need to back the fuck away and head whatever shit I'm feeling off at the pass.

My life is hockey. It's about being the best. It's about outrunning ghosts that will forever be a part of me.

Her job is profiting off athletes like me. It's about getting the biggest roster.

It's about acquiring them like tokens and cashing them in when all is said and done.

She's using me, and that gives me a justified reason to be pissed and push her away when I'd fucking kill to have her sitting beside me right now, quiet and comfortable waiting for the sunrise.

But I can't let that happen.

I don't deserve her.

I don't deserve anything.

She used you, Mad. She just showed her cards. She's in this for her. She can ply you with comments about how she wants to be your friend and be there for you if you need to talk, but the endgame is you being her client.

Another person to use me.

Another person to see me as a commodity.

Maybe if I keep telling myself that, I'll stop wanting her as badly as I do right now.

Maybe I'll find some other way to not be lonely.

Is this all there is?

Chapter
THIRTY-FOUR

Dekker

THE SUBTLE SORENESS BETWEEN MY THIGHS IS THE FIRST THING I NO-
tice when I snuggle deeper beneath the covers to hide from the sun streaming
through the window.

Last night is more than a distant memory. It's more like an in-the-face reminder of a pickle I need to figure my way out of.

I slept with a potential client. A current client all but caught me in the act.
And then I had a moment of panic.

A huge moment of panic that only took some tossing and turning in bed
when I couldn't fall asleep to figure out.

What I felt for Hunter—the reasons I pushed him away the last time we
were together—came back clearly last night.

And I wasn't sure how I felt about that. How can I purport to be this strong,
independent female who puts up with no one's shit, and after I spend one night
with a man, I still have those same feelings? How can I be proud of myself when
he was an ass to me at the club and I turned around and did what we did? How
can I do any of this when I haven't been up front with him about why I'm here?

I'm a chicken.

Isn't that what this comes down to? I'm an overthinking, nervous-nelly
chicken who doesn't have the guts to admit that I not only screwed up by sleeping with him for professional reasons, but also because I know I'm not gutsy
enough to tell Hunter being fuck buddies isn't good enough for me anymore.

I'm not the same person.

Three years does a lot to mature a person and after Chad, maybe I want
something more.

Maybe, my dad was right—not that I'll ever tell him.

Hunter Maddox. Complicated and multi-layered, incredibly gifted, a god
in the sack, yet troubled by something significant.

I'd ask myself what I want from him but I already know. *Just* sex won't be enough. *Just* being a client might never work.

Oh what a tangled web I've woven.

But at least I'm sexually satisfied for what feels like the first time in forever. There's always that very shallow tidbit to fall back on as the sky falls and more clients leave KSM, because one of their lead agents sleeps with clients and presumably gives them better treatment than all her other clients.

Even worse, they'll start thinking that sleeping with my clients is part of the KSM package.

Shit. The more I think the worse this gets.

I groan and flop onto my back, trapping myself in the comforter when I do.

"Woman up, Kincade," I mutter. Tell him the truth. Explain why this can't happen again. March up to him and say, yes, he's the player I'm here to recruit. And yes, we slept together. *Christ, Dekker*, he already knows that part. But maybe tell him it happened once, I own it, but I can't let it happen again because I want to win his trust as a client. And once he's a client I can't cross that line.

I take a deep breath and fight the urge to slide back into sleep like only a person whose body feels satisfied knows, when it hits me.

Oh shit. Oh shit. Oh shit.

I fling the covers off me and scramble to grab my laptop like a madwoman. I'm logged in within seconds, the connection accepting about the same time I'm patting down my hair and pretending I don't look like I just woke up.

"So glad you could join us," my father says through the connection as it goes from pixelated to clear where I can see him and my three sisters sitting at the conference table at the offices.

"Sorry. Late night."

Brexton's chuckle fills the room. "I hope he was worth it," she teases and has no idea how true that statement is.

"Funny," I feign. "I went with a few of the Jacks to a jazz club and then came back here to find a pipe had burst in the hallway. Late night," I overexplain when I need to just stop.

"Ha. Dare we ask *whose* pipe burst, exactly?" Lennox asks, staring at me through the screen.

There's absolute silence and then my sisters and I break out into laughter.

"Ladies," my dad says as he tries not to chuckle. "That's enough. We've already run through the status of all of our clients . . . your tardiness allowed you to miss that part, so you're up, kid. That status report remains blank so I'm beginning to get worried here."

"I'll update, but did we talk about what clients they're going after yet? Because I'm still miffed at my urgency and not theirs to pick up and leave."

"Considering Maddox is the one tearing up the charts and making scenes,

I agree with Dad that it was important for you to be there now. Get him on the upswing so you can show him why you'll prevent him from falling," Chase says in her clipped, professional tone as if she has no stake in any of this.

"Always the pet," I mutter, knowing that's what they say about me.

"And she finally admits it." Lennox laughs, to which I hold my hand up to the lens and flip her off.

"So has Hunter been receptive to your advances?" he asks, and I cough in response to fight the smile on my lips.

"We haven't gotten to that part yet." I bite my bottom lip as they all stare at me.

"Hence the blank status report," Chase mutters under her breath.

"And why not?" Lennox prompts.

"It hasn't been the right time."

"In two-plus weeks' time, you haven't found a measly moment to corner him and ask if he's happy with his representation?" Chase asks.

"Look, I'm here because you guys feel like he's a ticking timebomb you want me to manage. I have to use caution. His game is stellar, but he's a disaster off the ice, so I'm trying to be the one to be there to fix his fuck-ups right now. He's burned out, and I'm trying to help him see that. Trying to help him see what he fell in love with again."

There's a snort in the conference room and they all glance to Brexton, and I can only imagine what she said.

I clear my throat and continue. "I'm trying to show him I'm the one there when Sanderson's not or is too busy with his other clients. I'm trying to make it be me who Hunter calls when he needs something. When he needs someone to understand him," I say, knowing it's so much more than that. To them, this is our career and business, but to me, it's wanting to see him get over this. "I'm at the games with the praise, but it's the off of the ice part that will win him to my side."

"Smart. Let him get comfortable—umm . . . more comfortable with you," Chase says.

"Knock it off, you guys. Hunter and I happened over three years ago. We're both mature adults who've moved on," I lie.

"I hear Sanderson was there," my dad says before a fight can start.

"He was." I nod. "His warning was delivered and ignored." Their chuckles fill the room.

"And you?" my dad asks. "How are you holding up?"

How do I answer that with the four people who know me best? How do I mask my expression so they don't see I'm kind of a mess this morning, torn by emotions I can't even name myself?

Because now that he's asked, it's ten times harder to pretend it's not there.

Now that he's brought it up, all I want to do is crawl into his arms and get a fatherly hug that tells me it's going to all work out in the end.

"I'm good. Fine," I reiterate. "My goal is to get Hunter alone this week between the next set of games and pitch our case."

"Rumor is Finn's not happy with him," Lennox says.

"Rumor is a lot of people aren't." I pull my hair up in a clip, suddenly more aware than ever what I probably look like to them. "And I intend to exploit that to my advantage."

My father nods, his hands steepled in front of him, and lips pursed. "He's our in to Sanderson, Dekk. He's the influencer or whatever term you young kids use these days. He's the one who sets the bar. Get him over and it'll be easier to pull more hockey players who want to be him." He leans back in his chair and, as he looks me directly in the eyes, I feel both his challenge and confidence *in* me. "I know you can do it."

Chapter

THIRTY-FIVE

Dekker

"THIS SEAT TAKEN?" I ASK WHEN I SPOT HUNTER IN THE HOTEL LOBBY Starbucks.

He barely glances up from his iPad as he stands abruptly. "Now, it is. Have at it."

Ridiculously, I think he's standing to pull out my chair. Instead, he starts to walk away.

"Hey," I say after him, surprised and dumbfounded by his reaction. "Hunter."

"What?" he snaps as he looks back at me.

"I've texted and you haven't answered. I thought maybe we could talk, you know—about—"

"About what? Our *mistake*?" He scrunches his nose up and my insides twist at that stupid phrase. "No thanks. I'm sure Callum or another one of the guys will be along shortly, and I don't want to fuck up your reputation with them because you slummed it with me."

"Jesus Christ. Are you kidding me?" I stare at him dumbfounded, hands out, head shaking.

"Nope. I'm not kidding in the least." He takes a step toward me and lowers his voice. "You wanted sex, you got sex. You want to take the temperature on a new client, then put your damn toes in the water. Sleeping with him and bolting for old time's sake is a dick move."

His words sting and hurt and I stare after him, blinking. There's obviously so much I don't understand about last night.

I walked away trying to protect my heart.

He watched me walk away thinking I was using him?

I've really screwed up almost every aspect of this.

"You have this pegged all wrong. *Me* all wrong."

"Morning," Katzen says as he strolls into the coffee shop and then stops and looks from Hunter to me and then back. "We still working on that coupling thing?" he asks obliviously. "Because if you are, I think there should be a lot more lovin' and a little less fighting." He holds his hand up in mock surrender and laughs when Hunter glares at him. "Just saying."

"Whatever," I say with a roll of my eyes and a forced smile.

"I've got a phone call with Sanderson," Hunter says and holds his phone up as if that's his answer to why he keeps walking and doesn't engage.

Or maybe to throw it in my face who his agent is.

"Who pissed in his Wheaties this morning?" Katz asks with an over-exaggerated flip of the bird to his teammate.

"No idea," I murmur.

Me.

I did.

I'm the one who pissed him off and screwed this up.

"Well, shit," Katz says, sliding into the seat in front of me. "If he's not going to sit with a pretty lady, then I definitely will. I'm around way too many jockstraps these days and not enough G-strings."

I throw my head back and laugh. "If you're looking for G-strings, you're sitting at the wrong damn table," I say but then shift in my seat, considering the black lace one I put on this morning.

Chapter
THIRTY-SIX

Dekker

Kincade Sports Management
Internal Memorandum
New Recruit Status Report

*denotes urgent status
**denotes Diva Dekker is still making someone's pipe burst

Athlete	Team	Sport	Agent	Status
Carl Ryberg	n/a	Golf	Kenyon	In talks
Jose Santos	D-Backs	Baseball	Chase	face-to-face mtg
Lamar Owens	Bulls	Basketball	Lennox	Contracted. YES!
Michelle Nguyen	n/a	Soccer	Brexton	Coming to KSM Tues.
*Hunter Maddox	Jacks	Hockey	Dekker	**********
Vincent Young	Rams	Football	Dekker	First contact initiated
Garrett Zetser	n/a	NASCAR	Lennox	Face to face meeting

********** It means our dear sister is ghosting us. Dekker, Dekker, Dekker, Dekker . . . quit ignoring us.

THEY'RE BEING LITTLE BRATS, BUT THEIR COMMENTS ON THE SCOUTING memo give me a much-needed laugh.

And then I hit send, leaving the status for Hunter Maddox blank. Serves those nosy little punks right.

Chapter
THIRTY-SEVEN

Dekker

I SIT IN THE PRESS BOOTH IN WHATEVER DAMN CITY WE'RE IN AND AN-swer my messages. One after another. Email and phone call after email and phone call.

But I work through them as the Jacks practice on the ice below and work on a new defensive play that just might work in the coming weeks.

It would be smarter to work in my hotel room, but I'm distracted. Not by work that desperately needs my attention but rather the man on the ice who has consumed my thoughts since he left the coffee shop the other day.

Who am I kidding? He's consumed it much longer than that, but I'm not counting that part.

Maybe it's because we've never had a chance to be alone since then, my texts have gone unanswered, and my phone calls sent to voicemail. I've even thought about sliding a note under his door, but just my luck, a teammate would find it and more shit would hit the fan.

We really need to talk about why I left, about why I'm here, and about what his perception of it is.

This could all be solved with decent communication—in fact, if it were one of my friends, that's the first bit of advice I'd impart—but it's not as easy as that.

The minute I tell him why I'm here—whatever's happening or has hap-pened between us can be no more. Then he becomes a client. Then I must put professionalism before him.

And the struggle between pleasing my father and owning what I want makes the path not so clear-cut.

"You sure are spending a lot of time with the team."

I startle and look back to see Ian McAvoy standing with his arms crossed and shoulder leaned against the doorframe.

"The same can be said for yourself," I reply with a smile, hoping he'll smile at my joke. He doesn't. "Most GMs aren't fond of road trips."

"And most GMs' teams haven't been pulled from the depths of the hockey dungeon to the top of the division within two years."

"True." I nod, shut my laptop, and lean back in my chair to wait for him to talk about whatever it is he wants to talk about. Ian isn't one to hang and chat without having an objective in sight.

"Should I believe the rumors?" he asks.

"Depends which rumors they are."

"Why you're here."

"I have clients on your team. We're heading into unknown territory for some of them, and I want their heads in the right place come playoff time."

"And what about those who aren't your clients? Shouldn't it be said I need them to be left alone so their heads are in the right place too?"

"Let's not beat around the bush, Ian. If you've got something to say, then say it." I rise from my seat, never wanting to be at a disadvantage. Him standing over me puts me at a disadvantage.

"What do you want with Maddox?"

I purse my lips and watch the team practicing. Hunter moves with ease, and then something is said among them so their laughter floats up to Ian and me.

"He's not my client if that's what you're asking," I finally say, wondering if Ian would be having this same conversation with me if I were a man.

"I'm well aware he's not your client." His shoes squeak on the concrete floor as he takes a few steps past me and braces his hands on the desk the next row up. "It just seems like you've taken a special interest in him."

I draw in a deep breath and let the sigh of frustration be heard. "I have a vested interest in this team. Callum is coming off an injury, Stetson is trying hard to fight his way onto the roster, and Guzman is doing his thing. Like I told you when I cleared my being here beforehand, it was a good time to check on some clients. If something has changed, just come out and say it."

"I've known your father a long time, Dekker," Ian says, looking back at me over his shoulder from behind his glasses.

"So have I." My response sounds like I'm trying to be funny, but I'm not. I already know where he's going with this, and my guard is up.

"I've never seen him doing something like this."

"Like what? Road trip with a team to check in on clients? Funny. He's the one who insisted I come."

"It's different," he says.

"How so?"

"You're a woman. The team acts differently with women agents around. They—"

"With all due respect, Mr. McAvoy," I say and step beside him as Hunter scores a goal and the rest of the team taps their sticks to the ice in response. "This is my job, not a bar where I come to hit on men. I've never been anything but professional. I don't venture into the locker rooms to keep it that way, while male agents go in and out like a revolving door. Your implication is bullshit and unfounded," I lie through my teeth.

"Don't fuck with our season, Kincade. Maddox is a huge part of it."

"He's an old friend. I'm allowed to reach out and make sure he's okay, considering it seems like he's dealing with some shit. That's just the person I am, so you can either appreciate the help in taming your out-of-control star, or you can tell his agent to do his job himself. While I may be able to heed your threats, they only succeed in pushing your star further away."

"I need the Cup."

"I have no doubt Maddox is going to lead this team and get it for you."

Chapter

THIRTY-EIGHT

Hunter

I SIT ON A FROZEN METAL BLEACHER IN THE FREEZING FUCKING COLD and stare at the players.

My attention is rapt on the two kids on the ice. Two boys who are laughing as much as they're practicing. Two boys who every now and again skate past each other and wrap an arm around the other's neck in brotherly affection.

My decision to come here to try and remind myself how it used to feel rewarding.

You're burned out.

I watch them with tears burning in my eyes.

Two kids having fun. Learning to play a sport and love a game that has been humming in my blood for as long as I can remember.

Two kids pretending to be someone like me when all I want to do is go back and be like them. Innocent. Unjaded. With my brother back at my side.

Fucking fried.

What are you going to do, Maddox? Lie down and die? Walk away from the game?

Or win the Cup for Jonah with the club he told you to play for? Win the Cup he should have won in a game he was always so much better at?

My insides are a fucking jumbled mess. Shit stirred up I don't want to acknowledge. Shit Dekker's presence brought to light.

Fuck.

And thinking of her—hell, I feel like that's all I've been doing is thinking of her—screws me up even more.

I scrub my hand over my face and breathe out a huge sigh as the boys' laughter floats over to me.

"Nah-uh. Dad's never going to let us be on the same team," the taller of the two says.

"Why not?"

"Because then we can't both be stars, silly." He pushes his brother from behind so he's shoved forward, and they both start giggling hysterically and look over to where their dad sits in his truck, engine running, heater probably on, as he eyes the crazy man sitting by himself in the bleachers to gauge if he's a creeper.

I don't care, because all I hear is what the big kid just said: *because then we can't both be stars.*

Such a simple solution we never got the chance to figure out for ourselves.

The loneliness hits me even harder watching them, but so do the memories. The laughter. The secrets. The bond we shared on and off the ice.

It never mattered that he was the star and I was the second string. It only mattered that we were there together. It only mattered that we understood each other. It only mattered that I played the sport I loved with the brother I loved more.

I lift my head to the clear sky and close my eyes for a beat.

I'm so sorry, Jonah.

I'm going to win you that Cup you deserved.

I'm going to break every record in your name, because I know you already would have.

I'm trying to be the star for both of us before one or both of us burn out. "You can't go yet, J. Don't go until I finish the job you asked me to finish. Don't leave me yet."

When I rise from the bleachers half an hour later, I don't have all the answers, but I have more determination and clarity.

Chapter
THIRTY-NINE

Dekker

"Hey."

Hunter stops midstride and glances over to my car where I've pulled up beside him. "Go away, Dekk."

"What's that supposed to mean?" I keep driving slowly beside him as he keeps walking.

"Just what it sounds like. I don't want what you're selling."

"Lucky for you, I'm not offering anything," I mutter. "We need to talk about the other night."

"There's nothing to talk about," he says, still refusing to look my way.

"There's not?" There's a whole host of shit we need to talk about.

"Nope."

Nope? What the hell? I slam the rental car into park, hop out, and jog up beside him, but he still refuses to look my way.

"Hunter? What the hell?" I grab his arm and he turns on me with confusion and anger etched in the lines of his face.

"You're wasting my time, Kincade. I've got practice to get to. You know, *my job.* I haven't been avoiding you, I've just been throwing myself into perfecting my game. As an agent, you should appreciate that in a client."

His smile is tight and his words are cutting.

"I do, but I also know avoidance when I see it."

"What am I avoiding?" he asks and takes a step back and crosses his arms over his chest, throwing the ball back in my court and of course now that he has, I just stare at him.

Answer the question honestly and sound like a needy female. Lie and sound like a flustering idiot.

"Me." I choose honesty and feel so stupid saying it, but it's true, and it's better if we face this now rather than later.

"Bullshit," he sneers.

"You're not avoiding me?" I ask on the defensive.

"Nope. Don't think so highly of yourself. I have a Cup to win. I have a team to lead. I have consequences if I let them all down."

"You've always had a Cup to win." I take a step toward him as he takes one back. "I don't under—Hunter, talk to me."

"About what? How we got drunk. How we had a laugh or two. Then how we fucked." He throws his arms out to his sides and raises his voice. "Just like old times, huh? No harm, no foul—mistake made and realized until the next time."

His words should hurt, but for some reason, they don't. Maybe it's because it's been two days since we slept together and this is the first time I've been able to actually talk. It's been two days of overthinking and wondering if the sex was just sex or blowing it out of proportion to second-guess every nuance of his and wonder if there could be more. But now that I'm standing here, he's made it clear what the answer is, and I'm not exactly sure what to say.

"I—I just thought we should talk about it."

His chuckle is raw and brutal. "About what? The snow angels? The shit I said in the bar? Or someone seeing us together?"

"Because it could affect my job."

He chuckles and scrubs a hand over his jaw. "I expected more from you than that. I really did." The disappointment in his voice is like a knife to my heart. Here he is handing me the key to the door I need. But I know the minute I unlock and open it, everything I want will fall out of reach.

"I can't give you more." It's the only thing I can think to say as my professional world wars against my personal one.

"Why?" This time, he's the one who takes a step closer to me. This time, he's the one staring and demanding and wanting to know.

"Because I can't," I whisper.

"That's what I thought," he says and starts to stride off.

"Hunter. Wait." He keeps walking. "Truth. *Truth*," I shout, and this time he stops but doesn't turn around. I stare at him, the bright lights of the arena he's playing in tonight in the background. "I can't admit to you why I'm here because the minute I do, whatever happened the other night can't happen again. I can't tell you what you want to hear, because there's a blaring red line in the sand and once I cross it, all those things about you that made me want to come back to your room over and over once I left that night have to be buried and gone." My breath hitches on what feels like a sob, but it's really my fear in admitting the truth to both him and myself.

It's the fear in admitting that I had fallen for Hunter Maddox before, and being here, sleeping with him, just reinforced that I never got over him. That I chose mediocre options in the interim who never dimmed his sparkle, but rather made it shine brighter.

He turns slowly and stares at me, eyes burning into mine in a way I've never seen or felt before. The muscle in his jaw feathers as if he's trying to control any and all emotion from playing across his stoic face.

The hope I had that he might hear me drains away slowly.

I throw my hands up in a shrug and surrender whatever else I can't express. "I don't know what to do. I don't. My dad sent me here to win you over to the agency because you're you, and any agent would be crazy to not want you on their team. Now that I'm here, I don't know that I can follow through with it. I know you're struggling with something, and I would do anything to help you through it. But if I offer you that, you'll always be wondering if it's because I'm personally invested or because I want to profit off you professionally. The answer is I care, when it seems you don't want anyone to. So you tell me, Hunter, what am I supposed to do?"

The first tear slips over and I shove it away with the back of my hand as I stand before him, intentions exposed, emotions on the line, waiting for him to respond.

"I've got to get to practice."

He turns his back on me and walks toward the entrance.

And I watch him.

Every single step.

But this time through the blurred tears.

I now have my answer.

He walked away.

Decision's been made.

He left me.

I'm done.

It's time to go home.

Chapter
FORTY

Dekker

I stare at the memo and wish I could add more, but I can't. I've failed. My dad had faith in me, and I blew it.

Kincade Sports Management
Internal Memorandum
New Recruit Status Report

*denotes urgent status

Athlete	Team	Sport	Agent	Status
Carl Ryberg	n/a	Golf	Kenyon	Contract Mtg
Desi Davalos	n/a	Basketball	Chase	Contact initiated
Michelle Nguyen	n/a	Soccer	Brexton	In talks
*Hunter Maddox	Jacks	Hockey	Dekker	Recruited, no response
Vincent Young	Rams	Football	Dekker	Face to Face Meeting
Garrett Zetser	n/a	NASCAR	Lennox	In talks

I look at it one more time, and then I hit send.

Chapter

FORTY-ONE

Hunter

Dad: Worst game I've seen you play all year. Why isn't your head in the game, son? Think of everything we gave up for you to be there and prove you deserve it.

Me: Fuck you.

I STARE AT THE TEXT. AT THOSE TWO HOSTILE WORDS. AT THE CURSOR flashing. The pressure is mounting. I feel the exhaustion everywhere. Just. Fucking. Everywhere.

The suicide drills and the endless shooting challenges he made me perform until late into the night.

No breaks.

No sympathy.

Only the weight of the world on my shoulders. Only the knowledge that I'm the reason Jonah left that night. I was the catalyst who put him in the car and robbed *them* of *his* spectacular career.

I'm the *mediocre* brother forced to live out the dream Jonah no longer could.

Because living for Jonah is the only other thing they have. Even though I'm still alive and have dreams of my own.

And living for someone else is so exhausting, so daunting, so goddamn frustrating.

The cursor blinks.

The same two words I've wanted to respond with after every game I've ever played professionally.

Two words.

They say so much.

I'll never fill his shoes.

I'll never be as good as he would have been.

But I'm me. Fucking *me*. A man who rose to the challenge and have lived *my* every moment so that Jonah knows I'm sorry. That I'm so goddamn sorry for what I did that night. For how I lied. For not being responsible. For not being the one who took the keys.

The guilt is why I've always deleted those two words.

The guilt is why I've never thought I deserved anything—the praise, the accolades, the love.

The guilt is why I punish myself.

But hell if walking away from Dekker yesterday didn't shoot that all to shit.

Fuck if looking up in the owner's box and not seeing her there—as I have the past three weeks—wasn't a blow to my concentration. I thought of the ten other things I should have said to her instead of the one sentence I did.

The hurt in her eyes when I didn't acknowledge a fucking thing she said.

"You good, Mad Dog?" Callum asks as he walks by. I lean back against my locker, dropping my phone in my lap.

"Yeah. Just . . . that was a brutal fucking game." I glance at the bag of ice Saran-wrapped to my knee and shake my head.

"It always is. The Bandoliers are fucking thugs."

"Not going to argue."

"You were an animal out there."

I nod and replay the game in my head in the flash of time. All I can see are the shots I missed, the times I was stripped, the bullshit fouls called.

"Meh. I beg to differ, but it's not worth the argument."

He checks the bottom of his skates and busies himself before turning to look at me, eyes intense. "She leave?"

He doesn't have to say who *she* is, and I'll save him the bullshit of pretending I don't know who he's talking about. I have more respect for him than that.

"Not sure. I don't keep tabs on her." But I was looking. I was wondering.

"Huh."

"You got something to say, Withers?" I ask.

"Nothing you're going to listen to," he says. "Shit. We finally get to go home tonight. My bed is calling me."

"I'm listening," I say, ignoring his color commentary.

He pauses, stuffing his gear into his bag and stares at me. "She's obviously under your skin."

"What the hell is that supposed to mean?"

"It means, I've never seen you give a fuck about anything other than hockey and your family . . . but you give a fuck about her."

I blink and try to hear him—really hear him—and then like always, play it off. "I think that punch you took to the head tonight was harder than we all thought." I chuckle to sell the lie.

"You're indifferent with women. They're a dime a dozen to you because they're everywhere you go—"

"Whatever."

"But Dekker challenges you." He hefts the bag over his shoulder and walks a few feet toward me.

"Your point?" I ask.

"It's a good thing she does." He reaches a hand to my shoulder and squeezes. "She's a good person, Mad. She deserves to be treated right. Whatever happens, just remember that."

And without another word, Callum walks out of the locker room to our transport waiting to take us home for the first time in what feels like forever.

But I sit in the empty locker room. There are a few guys still in the trainer's room getting worked on and their laughter filters out to me, but other than that I'm alone.

So goddamn alone.

The worst part? The only time I haven't felt lonely is when *she's* around. Fucking Dekker.

Closing my eyes, I think about what Callum said. About Dekker and what she deserves and wonder what I've never allowed myself to wonder. About me and what I don't deserve, but hell if the moments spent with her haven't made me want. *An us.* About the opportunities I've passed up, the dreams, the happiness I told myself weren't merited.

Christ.

So fucking alone.

But this time when I stand to head to the bus, I don't delete the text like I normally do.

This time, I hit send. Finally.

Chapter
FORTY-TWO

Dekker

"It's midnight. Why are you here?"

I laugh as Brexton props her shoulder against the doorway of my office and debate how much I should tell her. "I guess the same could be said for you," I respond.

"I forgot a contract I need for the morning. Less traffic to get it now than to fight rush hour, and you know how I love my sleep."

I smile softly and wonder why brusque Brexton is being so kind.

"Smart," I say and look out the window to the city beyond. The Manhattan skyscrapers and their lights dot the distance. A city still alive, while I'm struggling with so much turmoil.

I walked away from Hunter, from my time with the Jacks, without saying a word. I walked away, knowing full well I left my heart behind. I came back home with the bitter taste of rejection on my tongue and knowing I was letting my dad—my sisters—down by not finishing what I set out to do. Letting Sanderson win.

"Wasn't there a game tonight?"

I nod and exhale a sigh. "Yeah, but . . . I decided to skip it. I have a shit ton to do and being in the press box isn't going to do anything toward getting Hunter to sign with us."

"Huh." She makes that stupid sound I hate that says *I don't buy a word you're saying*, and then twists her lips in thought as she studies me. "So you finally told him KSM wants him?"

"Something like that." I look at the papers on my desk and relive everything—my confession and his nonchalance—and wish my mom were here right now, as I've wished many times over the last fifteen years, so I could get her advice. I think I just screwed everything up. "He didn't react, so I'm not sure what to make of it."

I'm not exactly lying—he didn't react—so why do I avert my eyes and blink back the tears that threaten?

"Humph." She moves to the window of my office and looks out. Her hands are on her hips as she scans the skyline. I study her. "It never went away, did it?" Her voice is soft, gentle almost, when she's never gentle.

"What never went away?" My mind is thinking of clients and contracts I missed while I was on the road trip. What didn't I—

"The way you feel about Hunter."

I freeze and am grateful her back is to me so she doesn't see. Like with everyone else, I want to deny. Deny their observation. Deny my feelings. Deny it all. *Especially now. Why can't I tell the truth?*

"You're delusional."

Brexton takes her time moving to my desk before setting her hip on it. "I may be delusional, but I also know you have a habit of running the other way any time you get feelings for someone."

"I do not."

"Yes, you do."

My guard is up, my defiance front and center. "Name someone."

"Chad."

"What-the-hell-ever. Next."

"I'm being serious. You were fine with Chad—content with him—because you didn't feel anything for him. He was safe. He allowed you the appearance of having someone without you having to get emotionally involved." She picks up a trinket on the corner of my desk—a hockey puck given to me from a client a long time ago—and weighs it in her hand. "Chad is the latest casualty. Before him that software salesman who wore his pants too tight—"

"Come on. He wasn't that bad." She eyes me until we both start laughing and I nod. "Yes, I guess he was . . . but his pants were too tight for a reason," I say to try and get the focus off me.

"At least he had that going for him," she says and shakes her head. "And before him was the baseball player. Then Gene Harsket. I never understood what you saw in him."

"Brex—"

"No, I need you to hear me. To listen to me. I need you to see that you make a habit of being emotionally unavailable because you refuse to put yourself out there. You refuse to be hurt."

I open my mouth and close it, because it hits me how very right she is. And then to make matters worse, why can she see that when I can't?

"Look." She waits until I meet her eyes, and then it's a struggle for me to keep them there. But I do, and she continues. "It's okay to have feelings, Dekker. Mom died, and we all retreated into ourselves. It's natural to pull away and not want to be hurt when the last time you really loved something, you were devastated."

I clear my throat and rise from my chair, needing to abate the restlessness her words cause me.

"You're making me think I failed at this big sister thing. You're the one giving advice."

Brexton steps up beside me but we both stare at the streets below for a few seconds. "That's the thing, Dekker. We love that you're our big sister, but you became our mom and in doing that, you never allowed yourself to grieve. You never allowed yourself to rage. We did, and you were too busy holding us together to be able to do it yourself . . . so of course any kind of attachment scares you."

"I grieved."

"Sure," she says. It's her way of telling me she doesn't believe me.

"I did. I raged and screamed but I had to do it in a pillow so you guys wouldn't hear me." The wave of memories hits me. The loneliness. The fury. The unknown. The sadness.

"Okay, then why don't you let yourself love?"

I laugh despite the tears welling in my eyes. "Grieving for Mom and falling in love with someone are not mutually exclusive."

Her arm goes around my shoulder. "It never went away, did it?" she asks again.

I blink away the tears, but one escapes down my cheek as I think of how heartbroken I was three years ago when I walked away from Hunter, and how similarly I felt this time with his nonchalance and nod. "The first time, he didn't ask why the abruptness of it all. Why we went from seeing each other as much as we could to nothing."

"Maybe because he had feelings for you and felt scared about them too. If you bailed that easily, why is it hard for you to believe that he could do the same? If you're afraid of love, why is it unfathomable that maybe he's afraid of it for other reasons?"

I lean my head on her shoulder and breathe deeply, hearing her words but not wanting to believe them.

"What happened this time, Dekk?"

I let the silence settle as I struggle with telling her the truth. Their problems are my problems but my problems are no one's problems. So, I usually keep everything close to the vest.

"What happened this time?" I repeat. "He's like kryptonite to me." I give a self-deprecating laugh. "There's something going on with him he won't talk about, and of course, I want to try and fix it."

"No surprise there."

"No, I mean . . . I went there to do my job as an agent—what Dad asked—but when I saw him, I knew he was wrestling with something." I continue to explain his acting out, his hot and cold, his being completely burned out and finally admitting it.

"So you slept with him."

"Mm-hmm."

"And then what?"

"And then I bailed to my room. It was much easier doing that than trying to sort through my feelings with him sleeping right beside me."

"But you felt something, right?"

"I felt fucking everything," I admit without hesitation and know how stupid it sounds. To run away from those kinds of feelings, but the fact that she doesn't point it out makes me feel a little better.

"And when you confronted him?"

"He acted like I was asking him about the weather."

Brexton turns to face me and puts her hands on my shoulders so I'm forced to look at her. "The question is, what are you going to do about it, Dekker? Are you going to let him walk away a second time when you know damn well he's the only one who's lit your fire emotionally and sexually?"

"Christ." My cheeks flush.

"No. I'm being serious. What are you going to do? Rob yourself of the chance of seeing what happens because you're too chickenshit to try?"

"That's not fair."

"Why isn't it? Maybe what's not fair is how we've let you sneak by doing this and not really living for anything other than work and a false sense of security with people who put water on your fire like Chad." She gives a little shake to my shoulders. "So the question is . . . what are you going to do about it?"

"There's nothing I can do about it. I can't ask him to be a client and want to have a relationship at the same time. I can't—"

"Fuck that." She waves a hand at me. "We'll figure it out. Dad will have to deal. There are always solutions to every problem. We can handle him."

"But that doesn't fix the other problem."

"Other problem?"

"Like how other clients would perceive me sleeping with a client I'm going after."

"Then he's not with the agency or we pass him off to one of us to represent. Done. Next excuse." She flashes a dazzling smile my way, and I groan because the next one isn't so easy.

"You can fix all the things in the world on the professional side, Brex, but nothing will make Hunter see me as anything other than a no-strings notch on his busy bedpost."

"I think you're wrong."

"Good for you." I move back toward my desk and the stacks of paperwork, hoping that if I ignore her, maybe this conversation will go away.

"If Hunter didn't have feelings for you, do you think he would have gotten all butt-hurt when you left after Callum saw you that night?" She lifts her eyebrows and crosses her arms over her chest. "Do you think he would have been more of a dick and less dismissive when you confronted him in the parking lot? You made him feel like you put work before him . . . and I'd say that screams that he has feelings for you."

I see what she's saying but . . . "You weren't there."

"You're right. I wasn't. But if you want him to see you as more than a notch—which I already think he does—then force him to."

"He closes off emotionally before anyone can get too attached. It's like he doesn't feel like he deserves to be cared for or loved."

She coughs through a laugh and throws her hands up. "The irony."

"Shut up." But I laugh with her this time as my mind spins and whirls and contemplates if she could be right.

Could Hunter have feelings for me but not know how to show them? Could he be just as fearful of letting someone in as I am? If so, how do I push him past that—how do I push myself past that—to give us a chance?

"Say I buy into what you're saying—"

"You do. And you should."

"Then what do I do next?"

One side of her lip curls up. "Nothing. He'll come to you."

"That's a solid plan. Real solid," I say in frustrated disbelief. Just when I start to believe her, she pulls something like that? My sigh is loud.

"No. I'm serious. You've laid the groundwork. You were honest with him. You told him you wanted him personally and professionally and why the two can't mix. But he's a rule breaker, Dekker. He's going to push boundaries just because he can. He's going to want to be macho and masculine and prove he can have you and eat his cake too."

"I think you're crazy."

"And I think I'm right."

I stare at my sister, so similar and yet so very different from me, and wonder how she can be so sure. And I consider the many exchanges between Hunter and me. Over the laughter, his ability to be serious with me, and I wonder how I never saw it before. How angry he was when he accused me of *meeting* with my clients night after night. How he let his guard down ever so briefly with me on the hard-packed snow amid angel wings we had made. How his smile lit up when the ice became littered with tennis balls at the Dartmouth game.

And more so, I wonder how I've been harboring feelings for a man for over three years and never took charge of *them*, when I seem to grab every-thing else by the balls.

Because you're scared, Dekker.

You're scared because you know he's the most real thing you've ever felt and it terrifies and exhilarates you.

"I don't know," I murmur. How and when did my little sister become so wise?

"I do." She leans forward and drops the puck on top of the paperwork I keep staring at. "It may take him a few days—a week, or two—but with radio silence from you, he'll realize how much he misses you. How much he's gotten used to you being around, and how puck bunnies look boring to him now."

"You have an active imagination." That's just the visual I need in my head. *God, I hope he ignores the puck bunnies.*

"Either that, or I've had a client or two go through something similar be-fore going *holy shit*, I'm going to lose her." She clucks her tongue as if she had some play in these revelations. "He came back for you this time around be-cause he wanted to see if the feelings you both walked away from were legit. He's pushing you away now, because they are."

I lean back in my chair and close my eyes, letting her words settle and take root as she moves toward the door.

"Hey, Dekk?"

"Hmmm?"

"Falling for someone is never the plan. One day, you just wake up and it's there in full-freaking, high-definition color. You realize those unanticipated butterflies you got when you saw him, those frustrated late nights overthink-ing and overanalyzing every interaction, those automatic, genuine smiles when you received a text from him . . . they all add up until they become love. It's the little things that add up. It's the unseen that touches your soul. It's the unex-pected that makes you fall in love." She moves to the doorway. "I've got to jet . . . but you know I'm here for you. You know we only want the best for you."

I look at her through eyes blurred with tears and nod. "Thank you."

She smiles and then turns her back.

I listen to the door of the outer office click shut, to the lock engage, and to her footsteps down the hallway to the elevator.

When I put my feet up on my desk, lean my head back, and close my eyes again, I carefully examine her words.

I wonder what would have happened all those years ago had I not run from him that night. If I had just been honest instead of chickening out.

Is Brexton right?

If I wait, will he come?

Chapter

FORTY-THREE

Hunter

No text.

It's the first time in years that I look at my phone after my game and see nothing from my father.

There's relief and an odd constricting of my chest. Almost as if I don't know how to process my post-game cool down without the anger generated by them.

As if not having that negativity I've been a slave to for so very long feels like I've lost a part of me. As if it's no longer worth comparing me to Jonah . . . leaving him to him and me to me. *Untethered.*

I sit on the bench with the guys moving around me and simply stare at my phone.

This has nothing to do with Jonah, Mad, and everything to do with you. This is you realizing you can love your brother but not be beholden to our parents over life's fate.

Over fate's blind arrow shot in the night to ruin one person's life and change another's.

"Dekker? Hi." My ears perk up the minute Callum answers his phone, and fuck if I don't check my texts again to see if I missed one from her.

Nothing.

Almost as if she said what she said to me—confessed two things that could change my life in numerous ways like me sending that text to my dad did—but I'm afraid to face it.

Let her represent me instead of Finn. He's dogged and well-known, same as Dekker, and yet, I feel like she has more than just her bottom line in mind from how I've seen her manage Callum. I've seen her patience with him, Guzman, and Stetson, and I've talked to other players who she's secured endorsement deals for. All professional, no bullshit, all results.

And when it comes to me. Maybe . . . maybe there's even more than a bottom line and deals.

Maybe she could love me.

Fuck if that's not a hard thing to think out loud. Fuck if that's not the thought that has had me tied up in knots for days.

What am I going to do about it?

Live in the past . . . or realize I can't change the past and can only move forward?

Shit.

She followed us around the damn place and now that we're right in her backyard and our home turf, she couldn't bother to show up? A damn subway ride away from Manhattan to Jersey, and she couldn't make it?

If she wanted me that badly, wouldn't she have shown up? Tried to win me over?

So, you tell me, Hunter, what am I supposed to do?

Dekker's words replay in my mind. The confused desperation in her voice, the pleading in her eyes, the defeat in her posture . . . fuck. It killed me.

Why am I thinking about this now?

Why am I sitting in a locker room with my teammates and not celebrating being one game closer to clinching a playoff berth?

"Yes, it looks that way, doesn't it?" Callum says as he walks past me, his finger pressed to one ear, his cell to the other. *Because of her.* "But don't say the word. Don't fucking jinx it." His laughter rings out.

The playoffs.

She called him to talk about the playoffs.

Sanderson doesn't call me to talk about my games.

Shit, he doesn't call me unless it's to make me get in line. Unless it's negative and unsupportive, much like my old man's.

Fucking hell.

I lean my head back on the locker behind me.

Deal with her after the playoffs.

Deal with my representation and all the shit in my head and my questions after the playoffs.

Accomplish the one thing you need to—that you promised Jonah—and then maybe you can carve out more of a life for yourself.

"Hey!" I pound my fist against the metal locker behind me and the sound echoes across the chatter in the locker room. All the guys turn toward me as I climb on top of the bench.

Their hoots and hollers fill the room and mask my own groan as my knee aches from bearing weight on it.

"Speech. Speech. Speech," the guys begin chanting.

I motion with my hands to quiet down as I look at my teammates looking up at me. I looked at this team not very long ago and saw limitations and incompetence. *Just like my dad sees in me.* But when did I last congratulate *them* for a job well done? When did I last praise *them* for kicking ass? When did I last lead *them* off the ice like I do on the ice? The pressure to do right by them isn't as great as my own drive to do this for Jonah, but it's still there. In their smiles. In the excitement mixed with anticipation in their eyes.

"Way to kick ass and take names, guys. One more win and one more game down." I let them cheer, some fists going in the air. "I just wanted to give a shout out to the defense tonight. Killer job, guys. To the fresh legs off the bench, we needed you more than you know. To the guys up top—shit, you made it easy to do our jobs tonight. In short, keep it up."

"Great job, Cap," Katzen yells out from the back of the room, and I nod in response, because this isn't about me.

This is about them. It needs to be about them.

"One more thing," I say and hold my finger up to quiet them down. "I know I've been shit to deal with, play with—unpredictable as fuck. I'm sorry for that, but I promise you, my head's back in the game. My priorities are straight. And fuck if they're not fixed on winning the Holy Grail."

The small room explodes with noise and a palpable excitement as I climb down from the bench to finish getting my gear off.

"Glad to see you back, Cap," Jünger says just above the fray, then pats me on the back as he walks past me.

And each one of my teammates follow his footsteps.

A punch to my shoulder. A push to my chest. A bump of fists.

Each one stops and tells me in their own way that they're in it with me.

That they're ready to win it all.

And fuck, so am I.

Chapter

FORTY-FOUR

Hunter

16 years earlier

I JOLT WHEN TERRY STANDS AT THE FRONT DOOR OF THE HOUSE, HER dark-blue fancy dress with sparkles and her hair up in some flashy way that makes her look as old as you should be to do the things she did to me earlier.

Swallowing over the sudden panic mixed with immediate lust that hits me, I walk toward the screen and thank God I took a shower and changed.

At least she'll know I'm Hunter.

At least she won't realize I tricked her earlier.

On my best day ever.

Terry. Losing my virginity. The euphoric bliss over it feeling so much better than jerking off. Soap and warm water have nothing on what a girl feels like.

On my worst day ever.

How I've been beating myself up the past few hours over it. I know Jonah's going to find out what I did somehow—how I betrayed him—and shit's going to hit the fan.

I already know my parents are going to rail. Jonah's going to throw punches. I'm going to be dead. Absolutely fucking dead.

I'm guilty as hell. I feel like shit, but I also wonder why out of the two of us who are identical, why he's the one who gets everything while I'm left to pick up the scraps?

"What are you doing here?" I ask as I lean my hip against the jamb and stare at her. "I thought you were with Jonah at the dance."

She shrugs. "We were all supposed to go as a group. Gannon called though and said Jonah had to leave to do something. Pick someone up or something." She looks over my shoulder. "He's not here?"

"No one is," I say, ignoring the pang of guilt over making him get our mom.

"I'm all dressed up and nowhere to go." She smiles and fiddles with the hem of her skirt with one hand showing me more of her thigh.

I look behind me and debate asking her to come in. I know I should, but Jesus, isn't that inviting a disaster to happen? "I can call him. See where he is."

"I left him a text telling him I'll be here. I'm glad we're alone though, because I—uh"—a slow smile spreads across her red painted lips—"wanted to make sure what happened earlier stayed between us. I really like your brother and all, and I'd hate for him to find out that we—"

"Wait. What?" I shake my head as if my ears aren't hearing properly. "You knew I wasn't Jonah? You—"

Her laugh floats out freely, as I stare at her as if she's crazy. I should be thinking more along the lines that she's easy, that she's a bitch for doing that to my brother . . . but I'm sixteen, and that's my convoluted first thought about the girl I just lost my virginity to.

"Of course, I knew." She rolls her eyes. "I . . ."

Her words fade off as we turn toward the police cruiser that pulls into the driveway—its flashing lights are on but the sirens are off.

It's as if my body just tuned into everything around me—everything that has been faded by the high of sex—and there is the worst feeling in my gut and chest. *I can't breathe.* I don't know how I know it, but something bad has happened.

Even worse, when I walk toward the police car, an officer is practically carrying my mom out of the passenger seat of the car. She looks as boneless as her complexion is pale. Her face is swollen from tears but her eyes look completely hollow.

"Mom. Mom!" My voice breaks as I run to her.

"Jonah. Thank God you're okay," she says as she clings to me. I look at the officer, and then try to pull my mom off me so I can look her in the eyes.

"It's Hunter, Mom. It's me. What happened? Tell me what happened?" I yell at her as she stares at me with a slack jaw, almost as if she doesn't believe I'm me.

"Hunter?"

"Yes. It's me. What happened?"

"But you were the one who was supposed to be in the car." She grabs my hand and yanks me to the cruiser as the ever-present dread begins to weigh me down in a weight I've never felt before. "We need to get to the hospital. We need to—"

"What the hell happened?" I yell. Every part of me goes silent that moments ago felt off. And that scares me more than anything.

"There's been an accident, Jonah."

"Hunter. Mom, it's Hunter."

"An accident. Your brother was in an accident."

"What do you mean an accident?" I look at my mom and then to the officer. "What does she mean?"

"Your brother crossed the median and hit another car head-on." His voice is serious but his eyes, his eyes tell me they've seen way too much, and I fear what he's going to say next. I focus on the shield on his chest. The badge with the sun and rays of sunshine engraved on it. The letters of his last name, as I recite them in my head over and over and over . . . because if I stop, he'll tell me my brother is dead.

He'll tell me that my brother was drunk driving. That he was the responsible one. That when I refused to go get Mom, he went. *He couldn't refuse. He couldn't say no. He* drove to pick up our mom even though he'd been drinking.

Because I didn't . . .

I was the screw-up. *I didn't pick up the fucking cell.* His missed calls. Calls to tell me he couldn't drive because he'd been drinking. And the officer would know. He'll tell me that while I was having sex with my brother's girlfriend out of spite, I caused this. *I fucked up.*

"Is he okay?" I can barely speak as my body blankets with goosebumps. My words feel like they have to be pried from my mouth as I stare at him and hope and wait and already know.

"He's at the hospital. This officer—he picked me up from work to bring me there—to get you on the way—it's very serious, Hunter. Your brother. He's— and the other driver . . . she didn't make it."

I try to process.

I try to fathom.

I try to comprehend.

But none of it makes sense.

Except . . .

I caused this.

I'm the one responsible.

I'm the vindictive one.

I'm the one my mother thought she'd left at the hospital. *Alone.*

And then . . . I can't sense Jonah. I can't feel my twin.

I stare at the police officer as if I don't hear him, as if I don't want to hear him . . . then the bottom drops out.

Chapter

FORTY-FIVE

Hunter

SOMETHING'S AMISS.

My head's foggy.

My thoughts are lost.

I try to concentrate, but every time I try to manipulate the game plan, I fail.

Maybe I'm coming down with something.

Maybe this is burnout showing now.

"Tough game tonight."

I glance over at Maysen and nod. "Sorry. I . . . was fucking up left and right out there."

He shrugs, probably surprised that I'm not arguing or being defensive about it. "It happens, man." He pats me on the back as I head toward my locker. "At least we still won."

"True." I nod. I hate knowing I didn't contribute. Hate knowing that if there was a text from my dad, which there hasn't been for the last couple games, exactly what it would say.

"At least we have a few days to shake it off."

"My body could use it," I tease and throw my gloves into the locker, sighing when I see my screen light up with Dad on the message ID.

"I knew he wouldn't be able to resist for long," I mutter.

With a deep sigh, I pick up my phone. Panic hits when I see the three words on the screen.

Dad: Call. It's Jonah.

Within seconds, I'm out of the locker room, trying to find a place where I can hear and talk and have some privacy.

My mom doesn't pick up on the first call. I end it and try again.

"Hello?" She sounds like a ghost of herself.

"Mom? Mom. What happened? How is he?" My words sound strangled from part panic, part disbelief, part *just when I was trying to figure out a way to live for me, I'm sucked back into the darkness of shame.*

And of course, the self-loathing is like an old enemy—unabashed, relentless, and unforgiving.

"He coded. He—"

"He what?" I bellow. How the fuck do I get out of here?

I can't breathe.

"He coded and the ambulance came and . . ." The vibrato in her voice, the pure fear, hits me harder than any punch I've ever taken. "They revived him. He's at the hospital."

"Why? What happened?" *I need to get out of here.*

"Another bacterial infection in his lungs. His body, Hunter . . . it's broken and can't take much more. The doctors say his immune system is always on the defense and they were lucky to bring him back this time." She emits a sound I never want to hear again.

It's raw and abraded and sounds like her heart has been ripped from her chest.

"Mom. But he's okay now, right? He's resting and—"

"Yes. He is. He's under observation and will come home tomorrow most likely."

"Okay. Okay." I repeat the words over and over, almost as much for me as for her. Almost as if I need to talk myself into believing that everything is going to be okay when I know at some point it's not.

"Your father's heart," she murmurs almost in the same fashion as I just said okay.

Two people lost in the miserable grief and confusion we know is coming but want to deny.

"Yes, I know. His heart is okay?"

The same heart that went into cardiac arrest the night he found out about Jonah's accident. The heart that never fully recovered, but that only sparked to life when he pulled me onto the ice so he could somehow do something—boss someone else around and drive them into the ground, make them be what he thought Jonah was going to be—to save himself.

And I let him. Night after night. Day after day. Hour after hour. I let him break me down on the ice to punish me for what I'd done—for ignoring Jonah's request, for being the reason Jonah got behind the wheel drunk, for killing the innocent driver he hit. I cried and burned and prayed . . . with no idea if my brother would die that next day. My other half was gone. *I was alone.* In agony, I begged and bled and sucked it up because coaching me was the only thing keeping him going. Punishing me was the only way he knew how to manage the dreams he had for Jonah. *Dreams he'd never had for me.*

"I don't know what to do," she whispers. "What am I going to do?"

"I'll be there as soon as I can."

I find the exit just as I end the call and shove through the doors so they slam back with force.

I welcome the cool night air as it fills my lungs. As it burns my lungs and assaults my skin with its temperature and its indiscrimination. Taking huge gulps, I try to catch my breath from the thoughts that rob it.

Jonah's time is running out.

I felt it tonight. I felt *him* tonight.

That's why my game was off.

The other half to my whole was coding.

Struggling to breathe.

And I can't fix him.

I can't fix anyone.

Chapter

FORTY-SIX

Dekker

Kincade Sports Management
Internal Memorandum
New Recruit Status Report

*denotes urgent status
**denotes Diva Dekker is still making someone's pipe burst

Athlete	Team	Sport	Agent	Status
Carl Ryberg	n/a	Golf	Kenyon	In talks
Jose Santos	D-Backs	Baseball	Chase	face-to-face mtg
Lamar Owens	Bulls	Basketball	Lennox	Contracted. YES!
Michelle Nguyen	n/a	Soccer	Brexton	Coming to KSM Tues.
*Hunter Maddox	Jacks	Hockey	Dekker	**********
Vincent Young	Rams	Football	Dekker	First contact initiated
Garrett Zetser	n/a	NASCAR	Lennox	Face to face meeting

********** It means our dear sister is ghosting us. Dekker, Dekker, Dekker, Dekker . . . quit ignoring us.

Chapter

FORTY-SEVEN

Dekker

THE KNOCK ON MY FRONT DOOR STARTLES ME. THE PAPERS ON MY lap from when I fell asleep on the couch flutter to the floor with the jolt of my body.

I'm in that just-woken-up, confused and freaked-out phase where I wonder who in the hell is knocking on my door at one in the morning.

Who the hell did the doorman let in on my list that would come at this time of night?

Chad? My sisters?

Oh my God. Something is wrong with my dad.

My pulse pounds wildly as I run to the door, every horrible scenario playing out in my mind in those thirty feet. It's when I look in the peephole though that every part of me stops and freezes.

Hunter.

I almost want to laugh at the sight of him. I put him on my approved visitors list three years ago with the hope that one night he might make his way to my place. To fight for me.

I never took him off.

When I open the door and come face to face with him, my smile falls.

His shoulders are slumped, his face pale and hollow, and his eyes troubled.

"Hunter? Is everything okay? What are you—?"

He steps into me and holds on for dear life. His arms go around me, his face is buried into the crook of my neck, and his body shudders with an emotion I can physically feel.

"Hey. What happened?" I ask. His actions have taken me by surprise— especially from him, his need so palpable that I immediately slide my arms around him, hands running up and down his back, and my lips pressing a kiss to the side of his head.

We stay like this as he holds me, and I feel helpless.

"I just needed you." Those four words said in his broken rasp as the heat of his breath hits my shoulder, are all I need to hear for my heart to constrict. There *is* much more between us than just sex. So much more shared than a physical act meant to bring two people together.

"I'm here," I murmur to him. "I'm here."

My mind races over scenarios—he was cut from the team, something happened to his family . . . over and over—as we stand there in this silent desperation.

"Christ, Dekk." He runs a hand through his hair as he walks to the windows and then back to me. His shoulders sag. He stares at me with total defeat.

"Are you okay?" It's one of a million questions on my mind and the safest of them all. He'll talk when he wants to.

"Yeah. I think." Tears well in his eyes and the sight of them—of a man completely vulnerable when I've never seen him that way before—undoes me in ways I can't quite fathom.

They say he trusts me.

They say he needs me.

It's a poignant thought that gets thrown to the wayside to be thought about later when he's gone and I'm alone . . . but right now, *he needs me*.

"I was going to go home . . . but . . . it's just. I didn't know where else to go." His voice is barely audible, his admission mixed with the confusion in his eyes, enough in itself to tell me what he needs. To remind me out of the blue of something my mom used to say to us when we were at a loss for words. "*I needed you*."

Those three words slide around my heart and embed themselves in my soul.

He came to me.

He needs me.

"Come with me." I reach a hand out to him and even though he stares at it with question in his eyes, he takes it.

I lead him down the hallway of my apartment toward my bedroom. If I'd told anyone I was taking Hunter Maddox to my bedroom with no intention of taking my clothes off, they'd think I was mad.

But I am.

And he's so lost in his own head, in the heartache overwhelming him, that he doesn't think twice when I turn the covers of my bed down, climb in, and pull his hand for him to join me. With his eyes on mine, trying to relay a story his lips won't yet speak, he toes off his shoes and climbs in with me.

His arms go around my abdomen, he lays his head on my chest so I can rest my chin on it, and he holds on.

We lie like this without saying a thing, just me providing comfort and him taking whatever it is he needs, until his breathing evens out, and eventually he falls asleep.

With my hand running up and down the length of his back and the realization of how damn good it feels to be needed, I slowly drift off to sleep too.

Chapter

FORTY-EIGHT

Dekker

I WAKE WITH A START.

The sun is streaming through the blinds I never closed last night and the bed beside me is still warm, but I remember everything about what happened.

There's a thump in my living room and I slide out of bed, groggy, still sleepy, and still concerned for Hunter.

"Hunter?" When he doesn't answer, I head down the hallway just in time to see him walking toward my front door. He looks back over his shoulder and our eyes meet. "What are you doing?"

He still looks like hell—eyes red, brow furrowed, like he hasn't slept in years, when I know for a fact he just got a solid seven hours.

"I—uh—I've got shit to do."

"Hey," I say when he turns his back on me again. *He was going to skip out without saying a thing.* Hurt flickers through me that I try to justify and rationalize, and then give up all hope on. "What's going on?"

"It was a moment of weakness."

"What was?" I ask, but I already know the answer.

"Me coming here."

"Weakness?" I laugh, the irony not lost on me that his *weakness* is akin to my *mistake*. My temper fires on a dime as I study him. He's obviously still upset, but his choice to skip out is his way of using me . . . what feels like again. "You want to know what weakness is?" I take a step closer to him. "It's me baring my soul to you. It's me standing in a parking lot in front of an arena somewhere telling you exactly how I feel. That I'm willing to put my professional aspirations—ones dictated by my father and to benefit my family—aside, because of and for you. It's me standing there telling you that it's you. *It's always been you.* The one I walked away from three years ago because I was too afraid of how I felt for you, and the one I walked into this time still afraid but with a job to do. It's you, you asshole, and once again, I shouldn't be surprised that you're going to take the chickenshit way out and sneak away instead of face me and talk to me."

I suck in a ragged breath, because my body is trembling and my temper is wired as I stare at him and wait for a reaction—anything other than the pained look. *He's going to do the same thing as last time and let me go.*

"You don't get it," he says with a shake of his head.

"Then make me get it," I shout, closing the distance between us. After how he made me feel last night—suddenly afraid of losing him but knowing if he lets me push him away again, he wasn't good enough for me in the first place—I'm fed up. "You don't get to walk in here like you did last night and need me and then leave without saying a word."

"Or what?"

"Or it will never happen again." My voice is a low, threatening warning.

"What's that supposed to mean?" He laughs the question out.

"It means I'm not yours to use, Hunter. I'm the shiny toy in the store you can't have. You visit every once in a while so you can take me down and play with me so long as you put me back on the shelf when you're done."

"Fuck this, Dekk." He gives a shake of his head as he moves toward the door. "You wouldn't understand. You wouldn't want to understand."

"Then make me," I scream, as I stalk after him. "Make me understand. Talk to me and tell me what I need to know, because I'm here, real and bleeding emotion while you're standing there acting like it's not a big fucking deal when it's everything to me. When I'm realizing you're *more* to me than I want to admit."

"Dekker." He stops with his hand on the door and hangs his head, my name an apology I don't want to hear.

Tears well in my eyes. Just as I realize what I want—as I realize I want to see where things can go with us and, fuck yes, it's scary and the end isn't known and hurt is probably preordained . . . but I want to take a chance and figure that out.

Hurt reigns.

Embarrassment surges.

Anger wins.

"Then go. Get out. If you can't face me, I don't want to see you again either." Emotion drives my words as my heart jumps in my throat, and what's at stake hits me full force.

He turns and looks at me. His big body framed in the small entryway, and I swear to God if the tumultuous emotions in his eyes could be expressed, I'd be drowning in them. Every single one.

"You don't mean that." His eyes hold mine, the lines etched in his face so full of sadness that I look away when I speak my next words, my temper faltering despite my self-worth holding strong.

"I'm done being used. Just done." I turn my back on him and walk to my bedroom.

Let him leave.

Let him walk out.

Each time I repeat the words my heart hurts. Each time I say them in my head, I'm reminded how damn gullible I am. First to fall back in bed with him, then to let Brexton's words take hold and grow and evolve over the past two weeks. I began to believe that a true connection—a future—could be possible. The revelations last night with him in my arms making me think he realized there was more to us too.

And now this.

I brush my teeth with a vigor that might make a dentist cringe, but it's easier to focus on my hygiene than to chase after him in the hallway to the elevator like a lovesick woman with zero self-worth.

It's only when I dry my face off, when it's buried in the hand towel that I let the tears that have worked themselves up slip over. It's only when I let the disappointment hit me, and the hope I had worked up in my own mind to dissipate.

I stand there with my eyes closed and try to suck it up.

"Do you know what it's like to feel like you don't deserve anything?" Hunter's voice shocks my eyes open, and a gasp falls from my lips. *He didn't leave?* "Do you know what it's like to live a life where your every step, your every thought, your every action is driven by how you can make amends for the wrongs you created?"

I take a step toward him, shaking my head as I try to follow him. "What do you mean?"

"I mean, how do I deserve this life? How do I deserve someone like *you* when for as long as I can remember, I was told I don't? I made myself think I didn't." His voice breaks and the pain, God, the pain, is so palpable I can feel it ricocheting in the space between us. "How do I let you walk into and be a part of my life when everything I've done up until this point, every person I've pushed away, everything I've walked away from, is another way to punish myself for what I did to Jonah and my parents."

My body jolts at his admission and so does his. I watch him physically reject the words he just said, almost as if it's the first time he's ever heard them.

And just as quickly as I see it, Hunter pulls away physically by turning on his heels and jogging toward the door.

"No. Hunter," I call after him, and luckily, he's distracted by the emotions or else I never would be able to catch up to him and stand in front of the door like I do.

"Get out of the way, Dekker." His face is a mask of fury and shame, and it breaks my heart to see such distress in his every muscle.

"No. I'm not letting you walk out this door. I'm not letting you believe for another goddamn second that you don't deserve the success you have, the accolades you've achieved, or the love and affection you deserve." I'm breathless when I finally finish speaking, but I feel like I'm on borrowed time to keep him here and make him believe what I've said.

"No, I don't." He shakes his head and looks at me like a little boy wanting to believe but not trusting that he should.

"Yes, you do," I say and take a step forward.

"You don't know what happened. You don't understand—"

"Then make me understand. Sit down and tell me everything and get the weight you're carrying off your shoulders."

"I don't know if I can," he says in a whisper.

I don't care that he feels a million miles away from me, I take another step toward him and place his face in my hands. He tries to pull away, but I don't let him. "I know you're a good person, Hunter Maddox. I know you bust your ass day in and day out chasing a ghost no one can see, and I know it has to be a merciless burden that you carry." I wipe the lone tear that escapes his eye and slides down his cheek. It's devastating to see. But it's also a sign that maybe I'll be able to get through to him. Maybe I can help him. "Please, talk to me."

Chapter

FORTY-NINE

Hunter

I STARE AT DEKKER, AND MY BODY AND MIND REVOLT.

I'm terrified that if she sees what I did, she'll walk away for good and never come back.

Her eyes tell me to trust her and her words tell me to believe her, but fucking hell if that's not hard when all I know is regret. When all I feel is guilt.

I took away their star, their life, their hope.

"Hunter? Come on, talk to me. You can trust me."

My pulse pounds in my ears and my chest feels like it's on fire, like the space around my lungs is constricting and squeezing the breath out of me.

Betrayal comes with telling someone. A betrayal to my misery, to myself, to the way I've lived my life, and fuck, it's a hard thing to let go.

I open my mouth and shut it, the words so very hard to utter, that day so godawful to relive, but I know I need to.

I know that if anyone can help me, it's Dekk. She walked away from me before, knowing I would hurt her if she told me how she felt. I knew it. She knew it. It was so much easier to pretend like her leaving was no big deal.

But now? Shit, she's the only one who thought I was worth pursuing. *Being my fucking punching bag.* She's the only one who cared enough to dig beneath the surface despite my shitty attitude. Not Sanderson, who has a stake in my well-being, but Dekker.

She made me admit that I've burned out.

She forced me to acknowledge that I care.

She made me believe in the possibility of more.

I start rejecting the thought, and then try to push that ingrained response away.

I nod. It's slight, but it's there.

"It was supposed to have been me that day," I finally say.

Her breath hitches. She gently takes my hand and leads me to the couch.

Her papers are still where she left them last night, her laptop still open and no doubt the battery dead, but she sits me down in silence. She waits until our knees are touching and our eyes hold before she asks the one question that can break *and* free me. "Who was supposed to have been you that day?"

I stare at her for as long as I can before looking down to where I'm winding my thumbs around each other . . . and I tell her my story.

All of it.

Terry Fischer, and wanting to get back at Jonah for my dad's punishment.

Jonah driving buzzed to get my mother because I'd refused to.

The young mom of two little girls he killed in the accident when he crossed the median strip.

The way my mom became frantic in the driveway that day when she realized it was Jonah in the accident and not me.

My dad's heart attack when he found out about Jonah.

And then life after.

The endless hours on the ice where my dad tried to make me be my brother. How I felt—and probably still feel—like it's the only way we survived from the drastic change in our lives.

But did we heal?

My mom hasn't lived a day since then. Her every waking moment is for Jonah. My dad lives for him too, but also for me to actualize the dreams I robbed Jonah of.

And me? I've lived, but every accomplishment, every defeat, every critical text has been to reach my one goal, to win the Stanley Cup, because that's what was expected of Jonah.

Not of me.

Not for me.

But for them.

For him.

Because as stupid as it sounds, it's all I'm good for, and it's the only amends I can make.

Chapter

FIFTY

Dekker

WHEN HE'S FINISHED WITH HIS STORY, WITH THE GUILT THAT OWNS HIM and has owned him for sixteen years, tears are on my cheeks and so much sadness is in my heart.

There's also a healthy dose of anger too, but not at him. No way. His decision that day was of a young kid lashing out at a harsh father's favoritism. It was his way of rebelling for being made to miss a teenager's rite of passage. While consequences are consequences, the ones his father put on him that day, and Hunter's decision to refuse to collect his mom, are in no way worthy of a lifetime of devastating guilt and a life sentence of penance.

And he's borne the burden daily. Bullied to believe he must attain the things his brother *may* have achieved, because who knows? Jonah may have had an injury. He may have gotten into a different car at another time with alcohol in his blood. Who knows? But to be made to feel *less than* when *he*, Hunter Maddox, has achieved nearly every accolade possible, *is* the captain of an NHL team, *is* one of the highest paid hockey players in the US. It's . . . it's criminal.

The hardest thing to process though, is how to make Hunter see and comprehend the reprehensible injustice. It was Jonah's choice to get behind the wheel and drive drunk. No one knows what the future held for Jonah, so how could he be responsible for robbing him of something that hadn't happened yet?

But his words were so powerful. A life led with guilt and regret. Wanting to take back something that happened so long ago, when there's no way he can know what would have happened if he were the one in the car that day either.

"Hunter." I shake my head. "There is so much to say, so many comments I want to make; I don't know where to start." I reach out and lace my fingers with his, the tears on his cheeks dried long ago, but the pain they leave behind so very visible.

"Don't say anything. Please. I don't deserve any sympathy. I don't deserve to feel better or to rationalize it all away. I've spent years doing that. I've spent nights slamming the puck into the net as hard as I can to help and it doesn't, because when it all comes down to it, look at me and the life I have, and then look at Jonah and the life he's been left with." He goes to pull his hand away, but I hold on tight to it. "I definitely don't fucking deserve it."

"Survivor's guilt is real." My voice is a whisper, a small offer in the giant chasm that one incident left.

His chuckle is hollow. "It's so much more than that." He shoves up off the couch and moves to the windows to look at the morning outside. The city as it comes to life. His hands are shoved in his pockets and his shoulders are squared, as if he's about to go on the defensive after everything he's confided in me.

"You didn't make Jonah drive drunk that day, regardless of what happened before he grabbed the keys. You didn't steal his career, because who knows what could have happened—I mean, professional athletes are injured all the time. And you sure as hell don't deserve to live a life paying for things you had no control over."

My words hang in the air. My only hope is that they somehow cling to his soul and add some balance to the harrowing grief and guilt and gravity that have domineered it for so long.

"Maybe I hated him because he was better than me at everything."

"Siblings hate each other as much as they love each other. That doesn't mean you wanted or willed this to happen. That rivalry is a normal thing. There's jealousy one minute and horsing around the next. There's tattling to your parents one second and then sneaking into her bed the next to giggle and tell ghost stories when you're supposed to be asleep. It's a yin and yang that no one else understands unless they have a sibling."

"I was jealous of him. Plain and simple. Of the girls who fell at his feet. Of the constant praise he got on the ice. Of the grades that came easily, while I studied all the time . . . of fucking everything."

"Of the things your father pitted you against each other over." I'm quiet when I speak, afraid I've overstepped, but I heard the animosity when he shared his story. "That doesn't mean you're at fault. That doesn't mean you don't deserve to have a life. That doesn't mean you don't get to love and be loved. To laugh and have someone to laugh with."

"It's the fact that he was better than me," he says with a shrug, as if he didn't hear me. I don't take offense, because maybe he didn't want to *hear* it yet. It may be background noise to his thoughts right now but when the emotions settle, he'll remember what I said, and I hope he'll know it's true. "Maybe that's why I resented him. He was always perfect, and I was always the one who needed more work. Hell, maybe I secretly wanted the spotlight and was sick of being in his shadow." He chuckles, but there's so much sadness in the words. "Christ, that sounds stupid. We were the same in every way, but that he had more talent in his little pinkie than I did in total played a part."

"I find that hard to believe," I murmur.

"Go dig up our high school records. He still holds a couple that were made through our junior year. Could you imagine what he would have done if he had one more year?" He turns to look at me now, the city and morning sunshine at his back.

"I hear what you're saying, Hunter, but these are all normal things kids go through. I can tell you athletes peak at different times. Some people have natural talent while others have more heart and have to work harder to get it. But none of this"—I point to the space between us where the reasons I've pointed out are hovering like neon signs—"is why Jonah is paralyzed."

"How can you say that?" He raises his voice, but it loses its gusto on the last word.

"Because you didn't make Jonah get behind the wheel," I say so he might hear me again. "Sure, you were pissed at him and didn't get your mom like you were supposed to. Yes, you were duped by his girlfriend, who apparently wanted to brag she'd slept with both twins, but *you*, Hunter Maddox, didn't cause this. You didn't make him slide behind the wheel. He was already drinking, knowing he was picking up Terry Fischer and taking her to the dance. He had your mom's car, yet *he* was drinking." I pause, watching him contemplate something it seems he never considered—or rather, let himself consider. "And," I continue quietly, "you sure as hell aren't the reason your parents can't seem to step away from being Jonah's caregiver and be supportive parents to you."

Because that's the other crucial part of this he's not addressing. He not only lost his brother that day in the everyday sense he was used to, but he also lost his parents. They became so busy taking care of and cruelly coronating Jonah, that they forgot they had another son living and dying for the affection and approval any kid craves from their parents.

And the look on his face says I just hit the nail on the head with the other part of this whole tragedy—the little kid in him deserves love and affection instead of expectations and blame.

"But—"

"You didn't give your dad the heart attack, and you sure as hell don't deserve to live your life trying to make up for something you had no control over."

"Stop. Please, just stop," he says to me, covering his ears to prevent my words from hitting them.

"No, Hunter. No." I step toward him, toward his disbelieving eyes and shaking head. "I'm not going to stop, because you need to hear this." I reach out and grab his hands from his ears so he can hear me and whisper, "You need to hear you're not at fault. You need to stop drowning in guilt and burning in anger that's not yours to bear."

His eyes well and his chin trembles, and every part of me wishes I could convince him of the truth in my words. "You don't understand. No one does." He jerks his hands out of mine as his anger takes hold as his moment of vulnerability and need give way to self-loathing and fury. "It's like every time I see him there in that goddamn prison of a chair or bed, I hate myself even more. Do you know what it's like to sit there and know what he could have been? The incredible things he could have done? *I do.* I know a fraction of what he feels because it was like that when I was a kid. Sitting by while your brother did everything you were dying inside to do, but couldn't. No one was ever as good as Jonah. In our house, at our school, at our church. Not a single fucking person was."

"Is that why you're always angry?" I ask, trying to connect dots on a chart I can't see.

"You're goddamn right, I'm angry." His voice thunders around the small space, his hands fisting and his shoulders tensing. "Don't you get it? I've been running so damn long trying to chase the ghost of who he could have been, that it's the reason I'm burned out. That's why I hate the game I used to love but can't say a damn word, because who the fuck am I to complain? I make millions a year. I have records I'm chasing. I'm living the damn dream. All that's left is the Stanley Cup, and I'm going to win it if it kills me, because it's the least I can fucking do for him."

"But what about you? When do you get to have a life? When do you get to have someone to go home to at night? To wrap your arms around her and then lose yourself in when shit gets too tough? To laugh with, to fight with, *to live with*. When do you get to live, Hunter?"

Chapter

FIFTY-ONE

Hunter

SHE DOESN'T UNDERSTAND.

That's all I keep thinking as she watches me and says things to me I don't want to hear.

As I reject what I know are truths that she keeps saying, keeps repeating, keeps trying to rewire in my head.

When do you get to live, Hunter?

But there is so much anger, so much sadness, so much goddamn everything, it's hard to hear anything through it.

"You know the irony in this? I have all of this"—I throw my hands up—"to thank my dad for." I laugh, but there's no humor. "I wouldn't be here if it weren't for him and his punishments. That's the fucking blessing and curse, now isn't it?"

"It's whatever you want it to be. Make what used to be your curse, now be your blessing." They're words meant to fix but nowhere near as easy as they sound.

I know it.

She knows it.

And yet she says them anyway.

"If it were only that fucking easy."

"It's not easy. You're right. But it's also bullshit you've been made to feel like this life of yours isn't for you."

"I got out as fast as I could." I switch gears as the thoughts hit me. As if I need to purge everything at once. Maybe once they're out in the open they won't fucking hurt as much. "I love my brother more than the whole goddamn world. Hell, the twin thing is real—the connection, the feeling each other's pain—but looking at him is like a torturous, never-ending slap in the face. One minute I'm pissed at the fucking world, the next minute I'm pissed at myself . . . so the easiest thing for me was to get out, to not go back home. He's their world, and I'm just the fucking mistake."

"How can you say that?" I refuse to see the sympathy that fills her eyes even though it's sincere. "Look at the man you are, at the accomplishments you've made. Look at—"

"All they see is the one decision." I've never spoken truer words. Saying them out loud feels like a burden has been lifted from my chest. "All I see is him slowly dying, bit by bit, day by day, infection by infection. Christ, he's barely a shadow of who he used to be. He can't talk or eat or fucking do anything without my mom doing it for him. What kind of life is that, Dekker? What kind of fucking fate did I hand him?" My voice breaks and my shoulders shudder. "Like I said, all they see is the one decision."

"That's not true," she says, but I can see her struggle with wondering if it is. "You leaving them to have an NHL career made Jonah become their world. He's who they think about first and last . . . so it's natural for them to put him first now, but don't think they're not proud of you. Don't think they don't watch your games on TV and smile knowing that's their son. Don't—"

"Stop," I shout. I hate the tears that burn in my eyes. Tears I can't hide. I hate the silent hope her words are offering, but more than anything, the lifting of the weight that has been so damn heavy on my shoulders. *That I've carried alone.* I don't . . . I don't know how to stop believing. "Just. Stop." *Please.*

"Stop what?" she shouts getting in my face. "You have to learn that it's okay to be loved. You have to learn that you're not to blame. Winning a Stanley Cup is not going to take away the sting of what happened. It's not going to—"

"But Jonah will know that I didn't fulfill my promise to him and time is fucking running out."

When she reaches out to lace her fingers with mine, it takes everything I have to accept the gentleness of her touch. It was so much easier last night with the darkness around us to accept it versus now that she knows the truth.

But I crave it. And hate it. And feel like I don't deserve it, but all I want is to pull her into me and lose myself in her . . . but this time, not to forget. Not to use sex to numb the pain. This time it's because I want to feel. *I need to feel.* I need to think that for the smallest of seconds she's right, and I'm not to blame. That I deserve this.

That I deserve her.

"Dekker." Her name is a whisper on my lips, her touch a balm to my soul.

She frames my face and stares at me as she leans up on her tiptoes and presses her lips to my cheeks, kissing away the tears I wasn't aware I'd shed.

"Dekk." Gruffer.

Her eyes on mine. Her hands on me. Her words for my soul.

Our foreheads are pressed against each other's as her exhale is my next inhale, and her fingers tighten in the fabric of my shirt. The realization hits me.

All I want is her.

All I need is her.

She quiets the demons.

She sees me—the real me—and that scares the ever-loving shit out of me.

I lean forward and press my lips to hers. "Let me lose myself in you. Please. I need you."

They're the toughest words I've ever spoken. They're also the most honest.

And when she kisses me back, when she opens herself up to me after I bared every demon I have and she didn't back away, I'm overwhelmed.

She lets me set the pace. She lets me take what I need. Every sigh, every touch, every moan. She lets me evoke them from her.

She lets me be in control when I've felt out of control for so very long.

My hands slip inside her pajama bottoms to find naked skin. The strip of curls atop her pussy, the wet heat when I slide between her lips, the arousal that coats my fingers as I tuck them inside her. My groan is swallowed by her kiss.

How can I still turn her on even though she knows the truth? How can she still want me?

The thought is like a vicious eddy in my mind but with each touch, each sigh, each tightening of her fingers on my skin, it becomes more of a possibility. More of a reality.

The dance to undress is slow. There is no seduction needed. There is no desire needing to be awakened.

It's me as I grab her hips and sink down on the couch.

It's her as she lowers herself painstakingly slowly onto my cock and stills so I'm forced to feel everything about her. The warmth. The wetness. The tightness.

It's us as our eyes meet, fingers entwine, and Dekker leans forward to kiss me ever so slowly before begging to rock her hips over me.

Pleasure builds within. My balls tighten. My cock swells.

It's the shame that I'm now setting free.

Her tits bounce with each grind. Her teeth bite into her bottom lip. Her juices begin to cover wherever she touches.

It's the hope that I can believe them.

I reach out to touch. My thumb and forefinger over her nipple. My fingers bruising into her hips. My cock hitting the very depths within her.

And *it's the knowledge* that someday I might be able to.

Our pace is slow and sensual, her giving me everything I need, and God, she's so fucking sexy. Sitting atop me, working me out, with those innocent eyes and those vixen lips.

There's a connection I want to shy away from but she doesn't allow that. When I break my eyes from hers—to take in her fingers as she slides them between her lips and begins to rub slowly, to watch the pink of her flesh as it stretches to accommodate me, to watch her back arch as I run my fingers up the crack of her ass and tease the tight rim of muscles there—she moans my name and brings me back to her. To the emotions swimming in her eyes and the connection the two of us have that is so much more than the physical.

Hell yes, I need to lose myself here, but she's also showing me that I feel so much more.

She's showing me how to be found.

She's demonstrating that it's possible to find more than simple sexual gratification.

As my orgasm slowly builds, as our pace begins to pick up, as the frenzy starts to peak, I'm overwhelmed with a surge of emotions that bring tears to my eyes. When I try to turn away, when I try to close my eyes, Dekker leans forward, my name a moan on her lips before breathing life back into me with her kiss.

And I'm gone. Done. Restraint breaks and I empty myself into her—my head thrown back, my hips pushed up, my fingers gripped tight.

Jesus Fucking Christ.

She's a savior and a sinner, and I'm not quite sure which one I need to hold on tighter to.

But I do know one thing. *I want both.*

Chapter
FIFTY-TWO

Dekker

MY HANDS ARE THREADED THROUGH HIS HAIR AS WE LIE IN MY BED. His head is on my stomach, and the covers are thrown haphazardly over our bodies.

I know he has to leave soon. He'll need the time to take the train back to the Jacks arena in Jersey and get ready for his game tonight, but we don't talk about that.

We don't utter a sound about what he confessed to earlier and what we shared in the sex we had after that. Because it wasn't just sex. It was so much more than sex and I think both of us have our reasons for being scared to admit to it.

So we lie in my bed, where we've been for some time, and let things settle around us in a way that it no longer feels like confused chaos but more like something we might be able to work with. Something we might be able to make something out of.

"He's dying. My brother." They're the first words he's said, and I'm sure they're probably the hardest ones he's had to admit to himself.

Yes, everything else earlier was difficult, but admitting your brother is dying means you're acknowledging it. It means you're realizing it.

"I know," I murmur as I lift his hand and press a kiss to the palm. "I'm here for you. I'll be here for you when the time comes."

It's all I say. It's all I need to say, because that's the crux of everything. Hunter's anger. His urgency. His defiance.

He made a promise to his brother and he's worried Jonah might not make it to see it come true.

That's why this all makes sense.

Chapter

FIFTY-THREE

Dekker

HE PLAYS WITH QUIET CONFIDENCE TONIGHT.

There's steadfast arrogance to his touch that is trademark Mad Dog Maddox, but there's also a peace to him that I haven't seen in the longest time.

I know part of it is playing in his hometown arena for the first time after a long road stretch. The fans, the chants, the support.

But I like to think a part of it is because of what we shared in the past twenty-four hours. What he confessed and learned and heard.

I bring my fingers to my lips, the tenderness in the kiss he gave me before he left this afternoon still a memory there. The look in his eyes—gratitude, understanding, and something much more profound I cling my hope to—makes my heart feel so much happier tonight.

Wrapped with a blanket around me that smells like him still, I watch him clinch the LumberJacks first ever playoff berth, hoping somewhere in the suburbs of Boston that Jonah watched it too.

Chapter

FIFTY-FOUR

Hunter

Dad: It's about damn time. Good thing you had that Maysen beside you tonight or your three points would have never happened. Gonna need a lot of practice if you think you can make it through to the finals.

Dekker: Incredible. Every minute of every period you were phenomenal. Congratulations on clinching a berth to the playoffs!

THE ALCOHOL IS FLOWING FREELY IN DANTE'S INFERNO, OUR HANGOUT after the game. The bar is dark and crowded, but we're able to stay in the back room where the servers know us, know our drink orders, our occasional tendencies to get rowdy, and our penchant for leaving large tips.

I lean my head back against the booth and close my eyes. My legs are stretched out and my ankles are crossed, and the two texts keep running through my mind.

Oddly enough, one stands out more than the other. For the first time in forever, something is drowning out the negative.

"Hey Cap? You good?"

I look over to Katzen as he slides into the booth opposite of me and smiles. "I'm well on the way to being drunk so there's always that."

"Aren't we all?" He laughs that obnoxious laugh of his.

"You had some incredible saves tonight, Katzy."

"And you played like I haven't seen you play in a long fucking-ass time." He lifts his beer to his lips and mimics my posture on his side of the table. Then he angles his head to the side and just stares at me.

"What?" I ask.

"What happened? Did you figure out the answers to life's problems? Meet the Messiah? Eat some really good pussy that cleared both your head and your pipes? What?"

"Jesus," I say through a laugh and just shake my head, unfazed by my goalie and his crassness.

"Whatever it is, don't change it." He smacks his hand on the table with a resounding thud that startles me. "Superstition and shit."

"Fuck off."

"No, I'm serious. It's nice for us all to sit and celebrate instead of one of us having to keep an eye on you, worried you're going to throw a punch at some dude or fan or who the fuck knows who because they pissed you off."

"Huh." I don't know what to say to that if I'm honest. But suddenly I realize how much my poor behavior has affected my team. Has it really been that bad that one of my teammates has had to babysit me after every game? Even the ones we win?

Fuck. *And yet, they've stuck by me.*

Nothing showed me that more clearly than all the punches of encouragement they've thrown at me since I first stood up in the locker room and congratulated them last week. Is that the difference tonight? That *I* can celebrate? That I can believe *I* played a good game and led my team well?

The dynamic, the comradery, the whole of us. That's something I should feel guilty about. *Shit.* That's a hard pill to swallow.

Katz yells something else, but I miss it, no doubt distracted by my thoughts, the alcohol, and the noise level of the bar. "What?" I ask just as Maysen runs to our table.

A long, drawn-out, "Fuck yeah! We made the playoffs, baby," is yelled into the room as he slides two shot glasses our way. "Shots!"

I laugh with him. I drink with them. But the whole time I keep thinking about what Katz said and wonder why I played differently tonight.

But deep down, I know.

The weight was still there on the ice, just not as heavy as before.

The guilt was still there that I'm moving to the playoffs, I'm shaking champagne bottles in the locker room and not Jonah, but I could start to see around it.

The resentment of my dad's text was softened by the one right below it from Dekker.

Numerous changes in such a short time, but Christ, it feels so much better. I feel so much better. And that showed in my game. And in how I relate to my team. The emotions—sadness, guilt, anger, pain—are still there, but they're not as . . . loud. Consuming. After being bottled up for sixteen years, they feel lighter somehow. The change feels sudden, but I know it's been gradual . . . and because of one person.

One person who saw and believed in me.

I shove up out of my seat.

"Holy shit, you okay, dude?" Katz slurs as he looks my way, his eyes half-closed, and a stack of empties on the table between us. "You sprung up like you got a rocket in your ass."

"I'm good." I stumble when I walk. "I'm . . . I've gotta go."

"Uh-huh. Sure." His laugh carries over the noise and some of the guys turn their heads our way. "Don't lose this guy we had tonight. He—you—were fucking awesome."

I laugh and hold my middle finger over my head.

"Why you leaving?" Finch shouts as I walk past another table of teammates.

"Things. Gotta do things," I say, but it has nothing to do with things.

And everything to do with someone else I want to celebrate with.

This time, when I knock on her door at one in the morning, there's a need there, but it's different.

This time, it's because I want to share in something with somebody.

This time, it's because I want her near.

Chapter
FIFTY-FIVE

Dekker

When I open the door, I'm not exactly sure which Hunter Maddox I'm going to get. The knock alone at one in the morning was unexpected, but the sight of him even more so.

"Hi," I say. I don't fight the grin that comes at the sight of him all disheveled and glassy-eyed or the surge of emotions that hits me seeing him on my doorstep on a night that's obviously momentous for him. "What are you doing here?"

"I'm drunk." He shrugs, and it throws him off balance so he sways.

"So I noticed." I lean against the half-open door and hate that the sheepish grin on his face has me gripping the handle instead of pulling him into a hug I so desperately want.

"We won." Such a simple statement, but the emotion in his face is so pure, so relieved that it tugs on my heartstrings. It gives me hope that some of the words I said to him helped bridge the divide between his self-imprisonment and his eventual freedom.

"I know. I watched."

"And?"

"And you were *incredible*. One of the best games I've seen you play all year."

"I was? It was?" His cheeks flush red and that little-boy smile kills me in every way imaginable—all of them good.

"You most definitely were."

"I'm back," he says, and it sounds funny because he is physically back at my place but he means figuratively as in on the ice. He realizes the humor the minute it leaves his mouth and we both laugh.

But when the laughter fades, we're left staring at each other as how we left things between us hours ago replay in my head. There were no words spoken, there was nothing mentioned of where we go from here after this experience that no doubt drew us closer. There was just a bear hug that lasted so very long where words we both wanted to say were exchanged without speaking.

Thank you.

I'm here for you.

What is this between us?

Where do we go from here?

But when he left, we both had smiles on our faces—his eyes were still hollow, his shoulders still weighed down with the guilt I think he'll forever own—but I swear it was less than he walked in here with. And that's what I hope for. Each time I see him, to chip it away a little more. To lessen it bit by bit.

That he's here, tells me I might be right in my thinking. That I might have seen what I thought I saw as I sat astride him and rode him to bliss.

"Why are you here, Hunter?"

A scratch of his cheek. A lopsided grin. A rock back on his heels. "Because your bed is way more comfortable than mine."

And with that, he walks past me, into my apartment, and does a dive bomb onto my bed with the biggest whoop of laughter I've ever heard.

I stand there shaking my head at him until he notices me, grabs my hand, and yanks me down onto it with him. "Come here."

My shriek fills the room, and while I'm more than certain the drunken, chaste kiss he smacks on my cheek is going to turn into something more, it actually doesn't. Hunter pulls me against him, so his leg and arm flop over me, and pulls me in tighter.

"Mmm. I'm sleepy."

"Okay, drunk boy."

"I am drunk, thank you very much," he murmurs. "And you're just as comfortable as this bed."

And for the second time in as many nights, Hunter Maddox falls asleep beside me.

If this keeps up, I'm going to need stronger locks to guard my heart, because he already has a large piece of it.

Falling for someone is never the plan. One day, you just wake up and it's there in full-freaking, high-definition color.

How right my sister was.

Chapter

FIFTY-SIX

Dekker

Kincade Sports Management
Internal Memorandum
New Recruit Status Report

*denotes urgent status

Athlete	Team	Sport	Agent	Status
Alex Redman	n/a	Soccer	Chase	First contact
Desi Davalos	n/a	Basketball	Chase	In talks
Harry Osgood	Rays	Baseball	Brexton	Meeting set up
Michelle Nguyen	n/a	Soccer	Brexton	Negotiating terms
*Hunter Maddox	Jacks	Hockey	Dekker	No talks. Just sex.
Vincent Young	Rams	Football	Dekker	Contract sent

I STARE AT MY RESPONSE AND GO TO DELETE IT FOUR TIMES.

It's unprofessional.

It's not like me to write something like this and send it.

It's rather crass.

And while it might be true, they sure as hell don't know it. But they deserve it for razzing me over him. Between the status sheets and the ridiculous comments and innuendos over the past few Monday morning meetings, followed up by texts for juicy details, it's the least they deserve.

Let them read my comment—*no talks, just sex*—and I bet they'll either bombard me with questions . . . or leave me alone.

My dad will think I'm playing them.

My sisters? My bet's on them leaving me alone.

The question is whether they'll leave me alone because they think it's true or because they think I'm pissed.

Chapter
FIFTY-SEVEN

Hunter

"Hey Jonah. How are you, man?"

There's a quiet response on the other end—an R sound attempted—and even though the tears well in my eyes, a smile widens on my face.

"Can you believe it? The playoffs are next week. Next week. It's surreal and I don't know, J, it's crazy." I run a hand through my hair and look out the window to where the snow is falling. It looks so peaceful, but I know it's wreaking havoc for so many. "The Titans are a tough team, but I've been studying their films and have their defense and plays mapped in my head, so I think we can do this. You know if we make it to the finals you'll be there. I don't care what I have to do."

And I mean it. I don't care how much it costs, if I have to bring a traveling medical team . . . he'll be there.

"There's something else I want to tell you and I don't know . . . it's insane, but, I met this woman. I know. Don't be too shocked." I laugh, nervous over why I'm telling him. Torn over making him feel horrible and wanting him—needing him to know and be a part of my life more now than ever. "She's everything you'd say I don't deserve, but shit . . . I think she's actually making me a better person. A better man. I've known her for years but not until lately have things really clicked. And God, yes, it's scary as shit, but it's also pretty damn awesome to finish a game and be able to shut all the outside noise off because her opinion is all that matters. Her name's Dekker. Yes, *that* Dekker who I was having fun with a couple of years ago and who you met at the game, but, dude . . . this is a first for me. I'm at a total goddamn loss. She's . . . she's fucking everything and—"

"Hunter?"

"Mom?" I ask, startled and a little pissed at the interruption. "What—"

"What is it you just told your brother?"

"I—uh—why?" I fumble, not ready to tell this to anyone else yet. Shit, I haven't even told Dekker how I feel about her.

"Because he just got the biggest grin on his face, and I haven't seen him smile like that in the longest time." I can hear the elated relief in her voice, and my chest constricts at her words.

"He did?"

"Yes. What did you say?" she asks again.

"Some things are best left between brothers," I tell her, my own smile widening at the phrase I haven't used in years.

I hear her quick intake of a breath and know she heard it too.

And maybe, even if only for a second, we can both forget the accident, and I can revel in the knowledge that Jonah grinned about Dekker.

That's something to me.

When I hang up thirty minutes later and head to training, I couldn't be in a better mood.

Chapter

FIFTY-EIGHT

Dekker

"Why in the world are we here?" I ask Hunter as he glances at me. He's wiggling a key in what looks like an ancient door lock on a place that hasn't seen any attention in years.

The parking lot has weeds growing up through its cracks, the paint on the outside of the industrial-looking building is peeling in huge curls, while some spots are in hunks on the ground.

"Come on."

It's all Hunter says and curiosity gets the better of me—though I make him walk ahead of me in case the Boogey Man plans on popping out of its depths. But the minute I pass through the entrance, I know exactly what this place is— an old ice hockey rink.

Despite the outside looking well-worn, the inside is in fair condition. The walls and stands are gray, the barrier between what used to be the ice and the stands a faded and yellowed white, but there are hints of what used to be here.

"Well, it doesn't look like you'll be getting any practice in," I say, walking onto where the ice should be as he flicks on the overhead lights to brighten what the skylights in the ceiling don't.

"Nope."

"I thought you were taking me on a date to teach me some of your mad hockey skills."

"Mad hockey skills?" he asks as he takes a step toward me.

"Very mad, above-average, beanie-wearing Hunter." Instinctively, my arms slide to the side of his waist as he leans down and presses a chaste kiss to my lips.

It's that easy, the simple rhythm we've found ourselves in. Him at my doorstep after a game when he's in town. It's never talked about, never discussed, and yet he hops on the subway from Jersey to Manhattan and is there. We never make plans, but we end up hanging out together or taking a drive or talking on the phone till odd hours of the morning despite my work schedule and his games and practice.

It's fun and exhilarating and scary and overwhelming all at once—going from thinking only of yourself to suddenly thinking in terms of *we* when we've never really discussed anything.

As he walks around the vacant arena and moves toward the rink's center, I know he's changed in the few short weeks we've been doing whatever this is, and I like to think it's for the better.

"So is this your way of remembering where you came from before you start the first round of playoffs?"

"If I were remembering where I came from, I'd take you to an outdoor rink where your fingers would be frozen before you were able to put your gloves on. The lights would flicker on and off, and there'd be a chair near the edge where my dad sat with his whistle as he ordered us to do suicide after suicide." The soft smile on his lips tells me it's a good memory. "So in a sense, yes . . . just not the cold."

"This place could use some major TLC," I say as I walk around the rink's edge, my boots echoing around the space.

"I want to buy it." His words startle me.

"You want to buy it?" I ask with a laugh, but when he turns to face me with that lopsided smile of his, I know he means it.

"Yep." He shrugs as he takes a step closer, and there's emotion clogging in his eyes.

"What is it? Tell me?" I say, stepping beside him.

"It's a stupid idea. Never mind." He starts to walk away, and I grab his hand to keep him here.

"I think it's an awesome idea." I take a step away from him and can see it through the dust and neglect. When I turn back to face him, I can sense his discomfort. "Hey, why are you embarrassed? You can tell me anything."

"I believe I already have," he murmurs, his eyes as quiet as his voice.

I nod. "Fair enough." But it's not. Nothing is fair in this life, and while Hunter knows that better than most, the fear I still have of admitting I've let him get too close is in the back of my mind.

I take a walk to the other side of the rink and run my finger along the dust atop the wall at its edge. The memories come fast and sharp and are ones I prefer to keep in the dark recesses of my mind . . . but he shared his with me. He let me in while I'm still pretending I've kept him out.

The irony.

"For the longest time after my mom died"—I clear my throat—"I thought I was the one who killed her." Even the words are hard to say. I appreciate the fact that he stays silent to let me get them out on my own accord. "We'd been playing with those blow-up plastic baseball bats. My sisters and I won them at Coney Island in those games that cost like twenty dollars to actually win things."

My smile is bittersweet as I remember everything about the day. The scent of sunscreen and fried foods filling the air. The bickering between us sisters as my parents strolled in front of us, fingers entwined, their laughter easy.

"Anyway, we came home and were being pains in the asses—probably ungrateful . . . but I refused to get in the shower. I was too busy doing who knows what," I say when I know exactly what I was doing. I was texting the boy I had a crush on, because God forbid, my parents had taken us out for some family time instead of letting me stay home and stare at my phone waiting for him to text me. "My mom came upstairs to tell me I needed to get in because there were three others waiting for me . . . and one thing led to another. What started with her picking up the plastic bat and swatting me playfully on the butt ended with me grabbing my sister's bat off her bed and hitting her back. We had a fake sword battle with those stupid bats. We hit each other everywhere—heads, backs, legs, until we were laughing so hard we had to stop." I smile. I can still hear her laughter, can still remember her calling me Dekky-Doo, can still recall the drop in my stomach when I woke up in the middle of the night to the ambulance and its sirens and my dad's frantic tears.

"What happened to her?" Hunter asks as he steps up beside me. I was too lost in my memories to realize he'd moved closer.

"She had a massive brain aneurysm sometime during that night. For the longest time, I thought it was because I had hit her in the head with the blow-up bat. I hid it from everyone, thinking they'd all hate me for killing her."

"Dekker." My name is a resigned sigh as he places his hand on my lower back.

"I know now that it wasn't my doing, but back then, I was devastated. I worried the police would arrest me for murder, that my family would hate me for ruining their lives." I rest my head on his shoulder. "It wasn't until years later that I confessed to my dad that I'd killed her."

"What did he say?"

My sigh is heavy. "There were a lot of tears and hugs and reassurances that there was no way I was at fault . . . but I still worried."

"I'm sorry." He presses a kiss to my temple, and the warmth of his breath hits my scalp.

"Don't be. It's life, I guess. You live and you think you know one thing until you learn another. Guilt can be a nasty, ugly bitch, but it can also pull people together."

A silence falls between us. One full of mutual respect and understanding that we're each lost in our own pasts, our own memories, our own reasons for our guilt.

"No more sadness," I say suddenly, needing to shake the vibe. "Sadness is definitely not what you need before the big game tomorrow. How are you feeling about the matchup? You haven't really spoken about it."

"I'd name it after my brother, you know." His words give me whiplash and it takes me a second to realize he's talking about the arena. "'The Jonah Maddox Hockey Facility.' We'd make it the premier place to train for sled hockey," he says, referring to a modified version of ice hockey for those with physical disabilities. "We'd have camps for kids who are paralyzed, so they could forget the confines of their chairs for a while. No cost to their families. I'd get some of my teammates and friends in the league to come visit them. We'd make it easy for them. The equipment, the access—all the things most kids who want to play need but can't get at other places."

My heart swells, and I can't hide the tears over the purposeful thought he's put into renovating this place. And when he looks over at me, there are tears in his eyes too, and that heart of mine swells so large it virtually falls out of my chest, landing at his feet.

Not that I mind since right now, in this moment, I know it is pretty much already his.

"I think it's going to be amazing." I smile through the tears as he reaches out and links his fingers with mine. Such a simple action, but there's intimacy in the moment and it's perfect. Quiet and subtle.

"You do?"

I nod, realizing this is Hunter's way of letting his brother live on forever. This is his way of holding him close when the earth no longer can. "What better way than to let him be a part of the sport he loved while getting to be with his best friend?"

His smile is automatic. The bob of his Adam's apple reflecting the emotion that he's trying to keep at bay.

"I think you could even create a charity in his name, some kind of scholarship, or something like that. Something for your mom to be a part of. It might give her an outlet after. . ." *Jonah passes.* I twist my lips and hate that my mind went there, but I can't imagine living your whole life for someone and then suddenly having a life for yourself but a future without the person you cared for in front of you. I avert my eyes the minute my voice fades off, because Hunter knew what I was going to say and now I feel like shit.

"That's a good idea." His voice is soft but sincere.

"This place is not only going to be Jonah's legacy," I say and squeeze his hand, "but yours too."

Chapter

FIFTY-NINE

Hunter

"HEY MADDOX." HER VOICE JOLTS ME FROM MY FOCUS AS I WALK TO-ward the locker room and stops me in my tracks.

I turn and find her leaning against a wall. She has jeans on.

"Where's your Jacks gear?"

"Where's your Stanley Cup?" she asks, her smile wide, her tone playful in the reminder of the Dartmouth game when she told me she'd only wear it when I won a Stanley Cup.

"I'm working on it." I laugh and walk over to her. "What are you doing here?" I ask, confused and surprised as every emotion in between surges through me.

"Did you really think I was going to miss your first playoff game?"

"You said you had a client who—"

"I know what I said," she murmurs as she angles her head to the side. The sunlight highlights her hair and the gold lights up like a halo. There's a thump in my chest, and Christ if this woman doesn't do things to me I never expected. "But I'm here."

"Dropping your duties as an agent, huh? Poor client."

"No, dropping an agent's duty falls along the line of Sanderson," she teases.

But it's out there. The first damn time she's brought anything up about agents or my agent or any of the shit that's Sanderson's job since that night that feels like months ago. The night when we stood outside of whatever fucking arena and she told me the truth about why she was there. About how she feared telling me would ruin whatever this was between us.

"Sanderson drops the ball?" I ask with a smile on my lips.

"So I've heard." She nods.

"And you? Do you drop the ball?"

The slow run of her tongue over her bottom lip and the devious look in her eyes tells me exactly what she's thinking about. How the last time we saw each other, her lips were wrapped around my cock as her fingers gripped pleasurably firm around my balls.

"If you have to ask, Maddox, then I'm doing things all wrong." Her voice is liquid sex, the smile that crawls over her lips not far from it either.

I groan in response.

"You win tonight and we'll see if I drop the *balls* again or not."

"We'll win. No worries there. And I'll be the judge of your grip." I glance over my shoulder and lift a hand to Katz as he walks into the arena. "Hey Dekk?"

"Hmm?"

I take a step forward and lean in. "I never brought up the agent thing because you said it was either one or the other. You as mine or you as my agent. I'm not sure if that's still true."

"Oh." Her lips shock in an O, and I take the chance to steal a quick kiss before taking a step back and smiling.

"Thanks for coming." I wink. "I've got to go."

"Good luck," she says as I start walking away. "Hey, Cap?"

"Yeah?" I turn back to give her one more glance.

"Take a moment and let it all sink in. It'll go by in a flash, and I want you to remember it."

I nod and turn back toward the door.

"Stick, skill, finesse, Maddox."

I throw my head back and laugh.

⌁

Nerves rattle and I'm never nervous.

Sticks tap on the ice—the only kind of clapping we can hear while we're in the zone, and yet right now I hear everything.

The crowd.

The buzz.

I look up into the stands and see the people. The little kids wanting to be in my skates someday. The dads with their daughters teaching them the ins and outs of the game. The college frat boys needing an excuse to get drunk and heckle a player. The families wanting to be entertained.

I take it all in.

The sounds, the sights, the excitement.

This is for you, Jonah. And for once, I can see your smile.

I'm going to make you proud.

So maybe . . . maybe, this is for us.

Chapter
SIXTY

Dekker

ALL EYES FOCUS ON ME.

Brexton lifts her eyebrows. "Well?"

"Well, what?" I ask as I glance at the notes that have nothing to do with this status meeting on my notepad, but pretend to find them interesting.

"Hunter? The client you've been"—Chase coughs—"err . . . *not talks, just sex*, recruiting."

My cheeks flush with heat. "What about him?"

They're the queens of being difficult, so I'll take pleasure in being difficult for once.

"You've written a status sheet every week for the past few months, and it seems the only thing that's going down isn't your finger to the keys to fill us in on what's going on but rather"—she looks at our dad and shrugs apologetically before looking me straight in the eye—"well, *you on Hunter.*"

Her smile is cold and unmoving while the rest of us in the conference room choke back shocked laughter.

"Seriously, Chase? Should we go through your exploits? How about when you—?"

"Ladies!" My dad's voice thunders around the conference room, and the sudden bickering approaching DEFCON 3 suddenly quiets. We all turn to look at him. "Let's keep this meeting focused, as I'm sure you're all incredibly busy. Right?"

"*Busy*?" Lennox chokes on her laugh. "Sounds to me like Dekker's been plenty *busy.*"

Another round of laughter ensues followed by me scratching the side of my cheek with my middle finger. "Screw off."

Poor choice of words . . . I realize the minute I say them.

"There's that too," Brex chimes in.

"It's all fun and games until you have to face the music," Chase says in that singsong voice that annoys me. "So tell us, Dekk . . . just what's been going on with Hunter and his stick?"

I stand and pace to the window, hating, embarrassed, and feeling on the defensive that I really don't have much to report. *The favorite child has failed.*

I'm more than aware that they're all staring at my back as I watch the clouds building across the skyline, and I wonder if we'll get to watch the thundershowers sometime soon.

"Dekk?" my father asks.

Shit.

Time to face the music.

"I'm starting my conversation by reminding all of you that while your caseloads have remained the same, I've become the guinea pig for Operation Fuck You, Sanderson," I say as I turn around, cross my arms over my chest, and lean my hips against the credenza at my back. I meet each one of their eyes.

"Just give Sanderson that look and his balls will shrivel off," Lennox mutters. "Problem solved."

But it's the "*Pretty please*" that Chase murmurs that has us all laughing again.

"I have a meeting in twenty minutes in this conference room, so we need to get through this," my dad warns, and it still takes a few moments for our laughter to subside.

"Hunter Maddox." I draw in a deep breath and vacillate between the truth, somewhere close to the truth, and letting my father down wholly. "He knows I'm recruiting him. He knows we have a vested interest—"

"Vested, my ass." Lennox laughs, but I meet Brexton's eyes and her smile encourages me to continue.

"Truth be told, he knows why I was on the road trip. He knows why I'm there, but he's going through a lot of shit. I'm helping him through it. I'm . . ." *in love with him.* My breath catches at the words I've skated around in my mind for what feels like days but I've known for longer. I blink away the tears that flood and pray no one caught them. My hands fist where they're hidden beneath my elbows, crossed because I don't show emotion. I don't—

. . . they're on your sleeve when it comes to me.

Hunter's voice floods my head from those beginning days on the road trip, and I smile, because he's right. I do.

And isn't that part of this?

I twist my lips and meet each one of my sisters' eyes as I straighten my back. "He's currently in the playoffs and I don't think changing agents is where his mind is at." And it's true . . . but there is so much more at stake here.

For me.

"But he wasn't months ago when you started this, so that doesn't hold water," Lennox says and raises her eyebrows.

I refrain from glaring. It's hard, but I do.

"True, and all that time I've spent pursuing him, on top of my regular client load, and honestly, I'm not sure what's going to happen. I'm helping the human he is before the athlete everyone wants. I'm just being there for him." I draw in a deep breath and prepare myself to meet my father's eyes. When I do, the disappointment I expected to be there . . . isn't. Instead, his eyes are questioning but quiet. "I know I'm an agent and my job is to recruit him and help us on the whole, but I'm also a person who can't push another human being who is hurting."

His nod is just as reserved as his gaze, the muscle in his jaw ticks.

"So . . ." Lennox asks. "What does that mean? When all is said and done, I mean? Should I update that status on the recruit sheet for you?"

I open my mouth to give a vague response, but my dad cuts me off. "Ladies, can you give me a moment alone with Dekk?"

Feathers may be ruffled, but the conclusion of a meeting when they all have a million things to do overrides the irritation.

"Teacher's pet," Brexton says with a wink as she shuts the door so I'm alone with my dad.

"Take a seat," he says.

"I'm fine."

"Take a seat." It's the father tone and not the boss tone, so I begrudgingly slide into a chair at the complete opposite end of the table from him. If he's angry at my failure, I have distance, and if he starts asking questions, I can hope the space might mask the emotions in my eyes.

"What did you need, Dad?"

"Nothing."

"Nothing?" I laugh. "Then why did you ask me to stay?"

It's his turn to lean back in his chair and stare at me. He fidgets with the pen in his hand as the time stretches. "What is it you want to ask, Dekk?" he asks in that way where he knows exactly what I'm thinking—*and need*—without me ever saying a word.

And I do.

I have so many questions.

Ones that run through my mind as Hunter's soft snores fill my bedroom in the wee hours of the morning. Ones that nag at me as I watch him tear up.

"How come you never got remarried after Mom died?" He startles, and I know I've caught him off guard.

"I never found someone I wanted to marry."

"But you never dated."

He nods until his twisted lips spread into the softest of smiles. "I date plenty. I had girlfriends for months at a time," he says to my utter shock.

"When? Who? How come I don't know this?"

"Because the last thing I wanted was for you girls to ever think I was try-ing to replace your mother." He sets the pen down. "And I went out at night. Sometimes client dinners weren't really client dinners. Sometimes business trips were a little more than that."

Oh my God. I had no idea. How did I not know this?

"I'm stunned."

"Why? Because your old man had lovers or because—"

"Because I had zero clue, Dad. None. You had this secret life as a gigolo, and here I was feeling sorry for you for devoting yourself to your family." I laugh.

"Hardly the gigolo, but you and your sisters' well-being was more import-ant to me." His smile warms my heart as much as his words do. "What else do you have milling about in that mind of yours?"

"Did you ever love any of them?"

"A few, yes. Not in the same way I loved your mom. I mean, look at what she and I created together." His eyes fill with tears. "You and your sisters and this agency, but yes, I think I may have loved one or two."

"I don't even know what to say. My mind is blown."

"Why?"

"Weren't you scared to be hurt? Weren't you . . ." My voice fades off.

"Ah," he says, his fingers steepled in front of him, as if I finally got to the point he was waiting for me to get to.

"Ah, what?"

"Part of putting yourself out there, Dekker, is opening yourself up to get-ting hurt."

I stare at him for a beat and try to figure out how to put the jumble in my head at peace and turn the last key in the lock chained around my heart.

"Not that kind of hurt . . . the kind . . ." My eyes well with tears I attempt to blink away as my dad rises from his chair and moves toward the seat next to me. He turns my chair to face him like he used to do when I was a little girl, about to get a scolding or be taught a life lesson.

"The kind where the person dies and your insides feel like they're broken and your heart will never recover let alone beat again?"

I don't trust myself to speak. His words are too damn close to the truth, so I nod and when I do, the first tear slips over.

"It's always there in the back of your mind, because that's a pain someone never forgets, but Dekk, finding someone to love again is how you know you're not broken. It's how you know your heart can still beat again. It's the cure and the demise all at the same time. To be able to love again means you're still alive."

He reaches out and wipes a tear off my face like he did when I was a kid, his hands still feel so big even now that I'm older. I lean my cheek into his hand as his eyes meet mine. "Love is powerful, Dekker. It's why you're here. It's why you try so hard to please me. It's why you fight doggedly with your sisters. But it's also so very powerful when you find the one you want to give it to. Don't ever be afraid. You can't give half a heart, that's equivalent to giving someone your broken heart. No, you have to give them all of it and trust that they'll hold on to it and protect it."

The knock on the door shocks both of us apart to turn to look toward the interruption. "Come in," my father says.

And the shock that floods through me when Hunter opens the door and peeks his head in. "Mr. Kincade. Hi. Sorry for the interruption. I wanted to see if Dekker was free for lunch."

"No need to be sorry," my dad says. I wait for the shift from doting father to savvy agent as he crosses the distance toward Hunter to shake his hand. But it never happens. Instead he shakes Hunter's hand and pats the side of his shoulder. "Looking good out there. First round down, second starting, what? Tomorrow?"

"Yes, sir." Hunter nods. "We're headed to the airport in a few hours."

"Good luck, son. You're going to need it."

"Don't I know it."

My father looks back to me with something I can't read before nodding to Hunter and leaving the conference room.

I'm left to stare at Hunter as he leans against the shut door behind him and meets my eyes. He has a dark blue Henley on with jeans. His hair is styled and his grin is wide, and I'm sure the emotions I just shared with my dad are sitting on my sleeve for him to see.

For him to decipher.

For him to realize.

"You've got a lot of balls showing up here." I laugh as I close the distance toward him.

He shrugs. "Agents are a dime a dozen."

"Then switching agents should be no big deal," I tease and then am more than surprised when he tugs against my waist to pull me in for a soft kiss that steals my breath and incites my pulse.

"Hi," he says when he leans back.

"Hi." I'm breathless and my knees feel like rubber. How does he do that so damn easily?

"You look pretty." He fingers the lapel of my blazer. "Very *I'm going to bust your balls right after I suck them* pretty."

"Jesus," I bark out and laugh. "Only with you, Maddox. Only with you."

"Good to know." His hand slides down my torso and rests on my hip. "I thought you might want to catch a quick lunch before I head out."

I shouldn't feel overwhelmed by the gesture as it's quite simple, but he came here to ask me, knowing my family would see him, and that means he doesn't care what anyone thinks.

The panic I expect to ricochet through me like normal, doesn't flutter to life. No. It's too busy being soothed by my father's words and by the touch of the man whose hands are framing my cheeks.

"Lunch?"

"Yes, that meal between breakfast and dinner," he says as I stare at him, this feeling so very normal for us. "I'm hungry. I'm sure you're hungry . . . so, lunch."

"I'd love that. Thank you for asking." I take the initiative and press another kiss to his lips. "Be prepared for the shit my sisters are going to give you when we walk out of this door."

His grin is lightning quick and does things to my insides that shouldn't be legal. "I already got some, but you know as well as I do"—he winks—"I give just as good as I get."

I laugh as we open the door and Lennox is right there with her phone. "Do you mind taking a selfie with me? I think it'd be awesome to show you here at the offices on Instagram," she asks with a saccharine-sweet smile.

"Len," I warn as Hunter looks amused and confused.

"I can see the caption now. Hockey great, Hunter Maddox, touring the KSM offices." She holds her hands up as if she's reading it on a marquis.

"C'mon—"

"No, you c'mon, Dekk. You know Fuckface would croak if he saw Hunter here."

"Fuckface?" Hunter asks and then laughs when he realizes who she means. "You mean Sanderson?"

"Yes. Fuckface," Lennox reiterates, and I push her playfully away.

"I take it you met Lennox?" I ask as I tug on his hand to pull him toward the door.

"I met them all, yes," he says, and I'm not sure if I should be scared I wasn't here when they did.

"I guess that's our answer," Chase murmurs as I walk past her. I can only assume she's referring to their assumption that something more is going on between Hunter and me.

I'm just about to give a smart-ass comeback when I catch my father's eye in the back corner of the office. He's sitting with his arms crossed and the softest smile on his lips as his eyes hold mine. He gives the slightest of nods—almost as if it's approval—and my feet falter for the briefest of seconds as I hear him loud and clear.

Giving half a heart is akin to giving someone a broken heart . . . so give them your whole one instead.

Chapter

SIXTY-ONE

Hunter

Dad: Not horrible. Some of the best hockey I've seen you play, but there's still major room for improvement. You'll fall short if you keep that up. No doubt.

Dekker: Get off that road and come home to me. I'll show you just how damn proud I am of the way you played tonight. You were on fire.

"Now that's what I'm talking about, Maddox." I look up from my phone to see Sanderson bearing down on me on the far side of the LumberJacks' locker room. My gloves are off, my pads still on, and fuck if I haven't had time to take a seat before I have to talk to him. "You were a fucking lunatic out there. Way to go, man."

He goes to high-five me and I just stare at his hand and leave him hanging. Funny how the high fives are flying now. Interesting how I can see our relationship more clearly—when I'm good, we're good. When I'm troubled, he's with management and filled with threats. I get it's a business, but I'm finding more and more I need the people around me who care more about me when I'm at the bottom than when I'm at the top.

"Is there a problem?" he asks.

"No problem." I shake my head. "Just tired and hungry and ready to get home. It's been a long battle, and I'm ready to win the next two on our turf in front of a home crowd."

"You keep that shit up, you're going to have deals pouring in. I already have five messages on my phone."

"Great. I've got to hit the showers." I take everything he has with a grain of salt these days but nod, trying to give him the hint I'm not in the mood. He starts to walk away when I realize something. "Hey, Finn?"

"What's that?"

"No negotiations about anything during the playoffs."

"Come again?" he says as he takes a step back toward me, his hand curved around his ear as if he didn't hear me.

"I said hold off the phone calls and negotiations about endorsements. My game is dialed. Shit is sitting right in the universe. I don't want to jinx anything."

"I feel you on that. Not a problem. I'll send over who's interested but nothing else. You're focused on the Cup. I get it. I like the way you're thinking."

And when he walks away, I wonder if he'll still like the way I'm thinking when all is said and done.

It's late and freezing as I stand in the lot of the arena and wait for the rest of the guys to load the bus that will take us back to the airport with my cell to my ear.

"Hey." She sounds half asleep. Sexy. *Like home.*

How did her voice become the first thing I wanted to hear after every game? When did it start drowning out everyone else's?

"Did I wake you?"

Her sleep-drugged chuckle brings a smile to my face. "I fell asleep going over contracts." She shuffles papers, and I can picture her snuggling into that big blanket on her couch with SportsCenter on mute, and an empty glass of wine on the table next to her. Papers will be spread everywhere and her laptop will be half-charged on the pillow beside her.

"Sounds exciting."

"You gave me more than enough excitement tonight, thank you very much." She pauses. "I don't think I've ever seen you play this well. You guys are like a well-oiled machine. It was so much fun to watch."

"We've still got two games to win before we can celebrate anything," I say holding up my finger to Jünger who's waving me over.

"I'm all for celebrating every victory, no matter how big or how small."

"You are, are you?"

Her seductive chuckle vibrates through the line. "I'll show you just how much when you get home."

My balls tighten at the thought. Will I ever get enough of her? The prissy business side, the stubborn softer side, and the vixen I hope no one else knows about?

I hope not.

Because hell if I've ever felt at peace like this. I've still got a long way to go, but this—*she*—is definitely a really good start.

"I'll tell the pilot to hurry."

Her laughter is all I hear as I end the call and head toward the bus.

Chapter
SIXTY-TWO

Dekker

Kincade Sports Management
Internal Memorandum
New Recruit Status Report

*denotes urgent status

Athlete	Team	Sport	Agent	Status
Alex Redman	n/a	Soccer	Chase	In talks
Desi Davalos	n/a	Basketball	Chase	Signed!
Harry Osgood	Rays	Baseball	Brexton	Contract sent
Michelle Nguyen	n/a	Soccer	Brexton	Signed!
*Hunter Maddox	Jacks	Hockey	Dekker	******
Vincent Young	Rams	Football	Dekker	Walked away

******Whatever the heck it is you're doing to him *(or his stick)*, Dekk . . . KEEP DOING IT! He's on fire.

ALL I CAN DO IS LAUGH.

All I can do is hope he feels the same way.

Chapter

SIXTY-THREE

Dekker

HUNTER'S SITTING AT THE KITCHEN TABLE WITH THE SOFT GLOW OF the overhead fixture the only light in the room. He's slumped in his seat, but his attention is completely fixed on the laptop in front of him.

He's exhausted. I can see it in his eyes, in his posture, in the way he crashed when he hit the pillow earlier tonight.

So why's he up now?

This second round of playoffs has been grueling for him. With Finch out from a blown knee and Katz limping to the finish, if the Jacks can clinch a spot in the finals tomorrow, they'll have a few extra days rest while the other series still has at least two games left.

Regardless, the pressure on Hunter is tenfold, whether it's self-inflicted or not.

Not wanting to disturb him, but also wanting to be near him, I stand where I am at the bottom of the stairs and look around the common area of his house. Where my place is orderly and every piece has its place, his is an array of mismatched things that don't look cluttered when they should, and that shouldn't fit together, but do.

Kind of like us.

"Hey," he murmurs and pulls my attention to him.

"What are you doing up?" I ask as I move toward him. "You're exhausted."

"Can't sleep." He smiles as I lean my butt against the table so I can face him. My love for him is growing each and every day in ways I'm not sure I could ever have imagined. "Trying to crack their defense." His hand flicks to his laptop where he's watching film of the Eagles. "It looks so simple watching it but when you're on the ice, when you're bearing down on it, it feels fucking formidable."

"You're pretty formidable yourself, Maddox."

"I didn't feel like it last night."

I run my fingers through his hair and he lets his head fall back with a sigh.

His eyes close, and I can see the wear and tear from his need and will and want and drive for this to happen.

I know it's for him, but I also know it's for Jonah too.

"You're too hard on yourself," I murmur, and lean over and press a kiss to his lips. His body jolts with awareness and his eyes flutter open. "You know, you said your dad used to train you hard for hours and hours. Does he know the game as much as you do? Would he have insight you can't see being so close to the ice? Would he have any suggestions for you on how to break the defense?"

I'm not sure how he'll take my question, but a part of me feels like this fence needs to be mended if it can be for him to heal and move forward.

"Not an option." He moves the laptop out of the way and then uses his hands to guide my hips so I stand before him, his hands dipping beneath the hem of my shirt. "How about you sit right here and let me taste you."

Well, that's a change of topic if I've ever seen one. I thought he might be angry at my suggestion or stalk off and go to bed, but this? This is definitely him deflecting, and who am I to tell him no? Hell no. Not with a tongue like Hunter's.

I scoot up on his table, my bare ass feeling the chill of the wood beneath me, lean back on one of my hands, and spread my thighs.

That sigh. That smile. I'm thinking that sex might tire him out, relax him, and get him to sleep.

"You need some inspiration, huh?" I murmur as our eyes hold and I slide my finger down between my slit. A moan falls from my lips as my eyes close. My head falls back when I rub the pad of my finger on my clit and down to find myself already wet for him.

His groan matches how I feel sitting here, bared to him and so very aroused.

"Inspiration?" he asks, his eyelids falling heavy with desire as one hand reaches out and squeezes the tops of my thigh.

"Mm-hmm." The lazy friction mixed with his hands on me and his eyes a reflection of his own desire, is extremely arousing. Even more so is feeling comfortable to do this in front of him, the vulnerability of it only making it seem so much more.

"First little victories and now inspiration?" His smile widens.

"At your service," I murmur and sink my teeth into my bottom lip. "Inspiration comes in so many different places."

"Like here?" he asks, and I suck in a breath when Hunter's thumbs slide up and down the side of my sex. It's a hint of touch, but I feel it in every nerve all the way to my toes. "Or here?" His fingers push my hand out of the way and part me so the cool night air hits my most intimate parts.

Hunter looks up at me, a devilish grin on his lips and unmistakable desire in his eyes. They hold mine on the slow descent of his head between my thighs. "I'm thinking right here is an even better place."

And when his mouth touches me, when the warmth of his lips close over my clit, and then the heat of his tongue slides down its path to my core, when his fingers join the mix in an all-out sensual assault, all I can do is brace myself on the table behind me and let him find all the inspiration he needs.

Chapter

SIXTY-FOUR

Dekker

HUNTER DANCES DOWN THE ICE LIKE A MAN CLAWING HIS WAY OUT OF hell.

The clock counting down to the end of the game reads thirty seconds.

He weaves around one defender, then the next.

Twenty seconds.

He chases down the opposition, the forward heading straight for the goal unopposed by any teammate.

Ten seconds.

He swings his stick back for the shot toward the open net. Katz had tripped getting back to defend his goal and this is do or die. The opposition scores, and we're into overtime. They don't, and the Jacks go to the finals.

Five seconds.

Hunter dives across the ice the same time the puck flies. His body blocks it—a visible punch to his abdomen when it hits.

The buzzer sounds and LumberJacks Arena goes insane. The noise, the music, the cheering—they're like a symphony of chaos that has never sounded more beautiful.

But even better is the sight of Hunter being picked up by his teammates and celebrated. Tears blur my eyes and my heart soars into a dimension I never knew was possible.

It takes a second for me to catch on to what the crowd is chanting. It starts low and then becomes the heartbeat of the arena. *Mad-dox. Mad-dox.*

I think it takes even longer for the team on the ice to hear it because when they do, they slowly lower him to his feet, and one by one, they skate back a step and let Hunter have the limelight he hates.

But something about the moment is so poignant to me. To see Hunter standing center ice looking around with an incredulity on his face I could never put words to, hearing it. Taking it in.

He turns to each corner of the arena and puts his hand over his heart to let the fans know it's them that make it worth it for him. It's them who help motivate.

When he turns my way, the distance is great, but our eyes meet, and the slightest nod as he pats his hand over his heart is all I need to know. The feelings we've never addressed, the words we've never spoken, the future we've never discussed, don't matter.

Because that right there tells me how he feels about me.

And there's no question that I feel the same in return.

Chapter

SIXTY-FIVE

Hunter

"I'M NOT HAVING THIS ARGUMENT WITH YOU AGAIN, MOM. HE WILL be there for the first game and God willing the last game when we win if not every game in between. The arrangements have been made. You've seen them and his doctors have approved them."

"It's very gracious of you, but—"

"You don't have to come if you don't want to, but I will move heaven and earth for Jonah to be there. I have the means and I will do whatever it takes to make it happen."

"His health though. You don't understand—"

"But I do. I understand that you want to keep him within your bubble until the day he dies and while he's still alive that way, he's not fucking living."

"Don't you take that tone—"

"We had this dream since we were kids. Since we were teenagers, and we'd sneak out late at night and break into the rink and skate in the dark. We'd laugh and drink some of the beers we'd stolen from Dad's fridge in the garage and dream about the first time he'd get to play for the Stanley Cup."

"But he's not playing."

"Yes, he is," I shout, the emotion smothering my reason and respect. "We are one and the goddamn same. Don't you see that? I'm his legs because he can't walk. I'm his mouth because he can't speak. I'm his goddamn heart, and I can feel it beating still, so don't try to kill it because you're afraid of germs. Let him fucking live. Let him come see the dream he had, but that I promised I'd finish for him."

"Well," she says in the prissiest of tones. I've upset her. "I'll have to talk to your father."

"Don't you dare rob Jonah of this." When she remains silent, I continue. "The medical team will be there at nine to evaluate and prepare him for a safe transport." Steps that are way above and beyond what he needs but I know if I do this, she can't say no. "There are three tickets at the box office for you guys."

But when I hang up and toss my cell on the middle of the bed, I know not to hold my breath that my father will show.

Chapter
SIXTY-SIX

Dekker

"I'M SORRY. I WALKED IN. I DIDN'T MEAN TO EAVESDROP."

Hunter turns to my voice in his bedroom doorway and there's justifiable sadness in his expression that hurts me.

"It's just par for the fucking course," he mutters and laces his fingers behind his neck and exhales loudly. "Don't worry about it."

"But I do."

"I'm used to it." He shakes his head and forces a smile I know is masking his pain. "We still ordering food?"

"If you want." I pat my back pocket where I thought my phone was.

"Use mine," he says, pointing to the bed.

I'm distracted when I open it and it takes a second for me to believe what I'm seeing. The top of the iMessage screen says Dad, but there's no way in hell the messages on this phone could be from his father.

In just the static screen in front of me, there's word after word of negativity. Comment after comment of cruelty.

"Dekk? What is it?" Hunter asks, but when I'm so abhorred by what I see, I just look at him and hold out his phone.

"I didn't mean to. It was there when I opened it," I fumble. "What the hell?"

His sigh sounds like resignation and defeat as he takes his phone and tosses it right back to where I found it.

"I'll never be good enough for my dad." It's all he says. It's pained and raw and it rips my heart out.

"You play in the goddamn NHL, Hunter. You're the captain and have records and . . ."

"And I'm not Jonah."

Our eyes meet and hold, and so much is exchanged. So many emotions I think he's afraid to show come through loud and clear.

"Is it like that after every game?"

He nods. "I don't care. It doesn't affect me."

That has to be the biggest lie I've ever heard, because how can you play at the top of your game and your father, the man he probably craves approval from, not approve?

"You never respond to him. There's nothing from you back to him." At least not on the screen that I see.

"I did one time. I didn't get the satisfaction I thought I would from it, so I don't anymore."

I hate this. I hate seeing this the night before he's leaving for his first finals game. I hate that this is even a thing in his life when he deserves so much better . . . so much more.

"Why don't you block his number?" I ask, knowing it's much more complex than that. His parents are his lifeline to Jonah. If he cuts them off, he's cut off from his other half. It's complicated to say the least, but even harder is listening to his stoic tone when I know the words on these texts have to wreck him inside.

He chuckles. "You wouldn't understand."

"Try me."

He shakes his head, but I know he's going to tell me. "You know how you get used to something and it becomes a habit?"

"Yeah," I say, but I don't know how that can play into anything that's healthy for him.

"It's kind of become that thing I do. After I play a game, I walk in the locker room and look at my texts before I do anything else."

"But the comments are brutal. I mean, you played one hell of a game the other night and *that's* what he said to you?" My voice is rising as I realize so much of the turmoil inside him, of his long-term mental health, has to be affected by this. "My blood is boiling just thinking of it."

"*But he's watching.*" And there's something in the way he says it that stops the next comment on my tongue. It's sadness mixed with resolve, but it's something so much more. "It's sick and it's twisted and it makes no sense to anyone but me, but those texts at least tell me he's following me. It's not much." He stops when his voice breaks and another piece of me dies inside. "But it tells me he's still watching."

A scrap.

That's all Hunter wants from his dad. A scrap of love, of praise, of attention . . . anything from a father still hung up on a life that can no longer be lived the same.

I hate seeing him like this. I hate seeing him accept so much less than he deserves.

I tighten my ponytail and try to follow Hunter's logic, but God knows it's not normal. "He's watching but he's tearing you down. He's watching because he's trying to see if you measure up to your brother who hasn't played in fifteen-plus years." I get up from the bed and move from one side of the room and back, unable to shake the anger that's eating at me. "This is bullshit. You need to tell him that. But you don't need to because he can see it on his precious TV when he watches his son, the goddamn hockey star, score goal after goal."

But somewhere during my rant, the distress in his expression morphs to a soft smile. He's standing there with his shoulder against the wall of his armoire with amusement in his eyes, and it stops me in my tracks.

"What?" I ask.

"You're more mad at him than I am."

"Mad is an understatement. Mad is me wanting to pick up your phone, call him, and tell him he can take his texts and shove them squarely up his ass. Fury is—"

"Dekker." That smile. Those eyes.

"What?" I ask again.

"I love that you're so worked up about this on my behalf, but it's not going to change."

"Why not? Why can't he see you for you? Why can't he see the hours you put in studying film and the shot practice and the charity work and the way you love your brother and . . . Christ, Hunter, there are a million things that are incredible about you and a million more that I love about you . . ." My voice fades as my confession floats into the room before I have the courage to meet his eyes. This time when I speak, my voice is barely audible. A soft phrase spoken aloud, but it's been screaming in my head for weeks. "And even more reasons why I've fallen in love *with* you."

The tears that well in his eyes are blinked away but not before I see them. "That's not possible."

Months ago, he wouldn't have believed them, but not now. Not after we've spent hours talking about his past and his guilt and how he deserves the whole goddamn world.

"Yeah, it is," I say and take a step toward him. "It's more than possible because there are so many incredible things about you that it makes it hard *not* to fall in love with you."

"Dekker." He shakes his head back and forth, but there's a ghost of a smile on his lips that tells me he hears me. It tells me it'll take more time for him to believe it.

I frame the sides of his face with my hands and smile. "You don't have to say anything. Just hear me. Just know it. And while I'm sure your heart is pounding and your head is asking how this is even possible, know that mine does that every damn day I lay eyes on you. Without fail. And it feels pretty damn good."

Chapter
SIXTY-SEVEN

Dekker

THERE'S A PALPABLE EXCITEMENT WITHIN THE ARENA WHEN I STEP INTO it. With home-ice advantage, it's black and red everywhere you look—faces are painted and hair is sprayed to match. Instead of going straight to the manager's box, I take my time walking through the arena to soak it all in.

I think of last night with Hunter. My confession that I don't want to take back. Of how we spent the night making love before falling asleep in each other's arms. How a man who swears he doesn't deserve love sure knows how to give it.

I think of this morning—when he found out that Jonah had come down with another chest infection and wasn't cleared to make the flight here. The fact that it was Hunter's medical staff that made the decision and not his mother added validity to the outcome, but I know it still distressed him. But the calm I saw in his expression outweighed his disappointment. It's what I saw years ago in him, an inner strength not many have. But the difference was his lack of anger. In the past few months, his temper would have ignited. Yet he accepted the news about Jonah calmly, and my heart only grew deeper in love with him because of it.

I think of how he sat in his office for over an hour on the phone with Jonah. The conversation may have been one-sided as Hunter worked through the Cyclone's defense and offense and strengths and weaknesses, but you'd never know it. It's like they had their own way of communicating. You'd think he could actually hear his brother. Even more touching was when Hunter told Jonah to look closely on the coin toss when the cameras pan in and notice how he had written Jonah sideways in the one of his number thirteen so he could be playing with him.

And when Hunter walked out of his office and then house to join his team at the arena, I've never seen him more at peace.

Chapter

SIXTY-EIGHT

Hunter

EXCITEMENT HUMS THROUGH ME LIKE NEVER BEFORE.

I can feel the energy of the crowd and the anticipation of a game I've waited my whole life to get a chance to play.

"Let's do this, boys," I yell as I walk up and slap the shoulder pads of each player on my team. "Start with a win, end with the Cup! Start with a win, end with the Cup!"

They start chanting while we sit on the bench as my adrenaline begins to surge.

I take a glance up to the box. The owners are there. The GM beside them. Finn's there too. But it's Dekker I focus on. She's in the far corner, elbows are resting on the edge as she leans forward, but her eyes are on me.

She blows me a kiss, and I smile in return with a nod.

She loves me.

Me.

Fucking loves me.

"Start with a win, end with the Cup!"

The chant of my teammates brings me back. To the here. To the now.

To the ice beneath my skates.

To the feel of the stick in my hand.

To the chill of the arena on my cheeks.

Just like when Jonah and I were kids.

I've got you, brother.

I never stopped.

Chapter

SIXTY-NINE

Dekker

"What's this?" I ask, as I look at the gigantic box Hunter's carrying through my front door.

"Things."

"Things?" I ask with a laugh.

"Yes, things." He sets it down on the kitchen counter and pushes it my way.

"Can I open, said, things?" I ask as I toy with its edges.

"Yes." He presses a kiss to my lips. "I can only stay for your initial reaction and then I've got to get to work."

"Okay." I draw the word out as I lift the flaps of the box and then a laugh bubbles out when I see the team colors of the Jacks. Like lots of team colors. Black and red on hats and T-shirts and jackets and koozies and pens and everywhere. "Did you mug a vendor?" I ask when my laughter subsides and my sides ache.

"Perhaps," he says with a shrug of innocence but a smile like the devil.

"And these?" I ask as I pull out a thong—if you can even call them that—with the Jacks logo imprinted on the only spot of fabric big enough to hold it and dangle them off my fingertips. "These are sold in the kiosks?"

"We like to make sure everybody's covered."

"Covered being the operative word there," I say as I hold them with both hands to show how small they are.

"I wouldn't complain to see how they cover you." He quirks an eyebrow, and I roll my eyes. "Now there's no excuse why you can't wear Jacks gear to the next game."

"And I told you I only wear it after a team wins." I toss the thong back in the box and shake my head at the gear. "Besides, why are you pushing this? I thought athletes were superstitious and never liked to jinx anything."

"We are . . . but sometimes when you feel something in your bones, you just know that no amount of superstition is going to mess with your game."

"Getting cocky now, are we?"

He takes a step toward me and grabs his crotch. "Why yes, I have a cock."

"Jesus." I push against his chest and roll my eyes, but can't say it's not a hot sight. "Besides, *a lot* of players would disagree with you."

"I'm not a lot of players." He leans in and presses a kiss to my lips that is unexpected and heartfelt and stokes those fires he's damn good at sparking to life.

"Thank you for the gear, Mr. Maddox, but while you might not be superstitious, I, for the record, am." I wink and trail my fingernail down the midline of his chest. "Only *after* you win."

"Whatever." He exhales dramatically. "*After* we win, I'll make you wear them every day for a week."

"A week?"

"A week. And especially those panties."

I smile. "Deal."

He kisses me again, his hands wandering to places I want him to not let go of. Everything about the moment is perfectly right.

The Jacks are up in the series three games to two.

The game may be at the opponent's arena, but it's only a few hours away so I've been able to make every game.

Jonah's gotten the all-clear and will be at the game tonight.

I love Hunter Maddox.

How does it not get better than that?

"So I'll see you there?" he asks when he leans back.

"Wild horses wouldn't be able to drag me away." I squeeze his hand, glad he'll have this time tonight to be with his team and see his family before the big game six tomorrow. "And I just might have something for you too."

"Me?"

"Yep," I say with a nod as I walk over to grab the legal-sized manila envelope sitting on the counter.

"What's this?"

"You have to wait to open it."

"Why?" he asks.

"Because it's a surprise and if you don't like it, I don't want to see your expression." I laugh, my words partially true.

"It's that bad?"

"I don't think so."

"Okay, if I have to wait to open this, you have to promise me to personally go through this entire box until you find the surprise I left you."

I eye him, suspicious. "Deal." I lean in for one more breath-stealing kiss. "Good luck, Maddox."

"I'm gonna need it."

"Stick. Skill. Finesse."

And it's not until after he leaves and I settle down on my floor with this massive box do I realize just how much crap is packed in there. There are hats and socks and bears and you name it, along with my most favorite thing, a Maddox jersey.

In fact, there are two of them.

But it's not until I turn the second one over that I see my surprise.

My breath catches and I stare at it for the longest of moments. Tears blur and slip over and my soul sighs in contentment. I reach out with my fingertip and trace the Sharpie block handwriting that fills the number one of the number thirteen on the back of the jersey.

I LOVE YOU TOO.

I sit and stare at it for the longest time. A confession that just made me more whole than I ever thought I could be. An admission I didn't think he realized he could make.

It takes a few minutes for it to sink in. How hard that must have been for him to pen and probably even harder to admit to. But the minute it does, I run to get my phone to call him, and of course I can't find it. After a few minutes, I locate it on my bathroom counter and when I do, there's a text waiting for me on its screen.

Hunter: I didn't want to see your expression if you didn't like my surprise either.

My own laughter fills my silent apartment as I flop back on my bed and hug my phone to my chest.

My first call to him goes to voicemail. So does my second. My desperation to hear him say those words growing stronger with each second.

Hunter: We're reviewing film before we leave. Can't talk.

Me: I found your surprise. Tennis balls. Lots and lots of tennis balls.

Hunter: LOL. I meant what I wrote.

Me: I know.

I squeal into my apartment in elation. I probably scare the neighbors, but I don't care.

Hunter Maddox loves me.

Chapter

SEVENTY

Hunter

THE CHARTER COACH IS SPACIOUS. THE CYCLONE'S ARENA IS TOO CLOSE to fly and too far to get there ourselves, so we're all spread out among the seats of the bus, each of us in our own row as we make our way to what could be the final game of the series if we can pull it off.

I stare at the manila envelope for a moment, before curiosity gets the better of me and I open it. I spill the contents out onto the tray table in front of me and it takes me a second to realize what I'm seeing.

And when I do, I'm speechless. One of my dreams is coming to life before my eyes.

The renditions are in different colors with varying logos, but they're all the same thing—or rather the same place. Dekker had a graphic designer create mock-ups of looks and logos for the arena I told her I wanted to buy. *The Jonah Maddox Hockey Facility.*

I thumb through the fifteen or so versions, over and over, as chills chase over my skin at the sight of them. At the knowledge that she heard my dream and is trying to help me see it brought to life. Seeing the logos makes my idea seem that much more real, and I know come hell or high water, I will make this happen.

I grab my phone to text her, glad she understands that Coach has a no talking on cell phones rule on the bus.

Me: I'm speechless. They're incredible. I can't wait for you to help me pick one.

Dekker: See? Dreams do come true. Now, go out and achieve your other dream tomorrow.

Me: I love you.

Dekker: I love you too.

I stare at the text. At the three words and the weight they hold when I never thought I deserved them, and know I truly do mean them. Fuck, how can I not when it comes to a woman like Dekker?

She's everything I need and nothing I deserve.

She's strong, passionate, driven . . . and I love that she doesn't take shit from anybody, least of all me.

She's seen me at my worst and still loves me.

She champions my dreams when I doubt them, and she fights for me when I've stopped wanting to fight for myself.

How did I get to be such a lucky bastard?

Chapter
SEVENTY-ONE

Hunter

"Good meeting you, man," Katz says to Jonah before heading out of the meet and greet room where we've been hanging out in the underbelly of the arena.

"See you in a few," I say.

"My, he's handsome," my mother says with a smile and a fluff of her hair.

"I like to think more of his hockey skills than his looks, but that's just me," I tease, the strain a little less with each minute we visit. "You too, right, J?"

My brother looks so very weak—the pallor of his skin, the hollow lines of his face, his size—but it's his eyes when he looks at me that get me. He's proud. So very proud of me, and I refuse to let him down tonight.

I lean over to his ear and whisper what feels like I've waited a lifetime to say to him. "Tonight's the night, Jonah. We're going to win that Cup we promised each other when we were kids. You pushed me to be better and fuck . . . I'd give anything for it to be you out there, for me to be rooting for you. I would." I close my eyes to fight the tears so I can finish what I need to say. "I promised you I'd get here someday and that when I did, we'd do this together . . . so this game is for you, brother. Every shot, every juke, every block. I needed you here to win, because I couldn't do this without you."

I rest my forehead against his as my shoulders shudder with the weight of my words and the chance at my fingertips. When I lean back to meet his eyes, there are tears on his cheeks. He understands. He hears me. He forgives me.

He's with me.

"I've gotta get to the locker room." I turn to my mom and freeze when I see my dad standing in the doorway. "Dad." I sound like a child when I say his name.

You came to a game. To my game.

You're here.

"Son." He nods and takes a step forward. He extends a hand to me to shake and I do so, feeling detached and uncertain.

"Sir." I stumble over words. "Thank you for coming."

Another somber nod. "Good luck tonight."

Our eyes hold, and fuck if my chest doesn't tighten. "I've got to go."

And when I walk out of the room, I stop and brace my hands on my knees for a few moments to catch my breath.

The man I've called Dad for thirty-two years used to tower over me. Add in his anger, his shame, his . . . loathing, I've always felt so small.

But not now.

Now, I feel tall, like I tower over him.

Now, I feel proud, because I earned everything about this fucking moment. I'm the one who put the blood, the sweat, and the tears in. I'm the one who has sacrificed parts of my life for this chance.

Yeah, him showing up means something to me, but tonight I'm playing for something bigger than him and his relentless criticism. His presence doesn't erase anything . . .

I have a job to do. A win for my team to produce. A place in history to make. So, I straighten and turn toward the training room, ready to lead my team to victory.

Ready to achieve my dream.

Chapter
SEVENTY-TWO

Dekker

THE PRESS BOX IS NOT WHERE I WANT TO BE TO WATCH THIS GAME. I want to be with the fans. I want to be high-fiving when goals are made and booing on bad calls by the ref.

Tonight's game is definitely not one I want to watch from the expensive seats.

But I've spent the better part of the last hour up here as the countdown to the face off draws near. I've visited with Carla, since apparently Hunter has told her we're dating, I've talked at length to Jonah about how Hunter's conversations on the phone with him give him more clarity than I've ever seen, and I've been introduced to Gary, their father.

He's a hard one to read, but I'm sure my anger and resentment doesn't help much.

Uncertain what I'm going to say, but more than sure of my intentions, I step up beside where he's stood the whole time, arms crossed over his chest, as he watches the teams warm-up.

He doesn't acknowledge I'm standing there and for some reason, I don't expect him to.

"Your son is a good man, you know. Incredible, actually."

He nods, but doesn't say a word or look my way.

"He's lived a life trying to make you proud, trying to make amends for fate's cruel hand in the accident that injured Jonah that wasn't Hunter's fault to begin with. I understand your lives changed forever that day. I can't imagine how angry you are over it, and I can't imagine the pain and suffering you've all been through because of it . . . but while you lost the Jonah you knew that day, Hunter lost the parents he knew that day too."

When I look his way, there are tears welling in his eyes and his chin trembles, but he gives no other acknowledgment that he's heard what I've said.

"I'm in love with your son, and I will not stand by and let him be hurt by you any further. I won't let it happen. Are you prepared to risk losing your other son too or are you going to try and find a way through your anger to treat him how he deserves to be treated?" I take a step back. "Your call."

And without another word to Gary Maddox, I turn on my heel with so much more I want to say but restraint locked in place, and head toward my cheap seats.

Chapter

SEVENTY-THREE

Hunter

A GLANCE AT THE CLOCK.

Ten minutes left in the third period.

It's a tied game.

Ten minutes left to either be a hero or forgotten.

Two to two.

Ten minutes left to make something happen.

Katzen collects the puck and slings it out to me.

I pass it over to Finch then dodge around a defender. My grunt as his shoulder checks me is loud in my head.

C'mon, Hunter. Twenty bucks and me taking over all your chores if you can make this goal. Show Dad that you can.

The puck is stripped from Finch and we race back to help Katzen.

Withers cuts across the ice and intercepts the pass. We all switch gears and go back the other way.

We've been at this for fifty fucking minutes.

Our legs are tired. Our chests burn from breathing so hard.

We need to stay focused.

No more missed passes. No more checks turning into fights.

We need to focus.

We have to win.

I have to win.

Pass after pass we move down the ice. Withers to me. Me to Heffner. Heffner back to me.

A glance at the clock.

Time's wasting.

We need to score.

There is no sound.

There is no crowd.

There is no pressure.
It's me and the goalie.
It's the puck and the net.
It's Jonah beside me, pushing me to make this shot.
Daring me to prove that I can.

Chapter

SEVENTY-FOUR

Dekker

"Ten. Nine. Eight."

The Jacks fans in the crowd begin the countdown to the buzzer.

"Seven. Six. Five."

To them winning their first Stanley Cup.

"Four. Three. Two."

To twenty men a childhood dream is about to come true.

"One."

The arena erupts into chaos.

The men on the ice even more so as they pile on top of each other in an ecstatic frenzy.

Frozen in excitement, I stand in the midlevel seats in the arena with both hands covering my mouth in a state of shock myself.

They did it.

They really did it.

I can't take my eyes off Hunter as he breaks free from the pack and skates over to the edge of the rink that's closest to the box seats where his parents are seated. He stands there and points to the booth where Jonah sits in his chair, and I don't have to see Hunter's face to know that tears are streaking down his cheeks are elation, relief, and everything mixed in between.

He won Jonah his Stanley Cup. The one promise he could fulfill . . . he did.

I don't even realize tears are sliding down my own cheeks as I watch Hunter begin to search the arena, his lips moving as he reads the huge section numbers painted on the walls until he finds mine. It takes him a second but when he finds me, the look he gives me is one I'll never forget.

"We did it," he mouths, and all I can do is nod and watch him shine in the moment of his life.

He's quickly engulfed by reporters and teammates and his attention is diverted, but my heart is full beyond measure.

My attention shifts to the box seats where Hunter's family is seated. To where it's ventured numerous times tonight. To the man standing at its edge with his arms crossed over his chest in a formidable stance, but with a hand that's lifted a white tissue to dab beneath his eyes.

My anger is still there at Hunter's dad, it still burns bright. I don't think I will ever find it in me to forgive him for the years of agony Hunter experienced at the hand of his father. Perhaps a better woman would forget and forgive.

I'm not her.

But where does that leave us? By protecting the man I love and this man—his father—taking a step forward, when for so long he's refused to budge?

I'm not sure how to process his presence tonight as I make my way down the edge of the rink, but one thing keeps repeating in my mind. He showed up. He took a first step. He's the one crying, watching one son reach the pinnacle of his sport and fulfill a promise he made to his twin.

Maybe my words hit home.

Maybe this might change things.

Only time will tell.

I make my way to edge of the rink, wanting, needing to be closer to Hunter. Closer to the man I love.

Just as I get there, when I'm as close as I can possibly be while the TV networks are getting everything set up for the presentation of the Cup, Hunter skates over to where I am.

"You," he shouts and points to me as he climbs on the team bench so he can reach over the plexiglass partition. "Let her down here," he says to all the fans screaming for his attention.

It takes a few moments before fans realize what he's asking, so I can make my way to the seats right by the team bench. I climb up on the seat of the stands so I'm tall enough to be pulled into the arms that Hunter engulfs me in. His lips are on mine in a kiss that is one of pure jubilation.

"We did it, Dekk! We fucking did it!"

He reaches down to the back of his pants where he's obviously tucked something and produces a LumberJacks hat and places it squarely on my head.

I throw my head back and laugh, and then have to hold it to my head when I almost lose it.

"It's a good look on you," he shouts above the fray.

"I'm so proud of you," I tell him and kiss him one more time. "Now go celebrate with your team."

He steps down off the bench but his eyes still hold mine, and the goofy grin on his face tells me he's struggling to take this all in.

"I love you," he mouths.

"I love you more," I say, my words drowned out by the roar of the crowd as the Stanley Cup is carried out onto the ice.

Chapter

SEVENTY-FIVE

Hunter

Dad: Congratulations.

I STARE AT THE TEXT JUST DELIVERED TO MY PHONE AND THEN BACK across the room where my dad is standing against the wall with his cell in his hand but his eyes locked on mine.

I wait for the criticism to come. For my phone to alert another text where he tells me what I did wrong or what I could have done better. I expect the negativity that I've lived with all my life to come roaring in.

But he doesn't send another text, he doesn't say a word. He only gives a nod, but it's a nod that says more than I could ever ask for. It says things I've longed to hear for far too long and now that I don't need to hear them, I can probably appreciate them more.

But it takes me back. It challenges me to remember a time when there wasn't something negative to weigh down anything positive that has happened.

And still, the text doesn't come.

I struggle with how to feel. Relieved. Confused. Uncertain. At a loss. I'd think one of them would stand out, but it's been so long since I've been given a chance to have an emotion other than shame and anger when it comes to my dad, that I don't know how to feel.

And then there's the fact that he's over there staring at me but can't voice the word.

I should be angry at that. I should expect more . . . but I lost hope over that so very long ago.

So what now? How do I proceed?

While Jonah's body bears physical scars, mine are within, unseen, and just as devastating.

Some scars may never heal, but for the first time, it seems I've accomplished what he never thought I could. I won the Cup. I lived up to his ridiculous standards.

And a part of me suddenly feels free.

While I shouldn't give a fuck that I made my dad proud or happy because he stole or dominated so many years of my life, I have more to be thankful for than angry about right now.

I did this for Jonah.

I did this for me.

I did this for my team.

I've found Dekker.

Now I can really live.

A dream has been won. My heart is full because of the love of a woman I never thought I'd deserve.

I'm a winner in more ways than one.

And fuck . . . I'm thankful.

Chapter

SEVENTY-SIX

Dekker

1 week later

HE'S IGNORING ME.

Plain ignoring me.

Chase, Lennox, and Brexton are all out pursuing new clients, and I'm sitting here trying to figure out why he keeps getting up and shutting his door every time a phone call comes in.

Is it the doctor? Isn't that how this all started to begin with? My dad asking me to accomplish something and all of us in a panic that something was wrong with him?

I glance at my dad through the glass window of the conference room, but his back is to me as he talks to whoever has called him this time.

And it's not like phone calls are uncommon. That's all we do in here—talk and talk and talk some more.

So why am I on the defensive without him saying a word? Why am I panicked to talk to him and desperate to as well?

It's because he knows. It's because I failed him and his request. Sure, the status reports were cute and my sisters and I went back and forth with our facetious comments, but I failed to bring Hunter to the firm and now he's trying to figure out something else to keep this place afloat.

Overthink much, Dekk?

Jesus.

I blow out a breath and walk to the door, my hand ready to knock when he opens it.

"You got a sec?" I ask when he just stares at me. He looks frazzled. Hair mussed from his hands running through it, and cheeks flushed.

"What do you need? I'm kind of in the middle of something," he says, striding back to his desk and shuffling through his papers.

"Dad?"

"Hmm?" he says, completely preoccupied. "I have an appointment. They should be here any moment."

"*Dad*," I say more firmly.

His head comes up and sees me for what I think is the first time. "Sorry. Yes." He stops shuffling. "What is it?"

I shift my feet and stress over asking the question, a grown woman reduced to feeling like a little girl who's about to disappoint her father. "It's been a week since they won the Cup. Why haven't you asked me about Hunter's status on switching agents?"

Especially since you know I go home to him most nights.

He stares at me with an intensity that unnerves me. "I need you to sit down a moment."

"It's not a big deal. Forget I asked. I can see that you're busy."

I'm practically walking back toward my desk when he says, "Sit."

So, of course, I do.

He takes his own seat, his eyes flicking over my shoulder to where our receptionist Marge is speaking to someone, presumably his client.

"How do you think the Jacks won the Cup?"

What?

"The best team won?" I sound uncertain, even though I know my statement is true. The Jacks were the best team in the Cup. They peaked at the right time and the distractions and outside noise faded away. "This isn't about the Jacks. This is about Hunter and how I failed you."

His laugh is a low chuckle. *He knows more than I do.* "I'll ask you the question again. How did they win the Cup?"

I pause. I can see it in his eyes. This is one of his life-lessons moments. The last time we had one, he pushed me to find love—to give my whole heart. And I did. I let go of my fear, and I believed love was possible. I realized it was worth the risk.

And that's when it hits me.

"They won because they believed they could. They won because they played as a team. They won because they trusted their captain and wanted those endless hours of pain and hard work to count for something. They let go of their fear of losing and believed in themselves."

My dad's smile isn't something he gives quickly, but right now, I see my favorite one. *Pride.* He's proud of me, and somehow I don't think it's simply about my answer.

"You're right. They played as a team. Just like we do here. What you drop, another will pick up. What I drop, same goes. We'll survive without Maddox . . . but you're missing my point."

"What is your point then?"

"His point is that he sent you to recruit me."

I gasp at the sound and then the sight of Hunter standing in the doorway to my dad's office. He's leaning against the doorjamb, his thumb hooked in one belt loop of his jeans, and he has a sheepish smile tugging on the corner of his lips.

"Because he saw more in me than I could see in myself. He saw potential through my anger and skill through my antics. He saw something that most dismissed. He knew if I could get my head in the right place, that would be to my benefit. He knew that you'd see me as more than a hockey player when that's all anyone had. He knew that you'd help me see through the pain because like me, you were fighting your way through it too."

I stare at him as my jaw falls lax and my heart swells. And there are tears. For some reason, tears are welling when there's nothing to be sad about.

Because I'm not sad.

No.

I'm so damn happy, so fulfilled, that I never knew this feeling was real or possible or something I wanted to feel.

"Is that right?" I finally ask.

"Yes. That's right." I turn to face my dad and shake my head as I try to process what he means. "I didn't realize it at first." He chuckles as he stands and leans his hips against the credenza at his back. "I thought you were the right one to go after Hunter because you were dogged, and I didn't think you'd take any of his shit, but the more I talked to you, the more you questioned me, I realized everything Hunter just said was true. That you two were more alike than I'd ever thought. Funny how fate is that way."

I eye my father. I see the moisture he blinks away in his own eyes and can feel his pride for both me and Hunter.

He nods his head and smiles softly. "If you'll excuse me, I need to get ready for my client." He holds his hand out to shake Hunter's when he approaches him. "Good to see you. Congratulations, again."

"Thank you, sir."

"It's Kenyon."

Hunter nods as my dad walks down the hallway toward his office.

"What are you doing here?" I ask, rising from my chair.

A sly smile crawls onto his lips. "I wanted to make sure you were fulfilling your end of the deal."

"My end of the deal?" I ask and raise my eyebrows as he steps inside the conference room, shuts the door behind him, and proceeds to turn the blinds closed.

Just what exactly does he think we're going to do in here?

He puts his hand on the small of my back and tugs me into him. His lips find mine in an instant. He's warmth and arousal and comfort . . . and home.

Isn't that what I've come to realize over these past few months? That even though my dad sent me to find Hunter, I also found me?

I know I should be worried that I'm in my office—in the conference room—and being totally unprofessional, but it's so damn easy to get lost in Hunter.

In his touch. In his humor. In the way he makes me think about things other than the day-to-day. In the way he makes me feel.

My body heats from his touch, despite it only being hours since I slid out of bed beside him to come to work.

It's only when his hand tries to slip inside the waistband of my slacks that I push my hands against his chest to stop him. "Whoa, tiger." I laugh and press one more kiss to his lips. "Not here."

"Just trying to make sure you're holding up your end of the bargain," he says and wipes a thumb over his lip in case any of my lipstick transferred.

"My end of the bargain?"

"Mm-hmm." His eyes say he wants to devour me. "My LumberJacks gear?"

I laugh and take a step back. "Perhaps." I'm acting coy on purpose, because playful Hunter is always so much fun.

"Perhaps?" he asks.

"Maybe you'll just have to wait and see when I get home tonight if I have my Jacks panties on."

"Is that so?"

"It is."

"What if I have a way to let you out of your end of the promise." He angles his head to the side and studies me, humor mixed with mischief on his expression.

"I'm thinking I'll wear the panties." I sit on the top of the desk behind me. "I never trust someone who changes a deal midway through."

"Says who?"

"Says me." *What in the world is he getting at?*

There's that slow smile again that tugs on every part of me. "You're an agent. You know full well that negotiations shift. Change. Realign."

"Should I worry about what exactly it is you want to realign?"

"More like I want the terms to change."

"You're talking in circles, Hunter," I tease, and his grin widens.

"Good thing you're familiar with how to follow circles."

"True."

But he is talking in circles and it's making zero sense.

"What is it you want now?"

"*You.*"

Thud. My heart on the floor.

"Oh." I don't hide the shock or the stupid grin on my face from his un-expected comment. "In that case . . ." I grab the sides of his shirt as he takes a step toward me before framing my face and dipping down so he can meet my eyes. His are intense and alive with emotion.

"In that case?" He brushes his lips over mine.

"New terms accepted. Negotiation successful."

He laughs as I pull him against me, wrapping my arms around his waist. He rests his chin on top of my head and I revel in the feel of him and the knowl-edge that he's all mine.

Who would have ever thought I'd say that about the only man who ever truly broke my heart?

"I've been doing a lot of thinking, Dekk," he murmurs, his chin moving on the crown of my head. "Scary, I know."

"About?"

"Things."

"Like?"

"My career. My life. What I want from it." He leans back and our eyes meet again. "All of this—the clarity, your belief in me, you pushing me, the Cup—has me looking at things in a different light."

"I don't see how I had anything to do with that."

"How can you say that?" he asks. "You heard what your dad said. That it's your belief in me that allowed me to be my best me."

"I was just doing my job."

"No, you were being you." Those lips of his meet mine again in a kiss that lacks intensity but is loaded with tenderness. "I'm madly in love with you, Dekker Kincade. Maybe I always have been, but you helped me see the me I had lost. You allowed me to be the me who had hope. You allowed me to tell my darkest truths and instead of walking away, you held on tighter. You loved the me I hated."

"And I love the you that you now love too."

"I know." Tears well in his eyes, but he blinks them away just as quickly as they appear.

"If there's one thing I learned with everything, it's your next tomorrow is never guaranteed. I don't want to miss any tomorrows with you. I think we should take the next step. I think we should move in together and start build-ing that tomorrow and the day after that and the week after that together."

"You do?"

"I do." He laughs. "I'm getting confused where my toothbrush is and whether I'm coming or going from your house or mine. It's so much easier if I know I get to come home to you at the end of the day. That's all that seems to matter anymore."

"Says the league MVP."

"Exactly." He squeezes my hand. "We never made a bet on what I'd get if I won MVP and I did . . . and so"—he shrugs—"cohabitation."

"Cohabitation?" I laugh.

He nods. "I know I'll screw up. I know I'm stubborn and frustrating and will sometimes shut you out when all you want is to be held close . . . but I can promise you I want to do right by you. For you. For me. For us. I want to make this work because Christ, I'm miserable without you."

"But you haven't been without me for a while now."

"Exactly," he repeats, his voice softening, "because you're where I want to be."

I'm having trouble swallowing over the love that his words create, wrapping around my soul and taking root.

"Hunter."

"Don't cry." He wipes my tear that slips over. "No more tears."

"Just tomorrows."

His smile returns. "Just tomorrows."

I'm not sure how long I stay wrapped in his arms, settling into this idea of getting to wake up every morning next to him and getting to kiss him every night—but it's not a hardship to accept.

Not by a long shot.

There's a knock on the door and we jolt apart like kids getting caught.

"Dekk?" My dad peeks his head into the conference room.

"Yeah?" I pull the door open all the way.

"Can I have my client back now? You're messing up my schedule."

"What do you mean your client?" I look from my dad to Hunter and his stupid, wide grin and laugh that vibrates, then back to my dad.

"What you drop, another one of us will pick up," my dad says.

"Hunter?" I ask, confused but hopeful.

"He means *his* client. You once told me I could only have one or the other with you, and, Dekker, you sure as hell know which one I'm going to pick."

"Me?" I ask, an incredulity in my voice as my world comes full circle.

"Did you not just hear anything I said?" He laughs. "Of course, *you.*" He gives me a chaste kiss on the lips. "And then him."

He squeezes my hand as he stares at me, and I don't care that my father's there watching—I wouldn't care if the whole world was—because when Hunter looks at me, everything else is just background noise.

"I'll be in my office," my father says, leaving us alone.

"'Kay," Hunter says, but his eyes never leave mine.

"You sure you want to do this?"

"Do what?" he asks.

"This. Me. Us. KSM," I say with a nervous laugh, "because this is your only chance to bail. You know us Kincades, we never walk away from negotiations."

"Lucky for me, because I already let you walk away once, and I'm sure as hell not making that mistake again."

He leans in and kisses me with a kiss that's equal parts emotion and heat. But when he pulls back, the look in his eyes is one hundred percent emotion.

"What?" I ask softly.

"Just trying to fathom how you're here. How I'm here. How life happens."

"Skill. Stick. Finesse, Maddox."

He throws his head back and laughs.

And it's the best sound in the world.

Epilogue 1

6 months later

I ABSENTLY TOY WITH THE EDGES OF THE LETTER. IT'S LIGHT, BUT THE weight of it staggers me.

Unable to bring myself to look at the words typed on the page yet, I sit on the old dock and watch the lake sparkling in the sun before me.

"We'll own a cabin here someday," I say to Jonah. He looked over at me and skipped a rock across its surface. We both count as it dances five times on top of the water before sinking.

"Maybe." He leans back on his elbows and holds his face to the sun. "We might own a cabin and come here with our families. We might not. But this is where I want to die someday."

"Dude. That's fucked." I laugh. "Why do you have to get all morbid and shit? We're sixteen. Let's not think about that yet." I lift the beer we'd swiped from the cabin's fridge and take a drink.

I still think it tastes like piss, but I'm trying to acquire the taste.

And not get caught.

We'd be dead if we got caught.

"It's life, little brother. We live. We die. The earth moves on."

"You should drink that beer before Mom and Dad get back from the store or we're going to practice that theory when Dad finds us."

He laughs and takes a sip. I'm relieved to see his wince and that he doesn't like it much either. But guys like beer, so we'll figure out how to like it.

"Just think about it, though. What better place to be when you die? You're surrounded by everything that we love here."

"I guess."

"Right here on this dock. That's where I want to kick the old bucket."

My eyes blur from the memory.

My chest aches in a way I never thought possible.

My life missing a piece I have to figure out how to navigate without.

God, I miss you, Jonah.

My thoughts are filled with a million memories about this place. About that conversation. One I had completely forgotten until Jonah died and his lawyer told us his wishes were for some of his ashes to be spread here.

Just like his wish was for the lawyer to give me the letter I hold in my hand. The one he dictated to him over two years ago.

I'm not sure what my fear is. Is it that this is the very last piece of Jonah I have left? That if I read it, then this is real and he's truly gone? Is it because a small part of me feels guilty that I'm grateful he's gone so he's no longer in pain? Is it because I miss him and reading this will prove to me how goddamn much?

I shove the tears away and take a sip of beer. It's the same cheap shit we drank all those summers ago, and I laugh because it still tastes like piss.

With a deep breath, I look at the letter.

Hunter,

There's so much I've needed to say to you for so long, but I've known you wouldn't listen. You're a stubborn and determined little shit (yes, you'll always be little to me, no matter how old we get) and would probably walk out of the room if I told you any of this.

If you're getting this, I'm gone. Fucking sucks on both our parts. This wasn't how our life was supposed to go. We were supposed to be old, grumpy men on that rickety dock at the lake when we kicked the bucket. We were supposed to be Stanley Cup winners with kids of our own. Ones we'd teach how to play hockey if they wanted to. We'd argue over whose grandkids were the cutest before we'd fill them up on sugar and send them home. We'd have wives who were best friends.

We would have lived our lives to the fullest and without regret.

I no longer can, but I need you to promise me that you will. That you'll live for you. Every second. Every minute. Every day. Every year.

To do that, you need to hear this: what happened to me wasn't your fault. I've had a lot of years to think about this and plenty of time to play out all the scenarios that could have happened that day. Bottom line is, I'm at fault.

I drank. I got behind the wheel. I killed that woman. I did this to myself.

And I'd do it all over again if that meant protecting it from happening to you. That's the job of a big brother. Even now, I want to protect you. And the only way I can do that is by telling you I never blamed you, and the accident was not your fault.

I should have told Dad to go to hell that day, and that you were going to junior prom with us. I should have stood up for you—that time and so many other times—but I didn't. I failed you.

I've come to terms with that, and I hope one day you can forgive me for it.

I couldn't have asked for a better brother. You sat by silently while Dad put me on a pedestal when you were just as skilled and talented as I was. You cheered me on while being slighted. I see that now. Time has given me that opportunity to realize how wrong that was. I'm sorry. You are every bit as good as I could have been. I watch you playing now on the TV, and I'm so damn proud of you.

It's more than hockey though. It's about you. About how you've tried so hard to live for both of us. How you've made sure to include me in every step. How you've called and talked for hours when I know you had so many other things to do.

So what happens now, Hunter? I know you'll miss me as much as I'll miss you.

You live.

For you.

Without regret.

And every once in a while, go to that dock, crack open that cheap, shitty beer, and take a sip for me.

You were the one true thing I held on to all these years.

You were the one who kept me going.

You were my inspiration.

I love you.

Jonah

I hang my head as the sobs hit me. As the words my brother wrote crack every last chain of guilt I've grown so damn used to wearing.

It's just like him to know what I need to hear.

It's just like him to know that I'm struggling with how to move on in a world without him, and how to throw me a lifeline.

It's just like him to have one final say so there's no doubt in my mind how he felt about me.

In time, I know the ache will go away and the sadness will fall dormant, but fuck if it's not going to always hurt.

I let the tears fall, and when they subside, when I'm all cried out, I lift that crappy beer and take a swig.

My laughter is unexpected, but I can't help but remember him here that last summer before his accident. How crazy and carefree he was. How much we laughed. How much we loved.

I take the small container sitting beside me that holds my portion of his ashes and slowly pour them into the lake.

I give him what he wanted that day.

To be here when he dies.

To have the sun and the water and the memories.

I'm not sure how long I sit here, but I know she's here. I know she's been sitting here this whole time, giving me my space to grieve how I need to, giving me the time to figure this out.

But when I'm finally ready to go, when I get to my feet and turn around, I'm so very grateful to see her here. The blonde hair flying from the breeze and the compassion in her smile.

I know I'm leaving my brother here today, but I'm so very grateful to be walking toward her when I do. And I plan on carrying out my brother's final instructions.

I'll live.

For me.

Without regret.

Epilogue 2

Dekker

1 year later

Excitement fills the air.

I take it all in. The people milling around. The clusters of people sitting in the stands. The special staging area for kids to lose their wheelchairs and gain their sleds so they can skate. The staff in their bright blue shirts helping anyone and everyone who needs assistance.

And then I see him.

Hunter's standing on the far side of the rink. He's in the parking zone—a spot he created where parents park their kids' wheelchairs and then walk away to the stands. It's where kids can feel like kids. Where they can be entertained by clowns or talk hockey or anything really and have some autonomy. His grin is wide as he sits on his haunches talking to a little girl.

Everything I love about him can be summed up in this one moment—his passion, his drive, his kindness, his love, and his devotion.

The past year has been a hard one for him and so to see this—him—this alive as he immortalizes his brother's memory, is so heartwarming.

Someone comes over and taps him on the shoulder and hands him a microphone. The opening ceremony is about to start.

People hoot and holler as he walks out onto the rolled-out mat to center ice. My father's whistle being one of the loudest.

"Thank you for coming today," Hunter says and clears his throat. "What started as a dream of mine about eighteen months ago is now, today, officially a reality. *The Jonah Maddox Hockey Facility* is now officially open."

Applause fills the arena, but it's Hunter's eyes that find mine. There's a soft smile on his lips, and I'm sure I'm the only one who notices the tears welling in his eyes.

"This arena is for you. It doesn't matter what abilities you do or don't have, all that matters is that you want a chance to play and learn hockey . . . and I'll do everything in my power to give that to you." Another round of applause. "My brother was an incredible person and through this program, he will live on." Hunter bows his head momentarily to collect his emotions before looking up and finding me again. "Dekker, will you come out here and do the honors with me?"

I startle at his request but shouldn't be surprised by it. The two of us have been working side by side, nonstop, to get this place ready for today.

It takes me a few seconds to cross the carpet and make it to him. He links his fingers with mine and gives me that devil-may-care grin.

"In a lot of places, they cut a ribbon to officially kick off the start of something. But here at the Jonah P. Maddox Arena, we like to start things a little differently." Hunter glances at me. "You ready? Do you remember what we talked about?" Hunter asks the kids all around the ice. "Five. Four. Three." The arena counts down with him while I look around confused, as if I'm missing something. "Two. One."

And the minute one is said, the kids around the ice and the people in the stands, all start tossing tennis balls onto the ice.

"Tennis balls?" I laugh.

"Yep."

I laugh as I watch kids of all ages, ethnicities, and with differing disabilities toss tennis balls onto the ice. There is laughter and giggling, and chills chase over my skin at the sight of Hunter's dream coming true.

At this lifeline anchoring him.

I glance his way, fully expecting to catch his profile as he takes it all in, but I'm startled when he's looking straight at me. His eyes are serious, intentional. But his grin, wide and gorgeous, is a funny contradiction.

"What?" I ask just above the noise.

"Nothing." But the expression on his face dares me not to look away.

"I thought you hated the limelight," I tease as tennis balls bounce against our legs and feet.

"I do."

"Then why are we standing here in the middle of all these tennis balls," I ask.

"Because some things deserve the spotlight."

"Your brother most certainly did." I squeeze his hand.

His smile softens, his eyes sadden, and he reaches out to run a thumb down my cheek. "*So do you.*"

I go to refute him when I see the tennis ball in his hand. Except it's not a real tennis ball—or rather a useable one—as it's been cut in half. And when Hunter lifts the top off it, my mind goes blank. I have to remember to breathe.

Nestled inside is a diamond ring. I'm sure it's gorgeous and sparkly and everything, but what it looks like doesn't mean a thing. It dims in the shadow of the man who's holding it.

"Hunter?" I ask in reflex.

"Some things most definitely deserve the spotlight. And you, Dekker Kincade, have made every part of my life shine since the moment you walked into it. With your defiant will and your fiery temper. With your need to help and your love to fix. With just you. We've been through so much already, and all I can think about is how there's no one else I'd rather go through life with than you. Will you marry me?"

"Is this a negotiation?" I ask, fighting back my own smile and my urge to jump in his arms and kiss him a million times.

"No. This is one thing I'm not negotiating on."

"Whew. I taught you well, then."

"And?"

"Yes. Of course, the answer is yes."

And then I give in to what I want.

I jump into his arms and kiss him senseless.

With a whole arena watching.

Because today is a day for spotlights.

Today is a day for dreams coming true.

Acknowledgments

Hard to Handle was a chance to write my three favorite tropes all in one—sports, enemies to lovers, and second chance. I truly hope you enjoyed Dekker and Hunter's story as much as I did writing it.

I want to give a little shout out to my crew that keeps me on track: Christy for keeping things straight. Chrisstine for the honest feedback for that first 20% of a book where I'm constantly saying, "This book is horrible." Ali, Steph, Annette, Val, and Emma for keeping things running in the VP Pit Crew. Marion for polishing my words and cutting out all the repetition (and there's *a lot*). My proofers—Karen, Kara, Janice, Michele, Marjorie—for making sure my errors are few and far between. And lastly, to the readers . . . thank you for picking this book up and for all of your continued support over the years.

CUFFED

Cuffed
By K. Bromberg

Copyright 2017 K. Bromberg

Published by JKB Publishing, LLC

Editing by AW Editing
Cover Design by Helen Williams
Cover Photography Wander Aguiar

DEDICATION

To my Mom . . .
She is the one who showed me what strength is.
She is the woman who lifts me up when insecurity weighs me down.
She is my biggest cheerleader, my closest confidant, and my best friend all
wrapped in to one.
She is the woman I aspire to be some day.
This book is for you, Mom.
You'll know why, once you read it.
Head up. Wings out.

Grant

MY TUMMY FEELS ICKY, AND IF I LOOK AT EMMY, SHE'LL KNOW I've been crying. She'll know I told after I promised her I wouldn't. We even pinky promised on it.

So, I focus on *it* instead.

The glue on my hand and how weird it feels. It's crackly and tight and kind of cold. Kind of like what I imagine alien skin would feel like.

She's gonna be mad at me.

Except their skin would be green. Or purple.

She made me promise not to tell.

Mine would be green. Emmy's would be purple.

She's my bestest friend in the whole wide galaxy.

Her and her yucky purple.

How could I not say anything?

Malone Family Rules: If someone is hurting, you help them.

My dad's temper if I break a rule is much worse than Emmy's, though.

I'm only trying to help her.

The speaker in the room's ceiling crackles, and we all look up. The rest of the class is hoping for an interruption—an announcement for the winners of spirit day, a surprise assembly, anything—but I don't glance up. All I can do is hold my breath and focus on my alien skin.

"Mrs. Gellar?" Principal Newman says through the intercom.

"Yes?"

"Can you please have Emerson Reeves gather her things and come to the front office please?"

"Sure."

Ohhhhh. The whole class makes the collective sound, thinking Emmy's in trouble.

"Called to the principal's office," Cooper says.

But I know the truth.

I dare to look now. To see the worried look on Mrs. Gellar's face as she watches Emmy get her Strawberry Shortcake lunchbox and cram it into her yucky purple backpack. Emmy keeps her head down, but she misses the first time she tries to grab the zipper to close it.

Mrs. Gellar doesn't speak. She doesn't head to the whiteboard or ask us to pay attention like she normally does. Instead, she walks over to Emmy, puts her arm around her shoulders, and bends over to whisper something in her ear. Emmy nods but keeps looking down as Mrs. Gellar gives her a quick hug before standing back up.

When Emmy heads toward the door, I forget all about my alien skin and stare at her from my seat in the last row.

Look at me.

C'mon, Em. Look at me.

She stops right before she walks out the door and meets my eyes. There are tears in hers, kinda like how there are some in mine.

"You pinky promised," she whispers, her knuckles turning white as she clutches her backpack to her chest.

"Em—"

"I hate you. I never want to see you again." She mouths the words and walks out the door.

ONE

Grant

"10-4, OFFICER MALONE."

Her voice, smooth as goddamn silk and full of suggestion comes through the radio. I'm ready for the ration of shit from Nate when I turn his way. His grin is wide as he just shakes his head and chuckles.

"10-4, Officer Malone," he mimics. "Can I give you a side of blow job with that all clear?"

"Fuck off." I sigh.

"Dude, if she talked to all of us like that, the whole force would be walking around with permanent hard-ons."

"Liv does have a great voice," I murmur as a cheer goes up in the crowd to the left of us, drawing my attention. Drunken guys in board shorts, who are all sporting fraternity tattoos, are taking note of a group of tipsy girls with a skin-to-clothing ratio that should be illegal.

"A great *voice*. Yeah. Right. I'm sure that was exactly what you were focusing on . . . because hell if that body of hers isn't a fifteen on a scale of one to ten."

"I'd give it a twenty." I shrug, remembering all too well what she looked like as she straddled me. Goddamn perfection. "You're just a jealous fucker because I won't give you any details."

"You won't give me anything, Malone. For all I know, you're full of shit," he says as he adjusts his bulletproof vest beneath his uniform, both of us constantly scanning the crowd.

"We both know I'm not full of shit."

"Asshole," he mutters under his breath, and I chuckle in response. This is the same conversation we seem to have every time Liv and I interact on the radio.

"I think the hotline tip was wrong. I don't see any of Donnely's gang here."

"Neither do I. Just a whole lotta hot women in teeny, tiny bikinis, and I'm not complaining one bit."

"Pig."

"Well." He shrugs as he points to his uniform.

"Clever."

"Exactly. I'm the smart one. You're not, considering you're the one who walked away from Liv. Just one question, though, why exactly?"

"Too many women, too little time." I lift my eyebrows and grin. "To your right," I say with a subtle lift of my chin as a shoving match erupts between two men outside Hooligan's Bar. Alcohol. Testosterone. All day in the sun. Women to compete over for attention. It's never a good mix.

We shift our attention and assess the situation. Friends take care of it, pulling the men apart before it escalates. "Gotta love the annual Fourth of July pub crawl."

"It keeps us busy, doesn't it? Besides," I say as I glance at my watch, "we have about three more hours on shift in case you want to join them."

"No thanks. Give me a beer in my backyard with the fireworks overhead and I'm good. While the women are nice to look at here, I don't need the chaos of it. We get enough of that on shift." We glance to the left as a woman screams, but then it turns to a high screech of laughter. "You heading over to your dad's?"

"Yeah. Gray and Grady will be there. You're welcome to come if you want."

"*Help me, please,*" sounds off to my left and grabs my attention immediately. It's followed by what sounds like a laugh but is drowned out by the chaos of the crowded street. Hesitant that someone might actually need assistance, Nate and I move toward a group of women in a huddle about fifty feet away.

"Can we help you ladies with anything?" I say and remove my sunglasses as we approach to a hum of giggles.

"My friend here needs help, *Officer Sexy,*" the tallest of the women says, a brunette with a coy smile and legs for days. "She has a real thing for a man in uniform."

Nate snickers beside me as my sense of duty fades when I realize there is no need for help. These are just some women out to have a bit of fun. I stop before them, my thumbs hooked in my duty belt, and pretend like I didn't hear the comment that I sure as hell did. "So, everything is good here, then?"

"That depends," says a voice of the only woman whose back is still to me, "if you're going to give me mouth to mouth and resuscitate me . . ." her voice fades off when our eyes meet.

Holy mother fucking shit. It can't be her.

Can it?

"*Emmy?*"

Her eyes widen, and her lips part. And for that split second, I see the little girl from my memories. The one with the mess of strawberry blonde tangles and emerald eyes. The one who made pinky promises, mud pies, and agreed with me that Batman was far superior to Iron Man when it came to superheroes.

My best friend who told me she never wanted to see me again.

All the emotions come flooding back unexpectedly as I watch the familiarity flashing across her face vanish. Visibly flustered, she shakes her head and takes an abrupt step back, bumping into her friend behind her.

"No. I'm not her. She's not me," she denies.

"Emerson?" It's the brunette again, and hearing that name—*her name*—after all this time is like being sucker punched with a battering ram.

"I'm fine." She shrugs off the hand her other friend has put on her shoulder. Gone is the fun, flirty demeanor she had before turning to see me, Grant Malone—the boy she said she hated. Panic I can't understand, but desperately want to, has replaced it.

"Emmy—"

"It's Emerson," she snaps with a resolute nod before breaking our eye contact and looking at her friends. "I have to go . . ."

"What are you doing here?" I ask a question, but it's so much more than what it sounds like. *How are you? Where have you been? Why are you back? Tell me you're staying around.* But she just stands in front of me and stares as if she can't believe it's really me and, at the same time, frightened that it is me.

"Em?" I reach out, needing to touch her to make sure she's real, but the minute my hand touches her bicep, she jerks her arm back.

"I can't . . . I didn't want . . ." She shakes her head and then looks to the tall brunette before turning back to me with wide eyes as the color slowly drains from her cheeks. "Travis just texted. He needs me to help. I . . . have to go."

Travis? Who's Travis?

And with that, Emmy Reeves—the girl I haven't thought about in years—turns on her heel and walks away.

"No. Wait!" I call after her as she makes her way through the crowd, her mane of strawberry blonde hair the last thing I see of her.

Just like before.

"And you are?"

There's impatience in the voice that breaks through the cobwebs of memories suddenly spinning in my mind, but it takes an elbow from Nate to bring me back to the present.

"An old friend of hers," I murmur to the tall brunette, eyes glancing to the crowd Emmy melted into, as if she were a ghost I was trying to find again.

"An old friend, huh?" She crosses her arms and juts a hip out as her eyes narrow and she decides if she wants to believe me or not.

"From childhood."

"And your name is?" The other women lose interest in our conversation and begin chatting with Nate, but she's laser focused on me.

"Grant Malone." I stick my hand out. "Nice to meet you."

She stares at my hand for a moment before speaking, "Desi Whitman, and I'm still figuring out if it is indeed nice or not."

I look down to my hand and then back up to her with a lift of my brows, prompting her to reluctantly shake it.

"So, tell me, Desi Whitman, why is it you automatically believe I've done something to hurt Emerson?"

"First off, you called her Emmy. No one is allowed to call her Emmy. She hates it."

"First off?" I laugh. "It's been less than five minutes, and you're already suspicious enough that you've made a list?"

"Not suspicious. Curious. There's a difference," she says as she shifts her feet. "And yes, I like to make lists."

"Okay." I nod, fighting my smile. "Let's continue with that list of yours then. Why else have you assumed I did something to Emmy, er, Emerson?" I glance over to the crowd passing us by, making sure I don't see any signs of Donnely's crew and the rumored trouble they were going to cause before looking back to Desi.

"Because I've never seen her react like that to a man before."

"What do you mean?" Now I'm the one who's curious.

"Hmm." She eyes me cautiously.

"Look, there isn't much eight year olds can do to hurt each other besides steal each other's Legos," I lie, damn well knowing what I did to Emmy was a whole lot worse than that.

"Did you?"

"Did I what?"

"Steal her Legos."

"Jesus. Seriously?" I laugh, but it fades when I see that she is. "Perhaps. I don't remember. Are you satisfied?" She purses her lips. "Now, are you going to tell me why you said you've never seen Emerson react to a man like that before, or are you just going to rake me over the Lego coals for no reason?"

A slight smile curls up one corner of her mouth, and she looks over to her friends, making sure they're preoccupied with my partner before meeting my eyes again. "Em's a confident and in-your-face woman. A flirt. A female who takes no shit and can give as good as she gets. Strong. But when she saw you? It was as if she was a different person all together. Almost like she saw a ghost."

Funny, I felt the same way when I saw her.

"We knew each other in grade school is all. A lifetime ago." I shrug, hoping the explanation is enough for Desi when we were so much more than classroom acquaintances.

"Okay." She draws the word out, but her body language remains on the defensive.

"That's it. I swear." She moves her hands to her hips but doesn't speak, so I continue. "It's been over twenty years since we last saw each other, so I'm sure she was taken by surprise."

"Well, you saw her. She ran away. It seems to me she gave you her own answer whether she wants to continue your little reunion or not."

I nod, wanting to say so much more. Questions. Comments. Memories. All three collide, making me think she had the same reaction and that was why she bolted.

But my past is far different from her past.

Leave it be. Leave *her* be.

"You done chitchatting, Malone? We have a job to do."

"Yeah, yeah." I nod to Nate but hold up a finger before turning back to Desi. "Tell me something? Has she had a good life?" The question is out before I can stop it and is so very different from the one I had intended. I feel like a douchebag for asking, but I *need* to know. "Sorry. Never mind. Nice to meet you, Desi." I smile and walk away.

I take about five steps before she speaks. "From what I know, she has." I stop and look back to her. "The girl is a bundle of perpetual motion and laughter. Maybe it's a cover. Maybe it isn't. But it's how she's been since I met her ten years ago."

"That's good to hear. Thank you."

"Why would you ask that?" She angles her head and takes a step closer.

"When we were little, she was *that* friend. You know, the one who—"

"She's that to me, too. I get it. No need to explain." Her face softens, and her posture relaxes. "I can give you my phone number if you want."

My smile shifts to a grin. "Uh, well—"

"I'm not hitting on you, *Officer Sexy*. Although, while I'm sure you've charmed more than your fair share of women out of their clothes with your smile and uniform alone, you're not my type."

I choke on a laugh, loving this woman I've just met and her brazen personality. "My ego isn't liking you right now."

"Ego, shmeego." She waves a hand at me in indifference before digging in her purse and pulling out a business card. "Go on. Take it." She holds it out to me. "You know, just in case you change your mind . . . or if you want to check on her again."

I take the card she offers, and with one last look that tells me somehow she understands, she turns to her friends and they walk away.

"You ready?"

Nate looks irritated that I'm not reacting. "Sure. Yes. Sorry."

"Who was the woman?"

"Someone I haven't seen in a while."

"An old girlfriend?"

"Nah. We're talking third grade here."

"It's you, Malone. You probably had the girls lined up to play four square with you back then." He chuckles, and I roll my eyes. "Why'd she bail?"

"I'm not quite sure." I look down to where I'm turning the card over in my hand and stare at Desi's name but think of Emmy instead.

One thing is certain, Desi isn't here on vacation. The address on the card and area code are both local, which means she lives here. Does that mean Emerson lives here, too?

Forget about it. If Em lives here and hasn't sought me out, she doesn't want to see me.s

But I know I can't forget.

I've never been able to.

She obviously doesn't want this ghost from her past around.

That's the funny thing about ghosts, though.

You can't control when they appear or how they might affect you, but they always haunt you.

TWO

Emerson

THE ENGINE'S ROAR FILLS MY EARS.

I run through my mental checklist. Finish. Then begin it again as the rush of cold air dances around me and whips against my cheeks. My earplugs shift as I slide my jaw out of habit to equalize the pressure in my ears.

I glance over to where Leo is double-checking his own gear. "Head up. Wings out!" I shout over the roar. He gives me a thumbs-up, and with that, I loosen my grip on the door and dive headfirst.

My breath catches. My blood is flooded with adrenaline. My body spirals and hurtles and tumbles in a seemingly endless free fall.

But there is silence in my head. Peace. A bliss I can't find anywhere else as I gain control of my dive, stabilize, and master the arch of my body. The ocean in the distance and the rolling green hills of northern California laid out like a to-pography map beneath me are as stunning as the first time I saw them like this.

There are no demands from Chris and his bank.

There are no duties left to fulfill for Travis before I can call it a night.

There are no thoughts of Grant Malone and those brown eyes of his that met mine yesterday and surprised the hell out of me.

There are no demons from my past—the ones seeing him again brought out of hiding—trying to weasel their way in.

It's freedom.

It's just me hurtling toward the earth at what feels like a million miles an hour in what could be certain death.

It's my hand deploying the ripcord and my body jolting against the force before rebounding up as the parachute opens and saves me from that death.

Yanking me back to reality.

My parachute.

Saving me.

Grant Malone.

Saved me.

Stop it, Em. Don't think about him.

Look at the fields sprawled out.

I knew it was bound to happen when I moved back here.

At the waves crashing against the cliffs beyond.

He is from before. I'm only about the now.

At the cars on the highway in the distance that look like ants crawling home in the early evening light.

I close my eyes, hating that I'm missing a single moment of my descent, but I use the moment to refocus my thoughts and shift gears.

With another slide of my jaw to re-equalize the pressure in my ears, I open my eyes and force myself to admire the beauty of it all.

After a bit, sometime between the lull of the gliding and the serenity of the silence, I'm able to shut the world out and do just that. Enjoy the moment that will surely dissipate the minute my feet hit the ground.

I think about what I'll do with this place once Blue Skies becomes mine. Fresh paint on the sign. New marketing to tourists and locals. Convert the empty hangar into a clubhouse of sorts to entice the adrenaline junkies to stay longer and spend more money.

I have to get the loan first. Then I can dream.

My mental checklist begins again. The one I use to make sure I don't neglect a single thing. It's too easy to become comfortable when jumping out of an airplane day after day, so I use the repetition as my safety net.

My lone leash to sanity.

Plus it helps me to forget about Grant.

Well, in theory anyway.

"Desi's thinking of having another one of her barbecues again."

My jump coordinator's eyes light up and his lips spread into a huge grin. "Tell her thinking is not an option," Leo says. "She needs to pick a date and commit so my stomach knows when it's going to get treated to the good stuff again."

"No shit." I laugh and shake my head. Friends, food, and relaxation are just what the doctor ordered. Especially when it's *her* food.

"Just promise I won't be forgotten when the invites go out." He holds his hands together as if he's praying.

"I promise."

The phone rings on the desk before me, and Leo goes back to finalizing his schedules.

"Blue Skies, this is Emerson, how may I help you?"

"Emerson! Just the person I wanted to talk to."

"Great. Who's this?" I glance over to Leo, who's sitting at his desk laughing at something.

"It's Chris Severson with Sunnyville Trust and Loan."

"Hi, Chris," I say as I sink down into my chair and glance at the list of reports and paperwork he still needs for the loan. Of the ten items on it, I've only been able to cross two off as completed, and I don't understand what three of the remaining eight even mean or how to go about figuring them out. "What can I do for you?"

"I was just calling to see where you are with getting the information I'd requested."

"It's coming. Slowly." I chuckle because I already feel like I'm drowning.

"I know the list of requirements can be overwhelming, so know that you aren't the only one who feels that way." Sympathy resonates in his voice.

"That's good to know. Since I've never applied for a loan before, I thought I was the only one."

"No. Not at all. Is there anything I can help you with?"

My laugh is part mortification, part reprieve. "Really?"

"Of course. Since you decided to forego having a broker represent you—"

"Only because I know the owners of Blue Skies and they preferred not to use one," I feel the need to explain for what seems like the tenth time. What he doesn't need to know is the lack of a broker was my idea. I simply won't have the extra funds to pay them their fees once the deal is done. I'm stretched thin as it is.

"No need to explain, Emerson. It isn't always necessary to have a broker. Besides, I told you I'd walk you through everything step by step, and I will."

My shoulders sag in relief. "Thank you. I really do appreciate it. You don't know how much this means to me to have found—"

"No need to thank me."

"I still feel I should."

"How about this? How about we meet for a working dinner? It will give me a chance to review everything with you and answer the questions you have."

"I couldn't impose on you like that."

"Nonsense. It's just one of the many services I provide my clients."

I chew my bottom lip, torn between pride and necessity. The silence stretches. "That would be great. I'd appreciate it."

"Good. Then it's settled." He laughs, and I can hear a horn honk in the background. "I'm driving so I can't access my schedule. Let me check it and I'll email you some dates and times that will work."

"That sounds great. Again, Chris . . . thank you."

THREE

Grant

"YOU SMELL LIKE SMOKE." I GLANCE OVER TO MY LITTLE BROTH-
er Grady and make a show of sniffing the air before bringing the
beer to my lips.

"Occupational hazard," he says before lifting his chin to where our dad is
attempting not to burn steaks on the grill while he shoots the shit with Grayson,
our middle brother. "We were doing drills today over at the old gravel yard. I
guess I didn't wash all the smoke off."

"Hmm," I murmur, part listening, part lost in thought.

"So, you gonna tell me why you bailed on coming over on the Fourth? I
hope like hell she was worth missing out on Mom's apple pie." He chuckles. "I
guess you enjoyed a different kind of pie, huh?"

"You're the firefighter, why don't you go help Dad put those flames out."
Diversion intended to get conversation away from my sex life, but I'm not sure
he's going to buy it. My brothers are nosey fuckers.

He sits there silent for a moment, and I can feel the weight of his stare as
I look at the flames flare up on the old Weber again.

"So, you didn't get laid?" he questions.

"Nah." Another sip of beer. Another push with my foot to rock the porch
swing I'm sitting on.

"What's the deal, then?"

"Nothing really. It was a long day, and then I ended up chasing ghosts for
a bit and lost track of time is all." I shrug. It's close enough to the truth.

"You should have just told us you got lost in a call. Is it one I know about?"

"Nah."

He chuckles. "Are you being a dick, or are you trying to be vague on
purpose?"

I'm not trying to be a dick, but I know that once I say something to him,
it will become a Malone family free-for-all topic of discussion.

He doesn't push, which I'm grateful for, but my mind veers back to the
ghosts. To the wondering and questioning and wanting to know more.

There's the creak of my swing. The laughter of my dad and brother. The
sound effects Luke, Grayson's son, is making as he plays with Matchbox cars

on the grass. The squeal of kids a few houses down as they chase each other. The hum of a lawn mower somewhere down the street.

"You remember Emmy Reeves?"

Grady's bottle of beer pauses momentarily on the way to his lips. "Vaguely," he murmurs. "You two were like Mutt and Jeff. She was at the house all the time or you were at hers . . . and then something happened with her family and she moved, right?"

"Something like that," I respond, realizing he was only in preschool when it happened and probably doesn't remember the details. Having a father who was chief of police probably helped keep the facts quiet.

"Why are you bringing her up now?"

"I saw her the other day."

"No shit. How is she? Did she move back? Is she—"

"I couldn't tell you."

"No?" He reaches down and scratches Moose between the ears. The mammoth dog rolls onto his back without a care in the world other than wanting more affection.

"That's the thing, she wouldn't talk to me." I glance up as the screen door opens, and my mom comes out with a basket of buns for the burgers.

"How's studying going?" she asks, saving me from saying any more.

"It's going," I shrug, thinking of the stack of index cards with questions for my detective's exam on them. They are sitting on my nightstand collecting dust.

"Well, let me know if you need any help studying," she says, making me laugh. Once our mother always our mother, even when we're studying as an adult.

"I will."

"Time to eat, boys."

And eat we do. The mountain of food all but gone by the time we finish and sit back in our chairs with overstuffed stomachs.

"How was your night out?" Mom asks Grayson, leaning forward on her elbows, eager to hear that after one date he's ready to marry the girl and give her more grandchildren.

"It was fine." Grayson shrugs. "Nothing spectacular."

"He wore cologne," Luke says and then lifts his eyebrows. "You only wear cologne when you like a girl."

The whole table laughs. "Is that so?" Grayson says as he tugs down on Luke's baseball hat and then gives him a noogie.

"That's what they do on television."

"Are you going to see her again?" Mom fishes, relentlessly, but Grayson turns to me.

"So who do you have on the line now, Grant?"

I don't even have to look to know Mom's rolling her shoulders and getting that sour look on her face. It has become the norm when discussing my lack of settling down and giving her babies to spoil and dote over.

"I don't have anyone on the line." I glare at him.

"You always have at least one, if not four, falling hook, line, and sinker," he continues.

"That's such bullshit. I do not. I—"

"He has Emmy Reeves on the line," pipes in Grady, who then grunts as my foot connects with his shin beneath the table.

"Emmy Reeves?" Grayson says at the same time as my mom's head snaps up to look at my dad.

"Emmy, Emmy?" she asks.

"Fuck off, Grady," I mutter, knowing he threw me to the wolves to save Grayson's ass.

But when I meet the expectant eyes of my parents, there is a gravity to Dad's expression that I haven't seen since his days on the force. It makes me realize things were probably ten times worse for Emmy than I ever imagined way back when.

As an adult, I can decipher those expressions and understand the things I couldn't comprehend as a kid.

"Yes. Emmy, Emmy."

Mom's face brightens. "Did she contact you on that FaceWorld or InstaGreet everyone is using these days?"

"FaceWorld?" Grady says before letting out an exasperated sigh. "Mom, when are you ever going to catch up with the times? It's Facebook and Instagram. I told you I'd be more than willing to teach you how to use them if you'd like."

"And I told you that I'd rather remain happy and oblivious to all the ways people can stalk me online. I'm a cop's wife, Grady. You keep your personal information off the internet so you can keep your family safe."

"Yes, Betsy." Dad nods, trying to stop this bickering before it starts. "So, Grant," he asks and gives me his investigator's stare, "how did you connect with her?"

"I saw her in town the other day." This has my parents sharing another glance. "What's that look mean?"

"Nothing," Dad responds.

"Nothing?" I repeat.

"Just surprised to hear she was in Sunnyville. Her mom liked to move around a lot." Mom's smile softens. "I used to love that little girl as if she were my own. The daughter I never had. I used to joke with your father that you were going to grow up to marry her someday."

"Of course you would think that." I roll my eyes.

"How is she? Was she well?"

I take a long sip of beer and wipe my hands on my napkin before leaning back in my chair and shrugging. "No idea. I was working the crowd at the pub crawl when I saw her."

"And?" she prompts.

"She saw me, and then she had to leave, so we didn't really get a chance to talk." Emmy's shocked eyes flash through my mind. I'm not sure why I lie to them about it.

"Are you going to see her again?" Dad asks.

"It was so quick, I didn't get her phone number. Besides, if I wanted to, I wouldn't know the first place to look for her. She was probably here for the holiday or something and is gone now."

"You are a cop, dipshit. In case you didn't know." The kick to the shin I gave Grady moments ago is returned to me under the table.

"And your point is?" I grunt, glaring at my brother.

"You have all the stalking capabilities you need at the station."

"Nah, I couldn't do that," I reply, but that doesn't mean the thought hasn't crossed my mind a time *or a hundred*.

"Stick with that thought, Grant," Dad warns. "The last thing you need is to misuse city resources while being considered for the promotion."

"And the chief speaks," Grayson adds to lighten the mood with a laugh.

"Do you have more of that cobbler?" Grady asks, effectively shifting the subject, but not before I see one last glance between Mom and Dad that leaves me lost in thought while the conversation moves on.

I was a kid when everything happened with Em, so it was hard for me to reconcile how nice her dad was with what she said happened to her. Now, I'm an adult and have seen things on the job that have taught me that even the nicest of people could do the cruelest of things.

When I apply that knowledge to the little I know of Emerson's history, I can completely understand why seeing me may have caused some of the memories to rush back.

Chairs shift as the meal ends. The table is cleared. Dishes are washed. Luke helps, but he gets more water on the floor than in the sink. The night wears on.

My hands are on the railing, my body braced as I watch the sun begin to set in the distance.

My mom steps up beside me and slides an arm around my waist. "You're awfully quiet."

"Just thinking."

"About a dispatch or about Emmy?"

I should have known she'd revisit the topic. "A little bit of everything."

"It's okay to be curious about her, Grant," she says.

"Yeah, but for some reason, I don't think she wants me to be."

"What do you mean?"

"She bolted, Mom. She saw me, and I swear the look on her face went from happy to anxious. It was as if she was scared of me."

"You're a reminder of her past she's probably chosen to forget."

"Yeah. I guess." But that still doesn't explain why she's here in Sunnyville or why I can't stop thinking about her.

"Are you going to see her again?"

"Even if I wanted to, I told you I don't have any way to—"

"And I raised self-sufficient, resourceful sons. Don't give me your excuses," she says, putting me in my place before patting my shoulder and walking back inside.

Betsy Malone has spoken.

The only woman who can put the Malone boys in line.

FOUR

Grant

W HAT AM I DOING HERE?

I glance up at the sign that reads: Doggy Style, and I know this is a mistake right off the bat. I knew she seemed quirky, but this already sounds like a bad episode of *COPS*. Police officer stumbles unknowingly into a prostitute parlor.

Walk away.

I take another step up the stairs.

This is a mistake.

I knock on the door and am greeted with the baying of dogs and nothing else. No sound of a normally functioning business. No phones ringing. No customers talking. Just a yellow clapboard house I've probably driven past a hundred times and never noticed before.

Good. She's not here. Curiosity satisfied. Time to go.

And just as I begin to walk away, I hear the pad of footsteps on the raised floorboards followed by the sound of a woman's voice shushing the dogs.

"Officer Sexy," Desi says, giving me a wide smile when she opens the door.

"Ms. Whitman." I nod.

"To what do I owe this pleasure? Let me guess. You came here to convince me that beards and tattoos are out and clean cut and uniforms are in and that we're running away and eloping. Screw our parents and friends, because all we need is each other and the clothes on our backs because love is the currency of life. Is that right?"

I stare dumfounded, trying to process all she just said before laughing and shaking my head. "I was going to say hello, but I think your story is much more entertaining."

"So, you're telling me I can still like tattoos and beards?"

"You can like whatever you want." I turn down my patrol radio as dispatch talks. "Hello, Desi Whitman."

"Hello, Grant Malone. What can I do for you? I know I'm a law-abiding citizen, so I'm not in any trouble, unless you like to use those handcuffs for other purposes." She waggles her eyebrows.

The woman is hilarious. "A real man never kisses and tells," I say with a wink.

"But he does spank and flog," she comes right back without batting an eyelash, making me choke on air.

"Jesus."

"Would you like to come in? I promise all of my clients are locked up tight."

"Should I be worried about that statement?"

"Didn't you know I'm a Dominatrix? Wanna come check out my dungeon?" I just stare at her until she cracks a smile and laughs. "Dogs. They're all dogs. I'm a groomer and pet sitter."

"Ahh, and now the company name makes sense."

"I love a little tongue-in-cheek mixed with innuendo." She shrugs. "It gets clients to call, and why be serious? Life's too short not to laugh."

"Ain't that the truth?"

"In all seriousness, what's up? Although, I seem to think I already know." She motions for me to come in, and I shake my head.

"I can't. Thank you, though, I'm about to start my shift." We fall silent as she stares and waits for me to say whatever I've come to say. "It's about Emerson."

"I assumed." She crosses her arms over her chest and leans her shoulder against the doorjamb.

"Is there any way I can get her number or you can contact her and give her mine? I'd really like to see her again."

"Why?"

"To catch up."

"To catch up, or to pry?" she asks.

"Look, all I want to do is see for myself that she's happy."

"I already told you she is. Why would you think differently?"

"You should be a police interrogator," I deflect.

"Danger and I don't mix unless you consider the jaws of a Rottweiler hazardous."

"Sounds hazardous to me." The woman has a way of changing the topic like no one I've ever met before.

"I'm sorry, Officer Malone, but I can't give you Emerson's phone number without asking her. For some reason, I think if I ask her, she would say no."

"Why's that?"

"Because I saw how she reacted to you the other day. Then, when I asked about who you were, she wouldn't tell me, so now the onus is on you to explain. Who are you to her?"

"I told you the other day. I used to know her back in grade school. Anything else would betray her confidence," I say with a smile to ease suspicion. "I'm sorry, but that's all I can tell you."

"Are you sure that's how you want to play this?"

"I'm not playing anything, just stating the facts, ma'am."

"Smooth one, Malone." She shifts to put her hands on her hips. "My money's on you being her first kiss or first love. Something like that."

"Not quite, but you're getting warmer." My radio crackles to life again, prompting me to look at my watch to see I have a few minutes left until I'm on-call. "Thanks for your time, Desi, but I have to get to work. Sorry to bug you."

"I can't give you her number without asking her, but I could invite you to a little barbecue I'm having tomorrow night. And I might be able to tell you that a certain someone will be there . . . if, you know, you'd like to stop by and say hi or something."

"Or something." After Em's warmth toward me the other day, I can only imagine how thrilled she'd be if I showed up out of the blue.

"She could use a nice guy like you around."

"What's that supposed to mean?" I ask, now curious about the company Emerson keeps.

"Nothing. Oh, make sure you take that uniform"—she gestures up and down my body—"off before you come," Desi says, completely sidestepping my question. "My friends might get a little freaked if you show up in it. They're a little free-spirited, if you catch my drift."

"Seems like most people are these days."

FIVE

Emerson

"**P**ROMISE ME THIS BARBECUE IS NOT ONE OF YOUR ELABORATE ways to set me up with one of your friends." I take a bite of the carrot dipped in ranch and fight the urge to gag. *Nope,* still don't like vegetables. "Why do people eat this shit?"

"Because it's good for you," Desi says as she hums around her bright pink kitchen with a black-and-white checkered floor like she's freaking Martha Stewart.

"No. Sex is good for you. Chocolate is good for you. Wine is even better for you. They feed the soul. This crap," I say and hold up the carrot, "only serves to make you miserable."

"Says the woman who could eat nonstop every day and maintain her to-die-for figure." She rolls her eyes as she wipes her hands on a dishtowel.

I reach for the dish of M&M's and grab a handful with a grin. "Sucks to be me." I finish chewing them as she mixes something in a bowl. It looks nasty now, but I know will taste like heaven when she's done with it. It always does. "I'm serious, Des. You know I love your cooking, but it isn't enough to keep me here if you play matchmaker again. You try, and I'm gonna bail."

"Pfft. No you won't. My cooking is ten times better than anything you could make on the hot plate at your place."

She isn't making eye contact with me. That in and of itself makes me question whether I believe this whole party isn't a ruse to fix me up with one of the many people that come and go in her life. She's done it so many times, and yet, still has no shame.

"I mean it. I have plenty of men I can call up if I want a good time. I don't need your help in that department."

"Yeah. I'm well aware."

"What's that supposed to mean?" I narrow my eyes and stare at her until she looks my way.

"It means you purposely pick men you don't want to stick around."

Here we go again.

"And there's a problem with this . . . why?"

"Because, at some point in your life, you're going to want a guy who is around longer than just a couple of orgasms, that's why." Her tone is serious when I want to be anything but.

"But damn, those orgasms feel incredible."

"I'm serious, Em. What's so wrong with settling with one man instead of having many?"

I sigh audibly to let her know I'm done with this conversation. "Many? You make it sound like I sleep around. It's one man at a time . . . even I have standards. And nothing's wrong with settling down; it just isn't for me. You know me—no rings, no strings."

"You sound like a guy."

"I sound like me." I shrug. "Promise me, Des."

"Ah look, Leo's here. I'll get the door."

"Don't knock it till you try it, Cassy," I say to one of Desi's friends.

"There is no way in hell you're going to get me to jump out of a plane. No way, no how. I'd have to have about fifteen more of these to even consider it," she says as she raises her empty glass of wine and shakes her head.

"Drink up," I tease. "The offer stands, though. You wouldn't have to do anything other than enjoy the ride since you'd be strapped to me."

"That sounds like a bad porno, but it still won't get me to change my mind," she says through a laugh.

I lean back in my chair as the conversation wears on. Leo talks about his most favorite dive in Machu Pichu. Desi flits between the twenty or so guests, making everyone feel at home with her easy charm. The fairy lights in the trees add a soft glow, there's a welcome chill to the summer air, and the Carne Asada cooking on the grill smells like absolute heaven.

Even better, she's kept her promise. I don't see any unfamiliar faces she can try to set me up with. And while I don't know most of them other than a casual hello, I've at least seen them before. It's the perfect night.

"Don't you think, Emerson?" Leo's voice pulls my attention back from my thoughts, and I find eight pairs of eyes staring at me waiting for an answer.

"I'm sorry. I was in La-la Land. What am I supposed to be opining about?"

"We were talking about—"

I don't hear another word he says because, just over his left shoulder, I see Grant Malone standing in the frame of the door. He's wearing shorts and a cream-colored Henley, and his hands are shoved in his pockets while his eyes are trained on me.

I hate that the sight of him makes my breath catch and causes a flutter somewhere deep inside me. I despise that when I meet his eyes, I want to see the little boy I once knew instead of the achingly handsome man he's become. More than anything, I hate that he needs to go when all I want him to do is stay.

There's an awkward moment where everyone notices my blatant distraction and falls silent. They shift to look at Grant before, almost as one, they turn back to stare at me.

"Excuse me," I murmur as I rise from my seat, a mixture of anger and confusion rioting through my veins.

Desi broke her promise. And not only did she break her promise but she did so with the one man who made the dreams I haven't had in years come back. Last night, I woke in a blind panic: Pillow soaked with sweat, hands gripped in the sheets, and heartbeat out of control.

My rational self knows it isn't his fault, and yet, I blame him for scraping up the past, which is better left dead and buried.

If looks could kill, the one I shoot Desi would put her six feet under. The other guests murmur about who the stranger is as I make my way toward him.

"What are you doing here?" He smells incredible. Like soap and mint and why am I even noticing?

"Hi, Grant Malone. Nice to meet you." Cool as can be, he ignores the irritation in my tone and holds his hand out for me to shake.

"Seriously?" I eye his hand and then look back to him.

"Oh, you're going to remember that we know each other now? I'm sorry. I wasn't quite sure if you were still playing the 'I'm not Emmy, I don't know you' game like you were the other day."

I grit my teeth because I deserve the dig, but hell if I'm going to let him know that. "What are you doing here?"

"Okay, so now we're admitting we already know each other. That makes life much easier, don't you think?" He drops his hand. "Desi invited me. She said she's a good cook, and well, I like to eat." The shrug he gives me is casual, as if there is no other explanation needed, and that smile of his never wavers from its boyish slant. I haven't seen him in twenty years, and all the sudden, I cross paths with him twice in one week.

"In that case, she's right over there." I point to where Desi is sitting, cautiously staring our way. It's only then that I realize most of the guests are also watching us.

"That, *and* I wanted to see you again."

The words on my lips falter as I try to process why him being here has me so irritated, but it does. And just as bewilderingly, I can't stop studying him. I can't stop wondering about him and the man he's become. Is he anything like the person my mind had conjured him to be on the odd occasion I thought about him?

I can feel the weight of everyone's stares on my back and know they are wondering why I'm acting so bizarre. Normally, I'd hug whoever the new person was and welcome them into our transient circle without a second thought.

"Okay . . . well, then . . . beer is over there in the cooler and food is on the table. If you'll excuse me, I need to go to the restroom."

The kitchen is empty when I enter it, and I'm so very thankful for the silence to collect my thoughts. The irony is that the quiet doesn't last long. Someone turns on the radio and music drifts in through the open french doors, along with my friends' laughter and a voice that is unfamiliar yet familiar all at once.

I've come inside to get some distance from Grant so I can think, and yet I'm standing here studying him through the window. His dark hair and five o'clock shadow. How the sleeves of his Henley are pushed up to his elbows to showcase strong forearms. His natural ease talking with everyone and instinctual awareness of everything around him like his dad used to have when we were kids.

He's just like the little boy I used to know and nothing like him at the same time.

That's a brilliant thought, Em. He can't be both of those at the same time . . . and yet, he is.

"Watcha looking at?"

I jump back at the sound of Desi's voice and am shocked to find her standing beside me, admiring the same view I am. I was so lost in my thoughts that I hadn't noticed her come in.

"Nothing. Just thinking." Needing something to do with my hands, I turn on the faucet and begin washing them.

"Uh-huh. That nothing you're thinking of has a mighty fine ass, if I say so myself."

It's then that I realize I'm supposed to be mad at her. "You promised, Des." I drag my eyes from my hands to meet hers. "I said I was going to bail if you did this, so I guess it's time for me to leave."

"Have I tried to fix you up with him?"

"No, but I know that's only a matter of time." I cross my arms over my chest and follow her gaze. He does have a fine ass.

Oh my God. What am I thinking? I can't stare at his ass. Or notice how handsome he is. Or wonder if his hands are as strong as they appear. He was like a brother to me—my best friend—isn't it creepy if I agree with her? He's from memories I erased long ago.

And this is why I came into the house in the first place. All I wanted to do was have a few drinks and relax with my friends, but now my head's all over the place—courtesy of Grant Malone.

"I swore I wouldn't, and I intend to keep my promise." She bumps her hip against mine. "Besides, I made your favorite for dessert, so you can't leave yet."

Dessert? My ears perk up at the same time I try to fight the smile tugging at the corners of my lips. "Which kind?"

Her laugh fills the small space. "You like all my desserts, so does it really matter?"

"No." I laugh. And of course, now my mind is on whether she made a lemon tart or cheesecake or . . . crap, she's right. I'm not going anywhere. Not when her dessert is involved.

"Look, we ran into each other again, and I thought it might be nice for you guys to reconnect. What's the harm in that? He's *obviously* someone from your past. He's *obviously* interested in catching up. He's *obviously* drop dead attractive. He's—"

"You're *obviously* losing your mind."

"I meant no harm by it. I promise. I wasn't even sure he was going to show. We're typically surrounded by all my friends, so I thought it would be cool if you had your own friend here, too."

I eye her, knowing I can't argue since she invited him with nothing but good intentions in mind. "Your friends are my friends," I say exasperated.

"Exactly. He's my friend now, too. That means I was allowed to invite him." Her smile is smug as she expertly maneuvers me into a baseless argument.

"You're exhausting."

"And you love me," she says, refilling my glass of wine.

"Most days." I take a sip but my eyes are still fixated on Grant Malone, and my mind is still on the confusion seeing him again has created.

"All days."

I shrug and agree. "All days."

"Okay, well, I need to get back out there. You coming?"

"In a minute."

SIX

Emerson

"NO WAY IN HELL." GRANT LAUGHS, AND I HATE THAT EVERY-thing about the sound pulls on me to pay attention when I don't want to.

"C'mon. A bunch of us jump. We could teach you," Leo says with more slur than conviction after whatever round of drink he's on.

"I don't trust anyone enough, let alone myself, to jump out of an airplane and rely on them to know the parachute is for sure going to deploy."

Chicken.

I don't say the word aloud, but I think it, and for some reason reverting back to sounding like a kid makes me feel a smidgen better.

"Sounds like you have trust issues," Leo says.

"Yeah, how is that, Grant?" Desi pipes in while I just keep my head down and focus on picking at my nail polish. "You can risk your life every day doing your job, but you're scared to skydive?"

"My partner has my back," he states.

"So, you trust your partner, but you wouldn't trust a skilled instructor to tandem jump with you? They control the jump, pull the chute, and make sure you land safely."

Goddamnit, Desi.

I see the maneuvering going on here, and I don't want any part of the set up. I shift in my seat and try to find an out that won't be so obvious.

"Tell me something, Desi," Grant says as he leans forward and puts his elbows on his knees. "When was the last time you jumped?"

"Me?" She laughs. "You're all out of your minds. There's no way I would trust someone with my life."

"And you just proved my point," he says, and Desi just laughs harder. But that charming chuckle she has, which typically has all the men sidling up next to her, doesn't seem to affect Grant.

Talk quiets some as we finish our dessert and Leo brings another round of drinks for those who are ready.

"I swear every time Desi invites me over, I leave having gained ten pounds," Cassy groans as she adjusts the waistband of her pants and then points an accusing finger my way. "And, of course, you're going to have another helping and grin the whole time you're eating it."

My hand stops mid-cut into another slice of cheesecake, but the guilt is only momentary. It's too damn irresistible to pass up.

"Bitch," Desi playfully comments.

"You always did love dessert." It's Grant's quiet statement that has our friends turning their heads in his direction, the slow realization that he's from the past I never talk about settling over them.

But he isn't looking at any of them. When I glance up, his gaze is on me. Our eyes meet, and for a brief moment, I allow myself to wonder what it is he sees when he looks at me. His soft smile exudes warmth, but it's his eyes that draw me into places and times and thoughts that don't belong in this lifetime.

There's a stirring in my belly that shouldn't be there. The same one that has resurfaced each time the two of us have interacted in some way or another over the past few hours.

I need to stop thinking about the gold flecks in his brown eyes and how he still has the hint of a scar on his chin from when he tried to jump his BMX off a homemade ramp.

Familiarity.

That's what he is, and it's something I'm not used to outside the world I've created.

It's too much. Too unexpected. Too close.

"You're right. I don't need this extra piece," I say as I stand abruptly and begin to clear the dirtied forks that were discarded when the paper plates were tossed into the fire. My avoidance of eye contact only serves to compound the awkwardness and reinforce that I'm not acting anything like my normal self.

Once in the kitchen, I do things to busy myself. Wipe down the counters that have already been cleaned. Restack the dishwasher. Anything to settle the discord I feel.

"Emerson." The deep rumble of Grant's voice cuts through my thoughts. My hands still. My heart races. My feet turn to face him. "Is everything okay?"

Yes. No. I don't know.

I meet his eyes and struggle with how to respond. "I worked a long time to make this life, Grant." My voice is shaky, and I hate that it is, but there's no way I can disguise the emotion.

"Okay." He draws the word out as he cocks his head to the side, brows narrowing as if he's trying to understand. "I wasn't trying to interfere."

"Then what do you want?"

"To get to know you again. To be friends. I don't know, you're *my Emmy* . . ."

The endearment from our childhood tears into parts of me I didn't know existed anymore. "You being here . . ." I struggle to explain feelings I'm not even sure I understand. "You're from another place and time I've tried to forget."

He takes a step closer and leans against the counter, but his eyes never leave mine as laughter from outside floats in. He nods slowly, saying, "I didn't know that my being here would upset you. I'm sorry. It's just that since I saw you the other day, I haven't been able to get you out of my head. I thought maybe we could be friends again. That's all, Emerson. Nothing more."

"I can't be who you want me to be." My thoughts explode into words I can't believe I've said and want to take back immediately. For some reason, this conversation . . . *he* makes me nervous.

"Who's that? I don't want you to be anything."

"A victim," I whisper.

Those two words knock the wind from his sails. His shoulders sag, and he roughs a hand through his hair before releasing an audible sigh. "Em . . ."

"I don't need a hero," I explain, thinking of all the times he had talked about someday being like his dad, a hero who saves everyone from everything.

"No one said you did." The gold in his eyes burns bright as his temper surfaces. "I'm confused. Did I do something to offend you? Did I . . . Christ, never mind. Nothing's worth it if it's this much work. Nice seeing you again, Em. Have a nice life."

"No. Wait," I say against my better judgment, causing him to stop in the doorway and face me.

Sadness fuses with the anger in his eyes, and the expression on his face mirrors everything I feel but can't express.

"Am I staying or going, Em? You decide."

Words don't come, and we stare at each other for a few moments before he nods in resignation and leaves.

The front door shuts. Leo turns the music louder outside as Desi begins swinging her hips, but I remain in the kitchen with my chest hurting and my perfectly crafted world spinning off its axis. Even the half eaten cheesecake on the counter holds no appeal to me.

A part of me wants to chase after him and apologize. I was more than rude, and he deserves better. The other part of me has finally recognized the emotion I was feeling but couldn't put a finger on. *It's fear.*

I'm scared to death.

Grant scares me.

Out of habit, I run a hand over the inside of my arm and feel the ridges there. The reminders that fear can be overcome.

Drawing in a fortifying breath, I debate whether I should go back outside, drink some more wine, and waste the rest of the night away.

Something tells me that just might exacerbate the traitorous feelings I'm having. Alcohol, Grant, and fear are a dangerous combination that just might jostle things I've long forgotten and never want to remember again.

I've spent the last twenty years shutting myself off from all emotion—all feelings when it comes to anyone of the opposite sex—and in a span of one week's time, I've let Grant change that.

My black-and-white world has color seeping into its edges.

I love and hate it all at the same time.

It makes me feel alive inside when, until now, I hadn't realized I had been dead.

SEVEN

Emerson

"**N**ONE FOR ME. THANK YOU, THOUGH." I PUT MY HAND UP TO cover my glass as Chris tries to pour wine into it. *Again.*

"C'mon, Em. Just because we're working, doesn't mean we can't relax some and have a drink."

His cologne overpowers the scent of food in the restaurant, and there's a soft whistle in his nose every time he inhales. I try not to focus on it, but now that I've heard it, I can't unhear it.

"Where were we?" I clear my throat and lift the profit and loss statement we were talking about before the waiter came with the bottle of wine. This, of course, came after the three glasses he had already had.

"I forget. Where exactly were we?" he says in a playful voice as he scoots closer so we're shoulder to shoulder. *Again.*

Trying the same move I've done several times tonight already, I shift in my seat to put some distance between us. When I do, Chris reaches out and puts his hand over mine.

Alarm bells sound off in my head, but I do my best to appear unaffected. It isn't the first time a man has tried to flirt with me when I didn't encourage it.

I nonchalantly pull my hand out from under his to pick up the income statement. "We were talking about last year's net income of Blue Skies compared to the proposed loan amount."

"Yes, we were." He reaches across me to pick up an untouched glass of water, his elbow grazes against my breasts. I chock it up to being an accident, but I don't like it one bit. "But I think it's better suited if we talk about you and me."

"What about *you and me*?" I ask, befuddled where this conversation is going.

"You know I'm the only loan officer in town who would take a chance on you, right?" His voice is low, and he's so close that I can smell the wine on his breath.

"Yes, and as I've said before, I appreciate that."

"Nothing is guaranteed though."

"I know." I nod and shift my body again when he leans in closer. "Oh, you know what I forgot to ask about? What's it called? Crap. I forgot. Can you get the other papers off the seat?" I feign stupidity to try to get him to go back to his side of the booth. His excuse that he needed to explain a calculation in order to sit beside me was clearly a ruse.

"Forget the questions, Emerson. I know one surefire way to make certain you get that loan."

"Hmm? What's that?" I ask without looking at him, even though I'm pretty damn sure what he's going to suggest next.

"C'mon." He chuckles and the sound of it makes my skin crawl. "I'm always up for a little game of hard to get, but don't you think we're past that point?"

I choose my next words wisely because I'm in a precarious position. Do I tell him to back the hell off and piss off the only banker who would take a chance on me? Do I do that and risk losing my loan? Or do I just bite my tongue, politely refuse him, and bide my time?

"I'm sorry. I don't understand. " I decide to pick the second option and hope it works when every part of me begs to do the first one.

"This loan process would go much smoother and be a little more certain, if you'd just give into our chemistry."

I turn to look at him and startle when I find his face within inches of mine. His eyebrows are raised and his stare is unwavering.

"Let me get this straight. You're saying that, if I sleep with you, my loan will get approved?" I try to hide the disgust I feel and wonder if he senses it. Then again, it seems he's in an alternative universe if he's interpreted my indifference to his advances as my being interested.

His chuckle rumbles in the small space around us. "Now, now, I didn't say that, did I?" The smirk on his face and suggestion in his eyes says he meant exactly that. "Don't go putting words in my mouth."

"And if I don't *give into our* chemistry . . .?" His shrug is the only answer he gives. "I have a preapproval letter, Chris. The lender has already told me that so long as I get them the information they need and it's accurate, they'll give me the loan."

"Preapproval letters aren't a loan approval," he states, eyes hardening.

"I'm aware," I say with confidence while hating that his veiled threat only serves to intensify my anxiety over getting my loan.

We stare at each other for a few seconds. I refuse to back down or be intimidated by him. The man clearly isn't the type of person I thought he was.

"Oh my. Is it already six o'clock? Where did the time go? I need to get going." I begin putting the papers into a messy stack as a way to show him I'm serious about needing to leave. He doesn't budge. "Excuse me, Chris, can you please let me get out of the booth?"

He narrows his eyes and tilts his head to the side as he studies me. "I need the rest of this information by tomorrow night." His voice is cold when moments ago it was warmth laced with suggestion.

"Tomorrow night?" I laugh as if he's joking but then realize he's not. Panic hits me. It's going to take me all night to pull this together. "I don't understand. You told me I had until next Friday."

"Yeah, well, plans changed. I need it by tomorrow night."

"You're serious." I state the obvious, still dumbfounded by the personality switch he just flicked over to the *asshole* side.

"Deadly. *Unless of course* . . ." He leaves the words unspoken, but his fingertip trailing down my bicep says it all for him.

I yank my arm away and start scooting myself out of the booth, my hips hitting his to try to push him along. He relents but makes sure to stand well within my personal space as I gather the rest of my paperwork. I hate the feeling of him watching me as I bend over to grab my purse and briefcase from the inside of the booth.

All I want to do is get the hell out of here but I grit my teeth, force myself to face him, and sound cordial.

"Thank you for the dinner and for answering my questions. I'll do my best to get the documents to you by tomorrow night."

"Don't try, Emerson. Make it happen."

With bile in my throat and a film of disgust coating my skin, I walk out of the restaurant as quickly as I can.

EIGHT

Emerson

OW COULD I BE SO STUPID?

How could I have been so wrapped up in making sure I understood everything needed for my loan that I missed the signs Chris was giving off?

I press the pedal down harder. The speedometer hits seventy miles per hour, but it isn't fast enough.

First Chris.

Then the realization that I have no other options but to deal with him and his creep factor.

The needle hits eighty.

Nothing will ever be enough to outrun that feeling I get every time someone expects me to bend to their will. To be subservient. To play the victim.

Never again.

No way. No how. *Screw that.*

The long road is stretched out before me. Just fields, grape vines, trees, and flat asphalt, making me feel as if I were the only person on the face of the earth.

Hitting the outskirts of town, I push the envelope of safety, but when you jump out of airplanes for a living, that envelope is harder to breach than for most.

With each mile I put between myself and the restaurant, I feel the stress begin to shed. The pressure of making sure all my documents are in order so I don't lose the loan because of some stupid mistake eases. And with the clearing of my mind comes the clarity.

Despite it being so much easier to pick up and move when people started asking too many questions about my past, I let Desi talk me into coming back to Sunnyville. My need to put away the nomadic life I have been living and settle down to plant roots for myself was just a thought back then, yet, I'd been willing to try.

Then I found Blue Skies, which was in desperate need of some TLC, and decided that the girl, who liked to go where the wind blows her, suddenly wanted something permanent. A business. A fixture. Something to be proud of.

My desire to own Blue Skies and make it one hundred percent mine had made me stay to fight for something.

And fighting is what I'm doing.

The sirens come out of nowhere. Blue and red lights flash to tell me my fun—my reprieve—has been compromised and is about to be shut down.

"Shit." I pound a fist against the wheel, knowing this will be my second ticket in six months. The monetary fine. Points on my driving record. The increase in my insurance. All the consequences ghost through my mind as I pull to a stop and wait for Officer Asshole to walk up to the driver side and read me the riot act. I may even pull up the hem of my shorts some so when he's met with an eyeful of tanned and toned thighs, he might be distracted.

It's worth a shot.

"License and registration, please."

I look up to the gravelly voice standing outside my window and am met with my own reflection in his mirrored lenses. "Hi, Officer. How is your day going?" I'll try sweet-talking. I'm not good at it, but at least I'm not going down without a fight.

"License and registration, please, ma'am."

"What seems to be the problem?"

"How about going ninety in a fifty mile an hour zone."

"Oh. Was I really going that fast?" I feign innocence.

"Are you in a hurry?" I stare at him doe-eyed, unable to make my synapses fire so I can come up with some kind of brilliant excuse. "That's considered reckless driving. Endangerment of others. Should I go on?"

With each offense my eyes are seeing dollar signs that my wallet doesn't have.

The radio handset strapped to his shoulder sparks to life, and he responds in some kind of code that sounds like a foreign language. "No, Officer. The thing is I left my house in a hurry—"

"I think we've established that fact."

I look in my rearview mirror as another police car pulls up behind his, and my palms grow sweaty. Am I that dangerous that they need two units to handle this call?

"Anyway, like I was saying, I left in such a hurry that I didn't grab my wallet. I don't have my license."

He angles his head, and even though I can't see his eyes behind the lenses, I can feel them dressing me down. "Then your registration?"

"This isn't exactly my car." I hear the door of the second unit shut behind us.

And the award for Flake of the Year, ladies and gentlemen, goes to Emerson Reeves.

"Whose car is it then?"

"Blue Skies—the company I work for."

"Do you need any help, Off—*Emerson*?"

That voice. *His voice* has my whole body wanting to seize up and melt at the same time.

"You know this woman?" Officer Asshole says as I look to where Grant stands in his dark blue uniform with the setting sun at his back.

"I do."

"You want to handle this call?"

"Sure," Grant says, and after how things went between us the last time I saw him, I'm not sure if I'm relieved or worried.

"Thanks. You'll be saving me from John's wrath, coming home late from shift again."

"Husbands," Grant plays along and shrugs.

"Exactly." He lifts his chin toward the back of the car, and the two men step back there for a few minutes. They speak in hushed tones, before Grant steps toward me and the other officer climbs into his car.

"Christ, Emerson. Ninety?" There's a disapproving tone to his voice, but under it is something akin to amusement. "Seriously? You're lucky Lyle didn't haul you off to jail for reckless driving."

"We weren't quite done, but I'm sure that might have been an option."

"It *is* pretty serious. And hauling you off is a valid option for the safety of not only you but also everyone else on the road."

"But there is no one else on the road. No harm. No foul. Can I go?"

"You could have gotten yourself killed."

He takes off his sunglasses and hooks them in his shirt. I stare at them hanging from his neck because it's so much easier than looking him in the eyes. But he stands there, hands braced on the frame of my window and waits for me to meet his gaze.

While I had been certain sweet talking would have worked with Officer Lyle, at least until Grant mentioned the other officer's husband, I have absolutely no idea what to say to ease the situation.

"You always had a flair for the dramatic." The words are out before I realize it, and I hate myself for being the first to bring up the past when I don't want him to do the same.

"Dramatic is one thing, Em. Doing my job is another."

"Oh, I see what you're doing here. You're mad at me for the other night when you have no right to be and—"

"This has nothing to do with the other night and everything to do with the law and me enforcing it."

He always was a stickler for the rules. The longer this conversation goes on, the more irritated I become, and a big part of me wants it to continue. If I'm pissed at him, then I'll want him to go away instead of wondering what it would be like to see him again like I have been.

"Are you seriously going to arrest me?"

"Give me a good reason why you're in such a hurry you need to go ninety miles an hour."

Because I can.

The truth almost escapes but I stop myself before it does. Our eyes meet. Hold. Assess. Ask. And then I answer.

"I'm having a female emergency." I ignore the fact that I'm wearing skimpy white shorts no woman on her period would be caught dead wearing and give him the number one response guaranteed to make a man uncomfortable.

His lips quirk for a moment before he leans down so that his elbows rest on the door. "And?"

"Well, I was rushing to the store."

"And that's why you were going so fast?"

"Yes." I nod, hating that he isn't shying away like any man in his right mind would.

"What were you going to the store to buy? Tampons? Monistat? Astroglide?" he deadpans.

If I could die a thousand deaths right now I would. My cheeks burn, and I'd give anything to crawl under the steering wheel to avoid having to make eye contact with him. "Yes."

"All three? That's a feminine emergency if I've ever heard of one."

Already invested in my lie, I have no choice but to continue it. I clear my throat, but my voice comes out in a broken rasp. "Tampons. Just tampons."

"I see." He nods slowly. "Funny thing is, your car is heading in the wrong direction. All the drugstores are back that way." He throws his thumb over his shoulder as I cringe at my mistake. "But being new in town and all that, maybe you got turned around, huh?"

There's a smirk playing at the corners of his mouth while my embarrassment only intensifies. "Yes, that's definitely why." I squirm in my seat to try to sell it when I know he's probably not buying any of this. "Can I go now, please?"

"Go? To the drugstore? Of course you can. I wouldn't want your *situation* to worsen because of all this time we're wasting. Tell you what, Em, if it's such an emergency that you were willing to risk life and limb to get there, I think I should give you a police escort."

"No! That's okay—I—"

"Lights and sirens. The whole shebang all the way to . . . CVS, or is it Rite Aid? Which store has the brand you prefer?"

"A police escort, Grant? Really?" Irritation mixes with disbelief.

"Now that you're a resident of Sunnyville, I'm at your service. Here to protect and to serve." He flashes a grin that tells me he knows exactly what I'm doing and plans to make me pay for it.

And pay for it I do. With lights and sirens. Parading me the long way through town until we pull into the CVS parking lot.

His cruiser parks beside me, and I have every intention of running inside and buying some damn tampons I don't currently need just to get him off my back. So, I'm completely mortified when he climbs out of his car as I get out of mine.

"What are you doing?" I ask, eyes flicking toward the random people who are staring at the flashing lights and the police officer standing in front of me.

"Let's go."

I stiffen when he places a hand on the small of my back and starts ushering me closer to the entrance. He nods and murmurs a few hellos to people who address him by name, all the while I'm trying to figure how far we're going to carry on this charade. He's obviously trying to prove a point while at the same time, willing to make my life miserable in retaliation for my rudeness the other night.

When we enter the store, I immediately begin to scan the directory signs above the aisles to see where the feminine hygiene products are located. Anything so I can put distance between myself and him and this asinine predicament.

"Not so fast. Where are you going?" he asks as he grabs my bicep, keeping me in place.

"To find what I need."

"No worries. I have you covered. It's an emergency after all," he says, leading me to the front of the store.

"What are you—"

"Shh. It's under control." He points to his badge and smiles.

"No. It's okay. I can find them on my own—"

"Excuse me, where are the tampons?" Grant asks the service clerk at the front of the store. Some teenage boys waiting in line snicker, and the young clerk's face immediately turns bright red as he stutters a response. "Better yet, we're in an emergency situation here. *A ninety mile an hour* type of emergency. Can you get on the PA and ask one of your associates to bring up a box for us so this young lady doesn't have to search them out."

Oh. My. God. Is he seriously going to do this?

Yes, he is.

That irritation I was hoping for just hit full force.

"I can get them myself," I grit out between clenched teeth.

"Oh, no need to. He's got it under control." He lifts his chin to the cashier, who looks less than thrilled to be asked to do this. "Go on," he urges the clerk.

"Can I get some assistance to the front please?" the clerk asks, his teenage voice cracking on the overhead speakers. "I need a box of tampons brought up."

"Tell them it's an emergency," Grant says as the kid looks over to me and then down to my pelvis before realizing what he's doing and snapping his head up, more flustered than ever.

"It's an emergency." His voice booms over the PA system and draws the eyes of some of the customers waiting at the photo counter.

"Thank you." Grant flashes a huge grin his way. "Oh, wait. What brand do you like, Emerson?"

"You're joking, right?" I sputter.

"Only if you're joking." He lifts his eyebrows as he throws down the gauntlet to see if I'm going to come clean or keep lying. The problem is that I think if I don't continue, he might really haul me off to jail to prove a point. "I don't think generic will do for such a dire situation. Brand?"

"Tampax," I say defiantly.

"Tampax," he relays to the clerk, whose cheeks are burning brighter with each second that passes. When the clerk continues to stare at Grant as if he's crazy, which I'm beginning to think he is, Grant points to the phone in his hand. "Go on. Let them know so they don't bring the wrong one and then we have to start this whole process all over again."

The clerk goes to protest and then realizes that it's in his best interest to relay the message. "To the associate in the, er, woman's aisle . . . please make it Tampax."

I stare at Grant and his smug grin and know there is no way I'm going to let him get away with this. Funny thing is, I'm a woman, tampons don't embarrass me . . . but I know something that sure as hell will embarrass him.

"Are you still having that problem?" I loudly ask Grant, getting the blank look from him I was banking on.

"Problem?"

"Yes. You know . . ." I cringe and give him a sympathetic look before turning to the clerk. "While your associate is at it, can they grab one more thing for Officer Malone?"

The clerk's eyes widen. "Can't he go and get it himself?"

"No. He can't. He has a suspect in the car, and department policy says he can't be more than one hundred feet away from him at all times." I push Grant back as he tries to step forward and interrupt. "Please?"

"Yeah. Sure." The clerk looks at Grant and then back to me, uncertain how he became the ball in our ping-pong match.

"He needs his Viagra."

"Viagra?" The clerk's voice is suddenly soprano.

"Emers—"

"Don't be embarrassed, Grant. A lot of guys have trouble getting it up." I pat Grant's arm and return the smug smile as the muscle in his jaw clenches.

"Em," he warns.

"Viagra," I reiterate to the clerk ignoring the hand Grant squeezes on my bicep. "He's really embarrassed. I mean I wore lacy lingerie, high heels . . . everything, and he still couldn't get hard."

If the clerk's cheeks could get any redder, they would. "Th-that's a prescription. The phar-pharmacy—"

"Emers—"

"The urologist already called it in." I cut Grant off again, smile sweetly at the clerk, and point to the phone. "So just get on the PA and tell the pharmacy that you need the prescription of Viagra for Grant Malone to be brought up to the front."

Grant's hand tenses, and I swear I hear him mutter *son of a bitch* as the clerk stares at me as if I've lost my mind. I nod in encouragement to him.

He picks up the phone and keeps his eyes on mine the whole time he speaks on the PA system. "Uh, pharmacy, I need the prescription of Viagra to be brought up to the front."

"For Grant Malone," I say.

"The Viagra is under the name Grant Malone." His voice booms overhead.

Snickers of laughter from somewhere in the store echo up to us. The teenagers in line shift their feet and try to hide their smiles. The older lady standing at the Hallmark cards glances my way and then shakes her head in sympathy. I can only wonder if the sympathy is because I'm having a period emergency while wearing white shorts or because my assumed boyfriend can't get it up.

"Nice try, Malone, but I think I won this round," I mutter under my breath.

"Excuse me, Brian, is it?" Grant says to the clerk after looking at his nametag.

"Yes."

"Can you tell your associate that Emerson here needs the largest box of tampons you have?"

"The extra-large size box on the tampons?" he asks and looks at Grant with wide eyes.

"Yes." Grant smiles.

"Associate, please make that an extra-large box of tampons." Brian hangs the phone up and is about to turn his back when I speak.

"Brian, one more thing."

"You're joking right?" he asks exasperated.

"No, it's important. Pretty please?" I turn on my charm and bat my lashes.

"*What?*"

"The Viagra, can you make sure it's the extra strength?"

Poor Brian looks at Grant and then back to me for what seems like the tenth time. "You two are crazy. I don't want to be in the middle of your weird fight. Use the PA yourself if you need anything else." He holds the phone out to me. I'm more than tempted to make my request but figure we've caused enough of a scene, and by all accounts, I think I won this round.

"Thank you for your assistance, Brian, but we're good now," Grant says as he eases his grip on my arm and slides his hand down to the small of my back. I step away from him with the low hum of his chuckle in my ears.

Asshole.

The awkward tension only builds between us as the seconds tick by. Grant chats amicably with the cashier about how nice the weather is while the poor kid fidgets restlessly and refuses to meet his gaze. I glance around the store, waiting impatiently for the associate to bring the Tampax to the counter and wondering what is going to happen to my Viagra request.

Finally, the associate makes her way down the main aisle with the familiar blue-and-green box and holds it up to the male clerk. "Is this what you were looking for?"

Poor Brian blushes a darker red as Grant steps forward and takes the box from the associate. "Thank you, Eileen. You're looking wonderful as always," Grant says, prompting her to pat down her mass of gray curls. "How are the grandbabies? Is little Mario still as rambunctious as ever?"

Impatient to get the hell out of here, I force myself to watch the exchange between the two. Grant is holding the box of tampons in his hand, casual as can be, which is both surprising and unnerving. Not only am I privy to his personable skills with the nice lady who works at CVS but also I'm in the position to notice how perfectly well Grant's uniform pants hug his ass.

And what a mighty fine ass it is.

Stop it. Here he is dragging me through this stupid charade, and instead of being mad at him, I'm checking out his ass? Again.

But it's not just his ass. I'm also admiring the way his uniform sleeves hug his biceps and how broad his shoulders are.

But this is Grant Malone. He's the little boy I used to giggle with and play cops and robbers with. He was like the brother I never had . . . so how is it possibly okay to find him this damn attractive?

It isn't.

That's the plain and simple answer. I can't find him attractive. I can like him, but he's off limits. He knows too much. Him just being here reminds me of *before* too much.

He's too close when I've never allowed anyone to be.

I can be mad at him. I can be pissed as all hell that a little while ago he was threatening to haul me off to jail because I was a *smidgen* over the speed limit. I can also be livid that he called my bluff.

That's all I can be.

Oh, and I can be damn proud that I just met him tit for tat with his little plan to embarrass me.

"Right, Em?" His gravelly voice cuts through my thoughts—*of him.*

"Right, what?" I must look like a deer caught in headlights, and Eileen just smiles softly.

"He's such a good boy, isn't he?" Eileen says as she pats my arm.

I smile with so much saccharine that my teeth are going to rot. "He is."

And then she steps into Grant and lowers her voice. "No need to be embarrassed, dear. Having trouble getting an erection can sometimes be caused by stress." She pats his arm much like she did mine. "Try some good old fashioned pornography. I may have experience in knowing it does the trick." She winks and gives a knowing smile that leaves me biting back my snicker before she walks off as if she didn't just talk about porn.

Way to go, Eileen!

Grant blushes for the first time during this whole charade and blinks as if he's trying to make sure he actually heard her say what she said. I take his stunned silence and use it to my advantage by pushing a ten dollar bill across the counter to Brian. The poor kid is standing there trying to act like he didn't hear the exchange when he clearly did.

"I got it," Grant says with authority, taking my money off the counter and shoving it back in my hand.

"I can pay for my own—"

"No one said you couldn't." His lips quirk into a cocky smile, a clear indication he's regained his footing. "But it's the least I could do to help out with your . . . situation."

"Apparently, porn is what will help you with yours," I say nonchalantly, needing to get one last cheap shot in, before I turn and walk outside to wait for him in the fading daylight.

Within minutes, Grant strolls out of the drugstore with a bag in his hand and stops before me. We stare at each other for a moment.

"Viagra, Emerson? Really?" he asks, disdain owning his tone.

"I can go back in and wait for your prescription, if you'd like?" I bat my lashes.

"Cute. Very cute."

"You're not the only one who can dish it out."

"So it seems."

A new set of looky-loos slow their pace as they walk by, curious what crime I committed, and despite my little show inside, I'm not a fan of being the center of attention.

"Are we done now?" I huff as I hold my hand out for the bag.

We wage a visual war on the sidewalk in front of CVS. The lights on his squad car are still flashing and lighting up his face as he looks down at my hand and then back to me. "You tell me, Emerson. Are we done yet?"

"It's just a box of tampons."

"Oh, this is about so much more than *just a box of tampons*," he says, voice serious, eyes locked on mine. We stare at each other for a minute more, both of us wondering who will give in first. My wanting to believe the lie I tell myself that this is only about feminine hygiene products against his waiting for me to realize I'm wrong.

"May I have the bag, please?"

"Of course you can, so long as we get one thing clear." He steps closer to me and leans in. "Nothing's changed, Em. Don't you remember? I can always tell when someone is lying. Especially you. That's one thing about me that's still the same, so it's best you don't forget that. Otherwise, next time will be a whole lot worse than a box of tampons you don't need."

I grit my teeth as he leans back, those brown eyes of his laden with humor as he places the bag in my hand. "Is that a threat, Officer?"

"No. It's a promise."

NINE

Grant

GLANCE AROUND THE QUIET CUL-DE-SAC AS I STEP OUT OF MY CRUIS-
er. The street is a perfect picture of fictional Mayberry with its pristine cut
lawns, blooming flowerbeds, tidied houses, bikes left on driveways, glimpses
of swing sets above the tops of backyard fences.

Nate eyes me as we double-check the address of the house in front of us:
12662 Serenity Court. It's tan stucco with brown trim, above average in size. A
minivan is parked in the garage with the door open, and an SUV is parked behind it. The garage is clean but cluttered with toys on one side and a table saw
and drill press on the other.

Normal.

But that's the problem. Sometimes it's the normal that's deceptive.

Nate runs the plates while I keep an eye on our surroundings. When the
check comes back clean, we exit the vehicle. I glance over to the neighboring
house to the right and nod at the woman peeking out the window from behind the curtains.

"Is she the one who reported it?" Nate asks as we cautiously make our
way up the driveway.

I nod to tell him yes but don't confirm it aloud. "The caller wishes to remain anonymous."

"Mm-hmm."

It isn't surprising considering the call is a 10-16—possible domestic disturbance with a minor involved.

The pathway is lined with river rocks. Interspersed into the multi-colored
gray stones are some that are painted. There are a few that look like ladybugs,
others have indiscernible drawings on them, and still others with words written across the top, all obviously done by a child.

For the briefest of moments, I flash back to being a kid and making fun
of Emmy for painting the rocks on the side of her house. Just like a thousand
other kids have done. There's no correlation. Yet, I find it funny how she's been
gone for so long but, in the last few weeks, it's as if she's everywhere and there
is a memory of her in everything I see.

Nate's knock on the door is loud against the afternoon quiet. Standing about ten feet back with one hand on the butt of my gun, I wait for someone to answer, listening for the slightest sounds of distress inside the house as my eyes scan back and forth over my surroundings.

"Who is it?" a male voice asks on the other side of the door.

"Sunnyville Police Department. We'd like to speak with you for a moment," Nate says.

"About what?"

"Just want to make sure everything is all right in there. Neighbors heard some screaming going on, so we're going door-to-door around the cul-de-sac checking each house to make sure everything is okay," Nate lies in perfect good-cop fashion.

"Everything's fine here. Thanks for your concern."

"That's good to hear, sir, but I need you to open up so we can check for ourselves. It's a procedural thing."

There's movement to the right of me that catches my eye. A blonde-haired little girl peeks over the windowsill so all I can see is from her nose up. I smile softly to try to let her know we're here to help. She stares at me before ducking out from beneath the curtain and disappearing from sight.

"Jesus Christ," the man on the other side of the door mutters before the deadbolt slides and the door opens about a foot. "Everything's fine. See? Are you happy?" His voice is loaded with irritation as we get a glimpse of him for the first time. I take a mental rundown: Dark hair, blue eyes, a drip of sweat sliding down his temple. He's wearing a dress shirt with the sleeves rolled up to the elbows and tie loosened around his neck. His shirttail is untucked, and as hard as I try, I can't get a clear view of his hands so I can see what his knuckles look like.

"Thank you, sir. Your name please?"

"Ren Davis, but people just call me Davis."

"Thank you, Mr. Davis," Nate says, taking a step closer and placing a hand on the door to open it a little farther.

The man grunts in disdain. "You think I'm lying?"

"No, sir," Nate's smile is broad and disarming. "I'd just hate to lose my job for not crossing all the T's and dotting all the I's, if you know what I mean?"

"Goddamn government workers," he grumbles.

"Exactly." Nate moves his free hand from the butt of his gun and holds up two fingers behind his back.

There are two other people he can see in the house.

"I didn't hear any yelling."

"I didn't ask if you did," Nate responds, making sure the man understands he's on our time; we're not on his. "May I see the rest of the people in the house?"

The man's head startles at the request. "I'm home al—"

"I just saw a little girl run by," Nate interrupts. "I'd like to speak with her."

Davis exhales loudly, his irritation written all over his face before he steps back to reveal more of the scene behind him. There is a dark stain on the carpet where it looks like the plant sitting on the pony wall at his back had been knocked over and the dirt has yet to be vacuumed. From what I can see of it, the house seems clean, which makes that smear of dirt stick out.

"Keely, get over here," he yells, feet shifting, jaw clenched. With his movement, I can see one of his knuckles has blood on it and the others look a bit red. Nate notices it as well, and he slides a glance my way as I take a step forward.

"And your wife, too, please."

"My wife isn't—"

"There are two cars in the driveway, sir," Nate explains. "So I'd like to make sure she's okay, too."

"Was it that damn lady next door who called?" he asks. "She's so goddamn nosy. Always getting in our business. Last year, our dog pissed on her begonias and killed them so now she's out to get me back."

"No phone call," Nate says. "Like I said, we're just going door to door and checking to make sure everyone is okay."

Davis eyes both of us. His skepticism is etched in the lines of his face, but he shakes his head and calls back into the house. "Amelia. The police are here and want to make sure you're okay. Can you come down here to show them you are?" He steps back. "You happy?"

"Thank you, sir," I say, entering the conversation for the first time just as the blonde-haired girl peers out from the corner of the wall behind him. "What's your name?" I ask softly as I kneel to get on her level.

The poor thing is scared to death. Her eyes flicker to her father and then to me and then back to her father. She waits for him to nod before she responds. "Ke-Keely."

"Can you come here for a second, Keely?" I ask as her mother comes up behind her and places a protective *and* trembling hand on her shoulder. Keely looks back to her dad and waits again for him to consent before she slowly approaches the door. She reaches the threshold and just stands her hand clutching the arm of a worn teddy bear. There are matching smears of dirt on her cheeks that tell me she's been wiping away tears.

Her mother comes forward also but seems much more timid than her daughter. Amelia's hair is a mess and her red-rimmed eyes have black smudges under them from where her makeup has run. She crosses her arms over her chest to steady the shaking of her hands. Even though she remains several feet behind her husband, she never looks at him.

Alcohol or abuse.

It's my immediate assumption. It's definitely one of the two.

"Did you paint those super cool rocks over there?" I ask Keely, using the same soothing voice as before in an effort to earn her trust.

"Me and my mommy did." She barely nods, but it's enough for me to try to coax her away from her parents to make sure she is okay and not in danger.

"Can you show me which ones you did? I bet I can guess because they are so pretty like you."

She gives me a ghost of a smile, and the fleeting glimmer of happiness in her sad eyes breaks my heart. She looks up to her dad, who does not seem to be too pleased with my request. Those are the breaks, *asshole*. "Can I?"

He nods at her before shooting a glance over his shoulder to his wife.

Keely wrings her hands as she takes a few steps before looking back at her dad as if she's going to get in trouble. I gently place my hand on her shoulder to try to lead her over to where the majority of the rocks are—far enough away that I can ask her questions to make sure she's okay. My gut tells me she is—*for now*—but her mom's well-being is a whole other story.

"Which ones did you paint?" I ask as I squat back down.

She angles her head to the side and stares at me without responding, the willingness to talk to me moments before suddenly dissipating into the distance I put between her and her mother.

"I bet you painted that caterpillar there," I say, pointing to a rock and hoping I'm correct in my guess. The corners of her mouth softly turn up and her back straightens with pride. "And that one there?" I wait for her eyes to find what I'm pointing at. "That butterfly is so pretty. Is pink your favorite color?"

She nods but still doesn't talk.

I glance over to where Nate is talking to Mr. and Mrs. Davis, who are still standing in the doorway, and hope he is able to get Mrs. Davis alone for a moment.

"Ahh, there's a K on that one. I bet you painted that for your name."

"Yeah." Her voice is so quiet, and yet, I can hear the fear woven through it.

"That's what I thought. That definitely looks like a ten-year-old painted it."

She laughs, but there is no sound. "I'm not ten, though."

"How old are you then?"

"I'm five."

"No. Way. I thought for sure you were already driving. Are you sure the car in the driveway isn't yours?"

Another crack of a smile is followed by an adamant shake of her head.

"And that rock there . . . is that one of your teddy bear?" I ask, pointing to the rock and then her ratty bear.

She nods. "His name is Nemo."

"Nemo?" I smile. "I thought Nemo was a fish."

"Nemo can be whatever he wants to be."

"You are very right." Schooled by a five-year-old. "Do you know why my friend, Officer Nate, and I are here, Keely?"

She shakes her head, but her quick glance over my shoulder to her dad tells me she knows exactly why we are here.

"We're here to make sure you and your mom are okay."

"What about my dad?" Her brow furrows, and she wraps a finger in the hem of her shirt.

"Your dad, too. We're the police. It's our job to make sure everyone is safe at all times."

"Hmm." She twists her lips as if she's getting antsy, and I know I need to get to the point. It's only a matter of time before Mr. Davis gets smart and tells me I can't speak to Keely without a parent present.

"If you weren't safe, you could tell me, you know? Like if your mommy and daddy got into a fight, and it scared you, it's okay to tell a police officer like me. They're not going to get into trouble for it, but it would help me understand why you seem so upset." Her eyes widen. "Were they fighting earlier?"

"Mm-hmm." There is so much shame in her little expression that this hard-ass wants to pull her into my arms and give her a hug.

"When you get in trouble, does your mommy or daddy ever spank you?"

"Only when I've been really bad," she whispers, eyes downcast to watch her fingers, which are still twisting in the hem of her shirt.

"What's really bad?" Her eyes flash up, and then she shakes her head and bends over to pick up one of the painted rocks. She turns it over in her hand as she finds the words her innocent mind wants to use.

"When I come out of my room when they're fighting. Or if I spill my milk." She shrugs as if it's not a big deal but everything else about her posture says it is. "Or if I tell anyone about how they fight."

Fucking Christ.

"Well, I won't tell them that you told me anything if you don't. Okay?"

She stares at me with tears welling in her big blue eyes as she tries to figure out whether to trust what I'm saying or not. I slowly nod to reinforce what I've said. "Okay," she finally whispers, her eyes looking back to where her mom is speaking to Nate with her dad lingering close by.

"Does your mom ever get in trouble with your dad?" I ask, clocking her quick intake of breath.

"My mom doesn't spill her glass of milk." She breaks our eye contact and looks at the rock in her hand to avoid telling me more.

"Okay. Maybe she gets in trouble for other things though, huh?"

She nods subtly and then lifts her chin in pride as if she refuses to admit her mom is weak. She has no clue that her mom putting up with this might be a sign of weakness, but it is also a sign of strength to protect her daughter from the brunt of her dad's anger.

"Did anything happen earlier that you want to tell me about?"

"Keely? Tell the officer goodbye now," her mom says from the doorway where she stands with Davis's arm wrapped possessively around her shoulders.

Keely nods, her little blonde curls bouncing with the movement before she looks back to me. "I have to go now."

It's my turn to nod, even though every part of me is screaming to pick her up and put her in the squad car with me until I know for sure she's safe. "Can I give you something?" I ask.

She glances at them, torn between loyalty to her parents and the safety of a police officer, before looking back to me. "'kay."

I reach into my pocket and produce a sticker badge. It's left over from the elementary school appearance Nate and I made earlier today, and it's perfect. "I want to give this to you and make you a deputy officer."

"You do?" Her eyes widen and voice escalates with awe. Her innocence and willingness to trust is so palpable it breaks my heart.

"I sure do." I hand it to her. "I don't give these out to just anyone, either. It's an important job I know you can handle. This gives you the authority to call the police, dial 9-1-1 on the phone, if you ever get scared or are hurt or need help."

She stares at the sticker for a few seconds and speaks without thinking. "What about if my mommy needs help?" Her voice is back to being so quiet that I almost don't hear it.

"Definitely use it for that, too."

I hold my hand out for her to shake it. She giggles for the first time, and although I welcome the sound, I loathe it at the same time. Right now, I'm going to have to let her walk back into that house without knowing anything more about what happened other than the neighbor heard yelling.

"Nice to meet you, Deputy Keely."

She smiles again as she shakes my hand before turning on her heel and walking back to her mother, who ushers her inside and shuts the door on us without a second glance back.

Nate turns to meet my eyes and shakes his head as we walk down the front walkway.

"She walked into the wall," he murmurs with resignation, and I know he's referring to a bruise the mom must have had.

"She wouldn't give you anything else?"

"Nah," he says as he stares at me over the cruiser's roof. "She wouldn't step away from him so I could ask more. What about the girl?"

I know he isn't using names to keep the emotional distance, but for some reason, I can't do that this time. "Keely?" I reassert. "I didn't see any bruises, nor did she say she'd been hit. Daddy spanks her for telling anyone about mommy and daddy fighting, though. Or for spilling her milk. And probably just for breathing."

I grit my teeth as I rein in my anger. I can't stay detached. Not from a little girl with big blue eyes and soft blonde curls, who has most likely seen more than her fair share of adult things.

"Fucking prick."

"If only we could get Mrs. Davis alone to talk," I think aloud.

"We can try another time. Stop by for a well check when he's gone. Maybe she'll talk then."

"Perhaps." It isn't good enough. "He better not lay a hand on that little girl."

Nate eyes me for a second before nodding and sliding into the car to continue our day.

TEN

Grant

"WELL, THAT WAS CRAP."

I glance over to Nate as I crack the top of a Coke open and nod. "Sure was."

"And yet, we have shit to show for it. No arrests. No nothing."

"Makes for a long-ass day." I take a sip as I lean back and put my feet on the desk I'm currently occupying in the squad room. "If you want twenty-four hour lights and sirens, Nate, then you should move to San Francisco. I'm sure the guys there would kill for the slower beat we have."

"True. But I bet they're adrenaline junkies. They wouldn't be able to live without it." I nod at his statement. "Speaking of which, the fun stuff always seems to happen when I'm out sick."

"What are you talking about?"

"Lyle was just telling me in the locker room that you had a ninety five mile an hour-er the other day, but I don't see it on the reports anywhere." He leans his hip on the desk beside me and crosses his arms over his chest.

"It was an emergency situation. Lady speeding to get somewhere," I explain as I nod a hello to a few more guys coming in to roll call to grab their assignments. "I was trying to be nice and just gave her a warning."

"So, in other words, she was a hottie and you got her digits."

"Whatever." I roll my eyes and take another sip while thinking of Emerson. Her damn defiance and that haunted look she gets in her eyes every so often that makes me want to ask more questions than I know she's willing to answer. And then there were those little white shorts she was wearing the other day that make me think thoughts I shouldn't be thinking but can't help.

"Earth to Grant."

"Sorry. I was just thinking about that first call today—"

"The asshole husband and sweet little girl? Yeah, they got to me, too."

We both fall in silence for a second, and I hate that when I picture little Keely, an image of Emerson leaving school that day superimposes itself over it.

It's just because she's on my mind more than she should be. So much so that I'm projecting her situation onto another little girl when I know better.

"How about we liven up our day a bit and get some action?" he suggests.

"I get enough action. Thanks, though." I chuckle just to irritate him.

"Fucking, Malone. *Playboy cop.* One of these days a woman's going to come along and put handcuffs around that cold heart of yours, and then you'll be whipped like the rest of us fuckers."

"I'll be cuffed, huh?" I run a hand over my jaw and shake my head. "Sorry, I just don't see it . . . but if it makes you feel better about the white picket fence you'll be locked behind, then by all means."

"Some days I hate you, you know that?"

"Yeah, but you also love me," I tease as Liv, the dispatcher, walks down the hall and gives me a coy smile that makes parts of me regret walking away from her.

"Shit. I told you she still wants you," he murmurs as we both watch her hips sway.

"Me and my cold heart." I laugh.

"You sure you don't want to go out after shift is over?"

"Nah, I told the chief I'd stay and do some desk work." Like that's a fun way to spend the rest of my afternoon. "I'm reviewing the cold case files for him. Trying to prove how great of a detective I'd be. You know, gotta put a good foot forward if I want that promotion."

"You're kissing major ass with the extra hours you're putting in," he taunts.

"And I'm loving the OT pay. I can see a new patio and built-in barbecue in the near future."

"The offer stands. A bunch of us are meeting at seven o'clock at McGregor's if you get done in time."

"Thanks, but I have other shit to do."

"Ha," he says as he pushes away from the table. "Just make sure you remember her name in the morning."

"Whatever." I shoo him away as I sit up in my chair to play the role of desk jockey and tackle updating the stack of case files in front of me.

I shouldn't be doing this.

I shouldn't have let that old case file I went through get to me.

I shouldn't have looked at the picture of the victim and thought about both Keely and Emerson.

I shouldn't have let my finger hover over the search button on the file archives site where I had typed in "John Reeves, Emerson Reeves" and debated whether I should hit "find" so I could see what exactly it was that happened to her all those years ago.

And I definitely shouldn't be driving out to Miner's Airfield to where Desi said more often than not I could find Em.

But here I am, looking at the airstrip with hangars lining one side of the field and the airplanes parked to the right of them. On the far side is another parking lot and Blue Skies, an old skydiving business. It's been there as long as I can remember, owned by the Skies family, who last I heard, no longer had any family members in town to run or even care about the place. The lack of attention shows in the aged building and faded sign.

Why am I here?

Why am I chasing after someone who is clearly pushing me away?

Because I want to apologize to Emerson for the Tampax stunt? Yes *and* no, since she clearly beat me at my own game with the Viagra request. Or is it because every time I thought of Keely today, I kept seeing Em's face when she was little and I know it isn't going to go away any time soon.

More likely than either of those is the notion that if I see her, make sure she's okay, befriend her, then it might just ease the guilt I feel over breaking my promise to her when we were kids. My adult self knows it was the right thing to do. The little boy beneath the surface still feels the guilt every time I picture the look on her face as she walked out of Mrs. Gellar's classroom.

Em's always been there in my mind. Sure, it's been a long ass time since third grade, but in some sort of way, I knew I'd see her again. She isn't someone I could easily forget.

Great, now I sound like some goddamn Hallmark movie.

I scrub my hands over my face, and when I look up, there she is in full living color, walking across the tarmac as if she owns the place. In a flight suit with the sleeves tied around her waist and a purple tank top beneath it. If jumping out of airplanes is what she likes to do to relax after a long day, I can't imagine what else excites her.

As if sensing my attention on her, Emerson turns her head to face my direction, and I swear she knows it's me. It's the way she angles her head. It's the immediate straightening of her shoulders. It's the sudden stalking of her feet my way with a definite purpose.

I grin, can't help that I do. I love seeing her all worked up. After the day I've had, I'm more than ready for a good fight.

But fuck if she's not trying to distract me in other ways. Like that damn flight suit of hers. It should be the most unattractive thing on the face of the earth—dark blue, baggy, manly—but . . . goddamn. I'm a red-blooded male and would have to be dead not to notice how her tits bounce beneath that thin tank she has on.

I scrub a hand over my face to try to stop my thoughts from going where they shouldn't, but hell if they don't have a mind of their own.

They go there.

Oh, how they go there.

When she's about twenty feet away from me, she stops and plants her hands on her hips before calling out, "Airstrip's closed for maintenance. No one called for the police. You can turn around and leave now."

I stare at her behind my sunglasses with my elbow propped on the open driver's side window. "I'm off duty. And it's good to see you, too, Em." I grin just to irritate her.

"It isn't good to see you."

"Aww, now you're just trying to win me over with kindness."

She rolls her shoulders. "Sorry, we're all out of tampons today. You can take your emergency elsewhere." Sarcasm drips from her voice and only serves to antagonize me to draw this out.

"No emergency," I say as I climb out from my truck and lean against the door. "Just out for a drive and somehow ended up here."

"Convenient." She snorts. "You came. You saw. You can leave now because you won't conquer." She flashes me a dazzling smile that just might serve to warm that cold heart that Nate swears I have.

"And you used to be so sweet."

"And you used to not be so annoying."

"All this fire from you and I can't remember doing anything wrong."

There's a quick flash of something across her expression but between the distance and how fast it disappears, I can't read what it means.

But it's enough to know my comment got to her.

We stare at each other, both of us stubborn enough that we'd hold the line until someone looked away. While it might be fun to push her buttons, I know it isn't going to get me anywhere. That I know for certain.

"Is this where you jump from?" I jut my chin to the tarmac behind her.

"What's that?" she asks as she takes a step closer and furrows her brow.

"The other night at Desi's house, a bunch of you were talking about skydiving."

"And your point is?"

It takes everything I have not to tell her to stop when she begins to put her arms through the sleeves of her flight suit and zip it up. There's no need to cover up the perfection I was just admiring. And when I meet her eyes again, her knowing expression says I've been caught checking her out.

Can she blame me?

"Well?" she prompts drawing me back to our conversation.

"I assumed you guys are on a dive team or something."

She cocks her head to the side and chews on the inside of her cheek. "What do you want, Grant? You weren't just on a drive, and you just didn't happen to end up here . . . so what is it specifically that you want?"

Good question. It's one I need to ask myself.

I take a few steps toward her as she does the same to me until we're standing a few feet apart on the desolate tarmac.

"I'm not sure," I murmur, more to myself than to her, wishing she'd take those damn aviator sunglasses off so I could see her eyes. At least then I might have a clue as to what's running through that mind of hers.

"That's helpful. I'm sure the chief taught you that if you don't know what you want, there's no way you can get it . . . so, uh, good luck figuring it out. Like I said, the airstrip is closed." She lifts her eyebrows and turns as if to walk away.

My hand is on her arm in a flash. "What is your problem?" I snarl the words, and fuck if this woman can't rile me in a flash.

Why the hell am I chasing a ghost? Why do I even care?

She jerks her arm from my grasp but doesn't walk away. At least she's not running. "*You.* You're the problem."

"Why's that? What's so wrong with being friends?"

"I have plenty of friends, Grant."

"Not like me, you don't."

"Charming." She rolls her eyes and shakes her head. "Arrogance gets you nowhere with me."

"What is it, Em? What is it about me that irritates you so much? What did I do that was so wrong that when you saw me on the Fourth you already figured out you hated me?" I step into her, my thoughts flying and temper flaring even though I swore I was going to try to calm the situation.

"I'm not irritated," she sneers.

"Then what do you call it?"

"Hostile." She gives me a ghost of a smile.

"I call it being defensive." That one hit home. For a split second, her expression falls before she reins in whatever nerve I've hit.

"If you don't like it, then why are you here?"

"I keep asking myself the same damn question."

"Seems like we're at an impasse." It's that blasé tone of hers that irritates the fuck out of me. It's nothing but a mask she's hiding behind, and I want to rip it off so I can examine what's beneath it.

"I'm gonna wear you down."

Fucking brilliant, Malone. I went from swearing she was too much trouble to now vowing to wear her down.

"No you're not." Those hands of hers find her hips again.

"I know your type, Emmy. You're used to pushing people away the minute they get too close. You're used to calling the shots and being in control. News flash, I don't budge when I'm pushed and no one controls what I do."

"For the record, behind my sunglasses I'm rolling my eyes at your macho bullshit tantrum."

"You always did love to roll your eyes."

"Stop!" She clenches her fists and fights to regain her composure. "I told you, I'm not the same girl you used to know."

"Good thing," I say as I take a step toward her, "or else we'd be having this discussion while making mud pies in my parents' backyard and eating those gummy worms you used to love." There's a crack in her armor, a slight curl to one of her lips.

"There's nothing wrong with gummy worms."

I cringe in mock disgust. "And just like you're not the same girl, I'm definitely not the same boy. I won't try to sweet talk you into pouring salt on snails or covering your hand in honey to see how many ants we can collect. Bugs aren't my thing anymore."

She fights her smile, her ice melting. "What is your thing then?"

We stare at each other for a few seconds from behind the protection of our tinted lenses. I know I should walk away. This is complicated, and I don't do complicated, but instead of doing the smart thing, I dig in the front pocket of my uniform shirt for my card. "Here's my number should you ever want to call it and . . . I don't know . . . hang out at CVS with me."

This time, I'm granted her smile. "Thanks, but I'm all stocked up on drugstore supplies."

I deserve that. "Take the card, Em. I'd love to do something—as friends—and catch up on the last twenty years." I realize my mistake mentioning the past the minute I say it, but she saves me from fumbling with how to correct the statement when she takes the card from my hand.

"I'll take it, but I won't use it."

"Yes, you will."

"So sure of yourself, are you?"

"You've never been able to say no to me, Emerson."

"Oh. Please. Take your card back." She shoves it back at me, but she's laughing and that's a good thing.

"Nope." I take a step back. "You'll call. I know you will."

"I won't."

"You know you want to find out what happened to Miles O'Neal."

Her head startles as she remembers the little boy who used to have the biggest crush on her. "Whatever," she says as she slips the card into her pocket without looking at it. "For the record, Malone, I don't fall for sweet talk anymore."

"Then what do you fall for?"

Em freezes momentarily as she gets an odd look on her face that I can't read before shaking her head. "I have to get back to work."

Whoa. What? "*Work?*"

"Yeah. Work. I'm in the process of buying this place."

"The airport?"

"Blue Skies, the skydiving school."

"You are?"

"Yep." She turns her back to me and tosses over her shoulder, "Later, Phony Maloney."

So she is sticking around. Permanently.

Huh.

I watch her walk across the tarmac until she disappears inside the door of Blue Skies. Then I climb in my truck and start the engine but don't leave.

Fuck if I know why I'm working so hard for this woman.

But I am.

After a bit, I reverse, pull out of the parking lot, and smile.

She didn't correct me when I called her Emmy.

I guess I'll take any victory I can get, because I have a feeling when it comes to Emerson Reeves, they are hard fought and few and far between.

The question is, what the hell is the victory for?

ELEVEN

Emerson

"YOU REALLY NEED TO CLEAN THIS PLACE, EM."

I glance around the loft and shrug. I have a stack of clothes piled on a chair in the corner that I need to wash, there is a mess on the counter of the kitchenette—if I can call it that—and my bed's unmade, which is usual.

"You're the only one who visits, and since you already like me, it isn't like I need to impress you," I say to Desi as I pour some wine into her plastic glass.

"That's highly debatable," she says with a shake of her head and then begins to stack the paperwork on the card table, er, kitchen table—in some sort of order. "This place isn't exactly spacious. I'm sure it would look bigger if it were clean."

"Yes, mother." I lean back in one of my mismatched chairs and prop my feet on an opposing one. "Do you know how freaking exhausted I've been lately? Between Travis and Blue Skies and the loan, I feel like I don't have time to breathe."

"Then quit one of them."

"Easy for you to say. Travis manages the airfield. The odd jobs I do for him give me this glamorous roof over my head and the car to use. My job at Blue Skies pays the other bills. And the loan is going to hopefully be approved for enough so I can buy Blue Skies."

"And then what?"

"And then I can make it what I want it to be. Pull the rest of the money for the improvements out of my ass or something, but I have to have it first to be able to make it mine." I can see it all so clearly in my mind, but reality makes it hard to believe it just might happen.

"I have faith that you'll be able to."

"In the meantime, I'll deal with the exhaustion."

"But not too exhausted for sex."

"Huh?"

"Who's the flavor of the month?"

I nearly choke on my wine. "Who said there's a flavor of the month?" I laugh.

"Hmm . . . well the black pair of boxer-briefs over there in the corner tells me there was definitely a flavor—whether it be for the night or the week or the month is up for debate."

"Where?" And sure enough, when I look to where she's staring, there is a pair of Shawn's underwear bunched in the far corner of the flat.

"Which hot stud do they belong to?" she asks, holding her hand up to jokingly go through the possible names by ticking them off her fingers.

"Those would be Shawn's."

"Shawn? As in three months ago, Shawn?"

"Apparently." I bite my bottom lip and wonder how they got left there. "He hasn't stepped foot in here since asking if I minded feeding him a bottle while he wore a diaper."

"Shouldn't those be a diaper instead of undies, then?" We both snicker at the thought.

"Uh, yeah. I'm fearful of what else you might find when you actually do clean this place."

"It isn't that bad—" The lift of her eyebrows stops my response. "Okay, it is."

"Admission is half the battle." She laughs, but it's her eyes flashing and that mischievous smile sliding across her lips that gets my attention.

"What?"

"Nothing." Cue her cat-ate-the-canary grin.

"*What?*"

"You saw Grant, didn't you?"

And here we go again . . .

"Why would you say that?"

"No reason." She shrugs, but I don't believe her. "But you want to see him again, don't you?"

"Why would you say that?" I repeat.

"Because if you didn't want to see him again, you would have gotten rid of this." She lifts his card between her two fingers and hides her victorious smile.

"Uh, look around my place, Des, I obviously keep things I have no use for—case in point, Shawn's underwear. It's the same thing with Grant's card." I lift my eyebrows and hold her stare because I know she won't back down from this unless I do.

"I disagree."

"Great. Good for you." I rise from the chair, needing to move and think. My place is small, and all of a sudden, it feels like it's closing in on me. "He stopped by that airfield a few weeks ago. Gave it to me. If I cared, I wouldn't have thrown it in a pile of junk mail, now would I?"

"And if you didn't care, you wouldn't be so aggravated right now."

She's right, and she knows it, but I try to play it off as I grab a pile of clothing and toss it into the laundry basket. "I'm irritated because you won't leave this alone. He's become the main topic of conversation between us for the past few weeks. Why? Why is that?"

"You tell me."

"Don't give me your calm psychosomatic bullshit, Des."

"Remember when I came out to visit you on the skydive-my-way-around-the-country tour you took?"

Her change of topic gives me whiplash. "Where are you going with this?" Annoyed with her and this conversation when Grant already bothers me enough.

"We went to that bar in Podunk, Maryland. Remember that place?"

Of course I remember. Too many drinks and constant laughter. How good it was to see Desi again after meandering around the country for a few months while I got my head together after the death of my mother. "God, yes. We had fun that night, didn't we?"

She nods, her smile growing. "There was that bachelorette party there."

"Oh my God. Yes. They were so raunchy. And then the stripper showed up. We laughed so hard at how cheesy his moves were." I can still hear the hoots and hollers in my ears. "We thought he was a police officer coming to kick them out, and surprise, surprise, he was the entertainment."

"Yep. But he was sure nice to look at."

"Yes, he was."

"Remember when you saw him and said that there was something about a man in a police officer's uniform that you found super sexy and couldn't resist?"

Bingo. She just got to the point of this detour in conversation.

I stare at her from across the space where I've started to collect some of my clothes strewn about. "Desi," I warn.

"What?" she asks, voice feigning innocence as she blinks rapidly. "You can't resist a man in a police officer's uniform. Grant is a police officer. *In a uniform.* And yet, you're resisting him."

"There are a shitload of issues with your statement."

"Like?"

He lied.

And just like that, everything I've been fighting when it comes to Grant—every excuse, every bit of irritation, every bit of wanting him near but push him away—is summed up in those two tiny words. They have never before crossed my mind, but now they make perfect sense of why I've acted the way I have.

I'm immediately brought back to the pinky promise he made me. The tears in his eyes when I looked at him before I walked out of the classroom. The pressure in my chest that felt as if an elephant was stepping on it as I made my way to the principal's office.

Feeling like I'm suddenly lost in a fog I should have seen coming, I forget that Desi is sitting there staring at me and walk a few steps to sit on the edge of my bed.

It's stupid really. To hold that much resentment for so long over something. It's ridiculous to think that of all the shit I've been through, that is the one thing I've harbored subconsciously.

But it is.

He lied. He was the one person I trusted in that whole teeny, tiny world I had back then. He was the one place I felt safe. And normal. I believed him when he said he'd keep my deepest, darkest, most shameful secret, but he didn't. Instead, he told and tore my whole world apart.

Sitting here at the age of twenty-eight, I know what he did was right. Sitting here a survivor because of him, I know I should actually seek him out and thank him.

But it's so much easier to blame him.

It's much more palatable to pretend that he was the one who hurt me instead of the man I was supposed to trust above all others, my dad. It's so much simpler to blame my lack of trust or want for any kind of intimacy on the little boy I left behind.

"Em?"

The softness of Desi's voice is enough to make me blink. I'd been sitting and staring blankly at the dirty pair of Shawn's underwear for I don't know how long, and I look away. Panic claws its way up my throat as I try to process my epiphany without letting her get a glimpse of the past she knows only the gist of.

"Yeah. Sorry." I shove off the bed and begin collecting the rest of the clothes and shoving them into the hamper like a mad woman as I try to hide the trembling of my hands. "I just was remembering when we were kids is all. How his hair used to stick up all the time and how much I loved hanging out at his house after school."

"Hm," she murmurs, and I don't look up because I haven't quite gotten ahold of my unexpected emotions yet.

"I lost the train of thought. Where were we?"

"You were going to set me straight as to why you're resisting the hot guy in a police uniform. Then I was going to reiterate just how damn good he looks in said uniform and how if you're not going to let him get frisky, er, *frisk you*, then I'm willing and able to take your place. Then you were going to roll your eyes and tell me I'm jumping to conclusions and that he only wants to be friends, which we both know is a load of horseshit. I'd tell you when he looks at you, it's obvious he wants more than to meet you for coffee at Starbucks. You'd tell me I'm making it up, that you'd never meet him at Starbucks because you can't imagine spending that kind of money for a cup of coffee, but you know damn well you've thought about him in that way too and when he walks into the room your lady bits go all tingly . . . even though you won't admit it." She takes an exaggerated breath. "What have I forgotten?"

I laugh. Somehow, she has given me exactly what she didn't know I needed, her quirky and lighthearted sense of humor. It's drawn me back to the world I created for myself. One where the past is black, and day by day, I make my own future.

"Then I'd ask you why you're so invested in this person you just met and why you keep pushing him on me, your *best* friend, who prefers to keep shit with the opposite sex simple." I lift my eyebrows to challenge her.

Desi purses her lips and shrugs. "I'd tell you that he's nice and obviously safe. Besides, why is it so bad for me, your *best* friend, to want you to have another friend to count on should I walk out the front door and, I don't know, get struck by lightning."

"And out comes the guilt card," I say with gusto. "You forgot something, though, there isn't a cloud in the sky."

"It could be heat lightning."

"Whatever," I laugh. "You're just as irritating as he is."

"Oh, he's irritating, is he? That's a good thing. Pray tell." She props her chin on her hands like an eager child.

"A good thing? I call it a pain-in-the-ass thing," I say, playing along even though I'm the one who has been creating the friction with Grant. Then again, he did do the whole CVS stunt . . . so, I've earned the right to be pissed at him.

"But *why* does he irritate you?"

"Because he's a man. Because instead of writing me a damn ticket for going ninety miles an hour he called my bluff when I told him I was speeding because I was having a feminine emergency and took me to CVS to buy Tampax for me," I explain, fully expecting her to understand. When I look up, the sympathy I expect on her face isn't there. Instead, she's grinning ear to ear.

"Oh. *Wow.* So the guy saves you from a reckless driving ticket, a possible trip to jail, and is considerate enough to buy you tampons when he thinks you're having period problems. Man, he sounds like a *real* bastard."

"I assure you, it wasn't out of the kindness of his heart."

"You know what they say about boys who pick on you . . ."

"No. What?"

"It means they like you. And be careful, you're rolling your eyes so hard they just might get stuck there."

I do it again for show. "You forget, I knew him in third grade. He was much sweeter then."

"He still looks pretty damn sweet to me," she murmurs, her lips sliding into a mischievous smile.

"I told you, I'm not disagreeing with that . . . but he's *Grant*."

"Yeah, and I'm sure *Grant*," she says, mimicking the way I said his name, "wouldn't say no to a little fun with you." She rises from her seat and makes a show of tossing his card on the table before resting her hands on her hips and sighing.

"Uh-oh, should I assume you're going to finish the rest of our conversation for me?"

"You mean the one where you start making lame-ass excuses about why you can't call Officer Sexy back? Like how you think it's creepy to go out with a boy you knew in third grade, to which I'd counter with how there is *nothing* boyish about him now and who fucking cares? Is anyone keeping tabs? So what? You guys hung out, colored pictures of rainbows during class, and swung on the monkey bars together. None of those things matter when we factor in his hotness, his uniform, and his handcuffs, which I'd put a million dollars on him knowing exactly how to use. I reject that argument. It's moot. *Next*?"

I use a pair of tongs to pick up Shawn's underwear and put them in the trash while hating and ignoring the fact that everything she said makes perfect sense. But she doesn't know about how he fits into my past or the particulars. My mom is gone, my dad is out of jail and somewhere I don't care to know, so that leaves Grant and his family as the only ones who do. What about that? How does that make me feel?

I just don't know.

"I think you've pretty much covered the bases." I turn to face her.

"Good. Then my work here is done." She dusts her hands off as she grabs her purse, picks up the bag she set beside it, and holds it out to me. "I cooked for you."

My face lights up and my tummy growls. She really loves me. "Is there dessert?" I ask, skeptical as to why she had the forethought to bring me bribery. She nods. "You're forgiven for the inquisition."

"That's what I thought."

TWELVE

Emerson

"EMMY, SWEETIE, YOUR PARENTS HAD TO CANCEL THEIR PLANS. Your mom was called in to work. Your dad said he'd be by to pick you up in about an hour."

That icky, weird taste fills my mouth at the sound of Mrs. Malone's voice. "Okay." The word barely makes a sound when I speak it.

Grant nudges me. "That stinks, but at least we have another hour to play."

"You okay, Em?" Mrs. Malone asks from the porch. She has a funny look on her face that makes me want to cry and get one of her awesome hugs. But I know that will cause questions. According to Daddy, questions cause trouble, and trouble is punishable.

I don't like his punishments.

"Yeah. I was just looking forward to spending the night."

"I asked if you still could, but your dad said no. I guess you now have plans early in the morning, so it wasn't going to work. I'm sorry."

"'Kay." I shrug and lean back against the tree trunk next to Grant as she disappears inside.

My tummy doesn't feel good, and my hands are sticky with sweat.

"C'mon, Emmy, we can finish making our wine before you have to go."

I look at the mess we've made. The two bowls are full of smashed grapes Mr. Malone let us take off the vines growing in the backyard. My fingers ache from trying to mash the juice out of them. They made it look easy on our field trip to the grape vineyard last week, but for some reason, I don't think the clear juice will taste anything like the red stuff my mom drinks from her bottle.

"Nah, I don't want to make anymore."

"How come?"

Because I don't want to go home.

I close my eyes for a minute and just feel the cool breeze on my cheeks. I fight back the sting of tears burning against my eyelids and the sound of my heart beating in my ears. "Just cuz. I'd rather hang out with you."

"You never want to go home." He knocks his knee against mine. "How come?"

"This is our little secret, Em. You can't tell anyone or else it will hurt your mommy very badly."

My dad's whispers fill my ears and make my throat burn. I try to swallow over it, but I feel like I have one of the grapes stuck there, and it hurts.

"Just cuz." I pick up one of the rocks on the ground beside me and absently rub it against the inside of my arm until my skin starts to turn red. "Your house is much more fun than mine. You have brothers and a dog and stuff."

"Yeah, I guess. Stop it, will ya?" He takes the rock from my hand and tosses it. "We could always play at your house next time if you want. I'm sure we could find fun things to do there."

"Thanks, but . . ." I take a deep breath as I run my fingers over the red mark. "My house is kinda scary."

"You're just a girl. Girls are scared of everything. What's so scary about it?"

I shrug. "I don't know."

"You don't need to be scared, Emmy. I'm taking karate now. I could protect you."

There's laughter from inside his house, and we can hear it from where we're sitting in the backyard. The sound makes me smile even though my eyes are blurry with tears.

"My mom's drinking wine," he says. "You know what that means."

"Uh-uh, What?"

"Kissy, kissy."

"Ewww, gross."

"Yeah," he says as he picks up an escaped grape and throws it into our bowl. "She gets all giggly and then my dad will dance with her in the family room and sing horribly and then the grossness happens—they kiss."

"Ick." I giggle but hate that feeling in the middle of my belly that loves the idea of dancing and laughing. "My parents never kiss."

"They had to have kissed at least once because that's how babies are made and they have you, right?"

"True." I lean forward and grab a bowl as I try to forget what will happen when I go home in a bit. "But if your mom and dad kiss now, doesn't that mean they're going to have another baby soon?"

"That's not how it works, silly."

"Then how does it work, then?"

"I'm not quite sure."

THIRTEEN

Emerson

THE ASPHALT BITES INTO MY SHOULDERS AS I LIE DOWN ON THE tarmac in the chilly, early morning air. I needed to escape the loft and the fear that hung in the air from first my nightmare and then from the confusion I felt after the memory resurfaced of Grant and me as kids in his backyard.

"You don't need to be scared, Emmy. I'm taking karate now. I could protect you."

Guess I should have known he'd end up like his dad, protecting and serving—being the hero.

It suits him. The question is, does he suit me?

It's a tricky question, and one I'm not sure I'm ready to know the answer to. I've lived my life escaping my past, hiding it from anyone and everyone so that no one can ever look at me and blame my lack of success on *it.* Or just plain look at me differently.

But he knows.

He knows more than I might even know, and that's scary as hell to me.

So yes, I've blamed him unfairly, but it's so much easier to believe that truth—that he is more at fault than my own flesh and blood.

I've always thought of myself as a fair person.

There's no reason not to believe he isn't a good man.

And, as I sit here on the closed runway with the sun slowly rising in the east, I know I need to step outside the box I've carefully constructed and forti-fied around myself. I need to listen to Desi and her whacked logic and remem-ber what Grant said to me when we were nothing but kids.

I need to do the one thing I do every day in my professional life but can't seem to ever do personally: Leap before looking.

I need to follow my motto: Head up. Wings out.

FOURTEEN

Emerson

Me: For the record, I still think it's a bad idea, but you're right. You wore me down. Maybe we can get together sometime for a few drinks. Your call.

Grant: I knew you'd see my ways. How about tomorrow at six at McGregor's?

Me: That works.

I stare at the string of texts and feel as if my throat is closing up on me. At the same time, I'm excited and nervous and more than anything, afraid. My interactions with men are fleeting. I don't use them for their conversation skills. Sure, we go out and have a good time, but on my part, things are superficial. The first time they lie, they're gone. And if they can make it past that first test, then when they start wanting more . . . when they want to talk about our pasts and have that kumbaya moment where we realize we are meant to be together forever, they stop being of interest to me.

I only live in the now. I only live in tomorrows. I can only cope with the future I make for myself.

But there is something about agreeing to meet for drinks with Grant that is making me nervous.

"You are *not* chickening out. I will *not* let you," Desi says as she applies another coat of mascara to my eyelashes.

"I'm not chickening out. And I don't need all this makeup. It isn't as if he hasn't seen me before without it."

"Shush. Every woman needs to act like she cares on a first date." She takes a step back to admire her handy work. "If you don't act like you care, then you're not setting the standard of how you expect to be treated."

"But this isn't a first date, and I think you're off your rocker."

"You *are* hoping to be frisked and handcuffed at some point, aren't you?" I just raise my eyebrows at her when she gives me that motherly look. "Then shush and let me finish my masterpiece."

She busies herself with curling my hair when throwing it into a ponytail would be fancy enough for me. There's no use arguing with a determined Desi so I let her have her way.

"I may have done something in a knee-jerk reaction."

"What did you do?" She sets the curling iron down, plants her hands on her hips, and looks at me with warning in her eyes.

"You remember Paulo, don't you?"

"Hmm, that Latin lover you had fun with for a while."

"That's him." I begin to bite my lip, and she squeezes my cheeks to stop me from messing up my perfectly lined lips.

"Why are we talking about him, and why are you nervous to tell me?"

"Well, I kind of agreed to meet up with him tonight."

The reaction I expected is immediate: Brow narrowing, lips parting, eyes blinking, nostrils flaring. "Why in the ever-loving hell would you do that?"

I shrug, because now that I've admitted it out loud, it does sound ridiculously stupid. If I'm not afraid of meeting up with Grant, then why did I go and give myself an out for this evening should things get too serious? I don't shrink from her stare even though I want to.

Her eyes narrow as she pins me immobile. "You just showed your cards, Em." A broad grin slides across those heart-shaped lips of hers.

"My cards?"

"Yep. You wanted an out because you know tonight is going to be epic, and you're not used to epic. You're used to good sex with a pretty face but nothing behind it."

"I beg to—"

"Shush." She picks up my phone from the table beside me and tosses it onto my lap. "Tell Paolo thanks but no thanks. You're all Latin-lovered out for the time being and you're handcuffed to other obligations tonight."

"Fine." I huff out a breath as I pick up the phone.

She's right, but hell if I'll admit it aloud.

"Is this seat taken?" I ask as I slide into the booth across from Grant. Nerves idle within me, only serving to reinforce Desi's assumption that I'm already treating Grant differently from how I treat other men.

I'm not exactly sure how I feel about that.

"Hey there." Grant's face transforms with the warmest of smiles that makes parts inside me that I wasn't aware could tingle come alive. We stare at each other for a moment, almost as if there's a silent acknowledgement that the defensive banter we're used to has no place here tonight. "You look beautiful."

Uncomfortable with compliments, I blush. "You clean up pretty nice, too. Although, you can never go wrong with your uniform."

Did I really just say that?

"So I've heard." A smile plays at the corner of his mouth, referencing back to the first time we ran into each other, but his eyes hold so much more amusement in them.

A waitress comes and takes our drink order. There is ample chatter in the bar but an awkward silence between us. I play with the cardboard coaster, uncertain what step to take in the uncoordinated dance.

"Emerson."

"Hmm?" I meet his eyes.

"There's no pressure here. I just wanted to spend some time with you, have a few drinks, and catch up on what you've been up to. That's it."

Our eyes hold as I struggle with laying down my defensive shield and not running away at the mere mention of catching up. Catching up means talking about the past, and my past is dark as hell. And while he may already know the gist of my dark, it's hard not to be defensive over something I've always protected.

"I'd like that." I don't remember telling myself to say the words, but there they are, out in the open, making his grin widen and his shoulders relax some.

"Good. That's good. Because as stupid as it sounds, I've really missed you."

FIFTEEN

Emerson

BECAUSE AS STUPID AS IT SOUNDS, I'VE REALLY MISSED YOU.

Every time Grant laughs, I hear him saying those words. Every time he smiles, I hear him saying those words. Every time I want to clam up at a seemingly benign question, I remind myself that I only have to tell him as much as I want to and think of him telling me he missed me.

Those are words I don't think anyone has ever said to me.

"So tell me something . . ." Grant laughs as he slides next to me in the booth and then pushes a fresh drink in my direction. His eyes are a little glassy, but his smile is still kind and his humor is becoming of him. "What's a girl who's scared of heights doing jumping out of airplanes?"

"Who said I was scared of heights?"

"Oh come on," he says, patting my thigh with a tipsy flourish and then absently leaving it there. "This is coming from the girl who refused to climb Old Man Conner's tree because it was too high off the ground. You threw up all over his daisies just thinking about it."

I stare at him, flustered by his hand. *Warm.* On my thigh. *Contact.* When I should really be freaking out that Grant is talking about a memory I have no recollection of, but I can't. All I can focus on is the ache currently simmering a few inches from where his fingers reside.

"I don't remember that," I say and shift to face him in the booth. He moves his hand back to his drink and shakes his head.

"You don't? I made fun of you for weeks, calling you Daisy until you got so mad you told me you weren't going to come over to play anymore unless I stopped."

Daisy. The taunt ghosts through my mind, but I don't recall it. What I do know is that, even back then, we played games with each other. Sure, they were different games, innocent fun, which is a far cry from the one we are playing now. But just like then, I still feel the same sense of ease with him. The same level of comfort. I can't remember a single time I didn't want to go over to the Malone house to play. It was safe there.

I felt safe there.

"No. It's been a long time." I take a sip of my drink and hate how my fingers tremble ever so slightly.

"But skydiving, Em?"

I shrug. "It's my peace. For a few seconds, everything is there, laid out before me. It's calm. There's no noise in my head, just the wind in my ears, and I'm forced to only think of the present."

"The present is good."

"Mm-hmm." There's a look in his eyes that says a million things at once, and I can't pinpoint any of them, so I don't try. "So, a cop, huh?"

"Yep." He places his arm across the back of the booth, and his fingers automatically toy with a strand of my hair, as if it were the most natural thing in the world to do.

"I could have figured. All those hours playing cops and robbers on our bikes. You always had a hero complex, wanting to save anyone and everyone . . ." I'm stepping too close to no-go territory for me. Panic tries to find a foothold, but I ignore it and smile at Grant. "Remember that time we found—"

"The bullet shell smashed in the street, and we swore someone had broken into the Parker's house and robbed them?" His eyes light up.

"Yes! And we called 9-1-1 because we thought we were real detectives." I smile wider, thrilled to remember this memory and not draw a blank and feel stupid.

"Yeah good ol' Chief Malone read me the riot act for distracting officers from legitimate calls." He shakes his head and laughs.

"How is your dad?"

"He's good. Real good. He retired about eight years ago, and I think it's driving my mom crazy that he has nothing to do. Occasionally, the force asks him to consult on an old cold case, which keeps him occupied, but other than that, he's just busy being a grandfather to Luke. That's Grayson's son."

"Oh, I didn't realize any of the infamous Malone boys were hitched," I say with a wink.

"We're not. Gray's is a long story. Too long for right now."

"So no aspirations to be chief and follow in your dad's footsteps?" I suddenly want to know everything about him.

"In time." He shrugs and takes a sip of his beer.

"Give up the routine of sitting in The Donut Shoppe's lot and doing paperwork?"

"I actually despise donuts, and I'm more of a sit-in-the-parking-lot-of-Starbucks-on-Main-Street-and-do-my-paperwork routine kind of cop."

"A cop who hates donuts?" I hold my hand to my chest in mock horror. "Isn't that sacrilege? No wonder you haven't been promoted yet."

"It is. Actually, I'm up for detective right now. I debated for the longest time whether I wanted it—more responsibility, more politics, and less being on the streets, which is what I love doing the most. But, we'll see. It's a long process, and I'm not sure who else has applied for the position. Time will tell . . ."

"You're a Malone. In this town, that's gold, isn't it?"

"Depends who you ask." He angles his head and stares at me for a beat, curiosity owning his eyes. "So tell me, you're buying Blue Skies? Why that? Why now?"

I take a long sip of my wine and marvel at how easy it is for the words to want to spew off my tongue. It's unsettling; yet, I find myself wanting to tell him. I find myself wanting him to know I've been okay.

"My mom was a nomad at heart. We wandered around a lot, moved from one town to the next the minute she started to feel too settled." I smile softly as I think of her. Her crazy, colorful clothes. Her unconventional ways. Her fierce protection of me from everyone.

"That must have been hard with school and—"

"She homeschooled me for the longest time. Trust was hard for her." *As it is for me.* "If I was learning about American history, we'd take a road trip and live in Washington, DC for a while. We were fluid."

"That must have been hard, always moving around."

"It was isolating in a sense because I didn't have many friends, but it was rich in so many other ways." I shrug. "One year, we went through Missoula where the fire jumpers are based. It was hot and humid, but I sat and watched them practice their jumps for hours. I knew right then I wanted to try it."

"Did you?"

"Not then. I was too young, and if my mom wasn't willing to trust a babysitter watching me for an hour, she sure as hell wasn't going to trust an instructor to get me safely back to earth."

"True." He traces the line of condensation on his beer bottle with his fingers.

"I had to wait until I was eighteen for my first jump."

"That's a long time to wait."

"It was."

"As non-traditional as it was, it sounds like she taught you a lot."

"It was all I knew." I smile softly at him, the memories of my mom and the life she created for us so clear despite all the time that has passed. "We stopped moving around when I was a senior in high school. I could have easily taken my GED and opted out, but my mom refused to let me. She wanted me to experience high school for at least one year."

"That had to have been brutal."

"Yeah, well, when you live in a bubble, sometimes you don't have the cognizance to notice or even want to care. It was definitely an experience. Gone were the lazy days where we'd finish our lesson and then take a tube and float down river wherever we were to celebrate another day lived to the fullest. I fought her on it, but she wanted to settle for the first time in almost ten years. Little did I know it was because she was sick."

"I'm so sorry, Em, I didn't know." His hand covers mine and gives it a squeeze.

"How could you have?" I squeeze his back, loving that he keeps his hand there even when the moment is over. "She was fine for a while, but after I graduated, I spent most of my time taking care of her. She fought hard, but the years of being ill finally took their toll. During it all, the one friend I had made in high school was my moral support. That was Desi." I lean back in my seat and lift my eyebrows. "This is all a little too depressing, isn't it? Let's change the—"

"It's okay. I want to know."

I stare at him for a moment, hesitant to talk about one of my deepest sadnesses, but realize he loves his mom just as fiercely as I loved mine. He'll understand why the grief robbed me of so much for so long. And some days still does.

"When my mom died, I took to her ways to cope. The day she passed away, I headed to a local skydiving school and jumped. It was the only way I thought I could be free of all the grief I felt. At first, I couldn't concentrate, but then I hit this moment in my jump where there was silence in my head. It was almost soothing, and it forced me to think of what was next and where to go from there. It was liberating and sounds ridiculous . . . " I look down to where my fingers are fidgeting with the coaster. It's weird how easy it is to tell him about it when it's something I don't think I've ever given a voice to before.

"It isn't ridiculous at all."

I clear my throat and drop the coaster before continuing. "So, I said goodbye to Desi, packed my belongings, and traveled all over the country, going from jump site to jump site until the grief stopped drowning me."

"How long ago was that?"

"Eight months."

Grant lifts his eyebrows, obviously surprised that it happened so recently, and I laugh. "By some weird twist of fate, while I was on my adventures, Desi ended up moving to Sunnyville. It shocked the hell out of me when she told me. And then I found out Blue Skies was up for sale. I felt like all roads were leading me back here when it was the last place I ever thought I'd return to."

"Plus there was me," he says, adding a flash of a smile and tip of his beer against my wine glass.

"Plus there was you."

His finger twirls absently in my hair again, and I hate that it sounds so cliché, but my heart really does beat faster.

"I'm glad you came back, Emerson. I know it was probably hard, but I'm—"

I press my lips to his to shut him up. I don't want to think about how hard it was stepping foot in this town or how I expected everyone to point fingers as I walked by and remember me as "that girl."

I just want to feel now.

And I know I take him by surprise. It's in the hesitancy of his lips at first. It's in the tightening of his finger wrapped in my hair. But it only takes a split second for him to react, to part his lips and give me the taste of beer on his tongue. For him to consume my mind and shift it away from the hundreds of thoughts I don't want to be thinking.

He's heat and warmth and soft fingers on the underside of my jaw. A hand demanding more on the small of my back.

His kiss is thunder and lightning, a tornado and a tsunami, all in one fiery package that makes me forget about the here and the now, makes me want more when more with Grant scares the shit out of me.

The noise of the bar slowly seeps into my conscience as the kiss ends and we move apart. Grant's eyes are hazy, but his lips are turned up in a cocky but adorable grin that makes that sweet ache our kiss ignited burn bright. He shakes his head, and it mimics how I feel: *Holy shit, I just kissed Grant Malone.*

Our eyes hold for a beat as the bar carries on around us before I suddenly feel shy under his unwavering gaze. I look down to my empty drink and stare at the scars on the wood tabletop as I try to process the sensations running through me. Desire, surprise, and euphoria mix and meld as heat creeps into my cheeks as he studies me.

The realization hits that I have no idea what to do now.

Cue the nerves and unexpected panic.

Typically, I'd make the next move. We'd decide whose place to go back to and have some unapologetic fun.

But this is Grant.

Didn't I already know this—the emotion, the sensation, the fallout—would be different before I kissed him?

"Hey, Em?" Grant's voice calls through the haze of my overthinking. "I'm going to save you from the panic that's written all over your face." He scoots closer and lowers his voice. "I had a great time tonight. I'd love to do it again sometime—*soon*, but I think it's best if I go home now. I've had a long and crappy shift, but you were the highlight of the day."

He leans in, and I suck in my breath, thinking he's going to kiss me again. The ache in the delta of my thighs only deepens with the scent of him near, but he bypasses my lips and goes straight for my ear. "While I appreciate a forward girl as much as the next guy, you need to understand that you're not in charge here. I know you want to be so you can control the pace and set the standard—make sure you maneuver me into the next move so you can stay one step ahead and on the run—but that's not how I operate. I'm flattered you wanted to kiss me because, hell, if I haven't been staring at your lips all night long wanting to do the same, but next time, I make the first move. A man only has so many firsts in life, and I'm sure kissing you is going to be a damn good one that I plan on taking."

Without another word, he scoots out of the booth and stands to full height. I stare at him, fully expecting those flecks of gold in his eyes to be amused, but they are anything but. They are dead serious with a mix of temper and concern that I don't quite get. He smirks before looking over to the waitress and holding a finger up with a nod.

"Question is, Emmy, are you still stubborn? How bad do you want that next kiss? How long are you going to hold out just to make a statement while denying your body what we both know it wants?"

"You bast—"

"Next round's on its way. Have a drink on me, will ya? At least when you put your lips on it, you'll know it's from me."

And with another flash of that cocky grin of his, Grant turns and strides out of the bar without ever looking back.

"Arrogant son of a bitch," I mutter, angry at more things than I care to count. That he rejected me. That he maneuvered me. That he just put me in my place. That he called me out.

That he's leaving and all I can think of is how I want more.

"Thank you," I murmur as the waitress slides a fresh drink in front of me.

What exactly just happened? My head spins at the turn of events and my logic tells me I should be pissed off at him.

But I'm not.

Because as much as it pains me to admit, he was right. I am panicking. I am trying to figure out why everything seems so damn different when it comes to Grant. I don't do different. I run the opposite way from different.

Yet here I sit. I haven't run away. I didn't even protest. I just let everything that happened happen, and I know damn well I'd do it again . . . because that kiss of his felt like none I've ever experienced before.

And I hate that I love it.

And I detest that I want more of them.

The bar buzzes on around me as I focus on being angry with him. It's so much easier to be pissed off than to accept the fact that he scares me. And the good kind of scare.

So I look at the drink he left me in consolation. I fixate on that cocky smirk of his that makes me want to strangle him and kiss him at the same time. And I tell myself I need to stand my ground. I need to be the strong girl I've tried to be instead of allowing myself to fall prey to the way he makes me feel.

He's crazy if he thinks I'm going to drink this. I won't just out of pure spite.

No one handles me.

No one tells me what I can and can't do.

And no one walks away from me unless it's on my terms.

Lost in thought, I pick up the glass and take a sip. "*Shit.*" I just fell right into that one. I stare at the dark red liquid for a long moment before shaking my head and tilting the glass all the way up until it's empty.

SIXTEEN

Grant

"YOU HAVE A LIST OF CASE FILES ON YOUR DESK. THERE ARE A dozen highlighted and the remaining not. Do you need me to do anything with them?" Nate asks as I pull up in front of my house and sigh when I see Grayson's car there.

I'm not in the mood to deal with my brothers. Not after my sleepless night complete with requisite cold shower after thinking about Emerson and her damn kiss.

"Earth to Grant?"

"Sorry. I just pulled up and the assholes are here." Nate chuckles in my ear, knowing how much it annoys me when my little brothers show up unannounced and help themselves to my beer and food. "Um, the list of case files . . . do you have time to pull them up and request the rest for me? The non-highlighted ones. If not, I can do it tomorrow before shift."

"Nah, I'm killing time. Today's quiet as fuck. This will give me something to do. When's the test?"

"Written is in a few weeks. The interview, I'm waiting on the chief to decide. Stetson is making noise, though, and bringing up that crap with my dad—"

"Old fucking news that should have never been news."

"I hear ya." I roll my shoulders as I prepare myself for the onslaught of my brothers. "Thanks for your help. See you tomorrow."

I hang up the phone and push open my front door.

"Ah, look, asshole number one is here," Grady says as he lifts up a beer in greeting.

"And he looks grumpy," Grayson chimes in.

"What are you two pricks doing here?"

"It was a rough little league game," Grayson says, shaking his head.

"Seriously? That's what you two have to stress about? Get out." I throw my thumb over my shoulder but then realize Luke is nowhere to be found. "Should I be concerned that Luke isn't here?"

"Nah, he's with Mom and Dad. We were given a warning to go cool our jets because we were showing him a perfect example of what poor sports look like." Grady grins, and I can only imagine what happened to get that rebuke from our mom.

"So you decided to come here and crash my party?" I head to the refrigerator to grab a beer and grit my teeth over the stash they've already depleted.

"You were having a party?" Grayson sits up like a damn meerkat.

"No. No party. Go home." Shaking my head, I unholster my weapon and walk the few strides to place it in the gun safe before turning back to my brothers and lifting my eyebrows. "I don't see you moving."

"Oh, that means Grant has a *lady* coming over," Grayson harasses, drawing the phrase out and earning a laugh from Grady.

"No, it does not mean I have a *lady* coming over."

"Good thing," Grady says, "because she'd be sorely disappointed in your skills." He makes a show of trying to thrust his hips.

"Says the man who could fuck a cheerio without breaking it," I reply, just to shut him up, but I chuckle when Grady holds a fist over his mouth, points at me, and yells, "Burn!"

He never takes anything seriously.

"You really let him around Luke when he's like this?" I ask Grayson. "No wonder mom took him for a while."

"It's nothing like that," Grayson says, always one to defend whichever one of us is being picked on. "We treated the team to pizza after they won. We had beer and mom asked Luke if he wanted to spend the night. Of course he did—*it's Mom*—so we figured we'd come over here and bug the shit outta you."

"That is, unless you have a *wo-man* coming over," Grady chimes in.

"No, I don't have a wo-man coming over," I say and throw a pillow at Grady. "Get your feet off the table."

Grady laughs, tucking the damn pillow behind his head. "He so has a woman coming over if he's telling us to get our feet off the table and shit."

"You guys are fucking idiots." I plop down on the love seat and glare at Grady until he plants his feet back on the floor.

"So, big brother . . ."

Nothing good ever comes from Grayson starting off the conversation with those three words.

"It's been a long day, let's not start whatever it is you're trying to start," I warn.

"Why do we come here? It's nothing but abuse with him," Grady says as he takes another sip of his beer.

"Exactly. If I'm so abusive to you little shits, don't let the door hit you on the asses on the way out." I know they're not going anywhere, but I do our typical song and dance anyway.

"Not until we hear the scoop." Gray sits forward and rests his elbows on his knees. "Rumor is you were at McGregor's the other night with Emerson."

"And?"

I can still taste her kiss.

"Well, obviously, you tracked her down, so what gives? You bumping uglies yet?"

I can still see that panicked look in her eyes.

"What is it with you guys? Can't I go out with a woman for a few drinks and just be friends?" I ask.

I can still see the determination in her scowl when I walked away.

"No," they both say in unison, and it prompts me to sip my own beer because I have a feeling it's going to be a long-ass night.

The wood porch creaks as I sit on its steps and breathe in the fresh night air. It's the first time I've had a chance to think all day, and considering Mutt and Jeff are inside catching up on the Giants game, I'm taking the liberty.

It's fucking ridiculous that I have to go outside of my own house to relax, but it isn't like they've listened to me the thirty other times I've kicked them out in the past three hours.

"Needing a break?" My father's voice startles me.

"Dad?"

I look up to find him walking up my driveway. I was so lost in thought I didn't even notice when he pulled up across the street.

"I figured you might need help kicking your brothers out. They were quite the pair earlier." He steps closer, and his silver hair looks pale yellow under the porch light.

"I heard mom wasn't too thrilled with them."

He shrugs, as if to say boys will be boys. "You know your mom. She'll take any excuse to get Luke alone for a few hours so she can spoil him rotten."

"Thank God for him because that means she lays off me."

"True," he muses before taking a seat beside me on the steps. "What's troubling you, Grant?"

I glance over at him, and even though his face is etched with perpetual lines of worry every retired cop seems to have, he still has the impenetrable stare. A proud and defiant angle to his chin and jaw. "Who says something is wrong?"

He raises his eyebrows, as if to ask me if he's misinterpreted my demeanor, which prompts me to blow out a sigh, lean my head against the railing behind me, and close my eyes. He gives me a few minutes to gather my thoughts without pressing me.

"I saw Emerson the other night." It isn't much, but it's a start.

"So I heard." He nods but doesn't look my way. Damn nosy people already talking. "What seems to be the problem? Did you have a bad time?"

I chuckle. "Just the opposite, actually." His silence tells me he isn't following me. "It's complicated."

"Most things are. If they were easy, they wouldn't be worth figuring out."

Father logic is not what I need right now, and yet, I find myself needing to talk through everything.

"She kissed me."

It's his turn to chuckle. "And that's a problem, why?"

I push up from the step and walk back and forth on the sidewalk before shoving a hand through my hair. "Because . . . because I don't know how to handle it."

"You've never had trouble handling a woman kissing you before if I recall correctly."

"But this is different."

"Why?"

"Because it's her, and it's . . . everything she's been through and . . ."

"How do you know what she's been through? Has she told you? Has she talked about it with you?"

"No."

"Then how do you know?"

"Because I was the one who told Mrs. Gellar, Dad. I'm the one who turned her life upside down."

"You mean that you're the one who saved her." His voice is even but serious, and it stops me in my tracks. I stare at him with hands at my side and every part of me confused about one goddamn kiss amidst a million other kisses I've had.

"She saved herself, Dad."

"Good. I'm glad you know that. Because you're right. She did. But let me ask you this, son, if she hasn't said a word to you about what happened before, why does it bug you? How do you know it bugs her?"

"How can it not?" I raise my voice without meaning to. It's just that this is like talking to a brick wall instead of talking to the one person who should be able to give me insight on how to handle this.

"If you met her on the street, you would have no idea about what she's been through. So, if she doesn't tell you, then that's how you have to treat her."

I look at the moon above and shake my head. "Easier said than done."

"It is, but it's her past, Grant. Sometimes you have to accept the other's history and just leave it there—as the past. It isn't fair if you use it against her when she's never even brought it into the equation."

"I would never hold it against her."

"Aren't you already, though?"

"What are you talking about?"

"You wouldn't be out here stressing about Em if you didn't know her history . . . so that in and of itself says you're already using it against her."

I reject the idea immediately, but the longer he just sits there quietly and stares at me the more his reasoning makes sense.

"You're right." I walk to the end of the pathway and then walk back before throwing my hands out. "Never mind. This is just my crazy talking. A few drinks and a kiss should not amount to me stressing this much about a woman."

He gives a non-committal noise.

"What's that supposed to mean?" I snap.

"It doesn't mean anything," he says cool as can be.

He thinks I'm wrong. I take a sip of my beer but refuse to acknowledge he's right.

Because I am wrong. This is Emerson we're talking about. Of course, I'm going to think harder and be more careful with her.

Fuck.

"You don't understand. You wouldn't get it."

"Try me."

"There's this look she gets in her eyes. It's like she's perfectly fine. She's funny and outgoing and God is she feisty . . . but every so often, there's this sadness, this uncertainty that flashes in her eyes, and it fucks me up. I don't know how to make it go away."

"You always did want to save people."

"Not that again." I roll my shoulders and walk over to the bucket of ice on the porch and grab a new beer. I need it. This conversation is way more in-depth than I ever intended it to be.

"No. I'm serious. It bugs you because you want to fix it. You want to swoop in and take the pain away, but I'm sorry, that's something for her to deal with. You can't save her from something that happened twenty years ago."

"I know . . ." I hang my head and resign myself to this bullshit feeling I have. When I look back up, I meet his eyes with more certainty than I feel. "How bad was it?"

The widening of his eyes tells me my question takes him by surprise. "That's not for me to tell you, Grant." He glances back to the house where Grayson and Grady shout inside at the game, and he gets a ghost of a smile on his face hearing my brothers. "I'll tell you this, though. If it had been one of you, I would've stepped on the other side of the law."

Our eyes hold, and I know he means it. For Chief Malone to even utter the statement, it had to have been bad. Worse than I thought. Worse than I could even stomach considering. He slowly rises from the step, his still-fit body moving a little slower these days, and pats me on the back.

"You've always liked Emmy. I'm not surprised all these years later that you still do." He takes a few steps toward the screen door before turning back to look at me. "Tell me this. Is there any time you've been with her when she hasn't gotten that look?"

"Yeah." I laugh. "When she's mad at me." I think of the fire in her eyes when I left the other night. Her temper was hot, but it put color in her cheeks and made her spine stiffen some.

He smiles. "Seems fitting. She always did have a stubborn streak."

"She sure did."

"So how'd you leave things with her?"

"With her pissed off at me. She wants to be in control so she can keep her distance."

"Kinda like you," he muses and draws a quick glare from me that doesn't faze him. "And let me guess, you let her know you were the one who was going to set the pace?"

"Damn straight."

"Your mom would disagree with your line of thinking."

"So, don't tell her."

"I won't." His laugh rings out, and I know my brothers have heard him so our time is limited. "You already have your answer how to handle her, Grant."

"What?" I tip the bottle up again.

"Make her mad at you. It might be frustrating. It might not be pretty, but then again, matters of the heart never are."

No one said anything about hearts.

SEVENTEEN

Emerson

H E'S STILL THERE. I CAN FEEL HIS EYES ON ME.

I huff as I lay the first of six canopies out on the ground and inspect it for any sign of tears or any seams that might need to be re-stitched before I can repack it in its rig.

"Who pissed off Malone?"

I look over to where Travis stands with his sleeveless shirt on, his baseball cap bent at the brim, and a red rag fisted in one hand, and I am thankful that my sunglasses hide the glare I shoot him. The sweet, old man who manages the airstrip doesn't deserve my vitriol, and yet, his comment has fanned the flames of the irritation Grant is causing.

"How do you know Grant?" I ask.

"Everyone knows the Malones in this town. They're as much a part of Sunnyville as the grapes that grow on the hills around here." He adjusts the brim of his cap.

"For the record, I didn't piss off Malone." I walk to the other side of the canopy, which is starting to billow from the breeze, and force myself not to rush through the inspection. These chutes stop our falls, so it definitely doesn't pay to be hasty.

"If you didn't piss him off, why's he been sitting at the end of the runway for the past hour?"

"He is? I didn't notice." I don't even venture to look the way of his police cruiser where it sits blaringly out of place because I refuse to give either man the satisfaction of knowing I have been paying attention.

"Yep. Right out there." He lifts a chin and eyes me as he tries to figure out if I'm lying or not.

"Humph." At this point, the less I say the better.

"D'ya want me to go find out? Maybe he's interested in jumping. Having a Malone jump here might be good for business."

"Nah. He's not worth the wasted breath. Thanks for the offer, though." I squat and begin the methodical process of packing the first canopy into its pack under the scrutiny of both men. Each minute that passes only serves to annoy me further, until I'm huffing every few seconds to show some kind of resistance.

"Well then . . ." Travis's boots scuffle against the pavement until they are in my eyesight, prompting me to look up at him. "I put a to-do list on your desk. It isn't too long, but . . . it has to get done."

"I'll take care of it in a bit. Thanks." I focus again on the task at hand. After a minute, I hear him turn and head back inside, leaving me alone to ignore Grant.

Over the next hour, I work on the next five packs, well aware of Grant's presence. Reminded of the kiss we shared. Of the demands he laid down. Of the frustration I feel every time I think of him—*which is a lot*—when I don't want to think of him at all.

I don't get handled. I don't get played.

Even being firm in those beliefs, the scene from the bar plays in my mind over and over again. By the time I'm done, I'm hot, I'm tired, and I'm irritated to all hell.

"Whoa, where's the fire?" Leo asks as I slam into the front office of Blue Skies, stomping my feet like a tantruming toddler.

"Don't ask," I grumble as I walk right past him and into my office, shutting the door behind me. He stares at me through the glass door, completely confused, so I turn to stare out the window, which of course directly faces where Grant is parked.

For the love of God.

My phone is in my hand, and I'm pushing send without thinking this through.

"Officer Malone."

"Don't give me your 'Officer Malone' bullshit. How about Officer Stalker? Or Officer Asshole? It looks like you're a real crime fighter, sitting out there at the end of an empty runway."

His chuckle fills the line and grates on every nerve that isn't already shredded. "You never know where a crime may occur." There's a slow, relaxed drawl to his voice.

"Huh."

"Like it sure is a damn crime how good you look in that flight suit when you bend over and fold those parachutes."

I click end on the phone and stew as I pace the short distance of my office like a caged animal. He's going to sit out there for over two hours and that's all he has? *The jerk.*

I hit send again and grit my teeth harder with each and every ring. He finally picks up on the fourth one, right before it goes to voice mail.

"Seriously? That's the best you can do? You've gotta work on a better line than that."

"I knew you'd call back."

"You're infuriating."

"Perhaps."

"Definitely." I sit in my chair and then stand again, too antsy to stay still. "Why have you been sitting out there all day? If it's just to annoy the hell out of me, you've succeeded. Whatever else it is you're trying to do, it isn't going to work," I lie.

"Mmm."

"What's that supposed to—Oh . . ." The light bulb comes on. "I see what you're doing here, Malone."

"What's that?"

"You're trying to get the upper hand."

"I am?"

"Quit answering everything I say with a question, damn it." I throw my hands up in exasperation.

"Why does that bug you?"

"Grr. You just did it again!"

"Do you think I don't know that?" he says, and I can hear the smile in his voice, but I'm not going to play into his question carnival again.

"I'm not letting anyone control me or any situation regardless of what one particularly annoying male may think."

His chuckle fills the line again, and I hate that with as mad as I am at him, it's still sexy as hell. "You sure about that?"

"Damn sure."

"You might want to double-check that hill you're willing to die on."

"Why's that?" I narrow my brow as I stare out at his cruiser.

"Because I've already gotten what I came for."

"Yeah? What's that?"

"You to be thinking about me."

The line goes dead.

And before I can make it out of the building, temper leaving smoke in my wake, his cruiser is already pulling out of the driveway onto the main highway.

"You to be thinking of me," I mutter in disgust.

Because he's right.

I am.

And hell if he didn't just get the upper hand.

EIGHTEEN

Emerson

"HELLO?"

Crap. Why did I think calling him would be easier than texting him? That deep rumble of his voice. The memory of his kiss on my tongue. The thought of that smile that makes butterflies take flight in my stomach.

Get a grip, Em. It's Phony Maloney.

"Will you stop trying to win my friends over to your side?" Impatience owns my voice as I look through the sliding glass door into Desi's kitchen, where she is flitting around oohing and ahhing over the delivery.

"Come again?"

"The Williams Sonoma basket. The gift certificate for a cooking class. I mean, really?" I huff and put a hand on my hip.

"What? I'm not allowed to send a thank-you gift for having me over the other night? You know my momma, Em. She's real big on manners."

"Manners, my ass."

"What was that about your ass?" He starts with the questions as responses bit again.

"Nothing. Never mind."

"Were we hanging up now?" The humor in his voice sparks my temper, and I hate that he's getting exactly what wants from me—a response.

I can't help it.

"I forget. Were you always this annoying when we were younger?" I grit out as Desi pulls out a bottle of some kind of olive oil and holds it to her chest as if it's the Hope Diamond. I roll my eyes as I wait for his answer.

"Not that I know of, but I do remember you being a pain in the ass."

"I was not."

"Hmm, you sure about that?"

I hate that his comment gives me pause. That it leaves me standing in Desi's backyard, scouring my memories and wondering if he's right. I can't recall any one situation to disprove him.

"You there?" he asks, his voice full of humor and feigned impatience.

"Stop trying to distract me and stop trying to buy my friends."

"That's a steep accusation."

"What else do you call it?"

"Positioning?" He chuckles.

"This conversation is over."

"Okay." There's silence except for his breathing on the other line. "If it's over, why haven't you hung up?"

"Because you need to hang up first." Oh my God. I'm reverting to being a teenager here. Why does he make me act this juvenile?

"Ladies first."

If the phone was old school, I would have slammed it down, but it isn't, so I can't. There is absolutely no satisfaction in pushing end.

"This is absolute heaven," Desi calls from inside the house. "Come look."

"I'll pass," I say drolly as I move to the open door to watch her fawn all over what really is a gift tailor-made for my best friend. I can't be blind to his consideration, but I know deep down he's doing it to irk me and *position* himself in my life.

"Isn't this the sweetest thing? And all for having him over the other night. They don't make men like him anymore."

It's the second time I've heard that, but it strikes my ear differently from when she said it before. "The other night?"

Desi looks up, doe eyes blinking rapidly before looking back down to sort through the bagged pasta and gourmet sauces included. "Yeah. The barbecue."

"But that wasn't the other night." I step forward and brace my hands on the counter across from her.

She waves a hand my way. "Semantics, Em. The other night, a few weeks ago, it's all the same thing."

No it isn't.

And as she prattles on about this and that and truffle oil and terms that sound cook-ish but I'm not certain, the phrase "the other night" continues to replay in my head.

Have they gotten together another night to conspire about me? Desi told me she was busy last week when I asked her to go get some sushi, but she wouldn't tell me with what. Did she and Grant meet up so she could help him plan ways to win me over?

Correction—annoy the hell out of me.

Winning me over would mean he has a chance, which he doesn't. Okay, maybe he has a tiny one, but that's beside the point.

Another cry of pleasure from Desi comes at the same time a thought crosses my mind that makes my stomach drop. What if they weren't conspiring ways to win me over? What if I pushed Grant away enough that he moved on to Desi, and now they're seeing each other? My mind stumbles over the thought.

I'd like to say good riddance. That I don't care.

Not about how he delivered pizza to the crew at Blue Skies unannounced and for no reason. Or how a box of tampons with a blue ribbon tied around it somehow ended up on the hood of my car parked in the airport lot. Admittedly, that was so not cool, and while I'm sure every guy working that day thought it was strange, I still might have sat with it in my lap, fingers playing with the bow. I might have remained there, watching planes take off and land until sunset because I was so lost in thought and at peace that I hadn't noticed the day slipping away. I hadn't felt that way in the longest time.

My gut churns because as annoying as everything he's doing is, I hate the thought of him just . . . moving on. Would Desi do that to me? Would Grant?

"Nothing's worth it if it's this much work."

His words from the barbecue ring in my ears and cause a slight flutter of panic. But then I see Desi smile a mile wide and know she'd never do that to me, but that doesn't rule out a plotting session. And still, I hate that the thought of him charming someone else—because that is what he's doing to everyone else while he does nothing but provoke me—doesn't sit well with me.

Then I realize that . . . his plan has worked. He's maneuvered me. He's making everyone around me like him so when I tell him to take a hike, they'll all tell me I'm crazy.

Goddamnit, I've been handled. Positioned. Whatever he wants to call it.

Screw him. I'll find a way to outwit him. To put the ball back in my court. To take back control of the situation. The question is, when it seems he's always a few steps ahead of me, how do I do that?

I guess I could have started by accepting Josh's invitation last night to meet up for a little late-night rendezvous. But I didn't. I told him I was busy when in reality it was me, my hot plate, and *Big Brother* on television.

Did I seriously give up what I know from experience to be an incredible orgasm for Grant Malone? Or let's get real, multiple orgasms? It is Josh, after all.

I sure as hell did.

This is not good. He's already winning, and I haven't even read the damn rules yet.

"Em, look at this." Desi holds up some kind of kitchen contraption in glee.

Is that basket a bottomless pit of bribery?

"If you don't snatch that man up, I will."

Apparently, it is.

I groan.

How can I compete with this? How can I fight back when he is single-handedly persuading everyone around me to take his side?

He may think he's in the lead, but he hasn't seen me in action yet.

Now I just need to rewrite his damn rules and figure out a plan of attack of my own.

NINETEEN

Grant

"ARE YOU TRYING TO GET OFFICER OF THE YEAR OR SOMETHING?" Nate asks with a laugh.

"Huh?" I look up from where I'm lacing my boots to see him hauling two file boxes stacked on each other into my family room. "Are those the archived files?"

"Yep. Your patio cover."

"Ain't that the truth?" Those are some serious boxes.

"There are two more in the car, but please, stay where you are and sip your coffee," he says, holding his hands out in the stop motion. "I have nothing better to do than haul your shit around."

"I knew you were good for something," I say with a laugh as I make a show of sitting back into the couch, propping my feet on the coffee table, and making a loud *mmm* sound as I sip my coffee.

"Asshole."

"The one and only."

He laughs as the screen door shuts behind him while I get up to move the boxes out of the way. I have the lid off and am running my fingers over the tabs of the files to make sure they are the ones I asked for when he comes back in and drops the remaining two boxes with a *thud*.

"You got some dust on your uniform," I say as I point to nothing on his chest.

Nate lifts his middle finger as he makes his way to my coffee maker and pours himself some as if he lives here.

Cold Case File #865593: Jensen Darby Homicide - 6/12/2001
Cold Case File #628336: Mimi LaRuby Missing Person – 1/04/1995

"Make yourself at home. Oh wait, you already have." I say, only half paying attention as he opens the fridge and pulls out the creamer.

Cold Case File #458899: Matthew Larsho Homicide – 9/10/1992
Closed File #713920: Emerson Reeves – Sexual Abuse – 10/23/1997

Nate says something, but I don't hear him because I can't tear my eyes off the label on the file.

"These files . . ."

The green folder is several inches thick. Unfortunately, I know from experience on other case files I've looked through what it will contain. Evidence. Physical exams. Testimony. Psychological evaluations. Pictures.

Fucking Christ.

Pictures.

"Yeah, what about them?" Nate asks as my stomach revolts at the thought of what is contained in between the covers. The coffee that tasted like heaven minutes ago, feels like acid eating a hole in my stomach. "Is something wrong? They were the ones on the list on your desk."

"The list?" I ask absently but can picture it perfectly. The list of names where I was so preoccupied with curiosity about Emerson's past—what happened to her father and how bad it was for her—that I wrote her name down at the top of the paper. I can see it clearly. Her name in block letters with two lines beneath it. How Nate could have assumed it was for emphasis when it was nothing more than me doodling as I thought of her.

"Is everything okay, man?"

"Yeah. Sorry. I thought I forgot one, but I see it here," I say to distract him from coming over and inspecting the files.

"The boxes were ready to go when I picked them up, so if something is missing, blame the admin who pulled them. Not the messenger."

"No worries. I'm sure they're all here."

I had never intended to look up her case. Obviously, it had crossed my mind, but I had decided it was a line I wasn't going to cross. Now that the file, and the information inside it, is at my fingertips, I can't stop staring at it.

I can't stop wondering.

"Earth to Grant." Nate stands in the middle of my family room with his cup of coffee in hand and makes a show of looking at his watch. Our shift is about to start.

"What? Sorry." I shove the lid on the box and walk away from it.

For now.

I don't think any type of distraction is going to prevent me from thinking about the closed file nestled in the box.

"Something wrong?"

"Nah. I'm good." I force a smile and walk over to grab my cell and wallet so he can't look too closely.

"You ready?"

"Yeah. Sure. Let's go."

But as I shut the door, I give the box one last look.

Fuck.

TWENTY

Grant

"Officer Malone?"

"Yo." I shove my chair out and wheel across the aisle so the receptionist can see me.

"Delivery for you."

Nate eyes me from across the aisle of desks, and I shrug. "For me?"

"Who's subpoenaing you now?" he asks.

"Beats the hell outta me," I say as I grab the manila envelope and turn it over in my hands. There's no return address on it.

"Hey, Sue?" I call to the receptionist before she retreats back to her desk.

"Yeah?"

"Who delivered this?"

"Some guy. Kinda cute if you like the tall, dark, and handsome vibe." She flashes me a smile.

"Yeah, sounds just like my type." I roll my eyes and get a few laughs from the guys as I slide a finger beneath the flap and open the envelope.

There are waivers filled out with my name and yellow "sign here" tabs everywhere a signature is required. At first, I'm confused as to what all this is. Then the gift certificate works its way out from between the papers.

"Blue Skies Skydiving School Gift Certificate: Good for one tandem flight with lead instructor, Emerson Reeves. Unless of course you don't trust her . . ."

Look who just stepped onto the playing field with a Hail Mary right off the bat.

Took her long enough.

I chuckle, which has Nate narrowing his eyes at me. "I gotta make a call," I say as I stand and make my way out of the station away from the other officers who like to gossip like little old ladies.

"Blue Skies, this is Emerson, how may I help you?" Her voice sounds like goddamn sex. And she's doing it on purpose because her caller ID tells her exactly who's calling.

"You tell me. How can you help me?"

She murmurs a sound that I swear to God sounds like how I imagine her fingernails scratching over my balls would feel, and that thought alone tells me I'm so far fucked when it comes to her it isn't even funny. "I see you got my gift."

"I did."

"Just thought I'd pay a little token of appreciation to our officers who protect and serve."

"I think I'm the only one here who received a gift certificate, though."

"Yeah, well, you're a special case." She laughs. I can picture her standing on the tarmac with that damn flight suit on, her baseball cap pulled low as she peers down the stretch of runway from behind her aviators. "Are you calling to schedule your flight time?"

"Not hardly. I told you, I don't trust anyone, especially when it comes to jumping out of an airplane."

"Not even little ol' me?"

"Especially not little ol' you." I laugh, imagining she has a dartboard somewhere with my picture on the bull's-eye.

"What's wrong, Malone? Should I call you *Daisy*?"

"Touché."

"What then? Are you that afraid of a woman being in control?" Her voice is coy, playful, but I can hear the underlying tone of curiosity in it.

"Not in the least, Em. I actually think it's sexy as hell. What's even sexier is a woman who demands control from everyone else except for the one she's with behind closed doors because she trusts him implicitly. Now that? That's a turn on."

I hear her suck in a breath in reaction, and I love knowing that I've gotten to her somehow. "Well, I guess we both have control and trust issues we need to work through, don't we?"

"I thought that was what we were doing."

With a chuckle, I end the call and let out a long, controlled sigh.

Fuck. I may be getting the upper hand, but hell if I'll take any hand about now so long as it's hers.

TWENTY-ONE

Grant

"HELLO, ARE YOU OFFICER MALONE?"

What the?

I look out the open passenger side window to see a fresh-faced kid, late teens, dark features, about five foot eight, two hundred pounds.

"Can I help you?" I eye him. My immediate hunch is that he's harmless, but I don't like that I can't see both his hands.

"Yeah, I have a delivery for you."

"You what?" I sit a little taller in the driver's seat and study him closer.

"A delivery. Here." He shoves a pink box through the window. "From The Donut Shoppe."

"The Donut Shoppe?"

"Yes. There's a note on the top."

I eye him warily. "'Kay. Thanks." The kid starts to walk away. "Hey, wait." I dig into my wallet and pull out some ones to give him.

"Thanks," he says, but I'm already looking at the top of the pink pastry box. "Donut think you've won this battle – Emerson"

I stare at the writing and do the only thing I can, laugh.

"What's that?" Nate asks as he slides into the car.

"Emerson."

"She's sending you love notes on donut boxes now? I thought you were the one trying to get the upper hand."

"I'm trying, dude. Believe me, I'm trying."

"Well, try harder. If you play this game any longer, your balls will become bluer than your uniform."

"Fuck off."

He smirks. "At least someone would be getting some then."

"Whatever. Dude, you wish—"

"All units. 10-16 at 12662 Serenity Court."

I don't even have to glance over to Nate to tell him to respond. He already has the radio in his hand as I throw the car in gear and flip the lights and sirens on.

It's Keely's address.

We make it there in minutes, and I turn the siren off but leave the lights on as I turn into the neighborhood. We're parked in the driveway and out of the car, my fist banging on the door in seconds.

"Sunnyville Police Department, open up." I pound a few more times as Nate steps on the planters to try to see inside the front window.

"There was yelling and screaming." I round at the sound of a feeble voice, my hand automatically going to my weapon, but I ease off when I see the elderly neighbor from across the street.

"What else?" Nate asks as he steps forward, leaving me to man the front door. I hear words such as "shouting" and "threatening," but when it comes down to being a witness to anything, she didn't see much.

I pound again. "Mrs. Davis, open up. We just want to make sure you and Keely are okay in there."

Glancing around, I note that a few other neighbors are home from work already, a few even nosing out of their houses to see what the problem is. More rocks are painted in the entryway—hints of a normal, creative child or signs of a little girl escaping the fighting inside her house.

Just as I'm about to pound again, I hear the deadbolt slide, and the door cracks open. Amelia Davis stands there, tears staining her face and hair a mess.

"Mrs. Davis? Is everything okay in there?" I ask, voice gentle. I'm well aware that Mr. Davis might be on the opposite side of the door, judging her every answer and the according punishment.

"Yes. It's fine. Everything is fine," she says unconvincingly as she widens the door without my asking so I can see inside. My eyes scan her person for bruises, but she's wearing long sleeves mid-summer. "He's not home, if that's what you're worried about."

"Momma? Is everything okay?" Keely's timid voice calls from inside.

"Yes, sweetie. The nice officers from the other day stopped by. They wanted to see the new rocks you painted." She lies easily, and I'm not sure if I respect or detest her for protecting her child.

"He did? He is?" Awe fills her voice as she peeks her sweet face beyond the corner wall, blue eyes wide as a smile spreads on her lips.

"I did." I nod and play along with the mother as I eye Nate to take over the questions while I separate Keely from their conversation.

"I'm sorry, Officer. It was just a fight." I overhear Amelia say to Nate as I walk Keely down the path and away from the front door.

"Are you here because my mom and dad were fighting again?" she asks and breaks my heart.

I nod, not wanting to lie about the obvious and needing her to trust me. "Mm-hmm. It's our job to make sure everything is okay." I kneel so I'm eye to eye with her. "Is everything okay, Keely?"

She stares at me with eyes that have seen way too much, and her bottom lip trembles some before she nods ever so slowly.

I could kill the bastard for putting that look on her face. Wring his goddamn neck.

"You sure?"

She glances back to her mom and then down to her fingers, which have found their way to twist into her shirt. "Yeah." Her little shoulders shrug. "Mommy had me go in my room and be quiet. I don't know what happened."

"Okay." I nod. I can face down a six-foot suspect and know if he's lying or not, but give me a five-year-old little girl, and I'm lost in fucking translation. "What were they arguing about?"

"Stuff." She shrugs again. Twists her fingers. Shifts her feet. "Money and just stuff."

"Okay. Were you scared for your mommy or daddy at all?"

She finally lifts her eyes to meet mine, and I can see her fighting wanting to betray her parents. "Yeah. I don't like when they fight. Nemo and I hide under the covers and sing 'You are My Sunshine' so we don't hear them."

"That's my favorite," I say, thinking of how my mom used to sing it to Luke when he was a baby. "And a very *smart* move on your part."

"Did you really want to see my rocks?"

"Yes. Of course. That was why I came to talk to you. I've found some new favorites." I glance over to Nate to see where we are in the call, and his slight nod and stiff expression tell me he's getting no-fucking-where. "The poop emoji one is my new favorite," I say, trying to keep a straight face.

Her giggle makes me smile, though. "You know what a poop emoji is?"

"Of course I do. Don't let the uniform fool you. I know poop emojis like the best of them."

And every time I say "poop," I get another giggle, a sound that should be a norm for her but probably isn't. Déjà vu hits me in the moment, much like it did the last time I was here. I shake it, along with the image of the strawberry blonde little girl in my memories, away but come up with an idea.

"Tell me something, Keely, do you like to keep secrets?" I ask in a hushed voice.

"You mean like secrets that will get you in trouble or secrets like a super spy?"

"Like a super spy."

She nods, her smile widening. "I can keep super spy secrets. Of course I can."

"I thought so. I mean, I gave you the badge last time, but I was pretty certain you were spy worthy."

"I am. I am."

"Sometimes, when you're a secret spy, you have to leave coded messages for other secret spies so they know what's going on."

"You do?"

"Yep." I nod, knowing I need to wrap this up but also needing to get this point across. "Sometimes the littlest of signs tells other spies that things are okay or they're not okay."

"Really?"

"Definitely."

"So what does that have to do with me?"

"I need you to be a super spy for me. It's my job as a police officer to know that you and your mom are okay at all times." I can see her little wheels turning, and I speak before she can question it too much. "So, I'm thinking that we use your rocks as our secret code."

Her eyes and smile both widen, pride in her work replacing any skepticism she had seconds ago. "My rocks?"

"Yes, but you can't tell anyone else or else the secret spy code will be broken, and then we'll no longer be spies."

"I can keep a secret."

I eye her as if I'm doubting her, but then when I smile, she knows I trust her. "Good. I think we should come up with a certain picture or word, and if you paint that on a rock, then I know you're afraid and need help for you or your mom."

Skepticism is back, but it isn't as deep when she asks, "What word or picture?" Her voice is barely audible.

"You can pick it."

"Hmm." She twists her lips and thinks so hard it's adorable. "Watermelon."

"Watermelon?" I laugh, not expecting that answer in a million years.

"Yeah, watermelon. I'm not that good at painting, though. I know you're just saying it because I'm a kid and you're an adult so you have to say it so you don't hurt my feelings . . . but I promise I can really paint a good watermelon."

"I believe you." I love the little glimpses of her personality that are starting to shine through her fear. "Will it be green and—"

"No. It will be red with black seeds; although, mommy only buys the kind without seeds and those are no fun because there are no seeds to see how far you can spit."

"Got it. A red rock with black seeds." I glance at the painted rocks already there and know I'd be able to spot it in a second. "Good choice. Now, we need to decide on a place to put our secret signal. Where do you think?"

She bites her bottom lip and looks around. "How about right there at the corner of the sidewalk?"

"I think that's an excellent choice. See? You're already proving what a great secret spy you're going to be."

"How often are you going to check for the code?"

"As often as I need to," I say, not wanting to overcommit but needing her to understand she's safe.

"What are you two talking about?" Amelia asks as she comes up behind Keely and puts her arm around her daughter's shoulders.

"Secret spies and watermelon," Keely says.

"Is that a show on Nickelodeon?" Amelia asks.

"Yep." Keely looks back at me one last time with a soft smile before her mom ushers her to the house and shuts the door without another word.

"Did you get anywhere?" I ask Nate as we climb in the cruiser.

"You mean did she admit that the bastard hits her so she wears long sleeves in summer to hide the bruises? No. No matter how many times I told her that we'd protect her, that all she has to do is press charges to protect Keely, she kept denying anything was wrong."

"Son of a bitch."

"'Bout sums it up."

I pound my fist on the steering wheel. "I'm sure we'll be back again."

"We can't help her unless she wants the help."

"And in the meantime, the girl is in the crosshairs. That seems fair," I say, frustrated disgust edging my tone.

"Yep." He blows out a sigh. "At least we have donuts."

"No, you have donuts," I say, hating their smell currently filling my car.

TWENTY-TWO

Grant

"CALL EMERSON AND TELL HER YOU'RE RUNNING LATE AND then turn your car around and go home."

Desi sputters on the other end of the phone. "You're cute and all, but that doesn't excuse you for being a bossy asshole."

I glance over to where Emerson is sitting at the bar about fifty feet away. Her strawberry blonde hair is tucked behind her ear, her fingers twirl the straw stuck in her drink, and those long, tan legs call to every man in here. The thought alone has me itching for a fight or any excuse to get my anger over the Keely situation out of my damn system.

"I'll owe you one," I say between gritted teeth as another man sits beside her and offers small talk she doesn't encourage. But still, she smiles. Still, she's goddamn gorgeous.

"How do you know I'm meeting her for a drink?" Desi asks.

"Because I'm sitting in a back booth at Davenport's, drinking away my shitty day, and I'm watching Emerson sit at the bar and ignore every man who dares pull up a stool next to her."

Desi snorts. "So, in other words, you're pissed at every man going near her, and the sight of them has started the testosterone-laced caveman part of you to finally make your goddamn move instead of sitting on the sidelines, playing games like you have been."

"I am not playing games, Desi. I am making sure she knows she can't control this like she's controlled every other relationship she's ever had . . . at least according to you." I let that dig sit there to let her know if she talks about our conversations to Emerson, then I'll talk, too.

"Are you blackmailing me, Officer Sexy?" she teases.

"Just stating the facts, ma'am."

Another man. Another clench of my fists.

"Well, it's about damn time. I was getting dried up over here waiting for you to act."

"Yeah, yeah."

"Just so you know . . ." The four words every man cringes when he hears. "You're I'm-in-control shit doesn't fly with me any more than it flies with Em. I'm only calling her and doing what you ask because you two need to get over this cat-and-mouse game and eat the damn cheese already."

"Goodbye, Des."

The call ends, and I sit back and wait for Emerson to pick up her phone. As if on cue, the moment I think it, her phone rings. She looks at her watch while talking to Desi, and she shrugs, flinging one hand up as if to question Desi when she's nowhere in sight. She may be irritated, but that only serves in my favor in the end.

As soon as she sets down the phone, I'm already ringing her.

"Hello?"

"Hey, I'm heading out to you right now for my jump."

There's resignation in her sigh over the connection, and I physically watch as she slumps her shoulders back against the chair. "Not today. I can't."

"I thought you said any time, though." I push her buttons.

"Yeah, well, any time is not right now. Besides, I'm not even there."

"Where are you?"

"I'm meeting Desi."

"What's wrong?"

"Just a shitty day all around."

"You and me both. Wanna talk about it?" She's silent for a moment as a man sits too closely next to her and she shifts to regain her personal space. "Tell him to back the fuck off, Em."

It takes a second, but I can tell the moment awareness hits her. Her spine stiffens. Her fingers tighten on her drink. But ever cool, she takes her time scooting back and looking around the bar. She finds me right away. Our eyes lock. A smile flickers and fades before I hear her sharp intake of breath on the phone.

"Tell him, Emerson. Tell him you're with me."

Her brow narrows, but she doesn't move. "I'm meeting Desi," she says into the phone instead of taking the ten steps to tell me face to face.

"No, you're not. She isn't coming. I called her and told her to turn around and go back home." Temper stews on that gorgeous face of hers. "*Tell him.*"

She doesn't say a word to the man next to her, who is still eyeing her, but rather slides some cash across the bar, pushes her chair in, and then stalks over to me, phone still held to her ear.

She stands in front of me, and every part of me begs to kiss her. Fuck her. Anything with her because it feels like forever since we kissed and a lifetime of foreplay that has in no way been satisfying.

"You don't get to tell me what to do."

Okay. This is how she wants this to go. "Have a seat."

"No."

"Have a seat, Emmy."

"It's Emerson." She glares, her feet shifting as she lowers her phone from her ear. I eye the seat next to her and then look back to her.

"Sit."

"You're an asshole, you know that?" she sneers.

"Yeah. Probably. But I've had a shitty day, so fucking sue me if I want you to sit and have a few drinks with me and maybe see why your day was so goddamn crappy too . . ." I shrug. "Sit."

Her emotions wage a war across her face, but I can see reluctance flash through those eyes of hers before she lowers herself to the seat across from me. Without looking away, I lift a hand to the bartender and motion for another round. We don't speak until the drinks arrive, tension mounting between the two of us for some odd reason.

Foreplay.

I smile at the thought, and I know it pisses her off.

"Since when did you become such a stalker?"

"Me? Stalker?" I laugh, and this banter is just what I need.

"Yeah, word has it that you've been asking about where I live."

"You mean the one question I asked Desi?"

Her lips quirk as she fights a smile. "Yeah, that question."

"If I'm going to stalk you effectively, don't I need to know that info?"

She's still trying to make up her mind whether she likes this idea, just like I'm still trying to figure out if I like her living in the loft of a hangar doing odd jobs in exchange for rent and transportation. Even if it's for the harmless caretaker, Travis Barnhardt, it's still another thing on her plate to do when she already does too much.

"Being a cop and all, I figured you had better means than loose-lips Desi."

"I happen to have a soft spot for loose-lips Desi," I say just to irritate her.

"No shit. Give the girl William Sonoma, and she'll sing like a canary."

I laugh, which draws looks from others around us. "I'm afraid to know what else she confessed."

"That's for me to know and you to never know." Her eyes glance up from her drink and hold mine.

"So, you had a shitty day, too?" I prompt.

She shrugs. "Something like that. What about you? Why was your day so bad?"

"I had a donut delivery even though I hate donuts. My cruiser still smells like them."

There's her smile. "Must have been donut torture."

"Yep. It was. Waterboarding and the smell of donuts are right up there together." I lean back in the booth and take a long sip of my drink before pushing the bowl of pretzels and nuts across the table toward her. "A call we had today got to me."

"Want to share?"

"Can't . . . I just can't," I explain, when what I need is to talk about it. But not now. Not with her while I keep seeing her face in Keely's. Not until I can separate the facts from the past. "What about you?"

"You know what, let's not and say we did." She laughs and takes a sip, averting her eyes from mine. It's a gesture that only serves to remind me of Keely again.

"Nah. I'm not biting. What's going on, Em?"

She sighs and concentrates on picking through the bowl to steal all the cashews from it. I give her the time and smile at the prick who's glaring at me from across the way because she's talking to me and not him.

Maybe I'm taunting him because I'm in the mood for a fight. Maybe I'm just being an asshole. Then again, maybe I just want to kiss Emerson and know this is bad timing to be thinking about it.

"I told you I'm trying to buy Blue Skies, right?" I nod. "Well, trying is the operative word. In fact, my loan officer is a total prick."

"Is he not responding?"

Her laugh has my back up instantly. "He's responding, all right. I think the only reason he's responding and considering me for the loan is because he thinks he can get in my pants."

I don't like the fucker already. "Who is it?" I demand.

She eyes me and twists her lips. "He's a loan officer." She deadpans. "I can handle it myself."

Bullshit.

"Then go to a different bank." Simple.

"I wish," she says in a way that makes me want to move to her side of the booth and slide an arm around her. I'm not quite sure we're at that stage yet. "But they were the only bank even willing to consider my application. When my mom got sick, money was tight, so we used her credit, my credit, anything we could to pay for treatments. I've worked my ass off to pay it all back, took odd jobs everywhere I traveled to, and have sold off everything I own to do so."

"So, you have no collateral."

"Nope." She sighs, and I hate seeing the sadness in her eyes. "It's all paid off, but that doesn't mean my credit score has recovered. I just need a fresh start, and Blue Skies is my chance."

"Everyone needs a fresh start now and again. Besides, I find what you did—paying off the debt instead of declaring bankruptcy—very admirable."

"It is what it is." She rolls her neck.

"So, who's the prick?"

"I told you, none of your business. I've dealt with a lot worse than a handsy loan officer, Malone."

"Handsy?"

"Chill out. I'm a big girl."

TWENTY-THREE

Emerson

"**C**HILL OUT. I'M A BIG GIRL."

A look comes over Grant's face that makes every part of me come alive. It was an innocent comment on my part, and yet, the look in his eyes is suggestive as hell and perfectly fitting for this darkened, back corner of the bar.

"I'm well aware that you're a big girl, Emerson. You've gone out of your way to make me acknowledge it."

I'm not sure if it's a dig, but it's true, so I don't take it as anything other than that.

"I heard you dropped the donuts by the homeless shelter." His eyes flash up, and I'm immediately reminded of how I felt when I found out through the grapevine about what he did. "I have my own stalking capabilities."

"So I see."

"I think it was a super cool thing for you to do."

"Besides meeting you here, it was the easiest decision of my day."

I can see sadness in his eyes as he goes away from me momentarily. Back to his call? Back to the reason he is here, drinking in a bar by himself, perhaps?

"Tell me about your call," I prompt and reach out and put my hand on his. "I'd like to know about it."

His hand stiffens momentarily, and I know he's battling with whether he should talk or not—a blue blood through and through. He picks up his drink with his free hand, takes a sip before setting it down, and then laces his fingers with mine. But he still doesn't look at me.

And as the silent seconds tick by, my mind begins to wander. To how we just officially held hands and I'm not freaking out over it. To how it feels natural and pretty damn good. I think I'm more freaked out over that than the notion that we are sitting in a bar and looking like a couple.

"I used our rock thing today," he finally says as he meets my eyes, but I'm completely clueless as to what he's referring to.

"Our rock thing?" I ask, head angled as if it would help me understand.

"Yeah. It came to me today when I was on my call. I thought it might be a way to connect to a little girl, and I told her about it."

I'm so lost. Rock thing? What am I missing here?

"I don't understand."

"Yeah. Our rock thing. You know what, fuck it. Forget I said anything."

"No. Please. I want to know."

"My call today. It was a 10-16 . . . sorry, a domestic disturbance, and it wasn't the first time we'd been called out there. I think the dad is abusing the mom, but the mom is making excuses to protect him. It's a classic case of him beating her down enough, grooming her, so that she thinks he can't live without her and vice versa. I don't know. I don't get it, but I know it's real because I've seen it more times than I care to count."

"I'm sorry." It's all I say, but I squeeze his hand to lend him silent support as he thinks about something I can't even fathom.

"So am I." He sighs, the sag of his shoulders a visible manifestation of the toll the call has taken on him. "I want to help the mom, but I can't help her until she wants it, and I hope that it isn't too late. But what's even worse is that they have a daughter. She's five, and the sweetest little girl who is caught in the middle of a shit sandwich. She's defending a dad, who isn't nice, and loving a mom, who doesn't defend her. All this little girl wants is just to be a kid."

"That's rough. I don't know what to say other than I'm sorry. I can't imagine the things you see every day. The things you deal with," I say, really wanting to go back and find out what he meant about the rocks. Something is niggling at the back of my mind. I'm not sure what it is, but I'm too scared to ask.

"You know what? I think we should stop talking about our shitty days and go get ice cream."

"Ice cream?" I laugh. "We've gone from drinking away our sorrows to ice cream?"

"Yep. Do you have something against ice cream?"

"Umm . . . no. Who could hate ice cream?" My stomach growls at the thought of food, reminding me just how long it's been since I've eaten. "But then again, after my crappy day, this alcohol isn't so bad, either."

"There's my Emmy." He flashes me an irresistible grin that freezes when we both realize what he said.

I'm not going to lie and say those words don't make me want to give in on this silly game we've been playing—control be damned—and kiss him. Right here. Right now.

Our eyes hold and try to read what the other is saying. It's then that I feel his hand tighten around mine and realize our fingers are still interlocked.

"I know a way we can mix both ice cream and alcohol," he says, eyes never leaving mine.

"How?"

"Mudslides. They have them here." My stomach rumbles. "You want one?"

"Like you have to ask." I laugh when he raises his finger to the bartender before I even finish the sentence.

"I'm a big girl, Grant. I don't need you walking me home," I say and then giggle when I realize that I'm nowhere near the airstrip. But still. Saying it is like meaning it, right?

He swings our joined hands as he walks beside me. "I'm not walking you home. I'm walking you to my home since we aren't sober enough to drive." He veers off the sidewalk and up a short little path.

"Grant?" I ask as I take in the wood porch of the house in front of us.

"I know you're a big girl, Em. I'm well aware of it."

His words hang in the air, hitting my slightly fuzzy mind as I follow him up the steps to stand under the porch light. "Is that flirting, Malone? Are you flirting with me?"

He yanks on my hand, and I land solidly against him. It takes a minute for our minds to register what's going on—that our bodies are pressed together—because we're too busy making sure our wobbly feet don't give out.

But when we're steady, everything registers for me. The heat of his body against mine. The hardness of it, too. The hitch of his breath, answering the gasp of mine. The darkening of his eyes. The tensing of his hand on mine. The flick of his tongue across his bottom lip.

And, oh, how I want him to be flirting with me.

Better yet, I want him to be kissing me. All of me.

The thought makes me giggle as we continue to stand body to body, a lot a bit tipsy, beneath a dim porch light on an empty and darkened street.

"We shouldn't do this," he murmurs more to himself than to me. It cues the panic inside me, screaming that this insane display of foreplay between us needs to have the match lit before I combust from sexual frustration.

"Why not?"

"Because you're Emmy." He brings his free hand up and runs a finger down the side of my cheek.

That touch, skin to skin, is like a mainline of electric current to charge that slow, sweet ache burning inside me. It only serves to make me want more.

"And you're Phony Maloney."

"Exactly."

He steps back, and I tighten my hold on his hand and step forward with him. "Are you telling me there is nothing here? No lust? No attraction? No anything?"

He gives me that sly smile of his again, the one that lights up his eyes and does funny things to my insides. "I never said that."

"Then what are you saying?"

"I'm saying . . . Christ, Em, I don't know what I'm saying." He runs a hand absently up and down the plane of my back.

"Maybe you're saying we need to get each other out of our systems." I utter the words before I think them and then feel ridiculous.

"What?" He laughs. "Are you saying what I think you're saying?"

His body is against mine. His cologne is in my nose. His laugh is in my ears. He's everywhere all the time.

Too much talk right now. Too much *saying*. Not enough action.

"*Yes*."

A few seconds pass as he gauges whether I'm serious, and I wonder if he's going to take the bait. "And then what?" He angles his head to the side, silently asking a million questions my body wants to ignore.

"And then curiosity will be satisfied, and we'll be out of each other's systems."

"You think that's going to work? You think we've just met again after twenty years and it'll be that easy?"

He has a point, and I don't want to think about that or semantics or reality. I want to think about him. And me. And his mouth. And his hands.

So, I lean forward on my tiptoes and press my lips to his. "Enough talking, Malone."

He laughs, his lips vibrating against mine, but I don't relent. I want him. I want this. I know we're both buzzed, but maybe that's the best way for this to happen so I'm not nervous and overthinking and neither is he.

For a minute, I think he's going to reject me. It's in the way he stills for a brief moment, the way his lashes lower for just a second too long. Then he frames my face and leans back to look at me. Our breaths feather over each other's lips as an unspoken conversation passes between us. I can't put words to it, but somehow understand each and every syllable of it.

And then his mouth is on mine in a savage greeting of lips and tongues and hands on skin and history reconnected.

"Grant."

"Shh."

"Wait. I have rules."

He laughs with exasperation, a man being denied what's sitting at his fingertips. "Of course you do."

"No sleeping over. I don't do the sleeping together thing."

"No one said anything about sleeping, Em."

His smile sidelines me. The kiss he leans forward and brushes ever so tenderly against my lips makes me want to sag into him, even more so.

"No promises."

"I thought this was a one-night thing, right?"

"Yes, but no promises."

"I'm going to make you come. Can I promise you that?"

Another kiss. This time I take the lead and lick my tongue against his until I pull back and nip his lip. "I'll accept that promise."

"Good. Can we stop talking now because there are much more important things I want to be doing with my mouth, and every single one of them involves you and no words."

My teeth sink into my lower lip as our eyes meet. The door unlocks behind us. Our feet move in reflex. Our fingers link together.

Once over the threshold, we kiss again—his lips beginning their masterful assault of everything that is good and sexy and arousing and needed.

"God, yes."

His lips find my neck as my hand finds the door to push it shut behind me. As soon as the lever clicks, Grant has me up against it with one hand on my breast and his tongue licking its way up the line of my neck.

He laughs as he stumbles. I giggle as I grip his shoulders to steady us. But even when I do, the earth is still tilting beneath my feet from his desirous assault. Every sensation is welcome and wanted. Each touch of his another reason to temporarily ignore my history.

But he doesn't.

For some reason, the minute the thought crosses my mind, I can feel the sudden hesitancy in Grant's otherwise all-consuming and libidinous demeanor and know we are on the same page.

He is remembering.

He is wondering.

He is worrying.

"No," I gasp out in a desperate plea for him not to go there.

"Em." Regret. Fear. Uncertainty. All three meld and mesh in that one syllable of my name.

My hands are on his jaw, forcing his face up so that he has to meet my eyes through the dimly lit entry to his house. "No," I repeat. "I am not her anymore. She is not me. Don't do this, Grant."

With that simple statement . . . that simple devastating statement, I press my lips to his. I need him to see that I'm not a victim and that I refuse to be treated like one. I need him to know that he has no clue what I do or don't need, and therefore, I am going to show him.

As if he knows this is what I need, he allows me to take the reins. The man hell-bent on proving to me that he's in control, lets me take the lead in this dance that is uniquely ours.

"Show me," he murmurs, those two words as seductive as his touch.

And so, I show him.

With my hands and my tongue and my words and my touch.

This time, we start slowly. I tease and taunt him with the gentlest of caresses while my hands find the hem of his shirt and pull it from his pants. With the slightest of breaks of our lips, the fabric passes over his face and falls to the floor. I do the honors for myself next as we move slowly backward in that awkward dance of kiss, touch, retreat, repeat, until the backs of his legs hit the couch

"What do you need from me?" he whispers against my lips, unknowingly giving me the question I need and the willingness to take it.

I've never been shy about taking what I wanted from a guy before. I've never worried about what they thought because, in the end, we were both there for the same thing—pleasure. With Grant? I care. His ability to give me the things I need without even questioning is unnerving and comforting and makes me want this all the more.

"You. I just want you," I say as he hisses a breath when my hand slides inside the waistband of his jeans to find him hard and stiff and ready for me.

"Take me, Em."

And then our mouths crash together again in a torrent of desire that warns of its irreversible damage to my body and *my heart*. I push it away, focusing on his hands undoing my bra. The pads of his thumbs brushing ever so softly over the tips of my nipples. His fingers tugging at my zipper. The palms of his hands as they run down my sides and push my pants down over my hips.

My body reacts in every imaginable way to him. It wants and needs and begs and pleads. He pulls me against him so we're body to body. Skin to skin. Mouth to mouth.

"Christ, I want you," he says as he shoves his pants off and steps out of them.

"Then take me." I give his words back to him because control has given way to need, and hell if every part of me isn't ready and willing.

My hands are around his shaft, stroking him gently. I cry out as his fingers part me and find me wet, muscles vibrating, nerves stimulated and waiting to respond to his onslaught of touch.

He falls backward onto his couch—our laughs filling the room before they morph into drawn-out groans. There's the telltale rip of foil and then I straddle his lap. Our mouths meld again as I grind atop of him so that my arousal coats his cock, and the feel of him steals my breath.

Urgency becomes the name of the game.

I lift my hips so his hand can find its way between us, and his fingers press into me. I moan. My nails dig into his shoulders and score his skin. He doesn't seem to notice or even care as his fingers keep their even tempo.

"Grant. *God.* Yes. *Please.* I need. *Oh.*"

His chuckle is a murmur amidst the sounds I make, and at some point, I begin to beg. At least I think I do. Or maybe he does. I'm so caught up in the machinations of his fingers and the crest he's slowly building within me that I've lost all semblance of time and place. As long as he doesn't stop, I don't care where I am.

And in a practiced move that's both impressive and havoc inducing to every nerve within me, Grant withdraws his fingers from me and replaces them with the girth of his cock.

If I thought I'd felt pleasure before, I was dead wrong. This—his cock in me, his tongue licking against mine, the sexy groan in my ears—is pleasure. Pure, unadulterated pleasure like I can't ever remember feeling before.

"*Fuck.*"

It's one word, but it's long and drawn out and almost a growl as we begin to move together. He thrusts up as I grind down, allowing the base of his shaft to hit the nether part of my clit in a way that sends shockwaves to where his crest is working within me.

We don't speak, we react.

His exhale, my next inhale.

His curse—*fuck*—my want.

His tempo, my pulse.

We move in unison, each taking and giving and feeling, until every part of me burns bright with a desire I never knew possible.

His fingers press into my ass. My hands grab his biceps. The sounds of skin on skin fill the room with the constant undertone of our moans and groans and praise and pleas of bliss. His dick swells. I grind harder. My breath hitches then catches then gasps as the orgasm swells and surges. It hits with such forewarning, but I still lose myself as it drags me under its possessive haze, only to toss me up again just as Grant groans my name and loses himself to me.

My forehead rests on his shoulder. His fingers trail up and down the line of my spine. Our heartbeats bang against each other's through our rib cages. Our breaths remain labored. My mind too hazy from being overwhelmed by everything that is Grant Malone to think about next steps and what the hell line we just crossed.

"That promise wasn't so bad, was it?" He chuckles as he brings his lips to the top of my head, his breath heating my hair.

"No," I murmur.

He definitely made me come, all right.

At least I know he keeps his promises now.

TWENTY-FOUR

Emerson

THE ROOM IS BRIGHT, AND THE RAY OF SUN SLICING BETWEEN THE blinds hits me perfectly in the eyes. I snuggle deeper into the comforter, and then awareness hits.

My eyes flash open.

I'm not home. In my loft. In my bed.

I'm in Grant's bed. A bed that is way more comfortable than mine. And it's way past my typical six thirty wake-up time.

Grant's also nowhere to be found.

It takes a moment before it ghosts through my mind. *"Em. I have to go to work."* The gravel in his voice as he presses a kiss against my temple. The sound of his duty belt clinking. The metallic sound of the gun safe closing. The rumble of his chuckle as he runs a hand down my bare spine and makes me snuggle deeper into the bed that smells like him and is just as warm. "Stay as long as you like. Just lock the door on the way out."

Then falling back into an oblivious sleep.

I broke one of my rules.

Shit.

I'm here when I should be at work. I'm wrapped in the scent of him when I should be in my flight suit and focused on this afternoon's clients. Instead, I want to nestle back into this softness and remember every delicious thing he did to me last night.

No.

Get up.

I shouldn't do this. I don't get to throw my rules out the window for one man. One hotter than hell and more than skilled man named Grant Malone, but a man nonetheless.

I make myself sit up in his bed, the comforter held beneath my armpits to cover my nakedness, and take a look around. The room is classic and clean, light walls with dark gray and blue accents. Very male, but not in the bachelor monochromatic way. It's tidy and there aren't any clothes strewn about. He even took the time to fold my clothes on the chair in the far corner.

The walls hold a few black-and-white photographs of the ocean and cliffs—stoic, powerful, and moving. There are very few personal effects in his bedroom, but it's cozy and inviting.

Determined not to want to know more, I force myself from the bed. My debate whether to take a shower is short lived. One, it isn't my bathroom and that might be a little awkward just making myself at home. And two, I can still smell his cologne on my skin and I'm not certain I want to wash him away just yet.

If per my rules, I only get one night with Grant Malone, I ridiculously want to make it last a little longer. So, instead of thinking too much about how this is so unlike me, I force myself to get dressed in last night's jean shorts, tank top, and unbuttoned overshirt.

It's just when I finish making the bed—because as messy as I am, there's no way I can leave an unmade bed for Mr. Nice and Tidy—that I hear voices.

At first, I think maybe they are from next door and Grant left a window open, but after a few more seconds, I know for certain there are at least two other men in Grant's house.

"Dude, check it out," the first voice says. It's followed by a low hum of a chuckle.

"Looks like someone got lucky last night." There's a low whistle.

"Well, it looks like whoever it was, didn't want this nice setup of coffee he left for her. So, I don't mind if I do."

Coffee? Did he just say coffee? My ears perk up and my mouth waters at the thought of it. Did Grant really leave me a coffee cup and all the fixings? There is a God.

I just need to figure out how to walk out of this bedroom, surprise whoever the two guys are in the family room, and retain my dignity. But, then again, there is no dignity lost considering we were two consenting adults. Plus, who cares what they think?

My shoes. I don't have my sandals. They are most likely in the living room where I kicked them off last night. I look around Grant's spotless bedroom and change my mind. They are probably sitting side by side by the front door.

"Hey, Grady," the one voice says to the other.

It's the same time the voice says those two words that I know who is on the other side of the wall. It may have been a long time, but I would know that voice anywhere. Grant's brothers, Grayson and Grady, are in the other room.

"Shoes."

Crap. They noticed them.

Cue the panic. And not the run-of-the-mill, walk of shame type of panic, either. More like these men used to run around in their underwear with me in their sprinklers when we were little. We share a history of getting sticky from eating Big Stick popsicles that we bought from the ice cream man.

I snicker at the thought of Big Sticks and how that has a whole different connotation now.

Should I just stay here and wait them out instead of face them? But then what? They walk in here, find me, and I end up looking like a damn heel?

The longer I stand here and listen to the two of them bicker like kids, the worse my nerves hum with the thought of what they're going to think when they see me—little Emmy who suddenly up and disappeared years ago. That's the kind of attention I don't want or like.

So I react.

With a glance in the bathroom mirror, I grab some lipstick from my purse, do a quick fluff of my hair so I don't look like a complete disaster, and then suck in my breath. When I'm fairly certain I don't look like a hot mess anymore, I waltz out of the bedroom with my head held high and a smile on my face.

"I knew he was hiding something when I called him this morning. The son of a bitch."

"Hey, that's mom you're talking about," the other says.

"Whatever, dude. You know what I mean. Grant went and got himself laid last night. I wonder—"

"Actually, I was the one who got laid last night," I say as I enter the room and draw two pairs of eyes my way. I love the shocked O's their mouths fall into. Slack jaws on hot men are always a good thing—whether it's from some lacy lingerie or from putting them in their place. I walk right up to one of them—because they look too damn similar for me to venture which one is who after all these years—and grab the piping cup of coffee from his hand. "Thanks for making this for me. I appreciate it."

His eyes widen, and his lips sputter into a shit-eating grin as I take a tentative sip of the steaming heaven without breaking eye contact. "Hello, Emerson."

"Hi. And you are . . ." I feign ignorance to set the precedence that I have no past with them. It's hard enough as it is with Grant, so I need to make sure we start this off on the right foot.

"Grady Malone," he says and then lifts his chin toward Hot Malone number three. "And that's Grayson."

"Ah, the infamous Malone boys. Now, I've met you all again." I narrow my eyes and study both of them in the same way they are studying me. I can see the similarities. The little boys they were beneath the men they have become. "Thanks for the coffee. A little light on the creamer for my liking, but now you know for next time."

I flash a dazzling smile as they laugh. "He was right," Grayson says to Grady as if I'm not in the room. "She is feisty as hell."

"Always." I wink and walk over to where my sandals are perfectly lined up side by side near the front door. "I need to run so I'm not late for work. Grant asked me to lock up. Since you obviously have the keys to help yourselves as you please, can I trust that you can handle that instead?"

"We'll lock up. No worries," Grady says and then smirks. "It's the least we can do."

"Thanks. I'm tired." I turn the handle on the front door before adding, "Your brother really knows how to keep a girl up all night."

With that, I walk out the front door, shut it behind me, and don't spare a look back as I stroll down the street toward the bar where my car is still parked.

The ringer of my phone comes through my speaker on my car, and I know who it is before I even glance at the screen. I contemplate not answering. If I pick up, it will sound as if I want to go back on the rules I made last night. We shouldn't feel as if we need to do the obligatory *morning-after* call to make sure things aren't awkward.

Then again, if I avoid him, doesn't that just prove to him—and me—that I can't handle what happened when following my own rules.

"Get a grip, Em," I mutter as I jab my finger at the car's display and answer the call.

"Hello?" I say as if I can't already see it's him on the Caller ID.

"Good morning." I'm not sure why I expected there to be a smug sound in his voice, but there isn't. "Hey, I know you're probably on your way to work, but I just wanted to apologize for my brothers. Sometimes they come over and steal my coffee. Other times they just want to harass me for no reason. I didn't expect them to stop in this morning."

"It's okay," I say with a smile, remembering their shocked faces.

His chuckle fills the line. "I don't know what you told them, but somehow you managed the impossible."

"What do you mean?" I make a right turn onto the highway and smile when a police cruiser passes me. It isn't Grant, but it still feels like it is since his voice is in my car.

"The two of them can never agree on a single thing, and yet, when I talked to them earlier, they both decided they are head over heels when it comes to you."

"What?" I laugh.

"Yep. I believe *gutsy* was their word of choice."

"That's a good word." I let the word roll over my tongue and gladly own it.

"It is, and it suits you to a T."

"I may have played them a little bit." I chuckle.

"Oh really?" he murmurs. "I wouldn't know anything about that."

And there's something in the way that Grant makes the statement that catches my ear and puts my mind into overdrive. "What's the supposed to mean?"

"Nothing." I can hear the smile in his voice. "Break's over. I have to get back to work. Bye, Emerson."

TWENTY-FIVE

Grant

"YOU WANT TO EXPLAIN WHY YOU'RE IN SUCH A GOOD MOOD?" Nate asks.

I glance his way and then look back to my computer with Emerson front and center on my mind. "No reason. I'm always in a good mood."

"Bullshit." He snorts. "You got some action, didn't you?"

"Are you telling me I'm only in a good mood when I get laid?" I can see other guys tune in to our conversation.

"No, but it does help."

"True . . ." I muse as I request another cold case file from the archives to help Chief Ramos keep his promise to the public that the Sunnyville Police Department never backs down on crime, old or new. It doesn't hurt that it looks good for the promotion plus that patio cover I've been itching to build.

"So?" he asks in a verbal nudge.

"So, nothing." Much to his annoyance, I blow him off. None of the guys in the place need to know about my personal life more than they already do.

But that doesn't stop me from mentally reliving every single moment spent with Emerson. Every kiss. Each lick. All the moans. The groans. The orgasms. And every damn thing in between.

I shift in my chair, knowing I need to stop thinking about her or I'm going to be sporting wood.

But as I ignore the bullshit puppy-dog eyes from Nate and focus on calling up more cold case files from the archives, all I think about is Emerson. How sex with her was a mixture of familiarity and new and unforgettable all at the same time. Her rules she needs so she feels like she's in control but that I know I'll peel away one by one until it's just her and me and nothing between us.

And to add the cherry to the sundae that is most definitely her, she put my brothers in their damn place.

The woman is a force to be reckoned with and hell if I'm not sitting in the middle of her windstorm and waiting to be hit with everything she has.

"Malone."

"Yep." I look up to where Dyson is standing at the front of the squad room.

"Chief Ramos needs to see you."

I throw a glance to Nate, curious as to why he's asking for only me and not the two of us. He shrugs as I stand, make my way down the hall, and rap on the glass door. "What do you need, Chief?"

Chief Ramos lifts his eyes from the open file on his desk and motions for me to come in. "Shut the door, Malone." *Uh-oh.* "Take a seat."

"Sure." I sit in the chair across from him and wait for those dark eyes of his to study me. Nothing says a dress down is coming like the Ramos stare.

"How is the studying going for your exam?"

"Good," I say with caution. "Most of the stuff is second nature, but I'm reviewing it anyway."

"Do you have a test date yet?" he asks, glancing at his wall calendar before settling the intensity in his eyes back on me.

"End of the month," I reply. Twenty-two days. It should be more than enough time for me to spit shine my knowledge and ace the test.

"I'm sure your dad told you the test is the easy part, right?"

What is he getting at?

"So I've heard."

"Good. Good." He nods and leans back in his chair as he looks through the glass walls of his office and into the squad room. Even with his focus off me, he's still intimidating as hell when he wants to be. His sigh tells me there is more.

"What's the problem?" I finally ask.

"Your dad is a good friend of mine. You're important to this department. I just want to make sure you're prepared."

"Okay." I draw the word out, still lost to the purpose of this conversation.

"Stetson threw his hat in the ring a few days ago."

"What?" I feel like I've been hit by a two-by-four. "Fucking Stetson?"

"Yes. And I only have one opening."

I nod and clench my fists to hide my reaction. "Understood."

"You'll both pass the test easily. It's the interviews that are going to be tough. You each have friends on the committee, so the vote will be split . . . and—"

"And I have the bullshit lies Stetson and his dad spread about my dad and me to contend with." I finish his unspoken thought for him and hate to even have to say it.

"There's that." Another sigh. When he clenches his fists atop the file on his desk, it's just one last visual directive to have my shit in order. To not take any of this lightly.

"I knew it wasn't going to be a cakewalk," I say. "But I didn't expect to have to contend with a past I had nothing to do with."

"I know, Grant. It's bullshit, but it's shit nonetheless, and at some point, we're all forced to stand in it and try to wipe it off our heels."

"Thanks for the head's up," I say and stand, needing a moment to process this.

"Let me know if I can help with anything."

How about kick the fucker off the force?

I nod again and offer a tight smile before turning and walking out of his office. Nate catches my eye as I stride through the precinct without stopping. We've worked together long enough for him to recognize I'm about to lose my shit, and I know he'll be ten steps behind me as soon as others stop paying attention.

Once outside, I walk to the edge of the lot and try to calm the fuck down.

"Grant?"

"The asshole is coming after my promotion," I grit the words out to him.

"Stetson?"

"Fuck yes, Stetson." I roll my shoulders and walk a few feet away from him before turning and walking back. "He can't let it go, can he? His dad was a piss poor cop on a total power trip just like his bastard son is."

"I'm not going to disagree with you. But why now? He just up and decided he wanted to be detective?"

"Apparently." I laugh, but it's void of humor. "Is he trying to avenge dear old daddy?"

"Fuck that, Malone. His dear old daddy was crooked, so your dad kicked him off the force for misconduct and marred his reputation."

"Yep. And then he started spreading bullshit rumors about my dad to get back at him. *Fuck.*" I run a hand through my hair, the anger eating me raw inside.

"I know, man. I know. It was fucked up all around, but anyone who knows your dad knows the accusations are crap."

"Does it matter? He still stepped down over it and gave them the satisfaction of thinking they had won." The thought alone makes my body vibrate in anger. I know he didn't step down to avoid the smudge on his incredible career but rather to remove all drama so his son, who wanted to follow in his footsteps, could do so with a clean slate in front of him.

Yeah, I'm the selfish bastard who let him do that—not that anyone could have stopped him.

"Don't let your head go there, man. He stepped down because he had already planned on retiring, not because of you. We both know that."

"Yeah, well . . ." How do I go from the high of last night with Emerson to this shit? "Now I get to deal with Asshole Jr."

"He's doing it just to spite you."

"But he has friends in high places."

"So do you, my friend."

"Let's hope so."

TWENTY-SIX

Emerson

"**A**RE YOU AVOIDING ME?" DESI'S VOICE RINGS OUT THROUGH the red hangar, prompting me to lift my head without thinking and rap it smartly on the underside of the Cessna's wing.

"Shit." I rub a hand over the top of my head.

"Now, I know I was poking pins in the Voodoo doll I have to punish you for avoiding me, but I didn't think it would actually work."

"Very funny," I say as I roll my eyes, step away from the plane, and wipe my hands on a rag.

Desi stands with her hands on her hips, head angled to the side, and a scarf that looks like a rainbow threw up all over it wrapped around her neck. It's ridiculous and bright and girly, but she pulls it off and makes it look uniquely fashionable.

"So, are you?"

"Am I what?"

She huffs, as if she's trying to explain thermonuclear dynamics to a kindergartner, and takes a step forward. "Avoiding me. Not taking my calls. Not returning my calls. Pretending like Grant never called me two nights ago and told me not to show up at the bar because he was going to otherwise occupy your time. You know"—she shrugs—"that kind of avoiding me."

"No." I avert my eyes and finish wiping off the windshield of the plane with Windex to—_yes_—avoid her. "I've just been busy."

Her laugh is rich and bounces off the concrete floor and echoes back to me. "Like bow-chick-a-wow-wow kind of busy?"

I level her with a glare. "You're so childish."

"And you refuse to admit you slept with Grant." She'd be a really good interrogator. I don't plan on telling her that.

"Who said I slept with Grant?" I feign innocence, trying to keep the act up for some reason.

"You did."

"I did not."

"Uh-huh."

"If I haven't spoken to you, then I obviously haven't told you I slept with him."

"Your silence speaks volumes." She purses her lips as if victorious, and all I can do is attempt to follow her messed-up logic.

"Silence doesn't speak."

"Ah, but that's where you're wrong. It can scream sometimes, and honey, yours is louder than a sonic boom." I lower my hands from where I've moved on to the side windows and just shake my head. "Admit it. I need to hear it."

Another glare. A repeated sigh. A confession that I'm not sure why I'm keeping so close to the vest when I usually share everything with her.

"Yes, I slept with Grant."

"Woohoo!" She pumps her fists and jumps up and down as if I just completed an Ironman. "I knew it. He had sex all over his voice when he called me. It was so damn hot I almost had to get myself off."

"You're incorrigible."

"And you got laid. So . . ." She pats the makeshift bench of a two-by-six piece of wood sitting atop two spaced out sawhorses. "You better not leave out a damn bit of detail."

"You really want a blow-by-blow?"

"Ohh, you naughty girl!" She screeches. "You blew him, too. I love it!"

"No—I—oh my God, I can't believe we're having this conversation."

"So, you didn't blow him?"

"Desi!"

"Yes, that just means there's going to be another time to explore all other avenues you haven't ventured down yet."

"Slow down, Turbo," I say as I put some of my supplies back on the cleaning cart before taking a seat beside her. "It wasn't like you're thinking."

"It wasn't?" she asks, her smirk only growing wider. "Was it more swing from the chandeliers or more gasp for breath because your face is pushed into the mattress because he feels so good from behind?"

"Jesus," I choke out but shouldn't expect any less from her.

"Did you satisfy your curiosity then?"

"You know what they say about curiosity . . ."

"It killed the cat, yeah, yeah. But honey, by the grin on your face, I know your kitty meowed. *A lot.*"

"How about you stop or else you don't get any details."

Her face falls, and I know I've hurt her feelings when I didn't mean to. I love the woman to death but subtlety is not her forte and overboard dramatics definitely are.

"Okay. I'll shut my mouth so you can give me the 4-1-1."

I laugh. We'll see how long that lasts. "I don't know," I begin. "We had some drinks. We talked for a few hours. We were too tipsy to drive so we walked back to his house. On the way, we decided that if we got each other out of our systems, we might be able to stop this nonsense competition we seem to be in over who has to be in control. A one-time romp with no strings attached."

"Get each other out of your systems?" She guffaws and just barely manages not to laugh at the idea. "Because that's what normal childhood friends do when they reunite after twenty years."

"*Reunite*? Is that what it's called?"

"I am trying to be good here. What word should I use to describe it?"

"How about 'fucked'?" She isn't the only one who can deliver the shock value, and by the way she just choked on her next word, I'd say I was successful at it.

"*Fucked*. I can approve of that word." She laughs. "But the question remains: Did it work? Did you get each other out of your systems?"

I stare at her as I try to figure out how to answer.

Of course it didn't work. Being with him once only left me wanting more. Pride prevents me from acknowledging that every time my phone rings, I jump to see if it's him, only to chastise myself that it doesn't matter if it is.

One time. That's all it can be.

My rule. Not his.

And I hate that the only time we've talked was when he called to apologize for his brothers showing up unannounced.

"So, the *one-time thing*," she continues on, well aware that I haven't responded to her last question. "Was this his rule or yours? My bet is on you."

"You'd be correct. Don't act so surprised." I swat at her arm.

"I'm not surprised by the rule, I'm just surprised you fell for it." She swats my arm right back and gives me a look that makes me think she's privy to some type of knowledge that I'm clearly not.

"What does that mean?"

"You guys have been playing Control Wars for what? Two, three weeks?"

"Yeah. So?"

"Don't you find it awfully convenient that, all of a sudden, he let you call the shots when he's been vying for the top?"

"Are you saying he played me?" I hate that the coin she's just put in the slot drops down and hits with a loud, ricocheting *clank*.

"You're damn straight he did. Damn brilliantly, too."

She laughs, and her face has an incredulous expression on it I don't really feel like recognizing.

The smug bastard.

"Are you complaining about the outcome?" she asks after I sit quietly for a moment.

"Uh, no," I finally say. How could I complain about the skill of his hands and lips and marvelous cock?

"No?"

"Absolutely not," I assert.

"Then why do you look like you're about to call him and chew him out?" And she's right. I feel like doing just that even though there is no reason to because we both got what we wanted out of our little rendezvous, didn't we?

"I'm not," I concede.

"Good. You shouldn't be mad because he one-upped you."

"Are you trying to rub my nose in it?"

"Nope." She blows a bubble with her gum and it pops with a *smack*. "I'm just thrilled that someone finally beat you at your own game."

"I do believe that's rubbing my nose in it."

"Semantics." She grins with a shrug. "So . . . was all this trouble worth it?" She lifts her eyebrows, and the blush on my cheeks and laugh on my lips tells her all she needs to know.

"Definitely worth it."

"For a girl all about the orgasm, that says a lot." There's the sound of a plane's prop starting in the distance, and she waits a moment to continue. "We always get sidetracked when it comes to Grant and talk about all the swooniness that is him . . . are you ever going to tell me why the two of you stopped being friends in the first place?"

"No reason." I rise from my seat and head to the cart where I fiddle with things that don't need to be fiddled with.

"C'mon. There has to be a reason."

"I moved away." It isn't a lie. "It doesn't matter. He and I would never work anyway."

"I didn't know you wanted it to."

"I don't. I mean—It wouldn't—" I stop talking because I sound like a bumbling fool.

"Why wouldn't it work?" she asks. All I want her to do is drop it, which I know she won't. She's sunk her teeth into the point she's trying to make and won't let go until this conversation has played itself out.

"He's a player, Des. I'm a player. There's disaster written all over that," I say as I turn to look at her.

"You two could *play* together." I roll my eyes at her lame sense of humor. "But he chased you, Em. Players don't chase."

"Ha. They chase until they get what they want and then they're done. Besides, he didn't chase."

"Keep thinking that, sister, and I'll sell you some ocean front property in

Arizona." I level her with a side-eyed look. "Fine. I'll be quiet. Tell me how you guys left things."

"Other than saying it was a one-time thing, we really didn't leave it any way."

"There was no goodbye. No walk you to your car afterward? No, call me later?"

"No." I shift my feet because she's going to see right through this in a heartbeat. "He left for his shift at the break of dawn."

She leans forward, eyes wide, and full attention on me. "You were sleeping? In his bed?"

Yep, I knew she'd call me on how I broke that rule in a heartbeat. "It wasn't like that."

"Oh, so it was more like he sexed you up so good you fell into a sex-blissed coma and then he left you—a woman he doesn't really know—alone in his house when he went to work? Was that how it was?"

"You missed the part where he kissed me on the top of the head in the dark and told me to stay as long as I like."

She makes a show of shaking her head in mock disgust of my breaking my own rules, but I know she's secretly fist pumping beneath the surface. "Yeah, just minor details. Like sweet and endearing details."

I can't help the uncharacteristic smile on my lips or the warmth that spreads within me. I don't do tender or intimate. Hell, I don't do anything near the sort, but then again . . . this is Grant we're talking about. There is some level of comfort with him that I'm not used to.

It's only one night, Em.

"He obviously trusts you," she muses.

"Well," I laugh the word out, "it doesn't go both ways."

"What the hell do you mean?"

"Drop it, Des."

She angles me a look that says she's confused, and it matches how I feel inside.

It's amazing that no matter how many strides I take forward—how normal my life is—a simple thing like the word "trust" can force my past to come back and slap me.

Grant doesn't deserve it.

Then again, neither did I.

TWENTY-SEVEN

Grant

"**H**OT DAMN." NATE SMACKS HIS HANDS ON MY KITCHEN COUNT-er and scares the shit out of me. "I knew you got laid last week."

"What?" I look up from where I'm tying my boots.

Where the hell is this coming from?

"There's lipstick on this mug," he says as he lifts the coffee cup he was just taking a sip from.

"There is?" I mutter with a shake of my head. "My fucking brothers."

"Gray and Grady are wearing lipstick now? Wow. I thought they'd go for more of a red than a pink." He laughs as he dumps his coffee into the sink and grabs a new mug.

"No. They washed the cup after Emers—"

"I knew it!" Nate shouts from the kitchen. "You did get laid." He flashes a knowing grin that I ignore as I move to my other boot.

"I sure did."

"See? You can't hide shit from me."

"You're a real detective. Maybe you should put in for a promotion," I deflect.

"Nah, there's only room for one of us to steal center stage at a time. I'll leave it to you to put that fucker Stetson in his place."

I glance at my watch. "C'mon. Fill your cup. Our shift's about to start and there's somewhere I want to stop before we clock in."

"Sure thing." He puts the creamer back in the refrigerator. "And you can fill me in on all the details on the way."

"Humor me, will you?" I say to Nate as I pull the cruiser along the curb and put it in park.

His deep sigh fills the car. He doesn't have to say a word to let me know he thinks I'm way over the line.

He'll get over it.

The street is silent as I exit the car. The garage door is closed, and the driveway is empty. But there are new rocks painted in the planters along the walkway to the house.

One looks like a flag. Another is black and white like a cow's spots. One has a K in bright blue on it.

But there is no watermelon. Nothing red with black seeds.

No cry for help disguised as secret spy code.

I'm there for no more than a minute before I turn on my heel and head back to the cruiser.

"Everything okay?" Nate asks as I slide behind the wheel, his voice full of concern.

"Yep. Everything is okay."

For now.

TWENTY-EIGHT

Emerson

SLIMY BASTARD.

I can still feel his hands on my shoulders and smell his obnoxious cologne. I can still see the snake oil behind the lunch he brought with him to Blue Skies to conveniently offer to share. I can still hear the implied threat that if I don't acquiesce to the prick, then my loan might not be approved.

Or funded.

Or maybe if I dated a sturdy man of industry such as himself, the lenders would look favorably upon his stability and be more willing to bargain.

I'm well aware this is all total bullshit. He's out of his mind if he thinks I don't see that he's most likely holding back my loan from approval to string me along. To try to extort a date from me before he tells me if I've been approved or not. I've provided the correct documentation—a business plan, financial statements, an audit of the company—and yet I'm still dependent on him.

Dependent but not desperate.

No date. No way.

I may be a nomad in his eyes, but this nomad is smarter than he gives me credit for.

And then, of course, his departure was followed up by a phone call from the owners. Their weekly questions about our latest sales figures that segued into why I don't have the loan yet. That was followed by the casual mention—*threat*—that regardless of how hard I work for them currently, if the sixty-day escrow falls through, they already have backup buyers in place *just in case*. Oh, and naturally, the backup buyers are offering a higher buying price, which I find to be total bullshit. But if I call their bluff and don't play their game, too, do I risk losing out on my dream?

I slam around the training room, moving chairs back in place, resetting slideshows, wiping off the dry erase boards. Anything to calm my temper and rid the room of the slime Chris's presence left behind.

Everything about me is itching to put my gear on and jump.

"You okay?" Leo asks from where he stands outside the doorway. More than aware of my mood and prepared for a running start should my temper flare.

"Yeah. I'm fine. I'm just . . ." I stop talking, the frustrated tears threatening to make their presence known when I don't want them to.

"He's a prick, Em."

"Yeah, I know. I just wish I could tell him what I really think of him, but I can't risk the loan."

"My mom used to tell me never to wrestle with pigs. You both get dirty and the pig really likes it."

"Smart woman."

"Just know we all see it and admire you for dealing with him. It shows just how much you want Blue Skies to be yours."

"Thanks." I nod but avert my eyes, hoping it will prevent the sting of tears.

"You know Sully is taking one more flight up in an hour, right?"

He has my attention, which I'm sure was his hope. He knows me well enough to know that a jump is just about the only thing that will make me feel better. I've been so bogged down with loan stuff and instructing clients, that I need the release . . .

"He is?"

"Yeah. A fun run for some of the crew to get rid of some of the mid-week all-we-do-is-instruct-and-not-jump blues."

I laugh. "God bless him. What time is he going up?"

"In about an hour. Everyone's heading out to get a bite to eat and then meeting back here at seven. You want to come?"

I glance at my watch. That gives me seventy minutes to fill out a few reports for Blue Skies and complete the last few things on the new to-do list Travis gave me this morning.

"I can't go out to eat with you guys," I say, "but I'll be geared up at the plane at seven."

"Cool. It's been a long time since we just jumped for the hell of it."

"Amen."

Leo leaves me be, but I can still hear him rattling around and gathering his things in the office before the bells on the door ring as he shuts it behind him.

I'm not sure how much time passes before the bells on the door go off again.

"Sorry, we're closed," I call out to the front of the shop and mentally chastise myself for not taking the time to lock the door.

Then the thought hits that it's Chris coming back while I'm here alone.

"We're closed," I call again just as I turn the corner to the front office and run smack dab into someone.

"Whoa! Where's the fire?" Grant's hands are on my shoulders, holding me steady as I look up at him. I hate that I sigh in relief that he isn't Chris.

"No fire," I say as I catch my breath. "We're just closed."

"So you said." Grant's eyes narrow as he studies me, and I know he sees fluster. "Everything okay, Em?" Concern laces his tone, and the sound of it makes me step back quickly.

"Yeah, fine."

"You sure?"

"Nothing I can't handle."

Why am I suddenly so nervous?

"Em?"

"It's nothing, Grant. The loan guy was here earlier, and he was just . . ."

"He was just what?" The muscle in his jaw pulses as he clenches his teeth.

"I told you, I'm a big—"

"Girl who can take care of herself. Yeah, yeah. That doesn't mean that prick has the right to treat you how he does. Who is he, Em? I can take a quick stop by his house and—"

"No. You're not doing anything."

"All it would take is some asking around, a little detective work," he says, flashing me a smirk as he points to his shiny badge pinned over his heart, "and I could fix the fucker."

"Thank you for the chivalry. I really appreciate your willingness to be my knight in shining armor, but I'm a big—I have it handled."

He stares at me for a beat, our eyes warring over his hero complex and my independence. On any other day, I'd smile at the trait and think it was cute . . . but not right now. Not with my loan at stake.

"This is off your beat, isn't it, Officer Malone?" I ask with a smile and try to switch gears.

"You keep ignoring me." There is just a bit too much accusation there for his statement to be casual.

"No, I don't," I lie. "I've just been super busy."

"Too busy to return a text or answer a call?" He angles his head to the side, and his brown eyes pin me motionless as they try to read my body language and unspoken words.

"Just busy. I have a lot going on." A lot as in I'm trying not to want to talk to you as much as I've wanted to. I take another step back but bump into the wall behind me. "Did you need something?"

"I wanted to see you."

I've never known just how fine a line there is between want and need until this moment.

"That wasn't the deal, Grant." I reject his words immediately because they hit too close to home.

I wanted to see him, too.

"What deal?"

"The deal we made the other night."

"Oh, you mean your rules?"

"Yeah."

"Didn't anyone ever tell you not to believe any promises spoken when in the heat of passion?"

Heat of passion.

I level him with a glare. "Haven't you realized yet I'm not your normal woman?"

"If by 'normal' you mean the type of woman who jumps out of airplanes, loves to eat food without shame, gives as good as she gets, and has no problem wanting sex for sex. Then, no, I'm sorry. I didn't notice." His face is stoic, but his eyes hold the humor and sarcasm his voice is lacking.

"Funny."

"Perhaps, but it's true."

"The other night was a mistake." Lie. Lie. Lie. I'm just so unnerved that he sees me so well when most days I can't see myself.

"Nice try, but I call bullshit."

"You can call *it* whatever you want, Malone, but *it* isn't going to happen again."

The corner of his lips curl as he shakes his head. "I'm glad you have this all figured out."

"He chased you."

Desi's words come back and hit my ears as I stare at him and realize that he has the patience of a saint and she was right—he did chase me. He's still *chasing* me.

So, why am I pushing him away again?

Because rules are rules. Now, I just need to stick to my guns.

"Look, I'm far from typical. Anything you might need to do out of obligation after sleeping with someone is not needed when it comes to me."

"Like?" he asks as he folds his arms across his chest, leans a shoulder against the wall, and tucks his tongue in his cheek to fight from smiling.

"Like I don't require the phone call afterward to make sure we're both okay with the one-night stand thing. I don't need flowers or apologies when you move on to the next woman. I don't need empty promises or whatever else it is you guys do to soothe your egos. It's all crap."

"Every woman likes those things."

"I'm not every woman."

"So we've established." He holds his hand up when I start to protest. "But no worries, I don't do that. Just don't tell my mom."

"Good to know."

"Is there a reason for so much hostility, Em? I'm sensing you're mad at me, but if these are your rules, then how can you be?"

Silence falls in the small space as my tongue-tied thoughts spin and shift the conversation. "Look, we're attracted to each other. There's nothing wrong with that. We wanted out of each other's systems. We screwed. We're good."

"So eloquent." He lifts his eyebrows as his smile spreads.

"I'm serious. I barely have time to breathe most days, never mind have the time to deal with this kind of shit."

"Wow. Way to knock a man's ego—*and dick*—in the dirt."

I growl in frustration when I realize how he took my comment. "We're not talking about the sex part." I backpedal. "That was top notch. It's just . . . you're Phony Maloney. And I'm Emmy Reeves . . . don't you think we should let the past be the past and just be happy with knowing we turned out okay? With accepting our chemistry is great but that it will never work between us."

"What wouldn't work? The *screwing* part?" he asks, eyes narrowing as he mimics the way I said the word.

"Yes. That."

"But we already did that part, and what were your words? Top notch? So, I believe that did work." He knows he's irritating me and is enjoying every second of doing it.

"What about this?" I motion to the space in between us. "Isn't this weird?"

"It didn't feel weird the other night. In fact, it felt pretty damn amazing, so lay your next excuse on me. Why can't you pick up the phone and take my call, Emerson? I'm not buying whatever logic you're trying to sell. And frankly you're making absolutely zero sense, but please, continue. I'm enjoying this immensely."

"You're exhausting." I sigh.

"And you're infuriating, but we already knew that twenty years ago . . . so what's your excuse going to be now, huh?"

"I don't trust you." I know my comment is a low blow before it even comes out of my mouth, but I can't stop it any more than I can stop the sun from setting.

He staggers back as if I've physically assaulted him, and I can see hints of our past flicker through the anger sparking in his eyes.

Regret is immediate. How do I tell him not to think of the past when I just threw it in his face? I'm a goddamn mess. He doesn't deserve this. He has to know that much at least.

"You fooled me the other night," I say with a smirk, trying to make amends for the lingering effects of my childhood grudge.

Way to get my head straight. Tell him there was nothing to the other night and then admit to him that I'm thinking of it.

"Why ever would you think that?" He feigns innocence, but a smile plays on his lips.

"The agreeing to my rules but then turning around and saying I shouldn't believe anything said in the heat of passion. That type of thing."

He shrugs. "I agreed to your rules. We had sex. We got each other out of our systems," he says, but the way his eyes run up and down the length of my body has me shifting my feet to abate the ache the hunger in his look causes. It's like he's remembering every line and curve and flavor. "And now I'm here because I wanted to see you."

"But why? I've been nothing but bitchy to you."

He shrugs again. "Your words, not mine."

"I know, but they're true. We squabble like brother and sister and—"

"Not exactly like brother and sister, or else that would make the other night a little more awkward than you're already making it."

"You're a bucket full of laughs today, aren't you?"

"Always." And there goes the panty-dropping smile of his that makes me weak in the knees when I don't get weak in the knees. "I'm sorry. You were saying? Brother and sister . . ."

My concentration is lost amid his interruptions, leaving me to fumble with where I was going with my point. "Just why? That's all. Why would you want to come see me if I've been nothing but rude to you?"

"Because despite it all—or maybe because of it—I like you. And seeing as we got each other out of our systems, maybe I want to be friends."

"Friends with benefits," I retort.

"Not gonna deny the thought hasn't crossed my mind." His eyes lock with mine, those gold flecks dancing as my thoughts swirl, whirl, and tumble out of control.

"You're serious."

God, please let him be serious.

"As a heart attack."

Thoughts of us in the dim light fill my mind. The warmth. The pleasure. The comfort. The praise.

The breaking of rules.

"C'mon, Em. You know it's a good idea. We'll both be the beneficiaries of good sex—sex we've already proven to be *top notch*—and we don't have to deal with the complications of afterward. The clingy one who suddenly wants more. The frantic phone calls to make sure we're thinking about them. The randomly showing up where we like to hang out to make sure we didn't forget them."

I chuckle because it's as if he's repeating every scenario for why I've deleted names from my phone.

"See? You know what I'm talking about. You know that's all a pain in the ass."

"Kind of like you?"

"Yeah, but I'm a cute pain in the ass."

I can't stifle my laugh because he's wearing me down, not that I've put up much resistance.

"I have to think about this . . . without you in my face, badgering me like a little kid." Because I know he's playing me right now, and I'll be damned if it isn't a pretty brilliant play.

His laugh fills the room, and I know he knows he has me.

"Meet me here tomorrow after work. Like seven-ish. We can talk then."

"Deal." His grin is back and as disarming as ever.

And when he turns to go out the door, I hate that every part of me is relieved that I have an excuse to get to see him again. Whether I agree to his plan or not, at least I know he'll be here tomorrow. I spent the last week avoiding him, and I would never admit it aloud, but I'd missed him.

Friends with benefits.

Humph.

Way to stick to your guns, Reeves.

TWENTY-NINE

Emerson

STEP.
There it is again.
Step.
I dig my fingers into my stuffed bunny.
Step. The jingle of Rex's collar.
Don't make a sound.
Step.
Don't move.
Step.
My tummy hurts. I want to throw up.
Step.
Mommy. Come home. Please.
Step.
I can hear him breathing. I know if I open my eyes he will be standing there with his shoulder against the wall, watching me. Waiting.
I squeeze my eyes shut even tighter.
Please, God. If you make him go away, I promise to be a good girl from now on.
Step.
I promise not to sneak the M&M's hidden in the back of the pantry.
Step.
I swear I won't talk back and will make my bed every day.
Step.
Pretty please, God. I mean it this time.
The bed dips beneath me. His breath hits my face. The cold metal brushes against my arm.
I know what comes next.
"Emmy."
I want to throw up.
He moves my hair from my face.
"Emmy."
Runs his hand over my shoulder. Down my arm.

The sheets become wet as I go potty.

"Emmy." Angrier. Upset. Disappointed.

I've been a bad girl.

I know what comes next . . .

I jolt up out of bed, the sound of my voice filling the room. I'm disoriented and petrified. Confused. Sick to my stomach.

My heart is racing, and my pulse is pounding in my ears. There are tears on my cheeks, and my hands are shaking.

I don't remember anything about the dream.

Not a single thing.

Except the fear. I can still taste it on my tongue. I can still smell it clinging to my skin.

I know it has to do with *him*. I may not remember a damn thing from the dream, but I know this feeling. I've lived this feeling.

But it's been forever since I've felt this way.

Clutching the comforter tighter around me with one hand, I reach over and turn on the light on my nightstand. I don't like the dark.

The boogey man lives in the dark.

So does my dad.

Trying to settle the anxiety rattling around inside me as sure as the blood flowing through my veins, I stare out the window to the airfield beyond. To the yellow and red and green lights and pretend they are the lights on a Christmas tree. Something. Anything.

My fingertips run absently over the scars on the inside of my upper arms.

Over.

And.

Over.

And.

Over.

It's the only thing I can do to process the dream I can't remember and the nightmare I lived through.

THIRTY

Emerson

STARING AT THE BOX CUTTER IN MY HAND, I IGNORE THE CONTENTS of the open box in front of me. Its weight is as comforting as it is torturous.

My sleep-deprived mind drifts off and begs me to give into a need I haven't had in years.

Cut.

Feel the pain my mind has closed out.

Cut.

Take the blame I don't deserve.

The blade calls to me.

My skin begs to be scored.

To bleed out the guilt.

Cut.

My fingers itch to do it.

"You have a visitor, Em," Leo calls from the front of the office, making me drop the knife from trembling fingers. A quick glance at the clock tells me I've been standing here in La-la Land for way longer than I should have been.

"Okay," I say, but before the word is even out, Grant is standing in the doorway, looking like my own personal Heaven and Hell—a reprieve from the thoughts that have stolen my focus all day and the reason I think I had those thoughts. His smile is genuine, and I hate that every part of me craves to walk straight up to him and wrap my arms around him.

Comfort.

Distraction.

The need to feel anything other than what I'm feeling right now.

"Hey," he says.

"Hi." I infuse confidence into my voice when really I'm scared shitless over these emotions I'm not used to having.

"I'm early." He shrugs, his smile turning sheepish. "Can you blame me?"

My brow pinches, and I stare at him for a moment before what he's talking about dawns on me. The time and place I set. The offer he made that has, unbeknownst to him, been overshadowed by my issues he has no clue about.

"No. Um, no." It's his turn to study me, his eyes looking closer than I want him to. "I, uh, I have to bring a team up first. You're going with us," I ad-hoc. Dodge and weave.

"Like hell I am." He laughs and takes a few steps closer.

"Yeah, I think you need to cash in that voucher. I'm not tandem jumping with anyone, so I can strap you on." The words are out before I realize what they sound like, and the full-bodied laugh that falls from his mouth and echoes around the room is worth every ounce of blush that creeps into my cheeks.

"Thanks, Em, but strap-ons aren't my thing, and if they were, it wouldn't be you wearing one."

"I hear pegging is all the rage these days."

The look he gives me says he's having none of this conversation. "It'll be a cold day in hell, my dear."

Oddly enough, all it takes is talking to Grant about strap-ons to put me at ease for the first time all day. My smile feels real instead of forced and brittle. The ache in my shoulders eases some. The box cutter becomes less enticing. The weight of the unremembered dream fades.

"If that's your biggest fear, then jumping out of a plane should be a piece of cake."

"I didn't say it was my biggest fear—jumping out of a plane is. Heights and I don't get along."

"Still traumatized after going on the Ferris wheel, I see," I say, suddenly remembering him screaming to get down and trying not to cry as he clung to his mom sitting between us. The sour look on his face says he isn't thrilled I remember.

"Nice try, but I'm not biting. I hate the feeling of falling, and let's not forget the whole possibility of dying aspect."

"See? That's a huge misconception. There is no feeling of falling when you jump. Not one bit." I offer a huge grin.

"Not buying it."

"Don't you trust me, Malone?" I stand there with my hands on my hips, my head angled to the side, and my eyes issuing a challenge to that manly ego of his.

"No." There's no waffling in his voice when he says it, and while I should be offended, I'm not in the least.

"Oh, c'mon."

"Sorry, Em. Trust isn't going to save me when I'm hurtling to the earth at a million miles an hour and my parachute fails to open."

"Pfft. Such dramatics." I roll my eyes but smile when I realize he really is petrified of the idea. It's in the shift of his feet and the sudden shaking of his head as if he's physically rejecting the idea every time it gets brought up.

It takes a lot to overcome that kind of fear.

I should know.

"Dramatics? Life and death," he says as he pretends his hands are scales weighing each one. In his scenario, death wins. "I'll stay here and watch with my feet planted firmly on the ground."

"Suit yourself." I shrug as I slip my arms into the sleeves of my flight suit and zip it up over my red tank top. "You're gonna miss one hell of a ride."

"I know somewhere else I can get a ride," he murmurs suggestively as I walk past him and laugh.

"Head up. Wings out," I say.

THIRTY-ONE

Grant

THERE ARE HARD LIMITS.

And then there are *hard limits.*

Like watching the specks in the sky above me as they hurtle to the ground and knowing one of them is Emerson.

My hand shields my eyes, and my stomach churns when I think of the feeling of falling. It's total bullshit, there's no way you can launch yourself into thin air and not feel like your stomach shoves up into your throat.

"C'mon, c'mon," I murmur to myself as I wait for what feels like hours to see the parachutes deploy.

"A few more seconds," Leo says and startles me. I was so focused on Emerson that I hadn't realized he'd walked out.

I glance back to the sky in time to see the first parachute explode in a bloom of color. One after the other they open, dragging each jumper higher before slowly floating down again.

I want to say I breathe a little easier, but fuck if I'm not nauseated just watching the whole process.

"You really don't like this, do you?" Leo asks, giving me that look that says I'm a disgrace to the male gender for being such a pussy.

I glare at him from behind my sunglasses, saying, "You people are all fucking crazy."

"Yes, we are."

The phone rings in the office, and he heads back in to answer it while the parachutes continue to get bigger as they glide closer to the ground. From the corner of my eye, I watch the field person get ready to help jumpers if they need assistance, but I never take my full attention away from trying to find Emerson.

I mean, I know she's fine, but I need to see it for my own eyes. And when I do, my feet start moving on automatic to where she is standing amid the long grass of the field with a huge grin on her face.

"Great jump, everyone," she says as she goes from jumper to jumper and pats them on the back or gives them a high five. She takes pictures of a few of them, and some ask her to be a part of the shot with them.

"I have it, Em," Leo says, appearing out of nowhere when she begins to detach the parachute rigs for the clients. "You need to make sure Nervous Nelly over there's heart is still beating."

I open my mouth to make a dig of my own, but when Emerson laughs, it stops the words on my lips. She looks my way and waves animatedly before holding up a finger to tell me just a minute.

Leo may have offered to help, but the control freak in her can't simply walk away without checking all the rigs out. She heads to the pack nearest her and tugs on one part or another before moving to the next.

Definitely a control freak.

Which, of course, was why I let her think she was in control the other night. Anything to make her feel comfortable in the moment and keep what we had going.

And going it did. Very well, too. So well that I pulled the friends with benefits bullshit out of thin air yesterday as a way to get what I want—more of her, in any way, shape, or form I can get her.

She bends over and tugs on the last jumper's pack before laughing at something Leo says to her. And the adrenalized, carefree tone of it stops me in my tracks. Realization hits that I want to be the one who makes her laugh like that.

Christ. I know I want more with her—what that more is, I'm not sure— but until I heard that tone to her laugh, I hadn't realized how much I wanted it.

Studying her as she walks toward me, I know I'll pay whatever cost to make sure that happens.

"You have some serious balls," I say off the cuff the minute she's within speaking distance.

"At least someone does," Leo coughs out, and I lift a finger in his direction, but my attention is focused on Em—the flush in her cheeks, the lines around her eyes where her goggles pressed against her skin, the ear-to-ear grin on her lips.

She laughs and shakes her head. "We both know that isn't true," she says in a voice for only my ears followed by a wink. "You missed a good jump. Perfect conditions. Great visibility. Calm wind."

"I appreciate the hustle, but I'm not buying."

"You don't have to buy; you already have a gift certificate."

"You're relentless."

"And you're handsome as hell."

My feet stop moving as she keeps walking, her comment unexpected and probably one of the first things she's said to me that was complimentary. The thought makes me laugh because to most people that would sound odd, but they're not Emmy and me.

She's sunshine with a little bit of hurricane thrown in, and I'm willingly walking straight into her storm with nothing more than the clothes on my back.

She turns to face me, her brow furrowing as I just stare at her as the realization hits me again that I want to be a part of her beautiful destruction. All of it. Without a damn forecast to prepare me for what's coming next.

"What?" she asks.

"Why do you do it, Em?"

"Do what?" The setting sun plays against the strawberry highlights in her hair and pieces dance in the air like wisps of fire.

"Why do you push the edge?"

"I don't." She smiles and takes a step toward me so we're a few feet apart from each other. Airstrip asphalt stretches all around us, and the excited chatter of the other jumpers coming down from their adrenaline highs turns to background noise.

"What if the chute doesn't deploy?"

"Then it doesn't deploy."

The nonchalance in how she says it pisses me off. "Are you out of your mind?"

"Perhaps." She shrugs, as if it were no big deal. "But we can die at any time. What if I get hit by a car? What if I have a heart attack? What if a meteor falls from the sky and kills me? What if, what if, what if. No use going through life living scared."

"But jumping increases your risk."

"Living every day increases my risk." She laughs, but it's the look in her eyes that shuts me up. "Look, I could wake up tomorrow with cancer and never get to jump again. I'd rather take the chance, Grant."

"Em . . ." I know she's thinking of her mom.

"Look, the probability that something will malfunction is so small that it isn't worth even thinking about. Besides, I pack all my own gear, and unlike you, I trust what I do."

I take the jibe because I deserve it, but it doesn't help me process how casual she is being about this. "If it doesn't work, no one can save you."

"I'm well aware of that," she says as her shoulders straighten, telling me I've activated her obstinate defiance. I'm too pissed at how she can be so careless with her own life to care, though.

"Every time you jump, that probability increases. Don't you think that's something to consider? It isn't as if I could do anything standing here on the ground to help."

"There goes Grant Malone and his hero complex."

"I saved—" *I saved you once, and I'll save you again in a goddamn heartbeat without thinking twice.*

The thought screams in my head, but I stop myself from saying it, from bringing the past into the present. From treating her like the girl she no longer wants to be.

Yet, I remember.

And I wonder.

And I worry.

Just like that fucking case file sitting in my house.

"You saved what?" She grits out the words as she takes another step closer, posture defensive and full of challenge. Sure, she's angry with me. I'm questioning her, but fuck it, she needs to know I care. Too bad I'm a guy and am not sure how to get that point across without setting off that magnificent and infuriating temper of hers.

"Nothing."

"I can save myself just fine, Grant Malone. And not just in skydiving. At least in jumping there's a reserve canopy in case the first one malfunctions. Wouldn't it be great if life had a backup chute for those moments when you're falling without anything to catch you?" She shrugs with her hands out to her side.

"And if the backup chute fails?"

"Like I said, life fails all the time. The only way to deal with it is to roll with the punches. Besides, *living safely* is dangerous. It isn't good for the soul or the psyche." She flashes me a huge grin before turning on her heel and saying over her shoulder, "Come on, I've gotta close up."

Standing on the tarmac, I watch her stride toward the office of Blue Skies.

Living safely is dangerous.

Well, shit.

Just as I'm about to walk after her, my phone alerts a text. I groan when I read it and realize I just screwed up royally.

Talking about sex possibilities with Emerson or fulfilling obligations to my family.

I know which one I'd rather choose, and I currently can't take my eyes off her.

Emerson

"YOU DON'T HAVE TO DO THIS," GRANT SAYS AS HE PULLS DOWN the street I know so well from memory but have lacked the courage to venture back to since I returned to Sunnyville.

I'm not ignorant of the fact that he took the long way through the neighborhood. I am, however, silently relieved not to have to deal with seeing my old house for the first time since I left it twenty years ago.

I risk a glance his way, the anxiety I know visible in my eyes hidden by my sunglasses. "I know."

I don't know.

Needing to abate the nerves jittering through me, I slide my clasped hands between my thighs and squeeze my legs together.

Cue the panic.

"My mom is going to be thrilled to have a woman to balance out all the testosterone tonight," he says and reaches over to squeeze the top of my thigh. He doesn't remove his hand, though. I appreciate the silent show of support and wonder if he has any idea of the riot of emotions clamoring around inside me.

"It'll be good to see her," I murmur, eyes fixed on the houses as we pass.

Sally Glendale's house is still there and still that awful green color we used to say looked like puke. Then comes Adam Beecham's house to remind me of the hours we spent on the green transformer box out front playing UNO until the streetlights came on and it was time to go home.

Everything looks the same but so very different from my memories. I bet they've all moved out, moved on, and forgotten about the little girl, Emmy Reeves, two streets down who had the *unthinkable* happen to her.

Did their parents gossip about me for a long time after I left? Did they wonder if I was telling the truth, or did they just think I was making stuff up to get attention from my workaholic mother like little kids often did? Or did they not think of me at all because it was too unpleasant and might ruin the idyllic feeling of their safe neighborhood?

My palms grow sticky as the car slows down. My heart beats faster.

Why did I agree to come?

Because I know all of these people forgot about me a long time ago. I would bet that if I were to ask someone if they remembered the Reeves girl, they'd probably recall her name was Emily or Emma and have to think real hard about why the name sounded familiar.

Maybe I agreed to come because after the nightmare of last night, I don't want to be alone tonight. I'm so exhausted that I fear what other dreams will come when I finally let my subconscious crash.

"Emerson?"

I look over to Grant, only to notice that we were already parked along the curb in front of a place I remembered more fondly than my own, the Malone house.

My smile hides my nerves as I take in the exterior. It's just as I remember it being, but the paint's newer and the flowers are brighter. There's a woman's attention to detail in the colorful pots carefully placed on the stoop, and I can hear the wind chimes tinkle in the breeze as Grant opens the truck's door.

With a fortifying breath, I get out, but doubt shreds me apart with each and every step up the walkway. As positive as I am that most of Sunnyville doesn't remember Emmy Reeves with the pigtails and freckles, I am certain that the Malone family does.

I spent years going to psychologists, and every single one of them had the same exact look when they spoke to me. Pity. They all thought I was broken and irreparable. As soon as I convinced my mom I didn't need to go anymore, I promised myself no one would ever know about my past so that I'd never have to see that look again.

Now, for the first time since I made that promise, I'm willingly walking into a room, knowing full well I just might get that look again.

Grant must sense I'm about to lose my courage because he reaches out and links his fingers through mine, squeezing them in silent reassurance. He doesn't speak. He doesn't even glance my way. He just leads me up the last step as if this is an everyday thing for me.

"Hello?" he calls out as he opens the door, but his voice is drowned out by a cacophony of sound. A loud, baritone bark is echoing around the house, along with the screech of a little kid in what sounds like a tickle war. Laughter reverberates off the walls, and the faint chords of music playing in the backyard competes with the sound of an Indy race on a television no one seems to be watching.

Not only is it complete chaos but also it's exactly how I remembered it.

I follow Grant through the formal living room and stop when I see Betsy Malone. Her back is to me, and she's chopping vegetables on the counter I used to steal cookies from. Her hair may be shorter now, but everything else about her appears exactly the same.

"Mom," Grant says.

"It's about time you showed up," she says, but when she looks over and sees me standing in her kitchen, her lips fall lax. "Emmy Reeves. Well, aren't you a sight for sore eyes." She wipes her hands on a dishtowel and steps toward me since I'm frozen in place. "Grant said you were gorgeous, but leave it to a man to understate the obvious. My goodness. Get over here, you, and let me hug you."

Just like that, Betsy has her arms around me and is squeezing me so tight I can barely breathe, but it's okay because if I breathe the tears that threaten are going to fall. I don't want them to fall. Not here. Not now. Maybe later, but not now.

Her hand smooths down the back of my hair as if I were still a child, and I just close my eyes and sink into the feeling. It's like I've stepped back in time. The familiarity of her voice and the feeling of her arms provided more comfort than she could have ever fathomed. I know I was stupid for worrying about coming here.

Betsy Malone was my second mother.

This is the closet I've felt to being home since long before I never had an actual home to go back to.

"Let me look at you," she says, squeezing me one more time before stepping back and holding my arms out. When she meets my eyes, there are tears swimming in hers, and I enjoy knowing I'm not the only one who feels this overwhelmed being here again.

"Hi." My voice breaks with the single word, and it causes her to smile and pull me in for one more quick hug.

"Wine?" She punctuates the word with a decisive nod, most likely to prevent me from getting uncomfortable. "Wine is definitely what us two women need to combat the five testosterone-laced beings manning the barbecue."

And as if on cue, there's a flash of fur followed by a squeal of delight chasing after him. A little boy with sandy blond hair and dirt smudged on his cheek zooms through the kitchen before skidding to a halt and narrowing his eyes at me.

He looks just like the Grant I remember.

The thought knocks me back as I stare at him longer than I should.

"Who's she?" he asks Betsy.

"That's Uncle Grant's friend, Emerson."

"Cool," he says as he lifts a foot to continue his mad dash through the house.

"Luke," she warns, making him stop and causing Grant to chuckle.

With a resigned sigh like I'm ruining his fun, he turns to face me. "Hi, my name is Luke Malone, nice to meet you," he says in a monotone voice and holds his hand out. He's absolutely adorable, and I have a feeling he's also a bit of a hellion. The boy has Malone written all over him, which makes me like him because of and not in spite of it.

"Very nice to meet you, Luke. Is that your dog?" I shake his hand.

"No. That's Poppy's. He's big and slobbery and nice. His name is Moose and right now, he has one of my Pokémon cards in his mouth, and it's a Pikachu—a really good one—so I need to go get it back before he eats it."

Before I can say another word, he zooms out of the kitchen like his pants are on fire, leaving me with the glass of white wine Betsy's holding out to me and Grant eager to properly introduce me to the rest of the crew.

"See? That right there," Grant says with a laugh, "is why neither of you two bast—jerks have a girlfriend."

"This coming from the authority on women," Grayson says with a roll of his eyes.

My cheeks hurt from smiling so much, which tells me it was the right decision to come here with Grant. It had been against my better judgment, but obviously, I was wrong.

Luke is lying on his back on the grass about twenty feet away from us, Moose curled up next to him and dwarfing the five-year-old in size. The little boy seems to be talking to himself while he makes up stories about the aliens in the stars above him. I smile as I think of how many adventures I had in this backyard. It's the one place that holds one hundred percent positive memories for me, and that isn't easy to find.

"How's your studying going?" Betsy asks Grant, seemingly oblivious to the brief meeting of the eyes between Grant and his father.

"Good. I'm as ready as can be, but you know how it goes, there's always politics involved," he replies.

"Just remember, sometimes the high road can mean lying low," Chief Malone murmurs, piquing my interest.

"Once an asshole, always an asshole," Grayson chimes in, and I get the sense they are all talking about someone in particular, I just have no idea who. Even more peculiar is Betsy's lack of a reprimand over Grayson's comment, since over the course of dinner, most curse words were met with her rebuke.

No one can say this family doesn't have each other's backs.

"I have stronger words than that—"

"But you have a lady present," Betsy interrupts and gives Grant a warning glare.

"Yes, ma'am." Grant makes a show of looking properly reprimanded, which has his brothers snickering.

"Competition is healthy when going for a promotion," she says in the most motherly of tones, "even if that competition is a self-serving prick."

Everyone's eyes widen as they look back and forth at each other to make sure their mother really just said that before bursting out into laughter over her unexpected comment.

"You have a lady present," Grant mimics her.

"Yes, well, I'm sure Emmy's heard those terms before, haven't you, dear?" She pats my hand and smiles wider.

"So, Emerson," Chief Malone says. "Grant tells me you are buying Blue Skies out at Miner's Airfield."

"I'm trying to," I say. "After traveling for so long, it's finally time to put some roots down. It's been an adjustment staying in one place for this long, but it's a good change. Blue Skies has been neglected for a while now so I'm enjoying breathing life back into it. Now I just can't wait to make it mine. Fingers and toes crossed I get loan approval."

"You always were up for a challenge," Betsy says as she puts another piece of chocolate cake on my plate without my having to ask. "Eat up. You always loved dessert . . . but jumping out of airplanes? Really?"

There's something about the way she references how I used to be with such nonchalance that makes it ring in my ears. When Grant mentioned the same thing at Desi's, it made me uneasy. He was revealing a small part of my past to people unfamiliar with it. But this, Betsy bringing it up in the one place that was my safe haven, feels different to me. It's almost comforting to know I existed to someone when I was a child and that they remember me. Moving on a whim and living like a nomad, often doesn't afford you that feeling.

"Emerson subscribes to the living-safely-is-dangerous theory," Grant interjects as he bumps his knee against mine beneath the table.

"Well, if you're with that asshole"—Grady gestures to Grant—"then you definitely like to live dangerously. He isn't known to be one who sticks around longer than the quick—"

"Grady Malone," Betsy warns in that tone that brings a smile to my lips. "You know better than to talk that way when someone brings a guest over. Your father and I did not raise unmannerly heathens."

"Sorry, Mom," he says with no sincerity before looking at me. "See? Nothing has changed. We still bicker constantly like we did when we were kids. We're just older and the insults are more brutal."

That's the first time our collective past has been put out there in the open, causing an uncomfortable silence. Luckily, I've had enough wine that the mention doesn't trip me up like it might have if I were completely sober.

"Is it sad that I remember that? The names you used to call each other and how when your mom called you by your full name, it meant you really were in trouble," I say to try to ease the unspoken tension. "Being an only child, I never had to deal with that. The flip side was I couldn't blame something on someone else either so my mom always knew if I was at fault."

"How is your mom doing, Emerson?" the chief asks, and Grant tenses beside me.

"She passed away a few years back."

"Oh, Emmy," the chief says. "I had no idea. If my eldest would have had proper manners and let me know that, then we would have known not to ask. I'm so very sorry."

"It's okay. She was sick for a long time, and now her suffering is over."

"What made you decide to move back here to Sunnyville?" he continues.

"Blue Skies."

And possibly your son.

The thought has me lifting my fork and digging into the second piece of cake to clear the startling thought from my mind.

But it's true. I always knew that if I moved back I'd run into Grant Malone eventually.

Hadn't I wanted to?

Hadn't I always looked in every crowd, just in case I saw his face?

"Well, whatever reason it may be, we're glad to see you again," Betsy says, breaking the sudden lull in conversation and patting my hand. "It's like having my daughter back."

Those simple words are like resin being poured onto the cracks of my heart. A protective shield to ward off whatever lies ahead for it.

There's a crackling of a police scanner, and I smile at how all of them fall silent while codes are relayed over the radio. Their bodies still, heads all angle in the same mannerism that reflects they are related. Each so similar, yet so different.

"You're being rude, gentlemen," Betsy says and meets my eyes. "It's a full-time job keeping the Malone men in line and away from work when they're off duty."

"Shame on us for saving lives," Grady replies and has us all laughing.

"Always the class clown," Betsy mutters in jest as she stands up with her plate in her hand.

"Can I help you clean up, Mom?" Grant asks as he scoots his chair back. "Emerson and I need to be getting back."

"I thought you were off tomorrow," Grayson says.

"I am, but I sprung this on Emerson without asking, so I'm sure she has other, more pressing things she needs to do."

Every part of me wants to reject what he's saying. It doesn't matter how much I didn't want to come here, because now I don't want to leave.

There's a feeling here I've missed for so very long.

A feeling I craved in my childhood that this house—that this family—provided to me.

Security.

That isn't an easy thing for normal people to find in this world, let alone people with a past like mine. It's often fleeting and habitually false.

It's here and now that I've found it, I find that I'm scared to lose it.

THIRTY-THREE

Emerson

"HEAD UP. WINGS OUT. WHAT DOES THAT MEAN?"

I smile at Grant's question and lean back on my hands as my legs dangle off the tailgate of Grant's truck. "It was something my mom used to say to me. Originally, she told me that if I keep my head up and put on a brave face when I'm afraid, then the angels will put their wings out and use them to protect me." I smile at the memory. "Over the years, it became shortened to head up, wings out. The first time I jumped, she made me carry it on a piece of paper in my pocket, as if it would ensure I made it safely back to the earth . . . so from then on, I said it before every jump. When she died, it kind of became my way of reminding myself she's looking out for me. That it's her angel wings keeping me safe."

"Head up. Wings out," he murmurs. "I like that."

Silence falls between us for a few moments. "This is my favorite time of day to be here," I muse as I stare at the lights of the runway

"Why's that?"

"Because it's quiet. There's typically no one around, and if there is, it's because they've filed a flight plan ahead of time and I already know about it. There are the lights of the runway and the rustling of the trees from the breeze. It's even better when the moon's full and the shadows are everywhere." I fall silent, feeling silly but, for some reason, wanting him to know about one of the places I find peace.

"I can understand that. I have a place I like, too. It's up in the hills, and when I go there, I can stare at the city's lights below and the stars above for hours."

There's the baying of a dog in the far distance and then a reciprocated one from its echoes. This feels so normal, and I'm not sure why I'm not panicking that this is too close to breaking one of my rules, the one that demands I don't do anything that seems like a date. But there's a comfortable silence that I'm not used to, so maybe that's why the anxiety seems to be missing.

Though, I did feel the same way—normal—at the Malone house tonight, which was far from quiet. With Luke and Moose and their little boy-big dog relationship, the constant ribbing between three brothers close as night but different as day, and the constant love felt between all members of the family, it was the most welcoming chaos I think I've ever seen.

"Who would have ever thought the three of you would be what you are today—a police officer, a firefighter, and a rescue pilot," I muse, only realizing I've said it aloud when Grant's chuckle rumbles through the night.

"I'm thinking I should be offended by that comment."

"No. Not at all. It's just . . . kind of cool." My mind fills with memories I forgot I had. Of shy Grady and his books. Of loud Grayson and his daredevil stunts. Of responsible Grant always looking out for the two of them . . . *and me.*

He shrugs. "My dad instilled in us the need to serve."

"And what does your mom think about that?"

"She's tough."

"Yeah, she is." My smile is automatic when it comes to thinking of her.

"She's a cop's wife. She knows the drill. There have been a handful of times when I have known she has been really worried. Bad calls. Natural disasters. Accidents."

"You sound so casual."

"Like I said, she's tough. Just as any woman who decides to take one of us on has to be." He lifts his eyes to meet mine across the dimly lit night, and the look he gives me says the two words that don't pass his lips: *Like you.*

Chills race over my skin despite the warm night air, and I'm nervous and cognizant that we are talking about ourselves more than I typically allow.

"Thank you for taking me."

"The minute I turned into the neighborhood, I realized it might not have been such a great idea," he says, making me close one of the padlocked doors he'd just opened. "I'm glad you had a good time."

"I did. Um, I'd invite you back to my place, but there isn't much to it . . . but it is clean." It's the only thing I can think to say—when all else fails, talk about the physicality between us to prevent us from talking about anything else.

"You say it's clean as if it's a shock."

"It is." I laugh. "We'll just say it wasn't too pretty a few weeks ago. Or if Desi were here, she'd say *ever.*"

I shove up off the tailgate and begin walking to my loft, my mind set on the notion of if he follows, he follows, and if he doesn't, he doesn't.

That's a lie I knowingly tell myself. Truth is, I don't want to be alone tonight. I don't want to give my mind a single chance to get lost in itself and bring me back *there* again.

I have one foot on the stairs that lead up to my loft when Grant's hand lands on my bicep, turning me around. "Emerson."

He rubs his thumb on the inside of my arm, and I can see the confusion on his face the same moment I yank my arm away from his touch.

"Did you get hurt today?" he asks, and I cringe at my overreaction, but that's my ugly, and I don't want him knowing my ugly.

I've escaped him seeing them this far and now I scramble to figure out how to recover and take cues from what he asked. "No, not today. The nylon on the rig rubs me right there for some reason, so I have a few scars from always getting scratched. I'm so used to it that I forget it's even there until someone mentions it."

He stares, gauging whether to believe me or not. "I'm sorry, I didn't mean to . . ."

"No, I overreacted. It's okay." I lean in and do what I've been thinking about ever since we left his parents' house—I press my lips to his.

Grant reacts immediately. Hunger and the mint he had in the car are on his tongue. His hands run up and down my arms as he takes a step closer, bringing us chest to chest since I'm still one step up from him.

We sink into the kiss. There is no rush, just a sense that we are feeling each other out to see where we go from here.

A part of me doesn't want to know that answer.

I just want to enjoy the moment.

Live in the now.

Forget the complications that being with Grant Malone could cause in my life.

"Are we going to do this?" he murmurs against my lips.

A long, slow, mesmerizing kiss that leaves me weak in the knees when weakness isn't a thing I allow.

"Do what?"

A nip of my bottom lip.

"Do this. You. Me. *Friends*."

A hand runs languorously up and down my spine before landing on my ass and pulling me tighter against him.

"Friends don't do this."

His chuckle is muted against my lips.

"You and I have never been anything close to normal, Em."

A lick of his tongue against mine makes me press into him when he leans back.

"You're too sexy, and I'm too horny to walk away tonight without sleeping with you . . ." I murmur playfully. *And truthfully*.

"You're goddamn right . . . so is that a yes?"

"*Yes*," I grunt as his hand on my ass slides inside the waistband of my shorts.

The thumb on his other hand brushes the underside of my breast. A tease. A taunt. A promise of what's to come.

"But there are rules," I say before he goes to kiss me again, and I earn a chuckle as he rests his forehead against mine.

"I thought we already covered them?"

"We did, but—*ahhh*."

His teeth tug on my earlobe and cause an electric current to shock through my system.

"You were saying?" His breath is warm against my skin as he asks.

"Before was a one-night thing," I say, but his lips on my neck are making it hard to string thoughts let alone coherent sentences together. "And now we're agreeing to more."

"Em." It's part groan, part moan when his lips try to brush against mine as I take a step backward up the stairs. It's only a fleeting moment that we're apart before our mouths crash back together in a torrent of greed and need.

"No romance."

It's getting harder to remember the things I want to address as my body ignites with every kind of want imaginable.

"Naturally."

He places open-mouthed kisses down the line of my jaw, drawing goose bumps over my skin as we take another step up.

"No lovey-dovey."

"You're not the lovey-dovey type."

He pulls gently on my earlobe, the heat of his mouth only intensifying the sensation as the ache intensifies between my thighs.

"No overnights."

His hand slides beneath my shirt and begins working on the clasp of my bra as his lips close over the peak of my nipple through the fabric.

"Not unless we're doing this."

Another step up.

"No dates. No dating. No semblance of dating."

"You're talking too much," His words are punctuated with a nip before his lips find mine again and his fingers find the button on my shorts.

"Grant." I step up to get away and stand my ground, but I know it's for show. I'm too far gone, too lost in Lustville to push him away.

"Yes. No dates. Or dating. Or eating. Or talking. Or whatever you want so long as you shut your mouth unless it's kissing me and put your hand on my dick because, baby, I'm dying here."

I lean back and meet his eyes. There's humor there. And desperation.

My fingers find the button on his jeans, and he groans when I find purchase. After I tug the zipper down, I cup him and gently scrape my fingers outside and over the seam of denim, causing the sexiest sound I've ever heard to emit from deep in his throat.

"I know I'm forgetting something," I say as my lips find the curve of his neck, and he climbs the final step.

"Your keys. You're forgetting your keys," he says through a laugh as I go to pull my hand away from his dick, but his fingers are on my wrist in a flash. "That's not going anywhere, Em. Give me the keys, I'll open it."

In seconds, my keys are out of my purse and my door is open and we're standing in the dark with my hand on his cock and my rules wedged securely between us.

"No talking about our pasts. No sleeping with other people—just for safety's sake—"

"Woman, you could ask me to skydive and I'd say yes so long as I get to fuck you again. Shortly. Like in minutes."

He must be dead serious.

I draw his shirt over his head and then pull mine off, my bra falling to the floor as I lean forward and suck one of his nipples.

"More like seconds." His voice is strained and his hands grip tighter on my arms.

"This is such a mistake," I groan as his hands slide into the waistband of my shorts and push them down.

"Mm-hmm," he says against my lips. "You can call the first time a mistake. The second time, it's called a decision. Make the goddamn decision, Em. Please. Before I die of desperation."

I chuckle. "So dramatic." I kiss him again and love how when I pull back, he leans forward to take more. It shows what I do to him. It shows he wants me. "No . . ." I can't think of any more rules because his cock pulses against my hand, growing harder.

"What else can there possibly be?" he asks, exasperated as he shoves his own jeans down his hips so that his cock springs free into my hand.

"This," I say before I drop to my knees and look up to him as I take the entire, rock-hard length of him in my mouth.

"I fucking love that rule." He groans as his head falls back and his fingers sink into my hair, tightening when he hits the back of my throat.

THIRTY-FOUR

Grant

THE WOMAN IS INCREDIBLE IN EVERY FUCKING SENSE OF THE word.

She eyes me from where she stands in the kitchen—if I can call it that since it's little more than a hot plate, a mini fridge, a toaster oven, and a Keurig. It doesn't hurt that the only thing she's wearing is a pair of boy shorts.

No top. No nothing.

Talk about a morning view I'd like to revisit.

That fact makes it that much harder not to stare at her and her perfectly perky set of tits. I can remember so very vividly how her nipples feel against my tongue, and it makes my damn mouth water.

Fuck if my morning hard-on isn't begging to take advantage of everything about her again, but there's so much more at stake right now than coming again.

Like her not realizing that we've broken her first rule, not once but twice. *No overnights.*

I would be surprised if she doesn't already realize that and is making her coffee and plotting how to get control of the situation back. I'll gladly give it to her if I get to end up sitting here watching her shirtless in her kitchen again.

"How do you want yours?" she asks.

"I can get it."

"Relax. I'm perfectly capable of pushing a button and not screwing it up. If it were anything more than that, then you could be concerned."

"Black, please."

After putting in a fresh pod and pressing the button to start the machine, she pads to one side of the small loft and fires up her computer without looking at the screen. My attention stays on her as she checks her cell phone and gives it a roll of her eyes over something before flipping a file folder open and making a note in it.

A file folder.

Much like the one in a box on my table at home.

How the fuck can the little girl on that folder's label be this same damn

636 | K. BROMBERG

woman in front of me. Shouldn't she be fucked up? Shouldn't she be a mess of issues?

Maybe she is underneath and is simply doing a damn good job of hiding it.

Then again, it's hard to see a thing when her self-assuredness, confidence, and strength roll off her in thick waves.

Thankfully, the jiggling of her tits as she walks to get our coffee steers my thoughts away from any further psychoanalyzing. They mesmerize me as she crosses the distance, and hell if I'm not blatantly appreciating them. It's only when she stops at the edge of the bed and holds the cup of coffee out to me that I meet her eyes.

"You like what you see?" She laughs with a raised set of eyebrows, and I love that she is secure enough she can ask the question and make it sound sexy instead of conceited.

"No complaints here. I'm just trying to figure out how I can see this view more often."

"Such a typical male. You get blown, fucked, then fucked again, but you still aren't satisfied." Her smile is wide as she sits on the bed facing me with one knee bent beneath her and the other leg hanging off the edge. "What's it going to take, Malone?"

"*More of you.*"

There's a silent moment that passes where her eyes soften and her smile slowly falls, vulnerability written all over her features before she throws her head back and laughs as if what I said is the funniest thing in the world.

"Flattery will get you everywhere." She takes a sip of her coffee but leaves her eyes on mine from above the rim.

"It will?"

"It will."

"Good to know," I say as I lean back against the headboard and look around her place. It's small but has a pretty cool setup. The colors are muted, the furniture is modest, but it's a complete reflection of her. Practical and minimalist. The best part is the series of windows that face out to the field and trees opposite the landing strip.

"Who do you rent this place from, again?" I ask, already knowing the answer.

"Travis Barnhardt."

"I think I know him."

"You do know him."

"I do? Oh. Isn't he Dean's dad?"

"Dean?"

"Dean from Mrs. Gellar's class."

Her hand stutters in motion as she lifts her coffee cup to her lips. The quick aversion of her eyes tells me she doesn't like this topic.

I push anyway.

"I don't think so." Her voice is soft as she sets the cup down, picks it back up, and then straightens the sheets some.

"Sorry." I shake my head, hating that the simple mention of Mrs. Gellar's class puts her visibly on edge. "You're right. Dean's last name was Meyers."

I wait to see a reaction from her, but her expression remains stone cold. "Yes, that was it."

Silence falls between us as we both stare into our coffees, but questions nag me more than ever before since running into Emerson. It's her dig about not trusting me that she played off as one thing when she really meant another. It's her need to stay detached even though we're clearly sleeping together.

"About that day . . ." *Fucking Christ.* I'm so goddamn distracted by her incredible body sitting half-naked before me that I blurted out my thoughts.

"No," she snaps as she shoves up off the bed.

"We need to talk about it at some point, Em."

"Actually, no, we don't." She turns her back to me and walks toward the windows.

"Em—"

"Stop!" she shouts. "I've dealt with it. I don't need you bringing it up, so don't talk about it again. Now, *get out* before you break another rule because you're walking a fine line with me, Grant. The spending the night was a mistake. You bringing that up, wasn't cool . . . so, play time's over. The benefits have been used up for now. I have to get to work."

I study her for a moment—a silhouette against the morning light beyond—the curve of her waist, the shape of her legs, her strawberry hair falling down her bare back in tangles. There's so much shit I want to say, but the defensiveness in her posture tells me she won't hear a damn word of it.

In time.

In silence and with gritted teeth, I rise from the bed and pull on my jeans and shirt. All the while, she stares out the window, ignoring the tension settling into place.

With my keys in my hand, I walk toward where she stands. "Your past sure as fuck doesn't define the woman you are . . . and it isn't my business, regardless of how much I care about you and want to make sure you're okay. Em, I was there, and I feel like you hold it against me—"

"Or maybe I'm just this hostile with all men," she whispers, never turning to face me, but I can hear the pain in her voice and hate that I put it there.

I take the final step to her and hear her breath catch as I press my lips to the back of her shoulder. "Nah, I think it's particular to me." She nods but doesn't step away from me. "Can we somehow wipe the slate clean?"

"How, though?" Confusion laces her voice, and her willingness to even ask that question is telling. It doesn't matter how much I think I know about her past, I don't have a goddamn clue about the demons she still battles. And battle she does. Even now, she's fighting them with loud declarations of denial and softly whispered pleas for help.

"From here on out, we forget the memories and just chase the moments," I say with another press of my lips to her skin before walking out the door.

THIRTY-FIVE

Grant

"**I**F I HAD A SECRET, COULD I TELL YOU AND WOULD YOU PROMISE not to tell anyone in the whole wide world?"

"Huh? Yeah. Sure." I'm at the good part in my RL Stine book and don't want to stop.

"I'm serious."

She is serious. When I look up from my book, I realize she's been crying. Like red-eyes crying. But she's wearing her favorite purple dress with sparkly black shoes—the one she calls her "pop star" outfit.

"What's wrong?" She doesn't move other than to look over her shoulder toward where her house is and then back to me. "Emmy?"

"Never mind. I'm fine." She smiles as she sits beside me but makes a funny sound when she does. Like she's trying not to cry.

"You okay?" Something's wrong with her. Emmy never cries.

She bites her bottom lip and nods before looking over her shoulder again. Something's wrong.

"Em?" I nudge her with my elbow. "If you're gonna tell me, then you need to tell me quick because my mom's gonna come out soon with my lunch, and then we're going to have to walk to school. So what's wrong?"

"You have to pinky promise, Grant Malone, that if I tell you this secret, you won't ever tell another person, ever, ever, ever. If you do, I'll never be your friend again. Promise me. Cross your heart and hope to die."

"But I—"

"Not even your mom or dad or brothers or anyone." Her eyes fill with tears again. Girls and tears. I'd roll my eyes if she weren't so upset.

"Okay. I promise." I cross my heart and link pinkies with her. "Is that good?"

"Yeah. You really promise?"

"Yes. I promise. What's the big deal?"

"You know how my mom goes to work at night?"

"At the hospital? Yeah. It's super cool she gets to help people."

She nods and licks her lips and then looks down to where she's picking the skin around her thumbnail so it bleeds. "Well, when she goes to work, sometimes my dad hurts me."

"Hurts you? Like he spanks you when you get in trouble?" I'd give anything to have a mom like hers who doesn't believe in the belt on your bottom. My dad says it builds respect. I say it builds a sore butt.

"No."

"No? Then . . ."

"He comes in my room and holds a gun to my head and molests me."

A tear drops on her thumb, but all I hear is the word "gun." I don't know what molests means, but I know guns are serious. The million lectures my dad has given me and my brothers to never touch one fill my head, and I know this is bad, but . . .

"Emmy . . . why would he do that?" I look around the street and wonder if my mom can hear inside the house.

"Because he says I'm pretty and he loves me."

"But . . ." My dad has a gun, too, and he doesn't do that to me. I don't like the icky feeling in my tummy. My book slips from my hands, and I don't like what we're talking about, so I concentrate on the creepy monster on the cover as I shove it in my backpack. "I don't understand. I—"

"I don't, either." Another tear falls, and the way she says it makes tears burn in my eyes.

"We should tell my mom. She'd know—"

"No!" she yells as she grabs my hand and squeezes it so hard it hurts. "You promised you wouldn't tell anyone. He said it would hurt my mommy if I tell anyone, and I don't want her hurt, Grant. He said this is what daddies do and . . ." She hiccups over a sob, and I don't know what to do.

"Grant! It's time to get going," my mom calls from the house. "Oh, hi, Emmy. Look at how pretty you look today. Just like one of the Spice Girls."

Emmy smiles for the first time since she got here to walk to school, and I wonder if maybe she's fibbing. Sometimes she does that. Girls always want attention, or at least that's what Cooper says.

Em stays where she is on the sidewalk as I jog up the steps to get my lunch from my mom. After I shove it in my backpack, I give her a hug goodbye.

For some reason, when I hug her, I have to blink away the tears before she sees them.

"Have a good day, honey," she says and then she gets that line in her forehead like when she doesn't believe what I'm telling her. "You okay? What's wrong?"

Emmy's dad is mean.

"You have to pinky promise, Grant Malone, that if I tell you this secret, you

won't ever tell another person, ever, ever, ever. If you do, I'll never be your friend again. Promise me. Cross your heart and hope to die"

"Yeah. I'm good. Just got something in my eye is all."

She studies me again, but Grayson cries inside, saving me from more questions. "Don't rub it then, okay?" I nod before she says the same thing she says every day when we leave to walk the straight shot of a street to school. "I'll watch you guys from here until you get to the school gates, and then I'll meet you at the tree after class to walk home with you."

"'Kay."

When I jog down the steps, I hate that Adam from across the street is standing there with Emmy and waiting to walk with us. I need to talk to her and ask if she's really telling the truth. Her dad seems nice to me.

And he's not a police officer. Only police officers and bad guys have guns and he's not either of those.

But my tummy still hurts.

"You promise?" Emmy mouths to me from where she stands beside me in the girls' line while I'm in the boys' line. We're in the very back this morning because we were battling in two square and neither of us wanted to quit first and lose.

"I promise."

"If you tell anyone, I'll never be your friend again. I might even 'bad word' you."

"'Bad word me?'"

"H-A-T-E," she spells, and I forgot that her mom thinks the words hate and stupid are bad words worthy of television time being taken away.

"I promise, Em. I promise, okay?" I say loud enough that the kid in front of me turns around to shush me like I'm going to get the boys' line in trouble.

Emmy just stares at me like I told her we're getting to watch a Disney movie after lunch instead of doing work . . . I think the word for it is hopeful. I'm not sure, though.

But even as we start our morning paperwork, I can't stop thinking about what Em said.

"He puts a gun to my head and molests me."

Even after our circle time when we move into writing in our journals, I think about it.

But she seems fine. She seems like Emmy. The red in her eyes from crying is gone, and she's pulling out the dreaded composition notebook so she can write about Helen Keller. Just like we all did yesterday. And the day before. I don't care about Helen Keller because I already know the important stuff—that she was deaf and blind.

"Mrs. Gellar?" I shoot my hand up as high as it will go, hoping her answer will be the same as every other time someone has asked.

"I don't know the meaning of this word in our book."

"You know where Webster is," she says, using the class-decided name for our dictionary.

I walk to the corner of the room and open the book, struggling with the paper jacket when it falls off the hard cover. When I glance over my shoulder, no one is near me, but Emmy meets my eyes and smiles softly.

M.

It takes a few seconds for me to find the word.

Molests.

And it takes me even longer to figure out the definition.

To assault or abuse (a person, especially a woman or a child) sexually.

I snap the book closed, my cheeks red because there is the word "sex" in the definition, and I don't really know what that is except for it's what Cooper says only mommies and daddies do and he's never going to do it.

But I know the word assault. My dad uses that word all the time when I get to visit him at work and he talks cases with other officers. So, if he uses the word, then I know it means bad things.

Does Emmy have this same molestation disease these suspects my dad talks about have? But she isn't a suspect. She didn't do anything wrong.

Did she?

The bell for recess rings.

Guns. Mr. Reeves. Molest. Assault.

"Bet I'm gonna beat you at two square again," Emmy says, and I run to follow after her.

"Mr. Malone." Mrs. Gellar's sharp tone—like I'm in trouble—stops my feet from running when I know I shouldn't be running in the classroom.

"Yeah?"

"The word is yes, not yeah. We're working on grammar," she says as she walks toward me with her hand on her back and her big, pregnant belly—that Cooper says you get from having S-E-X—leading the way.

"Yes?" I correct.

"Head on out, Emmy. Grant's going to go back and put Webster in his proper place. He'll be there in a minute."

I grumble and shuffle my feet as the door to the playground shuts, taking the sunshine with it.

Guns.

Picking up Webster, I make sure the jacket is on . . .

Mr. Reeves.

Then I slide it into the bookshelf . . .

Molest.

Finally, I turn to head to the door.

Assault.

"Mrs. Gellar?" I ask, my voice breaking and heart beating so fast I can feel it against my chest.

"Yeah, sweetie? Oh, thanks for fixing Webster," she says, thinking I was trying to show her I did what she'd asked. "You can go play now."

"I have a question."

"You do?" She looks up from the stack of papers she is shuffling through on her desk. "Can it wait until after recess?"

"I'll never be your friend again."

"I don't think so."

She angles her head to the side and stares at me. "What's wrong, Grant?"

She's going to hate me.

"What if someone told you something and made you promise to never tell anyone but you think you should tell someone?"

"Are you tattling on them?"

"No."

"Are you saying something to make someone look bad so you look better?"

"No."

"Are you worried about their safety?"

I look down to the smiley face I wrote with Sharpie on my Converse and then look back to her.

Guns.

"Yes."

"Come over here, Grant. Pull up a chair."

With every step I take, I know Emmy is going to hate me that much more. She can't hate me. Dad says it's our duty to help people who are in trouble.

I move a chair toward Mrs. Gellar and sit. "Grant? What is it, honey?"

One of her hands is on her belly, and I stare at it, wondering if I'll see the baby move beneath her black T-shirt if I look long enough.

"Grant?"

"It's about Emmy." My throat is dry. Like if I played really hard during recess and the line was too long at the drinking fountain before coming back into class so I didn't get a drink.

"What about Emmy?" Her hand rubs back and forth and then stills again.

"She told me a secret, and I'm not supposed to tell, but—"

"What is it, Grant?

"She said when her mom goes to work at night, her dad has a gun and he molests her." Her hand jerks on her tummy, but I can't look up because I just broke my promise to Emmy and I'm scared she's going to hate me. "But I don't know what that means other than guns are bad and she's going to hate me and—"

Mrs. Gellar puts her other hand on my shoulder. It makes me stop talking and meet her eyes, embarrassed when a tear slides down my cheek because boys don't cry.

But it's Emmy.

"Grant?" Her voice sounds funny—different—and her throat makes a funny sound when she swallows. "When did Emmy tell you this?"

"This morning." I can barely get the word out. "Please don't tell her I told you."

"I won't."

I can't look at her anymore.

My tummy hurts so bad.

"Look at me, honey." I take in a deep breath, and I feel like such a wuss when I hiccup a sob, but I look at her. "This is what she told you? You aren't making this up?"

"No." I can barely get the word out.

"You did the right thing by telling me. Did you tell anyone else about this?"

I shake my head. "No. I promised her, and . . . I promised her."

"Oh, sweet boy," she says in a soft voice that makes me think she isn't mad at me for telling on my friend as she stands and gives me a big hug. It takes everything I have not to hold on tighter and cry like Emmy does when she scrapes her knee—super hard so she can barely talk—but I don't do it. Instead, I concentrate on trying to make my arms fit all the way around Mrs. Gellar even though her tummy is too big and my fingers won't touch. She leans back and looks at me. There are tears in her eyes, too, and that makes me worry. "You did the right thing, Grant. I know you're worried Emmy is going to be mad . . . and she might be for a while, but you did the right thing."

"Wh-what are you going to do?" Now that I've told her, I'm not sure what is going to happen next. How is she going to help Emmy without letting Emmy know I told her secret?

"I'm going to make sure she's never hurt again."

"She's hurt?" I know guns are bad, but I'm confused. How is she hurt? She looks fine to me other than having cried earlier.

"Grant, I need you to do something for me, okay? I need you to go out on the playground for a few minutes and get some fresh air. I don't want you to tell anyone else about what you said to me because it's important that Emmy has you as a friend. I'll take care of the rest."

"Are you sure?" How is she going to do that?

"I'm sure. Now, I need you to go out so I can do a few things in privacy, okay?"

I nod and then drag my feet all the way to the door. I swear I hear her sniffle, but her back is to me, so I can't be sure. Why would she sniffle? Just as I push it open, I hear Mrs. Gellar on the phone. "Principal Newman? I have a situation that needs immediate attention."

THIRTY-SIX

Emerson

WE FORGET THE MEMORIES AND JUST CHASE THE MOMENTS. Those damn words replay in my head over and over. All day. Before I close my eyes at night. When I'm staring out the window at the airfield, waiting for the next class of jumpers to get ready. Even while sitting here in a bar with Desi where I came to try to prove to myself that I don't care in the least why he hasn't called or texted me in over five days.

I glance at my phone again sitting on the table next to everyone's empty glasses and then hate myself for giving in to the temptation to look.

This is why I have rules. They are designed so I don't end up sitting here like some needy, whiny chick, which is exactly how I feel.

Maybe he's studying for his test like he should be. You know, he's doing important things. It explains the silence, since I made certain he knew not to count me as one of those important things.

Maybe I scared him off with my rules and shutting him out the other day.

Maybe I . . . shit, I don't know. It's me, so I'm sure I'm the one at fault.

"Earth to Emerson."

"What?" I snap at Desi, misdirecting my frustration at how I'm acting over Grant at her.

"Thanks for coming, but uh, maybe you can act like you're actually having fun instead of looking like I forced you to come," she says.

"You did force me to come." I groan as I stare at the dance floor, which is full of grinding bodies and alcohol sloshing over cups.

"Oh, quit being such an old lady. Live a little. Dance a lot. Drink something new. Pick a guy just for the night. Whatever floats your boat."

I glare at her for what feels like the tenth time in the past hour, but it holds no weight because she's Desi. I let her get away with everything. Case in point, I'm here when I want to be anywhere but.

"What, no guy for the night?" She gives me a double take. "Hottie at two o'clock has had your number since you showed up. He's just waiting for eye contact to make his move."

"Whatever. No he has not—"

Sirens screaming past the bar cut me off, and without thinking, I turn to watch the two squad cars as they navigate through the crowded intersection.

"Uh-huh."

"What?" I ask, realizing I've been caught.

"You do have a thing for uniforms, don't you? That, or you wish it was Grant."

"Hottie at two o'clock is all yours," I say as if she hadn't spoken at all.

"I know your game, Reeves. Hottie at two o'clock has no interest in me, but you're saying he does to throw me off so I don't go over there and play matchmaker. If I did, then you might have to tell him no. And telling him no would inform me, your *best* friend whom you're hiding things from, that you might like Grant a little more than you're letting on."

This time, the glare I level her with is real. "No one said I didn't like Grant." It's her turn to return the look. "He has skills in the bedroom department, and I sure as hell am not complaining about that . . . but I told you that we have rules and we're purely enjoying the physical aspect."

"The physical aspect," she mimics with a roll of her eyes.

"There are other terms I could use that would be more accurate, but I'm trying to be a lady." I smile a big, cheesy grin to let her know I'm going out of my way to annoy her.

"A lady." She snorts. "Well, if there is no commitment, then why aren't you out on the dance floor living it up?"

"Because I don't want to."

"Because you'd rather be with Officer Sexy."

"No." *Yes.* What the hell is wrong with me? "I'll dance in a bit."

"Ha." She scoffs. "You're such a liar."

She's right.

Grant Malone seems to be the only one I'll allow to upend my world.

First to save me.

And now to show me what it's like to feel.

THIRTY-SEVEN

Grant

"WHAT THE HELL, DUDE?"

Nate is barely containing the snicker, his face turning beet red as I stare at the blow-up doll positioned precariously at my desk. Someone—probably one of my brothers—put the thing in a skimpy female cop Halloween costume and used a Sharpie to highlight some of its better features.

"Grady and Grayson, I presume?"

"How could you tell?" He laughs as I finally see their self-portraits horribly tattooed above each one of her boobs.

All I can do is shake my head and take a seat at Ambrose's desk directly across from it . . . her? While I more than admire my brothers' creativity and attempt to make me relax after the long-ass exam, I'm already thinking of ways to get them back.

"Don't worry," Nate says. "All the guys already tapped 'dat for ya." He picks her up, and when he turns her around, there are signatures from all of the guys in the squad on her ass.

"Cute. Very cute. Thanks, guys," I say as everyone around us starts busting up laughing.

Fucking assholes.

"So . . . how do you feel?" Nate asks as if he isn't currently placing a blow-up doll back in my chair so that her feet are propped on the desk. No matter how hard he tries, her legs keep spreading open. Finally, he gives up and just pushes her out of the chair.

"I see how you treat suspects." I almost don't get the words out around my laughter.

"That's only if they're behaving." We both look down to where she's face down, spread eagle on the floor. "So tell me how it went."

"Good. It was pretty straightforward. None of the questions gave me trouble."

"Like I figured. Is the asshole still in there?" Nate lifts his chin toward the conference room where Stetson and I sat on opposite ends of the table to take our tests.

"Yeah, he—"

"Ah, boys, that test was fucking cake," Stetson says before emitting a whoop to his group of cronies—all of them newer beat cops not schooled in his knife-in-the-back-I'm-a-total-asshole ways yet—as he exits the conference room.

Nate makes the jacking-off motion and rolls his eyes at the sound of Stetson's voice. "May be cake," he mutters, "but Grant's gonna be the one eating it while you tank at the interviews."

"Thanks for the vote of support."

"I have your back," he says. It's his mischievous smile that worries me more than anything.

"I know you do, and I appreciate whatever it is that sick, twisted mind of yours is conjuring as a payback, but don't. I want this on my terms and because I earned it."

"Of course you do, but he's playing dirty. You know he's going to throw everything but the goddamn sink in because—"

I put my hand up to stop him. Not here. Not in the precinct where anyone can hear. The last thing I need is for it to become daily gossip that runs rampant in the squad room. "My record is clean, *unlike his*. Even if we both pass the test and do decent in the interviews, I'll beat him because I've kept my nose clean." It's the truth. Let's just hope the powers that be think that, too.

"'Kay. But if you change your mind, I'd do it in a heartbeat."

"I know you would," I say, rising from my seat and patting him on the back before heading outside.

There are a few texts on my phone that I glance over as I move to find shade from the blinding sun. My dad asking how it went. Grady wishing me good luck. My mom's simple text, asking how my day is so I won't think she is fishing to see how I did instead of just outright asking. Grayson asking if I want to grab a beer after shift.

I shoot them all back quick responses to get them off my back, but I know I wouldn't have it any other way. Family is everything. Even when it's full of nosy fuckers like mine is.

And then I text the one person I want more than anyone. The woman who I've spent far too much time thinking of with my dick in my hand when I should have been studying. She definitely would have been a better diversion, but if I had gotten lost in her body, the only preparation I would have been thinking about would have been how to have her again.

So, instead, I shut her out for a few days. I temporarily gave into her asinine rules and treated us like she said she wanted—bang buddies, which we both know is bullshit. Plus, after the way we left it the other day, I knew she needed time to wrap her head around what I said as I left.

Me: I apologize for not calling this week but calling leads to thinking about you and thinking about you leads to your tits and your tits are one hell of a distraction when I couldn't afford a distraction this week. But, guess what? I just finished my exam. Now, I can be distracted. Wanna meet up and distract me?

THIRTY-EIGHT

Grant

SITTING ACROSS THE STREET IN MY CRUISER, I STARE AT THE HOUSE. The lights are on upstairs. I can see Keely's shadow against the curtains as she stands on her bed and pretends to sing into a microphone, which is really a brush, and I breathe a little easier.

I shouldn't be here. I shouldn't be stalking this family. I shouldn't be wrapped around this little girl's finger, but damn it to hell if something about her doesn't remind me of Emerson and make me want to protect her.

It has to be the dream that had me driving this way without thought to where I'd end up. Even after a couple of days, I can't seem to shake the heartbreak I'd felt in my chest reliving the moment when I told Mrs. Gellar about Em.

Of course the dream—the clarity of it all these years later—only made the file folder so much more tempting to pull into bed with me and go through.

I can't do that to her.

Then again, wouldn't it be easier to know what ghosts I have to combat? *Shit.*

This woman is fucking with me. I don't get fucked up by women. I date them. I have fun with them. I move on when shit gets too serious.

But Em is . . . Em is different. She always has been.

I scrub my hands over my face, and admit that Emerson is right when she teases me about having a hero complex. Is there something so wrong about that? Maybe if I can save Keely, then I can make up for not saving Emerson sooner?

Even I know that's a whole lot of projecting.

Physical abuse is bad. Sexual abuse is horrid. A child shouldn't have to endure either.

So, I will make sure she's okay.

I pause and try to figure out which of the two females I'm referring to.

Needing a distraction to clear my head, I turn the engine on to leave, but I can't help myself. I can't come here and not look when I promised her I would.

So I'm out of the cruiser and across the street in seconds, trying to look inconspicuous as I jog up their pathway to check on the rock garden.

There's nothing new. At all. It all looks the same, and not just the same, but there has been no new ones added. There's always new ones added.

I'm not sure if that worries me or if it means things have gotten better.

Things never get better.

Abusers just don't wake one morning and stop abusing.

I walk back to the car, slide behind the wheel, and watch the light in Keely's window for a long time while I try to come to terms with all of the shit in my head.

The shit that tells me I need to see Emerson.

The part of me that needs to prove to her that her rules are going to be broken.

One.

By.

One.

Until she sees that sometimes sharing a past means you can build a future together.

It's a bitch that the only girl I've ever really loved is the only one it seems I'll ever really want.

I'm more determined than ever to prove it to her.

Her rules don't matter.

Her past doesn't matter.

It's just her.

It's just the now.

And it's about damn time.

THIRTY-NINE

Emerson

"WHAT ARE YOU DOING HERE?" I ASK, A LITTLE STUNNED to see him filling the space of my doorway. After his text the other day and our screwy schedules, we hadn't planned to see each other until tomorrow.

But I more than welcome the sight of him.

"I needed to take a break."

"A break from what?" I ask as he waltzes right past me as if I invited him in. I look out the front door and around the parking lot, hoping it will help me understand what the hell he is talking about.

"My brothers. Work. Other shit."

I turn and lean my back against the door I've just shut as he strolls over to the couch, drops whatever is in his hands onto it, plops down, and puts his feet up on my coffee table like he owns the place. He picks up the *People Magazine* on the couch beside him and starts flipping through it without a second thought.

The protest dies momentarily on my lips as I recover from the shock of seeing him. And it's a good shock. The kind of shock that almost made me jump into his arms, wrap my legs around his waist, and kiss him senseless. It feels like forever since I've seen him when, in reality, it's only been a week.

It's just because things were unsettled last time he left here, and I've had time to think it over and know I overreacted.

That, and the sight of him in that dark blue uniform has put butterflies in my belly and a bang of lust between my thighs.

"Don't you have your own house to escape to?" I ask as I push off the wall and cross the distance. He watches me, his stare unrelenting as I sit across from him on the edge of the chair.

"Yeah, but the view here is much nicer." He quirks an eyebrow, and the sweep of his eyes over my body tells me the view he's talking about is me.

I did tell him flattery would get him everywhere.

"Well, what if *I* want a different view?"

"We can go somewhere else if you want. The view I came here to enjoy is mobile." He flashes a heart-stopping grin.

"Good to hear you want to go somewhere else. Go ahead. I'll stay here." I match him smile for smile.

"Suit yourself," he says, tossing the magazine on the coffee table and shifting to lie back on my couch, feet hanging off one armrest while his head is on the other.

I rise and walk to the couch so I can stare down at him with my arms crossed. And as much as I'm playing the hard ass, every other part of my body is sizing him up and wondering how quick I can peel that uniform off him . . . then again, maybe he should leave it on. It is sexy as hell.

"Without you," I warn.

"C'mon. You know you like me." He closes his eyes and settles into the cushions.

"No I don't. I only like your cock."

He snorts and opens one eye to stare at me at the same time he reaches a hand out to rest on the back of my knee. "You like my mouth, too."

His thumb brushes up and down the backside of my knee and sends shockwaves through my body. "It is a pretty damn good mouth."

"Then there are my hands . . ."

"Mmm."

And within a second, he has pulled me down on top of him and his lips are on mine in a kiss to rival all kisses. It's hot and sweet and sexy and all-consuming, and when he pulls back, it leaves me breathless to the point that my chest is heaving and my eyes can't seem to break away from his.

There's a brief moment where I see something in his eyes—sadness, regret, I'm not sure—before it clears away. It makes me want to ask him what happened today that brought him to my doorstep.

I'd like to think he's here because he wants to see me. The kiss he just mesmerized me with says I'm at least part of the reason, but I'm also observant enough to know something is bugging him.

"Officer, is that your baton or are you just happy to see me?" I murmur.

His laugh rumbles through his chest and into me, and there is something about the moment—the ease of it—that makes me feel a bit better about whatever is bugging him.

"I'm hungry," he says, suddenly shifting our bodies so that he's sitting up sideways on the couch with my ass between the V of his thighs.

My laugh is instant. My desire well above a simmer. My body begging him to lie back down so that I can kiss him again. "You're hungry?"

"Yep. Let's go get something to eat."

"What? Where?"

"You're the one who said you wanted a change of scenery."

"I changed my mind." I run my fingertip down the side of his jaw.

"Unchange it. I'm hungry, and from what you've said, I can garner your cooking skills aren't that great."

"Like I offered." I scoff but smile.

"So, it's decided. We're going to grab something to eat. I just need to change first." And without another word, he shifts out from behind me and stands before he begins unbuckling his duty belt.

Then unlacing his boots.

Then unbuttoning his shirt.

Next his bulletproof vest.

When he's standing in my flat in nothing but his unbuttoned pants with a delicious section of happy trail on display, I have no qualms about appreciating the view.

Oh. My.

Sure we've already seen each other naked, but there's something different about watching someone undress when the taste of their kiss is still on your lips. There's a sensuality to it, an intimacy I'm not used to, so I take the time to admire him. His hard lines and tan edges. His broad shoulders and cut biceps.

With his eyes on mine and a smile playing at the corner of his mouth, Grant pushes his uniform pants down and then bends over to pick them up, giving me a very fine view of his boxer-brief clad ass when he does. So he's in my apartment, in nothing but his underwear, fresh out of that hot uniform, and he seriously thinks I'm going to be caring about food right now?

"Grant?"

He looks over to me and stands to full height, every fabulous pack of the six he has rippling for added effect. "What?" he asks with feigned innocence. The man knows exactly what he's doing as he makes a show of folding his uniform in some perfectionist way. Then he grabs the clump he dropped on the couch, which I now know are clothes.

"Food?"

"Yeah." He slips a T-shirt over his head—some Back the Blue competition—and then pulls on his jeans. "I'm starving." His grin appears again as he lifts his eyebrows while my tongue licks out to wet my lips. "You ready?"

"Yes." But I'm starving for a whole hell of a lot more than food.

"Well, Mr. Malone, no one can say you don't know how to charm the pants off a girl when you take her on a date." I take a bite of what's left of my French fries as I push against the sand, making my swing rock gently back and forth like his is.

He glances over to me, eyebrows narrowing as he finishes his own bite of hamburger. "Take-out and the park isn't where I normally take a lady on a date." My back is up immediately, offended by his response. He notices, too. "They're your rules, Emerson."

Those words snap me from the haze of my burgeoning temper. Me and my damn rule about no dates. Can't be mad at the man for listening to me, or for pushing my buttons to get me to realize how dumb said rules are.

"They are," I murmur as I toss the empty fry container into the open bag at our feet before scooting back onto my swing and beginning to pump my legs. Anything to get out the frustration at myself for being upset by his comment when it was my doing.

I lean my head back, close my eyes, tighten my hands on the chains as I swing higher and higher. The rush of the air against my cheeks, the feel of my hair flying behind me . . . there is something about being on a swing that's liberating. I'm under my own power. I'm the one who controls how high or fast I go.

There is no Travis and his to-do lists. There is no dread every time the phone rings over what Chris needs now or what proposition he has for me to assure that I'll get approved. There are no thoughts at all.

It's just the wind, and the effort, and it's just . . . juvenile.

"You can't outswing me, Reeves," Grant says beside me, prompting me to look to my left and see that we are swinging in unison, side by side.

I pump harder, for some reason needing to beat him, needing this release I don't understand.

Our laughter fills the empty park as we race each other. I'm so high now that as I reach the peak of the swing, the rubber seat beneath me falls lax for a second.

I'm not sure how long we race each other or if Grant willingly lets me win, but by the time we stop trying, I'm winded and my cheeks hurt from laughing so hard.

We slowly allow the pendulum of our swings to slow until our shoes are dragging ever so lightly on the sand beneath our feet. And when we come to a complete stop, I rest my head against my hand still holding on to the chain and look over to him.

His hair is mussed, and his eyes are as alive as his smile, but there is something else there that I wait for.

"You want to know why I brought you here?"

"Why?"

"Because the swing set was the last place I remember you before you weren't happy anymore."

My lips part as I stare at him, all the vigor we just used to beat each other gone. I think of that day. Of swinging with him on the playground. Of lining up after recess. Of the intercom call. Of telling him I hate him and that I never wanted to see him again.

My throat's dry, and I'm not sure whether it's because of the exertion or because of what he just said. The one thing I know for sure is that it's the first time that I don't want to run away when he brings up the past.

His reason is actually very sweet. And painful.

And just as quickly, the feeling of betrayal, I don't expect or know how to handle, comes back with a vengeance

"You lied to me," I say in a barely audible whisper.

His eyes fall, as does my heart. "I did." He nods, and the look on his face says he'd do it again in a heartbeat if he had to.

I'm not sure how I feel about that.

"It's hard for me to trust you because of that."

He laughs, but it's a short, gruff sound that dies almost as quickly as it begins. "I think your lack of trust has nothing to do with me and everything to do with what you've been through, Emerson."

"How do you know what I've been through, Grant?"

His head startles in confusion. At least I hope it's confusion. "I don't."

I don't relent on my stare because the sudden racing of my pulse has me doubting myself and if I should trust him now.

Hating this sudden unfounded uncertainty, I stand from the swing and jog over to the Merry-go-round. I grab hold of a bar and begin pushing it so that it starts to spin. When I think I have it as fast as it will go, I take a chance and jump onto the rusting heap of metal.

It's moving quickly and spinning out of control, but when I get on, I lie down. With one foot hooked on one side of the bars and my hands holding on to another over my head, I close my eyes and let the centrifugal force commandeer my thoughts from where our conversation brought them. I let the world spin out of control around me while I hold on for what feels like dear life.

There's a boost to the spin, and I know that Grant is there. He's pushing me now. I can feel the platform flex as he climbs on and the heat of his body as he lies beside me. I know that when he closes his hand over mine where it holds on to the bar, he's making sure not to let go for the both of us.

He brings calm to the chaos spinning out of control around me and within me.

For the first time in a very, very long time, I allow myself to accept that.

To accept him.

To welcome it rather than push it away.

FORTY

Emerson

"**D**O YOU EVER NOT HAVE THAT THING ON?"

"What? The scanner?" he asks as he turns onto the highway. "Yes."

He shrugs. "Does it bug you?"

"Not really. I just don't understand why you still listen to calls if you're off duty." I rub my feet together, and more sand from the playground comes off the soles of my shoes and dusts the floor mat.

"I have a few situations I like to keep an eye on. If a call goes out on one of those, sometimes I like to go so I can make sure what's going on."

"Hm."

"Hm?"

"Sounds to me like someone is attached to—"

"Possible 10-16. 12662 Serenity Court. Officers responding." The scanner interrupts.

"Son of a bitch," Grant says as he slams the heel of his hand against the steering wheel.

"What's a 10-16?" Whatever it is, it obviously isn't good.

"I jinxed it by saying it," he mutters to himself.

"Grant? Are you okay?" I stare at his profile and can see the disconcert in his posture.

"No. Yes. *Fuck.* This is the one case I'm worried about." He glances my way, and I can see the hesitation in his body language. "I need to . . . shit. My cruiser."

"If you're worried, just drive there now. I can sit and wait out whatever you need to do. Don't waste the time taking me back," I ramble, hating that he is so upset about this call.

"You sure?" He eyes me in a way that says he knows more than I do, which is obvious, and yet, I'm not sure why he feels the need to relay it.

"Yes. Positive. Go."

He grabs his cell, punches a few numbers, and then holds it to his ear, waiting. "Dispatch, I'm an off-duty officer responding to the call for 12662 Serenity Court," he says. "Yes. Grant Malone . . . I'm in civilian clothes but want it known to the guys on scene that I'm responding . . . No. It's an ongoing situation. I've been monitoring every call you have listed there . . . Yeah . . . I know, but I'm on my way. 10-4."

It doesn't take long to make it to the address, but that could be because Grant may or may not have completely demolished the speed limit.

When we pull onto the street and park beside two other cruisers, trepidation takes hold. I'm sure it will be cool seeing Grant in action, but at the same time, I feel like I'm eavesdropping on someone else's life.

As if I'm violating their privacy by being here.

"Goddamnit," he mutters as he slams the truck into park, flings the door open, and jogs up the front walkway.

Then I see her.

The little girl sits on a rock in the middle of a planter in the front yard with a teddy bear hugged tight to her chest. She's looking down at her bear's face, fingers picking at its eyes, as a big, burly police officer awkwardly tries to talk to her.

"Keely." I hear Grant say the name, and the minute it is out of his mouth, she looks up. A ghost of a smile turns up the corners of her lips, but something about her face expresses a sadness so strong I can feel it deep in my bones.

Big, burly officer visibly relaxes and has no problem stepping back. Grant lowers himself to the ground and sits cross-legged beside her.

"Oh." My hand flies up to cover my mouth, and tears sting my eyes at the mere sight of them. There is a comfort between them, a gentleness to him I never expected to see. He talks to her, pointing to her bear and the rocks in the planter around her. It's so obvious from the outside how hard he is working to make her smile and put her at ease.

Curiosity has me glancing to the backs of the officers standing at the front door, but I can't keep my eyes away from Grant and Keely for very long. There is something so precious and heartbreaking about their interaction. He dwarfs her, and yet, she seems completely at ease with him. They talk some, his expression so serious when she looks away and then warm when she comes back to him. He works for her smile, and when she grants it, there is a flicker of hope under all the shadows haunting her eyes.

It kills me. In every sense of the word.

Why does this little girl trust Grant so much? More so, why would a little girl know a police officer enough to trust him?

And then I remember the code 10-16—domestic abuse. Grant told dispatch that he'd been to every one of the previous calls to this address.

Every.

One.

How many times has he been here?

I push the thoughts and scenarios from my mind. I don't want to think or assume, but it doesn't stop the sting of tears in my eyes as he reaches out and holds her little hand in his.

Because it's *real*. Grant's hero complex and his need to save everyone is real, and I'm watching it firsthand.

He and Keely are pointing to the smaller rocks around them, and after a bit, I hear her giggle. It's the most adorable sound in the world. All I can do is stare. And wonder. And hope she's outside because whatever happened inside doesn't involve her.

I'm not sure how long I sit and stare at the two of them, but it's long enough that my feet are numb from their positioning and the sky has slowly faded to black. So lost in thought, I'm startled when Grant slides behind the wheel, starts the car, and pulls away from the curb.

"The fucker's lucky he wasn't home," he mutters under his breath but doesn't elaborate, and I don't ask for more.

I turn some in my seat so I can study him and try to wrap my head around how the man, who seemed so at ease moments ago with a little girl, now feels like a ticking time bomb. The lights from passing cars and streetlamps lighten and darken the features of his face, leaving me to wonder what's going on in that mind of his. I'd also love to pepper him with questions about what the call was all about, but for a woman who doesn't like to answer questions herself, the safe strategy is to keep my mouth shut.

We drive for some time, winding up through the hills around Sunnyville until Grant pulls off the asphalt and onto a graded road. We continue for a ways, and it's only when he pulls into a clearing that overlooks the city and all of its lights below that I know where we are: Grant's place he goes to think.

Our silence stretches, long and thick and heavy, but with the windows down, the sounds of the nightlife around us soften the tension in it. Every part of me wants to ease whatever is upsetting him but I have no clue how to even begin to do that.

"You want to talk about it?" I ask, hoping enough time has passed that he can think rationally about whatever happened.

His sigh is heavy. "I'm not sure that I can."

"Because it's a case?"

Without answering, Grant opens the door and gets out of the truck. I watch him pace back and forth, the moonlight above accentuating the tension seizing his posture. I slip out of the cab and find a flat slope of rock near the front of his truck and take a seat, cross my legs, and focus on the twinkling lights of the city. They almost look like embers burning in the bottom of a fire pit, and I wonder what each of those lights represent.

Is one of them Keely's?

How many of them hide the horror happening beneath their cover?

I shake the thought away. Too much thinking for tonight. Too much delving into a past I don't want to delve into.

"Remember the side of your house?" Everything inside me freezes. The minute I'm determined to get out of my own past, he brings me right back into it. "Remember how we used to go and sit there and play whatever the hell we used to play back then because you wanted to get outside? Sometimes, you'd paint those rocks of yours with silly pictures, other times I'd play Barbies with you. I hated it, but I played because you were always playing cops and robbers with me?"

"No." I whisper the word, not sure if it's because I don't want to remember or because I don't want to talk about it.

Either he doesn't hear me or he doesn't care, because he keeps talking. "After you left, I used to go there. I'd just sit there by myself because I missed you so much. I'd pretend that you were inside and you were going to come out to play any minute."

Every part of me wants to reject what he's saying. I want to cover my ears like the little girl he remembers would have done and shut him out. I don't want to know that he was hurt, too. It's so much easier to think I was the only one who hurt. It's so much easier to remember how much I hated him for pulling my world apart instead of looking at it like an adult and realizing he did the right thing.

But I don't lift my hands. I don't turn to face him. I need to hear this. I need to listen to him. I need to face what I don't want to know and am scared to death to remember.

"I missed you, Em. You were my best friend. You were the one I told all my silly secrets to. You were part of my every day, and then you were gone . . ."

I told him my secrets, too. But mine were far from any secret an eight-year-old should have.

I push up from where I'm seated and walk a few feet away from him, hating the hurt in his voice that somehow I had a part in putting there. But at the same time, I'm angry at him for driving me up here where I can't exactly escape the conversation.

Was this his plan? Trap me here and force me to talk?

"Do you remem—"

"What are getting at, Grant? What's the point to this conversation?"

"I just—" He shakes his head and runs a hand through his hair. "There are so many things I want to ask you, so many things that I want to know—"

"They're none of your goddamn business!" I shout in an explosion of temper I'm not sure he was expecting.

"No?" he shouts back, crossing the distance and getting in my face just as unexpectedly.

"No." I stand my ground.

"Oh, so, what? You'll open your legs for me but not yourself?" His eyes burn with anger as we wage a visual war of contempt.

"Fuck. You."

"That's the point," he sneers. "That's all you want to do."

"And?"

"And what?

"That was the deal, Malone. You agreed to the rules."

"The deal's changed."

"Then the deal's over."

"No. I call bullshit on you. Why can't you let me in? Why can't you just talk to me? I know you went through a shit ton of horror, but I was the one who was there. I was the one who cared about you. *Who still cares.* And maybe I need to talk about it to wrap my head around how you dealt with all of that and turned out so goddamn normal when it still fucks my head up some days . . . did you think of that?"

I fist my hands and grit my teeth as I try to calm the riot of confusion laced anger swirling around inside me. "So you'd rather I be messed up too just so you can feel better? Well, *I am*," I scream at him, hating to admit it but needing the catharsis of saying it. "Did that work? Do you feel better?" I sneer as every part of me vibrates with fury and shame.

"No." His voice is barely a whisper.

"You don't want inside my head, Grant. You don't want to know what's in the dark places there. It crippled me at one time. It sits there and waits for its moment to come forward and cripple me again. So, I shove it away. I don't talk about it. I try not to think about it. *Because if I do, then I can't function.* I can't be the woman you see when I live in the shadow of what happened to the little girl I was. That past doesn't exist to me. *It can't.*"

I walk away from him, needing to process my outburst, my confession, and how I can still seem strong to him when suddenly I feel so damn weak. Looking out at the city, Grant at my back, I cross my arms over my chest and dig my nails into my biceps. I welcome the bite of pain. I use it to calm myself and bring me back to the woman I pretend to be.

"Emerson." He says my name again. It's a plea. A request. It's *pity.* "I'm sorry."

"You don't get it do you?" His apology only serves to aggravate me further. To remind me of all those shrinks and their sympathetic eyes and the pity in their tones. The one sound I never wanted to hear again. My temper rages quietly beneath the surface, and I'm not sure if I'm mad at him for pushing me or mad at myself for what I said.

It takes all my effort to make my voice even and calm—unaffected—when I turn to look at him and speak, but there's still a bite to my tone. "Look, I'm sorry you can't talk about the little girl because it's police procedure, but that doesn't give you the right to start poking into my past. Into my life. I don't need to be saved."

"I'm not talking about her because it's police procedure, Emerson." He throws his hands up and laughs but there is nothing amusing in its sound. "Don't you get it? I'm not talking about her because I can't. I'm not talking about her because I don't want to upset you! A lot of fucking good that did me."

I startle at his words. "*Excuse me*?"

"I don't want to upset you," he says softer this time, his voice vulnerable, his body defeated.

"After everything I've been through, I assure you, you can't upset me." And I truly want to believe that, but I already know it's an untruth. Grant Malone serves to be the one person capable of hurting me the most.

"I can't? How is that—"

"Nope. Nothing does," I lie, hoping he leaves it be and doesn't call me on the fact that I just admitted differently moments ago.

He angles his head to the side and stares at me. His silent scrutiny unnerving.

"So, if I told you I think Keely's dad is abusing her but I have no proof to go on, you'd be okay with that? What if I told you I used our rock secret? That I stop by there more often than I should to make sure there is no rock painted like a watermelon, which is her signal to tell me she needs help. You're telling me none of that triggers anything for you?"

I stare at him with my head shaking and my mind rejecting everything he just said, even the stuff I don't understand. All I can think of is that beautiful little girl with the tear-stained face and the haunted eyes and wonder if that was what I looked like to everyone who saw me.

"No." I whisper the word, but my body burns with shame as I dig my nails deeper into my flesh.

"No?" he shouts, finally losing his cool. "How, Em? How is that possible?"

"Because it is, okay?" I yell back, itching for a fight to cover the emotions overwhelming me. "Screw it. Just take me home."

"No." The muscle pulses in his clenched jaw as his body visibly vibrates with anger.

"Yes."

"Why?" he demands.

"Because you make me feel, damn it! You make me feel when I don't want to feel, Grant. And being numb is how I deal, so please," I say, my voice breaking and almost turning into a sob, "take me home."

I see the minute my desperation hits him. His anger dissipates. His shoulders sag. His eyes fall vulnerable. And then he walks to the driver's side of the truck and climbs in, doing as I asked without saying another word.

FORTY-ONE

Emerson

"**W**HY ARE YOU OUT HERE?"

I shrug as I look over to Grant on his BMX, gloves on his hands and motorcycle helmet on, and know he's pretending he's competing in the X-Games. "Just cuz," I say, not wanting to tell him it's because my mom just got called into work for a patient and I'd rather be outside.

Outside is safe.

Outside is where I can hide.

"Whatcha doing?" He lays his bike down on the grass and begins to unbuckle his helmet as he walks over to me.

I look at the rocks in front of me, and my cheeks burn because they didn't turn out as pretty as I thought I could make them. The dog I painted on one looks like a big blob of brown. The smiley face I painted on the other is yellow, but the eyes are weird, and I couldn't fix them. Embarrassed, I take what's left on the paintbrush and just draw lines on the rock in front of me.

"Nothing. Just being stupid."

"Oh, those are kinda cool."

"You don't have to say that to be nice."

"No. Really." He drops his helmet onto the sidewalk with a clunk, and I know Chief Malone would get that line in his forehead like he does if he saw Grant treat his things like that. But I don't say a word because I'm too busy chewing the inside of my cheek and waiting for Grant to make fun of me.

He picks up each rock and looks at it like he does his Matchbox cars, and I fidget, worried about what he thinks.

"I think we should make a zombie one, too." I roll my eyes and begin to argue. "No, seriously. We can add stitches to the forehead and . . ." He takes the paintbrush from me and starts adding things to my smiley face rock.

I don't know how long we do this, but by the time we're done, my cheeks hurt from laughing so hard. We have about fifteen rocks in front of us that have all been boy-ified, and I'm okay with that.

"So, why are you really out here, Em?" he asks as we lean against the side of the house where the shade has fallen.

I shrug again but hate that my bottom lip quivers and tears well in my eyes.

"I just don't want to go inside." My tummy hurts, and I keep thinking about when it gets dark and I have to go to bed. Hopefully, my mom will be back before then . . . but most times she isn't.

"Is your dad in a bad mood? I always go outside when my dad's in a bad mood about work. That way, when he gets mad, I'm not in the way."

"Your dad gets mad?" I can't remember Chief Malone ever getting mad. Strict, yes. But not mad.

"My mom says he gets stressed when he worries about a case." He shrugs and picks up one of our rocks, stares at it, and then puts it back down. "He has lots of bad people he has to put away, and it's his job, so when they don't get put away, he gets stressed. What does your dad get stressed about?"

When I wet the bed.

When I cry.

When I pretend to be asleep and curl really tight into a ball.

When I don't do what he says . . .

I wake with a start, my own gasp still coming off my lips.

The room.

This is my room.

Not my old room.

In the dark.

There's the runway lights out the window.

There's the hum of the television I left on.

But it's the rocks that are front and center in my mind.

The painted rocks.

The ones Grant keeps talking about but for the life of me I couldn't remember . . . until now.

My hands begin to shake as memories I didn't know I had come flashing back to me.

Going outside to my spot on the side of my house to avoid my dad and finding a new painted rock there from Grant. Something silly that meant everything to me. Something to let me know he was there and checking on me.

To let me know he cared.

To make me smile.

The goddamn rocks.

Grant.

Memories I now remember.

So many more I don't want to.

Oh. Shit.

It's finally happening.

I can't let this happen.

FORTY-TWO

Emerson

THE NIGHT BLANKETS ME BUT DOESN'T PROVIDE THE REPRIEVE that I came out here to find.

There is no escape from my past.

There is no distance from the memories.

There is only the pain.

Only the isolation.

Only the need to make it go away.

I look down to where the blade of the box cutter rests against my scarred flesh. Just the sight of it there allows me to breathe easier. Just the feel of it gives me a tiny sip of control.

Shame has me squeezing my eyes shut. Fear has the tears leaking out. The incessant hurt has me pressing it against my skin.

And cutting.

The sharp sear of pain is instant and yet when I open my eyes and see the bright red blood highlighted by the moonlit sky, I feel like a weight has been lifted for the first time in forever.

The tears fall fast and hot down my cheeks as I watch the red bead up. As I inflict the pain on myself instead of letting someone else do it for me.

I stretch out my other arm, and my fingers itch to repeat the process.

To feel relief.

To gain control.

To match my pain with new pain.

Head up. Wings out.

My mom's voice rings in my ears and has me clenching the knife in my hand as hard as I can.

Don't do it.

The need owns every muscle in my body.

Don't give in.

The want has me vibrating with desire.

My mom's face flashes through my mind. The determination in her eyes. The encouraging murmur on her lips. The warmth of her touch as she'd hold my hand and wait with me for my urge to pass.

The promises I'd made to her that I wouldn't cut myself anymore are now broken. Shame blankets me. Smothers me. I wasn't strong enough to keep them.

My hands ache as I battle restraint. *So does my heart.*

I've let her down.

I promised her I would be strong. I swore to her I'd never cut myself again. *Don't do it, Emmy.*

With a wretched sob, I take the box cutter and chuck it as far as I can into the thick foliage at the base of the runway. It takes everything I have not to run in after it.

But I don't. I can't.

The shame is instant.

The regret immediate.

But the want still thrives despite knowing I broke my promise to her.

And to myself.

"I'm so sorry, Mom."

I double over and cry with every part of my body and repeat the words she used to whisper in my ear as she'd hold me after she'd find new cuts on my arms again.

This hurt doesn't take away my pain, only being strong will.

I am in control of me.

I will survive despite it.

I am loved regardless of it.

And at the end of the runway in the early morning, I rock myself back and forth, repeat my mother's words, and hope I can find my strength once again.

FORTY-THREE

Grant

"I FUCKED UP."

"Tell me something I don't know," Grady says as he pulls his attention away from the preseason football game just long enough to glance at me in the kitchen.

"No. Seriously." I look at my phone for what feels like the hundredth time and debate calling Emerson again. Her last text, the one from three days ago telling me she's super busy with a week-long jump class, still doesn't sit right with me. I didn't ask her to do anything. I didn't even text her. So her sending a random text to explain why she can't see me for a few days feels hinky.

Especially after how she asked to be taken home from the lookout and then jogged up the stairs, saying she had a stomachache. I was left to stare at the shut door to her apartment with my apology getting lost in the night around me.

Something is definitely off. Maybe she just needs some space. Fuck if I know.

"Hey, Romeo? You gonna finish your sentence or are you interrupting my date with the 49ers for a reason?"

"Are you in my house drinking my beer, watching my television, and eating my pizza?" I ask, and he nods. "Then shut the fuck up because I seem to be the one footing the bill for your romantic evening."

"Well, then get to the point and stop standing there like someone pissed in your Wheaties. What gives?"

"I don't know." I sip my beer as I cross the distance and take a seat across from him—my view of the backyard while his is of the game. "Watch those files, will you?" I say, pointing to the stack of cold case files I'm working on that are sitting on the opposite end of the couch as him.

"How can I watch them when they're freaking everywhere? On the couch. Falling off the couch. On the floor. On the coffee table. On the desk. I mean, Jesus, do you take them in the bathroom with you, too?"

"You make fun, but when you're sitting outside on my new patio with a built-in barbeque and flat screen television, you'll be thanking me."

"Doesn't seeing this shit every day ever get to you? Don't you need a break from it?"

"Sometimes." I sigh. "Recently, a lot of the time."

For being such a little shit, he's smart.

"Something's going on with her. She's shutting me out."

"I'd shut your ugly ass out, too." I kick my foot out to knock his feet off my table, more to antagonize him than for any other reason. "But considering you just switched topics and left me in the dark, should I assume we're talking about Emerson, again?"

"I'm serious."

"Apparently you are," he says as he smirks.

"What's that supposed to mean?"

"This thing with Emerson. You're supposed to be fuck buddies, right? Well, that was the plan anyway. Either you're getting too deep into it or she is because this is way more complicated than your normal run-of-the-mill one nighter . . . so what gives?"

"It isn't different." *But it is.* "She's not." *But she is.* "We're not." *But we are.* "We're just fucking." *But it feels like so much more than that.*

"Yeah, you keep thinking that's all there is, and I'll start putting money down on the 49ers to win the Super Bowl with this shitty ass team they have this year."

The game drones on, Grady groaning with every turnover—and there are a lot—while I stare out the windows to the backyard and watch the sky change colors as the sun sets. I'm supposed to be relaxing and preparing for my upcoming interview, but all I can think about is Emerson. Did I push her too far and get too personal when she is so obviously used to running away?

"Hey, Grant?"

"Yup," I say distractedly.

"I think I'm gonna head out."

"What?" I look at him, confused as to why he's leaving at halftime when I know the cable is jacked at his house. "What about the second half?"

"I have shit to do." I narrow my eyes at him at the same time he juts his chin toward the front door.

I turn around and find Emerson standing on the other side of the screen. Her face is expressionless and her hair is pulled back, but it's her eyes that are shadowed and sad.

"Em? You okay?" I'm on my feet as Grady opens the screen and gives her a soft greeting before jogging down the path toward his car. "Emerson?"

"I'm sorry. I shouldn't have . . . I just didn't want to be alone." Her voice is barely audible.

"No. Please. Come in." I have my arm around her shoulders and am guiding her into the house. She seems so frail when I've never thought her to be anything but the opposite. We move to the couch, and she sits beside me as if she's on autopilot. Concern rifles through every part of me.

Within seconds, I have the television off and the police scanner on the table beside me silenced. The overwhelming urge to hold her, touch her, soothe that look out of her eyes is too much, so I pull her into me—her head to my chest—and wrap my arms around her.

"What's going on, Em?"

"My head's messed up," she says.

"We all have messed-up heads," I murmur, my lips against the top of her hair, my fingers rubbing up and down her arms. It's only when she hisses that I realize my fingertips have run over the ridge of scars, causing me to jerk my hand back in guilt over hurting her.

"Not like mine," she eventually says.

"Want to talk about it?"

Her chuckle is despondent. "Do you know how many times in my life I've been asked that question? Therapist after therapist until I got so sick of being picked apart I just up and quit going."

"I can imagine," I say but know I have absolutely no fucking clue what she has been through. "Did something happen today?"

"Today? No. The other night? Yes." She lets out a deep breath. Her vulnerability transparent and haunting since I've never seen this side of her. "I can't stop thinking about Keely. I can't stop obsessing over whether her dad is doing to her what mine did to me. I can't stop wondering about what other horrible things he has done to her mother that she's been a witness to. It's messing me up, Grant, and that's really hard for me to admit."

"Sh. Sh. Sh," I say, guilt riding me hard over being the one to bring this all upon her. This is on me. The little girl I see as her, she does, too, and there's nothing I can do to reassure her that Keely will be okay. So, I just hold her a little tighter and press my lips to the top of her head while we both process the turn of events.

Her needing me, and my wanting her to need me.

"I'm going to do everything in my power to save her, Em, but without her mom pressing charges or the little girl admitting anything, I have zero legal rights. My hands are tied."

"And that's why you were talking to her about the rocks."

My hand stills halfway down her back. This is the first time she's reacted to any mention of the rocks. For a while, I thought maybe it was a fake memory I had created to deal with her leaving even though I know for a fact it was real.

"What do you mean?" I fish.

"The rocks. You were kneeling, talking to her, picking up rocks that I couldn't see but that I knew had color on them."

"Mm-hmm."

"I didn't remember, Grant. I didn't remember the rocks until I had a dream about them the other night." I can sense the hysterical confusion in her voice despite how muted it is. "You've mentioned them a few times, and I just thought . . . I don't know what I thought, but I just kind of let it go because it didn't make sense. Then I saw you with Keely and then that night I dreamed of the rocks. Of *our* rocks. The zombie rocks. And the ones you'd leave there for me to find when I'd come out to escape from my house and—" She loses a huge, heaving sob of a sound, her fingers grip into the fabric of my T-shirt, and her body shakes as she fights with every part of her to keep from breaking down.

"Don't be sad. It's a good memory. It was the only way I knew how to let you know I was there for you. It seems cheesy now, but we were eight."

"Not cheesy," she murmurs. "I looked forward to seeing if there was a new one every day."

"I didn't know what was going on inside your house, Em, but I knew it made you sad." I smooth my hand over the back of her hair and just pull her tighter against me, hating myself for doing this to her. "I'm sorry I brought you to the call. I didn't mean for it to upset you."

"You don't understand." She pulls away, her eyes red but not a single tear has fallen.

"Then make me understand." The confusion in her expression kills me. The vulnerability in it even more so.

"If I didn't remember that, then what else do I not remember?"

"It was rocks, Em. That's it. I'm sure there are a million things you remember about what we did or where we played that I don't. It's no big deal."

"It's not—you don't—you're here and I can't stop them," she says, flustered and visibly anxious.

"You can't stop what?"

"Nothing. Never mind." The first tear finally slips over as she runs a hand over her hair, and the chaos of her emotions hit her.

I just stare at her like a deer in the headlights. I can handle hysterical victims, I can manage crazy suspects, but give me Emerson's big green eyes full of tears and have her plead for me to give her answers I can't give her, and I'm a guy fucked in so many ways I've lost count.

"Talk to me."

"I'm so confused," she says. "It's you."

"Me?" *What did I do?*

"No. That's not what I mean." She squeezes her eyes shut for a moment and shakes her head. "I just—I don't want to know anything else."

"What are you talking about?"

She heaves in a breath that hitches as I reach out—needing to touch her—and use my thumb to wipe a tear off her cheek. The simple touch is nowhere near enough, the connection not strong enough, so I lean forward and brush my lips against hers, my hand on the back of her neck, our foreheads touching.

I stay like that for a few moments, caught between the push and pull of needing her to stay and never wanting her to feel pain again. Crushed by the realization that somehow I'm the one causing the discord in her life.

"I don't trust myself, Grant. I don't trust my memory. I don't trust that what I thought happened actually happened—"

"You didn't make it up, Em," I say, hating the defeat reflected in everything about her—eyes, posture, tone. I don't understand why she's so upset over this. "They were silly rocks."

"It's not just the rocks. It's *everything else*." The desperation in the way she says the words twists my heart.

I'd give anything to take her pain away, and for the briefest of moments, I consider telling her I have proof that her abuse happened. That I have the evidence to erase the doubt from her mind. Maybe if she had the choice to know the details, it would be helpful to her and make her feel more in control.

My eyes flash over the table stacked with blue and green file folders and know hers is somewhere in there. I've yet to open it, but I know it holds the detailed history of her abuse.

And as soon as I have the thought, I reject the horrible idea.

"I still don't trust myself," she whispers, the heat of her words warming my lips.

"I trust you," I say, scrambling for anything to take the pain from her voice. I'm far from qualified to give her the answers she needs, but hell, I'd walk through fucking fire if it meant I could make this right by her . . . whatever *right* is.

"It isn't the same."

"People trust you with their lives every day. Every damn day, they jump out of airplanes and put their lives in your hands, trusting that you'll get them back to the ground safely. How can you say they don't trust you?"

"They trust the name on the building. They trust the certificates lining the wall. They trust the reputation that's been around for fifty years. They don't know a damn thing about the woman behind the desk in the flight suit."

She looks lost, eyes wild, body language unreadable besides anything other than scattered, and I hate seeing her like this.

"It's going to be okay, Em. We'll figure it out. It'll be okay."

She pushes up off the couch, agitated and restless. "It isn't going to be okay, Grant. It will never be okay, and it will never go away. Fucking hell, I've gone twelve years without doing this, and now I have and what does that say about me? That I'm not strong anymore? That I'm no longer coping? That I'm just as fucked up as everyone would expect me to be?" She screams leaving me completely lost in regards to what she is referring to.

"Twelve years?"

"This!" She shouts throwing her arms out so the angry red marks on the inside of her right arm scream out to me. "This, Grant. I spent years cutting myself to cope. Years hurting myself because the pain I caused myself overshadowed the pain he caused me. It made me feel in control of something. I was the one responsible. I was the one who knew the ugly on the outside matched the ugly on the inside." Her voice breaks again, breaking my heart right along with it.

I'm out of my seat in an instant and by her side. "Em." I don't even recognize the grief in my own voice.

"You once asked me how I coped. This, Grant. This was how I coped."

"Emerson." My God. How did I not see this? I expect her to fight when I slip my arms around her, I assume she will resist, but she does everything but. Her arms are around my waist, and her head is buried in my chest as we hold on to each other and weather the torrent of emotion that is raging inside both of us.

"Emerson." I say her name again, needing to see her eyes, to know she is okay, maybe to know that I'm going to be okay knowing this, too. Fuck if I know. She tilts her chin and looks at me with red-rimmed eyes full of shame and sorrow before leaning forward and pressing her lips to mine. It's the last thing I expect, but the kiss is slow and hesitant—a woman trying to find her way through the power of the storm swirling around her.

I kiss her back. Gentle and tender. Giving her whatever she needs from me and promising that I'm going to do everything in my power to help her.

Salt from her tears is on our lips.

Her desperate need to lose herself palpable.

There's definitely pleasure in our kiss, but there is also so much more. Her well-being. My sanity. Our belief that we can see our way through to the other side of this.

My normally assured Emerson is anything but. She's timid, hesitant. She may have initiated this, but I know it's because she's trying to lose herself in the physicality like I now see she always has. She's trying to forget the ugly in her.

And that fucking kills me.

For a man who prides himself on being able to handle every situation—womanly or otherwise—I'm at a loss as to what to do.

God yes, I want her. Especially when she scrapes her nails against my abs under my shirt before lifting it over my head. The taste on her tongue. The smell of her skin. The knowledge of how goddamn good she feels when I bury myself in her. They all collide, vying for my focus.

And I may typically be a let's jump right in when it comes to sex, but something is stopping me from ripping her clothes off and giving her the exertion she craves.

If I do that, I'll be giving her exactly what she needs to run away from me again. I'd be giving her the tools to close off, when what she really needs is to know what I see when I look at her.

She needs to see the beauty in her ugly.

The thoughts are clouded with lust, lost in its haze, but when she reaches for the buttons on my jeans, I grip my fingers around her wrists.

"Em," I say, my breath coming in pants as my dick begs me to let her hands stroke it.

"No." She fights my hold, and I just keep my hands cuffed over her wrists as I lead her into my bedroom. "I don't . . . just please . . . I need—" she murmurs between kisses, her lips meeting mine over and over, each time more urgent than the last.

I push her back onto the bed, her mile-long legs working her body closer to the headboard as I crawl over her. She looks up at me with eyes so intense they steal my reasoning. My words. My breath.

Her lip quivers.

Her eyes well again.

When I reach down and pull her arms up so that they rest beside her head, palms up, her breath hitches. With my eyes locked on hers, I lower my lips ever so slowly and press them softly against the fresh and angry red mark on the inside of her bicep. She freezes, and I know it's taking everything she has not to pull her arm away from me. I know if she tries, I'll let her. But if she doesn't, then I'll know she trusts me, if only just a little bit, and a little bit is enough for now.

While I wait for her decision, I can see the shame in her eyes, the discomfort in my knowing, the struggle to let me in. Her inhale is shaky, but she doesn't move.

She puts her trust in me.

I lace a row of kisses across the scars on her right arm, my heart breaking and temper firing as my lips ghost over the ridges that mark her pain. There are so many, and all I can think of is how many times she's felt the need to cut herself to cope with what that fucking bastard did to her.

How much pain was she in that she needed to mar herself? Permanently scar herself to cope? With my lips against her skin and her perfume in my nose, I can picture her huddled in a corner, drawing a knife across her arm. Over and over. Tears falling like the drips of blood were. Alone and isolated from everyone and their help.

And then I realize it's not past tense. It's not how much pain she *was* in, because she just cut herself again. The pain *is* still there. Still prevalent. Still haunting this incredible woman.

My need to show her she isn't alone, that she's beautiful inside and out takes hold.

So I continue to worship her scars with reverent kisses. And when I'm done with the right side, the need to calm my ire leads me to kiss her lips again. To sip and take and soothe and know she's okay before leaning back, looking in her eyes to let her know my next intention, and then pressing my lips to the ridges on her left arm.

Call it my hero complex. Call it her being the first girl I've ever loved letting me love her now. Call it me being a fucking sap. I don't care . . . because put any man in my situation—with a woman who doesn't trust putting one hundred percent of her trust in him when she's at her most vulnerable, and for fuck's sake, it will change him.

Change him in ways he never knew possible.

As I slide my lips down the rest of her arm before pulling her tank up to expose toned flesh and pressing heated kisses across her abdomen, I know I'm changed. I know the taste of her, the sound of her, the feel of her will forever be seared in my goddamn memory.

I told her we should chase moments and not memories.

Enjoy the moment.

So I do just that. I take the trust that Emerson has bestowed upon me and slide my hand up her inner thigh, her flimsy skirt bunching up with it as I go. I lick over the cotton of her panties, prompting her legs to spread apart for me. I suck on her clit, the muted sensation of the fabric and the heat causing her hand to grip the sheets beside me and her hips to buck against my face.

I tug her panties aside with one finger and lick the length of her pussy, circling my tongue on her clit and sliding it back all the way down until I dart into her. She gasps, and her hands move from gripping the sheets to sinking into my hair.

My god. She tastes like heaven, like everything I want and need and desire. My lips are coated with her. My nose is buried in her slit as I lick and lap and pleasure and tease her nerves into a riot of sensations.

As I let her lose herself. As I make her feel. As I help her forget.

I kissed all of her pain away, now I want her to know I desire her, too. All of her. The scars. The beauty. The pain. The past. The future.

And goddamn, the mewl in her throat, the groan of my name, the desperate pleas for more as my tongue and fingers work her into a frenzy are an aural seduction all by themselves. When she gasps as I push her over that cusp where desire burns into bliss, I'm left reeling for her to come so I can push into her and join her.

"Grant." She pants as her body jerks and writhes under the pressure of her orgasm slamming into her. Her pussy pulses around my fingers and against my tongue. I suck ever so gently on her clit, pulling every last ounce of pleasure out of her . . . and fuck me if I don't want to get off the bed, yank her legs open, and fuck her into oblivion.

I just can't.

Not knowing how she came to me.

Not knowing that I'm the one who messed her head up.

Not knowing that she trusts me when it seems as if trust is something she never allows herself to give.

So, as much as my dick is begging to slide into her pussy, I keep my pants on. Fuck yes, my dick aches with the need to take her, and my balls burn for release, but I know this isn't about me. I'll be cursing myself later when I grab the lube and take to my hand, but this is the right thing to do.

With her addictive taste still on my tongue, I press a kiss to each side of her inner thighs then move up to circle my tongue around the rim of her belly button. Inch by torturous inch, I work my way back up her body. Every time my dick even remotely rubs against the mattress or her leg, I want to come like a sixteen-year-old boy.

"So beautiful," I murmur, raining praise between each kiss.

Up the side of her rib cage. Over the peaks of her nipples. Then I bring my lips back to the scars on her arms to let her know even those parts of her are beautiful.

I continue up to her shoulder and then follow the line to the underside of her jaw. It's her sighs that fuel me. Her sudden tensing as she guesses where my lips will land next followed by how she sinks into the mattress when she remembers that she trusts me.

It's when I find her lips again that I know she's calmed some. Her kisses, which were tentative before, are now laced with tenderness and satisfaction. They're still not one hundred percent the Emerson I've come to know, but they're enough for now—they're progress.

"Grant." She murmurs my name against my lips, and when I lean back and look down at her, a tear has slipped out of the corner of her eye and is making its way down to her ear and the pillow beneath.

"Sh," I say as I rest my forehead against hers.

"No one has ever treated me that way," she finally murmurs as she lifts a hand to rest against my heart.

It's only much later when she falls asleep in my arms that I really hear her words. I take pride in knowing I gave her that feeling.

Because while she's never been treated this way, I don't think I've ever paid that kind of attention to a woman before.

But then again, none of them have been Emerson.

FORTY-FOUR

Emerson

'M SHOCKED AWAKE BY THE DREAM.

I can't remember it, but the sensations linger in my mind. The darkness of the room. The scent of his cologne. The sounds he makes.

Fear consumes me in those first few seconds.

And then I realize it's Grant's arm that's wrapped around me. It's the heat of his body that is cuddled against mine. It's his even breathing that greets the still night air of his bedroom.

It doesn't matter, though. My heart still races from another dream. Another piece of my past unveiled. Another part chipped free.

I shift away from him, needing some space.

As if the distance will help me understand the constant dreams I've been having. Combat the fear that comes with each one of them. Untangle the nightmares where I'm Keely or she's me and my dad is coming down the hall. Things—little things—I hadn't remembered but that are now so vivid and terrifying that I can't breathe around them. I wish they would stay dead and buried.

But the fear reigns. It has owned me every day for the past few days and has taken a toll on everything in my life. I've messed up entering figures on my loan application paperwork, I've given misinformation to students during a class, and I've been scattered when I jumped.

Yet, even with all the distress and all the memories, the one I fear to recall the most remains silent. The blank spots in my memory that hide them taunt me and promise to reveal everything and destroy me in the process.

It's why I don't trust myself.

It's why, when I look at Grant, I know I need some space, and more than the foot of still-warm sheets I just put between us. Some time to think. A few days to clear my head and figure out where to go from here.

I slip out of bed and stand beside where he lies. The moonlight comes in through the window, dashing light across his abdomen but leaving his face in shadows. I take in the beauty of him, the kindness in him, and I know without a doubt I don't deserve him or the patience he has afforded me.

My heart hurts.

For so many reasons. It's why, when I lean over and press the softest kiss against his stubbled jaw, another tear slips over and down my cheek.

He thinks the ugly in me is beautiful.

I don't understand how he can. I don't understand how anyone could look at me and see beauty when it's edged with so much pain. When beneath the surface, I'm a disaster waiting to implode. The notion confuses me. The realization tells me I need to take a breather for myself.

To get perspective.

To figure out if Grant is the remedy or the cause of all the current unrest in my mind.

"Goodbye, Grant," I whisper. "Thank you."

And as I click the front door closed behind me, the tears continue to flow. I'm not sure if I feel vulnerable because I've finally opened up or because I fear I need to say goodbye.

FORTY-FIVE

Grant

"HEY, GRANT. YOU FINALLY DECIDE TO TAKE THE PLUNGE?" LEO asks as he leans back in the chair behind the desk and gives me a knowing grin that challenges my manhood, but I'll fucking let it.

"Nah. It doesn't feel like hell has frozen over yet, does it?" I laugh as I look around for any sign of her in a place where there is always a trace. "Is Em around?" The phone on the desk between us rings, and I make the go ahead motion with my hand.

Leo just glances at the caller ID and rolls his eyes. "The guy's an asshole. He can wait. And to answer your question, no she's not here. She took off for a few days."

Before I can ask where she went, the voice mail picks up and Emerson's throaty voice fills the space around us. "Thanks for calling Blue Skies. We're currently out jumping and can't get to the phone, so please leave a message, and we'll get back to you as soon as we can. Head up. Wings Out."

"Sorry, but the damn volume is broken or I'd turn it down," Leo says as the recorder beeps.

"You're not returning my calls, Emerson. I have a few more things to go over regarding the loan docs and need you to meet me for a late dinner tonight. There's nothing like a little wine to set the stage for success. I expect a call back within the next hour or else your follow-up paperwork might just get lost in the shuffle, if you catch my drift. One hour, Emerson. I don't like to wait."

Every part of me seethes at whoever the prick is on the answering machine. I mean, I know he's the loan guy and it's clear as fucking day what he wants in exchange for loan approval. It's just that he's using his position to try to take advantage of Em, and his boldness makes me think she isn't the first woman he's done this to.

"Fucking asshole," Leo mutters as his face reflects how my temper feels.

"Is this a typical thing?"

"The slimy bullshit? Yeah. It is. The guy's a grade A prick."

"Who is it?"

Leo stares at me for a moment, and I can see him gauging whether to tell me. "Emerson has him under control," he says after a prolonged second, not giving me the answers I fucking want. "If she needs help, I'm sure she'll let you know."

I give him my best cop beat-down stare, but it doesn't faze him. On one hand, I like knowing he has her back, on the other hand, I wish he'd have it a little more so that he'd tell me and I could help her.

"So she has the day off?"

"A few days off."

"Where'd she go?" I ask, hating that the fucked-up feeling I had in the pit of my stomach when I woke up to an empty house is back.

"She said she needed to get out of dodge for a while. She's probably jumping somewhere else for a change of scenery. According to Desi, she's known to do that from time to time when she needs to clear her head. I'm surprised it took this long, actually. With the pressure the Blue Skies owners are putting on her to get loan approval and this asshole holding it for ransom, I bet she just needed some space."

"Huh." His explanation does nothing to explain why my calls and texts to her have gone unanswered. "I thought she never left this place."

"It isn't often, but it does happen."

"Thanks. If she calls, can you let her know I was looking for her?"

"Yeah. I will. But don't expect her to. When she goes off the grid . . . she goes off the grid."

Fucking great.

I walk out of the office and stand with my hands on my hips as I look across the parking lot to where her car should be but isn't.

I have my interview to prepare for and cold case files to go through.

I have a life to live.

So, why I am at Miner's Airfield, wondering where in the hell Emerson is and why she left? I have no idea where she might have gone, but if I were a betting man, I would put money on her leaving having something to do with what happened last night.

Waking in an empty bed sucked.

The worry that followed was even worse.

FORTY-SIX

Emerson

"I MET A GUY—WELL, NOT REALLY *MET*, BUT MORE LIKE SAW HIM again—and I think you'd approve of him, but while you would, he's really screwing with my head. I don't know what to do."

My voice carries on the breeze as it whips through my hair. I tilt my face to the sun, close my eyes, and try to feel her presence beside me. One hand rests on her marker and the other twirls one of the wild daisies between my fingers that cover the top of her grave.

"It's Grant Malone." I smile at his name. "Yeah, I know. You always had a soft spot for him even though I wouldn't acknowledge him or the Malone family when you brought them up. But I ran into him again, Mom, and I'm really struggling like never before."

I watch a hawk soar through the blue sky over where I sit on the hill that overlooks my mom's hometown of Miltonville. She picked her resting place because, according to her, if she were on the top of a hill, she'd be able to watch over me no matter which direction I decided to wander.

"Things I don't remember, I'm remembering. Good stuff. Bad stuff. You were always so proud of how strong I was, but I don't feel so strong anymore, Mom. I feel like I'm losing my grip on reality. One day, all I'm trying to do is keep Blue Skies, get the loan, and keep on top of Travis's to-do lists, and the next day, Grant Malone comes barreling into my life, and it's as if none of that matters anymore."

"Why is that a bad thing?" I can hear her asking, just like she always used to, and the common refrain makes my heart twist in my chest because I miss her so damn much.

"It's bad because I need rules and structure and control, but all of that goes out the window when it comes to him, and I can't have that. Without the rules, my mind wanders, and it can't wander, Mom. I can't remember any more than I already do. I just . . . I can't . . ."

I can close my eyes and see her smile as she asks me, *"But why?"* while looking at me above the rim of her beloved cup of tea. If I hold the image long enough, I can even see the way the steam twirls up around her and her hazel eyes squint just a bit, as if she is trying to will the right answer into my mind.

"Because I can't need anyone. I can't trust anyone. You know that. It was you and Desi, and now it's just Desi." I take a deep breath, let it out slowly, and then admit, "I'm scared. I'm so scared because I don't know how long I can keep up the façade that I'm normal and strong when lately I feel like the little girl I used to be. The one who fell apart any time a stranger looked at her for too long and who just wanted to take a knife to her arms to prove that pain was all she ever knew . . . and is all she'll ever know."

I look down and play with a daisy as I struggle with the lie I just told her. How I pretended that taking a knife to my arm was more of an urge instead of a recent reality . . . and then I realize she already knows. Her wings were out that morning. That was why I was able to stop myself from cutting the second time.

Dropping the daisy, I trace the engraved letters of her name and know if my mom were still alive, she would tell me that I didn't mean any of what I said. That I was strong and resilient and beautiful, which was something he saw even if I didn't. She would tell me that was why I was really scared, and that it didn't matter if I remembered some of my past because we always knew it was a possibility.

She would set that tea cup down, reach out, and grab my hand before telling me that maybe I was starting to remember because I finally had someone strong enough to stand beside me and help me through it.

The words I imagine her saying hit my ears but don't grow roots. They're scary and unwanted and against everything I ever thought I'd allow of myself.

To let somebody in.

To share that part of my past.

One of the last things she said to me resonates with me in the moment.

Would she tell me that letting him in doesn't mean I have to stop being resilient and strong?

I smile because she totally would.

"I miss you, Mom. I miss you more than you could ever imagine," I whisper, tears falling as I lie down on my back atop of her grave and think of nights snuggling up in our van while we were between towns. The Reeve girls making an adventure for ourselves.

I stay there for a long while with the blue sky above me, the comfort of my mom around me, a map of possible jump sites circled in purple Sharpie beside me, and my mind fixated on the past and the two men who were such an integral part of it.

FORTY-SEVEN

Emerson

"STOP CRYING, EMMY." HE'S IRRITATED AND KEEPS LOOKING AT the clock on the wall, but he won't look at me.

"I want Mommy." My hands shake, and my body hurts, and I'm scared and just want my mommy.

"Knock it off. You're fine. Stop crying and get back in bed."

"You hurt me." I stare at him and watch that funny bump on the side of his jaw get hard as he bites his teeth together.

"No, I didn't."

My heart feels like it's in my throat again. The same way it did before I threw up and wet myself. I tell myself not to do it again. I think of the bath he put me in after. The warm water. The weird way he used the washcloth to clean my privates instead of letting me use it myself.

I feel like I can't breathe. "Yes, you did. Mommy would put you in so much trouble for what you did."

"No. You are the one who is in trouble. I don't think you want me to tell your mom about the phone call I got from Mrs. Gellar today about how you keep acting up in class. You know how much she hates when you act up."

"Mrs. Gellar called?"

"Mm-hmm. You and Grant weren't listening again. Do I need to ground you from seeing him anymore? Is he becoming a bad influence?"

Panic hits me. No Grant? He's my only friend. And . . . I don't understand, I didn't get in trouble today. I was good. I'm always good. "Dad, I didn't get in trouble today at school," I barely whisper.

"And I didn't hurt you tonight, now did I?"

"But you—"

"You were dreaming, Emmy." He looks at me for the first time, and his eyes look black to me. Black like the ghost in the Halloween book that Grant let me read that gave me nightmares last week.

Was I dreaming?

"I don't think I—"

"You were screaming. You had a nightmare. You were fighting against me when I woke you because I was holding you to calm you down. Then you peed the bed like a baby. Again."

I blink my eyes and know what he's saying isn't true, but I can't remember it all. I can't remember . . .

"You fell asleep on the couch while I was watching television. I should have put you in bed, but I thought you were sleeping, so I didn't . . . the nightmare you described was the exact same as on the show. You must have heard it when you were asleep, and then turned it into a dream." His voice is getting angry like it does when I don't do what I'm supposed to do.

I shake my head. I fell asleep in my bed. With my Strawberry Shortcake doll under my arm and my rainbow nightlight on the ceiling above me. I never get to fall asleep on the couch.

But my blanket is there. Next to him. Did I bring it out here?

"Mom would be so mad at me if she knew I watched that show with you when you were supposed to be in bed. She's going to be home any minute, and you know how mad she gets when you stay up late on a school night. Do you want me to bring you back to bed?"

"No." I can barely say the word. I don't want him in my room.

"Okay. Come give me a kiss."

I stare at him, my feet feeling like they weigh more than an elephant's. He reaches out and pulls me into him and presses his lips against mine. My tummy feels like it's going to be sick. The feel of his whiskers reminding me of earlier.

Not a dream.

"'Night, sweetheart. Do you love me, Emmy?"

"Yes, Daddy."

"Say it."

"I love you."

"How much?"

"With all my heart."

His smile makes me feel like ants are crawling on me. "Get to bed, now."

I hurry to my bedroom upstairs and shut the door. Then I open it because the darkness brings monsters.

But the monster is downstairs . . .

I struggle for air as I lie in bed and pull the covers tighter around me. The strange surroundings of the hotel room I'm in only add to my discombobulation.

I replay as much of the dream as I can in my head, and one thing stands out above all the rest.

With all my heart.

How could I tell a person who just molested me that I love him?

How could I spend years of my life cutting my arms to deal with the pain a man who was supposed to love me unconditionally caused me?

It all comes back to trust.

The Reeve girls.

I think back to how, while we were on the road, my mom didn't trust anyone. If someone showed the slightest interest in me—even in the most benign of ways—we moved on to the next city. To the next adventure. To the next place where no one would notice us for a while.

It all comes down to trust.

She didn't trust anyone with me.

And now? Now I don't even trust myself.

FORTY-EIGHT

Grant

"YOU'RE SLACKING ON THE JOB, OFFICER SEXY." DESI'S VOICE comes through the phone loud and clear. It causes me to perk up in my seat at the end of a monotonous day and a monster hangover after a few too many beers with my brothers last night.

"If it isn't my favorite nosy best friend," I say with a laugh, but I am relieved to hear from her. Maybe she's heard from Emerson since she sure as hell isn't returning my calls.

"You got that right. Nosy is better than nonexistent. Have you talked to our girl lately?" she asks, switching topics to exactly why I was drinking heavily last night. Worry does that shit to you.

"Not for seventy-two hours." More like seventy-eight, I mentally correct after I look at the clock on the wall. "But she's like that . . . when she feels like she's getting too close to me, she backs off a bit."

"So is she? Are you? I mean, she just up and took off for three days, should I be worried that you did something to her that I'm going to have to put your balls in a vise for and torture them until you beg for forgiveness?"

"Ouch." I shift in my seat and remind myself to never piss off Desi.

"Well?"

"No. I didn't do anything to push her away. She came to the house the other night upset about . . . a few things, and when I woke in the morning, she had taken off," I explain, not sure how much Desi knows about Emerson's past. If she didn't know anything, there was no way in hell I would be the one to divulge it to her.

"And you just let her go?"

"I was sleeping . . . so I didn't know she'd left."

"I'm going to be nosy here and ask, what are your intentions with her?"

"She's always been the one, Desi." My own answer stuns me. I say it off the cuff and before it's even out of my mouth, I know it's the complete truth.

It's always been Emerson. Every woman was a substitute, a way to pass time, because deep down, I knew she and I would meet again.

God, the fucking woman is gone three days, and I've turned into a sappy, sackless wonder.

Silence fills the connection, and I'm not sure if it's because Desi is letting me process my own epiphany or if she's just as stunned by it as I am.

"Well, it's about goddamn time you realize it. Jesus H. This whole dance was getting old. So, now that you know, what are you going to do about it?"

"I can handle my own relationship. Goodbye, Desi." I laugh as I end the connection and shake my head. I love the woman to death, but she is a royal pain in the ass.

True to my opinion of her, she calls me right back. I debate whether to answer it, but then realize we never got to the part where she tells me if she's heard from Emerson.

"I know you can handle your own relationship, you jackass, but the reason I called was to tell you that I talked to Emerson and something is going on with her."

"What do you mean?" I lean forward, worried and relieved all at the same time.

"She called me last night and she was a mess when normally—"

"She isn't a mess." My mind goes to the angry red scars on her arms, and I hate that I wonder when I see her next if there will be more. If the time away will have helped her cope or made it harder. A selfish part of me wants her to realize it's easier when she's with me. That she doesn't have to run because I'm here for her. To help her. To hold her.

"Exactly."

"What did she say?"

"She wasn't making sense, Grant. She was rambling on about doubt and trust and I don't know what else . . . everything about the conversation worried me. What was troubling her the other night when she came to your house?"

"*Shit.*" I sigh. This is all my fault. The damn ball started rolling because of me. "I took her to a call the other night. She didn't really see anything, but I think the whole scenario affected her and . . . *fuck.*"

"She's home now," she whispers, telling me what I need to know.

"I'm on my way there," I say, standing and grabbing my keys.

"If you break her heart, Grant, you'll break her spirit."

"No one said anything about hearts here."

FORTY-NINE

Grant

"E M?"

Emerson turns to me, her face a startle of shock, hair pulled back in a bun, and there are circles under her eyes. The minute she sees me, she begins to walk the other way.

"Emerson," I call after her and then jog to catch up.

"I don't have time for you," she says as she shakes her head and picks up her pace. "I've been gone for a few days, and I need to get caught up for the owners so that it's in good shape for any potential buyers."

"What?" My gut twists. "You didn't get the loan?" Here I am being an asshole, thinking all of this was brought on by me, and it had to do with her not getting the loan. It has to do with her losing her dream.

"I don't know if I did. It doesn't matter. I'm pulling my application."

What the flying fuck?

"What are you talking about?"

It's the first time she stops walking and turns to face me. "I'm a wanderer, Grant. I don't stick around. I get antsy and need to move on. It's obvious I can't trust my judgment anymore . . . I mean look at me . . ." She laughs. "I'm a twenty-eight-year-old woman trying to buy a skydiving school with money I don't have. I make rules that I never keep. I sleep with you then run away. I cut myself when I promised myself I was never going to again. I mean . . . who is going to put their trust in me to teach them to skydive, repay a loan, or live a normal life when I can't even trust myself anymore?" There's hysteria ringing in her voice, and the resignation from it is reflected in her expressionless eyes. "I have to get back to work."

And without another word, she turns on her heel and jogs toward the office and the comfort of company to prevent me from making a scene.

Panic hits me like a battering ram.

She can't leave me.

She's fucking crazy if she thinks I'm going to let her walk away and out of my life without a fight.

I guess it's time to make a scene.

"Hey, Reeves," I say as she pushes the door open. I follow her in, and Leo looks up from his desk, his eyes darting between Em and me as he leans back in his chair, watching the show. "Take me up."

It takes everything I have not to sound like I'm choking the words out, but I know the fear currently coursing through my body has nothing on how I'd feel if I lost her again.

"What?" she says as she makes a show of slowly turning around, brow narrowed, confusion morphing into surprise. "What did you just say?"

"I said I'm cashing in my gift certificate. Take me skydiving."

"But you're terrified of heights." She takes a step closer, as if she doesn't believe a word I'm saying, and honestly, I don't, either.

"Everyone has to face their fears sometime, right?" I shrug as she just stands there and stares at me. "Someone once told me that living safely is dangerous . . . I don't want to be dangerous, Emerson. I just want to be with you."

Her breath hitches, and she shakes her head back and forth. Her eyes say she wants to believe me, but her body tells me she's not certain.

I take another step forward, my own pulse racing and mind struggling to believe what I'm asking her to do.

"You're the only one I'd trust to get me down safely, Em," I finally say, my coup de grâce, that she needs to wrap her head around.

"No." It's a half-hearted sound, chock-full of disbelief but laced with hope.

"You don't get to say no." I smile as I catch Leo in my periphery laugh. "I have a gift certificate paid in full, and I'm cashing it in on you. Right now."

"No."

"The customer is always right, Em."

"Once you commit, you can't back out," she says, lifting her eyebrow and straightening her posture.

Exactly. *Once you commit, you can't back out.* I hope she realizes the same goes when it comes to me.

"I won't back out," I say, ignoring the way my feet desperately want to walk the other way . . . but everything about her changing demeanor stops me. The way her shoulders square. How her lips quirk. The placing of her hands on her hips.

She's back in her element, and hell if I'm not going to help her to stay there . . . whether it kills me or not.

Literally.

The growl of the plane's engine roars in my ears and vibrates beneath my ass, but it has nothing on the absolute terror owning my every nerve. Fuck yes, I'm a pussy.

But this is a plane.

And a nylon parachute is about to be responsible for preventing me from falling to my death.

And Jesus . . . I'm about to willingly jump out of an airplane door.

All for a woman.

For Emerson.

To prove to her she's just as fucking strong as she thinks she is. As I think she is. As everyone around her thinks she is.

Trust is an important thing . . . and I'm about to put one hundred percent of mine squarely in her hands.

How fucking stupid am I?

I go to run a hand through my hair but stop when I remember my helmet. I bounce my knee, close my eyes, and berate myself for not calling my mom to tell her goodbye and that I love her.

All of the things Emerson showed me in the classroom downstairs run on repeat through my mind. The initial jump at thirteen thousand feet. The belly-to-earth fall rate of one hundred fifteen miles per hour. Sixty full seconds of free fall. The arch of my back. The yank of the ripcord at twenty-five hundred feet above ground level. And then, of course, there is Emerson's reassuring refrain—if in doubt, whip it out—about the reserve chute in case the main doesn't deploy.

I've seriously lost it.

My ears pop, and I shift my jaw how she told me to equalize the pressure, but holy fucking shit am I nervous.

I can't hear what she's saying, but she's joking and laughing with the pilot as if she is headed to the park to walk the dog. As if she's not even giving this a second thought.

I try to be as calm as she is—which is pretty fucking impossible—and remind myself why exactly I'm doing this. For her. I took the one thing she knew I was absolutely terrified of losing—my life—and put it in her hands, telling her that I trusted her implicitly with its safety.

But doubt still reigns in my mind. Skill is one thing. Equipment failure is a whole other.

There's a nudge against my arm, and I turn to look right into her eyes. They are alive, and I realize in that moment that she needs this like I need my work. She needs the high from jumping just like I need to be the hero.

I guess we both thrive off endorphins and adrenaline but obtain them in extremely different ways.

"You ready?" she mouths, grin wide, eyes animated as she stands so that Leo, who is sitting on the other side of her, can hook the two of us together.

Ready?

No.

I'm not.

I swallow over the lump of fear lodged in my throat and force a smile. My legs are wobbly as I stand, the plane ride rougher than I had expected, but then again, that could be because the door is currently open and wind is rushing into it like a chamber.

The next few seconds are all a blur. My fingers gripping tightly on to the ropes fastened to the ceiling so I can steady myself. Emerson's body pressing against mine as Leo slowly begins attaching our harnesses so that we can tandem jump. The trembling of my hands as I look at the altimeter on my wrist to tell me we're almost at the point of no return. The churn of my stomach as I want to hurl but know there's no way I will be able to save face or my masculinity if I do.

Somehow, as I'm standing unsteadily, her hand finds mine. She links our fingers together and squeezes in silent assurance. It's a simple gesture, but fuck, if it isn't the lifeline I need to take those few steps forward to the open door.

Holy shit.

Holy shit, I'm doing this.

Holy shit, I'm going to step out of the plane.

We make it to the doorway, and Emerson moves my earplug and says, "Get ready to chase the moment, Malone." It's her laugh that rings the loudest. The carefree in it. The freedom. The ease and confidence. "Head up. Wings Out."

And then she pats my side in a signal we'd practiced when our feet were firmly on the earth to let me know it's time.

It. Is. Time.

She turns us around so that her feet are on the edge, her hands are beside mine on the opening of the door, and then before I can even blink, she lets go.

Head up. Wings Out.

Oh. Holymotherfuckingshitthisiscrazy!

Despite feeling like we are falling in slow motion, my brain processes everything—the fear, the euphoria, *my* mortality, the adrenaline—in snapshots of time.

The pressure of the air against my body. The rush of it in my ears. My initial gasp as we begin to fall. The lack of that stomach-in-your-throat sensation I hate, which she promised wouldn't be there. The feeling of being out of control until we hit our arch. The calming presence of Emerson at my back and her arms helping to guide the positioning of mine. Her confidence overpowers my uncertainty.

It's then that I find a few moments of utter peace.

Sure, the sound of the wind is roaring in my ears, but all I see is the whole valley laid out in its greens and browns with the ocean's blue not far beyond.

It's breathtaking and eerie and so serene that I forget that I'm falling over one hundred miles per hour.

Then, before I expect it, we are yanked violently upward as the canopy is deployed. It robs me of my breath momentarily, and I have just enough time to wonder what the hell happened before I'm hit with the sensation of floating.

The sound of Emerson's laughter is in my ears, and I follow her hand as she points to a few places for me to look at. And I do look, but my body has such a rush of adrenaline and nerves and disbelief that I just jumped out of a fucking airplane it's hard to concentrate on anything other than this. The moment. The knowledge that I just cheated death.

All I keep thinking as we glide the rest of the way down to the big orange X-marks-the-spot landing zone is: *I get it now.* Emerson's addiction to this high. Her need for it. Her use of it to escape her past that haunts her.

Before I know it, she's shouting instructions in my ear. Pull the guide left to steer us. Right a little more. Feet up so she can take control. Prepare for landing.

The excitement in her whoop is followed by the jolt of her feet as they run beneath us and take the impact of the landing. We are both sitting on our asses, my butt between the V of her thighs as we slide a bit on the ground and the parachute collapses.

Then there is silence around us. My head screams so many goddamn things, but I'm on the ground. Alive. Whole. And Emerson got me here.

She laughs when I try to turn to face her because we're still harnessed together and then makes quick work of unhooking us. Before I have a chance to process what the hell just happened, I turn around on my knees and kiss the life out of those lips of hers.

I'm riding a high like I've never known before. Cheating death. Proving to her I trust her. Facing a fear. *Everything.* And all I can think about is claiming the goddamn prize of Emerson Reeves because adrenaline definitely has my blood pumping and is intensifying my need to have her.

FIFTY

Emerson

I KISS GRANT BACK WITH A NEED MORE DESPERATE THAN I'VE EVER felt before. Right here in the drop zone, I deepen the kiss with my hands gripping the lapel of his flight suit and take every damn thing I need from him.

Leo chuckles somewhere near as he gathers his own chute, but I don't care. He gets it. He gets this. Post-jump sex is indescribable. Using the high of the adrenaline coupled with the bliss of an orgasm is a major inside joke amongst jumpers.

And more than anything, right now, I need Grant.

He showed up today seeing a broken woman ready to give it all up. Then with his simple request, he started putting my bricks and mortar back into place to prove that I am as strong as I thought I was. Sure there is doubt, and there always will be. But he knew that was what I needed—to be pushed back into my comfort zone so I'd find my confidence again. So, I'd wipe out my skepticism.

Grant leans back, the gold in his eyes dancing with excitement and lust, and I know he feels the same way I do. We shared something up there. I've jumped hundreds of times and have had the trust of the people I jumped with, but this was different. We both took what the other offered and used it to conquer something we feared.

I shove the rig off my back, leaving the parachute billowing in the breeze to pick up later, and without care of who else might be looking, I jump into Grant's arms and wrap my legs around his waist.

Between spurts of laughter, our lips find each other's, and God, how good it feels to laugh with him and kiss him. How good it feels to know my mom is looking down on me, approving of my taking a chance. How funny it seems that I want him to save me after all.

"I need you," I murmur against his lips as my hands thread in his hair and the heat of the sun does nothing to rival the fire in my body already burning bright.

"My dick's already five steps ahead of you." He chuckles as he begins to walk across the field with me wrapped around him like a monkey.

I wave over Grant's shoulder to Leo, who just shakes his head at us and rolls his eyes. I think he says something sarcastic like, "Sure, I'll take care of your parachute while you fuck," but I don't care, and I don't have any shame because it isn't like he's never experienced this feeling before.

"Hurry," I murmur as I nip the tip of his earlobe.

"Where? Keys?" His cock presses against me with each step he takes and makes the walk across the strip tortuous.

"Shit. My keys are in the office." I laugh as my mind scrambles. "Go to the left. Red hangar. Far side."

"Christ," he mutters, but only because with each rub over his dick he lets out a little groan. "Here?"

"Mm-hmm. The door slides," I say even though he's already pulling open the large barn-type door. Then we're into the shadows of the red hangar and he's shoving the door shut and slamming me back against it. His lips are on mine in a savage union of lust and greed and want and need and every one of the seven sins mixed in there.

There is no finesse. There are no niceties. We are all about how fast we can unharness ourselves from our rigs and step out of them so we can feel and enjoy each other's skin.

"Christ, Em."

"I know. Hurry." A laugh falls from my lips. "Post-jump sex is the best kind of sex there is."

"Oh really?" he says, leaning back to meet my eyes. His have darkened with lust and suggestion.

"Mm-hmm."

"You were holding out on me." A brush of his lips against mine. A cup of his hand against my ass pulling me against his hardened dick.

"Can't hold out on someone when they are the one refusing you." I quirk my lips, but then they fall lax as he tugs down the zipper of my suit and yanks down my tank so he can suck then graze his teeth over my nipple.

"I'm not refusing you now, am I?"

"I wouldn't let you," I challenge.

There is a quiet moment where our eyes lock and our bodies vibrate from our connection – mental, physical, emotional—and then within a beat, we are back into frenzy mode. Zippers on flight suits sound off. The shimmy of clothes being pushed down. The squeak of shoes on concrete. The begged pleas to hurry. Quicker. I'm desperate.

And then, as we stand in this massive hangar buck naked, his body a mouth-watering sight only serving to encourage my urgency for him, I realize there isn't really anywhere to have sex in here except for the concrete floor. The walls are lined with industrial shelving units. The tables are covered with plane parts.

"Where are we going to . . . crap."

He takes in the sparse space save for the Cessna in one corner and a Piper in another before turning back to look at me with a gleam in his eye.

"What?" I ask.

"Guess there's no time like the present to join the mile-high club, huh?"

Before I can process what he means, he lets out a whoop, swoops down, wraps his arms around my thighs and hoists me buck ass naked over his shoulder.

"Red or blue?" he asks, and I can only guess he's making me choose a plane. I don't have the heart to ask how he plans on joining any kind of club when there is definitely no room in either of them to have sex. "Decide."

"Blue," I say, and then cry out in shock when his hand smacks my ass as he makes his way over to the Piper. "Grant. What are—"

"Shush." He slowly lets me down so that I slide down the length of his body. The friction of my slow descent makes my nipples bud so hard they hurt, but it has nothing on the ache banging hard between my thighs. "We're chasing the moment," he says, flashing a smile before his lips are on mine again.

The trailing edge of the wing is at my back and he pushes my ass against it while we speak with tongues and moans instead of coherent words.

The adrenaline is a high, but so is the taste of Grant Malone. And, Christ, how I want more of him.

Our hands are everywhere and not enough places on each other. His fingers find their way between my thighs, and the groan he emits when they find me wet, willing, and wanting for him is enough to make me come on the spot.

But that's cheating.

If he wants to make me come, he'd better work harder than that to earn it.

"Turn around," he demands.

"Should I assume the position?" My eyes flash up to meet his, my bottom lip between my teeth as I make a deliberate show of turning around. I lay my torso and breasts against the wing and wiggle my ass in a tease as I hiss at the cool metal beneath my bare flesh.

"Christ, Em."

"Are you gonna frisk me, Officer Malone?" I say in my huskiest of voices.

His chuckle rumbles through the space as I wait for him. The sound of his hand working over his own cock is chased by his groan of appreciation, and just knowing he's doing that because he likes what he sees is fire to my blood.

"Frisking someone has never been so tempting." His foot knocks my feet farther apart before he leans forward. "Spread 'em," he says in my ear, the scrape of his chin against my shoulder as he retreats again causing chills to race over my skin.

Then there is an anticipatory silence as he stands behind me and I wait. Adrenaline begs me to rush this, my need paramount, but there's something about how sexy this is that has me biting my lip as I stand there, bare to him, aching for him to satisfy me.

I startle when his hands hit both sides of my right ankle before slowly sliding their way up my leg. When they hit the apex of my thighs, he rubs his thumb back and forth along my slit before pressing into me. The only sounds in the hangar belong to my hitched breath, his labored groan, and his thumb working me at a leisurely pace. And once he has me wanting enough that I'm pushing back against his touch, he stops, repositions his hands, and then starts his ascent up the other leg. But this time when he reaches the top, I groan when he removes his thumb without stroking me.

Then gasp when his tongue does it for him.

His tongue is hot and I'm wet and . . . holy hell. My eyes flutter closed at the feel of him. The tease of what's to come. The desperation for all of him.

I wriggle under his manipulation and plead when he stops. He takes one long, last lick with a libidinous groan before stepping back so that our only connection is where his hand runs back and forth over the curve of my ass.

Every part of me wants him.

"Is there a problem, Officer," I ask coyly, so very aware that he's allowing me to continue this charade of control he's afforded me for the past few hours.

I don't think he realizes that he could ask me for anything right now, and I'd give it to him.

Something changed between us today. Shifted. The fear I had over him, about him, is gone. I just need to accept it. Everything in me is whispering that a jumping-high orgasm slamming through my system to remind me how incredible his cock is will help do the trick.

"It seems I have forgotten my handcuffs." He chuckles and lands a smart slap on my ass.

"Oh, am I under arrest?"

"Definitely."

The palm of his hand slides down the line of my spine.

"What's the charge?"

"Making me want you. Every minute of every goddamn day."

His hands spreading me apart and then his mouth blowing ever so softly over me.

"What's the punishment?" I'm breathless, spent before we even start.

"I'm going to fuck you. Thoroughly. Properly. And hopefully slowly . . ." His words seduce me, but it's his dick slowly slipping into me that consumes me. It's the feel of his thumbs caressing over my ass before one of them presses unexpectedly against the tight rim of muscles above it that excites me. I part moan, part wriggle back against his fingers to let him know I want him. "But the way you feel right now, I can't promise the slowly part."

I purposely tighten my muscles around his cock and moan at how full he makes me feel. "No woman complains about thoroughly and properly," I murmur, the cool of the wing beneath me and the heat of what his dick is doing within me driving me to distraction.

"Good," he says as one hand twists around the length of my ponytail and tugs my hair back some to hold me in place as he drives into me harder this time.

"Yes." The word is a drawn-out sigh and each thrust brings a new round of pleasure, a new way to sustain the adrenaline of the jump.

"You like that?" He grunts as his thumb rubs circles to stimulate the nerves in my ass while the head of his dick expertly manipulates and taunts and teases the ones within me. With each touch, each graze, he pushes me up that welcome precipice between pleasure and pain.

"Please," I beg, and it's the last thing I have to say because he's as primed and desperate as I am and ready to take the fall.

Again.

"We are lucky everyone was gone so we didn't have to take the walk of shame back here," he murmurs against the crown of my head.

He is leaning against the headboard of my bed, and I'm resting my head on his chest. I'm comfortable and more peaceful than I have been in days . . . and I know it's because of him.

"Do you always take your suspects back to their place after you frisk them?" I murmur.

"No, but it sounds like you skydivers do after a jump." He chuckles, its vibration rumbling against my chest.

"Adrenaline has a way of doing that to you—making you need that extra release."

"Is this an occupational hazard I should be worried about?"

"No. God no." I pause and then add, "But I won't deny that all of my staff have had their fun at one time or another."

"And that's why Leo was laughing."

"Ha. At least we left plain sight," I say with a laugh as I think about Leo and that hot little number he all but mounted against the side of the Blue Skies shed after a particularly thrilling jump.

"I don't think I want to know."

"No, you don't." I can still hear the rest of the jumpers hooting and hollering for him to get a room, but the sweet, little thing he was with was so excited to have a catch like Leo, she had no shame.

We sit in silence for a bit, his fingers trailing up and down the line of my spine, moving the towel, which is still damp from our shower, down a bit more with each subsequent trace of his finger. I think of the day. Of how I came back determined to pick up and and go so I could escape the feelings and the memories I can't seem to stop. Oh how quickly that changed when he put his trust in me. He gave me his biggest fear and didn't walk away like I wanted to do to him.

Shouldn't I be able to face my biggest fear then, too?

"Thank you for getting me down safely," he murmurs as if he's reading my thoughts.

"Thank you for trusting me to do so."

"You needed a leap of faith, Em. You needed someone to prove to you that they trust you, so in turn, you should trust yourself."

"There are so many things you don't understand . . . things I wish I could . . ." My fingers draw absently on his chest over his heart.

"No. It's okay I don't need to know."

"I'm just not ready to explain—"

"You don't need to. I've done enough damage. I pushed you when I didn't realize I was. I guess I just want you to understand that I'm here for you. That I care about you. That whatever it is you need from me, I'll try to give you, so long as you tell me. I can't read your mind."

I draw in a long, deep breath as if I'm trying to digest and believe what he is saying to me. As if I'm willing myself to whole-heartedly trust him.

"Trust is hard for me," I whisper, feeling as if I just peeled back my soul and opened it to him. In reality, my revelation is nothing new but it's still huge for me to admit.

"Understandably."

Another deep breath. Another confession that needs to be expressed but that is totally unfounded. "I blamed you for the longest time you know."

"Blamed me for what?" he asks, trying to pinpoint what of the many things I could pin on him.

"My lack of trust." His fingers still for just a beat before they move to my chin and tilt my face so I'm forced to look at him. His eyes question me, but his lips refrain from verbalizing. "It was so much easier to blame you for everything than to blame the man who was supposed to love me."

He nods ever so slightly; the compassion in his eyes is truly overwhelming. "I can't tell you I understand, Em, because I haven't walked a day in your shoes, but I can tell you that I respect what you are saying. That I hear you. That I'll prove to you that you can trust me."

I feel so stupid, needing to hear him say those words, but now that he has, I feel as if a weight has been lifted off my chest. "Where do we go from here?"

"What do you mean?"

"I mean . . ." I pause and try to figure out how to put what I want to say into words. "Never mind."

He pulls me in tighter against his chest. "Where do we go, Emerson? First of all, you're not going anywhere. I love that you're a wanderer and free spirited—I wouldn't change that for the world. I'd never take that away from you. Though, I'd appreciate it if you keep the taking off without telling anyone where you are to a minimum. It makes the cop in me want to track you down to make sure you're okay."

"You wouldn't . . ."

"Don't tempt me," he teases but with a hint of an edge that tells me he'd do just that if need be.

"I won't. Remember, we're working on trust here," I say dryly.

"I'm aware." He plants a noisy kiss on my forehead. "Since you're staying put, then we keep doing what we're doing. You get your loan despite how much I'd like to punch that slimy fucker you're getting it through. I get my promotion despite the asshole trying to take it from me . . . and we . . . move forward. Together."

"This is all a huge change for me." I try to wrap my head around how two months ago, I was thinking about the next flavor of the month, and now, I'm sitting here discussing tomorrows with Grant.

"What is? The having someone care about you part or the feeling settled in one place?"

"Both. None. All of it." I laugh as I hook my leg over his. I meet his eyes and find myself admitting things to him I haven't yet digested myself. "I've survived this far by closing myself off and not allowing myself to feel . . . and then you enter my life with your lights and sirens blazing, and it's as if you've handcuffed me so that I can't escape from you. So that I'm forced to feel. So that I think in wants and needs. So that I wonder how I ever lived without it. I love it. I hate it. It's overwhelming, and it's just . . ."

"Well, get used to it because I'm not going anywhere and neither are you, even if I have to handcuff you and your nomadic ways." There's humor in his voice, but there is also an earnestness that tugs on my heart. It makes me just that much more thankful that he showed up today.

"Better make sure you bring them next time," I tease as my body reacts to the memory of earlier in the hangar.

"I'll make sure to put my extra set in the nightstand."

"Promise?"

He leans forward and presses the most tender of kisses against my lips. "Promise."

Our eyes hold for a moment. "You've pretty much obliterated my rules, you know that, right?"

He makes a non-committal sound. "I was wondering how long it was going to take for you to realize that."

I shrug. "I have a selective memory."

"Is that what it's called these days?" The way he says it makes my body become all too aware of how thin the towels wrapped around us are and how easily we might be able to slip out of them. He kisses me again as my fingers reach for the towel at his waist. "There is one thing I forgot to do earlier—you know, proper police protocol."

"Falling down on the job again?"

He chuckles against my lips. "Only if I'm falling on top of you."

"Cute," I say and then sigh as his fingers find their way between my thighs. "We were talking about following proper police protocol." It's hard to get the words out.

"Then I guess it's time to get this strip search under way," he says before his lips meet mine.

And just like that, we slip into something beyond my rules.

It should terrify me after the past week I've had, which was filled with doubts and questions, but there's something so comforting about the moment.

About being with someone who sees my scars and still thinks I'm beautiful.

FIFTY-ONE

Emerson

Roll your eyes all you want, but I'm breaking the rules again. Have a good day. – Grant

I look at the card in my hand again and then back to the arrangement of dahlias that were just delivered to Blue Skies. It's strange and sweet and crazy that he's sending me flowers on the day of his interview. Shouldn't it be me who is taking care of him today?

I smell them again. I want to be mad and say they're ridiculous, but I find it hard to stop staring at them. My cheeks actually hurt from smiling, and I know by the side-glances Leo keeps giving me, he's noticed.

"Did someone die?"

I look up to see Travis standing in the open doorway, ball cap in hand and eyes curious.

"Seems to me someone has taken a liking to Em," Leo says.

"Humph." Travis looks at the flowers again, then to the card in my hand, and then back to me with obvious curiosity. "When you get my age, you look at every flower like it's waiting to adorn your casket . . . so don't bring no flowers around me and jinx me."

"I won't." I laugh. "I promise."

"Well, you enjoy those then." He nods and offers a smile before leaving the office.

Leo and I both watch him retreat across the tarmac to the Skies' hangar. It takes a while at the pace he walks.

"What's going on with the loan and the prick?" he asks as he rubs his hands together in mock anticipation of when I own this place. "It feels like it's taking forever. When will you know?"

I blow the hairs that have fallen out of my ponytail away from my face and shrug. "Two, three more weeks? Your guess is as good as mine. We had to file an extension and get approval from the Skies family to do so because some paper had to be resubmitted or something like that. Honestly, I have this sick feeling that he's holding out, thinking the more desperate I get to have this close and fund, the more willing I will be to sleep with him." I roll my shoulders. "I'll never be that desperate," I say with a laugh as I look back down to the card in my hand and smile. "Thanks again for not telling Grant who the loan company was when he was in the other day."

"It isn't my business to tell." He shrugs. "Although, I'd gladly watch him go all badass cop on the fucker, if for no other reason than to prevent him from doing it to someone else. I know you can handle yourself, but you're a badass in your own right."

I look at him for a beat, his words striking me. Here I stand, always a mix of uncertainty beneath the surface, and yet, Leo is telling me he sees anything but.

His words remind me of something my mom might say to me and it makes me smile at the thought.

"You know what, Leo?" I ask, turning the card over in my hand again.

"Huh?" he says without looking up from whatever he's doing on his laptop.

"Can you cover my classes today?"

"Sure. Is everything okay?"

"Yeah." My grin widens. "I'm going to take the day off."

"*You're going to what*?" He looks as if I just punched him.

"I'm going to take the day off," I say as I grab my keys from my desk drawer.

"Take off or 'take off'?" he asks considering I did just disappear for three days.

"Take off as in the afternoon. Life's too short not to. I deserve it."

"You do." His laugh follows me all the way out of the office until I hit the stairs of my apartment.

I'm dialing my phone before I even take the first step up.

"Em?"

"Hey, wanna play hooky with me, Des? I need your help."

There's a chorus of barks in the background as she sputters. "Where is my friend and what have you done with her?"

"So, a week ago you were a wreck and now you're a damn ray of sunshine. Let me guess, you found a great new sex toy that's rocking your world and you haven't told me about it yet? Hm? Or should I guess his name starts with G and ends in a T with a whole lotta hotness in between?"

"Shush," I say as I laugh and lower my head as the elderly lady down the pasta aisle stares disapprovingly our way.

"She'll get over it." Desi waves a hand her way. "Well? The answer, please."

"What if they are one in the same?"

"God. Damn." She hoots throwing her arms up in a touchdown sign as we push the cart toward the end cap. "I knew he was packing. He is packing, right?"

"You're perverted."

"And there's a problem with that why?"

"Because you're supposed to be helping me shop for food, not getting me kicked out of the grocery store for offending the customers."

"Sorry. Not sorry." She shrugs unapologetically. "Grab that beef consommé there. We'll use that with the roast."

I follow her pointing finger and put the can into the cart. "You sure I'll be able to cook this by myself?

She stares at me like a mother does a child. "Is that your way of asking me to come over and make it for you and then leave so you can pass it off as your own?"

"I'm not saying the idea hasn't crossed my mind, but no. I want to do this for Grant on my own."

"Okay. Now we need vegetables." I scrunch my nose up in disgust. "It adds flavor. And while you may hate them, he may like them. He can't have all those rippling muscles eating crappy food all the time."

She grabs a plastic bag and begins putting some potatoes in it.

"So are you going to tell me why the sudden about face? I mean you went from running away from him, to struggling for control, to being a wreck last week, to being a giddy female when you're not a giddy female. I'm getting whiplash here, Em . . . but hell, I'll take it."

I want to argue with her and tell her there hasn't been a huge about face but realize she's right. I've been all of the above.

"This isn't like me, is it?" I ask but know I wouldn't change it for the world because it feels liberating.

"No, it's not." She holds up a rather large cucumber and giggles like a schoolgirl when she wraps her fingers around it and strokes it.

"Put that down!" I glance around, mortified that someone might be watching her.

"Can't blame a girl for liking a little girth." She sets it down. "I like this new you, though. I like the smile that's plastered on your face. I like the laugh on your lips. I love the confidence that's back with a vengeance but is still different. Care to explain?"

"I just feel like things are falling into place," I say over a mountain of apples.

"Okay." She draws the word out to let me know I'm making zero sense.

"I'm feeling confident about getting approved for the loan. I went and spent some time with my mom when I was a wreck, and it kind of cleared my head and helped me focus. I let Grant break every single one of my rules and—"

"Every single one?" she asks, voice incredulous, eyes wide.

"Yep." I flash her a huge grin.

"What prompted this?"

I contemplate how to answer her. While she knows I had a screwed-up past, she has no clue just how screwed up. I've let her assume what she wants to assume to avoid her putting a label on me like anyone else who has ever found out has. So, without giving her the correct context, there's only one explanation I can give her that she'll buy.

"You were right."

She accidentally drops the onion in her hands onto the floor. "Excuse me? Did I hear you correctly?"

I nod and let her have her moment of glory. "I let him in, Des. Instead of pushing him away, I let him in."

"You trust him," she whispers as if she's just unearthed the damn Rosetta Stone. She understands how huge this is for me.

"Yeah, I do." It feels so good to say it. It feels even better to think back over the past two weeks and remember all of the laughter Grant and I have shared. Whether it be taking his nephew, Luke, to an extra innings baseball game between the San Francisco Giants and the Austin Aces, or strolling hand in hand at the mall while eating ice cream, or snuggling up next to him while he prepares for his oral interview while I try to make sense of the Blue Skies financials to see where I can cut and expand once it's mine. Dare I say, we've felt normal?

And with the normal has come the cessation of more memories breaking through. It's almost as if the more I fought them, the harder they tried to make themselves known, and then when I decided to own whatever ones came my way, they stopped.

"Earth to Emerson," she says breaking through my own self-realization. "You were saying before you drifted off to thoughts of Grant and what he's packing . . ."

I scramble to remember exactly what I was saying so I ad-hoc. "I've been so busy trying to hide who I was and Grant wouldn't allow it. Instead he stepped in and told me that it didn't matter who I was—what had made me who I was—because I was who mattered. The moment was what mattered. Not the past." I groan and roll my eyes. "That's not right . . . it's hard to explain."

"I think I get it." She shrugs and laughs. "Basically, Grant is me, *but with balls.*"

I laugh so hard I snort. "Can we scrub that visual from my mind with bleach and finish getting the ingredients I need?" I glance at the time on my phone. "I need to make sure I have plenty of time in case I screw this meal up."

FIFTY-TWO

Emerson

"THANK YOU. I APPRECIATE IT."

"You need anything else?" Grady asks as he stands in the entryway of Grant's house.

"No. Here's to hoping I don't burn the house down." I laugh, knowing my attempt to cook anything could end up in a dire situation.

"At least you know a firefighter to call," he says before tossing me a wink.

"True."

"Well, I have to get back."

"'Kay."

He turns to walk out the door. "Hey, Em?"

"Yeah?" I look up from where I'm unloading groceries onto Grant's kitchen counter and hope I look somewhat competent.

"This is a really cool thing you're doing."

"I wouldn't say that yet. My post-interview, celebratory dinner hasn't even been started, so let's not jinx me. Cooking is not my strong suit."

"No, I mean it," he says, looking outside and then back toward me. "You mean a lot to him . . . and the fact that you're taking the time to do this is pretty cool."

I smile as he gives me one last nod and then closes the door behind him, leaving me to do this all by myself.

Sort of.

As soon as I know Grady has driven away, I FaceTime Desi.

"Are you sure you don't want me to come over there and help?" she greets me.

"No. I'm capable and competent." There is far more gusto in that statement than I feel. Inside, I'm secretly wishing she would. She may have written down step-by-step instructions, but even that isn't foolproof when it comes to me.

"He better appreciate the fact that you're risking life and limb to do this for him."

"It's cooking, Desi."

"Exactly. For you, that means life and limb."

"Hardy, har, har."

Oddly enough, the house actually smells delicious. And not the delicious that's really a cinnamon scented candle I lit so I could pretend I'd been baking desserts, but like real, honest-to-goodness, meat-and-potatoes type of food.

And despite how great the aroma is, I'm suddenly nervous. It sounds stupid that I've let the man see me naked, strip me bare, but letting him eat my cooking makes me anxious. Most likely because I half expect him to keel over and die because I screwed it up so badly.

So, I busy myself with straightening the stacks of case files on the coffee table. Then I shift the plant sitting in front of the window so the opposite side grows stronger toward the light. I wipe the counters down for the umpteenth time. I fiddle with the place settings on the table and debate over whether that seems too stuffy, but decide the candle I put in the middle negates that.

I pace the room a few times and then decide to fluff the couch pillows when I've never even fluffed my own. I'm putting a pillow back and pulling a throw blanket off the corner to fold it when the green of a case file catches my eye, and I smile. Considering how many times I have caught him nodding off amid reviewing stacks of them, I'm not surprised one has fallen into cushion oblivion.

But it's only when I dislodge it and go to set it on the table where the other stacks are that my heart stops. I shake my head to reject what I'm seeing.

It can't be . . .

My heart races, and my mind tries to comprehend what my eyes are seeing.

Closed File #713920: Emerson Reeves – Sexual Abuse – 10/23/1997

But I know what it is.

This is me. *The old me.* The little girl I was and don't want to be. It's the past I don't want to be reminded of, and yet, my file is sitting here—in Grant's family room—hidden in plain sight so I wouldn't see it.

These are the answers that could simultaneously cure all the doubt that plagues me and knock me so far down the rabbit hole I might not be able to find my way back.

Fuck having ownership of memories should they come. This is proof. Proof in ways I can't comprehend. There is no ownership of it now. There is only falling victim to it when I've been a victim enough in my life and . . . Oh. My. God.

Shock burns its way into anger. The fuse is so short it's combustible.

My hands tremble as I throw it down on the table like it's burning my skin. It hits the wooden edge and falls to the floor, causing a few items to dislodge.

Every part of me screams to turn around and run out of the house while my feet remain rooted. A little voice in my subconscious tells me, *"Look at them."*

Trepidation courses through me as I take the dare and bend over to pick up the piece of paper that taunts me.

What am I doing?

I turn it over, and it takes me a few seconds to have the nerve to open my eyes and look. What I see has a sob falling from my mouth as I sink to the floor.

The top of the page is labeled "Child Assessment – Emerson Reeves – Age Eight." Memories ghost through my mind of when I drew this—the light blue room that was cold, the nice lady with the gentle voice who asked me to draw a picture to show her what happened, my tears hot on my cheeks as I looked around for my mom.

The drawing depicts what I saw through my innocence. Now, I look at it with the knowledge of an adult. Tears well as I take it all in. There is a bed where two stick figures lie, one bigger like an adult with short brown hair and the other smaller with red hair. The red-haired figure, me, has blue dots falling from her eyes and making a puddle on the floor. The brown-haired man, my dad, has his hand over where the legs on my rendition meet. There's a black L-shaped thing on the top of the bed, a gun, and words line the left side of the page: No, stop, hurt, all my heart, I love you, daddy.

It hurts too much. *This* hurts too much.

I want to cover my ears and squeeze my eyes shut and block this all out so I can forget that I remember that day.

In haste and with a scattered mind determined to get the drawing out of my sight, I shove the piece of paper under the file's cover where it is on the floor. I pick it up to put it on the table, and when I do, I see the Polaroid beneath it.

I forget every intention I just had when I'm met with a picture of myself in a hospital gown. There is no smile on my lips. There is no happiness that every eight-year-old should have. Everything about me—my posture, my expression, my eyes—look defeated and scared.

I stare at the little girl in the photo and tell myself I am not her anymore. I will never be her again. But every part of me feels like her right now. Lost. Withdrawn. Petrified.

Betrayed.

A tear drops on the picture, and I realize for the first time that I'm crying. Tear after tear tracks down my cheeks as parts inside me I thought were whole again slowly crumble to rubble.

I tell myself to close the folder because I don't need to see this. I don't need to know more details. Don't I already know them somewhere in my mind?

FIFTY-THREE

Grant

IT'S AS IF MY DAY JUST KEEPS GETTING BETTER AND BETTER. I nailed my interviews and now I come home to find Emerson's car in front of my house and music floating out of the windows.

Grady's cryptic text earlier of "I let her in" makes perfect sense now.

Tonight seems like it's going to be even better than today.

What did I do to deserve this?

"Emerson?" I call when I open the door, but I see her before the word cuts through the room.

When she hears my voice, her body stiffens where she's sitting on the floor behind the coffee table. Her head rises slowly and the look in her eyes—a mixture of devastation and anger—is enough to have the hairs on the back of my neck bristling.

"Em?"

"So, what? I don't tell you what you want to know, so you figure, fuck my privacy. Fuck my need to quiet my own mind and deal with my own shit as I see fit . . . and take it upon yourself to figure it out on your own?" Her voice escalates in pitch with each word and warns me to proceed with caution.

"What are you talking about?"

"*I trusted you!*" she screams at the top of her lungs, and it isn't the sound of her desperation that kills me. It's the depth of grief in her eyes.

"I don't . . ." I step into my own house and begin undoing the knot of my tie. I'm fucking suffocating all of a sudden and have no clue why all the oxygen has been sucked out of the room. "I don't understand."

"Exactly. You didn't understand," she says as I round the couch and see it at the same time she speaks. "You didn't understand, so you dug up my old case file so you could."

Oh. Shit.

The green file folder—her file folder—is sitting squarely in the center of her lap, causing dread to drop through me like a lead weight.

"You had to call it up from wherever the fuck it was so you could pour over every goddamn detail there was about me. *About what he did to me.*

Anything you could find so you could satisfy that hero complex of yours and come to the rescue with your cape and save me." She stands and slams the folder down on the table with a smacking noise that sounds just like I feel. "Well, *fuck you*, Grant Malone. Fuck. You. If you think he violated me, what the hell do you think you just did to me?"

For the first time in my life, I'm at a complete loss for words, and yet, I know I need to find them.

"It was a mistake—"

"*So were you.*" Her voice is as cold as steel.

"It isn't what you think." I backpedal, trying to explain. "The file. It was a mistake. I had a list of files to pull to work on for Ramos. I was thinking about you. I doodled your name down—"

"And then what? Then you got the file and kept it? I've seen you move boxes in and out of here after a few days . . . but you kept mine. Why, Grant? Face it, you couldn't handle me not telling you what you wanted to know." She paces like a caged animal begging for either an escape or an attack. I guard the door, willing to take whatever she throws at me as long as it means I can explain what happened.

"At first, yes." My confession is barely audible.

"I hate you." The tears burning so bright and pain so raw in her voice it shatters every part of me.

"No, Em. No. It wasn't like that. I wanted to know. And then I realized that—"

"You don't get it, do you?" she shrieks, hysteria bubbling over in her erratic movements and flailing arms. "*I don't want to know.* I don't want to know every little detail. I don't want to hate the dark again like I used to. I don't want to lie in bed at night and listen for every damn noise because I think he's walking down the hall to '*love me*' again. I don't want to remember the feeling of the hair on his legs scraping against my bare bottom when he sat me on his lap." She covers her hands over her ears and emits the most horrid sound I've ever heard. It's part sob, part yell, part protest, and if I never hear it again, I'll be good with that. It renders me helpless. "I was fine until you, Grant. I had the memories I had and those were enough nightmares for a lifetime. But that wasn't enough for you, was it? My lack of answers wasn't enough?"

"Em—"

"Don't you get it? I don't want to remember what happened after the feel of his hair scraping against my skin. It was obviously so bad that my own mind has shut the memories out—repressed the fuck out of them *to protect me* . . . and yet, *you know*. I don't even know, but you know." A heart-wrenching sob breaks free from her chest.

I fumble for words, for a way to get her to see that I never opened the folder, but the truth she just told me is more staggering than that.

It was *so much more* than her remembering the damn rocks the other day.

She doesn't remember *anything*. At all.

How could I have been so stupid not to pick up on that?

"No, Emmy. No—"

"Don't you dare call me that! Just don't." She takes a step back as I take a step toward her. "Please don't." Tears continue to streak down her cheeks, and her mascara paints their paths. She's a broken woman, and I've done this to her. "Knowledge isn't power in this case. You can't use it to your advantage to save me from what already happened."

"Will you fucking listen to me? I did *not* look at it."

"I don't fucking believe you!"

"Christ." I blow a breath out and run a hand through my hair to stop myself from reaching out to touch her like every part of me wants to. "Will you quit being so goddamn stubborn and hear me? I did not—"

"How can I ever let you look at me again without thinking about how you know things about me that I don't even know? How can I ever be with you when you cared more about feeding your own need to be the hero than how it would make me feel?"

Her words cut into the room and ram like daggers into my heart.

"I trusted you, Grant. You pinky promised," she says, her words quietly followed by a hiccupped sob. "And you broke it. *Again*." With that, Emerson rushes past me out the door.

"Em. Wait." I jog down the path after her.

"I hate you. I never want to see you again."

It's those words—the ones repeated twenty years apart that hit their mark. I don't have the heart to stop her from going . . . because she's right.

Shell-shocked, I watch her get in her car and drive away without looking at me. I stare down the empty street long after the glow of her taillights have faded and the crickets have settled into their space in the night.

At some point, I walk into the house, turn off the oven, and blow out the candle as if I'm on autopilot. My eyes burn. My stomach churns. The pressure in my chest makes it hard to breathe.

Because she is right.

I wrote her name down. It may have been a doodle, but her name was there on the top of the list.

I held on to the file when I knew I shouldn't. My initial intentions might have been pure behind it—find out what exactly she experienced so I could . . . so I could be the goddamn hero.

Fuck.

I'm such a damn asshole.

I didn't want to screw this up and look what I just did.

Trust is hard for her.

And I just went and fucked that up.

I clench my fist and beg for something to hit.

The problem is, the only thing worthy of being punched is myself.

FIFTY-FOUR

Emerson

DRIVE.

I press the pedal to the metal and push the limits of the engine as I roar down the rural road. I use the rush of the air through the open windows to fill my ears and drown out my thoughts. And to dry my tears.

I don't know where I'm going.

I have no clue.

All I know is I need space and freedom and air that Grant Malone doesn't breathe.

All I want is to lose myself in something—*possibly in someone*—so I can remind myself why I don't let my guard down.

All I need are my rules back in place.

All I want is my chest to stop hurting and my heart back.

I know that, regardless of how determined I was to hold on to it, I left it back at Grant's house.

I gave my heart to him, and I gave my trust to him.

And he has just broken both.

FIFTY-FIVE

Grant

"YOU WANT TO TELL ME WHY YOU'RE BEATING THE SHIT OUT of the heavy bag like it has done something to you?"

I don't have time for Grayson or his shit right now. "I can punch you instead."

I grunt as I connect again. The jolt of my fist against the bag ricocheting up my arm and slamming into me is nothing compared to what I deserve.

"Who pissed you off?"

"No one."

Another grunt. Another unsatisfying slam against the bag.

"Ah, so then you pissed yourself off." He chuckles, and I don't respond. "Oh, shit, I'm sorry, man," he says suddenly, as if the wind has been knocked from his sails. And it's just enough to catch my attention that I glance his way.

"What?"

"Did you blow your interview?"

"No." I hit the bag again. "I killed the interview."

"Then what the fuck man?" A few seconds pass. "*Oh.*"

"Yup." A one-two combo.

"How'd you fuck it up?" I love that I have brothers who understand what's going on without my ever saying a word, but at the same time, it's annoying as fuck when I want to be left alone. A blessing and a curse.

A jab combo. An uppercut that I pretend is Grayson if he doesn't leave me the hell alone.

"Because I am a dumbfuck, is how."

"Tell me something I don't know," Gray says and dodges to his left as I miss the bag on purpose and come a little closer than I should to his chin.

My arms ache, but there's nothing I can do but blame myself.

"So? What did you do?"

It's his question that steals my air. I throw one more punch and then let my arms hang as I rest my head against the bag and try to catch my breath.

"I broke her trust," I murmur, not even sure I want to tell him. How could I have been so damn stupid?

"You *are* a dumbfuck." He slaps me on the back, and I jerk my shoulders back to get him off me.

"So we've established." I step away from the heavy bag and walk toward the bench where my water bottle sits, gritting my teeth when he follows.

"Considering you're here and beating the shit out of a bag instead of figuring out how to make it up to her, I'd say it's definitely been established."

"Leave me the hell alone, Gray. I can handle things on my own."

"You sure about that?" *Not at the moment.* "Because I may not know what the fuck you did, but the big brother I know doesn't give up without a fight. You're the hero. The guy who saves things . . . so, go save this."

I glare at him.

"I'm out of the hero business."

"Like hell you are."

"C'mon, Em. Open up." I pound my fist on her door. *Again.* The same as I've been doing for the past ten minutes.

"She obviously doesn't want to talk."

Leo's voice startles me, and when I turn, I find him leaning against the wall of the next hangar over, arms across his chest, eyes hidden beneath the shadow of a ball cap, body riddled with irritation.

"Thanks, but it's none of your business, Leo," I say and turn back to the door.

"It actually *is* my business."

I'm not in the mood for this shit. "You know what?" I say as I take a few steps down the stairs. "I love that you watch out for, Em. I do . . . I love knowing that when she's here alone, you have her back . . . but I'm not the prick from the loan office trying to get in her pants. I appreciate the whole big brother thing you have going, but it isn't needed. So, do you mind?"

Leo stands to his full height and takes a few steps toward me. Christ, here comes the macho bullshit.

"Choose wisely," I say with a lift of my brow. While I may not be in the mood to fight after hitting a heavy bag for over an hour, landing a punch on a real, live person might feel a lot more satisfying.

We stare at each other for a few seconds before he nods slowly.

"She isn't here."

"Where is she?"

He shrugs. "Not sure." *He knows where she is.* "She took off outta here like a bat out of hell."

"Christ." Emerson has gone, and I have no one to blame but myself.

"You're a good guy, Malone, but cop or no cop, you hurt her, I have no problem throwing a punch in her honor."

"I think she'd have no problem throwing one herself."

The entire day replays in my head. Over and fucking over.

Killing the interview. I nailed every question with such precision that when I walked out of there, I had no doubt I was going to get the promotion.

The highest high.

Coming home to what I thought was perfection—Emerson's car in my driveway and her waiting for me in my house—and then it turning to shit.

The look on Em's face. The accusations she hurled. The goddamn fucking everything I did to her all because I kept the file. If I wasn't going to look at it, then why did I keep it?

The lowest low.

Fuck me.

The rest of the night is a blur. The gym. The showdown with Leo. The coming home to see the file sitting on the table and knowing I'm to blame for all of this but having no clue how to fix it.

If she thought I broke her trust before—twenty years ago—and she had a hard time getting over it, then she sure as shit isn't going to get over this.

But what kills me more than anything is what happened this afternoon when I went to move her file into the storage box. I can't get it out of my head. The loose picture that slipped out and fell to the floor. The one of an eight-year-old Emmy Reeves—eyes haunted, skin pale, body language withdrawn, scared as hell—staring back at the camera.

The sight staggered me. My memory may have remembered a little girl with bouncy pigtails, freckles, a smile with missing teeth, and a laugh that came from her belly, but that was only the reality a naïve little boy could see. A little girl who looked so scared she might break if you push her shoulder with your finger is what she was.

And even two hours later, I can't get the image out of my head because that haunted look she had in the photo was the same one Emerson looked back at me with today before she left.

"Earth to Grant," Grayson says, throwing a pretzel at me. I don't react.

Leave me the fuck alone. I repeat it in my head for the millionth time but don't say a damn word. I want to wallow in my pity. I don't deserve to, but I'm going to.

"It must have been really bad," Grady says.

"You think he cheated on her?" Gray asks.

"I'm right here, assholes. I can hear everything you're saying, so why don't you just ask me yourselves?" I say it, but I don't want them to ask. I just want them to shut up. So, I slump farther down into the lounge chair in my back-yard and stare up at the stars above.

"You're not responding when we came here to try to cheer you up, so . . ." He shrugs. "We're gonna keep guessing until you start talking. You know it'll make you feel better."

"I didn't cheat on her," I mumble as the words she said ring in my ears.

"Well, that's good because that's one fire I wouldn't be able to put out," Grady says and then looks at me when I don't respond. "C'mon, you know that was a little funny?" He holds his thumb and forefinger an inch apart. "Just a bit?"

"Shit. He thinks he's Chris Rock now with the jokes," Grayson chimes in as the *crack* of a bottle of beer opening sounds off.

"Thanks for the visit, but you guys can go now." Their banter is not what I want to deal with right now, but it's obvious my statement falls on deaf ears. They don't move. "Okay, then I'm going to ignore you guys like you aren't here."

Grayson swears at me when I reach over and snake his fresh beer from his hand without asking. I take a long pull on it, lay my head on the back of the chair, close my eyes, and tune them out.

And think of Emerson.

It works for a little bit until something Grady says breaks through my thoughts and catches my ear. If he's purposely trying to get me to talk, it works.

"I bet you anything he couldn't handle it," Grady says.

"Couldn't handle what?" I ask, lifting up one eyelid to look at them

"You think?" Grayson interjects as if I'm not even here and hadn't spoken.

"Yeah."

"What the fuck are you two talking about?" I growl. I'm tired. I'm drunk. And fuck me, I miss Emerson, and for more reasons than just because. This guilt and regret are eating away at me from the inside out.

"You looked her up, didn't you?" Grady says, prompting me to close my eyes again and exhale. "Curiosity got the better of you, and you looked her up. Pulled her file or whatever the fuck you cops do so that you knew what you were facing."

Ignore him. He's just trying to goad you into talking.

"Just like *our Grant* to need all his ducks in a row so he knows exactly how to handle a situation, especially when that situation is a feisty, sexy handful who doesn't just fall into his arms like every other woman on the planet," Grayson adds with a chuckle that grates on my last nerve.

"Too bad a person isn't a situation," Grady says, the statement hitting its mark. Good thing I've had enough to drink that I'm mellow or I might just have landed that punch I was jonesing for yesterday.

Don't take the bait.

"True," Grayson muses. "I'm not saying that I'd ever follow through with it, but I can't say I blame him."

"What do you mean?"

"It's natural to want to know what you're dealing with. I mean . . . we all know whatever happened to Em was fucked up . . . so, maybe Grant was being a good guy and wanted to know what triggers to avoid or some shit like that for her own benefit."

"You're giving him too much credit," Grady says, and I clench my jaw. They may be enjoying making their damn point, but that doesn't mean I have to react to what they are egging me on to. "You know *our Grant*. He just wants to swoop in and save the day like always."

Another dig. Another bullshit dig.

"He did save our asses a few times," Grayson says.

"But this is different."

"It *is* different. It's Emmy. And Grant's in love with her."

Grady snorts. "Hasn't he always been?"

Patience snapped. Buttons pushed.

"Will the two of you shut the fuck up already? You've made your god-damn point even though you have no fricking clue what the hell happened," I lie because they nailed it on the head, which makes it even worse. That I'm that fucking readable and predictable. I shove up out of the chair to pace, and it takes me a few seconds to gain my balance. The beer is hitting me, and I already know I need it to hit a lot harder.

Because they're right.

I am in love with her.

Jesus Christ, when the fuck did that happen?

Probably about second grade.

FIFTY-SIX

Emerson

LOOK AT THE LIST OF TEXTS ON MY PHONE.

Grant and his apologies and explanations and hurt I don't want to deal with.

Christopher and his promises that we should have loan approval in a week or two, and since he's charging me a below the rate fee, how about I repay him by going out for a few drinks. At what point will the man understand that it isn't going to happen?

Desi and her daily check-in to make sure I'm okay and that I haven't fallen off the face of the earth.

Leo and his questions about the classes over the next few days and how to arrange staff since I'm the one who typically does it.

I scroll through them again and then toss my phone to the end of the bed before snuggling deeper under the comforter. It smells too much like Grant and so I pretend the world outside and everything that happened doesn't exist.

I know they all think I'm out jumping. That I closed my eyes and put my finger to the map and drove to that spot. That I'm chasing the wind and being the wanderer I typically am.

But I'm not.

My car's in the red hangar where it can't be seen.

And I'm holed up in my apartment. *Alone.*

The person I've become fighting the urge to cut myself, while the little girl underneath screams for more of the pain she knows. The pain she needs to feel again to know she's alive.

But I haven't cut myself.

And I won't.

If there's one thing I'm going to win in this whole damn situation, it's going to be that.

I don't even have a desire to jump.

Grant stole that from me.

Just like he stole my heart.

My trust.

But both of them have been broken before. Both of them have wounded me, and I have survived.

The only difference this time around is my ability not to feel *anything*.

Because hell if right now I don't feel *everything*.

So much so that it hurts.

It pisses me off more than anything because I can't turn them off.

That I can't run away from them when that's all I've ever known how to do.

FIFTY-SEVEN

Grant

"**Y**OU'RE RESTLESS."

"No shit." I look over to Nate, who has obliged me with a drive by of Miner's Airfield for no other reason than to see if Emerson is back.

"Just go talk to her."

"I've tried."

"Well, try harder. It's not as if she isn't going to notice the cruiser driving by several times this week."

"I know. It's just . . ."

"I know, I know. There's more to it that I don't understand other than you fucked up royally . . . well, royally unfuck yourself," Nate says and shakes his head.

"Gee, thanks, Dad." I roll my eyes and turn back onto the highway.

"Did you call her?"

"She won't pick up."

"Did you text her?"

"She won't reply."

"Did you stand there and pound on her door?"

"Ha." The image of Leo flexing his muscles comes to mind. "Yeah. Something like that."

"Did you send her flowers? Chicks always love flowers."

"Not this chick," I murmur, thinking I won't test fate by sending them to her twice.

"Then what is it she likes? What is it that is unique to you two? Use whatever that is. Chicks dig uniqueness."

"According to you, chicks dig everything."

"Be original," he repeats.

And I laugh. But as I glace at the Blue Skies sign one more time before we leave, an idea starts to form as a call comes across the radio.

FIFTY-EIGHT

Grant

"GRANT?"

"Mm-hmm."

"Don't you want to go out front and play?"

"No. I don't feel like it."

The screen door creaks. The wood of the porch flexes with each step she takes. The smell of her perfume fills my nose when she sits next to me.

"You miss her, huh?"

I nod instead of talk because my throat burns from trying to hold back the tears. Boys don't cry over girls, but she's gone, and all I want is to cry because I miss her.

My mom slips her arm around me and pulls me against her side. I concentrate on pushing the rocks on the porch beside me around with my finger instead of crying.

"Why did she have to go?"

I'm the reason she left.

She made me promise, and I told.

I'm the reason she left.

"She's gone for just a bit. She and her mommy are at the hospital for—"

"Is she sick?"

"No." My mom makes that one word sound so sad. "She's just   not feeling well."

"But why—"

"And then after they leave, they are going to go on a big adventure," she says in that funny voice she uses when she tells us the dentist is going to be fun. Like I'm supposed to believe her when she's not telling the truth.

"Where?" I ask, my hopes getting up that she'll send me postcards.

"I don't know," she murmurs and then sniffles as if she is crying, but when I look up to her, she shifts suddenly so I can't see her face. "Are these the rocks you were painting?" The dentist voice is back again.

"Yeah. I painted them for Emmy."

"That was nice of you."

"She likes rocks. Even ugly zombie ones. She's been really sad, so I've been painting them and putting them in her planter. She said they make her smile." I push the rocks around some more. "She's not going to have any more of my rocks, Mom. How is she going to smile now?"

"Oh, Grant." My mom hiccups real loud, and it sounds like she's crying again. Before I can look, she grabs me into a hug and holds so tight I can't breathe.

But I cry, too.

I miss my best friend.

Her and her yucky purple backpack and her Barbies and other girly things I hate but would play with her a hundred times if she would just come back home.

Bye, Emmy.

I'm sorry I told your secret, and it made you go away.

If I had kept my pinky promise, you'd still be here.

I'm sorry. Will you forgive me?

FIFTY-NINE

Emerson

THE KNOCK ON THE DOOR TO MY OFFICE STARTLES ME. THE PERson standing there does even more so.

I look like hell.

That's the first thought that glances through my mind when I look up to see Grant's mom in my doorway. My second is it's her son who made me feel this way.

"Betsy."

Is it bad that just the sight of her—my second mom—makes me want to hug her and just sob? I fight the tears burning my eyes because I will not fall apart. Not here in the office. Not at home. Not anymore.

"Em? You okay, honey?" She steps into my office.

"Yeah. Just . . . it'll be okay."

For a moment, she studies me as if she's trying to figure out whether to believe me. "I'm sorry for stopping by unannounced, but I called earlier, and it went to voice mail. I hope you don't mind."

"No, of course not. Come in and have a seat," I say as I stand from my desk and shut the door to my office behind her. The last thing I need is for the staff to hear any part of this conversation. I'm certain they're already wondering what's wrong with me since I've been snapping at everyone. I wait for her to get settled and sit in the office chair next to her.

"It's a wonderful little space," she says with a sincerity I know she means. "I can't wait to see how you improve it when it's yours. I won't stay long. I just . . ."

"What is it?"

"Grant will kill me for meddling, but I couldn't stand by and not say anything." I hold back my sigh when I realize why Betsy has come to see me. "He told me you've been remembering things you hadn't before."

I thought her opening statement was going to be about the file folder or some grand pitch about how I need to give Grant another chance—the same spiel I'm getting from Desi. So I'm a little taken aback by her statement. With anyone else, my guard would be up, but I find myself needing someone to talk to.

"Yes, they have. Ever since I saw Grant on the Fourth."

"And you assume it's because of him?"

I nod, curious but uncertain about where this conversation is going. "It isn't a coincidence."

"You know, sometimes it doesn't take a reminder to trigger a memory. Sometimes your mind just knows you can finally handle it. It knows you've found the right people, the right support network to protect you from the fall-out of the memory—keep you safe—and your subconscious just wants to rid itself of all of it and start fresh. Sure, the memory is going to screw you up. The devil is in the details after all . . . but sometimes, what you imagine might have happened is worse because your imagination magnifies it." She shakes her head and corrects herself. "That isn't what I meant. What happened to you was hor-rific. All I meant was that, maybe by knowing the truth, you'll stop feeling the need to run from the constant and probably nagging unknown. Because I don't want you to run anymore. You're the only daughter we've ever had, Emmy. You left such a big hole in our family when you left before, and we don't want you picking up and leaving again."

I feel like something inside me breaks from her words. I spent months missing Grant and his family after we left Sunnyville. They were the one nor-mal I could count on, and then they were taken away from me when I needed them the most. She has no clue how long it's been since I felt like I belonged somewhere or how her words are like salve on an open wound. They aren't enough to heal, but they are enough to soothe.

"I don't want to leave again, either," I find myself saying. The truth behind why getting the loan means so much.

"And since I'm being pushy, I might as well just get it all out. You can't leave Sunnyville. Plain and simple. Grant is the one for you, Emerson. He always has been." The stubborn lift to her chin is so similar to Grant's that it makes me smile. "He's patient and strong-willed and will put you in your place if need be, but he will also be the first one to pull you into his arms and hold you so tight that your demons have nowhere to go but out. I know you'll keep him on his toes and make him work harder to be a better man because that's what he thinks you deserve . . . but what do I know?" she says as she waves her hand dismissively. "I'm just his mom."

"I wish it were that easy, Betsy. Grant's a great man . . . but I have things I need to figure out first. Things I need to work through. I need to be able to trust him and . . ." I shake my head and exhale, unsure of how to explain it all to his mom.

"I know my son, Emerson. If he had looked at that case file, he would have been eaten up alive by what is in there," she says so matter-of-factly that it takes me a second to process he told his mom about the file

"You know?" My words are barely audible.

"Of course I know," she says, her eyes never breaking from mine. "You were like mine, Em. Your mom and I spent many nights together on the phone, sobbing one minute, screaming the next, and sitting in silence between so the other wasn't alone."

I blink rapidly, forcing back the burn of tears as my mind catches up with her words. With the piece of truth she just gave me.

I *remember*.

The murmured conversations in the back of the van when my mom thought I was sleeping. My eight-year-old self assumed it was my dad she was talking to, that she was apologizing to him because I had been such a bad girl, but it was Betsy.

"I didn't know."

"We both blamed ourselves, Em. How could the two of us—two intelligent, educated women—not see the signs that were sitting right in front of us? How could we be so busy with life that we failed you?"

"It isn't your fault," I say. My need to rid the pain in her voice all-consuming.

"You're right. It isn't. Just like it wasn't yours and it wasn't Grant's. Though, to this day, I think he blames himself for not saving you sooner."

Why would Grant blame himself?

The thought is staggering, and my head is so full of these new revelations all I can do is keep listening to her. "It was your father's fault. He was pure evil. To make you feel like it was your fault? To trick you into thinking it was all dreams? He was evil to the core."

My heart drops. How does she know this? How does she know the doubt I have and my mistrust of my own memory? "You knew about that?" My voice is barely audible.

"Who do you think sat and held your mom's hand as we watched you with the detective and therapist on the other side of the two-way mirror at Children's Hospital? It was me, sweetie. I know he tricked you. I know you doubted back then, and probably sometimes still do today, whether you were at fault or to blame. After all the games he played with your mind, that's more than understandable. Let me tell you that you weren't."

"I didn't realize that you were there after . . ."

"Do you think I would leave you and your mom when you needed me most?" She smiles a sad smile as she remembers. "I'm sorry for what happened to you. I'm sorry that you're remembering some of it. Will you keep remembering? I don't know. Your mind might continue to protect itself from the trauma . . . or it might not. Just know that we are here for you if you need us. You can call me any time, day or night, and I'll come to you, even if it's just to sit with you in the darkness and so you know you aren't alone with a new memory rattling around in your head. You're not alone anymore, Emerson. You never were."

"Betsy, I don't know what to say . . ."

"Don't say anything," she says as she reaches out to squeeze my knee. "Obviously, if you stay and want to be a part of our family—in all our craziness and bantering—it will be on your own terms, your own time frame. And the offer remains regardless if you are or aren't with my son." She stands. "But I have to tell you he's downright miserable right now. My bet is it's because he misses you."

SIXTY

Emerson

Y OU'RE NOT ALONE ANYMORE, EMERSON. YOU NEVER WERE.

Betsy's words still linger in my mind when Desi walks in a couple of hours later.

"You look like shit."

"Thanks," I say with a sarcastic smile as I brush past her without saying anything else.

"You talk to him yet?"

Jesus. Is this the Save Grant brigade? First Betsy. Now Desi. If Leo joins the party, I might just leave after all. It's really hard not to think about someone when they keep getting brought up.

"I have shit to do, Des. I have this class coming in to jump. I have . . . I just have shit to do."

"You think that's smart, Em?"

"What?" I busy myself with papers so that I don't have to meet her eyes.

"Jumping. *From an airplane.* You know, thousands of feet above the ground. I sure as hell wouldn't trust you to take me in the state you're in. Like I said, you look like hell. And distracted. Exhausted. And if I'm honest—"

"By all means, don't hold back."

"Sketchy."

"Sketchy?"

"Yeah," she says and then falls silent until I meet her eyes for the first time. "You look like you couldn't complete two tasks if your life depended on it."

"That's just because I'm trying to avoid talking to you."

"Well, at least you're being honest."

I stop fidgeting and sigh. She's right, and I don't want to admit it. "Look, Des. I'm dealing with a lot of shit. I appreciate you coming to check on me, but nothing has changed. Nothing is going to change."

"So, you're going to shut me out just like you're doing to him?" she asks, hands on her hips, eyebrows raised.

"How do you know I'm shutting him out? Did you talk to him?" My voice escalates in pitch, and when Leo walks in and sees the silent standoff waging between Desi and me, he backs back out of the office without saying a word.

"I didn't say I spoke to him."

She implied it, though.

"I'm not shutting you out. I'm just . . ." I look out the window to where I've noticed a cruiser drive by several times over the past week and hate that I hope to see it.

"Correction. You're not shutting me out, you just aren't dealing is what you're doing. In that head of yours, you're trying to figure out how you can rabbit out of here without messing up everything you've worked so hard for. The loan. Blue Skies. Me, your only family." Her voice softens. "I'm not going to let you run, Em."

I hate that my eyes burn with tears. I hate that the chocolate cake she brought me holds no appeal. I despise that as much as I hate Grant right now, I also miss everything about him.

"He hurt me," I whisper, the words barely audible, as if it pains me to admit it.

"Yeah, I know he did. And I'm sorry for it. I'm sorry you're hurt, but sometimes, when you're in a relationship with someone, that happens." I start to reject her notion of relationship, but she holds her hand up and nips it in the bud. "Have you considered giving him the benefit of the doubt?"

"Why does he deserve it?"

"That's up to you to decide, but in the meantime, you're miserable as hell, you look like shit, and in the end, you're only hurting yourself by not listening to him. Have you stopped for a single second to consider that maybe you're wrong? That maybe Grant is telling the truth about pulling the file accidentally and never opening it?"

I shake my head, not wanting to hear her reasoning because she should be the one supporting me. She should be the one telling me I'm in the right and to dump him.

But she isn't.

"I'm not wrong," I say, using anger to fuel my denial.

"Maybe you are." She shrugs with a challenging lift of her eyebrows. "Maybe you're willing to believe he hurt you because it's so much easier for you to be mad and shut people out than it is to believe them. Because believing him means you might have to put yourself and *your heart* on the line."

"I have my rules, Des."

She's wrong. She has to be.

She laughs, and I hate the condescending sound to it. "And look what happened when you threw them out the window. You came to life, Emerson. He made you feel alive. Anyone who can do that to you shouldn't be confined to your self-preservationist rules. They deserve the benefit of the doubt. They deserve a second chance."

"I have to get to work."

"Don't jump today."

"Head up. Wings out," I say as I walk into the conference room and away from the truth she's telling that I don't think I'm ready to hear.

And straight into Christopher.

Startled, I jump back, but he keeps his hand firmly on my arm.

"How did you get in here?" I ask, completely uncomfortable as I yank my arm away from him.

"The side door was open. I didn't want to interrupt your girl time."

My skin crawls with the knowledge that he was eavesdropping. "Next time use the front door please."

"Or you could answer my calls when I make them, or were you too busy sleeping around with the Malone boys?" He tsks. "Big mistake on your part."

"Mistake or not, it's none of your business." I grit my teeth for the ump-teenth time. Patience.

Only a few more days, and I'll never have to deal with this slime bag again.

His hand is back on my bicep without warning. "Apparently, you don't want your loan, Ms. Reeves?" he says, purring out my last name and causing my stomach to revolt.

"You asking me out for dinner has nothing to do with my loan."

"It has everything to do with your loan."

"Excuse me? I wasn't aware that when I signed the loan application with you that prostitution was part of the deal."

He runs the tip of his finger down my arm, and I want to slap his hand away. "*You* have everything to do with the deal. Don't forget that I am the only one willing to take a risk on you, Emerson. I'm the only lender even remotely willing to issue a loan with your credit history . . . so, I think it's *you* who should be bending to me."

"*No.* I don't bend for *anyone.* It's as simple as that."

"No?"

"You heard me, Chris. Your sexual harassment bullshit doesn't fly with me, and I'm sick of putting up with it. I'm sure the board of ethics wouldn't approve of it, either," I say without even knowing if there is such a thing as a board of ethics for lending practices. "Get the loan approved. Fund the money to the owners. Close the deal. Do your job."

His chuckle scrapes over my skin like nails on a chalkboard. "Your loan was denied this morning."

"What?" If I could get whiplash from the change in conversation, I would have it. "What did you just say?"

Is he fucking kidding me?

"Yep. It was rejected today. If you would have answered my calls or listened to any of my voice mails, you would have known that already . . ." He crosses his arms over his chest and leans one shoulder against the wall. "Don't worry, though. When the lender notified us, the Skies' broker said they were going to move forward and accept their backup offer. I'm sure if you ask nicely, they'll put in a good word for you with the new owners. Maybe they'll give you a job."

"How is that even possible?" I shout as every part of me rages in a disbelief I can't even process.

"Well, when you drag your feet and don't provide your loan officer the things he needs, it can happen quite easily." His smarmy smirk matches the tone in his voice. "One missing piece, one mistyped figure, is all it takes for the lender to throw it out."

"You bastard."

"Not from where I stand."

"You knew my loan was denied, and you pretended it wasn't to try to get me to sleep with you." My fists clench and body vibrates with anger. "Get. Out."

"Too bad, this place could have been all yours." He holds his hands out to his sides and winks. "Good luck finding someone to lend you the money now . . . but then again, it doesn't matter. Your dream is already being sold to someone else."

And with that, he slams the side door shut as I stand there and just stare at it.

With each breath, each beat of my heart, each tremble of my hands, the anger slowly morphs into disbelief.

Then disbelief gives way to shock.

Then shock to devastation.

"Em, you okay? It sounded like something fell," Leo says as he clears the doorway and looks around, his constant movement faltering when he sees me.

"Emerson?"

I just lost my loan.

"I'm fine. I just . . ."

I just lost my fresh start.

"I just need to get out of here for a bit. Can you handle everything?"

"Sure. Yes. You sure you're okay?" Concern laces his tone.

"Yeah."

I just lost my dream.

SIXTY-ONE

Grant

"HOW LONG YOU GOING TO DO THIS, MAN?"

"Do what?" I ask as I turn down Serenity Court.

"You're too close to this case," Nate says as I pull the cruiser to the curb and put it in park. There are cars in the driveway, the garage door is closed, and there are lights on inside. "How are you going to explain why you're in their front yard if Davis comes waltzing out? That doesn't exactly look good. I mean . . . what if he is abusing them, you snooping around constantly looks like a perfect case of police interference, planting evidence, discrimination—Jesus, just about anything people accuse cops of these days."

I hang my head and drum my thumbs on the wheel, knowing he's one hundred percent right.

"I promised her, Nate." It's the only explanation I can give before I hop out of the car and jog the few feet across the street to the driveway.

This is the last time.

Nate's right.

And just as I agree with myself, I turn the corner of the walkway and freeze. Sitting there in a garden of rocks that hasn't had a new one added to it for the past three weeks is a freshly painted rock.

It's red with black seeds.

Oh, shit.

And it's sitting prominently on top of all the others.

It feels like it takes me a second to register what I'm seeing, but I damn well know what it is because my fist is banging on the door without a second thought.

"Sunnyville Police, open up."

Bang. Bang. Bang.

"Open the goddamn door."

Bang. Bang. Bang.

"Mr. Davis, open the door. I know you're home."

Bang. Bang. Bang.

"What the fuck is going on, Grant?" Nate says, already out of breath as he runs up behind me.

The turning of locks startles me, even though it's exactly what I'm asking for. My hand is on the butt of my gun, my temper a rush of adrenaline that has that hand trembling.

"Keely, don't open the door—" Davis shouts from somewhere inside the house, but the sound drowns out to a white buzz when I look down to see her standing there.

Her cheek is bruised beneath her eye.

Her bottom lip is cracked, and there is some dried blood smudged in the corner.

And more than anything is the way she looks at me.

Haunted.

Like I failed her.

Withdrawn.

Like I didn't get to her in time.

Petrified.

Like I didn't save her.

For a second, the picture of Emerson that fell from the folder flashes in my mind and the two of them meld together.

Emmy and Keely.

Keely and Emmy.

They could be one and the same.

"Don't do it, Grant," Nate warns, already grabbing my arm and trying to drag me back a step. "Don't do it."

"Do you have a warrant?" Mr. Davis says as he stands there with a cocky smirk.

"I have probable cause," I say, lifting my chin toward his daughter.

"You don't have shit," he sneers. "She fell running up the stairs earlier. Got banged up real good, too, but we kissed it and made it all better. So, since you have no authority to be here." He strides the short distance to the front door. "Then good bye."

My palm is on the door slamming it back to prevent it from closing. Keely shrinks at the sound, and Davis curses at me.

"Grant," Nate cautions, but all I can think of is willingly letting this little girl go back into this house.

Her blood is on my hands.

Keely isn't Emmy.

I don't have probable cause.

She asked for help.

Emmy isn't Keely.

I don't have any cause other than a rock painted like a watermelon.

"Get inside, Keels," he demands, but never once looks at her. Tension ratchets with each second that we stare at each other, the predictability of what's going to happen next changes with each and every one of my thoughts.

"No." My hand is on her shoulder, keeping her put as she swivels those big, blue eyes of hers from her dad to me and back again, both of us wanting her for different things—I want to protect her, and he wants to hide his abuse.

"Man, we don't have the auth—"

"I don't care about parental privilege."

"Get inside the house," Davis growls.

I look at Nate and then back to Keely. I couldn't give a rat's ass about her piece-of-shit father, but I know what I have to do, and Nate is going to kill me for it.

Without warning, I stoop down and pick Keely up. "She isn't going back in there." I half expect to be attacked from behind as I walk down the path. I prepare for it, but it never comes. Though, Nate is swearing and Davis is shouting.

Or possibly Nate is holding Davis back while I jog away with his daughter. With the evidence.

I don't have a plan. I don't have anything thought out other than there is no way in hell I am letting her go back into that house with that jerk and her compliant mother. Keely's little hands grip my neck, and her sniffles fill my ears.

All I can say is, "I've got you, sweetheart. I've got you."

I press my hand to her back and make it as big as possible so she feels protected, but I fear there will never be enough protection for her.

The system fails.

Look at Emerson.

Nate's call from his on-person radio goes out for backup as Davis's shouts fill the quiet cul-de-sac.

By the time I reach the cruiser, my hands are shaking. I know I'm in the wrong, but I don't fucking care.

"What are you doing, man?" Nate says as he jogs down the path, out of breath and more than flustered.

"Where's the mom?" I say, worried about what else we'll find inside.

"Not home."

"Bullshit. Search the house. Make sure she's all right."

"On what premise? You know we can't do that." Nate blows out a breath as neighbors start coming out from their houses and standing on the curb as the blue and red sirens light up the night like a carnival attraction.

"Well check."

Keely clings to me, her whimper at the sound of her dad bellowing is all I need to hear to know I'm doing the right thing.

"Hey, sweetheart, is your mommy home?"

"She's in the shower," she barely whispers in my ear.

I glare at Nate as another cruiser burns down the street and comes to an abrupt stop beside us.

"Hey, Keely?"

"Yeah."

"I know you're scared right now. There's lots of shouting and lights flashing, and I know you're confused, but I need you to trust me," I say into her ear as Nate gives the new officers on scene a rundown of what's going on. "Have you ever wanted to see the inside of a police car?" She nods ever so slightly without lifting her head from my shoulder. "It's super cool. Can I show you mine?"

Another nod as I open the back door and slide into the backseat with her still clinging to me. It takes a minute for us to adjust and get comfortable, but her fingers never let go of their grip.

For a little girl used to seeing the worst in people, she is so trusting. The thought kills me. Her innocence has been tainted. Her ability to believe in happily ever after skewed.

"See? Nice and cozy." Outside the open car door I see Officer Lou talking to Davis on the sidewalk and assume Amelia is inside talking to Lou's partner. Nate's at the trunk of their car on his cell with someone—probably CPS.

"Maybe when you're not so scared I can let you turn the lights on and off and sound the siren." She doesn't respond. "Can I ask you something?" I say smoothing a hand down her hair. "How'd you get that bruise on your cheek?"

I feel her chest shudder against mine, and her fingers slowly release from around my neck as she voluntarily crawls off my lap and sits in the seat beside me. She studies her fingers for a long time before finally speaking.

"I fell on the stairs and hit my face," she murmurs.

"That's a big fall. Did you cry?" She nods but doesn't look at me in the eyes. "If you didn't fall on the stairs . . . you know, like if you got hurt in some other way, you could tell me and I wouldn't be mad."

"'Kay."

We sit in silence as I figure out how to get the truth from her. If she doesn't talk and if her mom protects her dad, then we have no grounds to keep her out of the house. Silence eats up the car as the crowd of onlookers grows.

"Keely?"

"Hmm?"

"Why did you use our secret code?" She shrugs, but I can see her bottom lip trembling. "Did something happen that made you think you needed help?"

Another shrug.

Another loss for how to talk to her.

"Is my daddy in trouble?" she whispers, and I fumble with how to answer.

"If he hurt you, then yes. Just like in school, you can't hurt people without getting in trouble. It's the rules." She nods. "Did he hurt you, Keely?"

She looks at me for the first time since I picked her up. Those eyes so wise beyond their years as she stares at me. Tears well until she finally blinks and releases them down her cheeks.

Tell me, please.

Car doors shut around us. Nate yells something to Lou. But I sit in the back of my cruiser with this little girl and will her to let me protect her.

To save her.

To do what I couldn't for Emerson.

After a few moments, she pulls her knees up to her chest, curls into a ball, stares out the window, and slides her hand into mine.

If I thought my heart was broken before, she just shattered it.

SIXTY-TWO

Emerson

I NEED OPEN SPACE.

I need the wind in my hair and the roar in my ears to drown out the devastation owning my soul.

I didn't get the loan.

I'm not going to get Blue Skies.

I tried to start over. To build a life. To stay put. To trust someone.

But it doesn't seem to be in the cards.

All this hard work. All this busting my ass, and I have nothing to show for it except that I'll probably be out of a job and most likely out of a place to live.

The thought hits me hard, and I press the pedal down even farther.

Anything to quiet my head, but it isn't working.

Nothing is working.

Me. Grant. Blue Skies. My attempt to make a life for myself. Maybe it just isn't meant to be.

So I drive. Push the limits of reason with a pedal and a full tank of gas and wonder what's next.

The sirens cut through my thoughts, and red and blue lights up the dark night.

"Goddamnit!" I shout to myself as I thump the steering wheel with the heel of my hand, and for just a second, I imagine flooring the gas and taking off.

Was he just sitting here waiting for me?

Nothing like abusing his power.

Because I'd bet anything it's going to be Grant walking up to my car and asking for my license and registration. It's going to be Grant trying to reel me in when all I want to do is run.

As I pull over to the side of the road and put my hazards on, I force myself to acknowledge that a small part of me yearns to see him. After the visit from his mom and the doubts Desi lit the match to in my mind, I finally feel ready to face him. The hurt is still there, still raw, but what if I was wrong?

I lean back in my seat and watch the swing of the flashlight as he walks, curious how he's going to play this. We still have a lot to say to each other, and the side of the road isn't exactly the place to do it.

Then again, he's the one who pulled me over.

I squint when the flashlight hits my eyes.

"License and registrat—ah, so we meet again," the officer says, startling me. It's the same officer who pulled me over before. The one who started the whole Tampax adventure.

"Hello, Officer."

"Do you happen to have lead in that foot of yours, Ms. . . ."

"Reeves. Emerson Reeves."

"Ah, yes. Emerson. Where's the fire tonight?"

I stare at him for a second, ready to bullshit my way through it but don't. "You know what? I had a really crappy day. That's it. No excuse. Sometimes there's nothing better than an open road and the windows down."

He chuckles. "Honesty. I like that." He nods as he leans his forearm on the top of my window. "So, what am I supposed to do with you—"

"Officer Roberts, what's your 10-20?" His radio interrupts.

"I'm out on Highway 43."

"We have a situation that needs assistance out on 12662 Serenity Court."

That address.

How do I know it?

"What's the 10-13?" he asks as he steps back from my door and walks a few feet toward the front of the car so he can watch me and also have some privacy.

"Malone and Nunez are on scene. The situation is escalating."

The minute I hear Malone, my heart jumps in my throat. *"Grant."* I don't know if I say his name aloud because all I hear is "situation is escalating" and dread drops like a lead weight through me.

"10-4. En route."

Is he okay?

"What's your ETA?"

What does escalating mean?

"Five minutes."

Please let him be okay.

Officer Roberts strides back to my window. "Today is your lucky day. Try to keep it below seventy."

I watch the beam from his flashlight as he jogs back to his car. The siren joins the lights as he pulls away from the shoulder and screams down the asphalt.

Grant.

SIXTY-THREE

Emerson

MY HANDS TREMBLE ON THE WHEEL AS I TURN DOWN SERENITY Court where blue and red lights explode in their dizzying array of patterns. They flash over the houses and cars and people gathered to watch the activity at the end of the street.

It's been nine minutes.

Nine minutes where I don't even remember purposefully taking the turns to get here.

Nine minutes where I mentally ran through every scenario possible and none of them were good. In every single one, Grant was hurt, and all I could think of was that I'd been stubborn and hadn't spoken to him. I hadn't made things right.

I haven't told him I want to take a chance.

Funny thing is that I didn't even admit that to myself until just now.

Tears blur my eyes as the realization hits me that this is his reality. His every day. His way to be a hero. I'm out of the car and running to where the crowd of looky-loos stands. My heart is in my throat and hope is in my hands.

"C'mon, Malone. We have to let CPS deal with this."

"CPS? Really, Nate?" Grant's laugh echoes off the houses just as I break through to the front of the crowd. I'm not sure what I expect to see—a stand-off, weapons drawn? I don't know, but this isn't it. Grant is standing in front of his cruiser, arms crossed and body taut, as Nate, the officer who was with him on the Fourth, and another face him. The tension between them is so palpable that if I didn't know better, I'd think Grant was holding someone hostage. Murmurs roll through the crowd about the little girl in the car, and there are questions about whether Grant is going to do it, whatever "it" is.

"CPS?" he says again, punctuating his incredulity with a shake of his head. My breath catches when I realize he actually *is* holding someone hostage in a sense. But only to protect her. *To help Keely.* "CPS's response was to put her back in the house so they could come and assess the situation at a later date because there is no immediate threat. Tell me that's not a fucking joke."

Nate rolls his shoulder, frustration evident. "I know, Grant, but there is nothing we can do. Without proof or her saying he did it—"

"Proof? You want proof?" Grant shouts. "Look at her cheek and lip. That's all the proof I need."

"It's her words we need to hear. We can't take her. We can't arrest him. We technically can't even be here since there wasn't even a call we were responding to! Nothing we charge him with will stick."

"I don't fucking care. When I leave here, she's either coming with me or she's going with someone from CPS. She is not going back in that house."

There is a determination in Grant's stance that matches the tone in his voice. The little girl in me roots for him. The grown woman in me can't tear her eyes away from him.

"You're too close, Malone."

"Did you see her face, Nate? That's not from the stairs. That's not from a fall. She's terrified. Of course she isn't going to rat her dad out. *He's her dad!*" He rakes his hand through his hair. "She still loves him regardless of how big a piece of shit he is. Then there's her mom, who sits by and lets it all happen. She's five. *Five.* Someone has to stand up for her, and fuck if I'm not going to be the one to do it."

"C'mon, man," the other officer says as she takes a step forward. "All you're doing is making a tense situation worse. We can stand out here all night long, but in the end, we're going to end up with the same result. Her back with her parents. Parental privilege."

"Just unlock the doors so we can get her out," Nate says, reaching out for Grant's arm, but he yanks it away.

"*Don't touch me.*" The two men face off, inches apart, duty versus morality.

"Grant, think about what you're doing here," the other officer says to try to cool the tension.

"I know exactly what I'm doing. I'm protecting and serving. I'm upholding my oath. I think you're the ones who need to ask yourselves the same question." Grant looks back to the car and shakes his head in disbelief. "Let me just take her to the police station. I'll sit with her all night until CPS can fit her in their schedule tomorrow. Anything. It's better than her being here." There's a desperation in his voice that brings tears to my eyes.

The man who blames himself for not saving me is trying to save her.

"Her parents are one hundred feet away."

"And they like to hit their little girl," he says.

"They are threatening kidnapping charges. Really, Grant? Is it worth it? Is your career worth it?"

"Yes." The answer is instant and unwavering.

Nate's shoulders fall as he pinches the bridge of his nose before saying something I can't hear to the other officer and taking a few steps away. Grant takes a step toward Nate and then thinks better of stepping away from the car. "The only way I'm leaving her is if you arrest me."

Minutes pass as Grant stands guard. He looks into the back of his cruiser and makes funny hand signals. The entire time, his face is a mask of calm, when I know he's feeling anything but.

The onlookers around me buzz about the standoff between officers. Opinions flow freely. Bets are wagered. Comments about how the little girl always looks so sad.

But it's Grant I stare at. It's Grant I want to look my way. It's Grant I want to know I think he's in the right.

Memories of when the police took me away for my evaluation ghost through my mind. The hard chairs. The white walls. The scary guns on belts I couldn't stop staring at. The perfectly sharpened crayons I made my drawing with. The constant fear that my mom was going to leave me there. Alone. The promise that she wouldn't.

Is Keely feeling any of this fear right now or is she just confused?

"I'm sorry, Grant, but I have to." Nate's voice startles me from the unexpected memory that has me shivering and pulling my arms around myself. He steps toward Grant, his hands going to his cuffs on his belt.

"Don't do it, Nate." Grant shakes his head.

"You've given me no choice. It's orders from the chief."

Grant stares at his partner as he reluctantly turns him around and pulls his hands behind his back. The first cuff clicks, and its then that Grant looks up.

It's as if he knows I'm there because he looks right at me. Our eyes lock, and I can see the fight in his gaze. The defiance. His want to be a hero for this little girl, and God, how I want him to save her. I want to wade through the ocean of emotion swelling between us and tell him he's standing for the right cause.

The cuff goes on his other wrist.

"I'm sorry," he mouths to me, and I don't know if he's apologizing for back then or for right now, but it doesn't matter. He doesn't have to apologize for anything.

Nate turns Grant so his back is to me and removes Grant's gun from its holster.

"Her blood will be on your hands," Grant says, causing Nate to falter; his statement making what his fellow officer has to do that much harder.

Nate pulls Grant's keys from his pocket and unlocks the cruiser, allowing the female officer to open the car door. The whole scene is hard to watch, but it's the look on Grant's face as he turns that breaks my heart.

Compassion. Grief. Anger. Disbelief. All four flash across his expression when Keely climbs out of the car. She's in a pink nightgown with a unicorn on the front of it. Her hair is a tangled mess, and she looks around shell-shocked at all of the strangers staring at her. Despite her hand being in the officer's, her eyes are big and terrified as they search for a familiar face.

I can sense her fear. Her confusion. Her uncertainty. And somehow, I remember the feeling of being lost in a maze of people when all I wanted was to be home curled in a ball on my bed.

Her terrified sob cuts through the air as she sees Grant and runs toward him, her arms wrapping around his thigh like he's her lifeline.

"Grant," I cry his name out, my heart shattering in a million pieces as she clings to him. And for a split second, he meets my eyes, and the look we exchange claws its way into my damaged soul and warns it that he's going to help heal it. The connection is quick and ends when he kneels down and says something in her ear.

Reassuring her.

Telling her it's all going to be okay when it isn't going to be.

Her life will forever be changed.

I remember the promise of a trip to Disneyland to try to dissipate the upheaval in my life. Every little kid loves Disney. I don't blame my mom for the fib, but I remember thinking back then how I didn't care where we went as long as she didn't leave me. And so long as my dad didn't come with us.

I'm jostled by the person behind me and it snaps me from the memory just in time to watch Nate grab Grant's elbow to help him stand. The female officer has the tough task of picking up a petrified five year old and walking her into a house that seems to be filled with fear instead of comfort.

Grant watches, too, defeat owning every part of him.

As Nate leads him to the police cruiser, opens the door, and guides his head so he doesn't hit it on the way in, Grant never once takes his eyes off Keely.

Officer Roberts slides behind the wheel, and the cruiser leaves with Grant in it.

I stare until I can't stare anymore.

I've only ever loved two men.

Both were taken away in handcuffs.

One because he hurt me.

The other because he tried to save her.

And in the end, save me.

SIXTY-FOUR

Grant

MY DAD PULLS THE BLINDS SHUT ON EACH WINDOW IN THE conference room. As he pulls the cords, one by one, the metal slats drop down with a resonating thud. The sound of my fate being sealed.

"I'm being interrogated now? I thought you were retired." I'm being a sarcastic ass, but I'm tired, and fuck, if I care about this police department right now when "To Protect and Serve" feels like a baseless catchphrase.

"This is professional courtesy extended to me by Chief Ramos to let me come down here and level with my son over why he was put in handcuffs tonight. You do realize they could haul you off to booking and charge you with obstruction, right?"

I slump back in my chair and sigh like a ten-year-old kid waiting to have his ass handed to him. "By all means. Let's get this party started."

"Would you rather do this out in the precinct where everyone can hear me ask you what the fuck you were doing?"

"Does it really matter? They all know why you're here so . . . ask away." I direct every ounce of anger I feel over the situation toward my dad. It's unfounded, and he doesn't deserve it, but the only thing that would calm my nerves right now is to know that both Keely and Emerson are all right.

Keely for the obvious, and Emerson because the last time she saw Keely, it messed her up. She doesn't deserve to be messed up any more than she already is.

When the last blind falls, he takes his time moving around the conference table before sitting directly across from me.

"What the hell were you thinking?" he finally asks as his brow narrows and his eyes demand an answer.

"My job," I state matter-of-factly.

"Your job?"

"Don't come at me, Dad, with the holier than thou bullshit. I did what I had to do, and I'd do it again in a heartbeat. You're lucky I didn't do what I really wanted, which was to beat the shit out of him, because I don't think I would have been able to stop once I started. So, yeah, it's a lot better than the alternative could have been. It's been a rough night, so if you came to give me a lecture, thanks but no thanks. I'm not in the mood for one."

He sighs and leans back in his chair shaking his head. "What you did was incredibly stupid and profoundly valiant."

I grunt, not feeling too valiant at the moment since I didn't accomplish anything. "I don't think Ramos is going to look at it that way."

"Probably not." He raises his eyebrows. "What did he say?"

I shrug, not wanting to think about the consequences when the actions were damn well warranted. "I haven't spoken directly with him yet."

"You suspended?" he asks.

"For starters."

"Your promotion?"

I laugh. "Most likely gone, too. Insubordination and obstruction aren't exactly looked upon in a favorable light when you're competing for a promotion."

"True."

"Sorry I didn't live up to the Malone family standards," I say with sarcasm he doesn't deserve.

"I don't give a shit about the promotion, Grant," he says, irritated by my cheap shot. "I care that you stand by the right principles and make the right choices. I care that, at the end of the day, you can hold your head high. So you tell me, if you had to do it all over again, would you do the same thing?"

"In a heartbeat," I say without hesitation. "It was the right thing to do."

I think of Emerson highlighted by red and blue lights. The look on her face solidifying I was doing the right thing. Her presence telling me the time she needed is up.

God, I need to know she's okay, but instead, I'm locked in this damn room.

My dad continues to stare at me, study me, mull over the thoughts I can see clear as day in his eyes.

"This doesn't have anything to do Emerson, does it?"

"Christ, yes, it does," I say with a disbelieving laugh, nervous energy eating me up. Too anxious to sit still, I shove up from my chair and pace the length of the room.

"Is she worth risking your career over?" I fall silent at his question, knowing the answer and not knowing it all at the same time. Certainty versus uncertainty. My routine versus her chaos. Alone versus loved. "Grant?"

"I didn't save her," I say, not answering the question, my voice breaking as the one truth that has eaten at me over and over finally has a voice. "I was her best friend, and I knew she hated being at home . . . and I did not save her." The guilt is real and raw, and I know that every time I've seen Em suffer through something, was because I didn't help her in time. It's my fault.

If only I had saved her sooner . . .

My dad sighs as he approaches behind me, his hand patting me on the shoulder and then squeezing there. "You were eight, son. There was no way you could have known."

"But still . . ."

"If anyone is to blame it's me. She was in our house day in and day out. I was the chief of police for Christ's sake, and I didn't see the signs because monsters aren't supposed to be your son's friend's dad."

I know he speaks the truth, but it's also hard to let go of the feeling that I still failed. Emmy then and Keely now.

"I saw Emerson when I looked at Keely tonight," I confess with a shake of my head. His exhale is long and steady and says his assumptions were correct. "I've seen Emerson in her all along, but tonight . . . she opened the door and had a bruise on her cheek and blood on her lip, and I lost it. They had the same haunted eyes. The same timidity. All that was different was the hair color."

"In order for you to draw conclusions, should I assume you opened Emerson's case file?"

His words stop my feet in place. The fuckers. Gray and Grady told him what I did after promising me they wouldn't. So much for all for one and one for all. "You gonna ride me for that, too?" I snap.

"Just asked a question," he says in the calm, probing way of his that tells me he's nowhere near finished.

And the longer he stares at me, the shorter my fuse becomes, until finally, I give into the pressure to explain.

"No, Dad. I didn't open the file. At first, I wanted to. I thought if I could just see the things she faced, then it could help me know how to best approach her."

"And it was your right to do that? Shouldn't you have waited to see what she did or didn't tell you? Wasn't that her choice?"

"Christ, yes." I shove my hand through my hair, hating the next words and knowing damn well they are truth. "I was afraid I was going to *hurt her*, Dad. We were sleeping together. How am I to know if there's something that bastard did to her that is a trigger? Something stupid and simple, but if I did it unknowingly, it would affect her? I've seen enough of these cases to know the kids are scarred for life . . . so fucking sue me if my first thought was how to protect her. How not to hurt her. Fuck it," I say as I sit and then stand again. "I'm so sick of explaining this."

The intensity in my dad's eyes matches how I feel inside. "I commend you for caring enough about her to think that far ahead. I can understand where you are coming from . . . but she doesn't get to look inside your darkest secrets without your consent, so can you blame her for feeling violated that you did hers?"

"But that's the thing." I throw my hands up. "I never opened it. I thought better of it, even when she was pulling away from me, I thought better of it. I only saw the picture because it fell out of the folder when I moved it to get it out of the house, but it isn't like she believes me."

"Can you blame her?"

I scrub my hands over my face and sigh. "I don't blame her for anything, Dad. Not a damn thing."

"But it makes you feel better if you blame yourself?" He gives me the same slow measured nod he's given me my whole life. It's the one that tells me he thinks I'm being dense and is waiting for me to see what's right in front of me.

"*Better*? Seriously? You think I feel better knowing nothing I did tonight matters because Keely is back in her toxic house where who knows what is happening to her because I can't get CPS to make time to help her out?" I pace the room. "I have to sit here, knowing I probably threw gasoline on the fire. If something happens to her, you're damn right the blame is on me. Add to that, there's all the hard work, the overtime, the everything, I put into getting the promotion, and now my chances are fucked. If those aren't enough, I hurt Emerson. I violated her trust, and I don't know how the fuck to make it right again . . ." I push out a deep breath and try to think around the chaos in my heart. "So, yeah, I'll wear the blame like a goddamn coat, but it doesn't mean shit because I can't do anything about anything to make it all right again."

"The Keely situation. The department will do right by her. It might not be tonight, Grant, but you made a big enough scene—reporters and all—that CPS wouldn't risk not dealing with the situation because they'd take the blame. It may not feel like it made a difference tonight, but you got the ball rolling and the attention piqued . . . so you did what you had to do."

"Not soon enough," I grumble but take a little bit of what he says to heart. Maybe I did make a difference.

"And the promotion." He shakes his head. "I'm not Chief Ramos, but I have walked in his shoes a time or two. You were technically in the wrong, but if the department is smart, they'll take the attention and turn it into good PR. With all the bad cop stories surfacing constantly, they'll have no problem highlighting how they had an officer who went above and beyond to protect and serve."

"I don't want the limelight dad. I just want my job." I sigh.

"You'll still have it. Take the suspension, enjoy the time off. I wouldn't be surprised if that promotion is yours within six months to a year. If it isn't, then it isn't. You still get to do what you love every day. There will be other chances."

I murmur in agreement, having a hard time believing him when I'm in the midst of the chaos.

"And then there's Emerson. She should be hurt by what you did. Intent matters, but it isn't all that matters. You know that. So, all she knows is your intent, even though she doesn't know your reasons behind it. You violated her privacy, Grant. It'll take time, but you'll redeem yourself."

The sound of Em's voice when she called out my name tonight rings in my ears.

Maybe I redeemed myself a bit already. If I did, it wasn't intentional, but then again, neither was loving her.

"Just remember when you're building a relationship, you need to hear what the other person *isn't* saying. Those are the words that are the most important."

I remember the look she gave me tonight. The pride and the pain. The will and the want. The apology and the blame. So many unspoken words I heard loud and clear.

"Do you love her?" The sincerity in his question throws me.

But the honesty in my answer does even more so. "Yeah, I do."

I'm not sure what I expected his reaction to be, but he just nods as if my answer is no surprise to him and gets a soft smile on his lips. "Then these little blips will be worth it. You'll recover from the fallout. She'll forgive you."

"Trust is a hard thing to earn back."

"Agreed." He gives a measured nod. "But remember, you don't need to know the details of her past to love her heart in the present."

I fall silent as I mull his words over and know they are truer than I care to admit. I think of all I've done thus far to prove to her I want her to stay and all the things I haven't even gotten to show her yet.

"You've always loved that girl," he says softly, as if he's remembering back, and I wish I could, but so many of my memories are of her not being there. "Have you told her yet?"

"I'm not sure she's ready to hear it."

Or maybe I'm afraid that, if she does, she'll run.

"You don't give her enough credit. She's tougher than you think, and maybe that's where you've underestimated her. You have to be all in or get all out. There is no halfway when it comes to love."

There's nothing I can say in response so I watch as he walks to the door of the conference room. "And there's no time like the present since she's been sitting out in the waiting room for the past several hours."

"What?"

"Ramos told me you were free to go when I was done with you."

SIXTY-FIVE

Emerson

THE LIGHTS OF THE PASSING CARS GLANCE ACROSS GRANT'S FACE as he drives to his house. They paint a vivid picture of the emotions roiling beneath the surface.

Or so I can guess.

Because other than saying, "Let's go," before he grabbed my hand and led me from the police station, he hasn't said a word.

He's been on autopilot. Get in the car. Start it. Seatbelt. Drive in silence—the pulsing of the muscle in his jaw, the flexing of his hands from gripping the steering wheel so tight, the dancing of his eyes between his mirrors and the road. Pull in the driveway. Park.

The house is dark when we enter, silent except for the sounds of our breathing, and we stand facing each other for the longest of moments.

We don't speak.

We don't move.

We just accept what has happened without ever exchanging a single word.

We absorb the moment and the weight of it.

That I'm here. In his house. Willing to trust him again.

We can barely see each other's eyes in the darkness, and yet, I can tell how emotionally drained he is from tonight and how emotionally stripped he is for me.

Without preamble or pretext, he makes the first move when he steps forward and pulls me into his arms. And just like that, we cling to each other as if we can't get close enough.

"Grant, I—"

"Shh," he says right before slanting his lips over mine. "Please." Another brush of a kiss. "I just need you, Em. Now. Here. All of you."

His lips are on mine again. It's the same man kissing me, but it feels so very different this time around. Something has shifted between us, changing us intrinsically without changing us at all.

It's just him. And me.

No past.

No future.

Just the moment.

I get lost in his kiss. In the feel of his skin and the taste on his tongue. In the unspoken need and unchecked desire.

We don't walk to the bedroom. We remove our clothes in subtle movements, as if we're afraid to ruin the magnitude of the moment, and lower ourselves to the rug.

We react in sighs and moans.

We feel in emotions.

We revel in the connection.

We make love for the first time.

SIXTY-SIX

Emerson

WATCH HIM.

The sun is barely peeking over the horizon, but I can't sleep.

And haven't been able to.

My mind won't shut off. I try to process everything that has happened in the last twenty-four hours.

I see Keely and the terrified look on her face and wonder if she slept last night. Did she have nightmares? Was she scared of the dark? Will someone show up today and make sure she's okay? In ten days? In six months?

I try to come to terms with the fact that the whole reason I came to Sunnyville is now gone. I wonder what I should do next. If I should let the wind blow me wherever it wishes.

But there's Grant.

I attempt to wrap my head around how I feel about the man snoring softly beside me. I itch to reach out and touch him, make sure the mix of emotions I feel are real, but if they're not, I don't want to ruin them with reality. They're scary and euphoric and I don't think I'm built to handle this.

I revel in how it felt last night to make love to him. To feeling closer to him than I've ever felt before without us having to utter a single word. To moving from the floor to the bed where he gathered me in his arms and didn't let go. To how it took well over an hour for his breathing to even out while I wondered what he could possibly be thinking about.

The clock tells me I need to get to work, my first class is coming in just over two hours, but when I pull open the covers, he reaches out and tugs me against him, my back to his front.

"Uh-uh," he murmurs as the heat of his body warms me in more ways than one.

Sinking into the feel of him, I'm reminded immediately of his raw and honest need last night. I settle my hands atop his on my waist and fill the silence. "Are we going to talk about last night?"

He rests his forehead against the back of my head. "What's there to talk about?"

"Well . . ."

"I did what I had to do, and it wasn't enough."

"It was everything," I say as tears spring to life. "You gave her hope, Grant, when hope is a scarce commodity for her. You showed her there are men willing to protect her instead of hurt her. And while she may have gone back into her house last night because that was what the law demanded, you also made it so no one will ignore her again."

"I didn't save her," he says, the statement holding so much weight in it.

"But you did. You let her know she's worth something." I link my fingers with his and pull his hand up to my lips so I can press a kiss to his knuckles. "You can't go around saving every little girl because you see me. It's honorable. It's admirable. It fills my heart in ways you could never imagine. It's why—" *I love you.*

I can't say the words aloud just yet, their power too much for even me to handle right now.

"Why, what?"

"It's . . . why you need to stop blaming yourself. What happened to me was not your fault. You couldn't have stopped it if you tried. It was my dad's fault. I've accepted that, and I'll continue to deal with accepting it the rest of my life . . ." I fumble with getting the things out I need to say so that he can stop beating himself up over this. So that we can move forward. "My dad stole so much from me, but I learned a long time ago that I can either let it define me or I can let it fuel me. I choose to let it fuel me, Grant. I choose not to let the fear own me or deprive me of what every woman deserves. Happiness. Some thrills. A good sex life.

"Am I perfect? No. Are there days when a new memory comes back and I'm rattled for a bit? Yes. But when it comes right down to it, I can't keep moving forward, I can't keep *chasing the moment*, if those around me who know about it keep looking to my past to manage expectations. That's not fair to me."

"You don't need to know the details of her past to love her heart in the present," he murmurs . . . or at least that's what I think he does because he says it almost to himself before pressing a kiss to my shoulder.

The words hit my ears nonetheless and give me hope that he heard and understands where I'm coming from.

"I didn't open the file, Emerson."

"I believe you." *And I do.*

"And I'll always blame myself for not saving you—I've been told it's called a hero complex or something." I can feel his mouth curve into a smile as he presses it against my shoulder. "But I'll use it to help others."

I snuggle in closer against him. My head is finally quiet, allowing me to fall into a dreamless sleep.

I wake with a start. For a minute I'm disoriented, but then I realize Grant's still behind me, arm draped over my waist.

Crap.

"I have to get to work," I say but make zero attempts to move.

"Call in sick," he says in a sleep-drugged voice that sounds as tempting as his morning hard-on pressing against my backside feels.

It has never sounded more appealing than right now. "I can't."

"You're picking work over me?" He chuckles.

"I'm picking money over you."

"Pretty soon, the place will be yours, so does it really matter if you're there today or not?"

The pang is instant. Having to speak the words aloud even more painful. "I didn't get the loan."

His body stiffens before he untangles himself from around me and sits up. "What did you say?"

"I didn't get the loan."

His face falls from shock to worry. "What does that mean?"

I slide out of bed. "It means I need to earn my paycheck while I can because I don't know who bought Blue Skies or what they intend to do with it, if anything. For all I know, they're going to raze the place and put something else in its spot."

"Em . . . I don't know what to—"

"There's nothing you can say. It's okay. Really. I'll figure something else out." I force a tight smile, always mindful of how my life goes from one extreme to the next, as I pull on my clothes. I haven't really even had time to process it all, so talking about it makes me itchy.

"If it's a money thing, Em . . . you know I'll—"

"Thanks, but from what I overheard in the station last night, you're suspended, so I assume you're not making a paycheck, either." I shrug and pull my shirt over my head. "I'm a big girl, Grant. I—"

"Can handle yourself," he finishes for me.

SIXTY-SEVEN

Grant

"CHIEF RAMOS," I SAY, SHOCKED TO SEE HIS NAME ON MY CELL. "This is an unexpected surprise."

"So is what you did," he says.

"What can I do for you?" I will not apologize, not even to my boss, for my actions.

"I know you talked to Deputy Chief Castro last night, but I have to give you the official company line. What you did was wrong. You went against protocol. Became the scene instead of managed it. Yadda, yadda, yadda. You got all that?"

"Sure," I say, biting back my smile at his cavalier attitude.

"Good. Now I can say what I want to say, off the record, of course."

"Of course, sir."

"You've caused quite a stir around here. So much so, that I have to have an official investigation, but before it even begins, I can tell you the results will be inconclusive. Were you in the wrong? Yes. Is there anything to charge you with or permanently ding your record with? No." I stand, suddenly needing to move. "Your suspension ends in five days, should I assume you'll be back here the following Monday?"

"What?" This is not what I expected. I expected weeks of internal affairs dragging their feet while I sat home, twiddling my thumbs bored out of my mind.

"Monday? Yes or no?"

"Yes. Definitely yes."

"Good. Now that I have your attention, I need to go over a few other things. Once reinstated you are not allowed to answer any calls—or non-calls—to the Davis residence."

"How is she?" I ask.

"Why are you so attached to this little girl, Malone?"

"She reminds me of someone I once knew." I think of Emerson's words yesterday as she lay in my arms. *Define or fuel.* She chooses fuel.

"She and her mother have been moved to a battered woman's home. They are undergoing counseling there for a bit while their family in Oregon makes arrangements for them to come live with them."

"And the dad?"

"We can't win every battle, Grant. We have to take the victories when we get them and hope the good guys win out the next time."

So, if I can't frequent the Davis residence, that means he still lives there. Still able to meet another woman and mistreat her the same way. The endless cycle.

But Keely is safe.

Keely is saved.

What I did mattered.

"I need your word that you'll avoid the residence in question?"

"Yes, sir."

"Good. Now, on to the promotion. I'm sorry, but I had to give it to Stetson," he says, regret heavy in his voice. "You were clearly the better candidate for the job, but I can't reward insubordination."

"It's on me," I say. Just because I knew this was coming, it doesn't make the sting of it any easier to take.

"It is," he agrees, "but that doesn't mean you can't go for it next time the position opens."

"Thank you, sir."

"Monday, Malone."

"Monday."

I end the call and put my hands on my hips as I look around my house and try to digest what I just heard.

It's good news.

It's great news, in fact.

Especially considering what I'm trying to pull off.

Glancing down at the papers scattered all over my table, I know I can't do this alone. I've been trying to these past few days, and now I need to kick it into overdrive.

I pull up my contacts on my phone and hit dial.

"If it isn't Officer Sexy."

"I need your help, Desi."

SIXTY-EIGHT

Emerson

"Seriously? That quick?" I look at Travis, who's standing in front of my desk, and my jaw falls lax.

"I know. I'm sorry. I tried for more but—"

"Thank you for getting me the two extra months. That's better than immediately." I force a smile as the bottom drops out and reality hits.

Not only is my job most likely going to be gone—because who knows what's going to happen since the new owner hasn't said—but my apartment is, too. I have two months and a savings I know will be gone before I can blink an eye.

"You okay, Em?" Leo asks after Travis leaves the office, shoulders sagging, to begin his task of emptying out the old owner's belongings to make way for the new owner's stuff.

"As okay as okay can be given the situation, I guess." I sigh. "I'm just having a hard time wrapping my head around the fact that this is all over. I've never stayed in one place for this long. I've never thought about tomorrows and futures, and it's like when I finally did, the universe tells me to quit adulting."

He chuckles, but the lines etched in his face tell me he's worried, too. "I'm sorry. I know that slimy bastard had something to do with it. You should have let me punch him, you know."

"You know what they say about hindsight."

He lifts his eyebrows and nods. "We could always try to start something ourselves. We could get Sully to fly for us. He'd give us a decent rate to bring people up. We wouldn't need much. Just some gear and a place to teach."

"I know. I've thought about it, too, but the insurance . . . that would kill us. There's no way we could take in enough to cover all the expenses, and I obviously can't get a loan . . . so, it's a good thought. Thanks for the vote of confidence, Leo." I smile through the hurt.

"I hear they're hiring at Fly High. Their crew had some infractions, so they're looking for a flight instructor and jump coordinator." He nods as he says the words, but I know we're both thinking the same thing: That's two hours away. "We could go as a package. Buy it out some day and make it our own."

"It's a possibility," I say, but my heart squeezes in my chest at the thought of leaving Sunnyville. Of leaving Grant. "Look at both of us getting old." I laugh. "I used to bail at the first sign of commitment."

"And I used to chase the next new city, the next great jump." He chuckles as he looks down at his hands for a moment before looking back to me. "Chasing the adrenaline rush does have that nomadic, will-jump-for-food type of personality it seems we both have."

"Maybe we should say *had* since now we're hesitating."

"True, but hesitating doesn't pay the bills."

"Maybe the new owner will pull through," I say, holding out hope.

"Or maybe he just bought it for the real estate and doesn't give a damn about Blue Skies and is going to demo it."

"Yeah. That thought has crossed my mind, too."

"Would it be so hard for the Skies to tell us if we have a future or not?"

"They don't care. They haven't cared about this place for a long time. Money is all they think about."

And that's the thought that is depressing.

Because I cared. Because I would have put the blood, sweat, and tears into making it work.

Even things that are worn down and ugly deserve love.

SIXTY-NINE

Grant

THE COLD AIR HITS ME AS I WALK INTO SUNNYVILLE TRUST AND Loan. I stop just inside and look around the place.

"Hi. How can I help you today?" the receptionist asks in an overly cheerful voice.

"I'm looking for—" And right when I say the words, I see him. The fucker is standing in an office in the back corner of the space, hands on his hips, back to me. "Never mind."

"Sir, you can't go back there!" I walk past her despite her protests and stride across the lobby. "Sir. *Sir.* Christopher!"

He turns around at the sound of his name, words fading, just as I enter his office. "Freddy, I'll call you right back."

Christopher pulls his Bluetooth earpiece off in a slow, measured movement while keeping his eyes locked on mine.

"Can I help you?" he asks, brow furrowed and a ghost of a smile on his lips that says he knows exactly who I am. The fucking bastard.

"Yes, you can." I laugh, but there is nothing even close to humor in its sound as I take a step toward him.

He takes a step back.

We continue this dance until he bumps against the wall at his back. I step well within his personal space so that I can smell the coffee on his breath and hear his startled gasp.

"How many clients did you threaten today, *Chris*? How many women did you tell that if they didn't meet you for drinks, *if they didn't sleep with you*, that you would pull their application or sabotage their loan? Huh, *Chris*?" I'm as close as I can be without touching him.

"Malone . . ."

"That's Officer Malone to you. Does it make you feel like a big man to play God with other people's dreams, *Chris*? Do you get off on their fear?"

"I do-don't know what you-you're talking about."

"Oh, but that's where you're wrong. You know exactly what I'm talking about." I shake my head very slowly, stretching the silence to unnerve him as much as possible. "Does the name Emerson Reeves ring a bell?"

His eyes widen, and his quick intake of breath is audible. "I'm not at liberty to discuss my clients or their applications."

"Funny how you become so professional all of a sudden when you've been anything but to her." I reach up quickly to scratch my chin and love when he flinches. The asshole should be scared.

"What do you want?"

"You will never, and I repeat, *never*, talk to Emerson, approach her, deal with her, or contact her in any way shape or form again." Our height difference allows me to look down at him with a threatening glare that makes my words more than clear. "And if you do, you'll have to deal with me. And *my whole* police department." That one little lie isn't going to hurt anyone.

He nods rapidly, his eyes blink, and his face turns red.

"And if I catch wind of you ever threatening another woman's loan because they won't sleep with you . . ." I shake my head and chuckle, long and low, as his Adam's apple bobs with his swallow. "The Sunnyville district attorney is a close, personal friend. I'm pretty sure this place would have to shut down after all the legal fees you'll incur trying to defend yourself from the dozens of charges she could pin on you." I take a step back with a cocky grin and cuff him on the side of his shoulder. "Did I make myself clear?"

The same nod again.

"I need to hear it."

"Yes."

"Yes, Officer Malone," I say and wait for him to repeat it.

"Yes, Officer Malone."

"Not so brave now, are you?" He just stares at me without speaking as the armpits of his dress shirt stain dark with sweat. "Good, then this little chat is done."

With another flash of a smile, I turn on my heel and feel pretty damn good with myself.

Time to go pay Leo back with a cold beer. *Or ten.* Thanks to his phone call earlier, I knew where to go to put this asshole in his place.

SEVENTY

Emerson

"**T**HIS IS DEPRESSING,"

Desi sighs from her spot beside me on the top step of my stairs that lead into my apartment. We are currently watching the small crane lift the Blue Skies sign off the top of the office. "I wish there were something I could do."

"There isn't." I take a sip of wine from my red Solo cup. "Sometimes you chase the dream and you catch it, other times you fall short." The words sound good in theory, but they feel like shit when they're reality.

"Are you really going to leave me?" she asks.

And leave Grant.

"What am I supposed to do, Des? In a month, I'm out of a place to live, and I don't have a paycheck coming in to pay rent."

"Easy. You move in with me."

"Thanks. You know I appreciate the offer, but then what? Where do I work? I'm not qualified to do anything other than jump. Sure, I could try, but being chained to a desk . . . not having that rush? It would kill me."

"Then maybe you do something else for a bit—help me with Doggy Style—and wait to see what happens out here with whoever bought this place. They might need help. It might not be jumping, but at least you'd be where you're comfortable."

"I couldn't do that to you."

"Pride doesn't pay the bills, Em."

"Neither does killing your spirit.

"The offer still stands."

"Thanks. It's generous of you, but how long can I hang on? It's as if I've spent all this time dreaming of making this place my own, and now that I have the idea, I don't want to settle. *I shouldn't have to settle.*"

"Have you told him?" Desi says, lifting her chin to Grant's car, which is heading down the highway toward us.

"Told him what?"

"That you love him? That you're leaving? Either or."

Tears spring in my eyes at just her words. "No to both," I whisper.

"I figured as much. You want to tell me why not?"

I shrug, my mental turmoil over the past few days returning. "He's been super busy. Doing all kinds of stuff for the chief to make amends for his suspension."

"Ah, so the truth comes out. You haven't been hanging out with me because I'm your first pick, but rather because you don't have him to hang out with. I don't do well being sloppy seconds." She laughs, and I know this is her way of trying to add levity, but I don't smile. "So he's been so busy you couldn't tell him you were going to leave? That sounds more like chicken shit to me than anything."

"I'm scared to," I say as his cruiser pulls into the parking lot. I know we still have time to talk because he usually has paperwork to finish before clocking off shift.

"Why? Because once you say it, you can't take it back? Or is it because once you tell him you're planning to leave, he's going to lose his ever-loving mind? My bet is you're avoiding telling him you love him but you aren't *in love with him* enough to stick around to save yourself from that hurt?" She purses her lips and gives me an I-don't-believe-a-word-you're-saying look. "Self-preservation."

"It isn't like I'm not going to try to make it work. I'll drive back on weekends—"

"Which are the busiest days for jumps."

"I'll make my off days match his so we can be together."

"Easier said than done."

"Desi, I love him, damn it. I want to make this work. I'm doing the best I fricking can, so stop the guilt trip, will you?"

She smiles. "I know you do. I also know you run when you're scared. You put the pedal to the metal and race the wind and follow wherever it takes you . . . but I'm calling you on it this time. I'm holding you accountable. I'm not letting you leave us without knowing the exact day you are coming back . . . and it better be less than seven."

"It's only temporary."

She stands, saying, "It better be," before walking down the stairs without looking back and stopping when she reaches Grant in the parking lot. She laughs about something, and there's an easiness between them—my lover and my best friend—that tells me I've built something here. A family. A place I belong. Every part of me wishes things didn't have to change.

I watch the crane lift the old sign, its beeping filling the air as it swings it to the far side of the building, and I hate it. Everything about it.

As Grant heads in my direction, I make my way down the stairs.

"Are you ready for date night?" he asks as he closes the distance. "I just have to change real quick and I'll be—what's that?" he asks as he notices the storage containers stacked at the bottom of the stairs.

"Hi." I pull him toward me and kiss him hello with an unexpected desperation that suddenly feels so real.

I don't want to lose him.

I don't want to lose this feeling.

But I also don't want to lose who I am.

"Whoa. Well, if that's the kind of greeting I get when I come here when my shift ends, then I'll be here every day at this time." He chuckles against my lips as I just pull him into me and hold on tighter.

How am I going to tell him?

How am I going to convince him I'm not going to leave again?

"Em, I can put these with my shit when I take this trip . . ." Leo says as he turns the corner, his words trailing off when he sees Grant standing in front of me.

"Trip to where?" Grant asks as he takes notice that the containers are labeled as kitchen, desk, and bathroom. Grant looks from me to Leo and then back to me. "What the hell is going on, Emerson?" He's already shaking his head, rejecting the notion that he already knows.

"That's what I wanted to talk to you about tonight," I say, my voice barely audible. In my periphery, I see Leo slowly slink away and wish I could go with him. If the look on Grant's face is any indication, our date night is about to turn into a blowout fight.

"You're not going anywhere!" The workers pulling down the sign turn to look at us, prompting him to grab my wrist and all but drag me up the stairs so we can have privacy, which is a huge mistake. When he enters my flat and sees everything stacked in partially filled boxes, the hurt is written all over his face.

I could have played it off before. I had planned to tell him I was prepping for the end of the month, but him seeing Leo and knowing Leo is moving on to Fly High is all he needs to draw the conclusion.

He stares at me, a plethora of emotions flickering through those brown eyes of his and every single one of them—hurt, disappointment, disbelief—is paralyzing. "Were you going to tell me, Em? Or were you going to leave in the middle of the night because you were too scared to face me?"

"I told you I was going to tell you tonight." I take a step toward him. "It isn't what you're thinking, Grant."

"It isn't? What exactly am I thinking, then?"

"I'm a restless soul. Blue Skies was my chance to settle, and now it's gone. The new owner hasn't said boo, and for all I know, they're going to raze the place. They've already cleaned out the hangar. It's written on the wall, my days here are limited."

"You don't know what the new owners are going to do. They're already starting to make changes, taking the sign down, what have you. You have a month left on your rent, why not stay here and see what happens first?"

"In theory, it sounds good. But everything sounds good in theory. If it is a new flight school, that takes time to set up. Certifications, insurance . . . I can't wait around for six months to see if I can start my life again," I murmur, as if speaking the words softly will make them hurt him less.

"What about me, Emerson? What about us?" The way he says it—the hurt emanating off every word—makes it hard for me to think.

"We'll make it work. It's only temporary. Hopefully, this will be a flight school and I can come back and figure out a new dream to chase, but in the meantime, it's only two hours away. There are days off and phone calls and FaceTime. We'll make it work." I'm pretty much begging for him to believe me, but the look on his face says he's not convinced.

"It isn't the same, and you know it."

"I know, but it's doable."

"What if I told you that you're not going? That I'm not going to let you go."

Every part of me surges with his words, already knowing he wants me to stay but still needing to hear it. I chuckle. "Then I'd tell you that you know me well enough to know the quickest way to get me to do something is to tell me I can't."

"Is it that hard for you to need someone, Em? Is it that hard for you to need me?"

"No." I'm just so conditioned not to need anything from anyone that my heart twists at the lie buried under all the truth in that one word.

"Then need me, damn it. Use me." I watch the hurt manifest itself to anger. "Stay at my house. Live with me while *we* figure this out. Do anything but run away because running away is the chicken shit way to deal with this situation."

There's the second time in ten minutes I've been called that.

"I'm not running, Grant."

"You sure about that?" His eyes bore into mine as everything about him screams defeat.

"I'm sure."

"Good, then you won't mind if I do this," he says as he steps forward and, before I can even process what he's doing, slaps a handcuff on my wrist and the other on his. "See? It's that simple. You're not going."

And just as quickly as my heart breaks, my temper fires. "Are you kidding me? What are you doing?"

"Did you really think I was going to let you go without a fight? I've lost you once before, Em. You're out of your mind if you think I'm going to let it happen again." Every part of me melts at his words and wants to surrender right here, right now to whatever he asks. I remember the emptiness I felt when I left him before. I remember how lonely I was, and I don't want that ever again.

"So, you're going to handcuff me?" I shriek, eyes wide and disbelief reigning. Amid the stubborn anger I have rioting inside me, a small piece of me wants to laugh at him. This is so *us* that it's ridiculous. But I can't. I won't. At least not outwardly.

"This is just insurance to make sure you're true to your word."

"My word?"

"That you're not running. So see?" He holds our hands up. "Now you can't."

I try to yank my hand away and am met with the bite of cold steel. The smirk he gives me and the feel of the metal is fuel to my temper. "The harder you fight against me, the closer I'm going to pull you."

"Let me go." Doesn't he know he's won?

He takes a step into me so his face is inches from mine, and as angry as I am at him, all I see are his lips. All I can think about is losing him. "This isn't how a relationship works, Emerson. You don't get to decide for yourself anymore. You talk to me. We discuss. Sometimes we fight. But in the end, we decide—*together*. Simple as that."

"And you think kidnapping me is the right way to go about that?" Despite the bite of pain I know it will cause, I yank my hand again, but this time it's more for show than out of anger. The look in his eyes and the determination in his words . . . how could a sane girl walk away from a man that resolute in his love for her?

"No, but apparently, it's the only way when it comes to reasoning with you." He quirks an eyebrow. "Do you think it'll be weird brushing our teeth like this? Or how about going to the bathroom. That might cause some problems." He chuckles and walks over to the couch without telling me so I'm forced to trail behind as he sits and puts his feet on the coffee table. "I could get used to this, couldn't you?" Then he gets back up and walks to the windows overlooking the backside of the airstrip, forcing me to follow again. He turns one way to pull me and then back the other way.

"You're infuriating, you know that?" I say, trying to stand my ground when I'm not really sure what we are fighting about anymore. "We're talking about the same thing here."

"No. We're not. You're talking about going, and I'm talking about you staying. That's as different as night and day."

"It would be temporary."

"I don't do temporary. See?" he says, lifting our hands again. "I like sure things."

"I am not running," I grit out. "I didn't want this. I didn't want to lose the loan and have to leave. I wanted roots for the first time in forever. I want you damn it. That's all I really want. You and my jump school. That's it. So, stop turning this on me. Stop acting as if this is all about me. *I love you,* and as much as that scares the shit out of me, not having you terrifies me even more. *You win.* Tell me what you want me to do, and I'll stay." I heave in a huge breath because I used it all. When I look at him, he's blurry because tears are in my eyes, and I don't care. This . . . he and I . . . is what matters.

But his fingers on his handcuffed hand link with mine. He stares at me, eyes blinking, a ghost of a smile on his lips and relief easing the lines etching his features.

"It's about time," he whispers.

"What?" My head spins from the mental whiplash.

"I don't need convincing about how you feel about me, Em. Hell, I don't even need the words. I already knew. I just needed you to know. I needed you to admit it. I needed you to believe it. You're the most honest when your back is against the wall . . . so, I pushed your shoulders some to get it there."

"You maneuvered me."

"I believe the correct term is positioning," he says as his smile inches up a bit more. I want to be indignant that he can read me so well, that he knows me so well. And then I realize that I told him I loved him. He sees it the minute it hits me and reaches out to pull me against him.

"It's okay to need me, Em. It's okay to love me. God knows I think I've been in love with you since we were six years old. You're maddening and frustrating and stubborn and the biggest challenge I've ever faced, but seeing you is the best part of my day and where you are is the only place I want to spend my nights. Losing the loan was a curve in the road we didn't see coming. But you like to speed, so we can ride this out. We adjust the wheel and take the curve. We talk, and then we work together to create another dream for you to chase." He leans forward and presses his lips to mine in a kiss to rival all kisses that I feel all the way out to the tips of my toes and back. "Two hours is too far away from me when we have twenty years to make up for . . . so, please trust me when I say we can make this work. Trust me when I tell you that making this work might be the hardest thing we ever do, but the payoff will be worth it and then some."

I'm rendered speechless. I open my mouth to speak but know words won't do any justice. So, instead, I press my lips against his.

"I love you."

God, it feels good to say it.

To know it.

To know it's returned and then some.

Grant Malone loves me.

We stand like this for a few minutes before there's a honk of a horn somewhere outside that interrupts our moment.

"Seeing those boxes really upset me," he admits. "Can we bring them inside now? Can we tell Leo you're not going?"

I roll my eyes and shake my head at the silly request after such a poignant moment between us. "If it makes you feel better."

My laugh turns to a shriek when, without warning, Grant swoops down and picks me up and hauls me over his shoulder, our handcuffed hands making it a tad more difficult.

"What are you doing?" I laugh.

"I told you, we're going to get the boxes."

"Right now? Wouldn't it be easier if we had both of our hands free?"

He smacks me on the ass. "Yeah, but I kinda need you to get used to the fact that you aren't going anywhere before I take them off."

"You're being ridiculous. After what you just said to me, any woman would be stupid to walk away."

"That's good to hear." He laughs as he makes his way down the stairs. "But it doesn't hurt to have a little insurance." He sets me down on the ground and then says, "And a backup plan."

"A backup plan?" I ask, using my free hand to flip my hair out of my eyes so I can see. And when I can, he lifts his chin in the direction over my shoulder.

I turn to look at what he's talking about and blink. It takes a few seconds for it all to register. To understand what it means.

The new sign on top of the office. It's a deep purple with the words "Wings Out" written in some fancy font atop a pilot's wings.

"Grant?" I take a few steps forward, my free hand to my chest, my lips parted, my mouth dry, and my mind spinning.

The door opens, and I watch all the important people in my life walk out. Desi. Leo. Grayson. Grady. The Malones. Sully. Travis. One by one, they file out and stand beneath the new sign.

I blink several times to make sure I'm really seeing what I'm seeing. "Grant?" I ask again as I look at him standing beside me.

"It isn't a painted zombie rock, but I think it will make you happy all the same."

"This can't be . . ."

"My backup plan." His smile is wide as his eyes dance with excitement.

"What did you do?"

"I've been doing a lot of overtime for the department, so I figured why not use it as a down payment on a new business venture. It's always been a dream of mine to own a business. You know, have something to fall back on when I retire from the force."

"Grant," I say his name again as I shake my head in disbelief. I must be freaking dreaming right now.

"I have some confessions to make," he murmurs as he shifts and wraps his arms around me from behind as we both stand and stare at the new sign. "They were all in on it. Every single one of them, even poor Leo. I haven't been working late because of the station, I've been madly scrambling to convince the owners of Blue Skies I'd be a better fit than the backup offer they were just about to sign on. That, and paying them a little above asking price had them changing their tune on which person they thought would be the best buyer. Then I had to get paperwork for loan docs. Desi was enlisted to keep you busy and away from my house. Leo has known for the last few days and played along so he didn't spoil the surprise."

"So, there is no Fly High?"

"There is, but not with you two. I've already called them and told them you wouldn't be showing up."

"Grant . . . I don't know what to say."

"You don't have to say anything."

"I need to say everything." I laugh as none of this sinks in.

"No, you said all I needed to hear upstairs." He presses a kiss to the back of my head as Leo whoops at something, and Desi's cackle rings across the tarmac.

"This is too much, Grant. I can't—the money—"

"I figured I didn't need a new patio after all."

"But you put in all that overtime."

He shrugs sheepishly. "I assumed if you had a place of your own, you'd be stuck with me. You can't be a nomad when you have roots. And I want you to have roots, Em. Here. With me. Ones that tangle with mine and can never be ripped out. Lazy Sunday together ones and white picket fence ones."

"I'm stunned. Shocked. Overwhelmed."

"This is yours, Em. Your school. Your dream. Yours. My dream has always been you, and I have you. Your dream is the school, and now you have it. Oh, but there's one caveat."

"Anything," I say, still thinking I need to pinch myself.

"The new owner says it's against code to have someone living in the hangar."

"He does, does he?" If I could smile any wider, I would.

"Yeah, he's a stubborn SOB, so I don't think I can get him to change his mind . . . but I happen to know one half of a king-sized bed that's unoccupied."

"I snore."

"I know." He laughs.

I turn to face him for the first time and know I could never repay him for what he's given me. The safety. The security. The love. The friendship. The humor. The opportunity.

"I'll pay you back. I'll work harder than—"

"I'll count on it," he murmurs as he presses his lips against mine.

"I'll sign an agreement to—"

Another kiss.

"No worries, I have insurance." He laughs as he holds our handcuffed hands up. "You're not going anywhere."

EPILOGUE

Emerson

Eighteen Months Later . . .

THE CITY'S LIGHTS BEGIN TO COME ALIVE AS THE NIGHT GROWS darker. I sit and stare at them because it's all I can really do since Grant is sitting solemnly beside me without saying a word.

"Do you want to talk about it?" I ask, knowing the case he's investigating has been upsetting him. He won't admit it, but it's in his snap of temper and silence when he comes home after work.

It's taken some getting used to him being a detective and having cases to become invested in versus his old job where he responded to a call and then left.

"I'm fine."

When he asked if I wanted to take a drive and we ended up here, I wasn't surprised. His thinking place. His temporary solace.

"When you look at those lights," he finally says, voice gruff and eyes fixed ahead, "what do you think of?"

I look at him with a narrowed brow and try to figure out where he's going with this. We've been up here dozens of times, and this is the first time he's ever asked me that.

"I think each light tells a story of the person living beneath it."

He nods slowly and falls silent again for a bit. "You know what I think? I think each one of those lights represents someone's dream. Sometimes they flicker and fade and die out, and other times they grow brighter and stay lit forever."

I startle at his statement, finding his thoughts to be quite profound. "I like that," I say softly and lean my head gently on his shoulder.

Grant points to the far west where the skyline is lit up with lights. "What dream does that sparkle over there represent for you?" he asks.

"There are thousands of them." I laugh. "How do I know which one you're pointing at?"

"Just pick one."

I do as he says and stare at it for a beat before I answer. "Wings Out. That's definitely Wings Out because it's the brightest one."

He nods in acceptance of my answer. "And the sparkle over there?" He points to the east.

I play along and pick one out and stare at it. "That's happiness. I never thought I'd find it and I have. You've helped me find it."

"And that sparkle?" he points straight ahead of us.

"Wait. That's not fair. It's my turn to ask." I pick a location he hasn't done yet and point. "What dream of yours does that sparkle represent?"

He falls quiet for a moment as if he's deep in thought. "*You.*"

"What? *Oh.* Grant. That's so sweet." I press my lips to his shoulder, my heart a jumbled mess of love for the man beside me.

"What about that sparkle over there?"

"You." I smile, wanting to return the comment because I really do feel that way.

"Nope, you can't steal my idea. I get to win the romance award tonight," he says and chuckles as he presses a kiss to the top of my head. "Pick another dream."

"Hm. It's stupid and isn't realistic . . ." I begin to explain.

"It's a dream, Emmy, there is no such thing as reality. There's just possibility. What is it?"

"That no one ever has to go through what I went through." My voice is barely a whisper, but I know he heard me.

"I agree."

"Okay. My turn," I say, wanting to keep this mood upbeat so I can help cheer him up and pull his mind from work. "What dream does that sparkle represent for you?"

"You."

"You don't get to repeat the same one."

"Says who?"

"Says me."

"Well, since I made up the game, I get to make up the rules, and I say I get to repeat the same dream." He purses his lips and lifts his eyebrows, looking like the defiant little boy who saved me so very long ago.

"You never did play fair." I laugh while he just grins. And I love the sight of it since he's been so serious lately.

"Next one," he says as he peruses the skyline for a location and points. "What dream does that sparkle represent?"

"Endless possibilities," I murmur.

"Getting all philosophical on me, are you?"

"Yep. My turn." I point to the south. "What dream does that sparkle represent?"

"You," he says again, and when I look up to scold him, his lips meet mine.

They're warmth and comfort and familiarity and desire. Everything I could ever want. I melt into him as his hands frame my face and our tongues dance intimately. When the kiss ends, he presses his forehead to mine and we just sink into the silence of each other for a bit.

"I want to pick one more sparkle that you need to pick your dream for."

"Can't we just sit like this and ignore the sparkles?" I murmur, loving the feel of his hands on my face and the warmth of his body against mine. I almost groan when he removes his hands and runs them down my arms.

"What about this sparkle?" he asks as he leans back, eyes locked on mine for just a second before he glances down.

I see the ring immediately, the sparkle of the diamond off the moonlight, the shine of the platinum against it, but I'm unable to form words.

I have so much passion and joy and every indescribable emotion inside me that I'm not sure how to manage it. So, I do the one thing I know will calm me. I thread my fingers through his hair and press my lips to his until I've knocked him backward onto the ground with me on top of him.

"Yes." Kiss. "Yes." Another kiss. "Yes times infinity," I tell him as I smother the laughter on his lips and deepen the kiss.

"Is that a yes?" he murmurs when I finally let him up for air.

"Yes." This time, I yell it so loud that he winces before laughing as I kiss him again.

When I lean back and sit astride his hips, all I can do is stare at him. At his mussed hair and his crooked smile. At his eyes that hold more than I could ever ask for. I see love in them. I see pride. I see tomorrows.

I see forever.

"You know I had a whole speech planned out, right?"

"You did? I'm sorry."

"I should have accounted for the squeal factor."

I swat at him and then lean forward and kiss him before sitting back up. "This is far beyond the squeal factor. This is more the best-day-of-my-life-need-to-tell-you-yes type of urgency."

His grin grows wider, and the gold in his eyes lights up. "The best day, huh?"

"By far." I lace my fingers with his, needing more of the connection we already have.

"How about I tell you this is only the beginning. From here on out, you're going to have best days top best days top best days because that is what you, Emmy Reeves, deserve."

"Grant—"

"My turn," he warns as he lifts his eyebrow and a ghost of a smile pulls at his lips. He sits up so that I can settle onto his lap with my legs wrapped around him. We are face to face, and the temptation is too hard to resist. Another brush of lips. Another chance to get lost in him.

"Emerson Reeves, you know I've always loved you. What you don't know is that since you've walked back into my life, I've realized just how ready I was to settle in all things—relationships, jobs, *life*. You always say I'm the hero, but you're the one who saved me. From a life without passionate fights and incredible make-up sex. From a life without nonstop laughter and friendship and unconditional love." He leans forward and brushes the most tender of kisses to my lips that makes every part of my body want to sigh. "From a life without you, Em." The sincerity of his words weaving their way through my heart and wrapping themselves around my soul.

"Grant . . ." His name is a plea. A promise. An answer.

"I love you, Emmy. I want to spend a lifetime chasing moments with you. I want infinity to love you. I want you to know you're my sparkle. My dream come true. I just want you. Will you marry me?" he asks, every part of my body captivated by the sound of his voice and the words he speaks.

His eyes are swimming with emotion as he waits, but I take a moment to take it all in. To take him in before I give him my tomorrows. "Yes," I say on a whisper. "Yes to infinity and sparkles."

I wrap my arms around him and cling tight. My face is buried in the crook of his neck, and all I want to do is breathe him in.

Breathe the moment in.

Tears blur my vision as I lean back and look at him. My rock. My sparkle. My everything.

To think I wanted to run from this. From him.

To think if I had never taken the chance.

Head up. Wings out.

Want more of the Malone brothers and the town of Sunnyville? You can read more about them in the remaining standalone books in this series, out now.

Combust: Firefighter Grady Malone has met his match when songwriter Dylan McCoy rents a room in house. Dylan needs time to come to grips with walking in on her now ex-boyfriend and her replacement. Grady needs time to recover from a tragedy at work that has scarred him. Together, they just might be what the other needs.

Cockpit: The last person Medevac pilot and single dad, Grayson Malone, wants to see on his doorstep is Sidney Thorton. She's not high on his list of high school classmates he ever wished to see again, and now she's telling him he's in the running for the title of Hot Dad with her magazine. Can he win the contest for his son and keep her at an arms' length while doing so?

Control: Desi Whitman loves her messy, chaotic life. But when SWAT office Reznor Maybe moves in next door, he's about to show her how good control can feel.

NOTE FROM THE AUTHOR

Dear Reader,

Often times, authors use events that have happened to them in real life and tweak them to fit in a story. How better to write about a situation—to get the emotion across to the reader—than to have actually walked in the shoes of your characters. From there, the author takes the situation and builds on it by adding the fiction to complete the story.

Cuffed is that book for me. I may have changed the names, but when I was in elementary school, I knew an Emerson.

And I was the Grant.

No, we weren't best friends who basically lived at each other's houses like Emerson and Grant do in *Cuffed* (that's my added fiction), but we were friends nonetheless. I will never forget the day we were walking around the playground and Olive (that's what I'll call her for this) told me the exact words Emerson told Grant. "When my mom is gone, my dad holds a gun to my head and molests me and my brother." I can still picture the look on her face and the sound of her voice. And then, of course, she went on to say he'd told them he would hurt them if they told anyone else.

It's been over thirty years since that day, but I still remember so much about it. I remember going home and asking my mom what "molest" meant and her shocked reaction when I wouldn't tell her why I'd asked the question (there is a lot more to this part but for the sake of this note, I'm keeping this short). I remember worrying about my friend all night long because, while my mom's explanation of the word wasn't scary (remember she was explaining to a young child), I knew "gun" was a bad thing. I remember going to school the next day and Olive telling me that it happened again.

And then I remember telling my very pregnant teacher when everyone was out at recess that I had to talk to her. That in and of itself was hard to do, so you can imagine how nervous I was telling her what Olive had told me. I can picture her face when I told her and how when she hugged me, I couldn't fit my arms all the way around her pregnant belly.

What happened next was the same as the story. The principal came over the intercom, called Olive to the office, and as she walked out the door, she turned to me and said, "I hate you. I never want to see you again."

Over thirty years have passed, and I still think about Olive off and on. I never saw her after that day when she walked out of the classroom and told me she hated me. She never came back to the school. Through the grapevine, we'd heard she and her brother were removed from the home and adopted, but we never knew more than that.

When I think of her, my main hope for her is that she has had a good life. I wonder if she ever thinks about the chubby little girl whose name she probably doesn't even remember but who pinky promised her she wouldn't tell and then broke that promise. Does she still hate me for tearing her family apart despite getting her out of that situation? Even if I found her again, I would never approach her but rather would just want to know she's okay. That she's happy.

That she doesn't blame me.

Or hate me anymore.

Sound familiar? There's a lot of how I feel in Grant.

In a perfect world, there would be no Olives, but unfortunately if there is one, that is too many.

This book is dedicated to all of the Olives out there. Wherever you are, remember we are rooting for you. To succeed. To thrive. To battle. To overcome.

And to my Olive, I hope you have found happiness.

ABOUT THE AUTHOR

New York Times Bestselling author K. Bromberg writes contemporary romance novels that contain a mixture of sweet, emotional, a whole lot of sexy, and a little bit of real. She likes to write strong heroines and damaged heroes who we love to hate but can't help to love.

A mom of three, she plots her novels in between school runs and soccer practices, more often than not with her laptop in tow and her mind scattered in too many different directions.

Since publishing her first book on a whim in 2013, Kristy has sold over two million copies of her books across twenty different countries and has landed on the *New York Times, USA Today*, and *Wall Street Journal* Bestsellers lists over thirty times. Her Driven trilogy (*Driven, Fueled*, and *Crashed*) has been adapted for film and is available on the streaming platform Passionflix as well as Amazon.

You can find out more about him or chat with Kristy on any of her social media accounts. The easiest way to stay up to date on new releases and upcoming novels is to sign up for her newsletter (http://bit.ly/254MWtI) or follow her on Bookbub (http://smarturl.it/KBrombergBB)